ETERNAL *Gold*

Ildiko Szekely

First Edition

NEWMAN SPRINGS PUBLISHING
320 Broad Street
Red Bank, NJ 07701

First originally published by Newman Springs Publishing 2021

ISBN 978-1-63692-723-7 (Paperback)
ISBN 978-1-63692-724-4 (Digital)

Printed in the United States of America

To my father who, for my sixth birthday, gave me his old "portable" Olympia typewriter (for portable, read, about fifteen pounds), thereby launching my writing obsession.

Contents

Introduction

Gold is the most precious of gifts the earth can give to humanity and the most precious of gifts which humans can offer to their gods or give to one another. It will last, unchanging, through all the ages but can be altered by the artistry of human hands. Its beauty stands alone, its color and shine give an incomparable soft warmth, and when shaped by the hands of humans, its beauty can be beyond compare. People have desired it, cherished it, prided themselves in its possession, and sold their souls to possess it.

This is the story of a lump of gold mined out of the bounty of the earth and its passage through the generations and centuries of humanity. It is also not so much the story of the lump of gold and its transformation from one object to the next but rather the stories, however episodic, and the fates of some of those people, lucky or unlucky, happy or unhappy, who possessed it. As such it becomes a prism through which one can view the passage and fate of generations and nations which had been or are still present on the stage of our existence.

By the very nature of telling such a story, one can only seize moments out of the whole texture of centuries. I admit that I have chosen periods of history which have a particular fascination or meaning for me—one individual's special fancy. Any number of other stories could be added or inserted into this list, like pearls to a strand of a necklace. By that very assessment, this story will never be complete and awaits additions, if not by the writer then by the reader's imagination.

The Pyramid Builders
2575–2465 BCE Egypt

The skies cloud over, the stars are obscured.
The vaults of heaven shake, the limbs of the earth god tremble.
All is still.
When they behold the king in all his divine power,
The dwellers of heaven serve him.
He moves across the heavens.
He roams through every land.
He, the most powerful, who has might over the mighty,
He, the great one, is like a falcon who soars above all falcons.
A god is he, older than the oldest.
Thousands serve him, hundreds make offerings to him.
His lifespan is eternity.
The borders of his power are infinity.

—Contemporary Egyptian poem

Prologue

The mine had been there since time immemorial. It was located in the Eastern Desert, between the sacred life-giving Nile and the salt waters of the Eastern Sea. The mine had always served the mighty and the rich of the land. Out of the barren rocky soil, under the searing desert sun, workers, since time immemorial, had dug out the gold, a never-ending, toiling mass of wretched humanity bringing forth an endless supply of gleaming yellow metal to adorn the bodies, the homes, the temples, and the graves of the great of Egypt.

Gold was, after all, the blood of the gods and, as such, the exclusive property of the Living God of the land. If Pharaoh wished to give some of the gold to others who, by deed or by ancestry, had distinguished themselves sufficiently to merit this honor, then that was Pharaoh's right by virtue of his divinity. No one would dare question this; it was a law brought down from the heavens to earth at the time of creation—it was the will of the gods.

The gold that was brought up to the surface was heavily mixed with rock. It became necessary to separate gold from the impurities brought with it up to the surface. Transport through the desert was dangerous and difficult, and the need urgent to carry only that which was of value or was necessary to sustain the camels' and camel drivers' lives. Thus the gold was then smelted in furnaces burning day and night to separate the ore from the other impurities. Those who worked the furnaces were, because of the immense heat, not able to last longer than a week or two, and so the ones sent there to work had committed some infringement such as stealing whatever meager food there was from one of the other workers. For the sake of ease of disposal, the bodies were thrown into the furnaces to feed the ever-hungry flames.

The workers were slaves and condemned criminals under life sentence. Most of the criminals were earless or noseless. From dawn to dark and from year to year, they labored until they dropped in their tracks or curled up one night in their tattered cloaks, never to rise again in the morning. The rule in the land was mild and humane, for it allowed such wrongdoers, as would have been killed anywhere else, to live and to toil for the glory of the gods and the wealth of Pharaoh.

On the gods' feast days, the men were allowed women, if any such were willing to go, and since such women were few, they were wildly fought over by the stronger and more aggressive of the workers. They fought over everything, especially over water. Water was even more precious than a woman's body, for in their marginal existence, it often determined who lived and who perished.

The men in the mines had no names. Their rightful names had been shed and long forgotten, along with every aspect of their earlier existence. Rather the Egyptian guards called them by some distinguishing trait or attribute of appearance. They were One-Eye and Toothless and Sloth and Crab and Hunchback.

Among the men was one called Bruiser, a great giant of a person, strong and black as one of the bulls that were kept for the gods in the city of Memphis. Bruiser had been captured in the land of Punt, to the south, and, because of the strength of his arms and his back, had first been recruited into the army. He had run away, was caught and flogged, and promptly escaped again. This time when he was recaptured, he received the just punishment of a runaway slave—his ears and, for good measure, his tongue were cut off, and he was sent to work in the gold mines.

It was here that, one day, Bruiser met a young woman called Midnight, for both the color of her skin and the nature of her activities. Midnight was a lovely girl with a round moon face, gleaming teeth, and a smile that melted Bruiser's heart. They soon came to love each other, and though Bruiser could not speak, they agreed to run away together and made elaborate and careful plans. Over the next months, Bruiser managed to secrete away a gold nugget the size of Midnight's little finger, and then another such. She, in turn, stole a goatskin partly filled with water. They knew not where they were nor how far home was, only that it was to the south. Thus they fled one night, taking care to keep the setting sun to their backs.

Luck was with them, and for two days and nights, they traveled unmolested, stopping only to rest and sleep briefly, eating such insects as Midnight was able to dig up and drinking sparingly. On the third morning, at dawn, a caravan stumbled upon them. The caravan was Memphis-bound and carried huge blocks of salt. These had been taken from the surface of the earth far to the south, in the land of the Danakili, and then transported northward partly by way of the Eastern Sea, partly over land. The camel drivers were evil men and greedy, as such usually were, for none but ruthless adventurers, thieves, and murderers were willing to undertake such a long and perilous journey with only a tenuous hope of rewards.

Bruiser's disfigured face gave sufficient evidence of what he and Midnight were, and the camel drivers behaved accordingly. Though Bruiser slew one of them with one strike of his massive fist, he was overpowered in the end and bound. They pried the gold nuggets from his fingers and then slit his throat, leaving him to feed the parched soil with his blood. The men took turns to enjoy Midnight and clubbed her to death only after she had repeatedly served them all, for to take her with them would have meant to share their precious stores of food and water.

In Memphis, Bruiser's gold nuggets were sold to one of the capital's leading artisans, whose workshop had recently been commissioned to prepare several items of gold and gemstone ornaments for the royal household. Among these was to be a delicately worked cosmetic palette with raised designs on front and back and little wells for paints and creams on one side. It had been ordered on behalf of the young Pharaoh and was destined as a gift for one of the young princesses whom he was shortly to marry. The owner of the workshop was well pleased with his purchase, for he paid less for the nuggets than what he would have had to pay for gold transported directly from the mines. The latter were heavily taxed by the administrators of the royal treasury, and he was only too happy to outwit the tax collectors whenever the opportunity presented itself.

The Queen Mother was dying.

Hetepheres lay upon her bed, her exquisitely beautiful gold-gleaming bed, gift of her husband oh, so many years ago, fighting for breath. Each gulp of air barely raised her breasts, and each gust exhaled diminished her until she almost disappeared under the coverlets. She was fighting for breath; she was fighting for life.

Her eyes, not quite alive, not yet dead, looked at the dark statue of Sekhmet across the foot of her bed. The statue came to life in the light of the torches. It frowned at her as the lion's head on a woman's body slowly turned from side to side. It breathed—oh, how lightly and easily—the chest moving slowly with the rhythm of life. To her the statue was more alive than any of those gathered around.

"How my husband had hated you," Hetepheres told the statue. "Had that been the reason I had you placed in this room, by my bed? To tell him to keep himself apart? Perhaps, perhaps…but long ago—oh, so long ago—I cannot remember any longer.

Why keep him away from her bed? The bed which had been his gift to her, her pride, the bed in which she had conceived his children? He had been her brother, her playmate in childhood, her husband, her divine lover and companion, her Horus-Falcon. To keep him away was unnatural, like separating her body from her soul. Why then do so?

To remember, to remember so many things! She must remember—it was important that she do—for she could not tear herself away from here until she did. She was tired. She closed her eyes in frustration and allowed her mind to dive deeply into buried memories. A whole abyss of memories, filled with layers of swirling mist.

*****

Sennefer. There at the bottom of the abyss she stood, looking up at her with smiling wide-set eyes, her mouth turning delicately with her smile. It was the day of The Shaving of the Head for both of them; that wonderful day of growing up and receiving their first wigs. Sennefer had sparkled with delighted expectation since sunrise. She crouched upon their bed and peered through the bed curtains waiting for Atet, the first mistress of the royal daughters, to arrive with the servants.

"Look, sister," Sennefer whispered, turning back to Hetepheres and catching her hands in eagerness, "look, no clouds in the sky. Ra has banished them today so that all the heavens can belong to him and to us alone!"

She scampered off the bed and knelt by the beautifully inlaid ebony chest which held their jewels. When she returned, she held a flat golden object in her hands.

"Look, look," she whispered again, flushed with childish pride and urgency, "what he gave me yesterday! With our names entwined together on the back!"

Hetepheres stretched out her hand and took the gift to see it more closely. It was a gold-gleaming cosmetic palette, and there on the back, she could recognize Sneferu's Pharaoh cartouche and another one next to it, which must have been her sister's.

She dropped the palette on the bed. Her own thin brown arm lay next to it, and she watched her pulse beating furiously.

That must have been yesterday afternoon, when Sneferu had come to pay them the required official visit on the eve of their celebration. As eldest daughter and future consort of the divine boy king, Sennefer had the privilege of walking alone in the gardens with him. Hetepheres had felt excluded and miserable, but in a way, she had been glad not to be with them, for it would have been difficult to hide her feelings adequately.

Now Sennefer's chatter splashed over her in a shower of breathless whisperings and subdued giggles. She hardly listened, only adding an occasional nod. How good she had become at this game! Long ago she had learned to guard her words and especially her eyes, not only from Sennefer but from all others at the court as well. It was the only way to keep apart, for she sensed that Sennefer had, at times, as much insight into her being as she had into her sister's. But then maybe not; Sennefer had never been a very observant person.

What a curse of the gods it was to have been born twin sisters! She was only too aware of the mysterious bonds, and she recoiled from that togetherness, that very sameness which the family had forced upon them and expected of them. She yearned for privacy of the body and especially of the spirit. At least the gods mercifully allowed her not to think and act as her sister did. She had always found an odd comfort in that and in the fact that they did not look alike, even though that was to her disadvantage.

Not for her the gaiety, the breathless giggles of coy girlishness, the carefree heedless living from day to day, that casual acceptance of privilege, honor, deference, and admiration—all that which came only because of a few heartbeats' difference in time. Such a brief span by which to be second, always and forever and unalterably to be second.

For the only thing that mattered was to be first, Hetepheres thought fiercely. To be born second, by however short a margin, means nothing, nothing, nothing. Only the firstborn would become heiress to the throne of the Two Lands and thus, by her marriage, confirm her husband's right to rule. Only the firstborn would become Great Wife of the Living God. Only the firstborn would be embraced as equal by the Lord Osiris in the afterlife. *And*, she thought bitterly, *only the firstborn receives the gift of a golden palette from Pharaoh.*

Hetepheres dropped her eye to her lap, as with deliberate care, she withdrew her hand from the golden object. Those who were born together—soul sisters—were too much attuned to each other. It would never do for Sennefer to even guess her thoughts. She withdrew into herself, the only place she knew where she could hide from others and be alone. She murmured "how pretty" to Sennefer and to the palette lying on the covers, drew her legs from under her, stood, and then walked slowly to the door and, from there, to the gardens trailing down to the edge of the river.

Rage and bitterness were choking her, but her eyes were calm and her brow smooth. The Lady Atet, arriving to greet the girls, thought how odd this younger princess was, so contained and serene, even on a day when girls should chatter and flutter with self-importance and excitement.

*****

The Queen Mother stirred faintly. Keser-khaf, the high priest of the Great Temple of Ptah in Memphis, signaled his acolytes to fan the incense burners into new life and stepped closer to the deathbed to peer at the old mistress. Outside the gold-worked cart, with its garlanded bullocks, stood ready for the short trip to the House of the Dead.

*****

After the head-shaving ceremony, feeling very much the adults, resplendent in their new wigs and wearing their best jewels, they were escorted to the temple of Isis for the sacred ceremony of adulthood. For the first time, they were allowed to participate in washing and clothing the image of the goddess in the holiest of holies, and then they took turns to raise the figure of the goddess Ma'at, guardian of the divine order, to the altar. *Our mother was still living then*, Hetepheres remembered, *and she shed tears of joy when she saw us thus, all festive and grown-up, standing there solemnly while the priests sprinkled water from the Sacred River on our heads.*

How strange, Hetepheres thought, *that our mother was so altogether different from either of us! Quiet and gentle and self-effacing, seemingly without ambition or desire, except to please my father, her brother, while he lived. So full of warmth and tenderness toward all living things that she could not bear to hear a slave girl scolded, would not even bring herself to eat the flesh of an animal. How could she ever manage to bring forth two such alien beings, her twin daughters?*

After the ceremonies, there was a great celebration on the river. There were flower-bedecked barges, there was music and dance and a great big banquet with columns of bearers bringing up the food. There were also gifts: bracelets and matching collars in gold, inlaid with turquoise, chalcedony, onyx, and lapis lazuli from their mother, Meresankh, beautifully worked filigree amulets and a caved ivory senet game box for each of them from Sneferu, and all manner of lesser gifts from the various relatives and the ladies of the royal harem. But the best gift was when Sennefer—too full of excitement, food, and wine—had to be bustled back to the palace and laid to bed before the evening was over, and she and Sneferu were left alone for a while, standing in the prow of the royal barge in the gathering darkness.

"You did well to restrain yourself, unlike our sister," Sneferu said, and although his face was indistinct in the dark, she could hear the smile in his voice. "For it would be a sorry evening indeed if both celebrants would have to miss their festivities. Perhaps," he added, and now she was certain that he was laughing, "perhaps the ceremonies of adulthood were planned a little prematurely?"

Hetepheres turned her body toward him. "My sister's actions are hers, and mine are my own. Do not confuse us, my brother! I am as little given to excesses of the body as Sennefer is to moderation. My sister acts before she thinks, while I think and then do not act at all."

Sneferu had also turned, and he now was contemplating her with a slight frown, trying to penetrate the dark. "So you do, indeed," he agreed. "Do you know what our father used to say about the two of you? 'Sennefer will grow up to remain a child, and Hetepheres was born old.' Does that surprise you?"

Somehow this assessment of a father only dimly remembered pleased Hetepheres. She shrugged her shoulder. "Ah, but I wish they were the only differences between us, dearest brother. Yet we have differences much more readily perceived by anyone!"

"Meaning?"

"Dearest brother, you do not have to be that kind to me, even on my festival day!" She laughed. "Only the blind would not see that Sennefer is slim and lovely, that her eyes shine, and her mouth smiles. I, meanwhile, am thin and scrawny and brown like a nut and have no grace whatsoever."

There was a sudden splash in the dark water below them—a fish, maybe, or a crocodile—and Sneferu leaned over the railing.

When he straightened, his voice was serious. "You are the daughter of the Eye of Ra, my sister. You must never look at yourself with the eyes of mortal humans."

"And do you think I could be unmindful of that, brother? What we are, we are. Yet I cannot but feel that the man who will enter my bed will have the choice of the lesser of two women."

"Hetepheres! The man whom you will accept will have a companion of sense and wisdom. You, my dear, are also perceptive and intelligent, calm in the face of danger, and wise in judgment. Can you not be proud of those accomplishments?"

"Common sense! Wisdom! Judgment! Pale substitutes they are to beauty when one is but a young woman."

"Wherever you reside, nothing will be pale, sister. The man whom you take for husband never need complain of boredom. You will add savor to his days and spice to his nights."

"And Sennefer?"

"Sennefer is full of gaiety and sparkle. It lifts my spirit to hear her laugh. It pleases me to see her move. It rests me to listen to her chatter. She is my wife-to-be and so dearer to my heart than all others. But you, my dearest, are like this river, strong and dark, filled with mystery one moment, seemingly transparent the next, life-giving and death-dealing all at the same time, with hidden depths and dangerous whirlpools yet calm and smooth on the surface!"

Hetepheres had lowered her arms from the railing. She listened with slightly bent head, avidly trying to catch his every word spoken into the breeze. Her hands were pressed together and to her body, as though trying to clutch his sentences to herself. For once she did not dare speak, so much was she afraid to trust her voice. When she did speak, after a few moments, it surprised her to hear that she was able to steady her voice and even to make it sound light and mocking. "I dared not have guessed that the Divine Lord, Eye of Ra, would find time to think of his younger sister. I am flattered, my brother."

"Is not your flesh and blood the same as mine, Hetepheres? Were we not given life by the same parents? I think of you both much and often, and though Sennefer's future is known to me, I am disquieted about what your life will become, my dear. Yes, and about the day when we shall part, and you leave this house. Even yesterday, that day had seemed so far away, but now, seeing you so grown-up makes me realize that we shall soon lose you, and the thought makes me sad." He sighed and went on.

"At least it is a familiar sadness...Do you still remember how we used to play in our mother's house? You loved to hide behind pillars and draperies, while I had to sing that silly little rhyme. I had to play-act that I could not find you anywhere and go search through all the rooms and hallways. Then I had to tell Atet that you had disappeared or run away and put up a great wailing and crying for you. Or I would tell Atet that I would command the army to go rescue you from some evil spirit's clutches. Sennefer always believed us and cried in earnest, until you jumped out from some hiding place with a terrifying noise, and we cowered in pretend fright. You would run after us, screaming, 'It is only I, it is only Heteres,' for you couldn't say your name right.

"And do you remember when we were older, how I tried to teach both of you to swim in the lake off the palace gardens at Tinis? Sennefer was always afraid and clung to my neck, but you just furrowed your brow and kept at it until you were able to traverse the whole width of the pond.

"Then one day it all changed. Our father decreed that I was too old to remain among the women in our mother's house. The court came with great ceremony, and I was bitterly afraid but dared not show it. For many days thereafter, I would cry for my mother, for both of you, and for the only kind of life I had ever known, but only when no one would see me, for I was a boy old enough to be shamed by tears. Oh, yes, I was sad for a long time, and lonesome. Now I feel the same sadness when I think of you leaving this house, even though I know that one day soon, you must."

For many months, Hetepheres cherished that conversation, while a mutinous thought slowly crept into her mind. Indeed, why did she have to leave? Sneferu could well marry two sisters; this was not something very unusual, and she knew for a fact that several of her ancestors had done just that. Ah, how lovely it would be to remain here forever, as Sneferu's wife! But then it occurred to her that such an arrangement would also be unalterable, as pleasing as it seemed today. To be forevermore in second place behind Sennefer—that would be torture, totally intolerable! To share Sneferu with anyone, especially with Sennefer, would be unthinkable!

Presently her musings were interrupted by the arrival of courtiers, and shortly thereafter, Sneferu took his leave. Hetepheres, together with the other ladies, was borne back to the palace. Sennefer was asleep and, in the morning, complained of an aching head.

*****

One day followed the next in their ordinary set pattern. Night followed day, and a new day followed the night. Akhet, the season of flooding by the Great River, arrived, and in time, the waters began to recede during the season of Peret. Sneferu started on his annual festival tour, setting out to visit parts of the country to bring divine blessings upon the fertile fields to assure their continued fertility before the spreading of the new seed, and also to perform the ritual of Cutting the First Sod and to ceremonially open the water channels.

At such times, the palace was quiet, almost somnolent in the heat. With the absence of Pharaoh, there were no banquets, no festivities, no ceremonies. In the royal harem, the ladies retired indoors, spending much of their time finding relief in the coolness of marble floors, high ceilings, and such drafts or breeze as the efforts of their fan bearers afforded. Their mother, Meresankh, was ailing. Of late she had developed a terribly fierce pain in her chest, which attacked her at unexpected times and left her shaken and ashen-faced, painfully panting for breath. The physician priests came, first those of the temple of Isis, who was known to be the especial protector of women; then those of Hathor, the life giver, cow-headed goddess of love and motherhood, but all of them remained powerless in the face of this infirmity.

Then one day, Ahhotep, who bore the titles of first lady and unique friend to the queen, begged her to allow the priests of the goddess Mut into the august presence. Ahhotep had come to the court from faraway Thebes, and she recalled how, in her childhood days, Mut was revered as the mother of the universe who had great power to heal the sick of the Upper Kingdom. Arrangements were made finally, for there was no temple of Mut near Memphis, and a special detachment of the royal guards was dispatched to bring the statue of the goddess and her priests to the queen's presence.

Hetepheres did not know what transpired in the royal chamber, for she and Sennefer were not allowed to attend, but soon thereafter, the queen started to recover her strength and eventually returned into the presence of the court. She was somewhat paler and quieter than before, more cautious of step and slower of movement, but well enough to call forth thanksgiving celebrations. One day she explained to her daughters that the goddess had given her a basket of flowers and commanded her to have the blooms dried and to drink drops of a bitter brew made from them, and that hence, whenever she felt ill, drinking from this miraculous concoction would restore her.

Thus a small temple was soon established to Mut and her priests and attendants, quite close to the palace gardens; although in truth, the common folk, in their plodding ways, as always, resistant to change, continued to ignore the goddess and her blessings.

Throughout this whole time, Hetepheres lived as though in a half dream. Once long ago, in the lake at Tinis, she had tried to swim underwater. Now she had the same sensation, one of curious detachment from her surroundings, even from reality. Sounds and voices reached her faintly, people and events floated by dimly, and she felt separated from them as by a curtain of water.

The only true reality was Sneferu's remembered voice talking to her, his words engraved on her mind, the sentences rolling and tumbling about in her brain. In typical small girl-child fashion, she had always idolized her big brother because he was older and thus infinitely wiser—a boy and the heir. After he did become Pharaoh, the distance between them widened, and her admiration increased.

That he should not be able to expect more than a pretty-looking scatterbrain for his consort had always rankled. That such a scatterbrain should unquestioningly accept this good fortune as her due became increasingly intolerable with the passing of each day. That everyone at court should look upon this matter with uncritical equanimity became unbearable. She wanted to run to them and shake them and cry, "Look at me, see me, recognize my worth, and see my sister's unworthiness!"

But of course, she did not; she could not. She behaved as ever before, self-possessed and cool, only perhaps a little more withdrawn and vaguer. The ladies gave one another knowing glances and whispered behind their fans that she was growing up too fast, that she needed a husband and children to occupy and fulfill her.

So the days passed. The first arrangements were made for Sneferu and Sennefer's marriage. When the Divine Pharaoh returned, they said he and the priests would select the day for the august occasion out of the list of auspicious days presented by the seers. The sisters saw less of each other, as Sennefer occupied herself with selections of furniture and furnishings, robes, jewelry, and servants. Hetepheres was increasingly left alone, and that too was well enough with her.

There was a place within the palace gardens, less known than other places and infrequently visited, to which she liked to retreat, sometimes spending long periods of the lazy afternoons there. It was well out of the way and down by the river's edge. She would sit there for hours, observing the flow of the water and the sacred ibises wading on the shore. The river made a slight bed there and had gouged a hollow beneath a little ledge on which one could stand and look below.

Idly she would watch how the water swirled and circled in a whirlpool beneath her feet, watch fish, like silver streaks, swim by under the shadowy surface, sometimes break through the surface with a sudden splash. The whispering of drying papyrus stalks, the droning of insects over the reeds, the slight hissing of the river, the soft lapping of waves, all combined their sounds and, together, created a special somnolence, a lassitude of body and spirit. In the turmoil of her rebellious soul, this place became her refuge, the quiet there her balm.

Here she would sit on the grass or on a broken-down bench, idly counting the clouds in the sky, or trying to guess their shapes in that ageless game so gladly played by countless other humans. She would think of everything and nothing, her thoughts half-submerged like those reeds by the water's edge. Her shift became grass-stained, her face bronzed by the sun and her hair streaked with lighter shades. The Lady Atet had scolded her several times for arriving home—as she put it—like a witless peasant girl who had just had a good roll in the rushes, but Hetepheres only smiled absently, lifted her shoulders, and went her way. The Lady Atet did not dare say anything more and was grateful that her scolding was accepted without demur. Her influence, she thought sourly, over the twins was waning rapidly, as their roles gradually became inverted that of the girls becoming more and more exalted with their early adulthood, and hers, in contrast, reduced to nothing more than that of a glorified retainer.

Here by the river's edge, on a day shortly before Sneferu's return to Memphis, Sennefer surprised Hetepheres in her solitude. She had stalked Hetepheres and followed her, half in game, half out of curiosity, and suddenly emerged out of the shadow of a group of palms. Hetepheres reddened at her unexpected appearance. She had let her guard down and now felt exposed and vulnerable, thinking that her innermost thoughts must be laid bare upon her face. But almost immediately, she composed herself, realizing that her sister had other matters on her mind and, besides, was not a keen observer.

As indeed she was not. She had been petulant and cross; now the reason became apparent.

"Ah, so this is the place where you hide yourself all day long, sister! The secret of Hetepheres's days!" She giggled and lifted the hem of her finely pleated shift to step over some wet stones. "Why, this place is nothing but an unattended corner of the garden with a tumbledown bench, not even sufficiently comfortable to sit upon! Yet you prefer it to my company." She pouted. "You go around wrapped in your mysterious silence as though no one else is around you. Everyone is full of the anticipation of my wedding day, but you pay less attention to me than to those fish." And she jutted her chin in the general direction of the river.

Hetepheres sighed and was going to give some simple explanation, as though explaining to a child, but for once, her words were sharper than she had meant them to be. "It is exactly because everyone is so busy fawning over you that I keep myself apart. Pharaoh's daughter does not wish to compete for her sister's ear."

"Well," Sennefer countered angrily, "I am as much Pharaoh's daughter as you, and I also should not have to compete with fishes and reeds for your attention!"

Hetepheres, sitting on the ramshackle bench, pulled her legs under her. She contemplated Sennefer quietly, then made a swift gesture of appeasement. "Sister! You are tired and on edge. All this planning and excitement must be exhausting. You see things that do not exist. I only tried not to be underfoot while your days are taken up with your and Sneferu's wedding plans."

Warily Sennefer eyed her, indecision on her face. Then her basic good nature won out.

"Truly? Why, Hetepheres, I shall always be glad to see you, even when I am Great Wife. You know that."

What had been said was well meant, but the unintended condescension brought the blood rushing into Hetepheres' cheeks. She jumped up and moved swiftly to the river's bank, averting her face. For a while, she struggled for composure. "It is very peaceful here, and my spirit craves the quiet. I suppose our mother's illness had upset me more than I expected."

"Oh, that, but she is so much better now!" Sennefer exclaimed with a careless shrug of her shoulders. "There is no reason to fret any longer!" Sennefer's mind quickly discarded the unwelcome topic like a piece of worn clothing, only to return once more to the matter occupying most of her thoughts.

"Look, I have been planning a surprise for Sneferu when he returns. I want to tell him that we should not have to stay in this big old palace. Once we are married, we should have our very own house, not just a separate household but something entirely built and appointed to our wishes—a newer place of greater comfort and elegance. Last year, when the first of those forty ships of his returned from the Northern Sea with their loads of cedarwood from Byblos, remember the wondrous tales we heard? Of the great richness of colors used there, of floor designs laid out in little bits of colored stones, of hangings woven with gold thread, of furniture carved out of fragrant wood, of pools everywhere within the houses, and of cascades of water falling from basin to basin, the water perfuming the air? That's the kind of place I want for us, different from anything we have here. Who wants to live in a place built to the taste of men long dead and buried?"

"But, sister, where would you build such a place? And what would become of this palace?"

Sennefer shrugged. "Oh, well, I don't know where? That's for Sneferu to decide. Maybe—maybe somewhere closer to the sea, where the breeze is cooler, or perhaps farther upriver, closer to the mountains? All I want is a place away from here, where he is forever called to do some duty, where the priests always remind him of his obligations, where there are a hundred curious and disapproving eyes molesting us, and the old biddies of our father's harem would love nothing better than to snoop on us day and night! Everything is so old, boring, and worn here, just like they are! We could still keep this palace, of course, for the people who—well, for you, for instance, until you go away to marry, that is, and for Mother and all the others..."

Her voice trailed away in the rush of eager anticipation, unaware of the thoughtlessness, the hurtfulness of her words, of the implicit unuttered slight. Unseeing, she stared across the water, chewing her fingernail, then roused herself and turned to Hetepheres.

"You will help me, sister, won't you? To persuade Sneferu, if he becomes balky? He is so wrapped up in planning his House of Eternity. Gods! I cannot bear to think of him dying. Why, it's silly when one is as young as we are!"

"But, Sennefer, you know full well how many years it takes to prepare a proper house for him in death! Always and always, Pharaoh's funerary monument was begun as early in his life as possible. How else do you imagine it could be completed in one lifetime?" Hetepheres remonstrated, then added with a little laugh, "Since when do you think you need my support with Sneferu? You have him wound around your little finger! One smile and a tear from you, and he will do what you wish."

"Maybe." Sennefer was still in thought. "Maybe, but still..." She stopped herself short, then ran the few steps to Hetepheres and hugged her impetuously. "Oh, sister, isn't this exciting? Are you not excited for me? From now on, once Sneferu returns, there will be nothing but feasts and celebrations, and everyone will be joyous for us—think of it!" She glanced at Hetepheres and made a face. "But you are not even listening to me! What is it that interests you so much in that silly river?"

Hetepheres was truly shocked. "For shame, 'Nefer! Never, never! Never call the great life giver a silly river. How could you? May that the gods did not hear you! Your husband-to-be even now toils to bring divine blessings upon it and upon the fields it feeds. Without it we should surely perish. What would our mother, what would our dead father say, if they were here to hear you insult the gods so?"

But Sennefer was not to be deterred. "Well, Mother does not hear me, our father even less, and neither does Sneferu." She shrugged. "Honestly must you be so tiresome about everything? You are so pompous, self-righteous, and stuffy, just like an old maid. Can't you have some fun? No wonder Sneferu thinks…Oh, look! Look there! A bird's nest! And there are three dear little eggs in it!"

Sennefer bent forward with curiosity, her hands on her knees. The nest of some waterfowl was wedged into the crumbling corner of a flight of ancient steps, half-buried, half-overgrown with weeds. Originally the steps had led down to the Nile, but by now, only some broken fragments remained. Underneath the steps, there was a bank of loose gravel and shale. Below the water foamed and swirled and gurgled.

Hetepheres wanted to ask what it was that Sneferu thought or said of her, but then she saw Sennefer stumble, as one of her sandals caught on the jutting stone edge, watched her throw out her arms to regain her balance. She wanted to call out a warning but did not, for at the same instant, the cracked piece of stone detached itself, giving way under the weight of Sennefer's body, and, with sucking noises, began to slide down the curving wet bank, smaller stones, gravel, and wet clumps of earth rolling and tumbling down with it.

Hetepheres heard her sister cry out, watched her fall to her knees, then flat onto her stomach, her arms and bosom becoming streaked with mud, her fingers trying to clutch at a tuft of weeds.

With utter disbelief, she realized that this was not playacting or a silly game and that Sennefer would be unable to halt her fall and inevitably slide into the river.

But not, how ridiculous! This cannot be—it all happened too fast, in the blink of the eye, almost! On such a peaceful sunny afternoon, with bees droning about and butterflies fluttering above the reedbeds! This was just such an inconsequential little misstep. All sorts of people did occasionally stumble and fall; she had too—that's all there is to it. At the same moment, two other thoughts flashed through her mind: the whirlpool below and Sennefer's inability to swim.

Quickly Hetepheres stepped forward, intending to reach down and try to catch one of her sister's hands. But she did not move fast enough—could not—would not—move fast enough, and Sennefer's body slid inexorably into the water, her mouth a soundless distorted O, her eyes wide, the laughter of finding the nest mingled with surprise and fright. As her distance from the shore widened, above her, Hetepheres stood on the bank, stood mute and motionless, and stared down with unseeing eyes, her arms hanging paralyzed by her sides, her face closed like a statue, her eyes veiled. Sennefer's gaze clung to her sister's while her body turned, sluggishly at first, then faster, as the swirl of the current caught, her gown billowing about her, her arms slapping the water. Then the head disappeared below the water, bobbed up again, but unexpectedly even farther from shore. Hetepheres, unable to open her mouth or utter a sound, watched the ineffectual splashing. She watched the head disappear again. A pale pink wisp of cloth still floated upon the surface but briefly, then that disappeared too.

Further downriver, a heavy splash sounded, then another, as the bodies of sunning crocodiles slipped into the water.

Hetepheres could never give an account to herself of how she got back to the palace. Despite the heat of the late afternoon, she felt chilled, her hands and feet icy. She moved calmly through hallways and rooms, ordered herself a bath, and, for a long time, lay quietly in the perfumed water, allowing her mind to drift aimlessly. She felt numbed, but already underneath the numbness of feeling, she could sense the stirrings of excitement, first suppressed, then growing and blossoming like some secretly nurtured flower. It was like a door opening in silence upon vistas which she had never before allowed herself to contemplate, her spirit suddenly escaping its accustomed cage. The chattering of her maids rose dimly to her ears and, from somewhere more distant, the sounds of a flute. She closed her eyes and listened to the swelling thuds of her heart.

Those were to be the last moments of solitude she would remember for a long time, for the world closed in and claimed her soon enough. Sennefer began to be missed; no one could quite recall where they had last seen her. Earlier she had been observed playing senet with the Princess Khnumet, her half sister and one of her favorite friends. She had also been seen playing with her pet monkey, but then she had withdrawn to rest, it was assumed. First gaily, then with increasing concern, the ladies and servants went looking for her, going from room to room and through the darkening hallways, searching through the long terraces and, finally, the gardens below, calling out her name.

Still later, the palace guards were summoned, and they went through the now-dark and quiet gardens with torches, while indoors, the women looked at one another in sudden consternation and fear. No longer was this a game! The Divine Pharaoh would be back soon, and what account could be given for the future Divine Consort's absence? In time, the queen was notified, though reluctantly, for no one wished to subject her frailness to unnecessary stress and anxiety.

Much later, long after nightfall, when Hetepheres and her mother stood on the terrace, watching the flaming torches move to and fro in the darkness, they began to hear voices raised, first far away, then nearer and nearer, and finally hurried footsteps. One of the guards approached at a run. Up, up the steps he came, carrying something in his hands upon which the moonlight glinted. It was Sennefer's sandal, caked with mud, found down by the river. The queen just stared down upon it for a moment, her hand going to her breast. She only uttered a little sigh, then turned and fell to the floor.

All the events of the following weeks remained in Hetepheres's mind, a kaleidoscope of movements and color, fragments of words and sounds, disjointed from one another as in a dream. She saw Sneferu before her, his eyes red-rimmed, tears rolling down his cheeks. She saw her mother's body as the priests came to bear her away to the House of the Dead to prepare her for her great journey into the Western Land for her life of eternity. She did not utter any laments. Dry-eyed and silent, she watched the comings and goings, ebb and flow of people around her, doing what was needed, speaking what was expected of her.

She remained dry-eyed even when, more horrible than all else, what remained of Sennefer's body was found and brought in, mutilated beyond recognition by the fish and the crocodiles and recognized only by some wisps of clothing still clinging to it.

*****

The Queen Mother, on her deathbed, stirred and uttered a low moan. She closed her eyes, and her lips moved in soundless soliloquy. These shapes around her, were they dream or reality? Her mother's half-forgotten image, her sister's smile—were these only her imagination? Yet she remembered now, how long gone from this world, and gone because of her? She frowned with the effort to think. To recall those events which, most of her life, she had submerged because they were not to be thought about were indeed unthinkable. *Go away, go away, shapes, and leave me be…leave me be alone with Sneferu!*

*****

Ah, alone with Sneferu!

After all the laments were sung, after all the burial ceremonies were acted out, they had returned to the business of the living. And the business of the living demanded Pharaoh's marriage to his exalted elder sister or, if such a person did not exist, to the most highly placed living female relative of marriageable age. Such a marriage was necessary; it was the affirmation of Pharaoh's divine right to rule. The sister-wife of Pharaoh confirmed him in his right to rule the Two Kingdoms, much as the goddess Isis by giving new life to her slain brother-husband Osiris, had once allowed him to reign over the Underworld. Thus Sneferu and Hetepheres's marriage had to take place, and did, in due time. There was little need for much-added preparation, for most of the preparations for a royal wedding had already been made.

Only the divine name of the Great Wife had to be changed. But to the people of the land, one name was as good as another. The scribes and stonecutters carefully erased Sennefer's name from the carved cartouches, from written documents, and from the messages to be sent and substituted that of Hetepheres. On the vases, urns, plates, trays, on all manner of lesser decorations, the artisans reworked Sennefer's symbols for those of Hetepheres within the ovals of the Great Wife's cartouche. In Maidum, where the construction of Sneferu's House of Eternity had been in progress since his accession, the stonemasons obliterated Sennefer's cartouches wherever they appeared and sought to replace them with Hetepheres's as speedily and inconspicuously as possible.

To the people, the name of the queen may not have mattered, for they knew little of royal personages and cared only that there be a queen in accordance with divine law, but in the palace, it was altogether different. There years of friendships and allegiances had been destroyed and many an aspiration fractured by the sudden deaths of two royal women. Yet for the most part, the ladies took pains not to cast a shadow on such an auspicious event as a royal wedding. Even the Lady Ahhotep, whom Hetepheres had allowed to retain her position as first lady and unique friend, had made valiant efforts to be gay and to smile when she and her entourage entered Hetepheres's bedchamber on the morning of the great day.

"Our Divine Lord has already returned from making his devotions at the temple of Ptah, Mistress." She smiled while casting a judicious eye over the wedding robes spread out for her inspection. "In fact, I was told he hardly slept at all last night—no, not those sandals, take the gold ones with the amethyst stones and the gold Horus emblem to match the collar, over there! But no wonder, there is such an air of excitement everywhere—take care, girls, and wrap cloth about your hands before you touch that headdress, or it will show all your fingers' marks! The priests are all assembled in the outer court, waiting to serve on both of you as soon as our Lord arrives, so we must make haste!"

Khnumet, Hetepheres's half sister, giggled.

"They will be happy enough out there, I should think. They will spend their time still arguing to the very last minute about who takes precedence over whom when addressing you." She looked about herself. "Who is willing to bet with me that the priests of Ptah will go second after those of Isis?"

And to a chorus of "how do you know?" she solemnly ticked off her reasons on her fingers. "First, the priests of Ptah are all old men and so fat that they can hardly step quickly. Second the servants of Isis will—quite rightly—claim that their goddess is the true protector of marriage and family. Just wait and see how they will jockey for the best position!"

"Perhaps," the princess Radji, Khnumet's sister, continued, "perhaps with the same reasoning, they should let the priests of Taueret come first of all, now that should then really be fitting!"

And again a chorus ensued, this time of laughter, for Taueret, who had the shape of a pregnant hippopotamus, was the patroness of childbirth and motherhood, and Radji, who had been married recently, was heavy with the burden of her own pregnancy and felt very close to that enormous goddess. Seeing even Hetepheres's solemnity dissolve into smiles, Radji looked about herself with understandable satisfaction.

The night before, Hetepheres had carefully gone through all of those things which were Sennefer's belongings that had not yet been disposed of. She had sorted out some minor jewelry, to be given as mementos to several of Sennefer's young friends. For herself, Hetepheres had not wished to keep anything. Then she had come across the gold cosmetic palette which had been Sneferu's present to their sister.

Hetepheres could still remember her emotions on that day of head-shaving. Now she held the thin gold oblong in her hands, slowly turning it, letting her fingers trace the raised design on the front and back. Suddenly she removed a heavy gold and turquoise bracelet from her arm and, with furious concentration, began to rub the bracelet's edge against Sennefer's cartouche. Gold against gold had little effect, but eventually a stone dropped out of the bracelet, and she used this to scour the palette's surface, until most of the design on it was scarred and marked and obliterated beyond any recognition. Resolutely she stood and, taking the ruined palette with her, dropped it into a high woven reed basket, which held such odds and ends from their childhood days—assorted dolls, marble balls, and other bits of toys—which had been saved by the girls from oblivion for the sake of the various memories associated with them.

Carefully she replaced the basket's lid, and for a long while stood, lost in thought, staring into the flame of a flickering torch, before summoning her servants to assist her in going to bed. She had slept a sound and undisturbed sleep, the first in many a day, and awoke calm and refreshed on the morning of her wedding day.

That evening, Sneferu, the lovingly concerned, the simple-thinking solicitous brother-husband, came to her and found her in their wedding chamber, dissolved in tears. It was the first and only time he saw her cry since the tragic events so recently passed, and he thought her tears were those of sadness for the dead and apprehension for the future. Having had a fair amount of passing experience with the more attractive young virgins of the royal harem, he had learned that girls could be so odd at such times, timid, and fretful, evidently even if they were one's sister. So he embraced her and comforted her and soon made love to her in his own, at first, hesitant, probing, halting, and finally youthfully tumultuous way.

Sneferu had never been a womanizer. Of course, he had been given his own harem at his accession, and the younger women, both of his mother's and his sisters' households, were available to the wishes and desires of the god-king, but he had had relatively little experience with how to deal with a young woman's emotions. When he approached his wife, it was with gentle clumsy tenderness at first, giving way to the impatient urgency of a healthy young man, but with little true passion. Perhaps the lack of passion was to be expected while—however subconsciously—in his mind, the role of a sister was being molded into that of the lover. For Hetepheres too, passionate though her nature was, passion was not a feeling as yet connected to her lovemaking. She had never had a man close to her or touch her; but this man, after all, was her brother. His presence did not threaten or intimidate, but it also did not arouse her. Their intimacy felt strange to her but not unpleasant, even oddly comforting. Always she had adored Sneferu and yearned for him because he had been unattainable. Now he was hers, and she was Great Wife and happy in that knowledge. Passion, for the time, could wait.

Toward dawn, they talked. Hetepheres, feeling hot and rumpled, eased herself from bed and walked to the doorway open to the terrace. On silent feet, Sneferu followed her. Outside dew covered the grounds with silver glistening sheen, like gossamer cobwebs. In the distance, where the rows of trees and shrubs marked the course of the Nile, the early mists hung low over the river. A light breeze from that direction occasionally lifted the hangings over the door. The breeze brought with it the smell of water and marsh and the sleepy chirpings and rustlings of waterfowl. A goose in the reeds honked deep and low. It was a magical time, unearthly and fleeting.

After a long silence, Hetepheres stirred and moved to a low-cushioned bench close to the window. She settled herself comfortably so that she could have a view of the gardens and be in the path of the breeze, and then extended her arms to Sneferu. He sat on the floor in front of her, propping his head in her lap with a sigh of contentment.

"Gods! My neck still aches from the weight of that infernal collar they made me wear to the ceremony!" He groaned, massaging his shoulders. "When I was finally fully dressed in the morning, I could hardly move at all. I swear I was wearing more ornaments than Hathor does on her feast day!"

He stretched himself and sighed again. "How fortunate," he continued, "that I need to marry only one consort, my dearest! Nor would I wish for another one. I hardly think that I could survive one more such day as this. I'll have to just make do with you." And as a proof of his good intentions, he caught her hand and, turning it over, kissed her palm.

"But I am happy that it is over now," he continued in a more serious tone, "and the household can recover from all of the recent turmoil. There will be several things which need my decision, and I wish to consult about them with you, Hetepheres."

"With me, my brother?" Hetepheres asked in surprise, still calling her new husband by the name she had been accustomed to all her life.

"Yes, wife, with you." He put a bit more weight on wife than necessary. "Have I not always told you that I think you to be sensible and wise? I consider myself lucky to have such an adviser by my side. Well, now I shall avail myself of all that wisdom and sensibility. Why else do you suppose I have married you?" he asked in that bantering older brother tone, which had always melted her heart because it made her feel included into his exalted sphere and equal to him.

The idea of being needed and valued was so novel to Hetepheres that it startled her. She felt its warm glow rise to her heart. She snuggled herself more deeply into the cushions and closed her eyes.

"Yes?"

"Well. First off, there is this matter of an expedition to the south." Still holding her hand, he began to play with her fingers. "It is, I am convinced, long overdue. The Nubian settlements there have become increasingly restless, even often hostile, ever since our father's death. They need a strong fist, and I would guess they feel that they have nothing to fear from a youngster like me. There have been incidents of burning and looting, tax collectors have mysteriously disappeared in the darkness of the night, but most importantly, our shipments of granite and diorite from the hills around the First Cataract are imperiled. They simply have to be taught a lesson, a lesson most especially administered by me.

"Then secondly, there is the construction of my House of Eternity at Maidum. I am told that work on it has all but stopped since our mother's and—well, since…recently…" He faltered." It is probably my fault, for they have lacked direction as I was…preoccupied…but then I also do not have an architect the stature of the divine Imhotep…How blessed our father's grandfather, the most divine Djoser had to be in having him! Imagine, Hetepheres, such divinities, such greatness in one lifetime!

"The outer pattern of stone blocks had been laid down, as you probably know, but the architects cannot go on without further directions by me. None of them have the great knowledge of an Imhotep to design and improvise of their own. They dare not for fear that it will lead to some calamity or that I will be displeased... so far they have built it almost straight up with little decrease from the vertical. That is how our divine Djoser's had been built as well. But—and here is the rub—the structure cannot go higher and higher without, at some point, collapsing what they have constructed so far, or so they tell me—"

"That means that at some point, they have to do what also was done at the tomb of the Divine Djoser—make it a stepwise pyramid, or at least, one or two steps of decreasing size. I really have little liking for it because I am set on a smooth limestone facing on the outside. I think a smooth expanse of limestone covering on the outside would look ever so much more attractive and imposing. Also it would lend itself to embellishment such as painting or covering parts of it in gold wash, don't you?"

"Basically what has to be decided is this, should the final appearance of the structure follow the lines of the Saqqara Pyramid, or should we deviate and do what I am much more attracted to because of its beauty, but then break with tradition?"

"Also sometime soon, I must begin to give thought to the construction of the funerary temple at the foot of the very causeway which will connect my house to the river, upon which my body shall be taken—" He stopped in midsentence, seeing Hetepheres's stricken expression. He smiled and shook his head. "Don't worry, my dearest, not just yet!" And turning toward her, kissed her chin because it was the only part of her face he could easily reach from his position where he sat on the floor.

When he resumed, it was in a different direction altogether.

"There also remains the question of Ankh-haf, you know him, we played together as children. He is a deserving fellow and my friend and comes from an excellent family, although unrelated to us. He has lately been plaguing me by hints and gentle reminders that he wishes to become the high priest of Ra in one of the delta cities, in Bhuto perhaps, or in Saïs. His wife is from there, you know, and he himself, I believe, is being nagged into settling there. It would certainly make worthy living for him, and why not? The problem, of course, is the presence of the two current high priests who would have to be dislodged without causing undue bitter feelings."

"But, my lord, why should their feelings worry you? Your command is above them. They will do as you say. One cannot resent the wishes of the Living God any more than one resents the heat of the sun or the chill of the night in the desert. They would act as you demand."

"They would. But in their heart of hearts, they would also know that I am doing this to give favor to a personal friend. Even gods do not need enemies, Hetepheres."

"You are stronger than your enemies, my husband." Hetepheres stirred impatiently, for the first time addressing her husband by his new appellation. "What kind of men are they, anyway?"

"The one in Saïs is an old man and of great merit, I believe. His name is Methety. He has always served our interest faithfully. I cannot just dismiss him!"

"You do not need to, Sneferu. There are ways…" She hesitated for a moment, then went on rapidly. "Can you not send him your greetings and a message that you have considered his great value to you and wish to have him closer to your person to benefit by the wisdom of his years before the days of his life run out? You could even reward him by making him master of secrets or master of the secrets that only one man sees?"

Sneferu twisted slightly in his position to look at her. The pale moonlight from the gardens glinted in his dark eyes.

"You wicked little conniver! That would certainly absolve me from slighting the old goat! He might even turn out to be of real value to me. Not bad at all…"

"And the other?"

"The other you also know well. He is Lady Ahhotep's brother-in-law, Sahure."

"Ah, is he the one whose wife is always sickly? Ahhotep is always in a tizzy over her sister!"

"The same."

"Well, then that's so easy! Tell him that you do not wish to expose his lady any longer to the morbid air of the flat riverbeds and swamps there. They do breed all manner of disease, you know! Send him and his lady south, to Maidum maybe, or to Dahshur. Or better yet, send him to Fayyoum. Does not everyone say how beautiful it is there, and how beneficial its climate is to the ill? That way," she mused, "both men would be in your debt."

A sudden thought struck her, and she proceeded more swiftly. "If you send both men from their present positions, they will both serve you with gratitude in the future. You could then make Ankh-haf high priest in both cities. After all, they are close enough together, it would not be such a difficulty. And even if it were, getting twice the riches would indebt Ankh-haf to you sufficiently to make that much more of an effort. Also did I not always hear complaints that the coastal cities are too independent on account of being too close to the Great Salt Sea, where they would love nothing more than to do some independent trading? Well, one joint high priest of Ra for both cities, well placed, who is supported by and indebted to you, and they would be better controlled and willing to abide by your wishes."

Sneferu laughed out loud. "I always knew you were a scheming little witch, woman! Shame on you! One day I will tell our grandchildren that on our wedding night, you were arranging men's lives like pieces of a senet board, and then they shall despair of our sanity!" His arms went around her, and his voice grew husky. "Come here, little sister! Have we nothing better to do now than to manage the fates of cities?" And rising, he kissed her and pulled her up from her seat to draw her back to the soft darkness of their bed.

There was magic in those days. Hetepheres was content and happy—yes, whenever she could be with her husband. Being with him, laying claim to him above anyone else, even the simple act of saying my husband filled her with joy and pride. He was her prize she had always wanted without any hope of attainment. Now the vain wish had turned to reality, and just thinking of this unutterably sweet reality made her heart soar and her lips smile.

She found pleasure in talking to him, walking with him, waking in the mornings next to him. She found pleasure in listening to his plans and having a part in his life. Slowly a whole new world opened to Hetepheres. She, who had been accustomed to secretiveness and withdrawal, now dwelled in the center of the court. Her wishes were anticipated, her opinions mattered. Her husband, the God-Pharaoh cherished her, and through him, she became in her own eyes—not just symbolically—the earthly representation of Isis, the eternal wife of Hathor, the great goddess of fertility, and of Nut, mistress of the sky, who, in her union with her husband, Geb, god of earth, had given birth to the universe. Heady stuff, indeed, for a young girl whose aspirations as a royal princess, in the normal course of her life, would never have brought her farther than to become the wife of a provincial governor or that of one of the realm's vassal princes.

In those to-be-treasured early days of their life together, Sneferu was devoted to her as to no other. How much he loved her, Hetepheres could not measure, but she knew that he desired her body and enjoyed her mind. Obviously having a consort of wit and intelligence was a pleasantly unexpected new experience for him. More and more, he had the straightforward sexual appetites of a healthy young boy-turned-man, and although for herself, Hetepheres found neither passion nor release in his embraces, she was happy in the prestige and security of their union. Life for her was good and serene and became even more complete after the birth of a son, whose name Sneferu immediately decided should be Khufu.

As men will always be, Sneferu was overjoyed and filled with the pride of accomplishment, which he considered entirely his own. With overflowing generosity, he pampered Hetepheres, giving her more jewels than she could possibly wear until she laughed and begged him to stop. His most precious gift to his young wife, however, became a magnificent set of gold-sheathed bedroom furniture, the beauty and exquisite workmanship of which surpassed anything any living person had seen. Hung with the most delicate of translucent linen draperies and worked in gilded ebony and cedarwood from Syria, the furniture became Hetepheres's most prized possession and a daily seal to her of her husband's devotion.

*****

The land prospered along with the royal couple. Floods enriched the blessed soil, which bore heavy harvest year after year. The building of the pharaoh's House of Eternity at Maidum progressed since the great architect Menkau-hor, uncle to both Pharaoh and his consort, had been put in charge of the construction. Seasonally his reports of the work arrived at the royal palace in Memphis.

Nevertheless, Sneferu enjoyed traveling south occasionally to personally oversee the work site; it was a welcome break in the accustomed pace of his duties, as were the brief but successful armed forays he undertook to the southern perimeters of his realm. Those incursions always proved to be not only successful in a military sense but also greatly enriched the country's and the rulers' coffers. Much to Sneferu's pleasure, for he was no less adverse to praise than any other man, an overzealous court scribe fashioned the following narrative in honor of his master, which then was spread far and wide through all the provinces:

> In the reign of the glorious ruler Sneferu
> was the building of Tuataua ships of mer wood
> Of a hundred capacity; and sixty royal boats
> of sixteen capacity. Raid in the land of the
> Blacks, and the bringing in of seven thousand prisoners, men and women, and twenty
> Thousand cattle, sheep and goats. The
> bringing in of forty ships of cedarwood...

Peret, the planting season, was over. The festivals of Shemu, when the crops were harvested, would follow in about two more months. This was the ideal time to visit the Maidum building site and to discuss plans and alterations, for at this season and until the end of Shemu, only the master builders and the specialized artisans worked on the enormous edifice. With Shemu over, however, when the Nile dropped to its annual lowest level and fields began to parch and to crack open, farmwork ceased, and the farmers could only wait for the next flood season. That then was the part of the year when workers were conscribed by Pharaoh's emissaries from each village, to contribute their labors to the House of Eternity for their Living God, from whom all good and all power flowed.

Thus when the sun was at its most tender, and the bloom of late spring lay upon the land, when papyri bloomed along the Nile and lotus flowers perfumed the air, the royal barges were fitted out and the household packed up for the voyage to the south.

Hetepheres loved these excursions. Her restless spirit welcomed the changing scenery, the ease of their daily lives and lack of ceremonial constraint during the confinement of the trip. She especially loved Sneferu's prolonged proximity. There were no duties to call him from her side, and she took great pleasure in his nearness over the long lazy hours.

She leaned over the rail of the barge and shaded her eyes against the blinding glare of the sun and water. Storks waded near the shore or stood motionless, one leg pulled up under their bodies. Ibises waded up and down in the mud of the riverbank, moving their long curved bills impatiently from side to side in search of food. Spoonbills snapped at small crabs, threw them in the air to twirl them around for easier swallowing. Great clouds of river birds circled overhead to start their mysterious journeys northward to the open sea. A herd of gazelle had descended to the river's edge to drink and now were jostling one another for the best position. Behind the brilliant band of water, a narrow strip of vegetation wound its way, like green cloth wraps around a body, following each bend and turn as far as the eye could see. Thickets of reed and papyrus alternated with fields of wheat, barley, and millet, their tender shoots a delicate green.

Everywhere near the little villages, with their mud-brick and thatch-and-wattle houses, men and women were at work. A group of women, slim and graceful with the flowing robes of the desert folk, walked along the bank, rush baskets filled to overfilling on their heads. They stood and stared as the ornate barges pulled by, obviously too ignorant to realize who they were looking at. A short distance away, a young boy herded goats past an ancient creaking waterwheel pulled by a camel and a donkey. Just past the village, at a fork in the road, a group of four camels, heavily laden with bales of rushes, stood while their masters conferred or argued. The camels grew restless; one of them threw his head back and bellowed, spraying the nearest bystanders with spittle, the sound floating to Hetepheres over the rhythmic slapping of the oars.

Beyond the village, with its fields and orchards, stretched the desert, rolling endlessly toward sunset and sunrise. The sand was like a living thing, it moved and sighed in the breeze, it glowed with hues of the most delicate pale shell to brilliant gold to deep rust, turning from pink to soft purple to slate in the crevices and folds, where the sun's rays did not reach. Hetepheres thought that no effort of man could possibly achieve such beauty of colors, such delicacy of shading. Truly this was the land of the gods, the center of the world, lovelier and richer than any other place.

The passage of years had been good to her. There was a softer quality to her face, assurance and authority to her movements. She was not pretty, but her eyes were bright with intelligence and alertness, and her cheeks were now rosy with the breeze. She was still slim, too slim perhaps, although she had borne four children: two girls, Henutsen and Meritites, after Khufu, and then another little boy who had not been named yet when he died of the swamp fever. She was with child again; indeed, she was a fertile field for her lord's labors, she thought with a smile. Although not heavy yet, she was—the gods be thanked—past her first few months, which inevitably made her ill and snappish.

The children had been left behind at the palace in Memphis, for it was deemed unhealthy for the little ones to travel such distances, except for Khufu, who approached his eighth year that spring.

How fortunate, Hetepheres mused, that it was Khufu who resembled her, while the little girls took after their father. A boy, after all, needed no handsomeness, especially one destined to be Pharaoh one day. Instead of looks, she had passed on to him her tenacity, her ambitious drive, her fierce will, and resourcefulness; *those*, she thought, *he'll thank me for one day.* She was well pleased with his agile mind, quick wit, his curiosity, and self-reliance. It even pleased her that he was smallish, thin, and olive-skinned, for in him, she saw a miniature of herself.

Someone stepped close and touched her arm. Hetepheres roused herself from her reverie; it was Sneferu. With some irritation—it always irritated him when she retreated into her own world—he reminded her that she should get ready. They would be arriving in Maidum within the hour.

"I am ready," she countered, looking down at her sandaled feet, her filmy gown of Nile-water blue delicately pleated under her breasts and secured with thin bands of gold.

Sneferu made a gesture of impatience. "You look like one of your servant girls! Your face is unpainted and your wig disheveled. Did you not bring one that is more befitting the occasion? After all, in their eyes, you are the Great Consort of the Living God, and you have come to visit them, not for a romp with the children. For the sake of Horus, give them something to look at! They expect to see you and I look like gods, or why else do you think they turn out in such numbers?"

Hetepheres sighed. Oh gods, why did he have to be so pompous and proper, so self-righteous, so always conscious of status and criticism? Why did he have this constant need for approval? He was Pharaoh; he was the Eye of Ra, the Horus-Falcon come down to earth. If he chose to appear unadorned or even with just a loincloth, who would dare to question him? She dropped her hands from the railing and turned to go—as she used to think of it with some irony—embellish herself.

At the landing place, the dignitaries of Maidum and of Dahshur were lined up to receive their master and mistress. Menkau-hor, their uncle, waited at the head of the delegation, a little round man, browned and wrinkled by the desert sun, with quick shrewd eyes, a great commanding hooked nose, and an almost toothless grin. Hetepheres had always liked this uncle, an outstandingly capable, though unprepossessing, gentleman and wise enough to allow himself to be witty and unpretentious. The Lord Sahure stood by his side, massive with self-importance, fleshy with good living, his round bald pate shining with perspiration, his soft beringed hands holding the folds of his robe. Evidently he had undertaken the arduous journey from the Fayyoum, anxious not to miss the opportunity to make his obeisance to his lord and benefactor. A young man in military uniform, handsome but stern-looking, stood stiffly off to the side, at the head of a detachment of soldiers.

The royal couple disembarked and, scantly shaded against the fierce glare of the desert sun by the umbrellas held over their heads, commenced to listen to the glowing phrases of welcome. Surreptitiously Hetepheres glanced around her. There stood Sneferu, impatiently shifting from foot to foot. Sweat ran down his cheeks in rivulets; every once in a while, the royal linen-bearer would step up and wipe his face and neck with a linen kerchief. It must be devilishly hot under that headdress he is wearing, Hetepheres thought, eyeing the white conical hedjet, crown of Upper Egypt. *Thank the gods*, she thought that after all, this was an informal family outing; he did not have to wear the deshret, the red cylindrical crown of Lower Egypt, as well. In fact, he could have dispensed with wearing a crown at all. *The fact is*, she thought sourly, *with Sneferu, there are no informal family outings; he is driven by the necessity to exhibit his royal authority unreservedly*.

Ever since he had led three expeditions—they really were not wars—into the deep south of Nubia and roundly beaten the tribes there, he fancied himself a warrior king in the fashion of the Great Djoser and their father, Huni, of blessed memory, or even that almost mythical figure the Divine Narmer who was supposed to have united the Two Lands in the distant, distant past. As a warrior, he greatly favored the hedjet, symbol of the warrior tribes of Upper Egypt, over the red deshret crown of the delta cities. Exactly like a little boy, Hetepheres smiled inwardly.

Letting her attention wander from her husband to Sahure, who had just stepped forward to commence his homage, she caught some of his lofty phrases. "Great and omnipotent Horus-King, glorious sun of Ra over Egypt" and "thrice-blessed consort of the Living God, fertile mistress of Creation." She sighed. Gods, she had heard all this so often; was there really a time in her life when she had yearned for this, when she could not hear it often enough? Why can't they get on with it? Can't they see that we are hot and tired? Can't they understand that I am with child, and my back is hurting? What business of mine is it to listen to this pompous fat priest who is in love with the tiresome sound of his own voice? Her eyebrows went up a fraction, the corners of her mouth down, while she tried to concentrate upon the heavy gold chain and pendant hanging from the man's neck, which he alternately clasped and unclasped with the fervor of his oratory.

She felt someone watching her, and her eyes searched the crowd. There, it was that young soldier, and—how dare he—he was looking at her boldly and openly. Their eyes met, hers cool now, disdainful and impersonal, his searching and weighing her. Then a fleeting shadow of a smile passed over his face. He glanced at Sahure and then back to her. The smile widened to a grin, accompanied by a gesture almost of apology. Hetepheres could not help herself, she had to smile back at him. *I like him*, she thought, *he is impudent and quick, and I like him a lot.*

She liked him sufficiently to inquire about him after the reception. She was told that his name was Merneptah, that he commanded the local garrison, and that he was the son of the court scribe, Herihor, master of the royal archives, by one of his minor wives.

*****

"Merneptah." The old Queen Mother's shrunken lips mouthed the word soundlessly. "Merneptah, oh, how I loved your laughing eyes, your stern face, the set of your head on your shoulders, the sound of your voice, the pressure of your lips upon mine...Was that how it started? At Maidum, standing under the desert sun with the desert sand under my feet? No, it started much later, for I did not see you then for a long time. Or maybe it started before, when Sneferu took Merit into his harem? Sneferu, who still had the power to please me or hurt me..."

Someone leaned over the dying woman—one of the court physicians. He offered her a drink from a goblet by the bed stand. The strong wine slopped over and dribbled down the ancient chin, unnoticed. The Queen Mother's breathing was a harsh rasp filling the air of the bedchamber. The physician placed his palm under the shriveled breast. Only moments later, he withdrew it, backed away, and raised his shoulders. "Not much longer, I believe," he murmured.

*****

Sneferu had brought Merit home to Memphis from the fourth of his military campaigns into the south. He brought her back with him and installed her in the royal harem. The daughter of some rough and plain local village chief around Edfu, she was an insignificant person in her own right, Hetepheres judged, but she had pretty round breasts, large moist black eyes with a constant expression of wonder and admiration in them and gleaming white teeth. Long ago, Hetepheres had tried to make her peace on the subject of the royal harem, even though it stung her pride and self-esteem, but the same pride and self-esteem would not allow her to show the hurt. Sneferu's harem, after all, had existed long before her marriage, even before his accession to the throne of their father, Huni. According to custom, when a prince of the blood, especially the future Pharaoh, left his childhood and moved out of his mother's circle to establish his own household, he was entitled to maintain his own selection of concubines and even minor wives in the royal harem. Until now, such women had been fleeting episodes in Sneferu' life, no more than convenient subjects for his nightly visits and to relieve his urges. She had invariably and always been the constant in his life.

When Merit entered their lives, Hetepheres was pregnant again, having lost their fifth child when she slipped and fell while carrying it. She had been ill for a long time, and when she recovered, thinner than ever, the bloom of youth had been wiped from her face. She had been counselled against another pregnancy by the royal midwives and physicians but was happy and hopeful for a boy child after she got pregnant again. She had not minded Merit so much at first, for during her pregnancies, her husband was in the habit of seeking his diversions elsewhere.

Merit, however, became more than an episode. She was a tiny placid girl of little spirit and less intelligence to whom the gods had simply seen fit to assign the most luminous of dark eyes, the longest lashes lying gently on her cheeks, the most generous of mouths, and the sweetest of smiles. Her awe and admiration of Sneferu were boundless, and Hetepheres had no reason to suspect pretense since Merit did not have sufficient mental resources to successfully carry out a long-term subterfuge. Her gentle bovine eyes followed him with adoration, and she flushed every time he addressed her. She was the most perfect foil for a man's vanity, a constant affirmation of his virility, a living breathing manifestation of his power. What man would be able to resist such a person?

Hetepheres grew to detest her. Not because she was a threat—the privilege of her birth and marriage protected her from that—but because the man on whom she had, since childhood, lavished all the attributes of divinity, whom she had clothed with such nobility of spirit and loftiness of mind had, after all, tuned out to be just an ordinary mortal who could be chained to such a one as this—low-spirited and trivial. Thus did Merit become the living symbol of her slowly unfolding sense of disillusionment.

Only through slow bitter months did Hetepheres come to terms with her feelings. Layer upon layer, like the skin of an onion, she peeled away her image of Sneferu from the real person. What remained was a young man approaching his middle years, tall, handsome, and vigorous still, his jawline rounded from good living, clothed in the overpowering aura of majesty and command. But beneath the liquid black eyes, she detected shallowness and vanity, around the full curving lips, petulance. No longer the invincible solicitous brother her child's mind had created, no longer the divine lover of her young womanhood, he was but a slightly balding man given to fleshiness and a double chin, who could be kind and generous in his pleasure but also vicious and vindictive when opposed.

"I will not allow you to slight Merit in public," he screamed at her, pacing up and down in her veranda in agitation. "How dare you look through her as though she were no better than an insect? Has she ever hurt you to merit such treatment at your hands? Has she ever been anything but obedient to you? No, on the contrary, she is forever asking me why you hate her so! And what am I to tell her? She has told me repeatedly, and with humility, how much she wishes to become your friend." He advanced on her angrily. "Your friend! But does she ever find friendship in you or even a friendly word? No, I tell you, and I will not stand for it! I want harmony and peace in my house. In the days of our mother, she had the grace to accept things as they were and not to feel threatened in the position which she held and which was unalterably hers. She created harmony and even friendships wherever she could. But not you, of course, that could never happen! I tell you, I will not stand for this any longer!" He drew a quivering breath and stopped, momentarily at a loss for words.

Hetepheres's chin went up a fraction. "I am not accustomed to being solicited or selected for friendship, my lord," she said quietly. "The friends I have, I seek myself. I am queen, I am the consort, your wife and sister and mother of your children, mother of the heir, but I am not this person's friend." Her face was pale, except for two red spots on her cheeks. "Besides," she added, "I am assured that the Lady Merit can find companionship elsewhere, more suited to her, ah, personality and interests."

"But she feels daily slighted by your behavior toward her. She is just a child, Hetepheres, and she feels lost and frightened here and out of her depth. You could help her and guide her and be an adviser to her."

"Be a mother to your concubine? Truly your passion has impaired your judgment, Sneferu! I have my children—your children—to be mother to. I have no intention to be anything but mistress to this—or to any other—such person you may wish to bring into this house, not mother nor sister nor any other such thing! Go away from me! Go!"

There was stillness, then she heard Sneferu heave a sigh, trying to calm himself. Slowly he walked over to her side and sat down heavily. She stood there in front of him, eyes flashing, breasts rising and falling rapidly. He looked up at her for a moment, searching her face, trying to gauge the depth of her distress. Then he caught both of her hands into his.

"Hetepheres, I entreat you, listen to me. All I desire is some measure of peace and tranquility. Merit makes me feel good, she is quiet and restful. She does not argue, she does not instigate, she does not manipulate. She is neither clever nor witty nor very entertaining, I am afraid, but rather like a placid lake into which I look and see myself reflected. Did it ever occur to you, sister, that I may need and enjoy the company of such a person? This—this undue harshness of yours is unbecoming a woman, women should be soft and pliable." He stopped, then went on ruefully "I am afraid, my dear, that you were never a very soothing presence, you know. Sometimes you are like a burr in one's sandal!"

Hetepheres pulled her hands away. "What you do with this girl, my brother, or where you do it is your affair. I have no right to meddle into it. But I will not now, nor knowingly in the future, have any association with her. Keep her, if you wish, wherever you would, for your word and your wish is law in this land. But do not keep her near me, I pray, nor force her upon me. I am Pharaoh's daughter, Pharaoh's sister, Pharaoh's wife, Pharaoh's mother. You may find something in common with her, but not I!"

Sneferu jumped up in anger. "Am I to be thwarted and crossed by you forever?" He stormed at her. "Am I to be worn to bits in this silly bickering? As you say, my word is law everywhere! Why not so under my own roof? Am I to be pulled and torn this way and that by a silly girl and an obstinate woman? By the gods, I mean to put a stop to it! I will have no more of this, hear? I will not tolerate it any longer!" And he turned and slammed out of her apartment.

He did put a stop to it too in a compromise sort of a fashion. He had a separate wing built for Merit, at the far opposite end of the women's courts. But all his attempts at appeasement failed, foundered, and broke on the rock of what he called Hetepheres's infernal obstinacy. In time, however, he began to tire of Merit's bland placidity and even commenced to spend more and more of his time in his wife's company.

Hetepheres, on her part, continued to ignore Merit's presence. After long reflection, she did, more or less, absolve Sneferu, though, because she realized that what he had said about her was true, and because she understood that, in all fairness, she could not reject him for failing to live up to the image of her youthful phantasy of him. Still this absolution left her sad and empty, like the sight of an old and damaged toy of one's childhood.

She attempted to find enjoyment in her children but found it difficult. By nature she was not a very motherly person, and little children wearied and irritated her. Khufu, to be sure, was growing up. He was seven by then, almost eight and almost a man, certainly a thoughtful mature boy for his age. Hetepheres had long quiet conversations with him, teaching him to appreciate the land that would become his one day, and to value its inhabitants who were all placed here by the gods for Pharaoh's service. She tried to teach him to curb his impatience and temperament and to act advisedly. But Khufu was increasingly called away from the women's quarters, and Hetepheres knew that the day was near when he would leave it, and her, permanently.

It was because of the children that she remembered the old reed basket, now gathering dust and sagging with age but still standing in the far corner of her bedchamber. It ill fitted the splendid room with its elegant furniture of ebony and gilt, yet Hetepheres had never allowed it to be removed.

On this day, the younger children were in her apartment, and while the twin toddlers Nefermaat and Kanefer slumbered peacefully, Henutsen and Meritites romped about, their piercing shrieks of glee rending the air. Nursing one of her nagging headaches, Hetepheres went in search of the ancient senet board which she recalled reposing in the gloomy depth of the basket. Maybe allowing the girls to play senet, a grown-up game, with her would quieten them somewhat, she thought.

She rummaged around in the basket, hallowed repository of childhood memories, and as her fingers touched an object or another, a gentle smile began to play about her lips. *What a wonderful balm the distance of years was,* she contemplated. *It allows us to forget the bitter, the awkward, and covers everything with a gentle golden mist.*

Then she touched something flat and cool, something which, by its weight had dropped to the very bottom of the container. As she groped for its edge to grasp and pull it out, its identity flashed through her mind a second before seeing it—Sennefer's gold palette. Hetepheres paled, felt the blood drain from her heart. She struggled for composure and, regaining it to some extent, dropped the palette back into the basket and forced herself to go and spend the remainder of the afternoon playing with her daughters.

That night, after quiet had descended upon the queen's apartment, Hetepheres went back to the basket. Dropping to her knees in front of it, she withdrew the palette and held it in her palms. In the dark room, moonlight glinted on its pale surface. Again, like on the eve of her wedding so many years ago, her fingers traced the design. She stared, her face turned to the pale oblong of the window, tears flowing unchecked down her cheeks, while she rocked back and forth, and misery shook her body. She wept for Sennefer's lost youth, for the terrible image of her mutilated body; she wept for Sneferu, deemed unworthy now of such sacrifice. But most of all, she wept for the girl she had been, able to do this—this—oh, horrible confrontation with herself! And did she indeed do it? And do it deliberately? Or is it all a chimera? And for what? For what?

Hours may have passed, or perhaps only minutes. She was oblivious to time. Finally she roused herself, gently laid the palette back in its crypt, and dashed some cold water on her face. *We all have our private monsters to grapple with,* she reminded herself, *and only we and the gods know where they lurk in the depths of our souls. Bury them, bury them with the dead, for otherwise they will rise up and devour us at the moment least expected!*

There are periods of lightness and joy in life, when laughter comes easily and one's step is light, when days flow by pleasantly, and success is effortless. Then again, there are the dark days of terror and sorrow, of anguish and remorse and despair, when events close in, and no path of escape appears to the mind's eye. This was such a time now for Hetepheres. Her apparent inability to come to terms with the real person of her husband, her gnawing jealousy and disappointment, all now coupled themselves to her mounting feelings of guilt and self-reproach. It was no use to tell herself that in all likelihood, she would not have been able to save her sister. Inevitably the next thought attaching itself to the first one was, but did she indeed want to save her, and even if she would have acted immediately—and there was no avoiding this self-reproach. She lost interest in all the things she had relished until now, her part in statecraft and governance, plans for her own House of Eternity, the plans for new gardens for their summer palace in Abydos—all were dropped as she turned from them to her solitude, her meditations.

Sneferu hardly noticed. He was engaged in plans for leading his army on another foray across the Eastern Sea. He was anxious to protect his extensive turquoise and copper mining operations in the mountains, on the sunrise side of the Eastern Sea, from the belligerent nomadic tribes.

"I cannot imagine that these would be Sinai nomads supported by some others even farther north and east from the mountain regions of the Assyrians," he explained to Hetepheres when he stopped by at her apartment before departure. "There has been a lot of movement reported from there, a lot of movement down to the sea. They have become bolder and bolder lately. I should have put an end to them before, I suppose, but I did consider them to be only a nuisance up to now. But when they dare attack the royal mines and impede the transport of my goods, then that becomes another matter altogether! We simply must put a stop to them now before they become even more emboldened."

He frowned and threw himself onto a chair. He stretched out his legs and moodily contemplated the lacings of his sandals. Quiet enveloped the room. Then he looked up at Hetepheres and proceeded swiftly.

"There is another matter of concern. Isn't there always? You know, of course, that we have not paid yet for those last two shipments of cedarwood out of Byblos, don't you? It is absolutely essential that we have an uninterrupted flow of turquoise, and especially copper, from these Sinai mines. How would we be able to refurbish the army's weaponry without sufficient copper and, moreover, a guaranteed supply of it? If payment is not forthcoming soon, we can say farewell to our imports of wood from the Levant. And try as hard as possible, we cannot seem to grow those damn trees on our soil. As it is, I am told that the amount of wood brought in ought to be doubled, or even tripled, if I am to finish furnishing my House of Eternity on time. Also we need the turquoise, not only as payment for the wood but my architects tell me that the design and decoration of the interior chambers need the color derived from ground up and filtered turquoise rock. Lots of it! I swear, my dear, those thieves at Maidum must sell half, or more, of what I send them! Great Isis! Damn them all!"

Hetepheres watched him in silence. Presently Sneferu became aware of the quiet and raised his eyes to her, scanning her face.

"What is it? Say something!"

"What is there to say, husband? What can I say? You have a problem but not of the kind that I can help you with, can I?"

"No. I don't suppose you can." He growled speculatively. "Still you have been very out of sorts lately, haven't you?" He sat up straight and focused his attention on her. "What is it?" he repeated. "Are you pregnant, lady? Do you feel ill, Hetepheres?"

She shrugged. "No, not pregnant. I just feel—tired and listless, I suppose. It is nothing."

"Nothing? Nothing is just nothing when it concerns the body! In all my life, I have never known you to be tired and listless! Never! If the children give you trouble, for the love of Isis, get yourself more servants for them!" He halted, still examining her with a worried look, and then he got to his feet and walked over to her and grasped both of her shoulders.

"Hetepheres, are you ill? What ails you? This is not at all like you!"

Hetepheres extricated herself from his hands and forced a smile on her lips. "It is all right, dearest husband. I am fine. Do not concern yourself with it."

"Do not concern myself with it—do not concern myself with it? What do you mean? Of course I am concerned! You do not look well, and I see you have lost weight again. I'll have my physicians look at you, I am convinced they are better than the ones you women usually avail yourselves of. Perhaps you need a potion or a tonic to strengthen you. How can I leave you here alone unless I know you are well and able to carry on in my absence? You know I cannot trust anyone else! I shall want to have word from you daily on how you fare, hear?"

Hetepheres was genuinely touched by his concern. She ran her fingers over his face. "To consider that I am ever alone here is a great exaggeration, my dear. When you are absent, I practically have to shoo my ladies—and many of your gentlemen—out of my presence. None of them ever want to be accused of not paying enough attention to the queen! Please be at ease! I will send you daily messages, Sneferu, I promise. By the time you return, I shall be as good as new! You know that women have these passing little malaises of body and mood. They do not signify." She caught herself. I act and talk as I would to Meritites or to Henutsen, she thought. Yet her words apparently calmed him.

"Well, I shall be off then, within the hour. Will you look in on the doings at the weighing house while I am gone, my dear? We have a new overseer there, who is well recommended but untried. I want no shortchanging when grains are weighed out. Especially not when it is grain destined to go on sale to the population. Things are hard enough for them, anyway. As far as this overseer is concerned, I am sure the scribes would not risk their positions to report him, were there anything to report. Should this fellow turn out to be a scoundrel, deal with him accordingly in my absence do."

He leaned toward her and kissed her pale cheeks and her mouth. "Farewell, sister, may the gods be merciful to you and preserve you. Keep well!"

Hetepheres's arms went around his neck. She drew him to herself and rested her head on his shoulder. Then embarrassed by her sudden softening, she commenced to fuss with his neck chain, adjusting the broad pectoral almost covering his breast. "The gods preserve you, father of my children," she murmured. "May they stay the hand that would be raised against you and the arrow that would smite you! May you and your land prosper together all the days of your life. Farewell!"

Briskly Sneferu walked to the entrance. In the last second, he hesitated and, reminded of something, called back to his wife. "You know, Hetepheres, don't you, that I have called a new detachment of soldiers to Memphis? They are here to replace the guards I am taking with me. If you should need anything in the way of assistance or service, turn to their commander. You will find him a very capable and loyal fellow. His name is Merneptah."

And he was gone out of the room.

*****

Merneptah? What was so familiar about that name? She had encountered so many names during the past nine years of her life; it was difficult to sort out one from the other. Then in her mind's eye, unexpectedly, there arose a memory: the picture of a young woman standing, back aching from standing too long, bored by long-winded talk, and made sleepy by the desert heat; of a serious young soldier, of a quick flash of kinship and understanding, like lightning, across the gulf of rank and custom separating them. A playful moment it was, surely nothing more than that, yet—yet—why did the remembrance bring warmth to her heart and softness to her cheeks?

For days following Sneferu's departure, she played with the idea of seeking out this man. Like a child, she devised elaborate plans, only to reject them again. Then again she chided herself, what business of hers was this person? Just because of the recollection of what was no more than a fanciful notion, was she going to waste her precious time on an unknown underling, the son of a scribe? She plotted, she hesitated, she vacillated, she reasoned, she ridiculed herself, then again she daydreamed. In the midst of talking or listening to someone, her mind would wander so that not once, not twice, she had to call herself back to the present.

Then unexpectedly, her indecision was resolved for her. Sneferu had recently commissioned the master of the royal archives to execute a biography of their august father, the Divine Pharaoh Huni.

He had followed progress of the work with his customary dedication to detail that he gave to all his widespread projects and was most anxious for the work's timely completion. Recalling this now, Hetepheres decided to surprise and please him with an account of the work and, one day, made her way to the library housed in a large and airy building on the palace grounds.

Her visit had been unannounced and, therefore, no reception or ceremony expected. Before entering, she had a moment's glimpse into the normal work rhythm of this curious place: scribes bending over scrolls of papyrus, brushes at the ready, others working on smallish clay tablets into which slowly, and with great care, they proceeded to etch word symbols. Still others were crouching on the ground over crocks of pigments to be ground. Bits and fragments of papyrus littered the paint-spattered stones. Here two men were consulting over a scroll by a casement, there another one was reaching high to fill tall shelves with a stack of scrolls under his arm.

Suddenly all this activity came to a halt. One of the scribes had glanced at the entrance and recognized the royal retainers standing there, next to a now-empty litter with the royal emblem on it. There in their midst stood a small slight woman wearing a heavy wig encircled by a gold uraeus diadem, an ornately bejeweled collar, and a light pleated dress the color of the desert's soft blue gray at sunset. Recognition dawned; the man called out to his companions and threw himself to the ground.

One by one, brushes were laid aside, mortars, pestles, and chisels abandoned as men looked up from their work, rose, and prostrated themselves. The one holding the scrolls under his arm turned, his eyes falling on Hetepheres, then he too fell to his knees, then to his face, the scrolls scattering on the floor and rolling away from where he had stood.

An elderly man was now advancing toward Hetepheres, weaving his way around tables, baskets, and containers, until he came face-to-face with her. His eyes were restrained but questioning, alive with intelligence, a genuinely warm and happy smile on his lips. He bowed deeply, then knelt, touching his forehead to the stones.

Hetepheres looked down on him, suddenly recognizing the son's smile on the father's features.

"Arise and be at ease," she said kindly, for she decided that she liked this old man a great deal. "I am persuaded to think that you must be the master of our libraries and of my lord husband's archives, are you not?"

"The very same, divine lady, and your insignificant servant, Heri-hor by name. Will you not enter and grace us with the radiance of your presence?" And standing aside, he gestured her in gravely.

"I have come to look at the progress of your work, Master Heri-hor, to both satisfy my curiosity as well as my dear husband's impatience."

Heri-hor bowed again. "It is my honor, Divine Mistress. If you but follow me to my chamber in the back of this workshop, I shall deem myself to be the most fortunate of your servants to explain to you how and how far we have progressed in this project so well blessed by the gods. Please! This way!" And bowing repeatedly, he preceded her across the vast room to his own cubicle. Most of the space there was occupied by an enormous table on which rested piles and piles of papyrus rolls and stacks of clay tablets.

Heri-hor quickly swept some of the clutter to a corner of the table, then pulled out the only armchair in the room for his queen. Hetepheres seated herself, while Heri-hor began his explanations. Her eyes roamed around in open curiosity. They ran along the high walls entirely covered with pigeonhole-like openings accommodating more and more rolls: documents, deeds, accounting and inventory lists, death registers, battle accounts—all things that had become familiar to her over the years. In addition to those, as Master Heri-hor quickly explained, there were sections of shelving assigned also to books: poems, legal, medical, historical, geographic, biographic, and theological texts, all the accumulation of data for the world's greatest most well-ordered and civilized nation.

Then standing in the semidarkness of the small room's corner, half-concealed by the heavy draperies which divided the master's office from the gigantic vault beyond, where finished documents were stored, her glance detected the figure of a man. A tall soldier, she could tell by the uniform and the weapons that were laid on the floor by his feet, leaning against the wall with his arms across his chest. Although his face was in the shadows, Hetepheres knew instantly who he was.

The figure moved, stepped forward, and knelt before her, head bowed in obeisance. Heri-hor, only now recalling the man's presence, made a flustered gesture of apology and introduction. "Forgive me, Shining Magnificence! My son, who has just come to visit his old father. He shall leave immediately."

Hetepheres smiled, shook her head, and leaned forward. "By no means, old master. I am indeed already acquainted with him. His name is Merneptah, and he currently commands the Memphis garrison."

Merneptah raised his head and looked boldly up at her. "Gracious consort and sister of Horus, you do me more honor than I deserve." He bowed his head again, then rose to his feet, turning to his father. "Our Divine Mistress, the Lady Hetepheres, and I met once before, many years ago, in Maidum. Not ever would I have presumed to hope that she would remember this least of her servants."

"I have not forgotten. You were once concerned that I weary of a long oratory. We shared a passing moment of mirth over that oratory. Was that not so?"

"Truly it was, Majesty. Your memory merits admiration, like every aspect of your gracious person." And an impish glean appeared in his eyes.

Hetepheres's smile broadened. "No, Commander," she confessed. "Only on certain occasions."

"Then I bless the occasion which has brought me such honor and joy! I shall make a gift and do devotions at the altar of Nephthys, patroness of the desert, in grateful remembrance."

Hetepheres shook her head. "Commander, I must make a confession, lest your admiration of my memory carries you into greater raptures. Before departing, my lord husband did inform me of the change of palace guards to occur during his absence."

Heri-hor cast an anxious and wondering glance from one face to the other. These two, it passed through his mind, they talk as though they were alone together. In some confusion, he cleared his throat.

"If your august magnificence would allow me, I shall endeavor to enlighten you on our work here," he commenced, adding rapidly, "and also concerning the progress of the life history of our long lamented great and glorious god, the Pharaoh Huni, whose memory shall be blessed forever." He took some scrolls off a nearby shelf, and one by one, spread them out in front of Hetepheres. "First of all, with your gracious consent, Divine Consort of the Living God, allow me to explain the process whereby the materials needed for our work, namely the precise documents and descriptions of his deeds on the one hand, and on the other, the sheets of papyrus and the pots of color base are either acquired, collected, verified before…"

His voice droned on, while his agile fingers pointed first to this, then to that item. The room was closed and warm, and a feeling of dreamlike somnolence, almost of unreality, descended upon Hetepheres. She tried to concentrate but could not. All her awareness seemed to be centered upon the figure next to her. Without looking, she was aware of his posture, the expression on his face—so grave and attentive yet able to smile so readily, his strong hands, holding back the folds of his cloak as he leaned toward the table, and his sandaled feet, somewhat worn and dusty now. *He had probably come here on foot, stamping through the dust of the streets to visit his old father*, she thought, *for soldiers, even commanders, were not paid richly*. There was a deeply gouged scar on his calf; inexplicably she longed to extent her hand to touch it.

In a trance, she rose in response to Heri-hor's invitation, and the three of them walked through the storage vaults. She listened, she nodded, she questioned, hardly knowing to what she was responding. When they reached the outer workshop again, she remembered her escorts and litter-bearers, still standing at the entry. On an impulse, she beckoned to their leader.

"Commander Merneptah will have the goodness to accompany me. I have news to receive from him and other matters to discuss. Go, you may leave." Then she turned to Merneptah with a questioning look. "Commander, will you oblige me? I am persuaded that you may have more detailed news about the progress of my lord husband's warfare. The messages I receive from him are long on solicitousness but scant on detail of the events that occur there. Perhaps his scribes think such information too indelicate for a woman's ears. I am anxious to hear all you can tell me."

Merneptah's eyes rested on her. His face was inscrutable. Wordlessly he bowed. Later as they walked from table to table, she repeatedly felt his speculative glance questioning her.

Finally she grew restless and weary and made her farewells, the formal phrases of royal favor flowing from her lips of long habit. Then they were outside, she and her quiet escort. The air from the river was sweet and fresh. The well-kept paths to the main building of the palace wound along hedges and beds of flowers, all giving off their sweet scent in the evening breeze. The sun had moved to the west across the river, toward Saqqara's Place of the Dead, streaking the sky with bands of gold and pink and dusky blue. Between the fronds of the palms, the river glinted with pale metallic sheen, its surface dotted with homeward bound watercraft. Birds were arguing and screeching noisily in the trees as they settled for the night, and from the kitchens far away behind the palace, a woman's high-pitched voice shrilled, "Sinuhe! Si-nuhe!" Probably a servant girl from the kitchens, Hetepheres thought, calling for a water-bearer.

They walked wordlessly, Merneptah a few deferential paces behind his queen, until Hetepheres turned and motioned to him. "Come closer, Commander, for I shall get a crick in my neck from talking to you over my shoulder! So. What news have you of my husband?"

High overhead, a falcon wheeled and circled, suddenly emitting a fierce shriek. Merneptah looked up and smiled. "Your lord husband, my master, seems to command me." Then he sobered. "All is well with him, he is victorious."

Hetepheres tossed her head impatiently. "This I know, Commander, from his messages. But I would know this, was his victory at great cost? With many lives lost? Who are these enemy tribes, anyway? Whence did they come? How do they do battle? With what kinds of weapons? How was my lord's victory won?"

Quite irreverently, Merneptah burst out in laugher. "Your gracious pardon, my lady, forgive me! How can I answer all your questions when they cascade over me like water spilling over a cataract? You see, I know little more than you do, magnificence. But I do know that the king, my master, is well and unharmed in any way, although there were heavy losses. There is also illness in the camp of—well, of…" He hesitated, embarrassed and at a loss for words. "Of an unpleasant and prostrating nature, owing to the fetid waters of the Eastern Desert and the food, which is difficult to preserve and therefore spoils too easily in the heat.

"The foreigners are gross and stinking tribesmen who originate from the wild mountains far to the east of the Eastern Sea, rough-hewn, coarse, and thieving but greedy and, because of that, fierce fighters. They have become bold and ever bolder to enter into the very confines of our sacred land. What weapons they use, gracious Queen, I have no knowledge of, but it is evident that they cannot be superior to ours. I think our great lord's victory was inevitable, though not easily won. I believe he shall soon return in victory and glory, though I hear he plans to move south first. He means to crush those of the retreating tribes who have fled in that direction."

Hetepheres did not reply. They walked on, listening to the gravel crunch under their feet. Hetepheres stumbled slightly and felt his warm hand under her elbow, steadying her. This gesture in itself, she thought, was sacrilegious and never to be done. Men have died for less, she thought, and then, that the touch of a hand had never been so meltingly sweet. She lowered her head and looked down at the path ahead of her, afraid now to break the silence, almost afraid to breathe.

Merneptah had begun to speak again, in a voice as calm and impersonal as before. "When you came ashore that day at Maidum and had to walk across that narrow board laid between ship and shore, I was afraid for you that you should stumble and hurt yourself. No one dared extend a hand to you to help. Did they believe your divinity would scorn assistance or that you were incapable of human frailty? They saw only the queen, splendid and forbidding, but I saw you. Your frailty, your weariness, your impatience, and your humor—your humanity. And I also saw the strength and the tenderness, the concern as you looked at your husband. I felt your ka, your soul, and recognized it. From that day on, your image has never left me for an hour. I may not speak to you like this, I know. Call your guards and have done with me as you wish, but your image will be with me in the afterlife and my ka with you in all eternity."

There was a roar in Hetepheres's ears, like the breaking of waves after a storm. She listened with disbelief, sensing the world slowly turn upon itself. Reality suspended, she could not have told if she was dreaming or awake. She walked on mechanically, setting one foot in front of the other. When she looked up, they were in front of the steps leading to her private verandah. She found it impossible to say how she got there.

She caught one of the pillars supporting the flat roof, felt its roughness under her palm. The roughness felt real; it validated her reality. She leaned her forehead against it, then with a slow effort of will, she turned around. Merneptah stood three paces away from her, doggedly staring at the stone flags under his feet. Beneath his bronzed skin, she saw his deathly pallor, the working of the muscles of his jaw.

"Merneptah," Hetepheres said softly. He glanced up and made a hasty motion toward her, but she warded him off with an urgent almost imperceptible gesture of her hand, her head. She turned and fled into the building.

*****

For two days, Hetepheres did battle with her thoughts, her desires. On the third day, she laid her plans. That night, after the palace had quieted, after the moon had risen, and a freshening wind was pushing the clouds across the sky, a curtained litter made its way through the royal gardens and, from there, along the bank of the river, toward the edge of town. The litter-bearers moved noiselessly on bare feet. They were Hetepheres's most trusted, most loyal servants, whose devotion to her, she knew, was boundless and unquestioning.

Hetepheres had left guards at her apartment too. They were not to admit anyone; she was feeling ill and indisposed. Indeed, she was feeling ill; her heart thundered and her hands shook. She could hardly breathe in the airlessness of the litter. What was she doing here, merciful gods? The queen of the realm, stealing herself through hidden byways, across the stench and filth of unknown alleys, where mangy dogs slept next to urine-stinking puddles and human excrement, or stood, scratching their flea-bitten hides; stealing herself in secrecy to a man's house like some loathsome tramp, like a prostitute? She shrank deeper into the shadows of the cushions and closed her eyes, trying to exorcise her shame.

The litter halted and was lowered to the ground. They must have arrived. Cautiously Hetepheres lifted the curtains and saw the garrison grounds, rows of tentlike mud-brick huts half-visible by the light of scattered campfires, and a spear-throw away, a building of greater permanence, thatch roofed and surrounded by a fence. Light shone through a gap in the doorway and illuminated a narrow strip of ground in front of the entrance. One of her men was going in that direction. She saw him stop and briefly talk to the guard standing in the strip of light. The guard nodded his head, then raised his palm in the unequivocal gesture of taking a bribe. He nodded again and, with a brief glance toward the litter, walked off in the direction of the nearest campfire.

He thinks I am a town whore come to visit his commander, Hetepheres thought, her face aflame, wanting nothing as much as to turn and flee. But the time for hesitation was past. Silently she slipped out of the litter and walked to the entrance. She stopped there and, lifting the draperies, leaned weakly against the doorpost, her pulse beating in her throat and her knees threatening to give way under her.

The room inside appeared to be half office, half living quarter, with rush mats on the beaten earth floor and some rough-hewn benches against one wall, weapons, shields, and armor on pegs on the opposite. A torch burned, illuminating most of the interior, except for the darkened corners.

Hetepheres stood irresolutely, not quite knowing what to do next, when she heard hurried footsteps and saw a man appear from some inner chamber into the torchlight. The man strode purposefully to a bench and, bending over it, began to sift through a stack of papyrus scrolls lying there. He wore nothing but sandals and a short white linen kilt wrapped about his hip. The light of the torch touched the muscles of his arms and back.

A sudden brief draft from the open doorway caused the flame to sway, and the man's hands stopped in his work. He straightened and glanced toward the door. Frowning, he advanced, then halted abruptly. It was Merneptah.

Hetepheres watched the play of emotions on his face, wariness giving way to surprise, then incredulity, and finally consternation. In two quick strides, he reached her, caught her hands, and drew her inside. He went back to the entrance and peered out into the darkness, to see if anyone watched, before dropping the draperies into place. Weakly Hetepheres allowed herself to be led to a chair and sank down on it gratefully.

"My lady," Merneptah murmured, "my queen…"

The tears began to course down Hetepheres's cheeks, finally giving her release from all the nameless emotions of the past days, from desire, tension, shame, and fear. "No-no," she stammered, her voice catching on a sob, "no, do not call me that, not your queen, not your queen…" She covered her face with her hands and then looked up. "I had to…I could not just let life go by without—without…and I could not let you endanger yourself to—to…don't you see, you couldn't…you must not have…I had to… I had to be one to act…" she stammered.

Merneptah knelt on the floor in front of her. Simply he took her face and kissed her eyes, her mouth, her forehead. "Hetepheres," he whispered, his voice rough with emotion, and then again, "Hetepheres". His arms went around her, and he strained her to him, rocking her gently and tenderly, like a child, stroking her hair, his cheek against hers. He unclasped her cloak, rose, and laid it carefully down on the bench. He only hesitated for a second before turning back to her.

Never had Hetepheres seen so much love, so much devotion, gratitude, and passion on a face as now. She reached for his hands extended to her and stood up, swaying slightly toward him. Neither of them spoke. Slowly, obeying more the command of his body than that of her mind, she allowed herself to be led into the inner room.

Inside Merneptah released her and stepped back to look at her long and ardently. "I cannot yet believe it"—he breathed—"that you would come, that you are here." And with a sudden laugh, he gathered her into his arms, lifting her off the ground to swing her around until she smiled too. Kicking her feet and drumming her fists against his shoulder, she begged to be put down again. But he only shook his head.

"Oh, my own love, have you not ever been young? Do you not feel young again, now? Did you not ever laugh and play and romp? Were you always so solemn, so dutifully grave? I want to see you laugh and sing, to be young and forget the world and yourself. At least for a little while, my heart! I want to see your cheeks glow and your eyes sparkle! Oh! I want to see you as happy as I am now!" And his eyes sobered again and filled with tenderness. "Oh, Hetepheres, my queen and my love, I want to serve you and love you all the days of my life! And if that life be short but glorified by your love, with your mind and body next to mine, is that not much greater than a long lifetime of solemn loveless restraint?"

Those days, those weeks, became the most incredibly felt magical time in Hetepheres's life. Her thoughts, her mind, her body, her whole being was centered in Merneptah. How could she have known, how could she have ever dreamt that love would be like this, this sweetness and agony, this joy and pain all at the same time? When he touched her, her heart turned over, and her whole body seemed to melt. When she heard his voice, looked at his body, she was consumed with desire. He had aroused passions in her she never suspected to possess nor even that they existed. Her husband, her children, her accustomed life, all disappeared into insignificance.

Reality became Merneptah's tender endearments, his laughter and gaiety, the look of desire in his eyes, his caresses in the heat of their loving, the feverishly whispered words in the shelter of his arms.

Reality was Merneptah's presence, lying next to her, sated, and made somnolent with lovemaking, or—oh, to have such power over someone—aroused and passionate from her touch, her kisses.

In Merneptah's love, Hetepheres felt totally secure for the first time in her life. Much later on, she would find it incomprehensible that she should have had no fear of discovery, no sense of apprehension. So wrapped up was she in loving and being loved, so much did all her emotions telescope into those hours spent with Merneptah that all other aspects and events of her life became secondary.

She lost her sense of guilt and shame. With her love for Merneptah, she gave the truest, the purest, the most selfless and generous part of her being, unadorned by subterfuge, unembellished by pretense or ambition. How could such feelings become the cause for shame or remorse? Although she still followed the dictates of prudent caution, never ventured to meet him in daylight and took the same pains to hide her nightly visits as on the first night, she did not do so out of fear. Rather so precious had those hours in Merneptah's company become that she desperately wanted to keep this part of her life untouched by her surroundings, by her normal daily existence. Like the collector guarding his treasures, like the miser hiding his wealth, she sheltered this sanctuary of her life from intrusion and prying.

For Merneptah did become her true sanctuary, not only the joy of her body, the answer to her desires. He became the only person in her life to whom, in the darkness of the night, she made halting whispered confession of her sister's death. She gave him the gift and burden of her guilt, expecting that he would draw away from her in revulsion. But he did not—oh, unimaginable wonder—he did not recoil and turn away. Even then, sinful and fallen mortal that she was, no longer a living goddess, he continued to love her.

He listened gravely, not interrupting once. When Hetepheres had finished, there were tears and pity in his eyes, and he gathered her to himself. "My poor darling," he whispered sadly, "to have been so young and saddled with such vehemence of feeling. To have carried this dreadful secret, this poison, with you for so many years and never have received absolution!"

"Merneptah, I do not deserve absolution. She was my sister!"

"No? Everyone deserves absolution. We are all weak and sinning mortals. Does your torturing yourself bring life back to Sennefer? Is a twenty-five-year-old woman responsible for what a sixteen-year-old girl did, blinded by infatuation and jealousy? Could you have saved her then? Can you tell? Can you even remember? Can you admit to yourself more than the sins of weakness and hesitation? And, my dearest love, even if you would have acted immediately, could you be assured of success? Or would you, more than likely, have died with your sister, causing the added grief and consternation of losing two young royal women?"

"Merneptah! The passing of the years and my growing older does not erase the guilt. The deed was done."

"Yes, it was done. And it cannot be undone. All your self-reproaches will not alter that. Do you think others have not sinned? Do you believe yourself to be above mortal failings? Truly your greatest sin then is your excess of pride. Look to the heavens, into the seas, to the stars. All of our gods, when they had mortal forms, have sinned too! Look at yourself, a sister of the gods you may be, but in life, you wear a mortal body and are subject to mortal weaknesses and passions, as are we all. Were it not so, you would not be here, now, with me! Be done with the past. Close the door on it. All your remorse will not add one whit to the enrichment of your people, your land. That is where your duty lies. Your land needs you. Serve it instead of serving your guilt! Your husband needs you. He is a good and noble lord, a worthy warrior but often hasty in his decisions and unyielding in his anger. He needs a wife's understanding heart, needs to be tempered by your wisdom.

"And lest you think, my love, that the future is some distant far-off day, consider that the future that was yesterday is the now of tomorrow. Consider also that all our lives are short, not just your sister's. Once we complete the assignment the gods gave us, our life will end, one way or another. My life has almost carried me to that point—no, do not contradict me—but yours will still have many years of service ahead."

"You do not despise me, then? You will still love me in the future?"

"Hetepheres, whom I call my life, my sister, and my only love, the first time I spoke to you freely, I told you that I will always love you and you only. That love will last longer than my life, longer than the desert, the seas, and the mountains, for it will last forever in the world of the dead. And if the Lord God Anubis, as he weighs our guilt against a feather, will graciously allow it, then we will truly be together for all eternity. I do not love you because I think you pure and perfect, nor can I unlearn to love you because you are less. I love you for yourself, my dearest. Where could we humans find love in this world if we could only love the sinless, the perfect?"

How could she fail to love such a man as this? His words had healed her, renewed her strength and confidence. That he spoke the truth, she doubted not for a moment. Had she not also loved him long before she knew him, knew the kind of person he was?

On the day after her confession, she brought Sennefer's defaced palette to him. She gave it into his keeping as she had given him her most secret being. She felt whole and sound and free.

If she looked, moved, acted differently in her happiness, she was not conscious of it. Yet others saw it: the glow in her eyes, the softness of her mouth, the serenity of the brow. They saw it and wondered what had befallen their queen. Nor was she the exacting demanding mistress of the days past, whose mere presence could make those around her to move more quickly and act more advisedly.

They noticed, and the first murmurings of gossip, like the sighing of wind through open windows and doorways, ran through the palace.

Weeks passed. Two months, then another. Then suddenly two events occurred in rapid succession, each of which was destined to destroy the placid little cocoon the two lovers had spun for themselves.

The first of these happened on a sweltering hot night, when the full moon hung pale in the cloudless sky. Hetepheres had just alighted from her litter in front of Merneptah's house. She had thrown back the heavy cloak, with which she usually shielded her face and her body from prying eyes, because she had found the heat inside the close confines of the litter unbearable. She was in too much of a hurry to rearrange the folds of her covering before emerging. Too late—her eyes fell upon the familiar figure of one of the officers of the palace guard who had departed with the rest of his detachment to follow her husband. Too late, she saw the flash of recognition, consternation, then doubt on his face.

When she entered Merneptah's house, she was frightened and shaking. It took all of his powers of persuasion to calm her. How could that man think that the person he saw was his august queen? Of course he looked startled, startled by a prostitute's resemblance to the queen. Would she not have been similarly startled to see Sneferu's likeness among a group of townspeople? Hetepheres resembled her father. Was it not said of his glorious reign that he had an eye for female beauty? That untold numbers of women had drifted through the palace and the royal bedchamber? That he had sown his seed hither and yon? There could quite well be one or two young women in Memphis who bore a marked resemblance to the royal visage! Who in their right mind could envision the great Queen Hetepheres going abroad at night, traveling in a plain litter, wrapped in coarse brown cloth? No, she needed to put this worry out of her head and think only thoughts of happiness and love!

It was only too easy to be persuaded by him. In the end, she relaxed and let herself be lulled into security. But a gnawing sense of foreboding did steal into her heart, especially when she found out that the man had only been in the camp briefly, bringing a royal message, and that he had immediately returned, that he would see Sneferu and give him his report in a few days' time. Every so often, during the most unexpected moments of her days, she felt the chill of premonition.

The second event, though not sinister in itself, was nevertheless fraught with sadness and heartache and came as a shock. Among Sneferu's messages was one to her, telling her that he had arrived in Thebes. He intended to rest there and to rest his victorious but weary army. He wished to have his family near as soon as possible. Would Hetepheres commence all the preparations for travel and join him, together with the children, as soon as she could arrange it? He missed the children greatly and was sorely weary of camp life, the message said, and closed with some allusions to the emptiness of his life and his bed.

Hetepheres was stunned. Somehow she had managed to keep Sneferu out of her thoughts, out of her mind, and the last thing she expected was shortly to see him face-to-face. She could hardly curb her impatience until night came, until she could impart her grief to Merneptah. She realized that she was behaving badly, irrationally, that this day was bound to have arrived at any time. More than anything else, she now recognized how much she was dependent on Merneptah. He had become her strength. She who had always prided herself of not needing anyone! How could she let this happen to her? How could she, mother of five children, like a child, run to him with her hurts, her problems, her anxieties?

In a short few months' time, he had entered every part of her life. He had listened with consideration and understanding and had advised her thoughtfully and with humor. She had shared with him not only her past but her present worries as well: her aspirations for her son, the Pharaoh-to-be, her concerns about her daughters, her ambivalent feelings about Sneferu, her jealousies about his women, the joys and disappointments of her days, all this she had brought to him. And burdened him with it? Until now, Hetepheres had never considered that that might be exactly what she had been doing. She had felt freed and lighthearted, but was that not at Merneptah's expense? And what had she given him in return? Her love, to be true, but that was no more than what he had given her; and he had given her so much more!

Beyond the hours spent together, she still had her family, her country, her people, her position. What did Merneptah have other than herself for a few brief hours each day? His aging father? The prospect of a successful military career? But did that not preclude having a family, a wife, or at least a concubine, children, some kind of a home? Except for the very top layer of ranking officers, they had to accept an almost nomadic life from garrison to garrison. If he really distinguished himself—and lived—perhaps he could aspire to the local governorship of one of the nomes, or such, as the reward for a lifetime of service? And even all that, he was placing in jeopardy for her sake, for the privilege of loving her!

When she finally stood face-to-face with Merneptah, his arms around her, his mouth warm on hers, she was unable to tell him her news. For a little while longer, she wanted everything to be as before, carefree and untouched by the outside world. But her heart was heavy and her throat constricted with the misery of hurting him. She could not dissemble—to him, she never could; for he was too keenly attuned to her emotions, too much aware of every changing nuance of her features.

Merneptah waited until they entered his bedchamber, until she had removed her cloak, to ask her if aught was worrying her. Hetepheres threw her arms around his neck with such unexpected vehemence that it made him stagger. Gently he extricated himself from her embrace and, catching her shoulders with both hands, looked down on her with deep concern.

"Hetepheres, my sister, what ails you? You are trying to hide tears, don't you think you had better tell me?"

She tilted her head and laid her cheek against his hand. In the stillness of the night, in the quiet of that room, which had harbored their love, she wrenched the words from her heart.

"Oh, my heart," she whispered, "I have to leave you."

Merneptah did not move nor did he answer. The only indication he gave of having heard her was the sudden constriction of his fingers upon her shoulders. Then slowly and with deliberateness, he released her and stepped back from her.

"Your husband." It was a statement, not a question.

Hetepheres nodded in silent misery. Feeling the tears welling up and beginning to flow, she averted her face from his searching eyes. There was perfect silence. Then Merneptah turned and walked over to a table in the corner. He lifted a heavy earthenware wine jug and poured a cupful, brought the cup back to her.

"Drink this," he said, and it was not a request, "it will calm you."

Obediently she drank and gave the empty cup back to him. Her eyes followed him as he went to the table again, poured again, and downed it. When he returned, he pulled out a chair for her. Gratefully she sank down on it, while he seated himself on the ground at her feet. He reached for her hands and commenced to question her quietly.

"Has he found out?"

Hetepheres shook her head. "No, no, I cannot imagine. He is in Thebes."

"Has he sent for you?"

"And the children too."

"When?"

"Immediately. He—he says he is so lonesome." And she drew a shaky breath that ended in a sob.

"I do not doubt it," Merneptah murmured absently. He remained silent, apparently following his own thoughts. Then he rallied, sighed deeply, and began to talk to her earnestly.

"My beloved sister, we have always known that this day would arrive. We did not talk about it because it would have been too painful. Perhaps we did not even want to acknowledge it, but we knew, did we not? Now or later, at some time in our life together, we must look at it squarely and come to terms with it. With the fact that you are Great Wife and Pharaoh's Consort and mother to the next ruler, and that your life belongs there and not here. In that sense, you do belong to him. You two had grown up and been together since childhood. The love you bear for him may not be passionate like ours, but it is equally real, you cannot deny it. This—I have no claim on you. That I love you is my pain and my blessing but does not make my claim rightful. That you love me has been the greatest gift the gods could have bestowed upon me but cannot change the direction of our lives. We must be thankful for what fate has given us. For me, it is more than I would ever have dared to hope. For you, my dearest, perhaps it is too."

"Oh, Merneptah, how can I be grateful when I am losing you?"

"Hetepheres, my love and my life, you shall never lose me. I shall be with you always. Be certain of that!"

"But perhaps never to see you again! Never to talk to you again! Never to feel your love—"

Merneptah laid a finger on her lips. "Ssh, sister! Life's roads are tortuous. Who knows what paths they lead us on and where our paths shall cross again? You are only going away for a little while. Let us believe that we shall meet again soon thereafter. To contemplate a brief separation is sad but bearable. To face a lifelong farewell is monstrous, is intolerable. Think not of it!"

He rose and managed to smile. "Remember, all life is but a brief passage on our way to the gods. All our pain of today is tomorrow but a memory. Come, Hetepheres! Let us love one more time before we leave each other. Then let us pray, each one of us, to great Isis, and to Hathor too, to beg their mercies for us."

Hetepheres rose. Mutely she turned and presented her back to allow Merneptah to unfasten the clasp of her gold collar. She felt his warm hands on her neck, her shoulders, then, with unusual tenderness, slide down to her hips, indicating the direction of his desires. She closed her eyes, leaned her body against him, then turned in his arms. With infinite care, he lifted the collar from her, bent and kissed her shoulders and her breasts. She sighed, lifted herself upon her toes, and wound her arms about him. Burying her face in the curve of his neck, she felt herself lifted up and carried to the pillows piled high upon his bed.

Later, much later, as she lay next to him, with her head pillowed on his shoulder, she heard him speak again, not the disjointed cries and hoarse whispers of their lovemaking but softly now, and composedly, but with ineffable bitterness.

"To think of him where I am now is the most poisonous thought of all. I know I must yield because he is your husband and my lord, but I will need all my strength of will to do so."

Her sadness wound itself around her heart and choked her. She turned her head, searching for his lips. "I cannot go back to him, Merneptah, I cannot!" She moaned.

"You shall and you will—you must. We will have done with this crying and wailing! It is not worthy of either you or me. Tomorrow or the day after, you will leave, Hetepheres. May Horus guard you and Ptah guide you, and if it be so, may he safely guide you back, even if not into my arms, at least before the sight of my eyes. That shall have to suffice then."

"Can you not accompany me?"

"No, dearest, I cannot, for no such orders were brought to me from my master who is your husband. Nor should I, it is too dangerous for both. Especially for you because you, the queen, are always more closely watched than I am. For even if we were silent and not to move a limb, our eyes would speak for us clearly enough for everyone to see. I have brought you enough of danger as it is."

"Why? The danger is yours, not mine. Who would dare lift his voice against the queen? It is I who have endangered you since the day I first recklessly sought you."

"And I bless that day and shall forever! In my heart, there is no fear for myself, only for you, my queen, and gratitude to you."

Hetepheres sat up, clutching the covers to her bosom. "My love, do not speak to me of gratitude! All gratitude is mine, not yours. See, and I have never yet told you so. Will you forgive me, my Merneptah? I have been selfish, thoughtless, foolish, and as willful as a silly child. Not only did I bring danger to you, but I have abused your love. I have abused your understanding, strength, and kindness. I did not mean to, I swear. I did not mean to, only it happened because… because you allowed it, and I needed you so much!"

"My dearest love, whatever are you speaking of? How did you abuse me?" He sounded puzzled.

"Before I met you," Hetepheres explained earnestly, "I was ignorant even of my loneliness. I believed that every life must be such. I was like a sealed wine jug with the wine fermenting within. I was insecure, and you gave me confidence. I was isolated, and you showed me the world around all of us. I was frightened, and you soothed me. I was unhappy, and you gave me happiness. I—I was damned, and you forgave me. Do you not know how you have truly given a new world and a new life to me?"

Merneptah caught her shoulders and pulled her down upon him. He kissed her with increasing passion, his hands roaming over her naked back. "I love you," he murmured into her ear, "and when one loves, one does not weigh and measure what is given to the other.

One gives because giving means happiness. One aids because helping bring shared joy. You must surely feel that, Hetepheres." His arms went around her with sudden ferocity.

"I want you, Hetepheres! I shall never have enough of you! But you shall leave this bed now, dress, and walk away without another word, without looking back."

And so she did. She never looked back as he asked her. It had been the hardest thing she had ever had to do to that day.

*****

In the room of the dying Queen Mother, there was a sudden flurry of motion. Great Pharaoh himself had arrived. He walked into the room with his customary hurried stride, bringing youth and vitality even to the death chamber. Not looking left or right, only at the dying woman, he knelt by her side and took the withered hand into both of his, then put his lips close to her ear.

"Grandmother," he whispered urgently, "Grandmother, do you hear me? It is I, Djedefre."

Presently, miraculously, proof for every one of the divine powers of Pharaoh, the old woman slowly opened her eyes, her gaze as clear and piercing as ever. She seemed to rally, as she looked straight at her grandson.

"Djedefre, son of my son," the old lady mumbled between agonizingly drawn gasps, "it is good…it is good…you have come to… see me off…"

"I came as soon as I heard, Grandmother, and as soon as I could. Not to see you off, only to visit. You are only a little ill, darling, but do not worry, the physicians—"

Hetepheres made a weak gesture of impatience. "No, no. They are…idiots all…They do not know. But I—I know! It is time…long past time…it is good so…" Exhausted from speaking, she lapsed into silence, then roused herself again.

"I want…sit up," she murmured.

Again a flurry of activity as pillows were fluffed to prop up the ancient back, the shrunken shoulders.

Hetepheres looked around herself with sudden clear and alert glance. *Someone must have removed those curtains in front of the bed which obstructed my view*, she thought. *But no, I have heard it said that dying people rally before death, and surely I must be dying. Pray, Osiris, that I am dying. It is good*, she thought, *to see clearly once again, to look at everybody one last time. One last time*. She sighed and thought, *Gods, I am tired, so very, very tired!*

There, in front of me, stand the grandchildren, some of them. Did I and Sneferu really produce them, flesh of our flesh? How very peculiar... But yes, there is Djedefre, he is now Pharaoh, the Living God, is he not? And there is Khafre, both so tall, so handsome and earnest of face, so like their grandfather was in his youth, especially Djedefre. But now his head is bowed and his eyes red-rimmed. That charming smile which is so much his heritage, which was my father's and Sneferu's and Sennefer's, but never mine, it does not lurk at the corners of his mouth. He is sad—is he crying? Why? For me, I suppose. The fool, but he should be glad for me!

And there, a little behind his brother Khafre are Khufu's younger sons, Kawab and Djedefhor, the twins. Twins again? Terrible heritage! But no, she recalled, not these two, it is different with them. They are so much alike and so devoted to each other!

Hetepheres knitted her brows, and her hands moved searchingly across the cover. *Khufu*, she thought, *where is Khufu? Why is he not here? He is ill*, she recollected, *terribly ill and shriveled up and screaming in pain—no, no, he is dead. My son is dead, and I accompanied his body to his House of Eternity, that gorgeous miraculous wonder of a structure at Giza. That was three years ago, and now he is gone, and so is Meritites, his consort, who is my daughter...so many...But there is another yet, another son...*

The wandering eyes searched, hesitated over the bowed heads of the young people, then moved slowly over to the other side of the bed. There they found what they were looking for. The pupils dilated, and the shrunken lips began to tremble. "Merneptah." Hetepheres moaned softly. "Merneptah."

The man standing there shot a questioning look at his nephew, the young Pharaoh, and saw Djedefre raise both shoulders and eyebrows in puzzlement. The man stepped up to the bed. Hesitantly he laid his palm against Hetepheres's cheek. He was a handsome older man, with close-cropped graying hair, the custom of priests, in contrast to the shaven heads of most men.

"Mother, it is I, Rahotep, your son, look. There is no Merneptah here, it is only I, see? Who is Merneptah?"

The Queen Mother's head rolled impatiently on her pillow. *Merneptah, my love, you need to hide your name no longer*, she thought, *Sneferu is dead. He is dead and can nevermore harm you.*

The man was stroking her cheek, drawing her hair from her forehead. "Mother," he insisted, "Mother, look at me. I am Rahotep. There is no Merneptah here!"

Hetepheres's eyes were glazing over. There was a roar in her ears, like the noise of a hundred cataracts. She wanted to slide back into her dreamworld, but something, some unfinished deed was nagging at her memory, was prodding her consciousness. With a tremendous effort of will, she pulled herself together, saw Rahotep, her Rahotep leaning over her. The same liquid black eyes, alive with intelligence, keen, alert, and guileless, full of compassion now, the same bold nose, full, sensual mouth—the way he holds his shoulders, bends his head to listen, the same, the same, the same!

"Rahotep," she whispered, "the gold palette...in my jewel box...old palette, all scratched and marked...Do not toss it away! It is yours, your finest inheritance...keep it to remember me... to remember your father. Keep it..." The lips continued to move soundlessly. Rahotep bent closer, listening intently. No more words came, only the sound of her rasping labored breathing, and even that became more halting, more hesitant, and more infrequent, until it stopped altogether.

*****

By the time the barges arrived at Thebes with the royal household, with Hetepheres and the children, Hetepheres knew she was with child. Sneferu was waiting for them as they docked. The children all flocked about him with glad cries, for he had always been a kind and indulgent father on those occasions when his time and duties permitted it. After he was done with their hugs and kisses, he extricated himself laughingly and walked to his wife. He laid his hands upon her shoulders, kissed her, then looked at her with a frown. "You look pale, my sister," he commented with some concern. "Have I laid too many burdens upon you during my absence?" His hands still on her shoulders, he commenced walking with her up the palace steps. "Come and rest from your travel. We can talk later."

Indeed, Hetepheres looked pale and frail, weary from the voyage and heartsore. She had all she could do to hide the periods of illness and nausea, which would overcome her from time to time. For Sneferu's sake, she forced herself to smile, to talk with animation, to be attentive to his long and rambling tales of war and battles, to eat and drink when all she wanted was to turn and run from the food-laden table.

Hetepheres had expected the nights to be more difficult still. She had dreaded the renewed sharing of his bed and her body, had feared that somehow she would give herself away. Yet no such thing happened—nothing happened. She accepted her husband's embraces with the same cool equanimity with which she allowed her servants to bathe and dress her. She accepted him of long habit. His body, his hands, his voice had the same familiarity as her own, and she found nothing, nothing at all within herself to connect this act with her emotions for Merneptah.

Once she had settled herself into her new surroundings and had gotten over the early weeks of her pregnancy, she had to confess to herself, in all honesty, that she still enjoyed her husband's company, perhaps because her relationship with Merneptah had never allowed them the luxury of leisurely togetherness, with conversation about anything and everything. Sneferu had seemed to be quieter, more settled, almost appearing to approach middle age—too soon, she thought—and even more sedate than she remembered. He was apparently genuinely pleased with the turmoil of family life surrounding him. They took long walks in the park along the river, sat on the old stone benches which, judging by the weeds growing out of the cracks and broken pieces of ornamentation, had seen little use or care lately. They talked, quietly, more like in the old brother-sister days, Hetepheres thought, while the younger children romped about them, playing tag or ate platefuls of sweet grapes and sticky honey cakes, and the twin boys crawled around in the grass like diminutive crabs.

Occasionally Khufu came to visit them, feeling very much the odd man out, not young enough to sacrifice his dignity and join into his sisters' boisterous games, not old enough to feel at ease with his parents. He was a studious serious young man, who made Hetepheres worry because she detected such a degree of single-minded determination in him as to border on ruthlessness, but she reassured herself that this would disappear when he was really grown-up. For now, however, Khufu would talk to his parents with great seriousness about his studies in history and geography, philosophy and literature, but most especially in architecture and with great diffidence about religion and his military training. There was a degree of constraint between father and son, Sneferu making it amply evident that he expected any son of his, most especially his heir, to be more of a daredevil and less of a scholar. At the same time, Hetepheres believed she could detect in her husband the beginnings of a healthy new respect toward his son, a new insight perhaps, that this studious young man was a well-rounded individual in his own right, not just a clay figurine to be molded into his father's image.

At times, Hetepheres caught her husband's speculative glance on her. She knew, that despite the pain of separation from Merneptah, she had become more tranquil, mellower lately, ever since the catharsis of her confession to him. Once, Sneferu alluded with a smile to having gained a brand-new wife. Quickly—perhaps too quickly—she assured him that it was only because she was now "getting on in years, a veritable old lady." After some weeks had elapsed, when she told him of her pregnancy, he immediately began to attribute her changed manner to her condition.

What occupied her thoughts, a great deal more than her current relationship with her husband, was her anxious desire to inform Merneptah of his child-to-be. A hundred times she toyed with the idea to send a message with one of her trusted servants, a hundred times she rejected it as too dangerous. No, she could trust no one, for both the carrier and the recipient of such news could face certain death if the message was intercepted or the messenger caught. No, she must be content, she told herself, until her return to Memphis and then contrive some way to notify Merneptah, if in fact he was still in the capital city, which was not at all assured. She was aching to share this gift of his with him, aching to alleviate the loneliness she knew he must feel but knew too that she had to be patient and prudent.

Then finally, when the Nile flooding was imminent, the household made plans to return to the capital before the floodwaters made water travel impossible. Sneferu had decided to remain and to start his annual Jubilee journey as soon as the waters receded. He took this task very seriously, feeling bound by traditions, which stretched back to the mists of history. Since the country had existed, and people had lived on it, Pharaoh would travel through the land and make sacrifice to his fellow gods for the success of the crops. Being a divine person in his own right, he would bless the fields, the villages, and towns of the realm. It was an archaic custom, which several of Sneferu's ancestors had begun to neglect for the love of their own comfort.

Sneferu, however, ever conscious of duty and tradition, feeling the need for contact with his people, had renewed the custom during the early years of his reign. Early on, he had also discovered that there was great economic significance to this contact and that it usually increased his revenues, which needed constant infusion in view of his grandiose and expensive building schemes. Since all taxes levied on crops depended altogether on the annual blessings of the Nile, and on whether flooding occurred yearly or only occasionally, it was important for a prudent ruler to be personally aware of the extent of each annual flood. True, steps had been carved into the riverbank of one of the islands at the First Cataract, and this measure had traditionally been accepted as the indicator for the level of floodwater, but at best, this was an inaccurate method. The word of Pharaoh, the Eye of Ra, at any rate, superseded any other regulation or measurement.

There was also a more immediate and practical need for getting as much revenue out of taxation as possible—after years of work on his House of Eternity at Maidum, the project had been abandoned. Sneferu's attraction to the concept of a smooth-sided pyramid won out, and after some initial experimentation with redesigning the existing structure, it was decided that it would be a better solution to abandon that building altogether. Thus construction had begun a few years earlier on a new building at Dahshur, closer to the river. There the connection between the funerary temple and the river was short and construction of a river channel to the temple and a causeway from temple to pyramid less difficult. The building of the pyramid was progressing well, but all this cost great amounts of money and great effort on the part of the conscripted population.

On the day before their departure, Hetepheres was reclining on an ottoman placed for her comfort on a shaded verandah. She was overseeing the sorting of items to be packed by her servant girls. The day was hot, and she was clothed as lightly as possible, in filmy white linen, which left her throat and part of her breasts, her arms and shoulders, her calves and ankles bare. Her pregnancy was well over halfway to its completion, and she was showing it. Sneferu, counting the days of her pregnancy from a different inception than she did, had remarked that this time, she was going to give birth to a veritable giant of an infant. Now that the decision for the return had been made, Hetepheres's eagerness increased day by day; she wished for nothing so much as to be able to push ahead the hours until departure. Already she wanted to be on that barge, floating down the Nile to Memphis.

She heard voices below in the garden, and raising herself upon her elbow, she looked down to search for the speakers, shielding her eyes against the glare of the sun with an ostrich-feather plume. She recognized her husband talking to another man, judging by his clothing, an officer of the guards. The men had their backs turned to her and were slowly pacing down one of the palm-lined paths. They stopped, the man apparently talking more vehemently, while he swiftly nodded his head. She could not make out his face. She called out and waved gaily. Sneferu looked up but did not acknowledge her greeting. Instead he turned back to the officer, said something to him briefly, and then dismissed him with a genial clasp upon his shoulder.

The soldier knelt, touched his forehead to Sneferu's sandal by way of salute, turned, and walked away briskly.

For a long time, Sneferu remained standing there, not looking at the retreating back of the soldier, but instead staring at the path under his feet, deep in thought or agitation, as a bull will stare ahead before charging. Even from the distance, every sinew and muscle of his body appeared taut with some suppressed but barely concealed energy. Hetepheres frowned, finding his behavior puzzling. Again she called out to him and saw him shake himself, as someone does who wants to throw off a bad dream or an unwanted thought. He did turn then, abruptly, and commenced to walk briskly toward the palace entrance. When he was near enough, he looked up, his gaze resting on her for a long moment but apparently without recognition. Then the stormy dark eyes slid off her face, and wordlessly and still without any sign to her, he entered the building.

Hetepheres shrank back. Never had she seen his glance so dark and forbidding, his mouth so set in lines of bitterness and fury. The pale skin was stretched taut across the frame of the cheeks, the face almost distorted with rage and golden lights of a near-murderous fury lurked in the depth of his eyes. Never had Hetepheres seen her husband look like this. She hardly knew what to make of it. Some unwanted news, she guessed, some kind of angering message from that man, must have aroused him to such fierceness. She had known him long enough and well enough to know that she best not approach him at such times. Let him work it out by himself, then before long, he would come to discuss it with her; she was the usual sounding board for his varied problems and grievances. Sneferu was not, by his nature, a person to hold his anger or, for that matter, any of his emotions to himself for long. The next thing that usually happened would be a string of explosions from him, and then the matter would be forgotten or dealt with in a more rational manner. Nevertheless, for some reason, this whole episode left her disquieted and with an unreasonably dark sense of foreboding.

Throughout the voyage to Memphis, Hetepheres could not shake off her pervasive sense of unease. Amid the noise and play of the children, she felt alone. Under the heat of the late summer sun, she felt chilled. Her sense of urgency only increased as they drew closer to Memphis, and once arrived there, her most urgent wish was to contact Merneptah in some fashion.

Yet she hesitated, she delayed. An undefinable feeling again and again stayed her hands, her feet, her lips each time she wanted to act upon her impulse. She felt that she was watched by day and knew so by night; evidently in his concern for her well-being, Sneferu had decreed that one or another of her servants should sleep on the floor of her bedchamber and in readiness, should she feel ill or in need of assistance. A month went by in this fashion; she was close to the end of her pregnancy.

It was incomprehensible that Merneptah did not somehow contrive to reach her, she thought, pacing about in her apartment. Surely he must know that she had arrived! Surely he must guess that the reason for not hearing from her was due to necessary caution on her part! Surely if he assumed that she could not, or did not dare to reach him, he could use some pretext, some opportunity! Officers of one or another of Pharaoh's armies kept coming and going to and fro; often the palace became a beehive of such activity. Surely among them, Merneptah would not have become too conspicuous! Once here, surely he could have prevailed on one of the servants or guards to bring a message to her, or even just a greeting. Just a greeting! If nothing else availed, surely he could have come to visit his father at the royal archives.

The royal library! Heri-hor! Hetepheres stopped her pacing. Oh, how could she have forgotten? There, there was the perfect pretext, the golden opportunity—she would go and inquire again about the progress of the biography of her and Sneferu's father and then please Sneferu by sending him the report. How was it that she had not thought of this before? Perhaps even a meeting there could be arranged, her heart sang, *And I could see him, and if he could see me now, he would know in his heart...he must know that this is his child...*

That same day, not wishing to walk the distance in the heat and in her condition, she had herself carried to the building of the royal archives. She had sent a messenger ahead so that she would not burst in on Heri-hor, as she had done the last time. When her chair stopped in front of the building, and she alighted, several men were assembled and waiting to greet her. Her eyes moved from face to face. To her consternation, none of them belonged to an old man.

Hetepheres suffered through the polite phrases of welcome and was bowed inside. Perhaps, she reassured herself, the old man was getting too frail to stand outside in the baking sun? She was seated and offered a cooling drink of milk and honey and a bowl of fruit. She tried to curb her impatience, nibbling on some figs, letting her eyes wander over the by now-well-known expanse of the workroom. She was not ushered into the inner chamber belonging to Heri-hor. Instead the work in progress had, in advance, been spread on a table in front of her.

A middle-aged tall man of great dignity, who must have been handsome once before rolls of fat began to obscure his features and disfigure his frame, commenced a lengthy explanation of the manuscripts. He had introduced himself earlier as Itethy and spoke with a slight nervous stammer, which somehow disconcerted Hetepheres. Again and again, her eyes roamed the great room without seeing what she wanted to see. Finally at a moment's break in the flood of explanation, she held up her hand and, leaning forward, asked, "Master Itethy, as you know, I was here a year before now and saw much of the proceedings, which Master Heri-hor had explained to me at length. I am curious, where is the master of the libraries and archives today?"

Itethy looked up in surprise. He moistened his fleshy lips and answered with a stammer, "Divine Mistress, forgive me, for I am but dust under your feet. I am now the master of the libraries and archives."

Hetepheres's heart skipped a beat. She forced as much casualness into her voice a she was capable of. "Oh? Then I suppose the old master was retired out of respect for his age and gratitude for his accomplishments?"

"He has retired, yes, not because of his age, for despite his years, he was vigorous still. He was struck down with the sudden paralysis, divine lady, on hearing...on receiving bad news."

Hetepheres's hands gripped the armrest of her chair. She felt a pulse beating in her neck. "How sad! What manner of bad news was it he received which so affected him?"

Itethy hesitated, his eyes shifting to his colleagues in consultation. His reluctance to talk was apparent. Obviously he did not wish to weary or upset his queen in her delicate condition and thought this matter to be too minor, anyway, for her exalted attention.

"He-he," Itethy stammered, "he—it was a family problem..."

Hetepheres felt her lips grow stiff and numb. She pressed on. "Family? The old man told me he had no family, only a son in the army. I met him in this very place, for he had been visiting his father when I arrived." She amazed herself with her ability to dissemble. "A son who was called, I believe, Merneptah."

Itethy brightened, seeing that she had some perfunctory interest in the matter and was now eager to oblige her. "Just so, Divine Consort!" The fleshy jowls wobbled with his quick nods. "Blessed indeed are your subjects that your magnificence should so honor them by remembering their lowly persons and even their names! As you say, it was Merneptah, his only son. A great calamity befell him, gracious goddess.

"On a night little less than one moon ago, he disappeared. Disappeared from the encampment of his soldiers where he had housed himself. It may please your blessed magnificence to know, great lady, that he lived by himself for he had neither wife nor child. No one missed him immediately, therefore, not for another day and night. The following morning, however, his detachment was to move out on a hunt. It was then that his disappearance was officially noted.

"A search was made of his quarters but to no avail, for nothing appeared amiss there. A search was made of the campground and environs, also with no results. His soldiers were going to leave without him, expecting him to join them at the hunt, when one of his men discovered him lying in the thickets of the reedbeds by the blessed Nile's edge. The river must have carried him to the shore. He must have become victim to the juice of the grape, although those of his men who knew him better swore that he never did that in a greedy manner. Maybe he succumbed to some sudden illness or dizziness and fallen into the water, where they say he had developed a habit of walking back and forth on those nights when sleep eluded him. Perhaps it was for the best. They say he was sleepless much of the time and often behaved like a madman. They say perhaps some ill spirit had invaded his body. When he fell into the sacred river, he must have hit a stone, for they say his skull was cracked open like an egg..."

Hetepheres sat motionless, her hands still gripping the arms of her chair. The words splashed over her, some entering her consciousness, others dissipating into the air around her. Her mind struggled to accept what she was hearing. Waves of nausea and weakness flooded her, while the room spun around, and the figure of Itethy danced and advanced and retreated in front of her eyes. She opened her mouth but could utter no sound. She wanted to lift her hand to make him stop, but the hand lay still and did not obey her will. None of the muscles of her body seemed to obey her will at all.

"When it was ascertained that the poor creature was quite dead, stone-cold dead, Great Sister of Hathor, a message was sent here to the hapless father. I myself happened to be in this very room, although it was already late in the day, and the workmen had left. But Master Heri-hor had wanted some corrections to be made in the newest documents of your glorious husband's most recent victories. These he was discussing with me just then. The messenger arrived—I saw it all. Master Heri-hor received the message. He prostrated himself in his grief, uttering great sobs. I left him briefly to bring him a drink of water and could hear his groans even by the garden well, then the wailing stopped. I hurried back, fearful that the old man had fainted, and found him lying on the ground like a dead person. I knelt by his side and rolled over his body. It was then that I saw how he had been stricken, for his eyes stared without seeing, his jaw was slack, and his mouth drooping and distorted. On the left side, he could move neither arm nor leg. It was a terrible calamity, truly, truly, and a pitiful ending for such a great scholar."

Slowly, by degrees, the numbness left Hetepheres. She moved her fingers, her wrist, her arms; she stood up, swaying a little. A terribly tight band was constricting her chest, her neck. *If I can only catch my breath*, she thought, *just long enough to speak, to stop this fool and his torrent of words! If I can only force my legs to move and to take me out of here. Once I am outside, I will be well, and this nightmare will disappear…Oh, great Ptah, give me strength! Sekhmet, Divine Wife of Ptah, assist me!*

Somehow, miraculously, she had found her voice, she had been able to piece together the appropriate words, she had been able to nod and to thank and to nod again. Somehow, miraculously, she found herself outside, she was again in her litter, was borne back to the shelter and safety of her apartment. Somehow, miraculously, she was standing inside her bedchamber, alone at last. She felt deathly ill. She took a few hesitant steps toward her bed, blindly reaching out to clutch at the draperies around it. Darkness enveloped her. Slowly her knees gave way, buckled under her, and she sank to the ground, pulling down the draperies with her.

It was thus that her women had found her, in labor. For weeks thereafter, Hetepheres floated between life and death. After her struggles to bear her son, she continued to struggle with no one knew what kind of phantoms of death, demons of destruction. At first, everyone believed that both mother and son were doomed, for the infant, a wizened little boy, was premature, small, weak, and hardly breathing; and the mother had almost bled to death in giving him life. The child was placed into the warm wet body cavities of freshly killed goats and sheep. It sheltered there, barely moving, mewling occasionally like a sick kitten.

There was less that could be done for the mother, once the court obstetricians declared that their science was inadequate to her needs, beyond prayers and sacrifices. For a while, there was talk for the royal surgeon to open her skull, a time-honored practice when all other means of healing failed, but a post-haste message from Pharaoh absolutely forbade such an action.

Then slowly but inexorably, her tenacious constitution asserted itself. Despite herself, Hetepheres began to recover, by painful stages, though this mending involved only her body. She felt bruised and beaten to the very marrow of her soul, but that soul was under the command of her body, and the body triumphed in its will to live. She accepted life, though not willingly but because she was too passive and dazed to do anything else.

She spent hours and days on her verandah, lying quietly on a couch, her dark eyes, enormous in her gaunt face, following the flight of a flock of birds, the shapes of passing clouds, or the play of palm fronds in the breeze. The first sign of animation appeared on her face when her infant son was finally brought to her.

His progress was nothing if not miraculous. He had long left the steaming womb-like enclosure of his early days and now, sucking with ferocious hunger on his wet nurse, grew and developed by leaps and bounds, as though intent to make up for lost time. Hetepheres watched him too, with the shadow of a tentative smile on her face, and gave him her little finger to suck and to hold on to. She named him Rahotep, ignoring the custom which accepted the father's right to name a male child.

*****

In the early days of Peret, after the sowing of the fields, Sneferu returned to Memphis. Kept informed of the birth of his son and his wife's illness, he had not deemed it necessary to shorten his absence. Women, after all, often fell ill when they gave birth; it was their lot to lose their blood and even their life for the purpose they were made, just as it was man's fate to bleed or die in battle. Such were the laws of life laid down by the gods, and even the will of Pharaoh could not alter them.

Nevertheless, after he arrived and when he first saw Hetepheres, he was shocked by her appearance, the deep dark circles under her eyes, her haggard sallow face, her thin hands through which the light of a candle could be seen. Yet he showed little emotion, bending down to kiss her forehead and murmuring some commonplace words of concern to her. The child interested him hardly at all, and when he heard that Hetepheres had named him already, he shrugged and only fleetingly glanced at Rahotep, then lifted his eyes to his wife's face. His eyes rested on her in silent contemplation; then he turned and walked away without another word.

Had Hetepheres been inclined to be more observant of what was happening around her, she would have noticed Sneferu's aloofness. But she was too deeply wrapped up in her own misery to be aware. In fact, in her mute torpor, she had dreaded Sneferu's worried questions, his insistent attempts to cheer her. She was thankful that he went his own way and left her alone, except for periodic brief visits. She did not notice the clouded brow and the petulance lurking around his soft mouth, did not see how his eyes avoided her, nor the subtle tension implicit in his bearing, in his stride.

It was the first time in the life of the palace that the royal couple conspicuously went their separate ways. The air became charged with gossip, which was quick to spread not only through the servants' quarters but diffused all the way to the galleries and reception rooms of the august inhabitants. They seemed unaware. Hetepheres cloaked herself in the mantle of her grief, while Sneferu renewed his frequent visits to his minor wives and concubines in the royal harem, especially to Merit's apartment.

The day of eruption from this state of latent tension commenced like any other preceding it, with Hetepheres settled on her couch on the verandah and Rahotep somewhat removed from her in his cradle under an awning. Hetepheres had dismissed the nursemaid and was contemplating the infant, trying to discern something of the beloved features in his face. She heard the crunch of footsteps upon the gravel and saw a shadow fall upon the marble flags of the verandah. She looked up—it was her husband. He nodded toward her by way of greeting, then walked over to a low table and selected an orange from the deep fruit bowl. Toying with the fruit, he stepped to the child's cradle and looked, a long and lowering look, while a frown creased his forehead. Finally he sighed and turned, and leaning against the balustrade, he began to peel the orange with deliberate concentration. He seemed abstracted, and a long silence ensued. Then he glanced at his wife.

"How long, Hetepheres?" he queried.

Hetepheres shifted her position and raised her eyes to his. "How long what? What do you mean, Sneferu?"

Suddenly he dropped the orange and strode over to where she lay. Leaning down over her, he braced both arms upon the sides of her couch. His eyes, dark and stormy, bored down into hers.

"I mean, how long will you persist in this inane state of lethargy? How long until you take your assigned place as my wife and mother of all our children? However much the birth of this—this child of yours has affected you, don't you think that you have now had sufficient time to recover? How much longer? How much more time do you need to be done mourning for your—your…to be done with this mourning?"

Hetepheres raised her head. She felt a sudden aura of threat to herself, to the child. She had been unprepared and now felt vulnerable and exposed.

"Mourning?" she stammered, trying to rally her wits. "What makes you say I am mourning?"

Sneferu's fists struck the arms of her couch with sudden vehemence. He pushed himself up and straightened. She saw the flash of anger in his eyes and the compression of his lips, the tightening of the muscles of his neck. For a moment, she expected him to strike her. But instead he just reached into the bosom of his short tunic and withdrew something. Something thin, wrapped in a piece of cloth. He weighed it in his palm, then threw it onto her lap.

Hetepheres did not have to unwrap the package to know what it contained. She herself had wrapped it into that strip of linen. She uttered a cry and jumped up, the package clattering to the stones. The binding unwrapped itself, releasing its contents, a flat golden object, much scratched, marked, and defaced to the point that its design no longer could be made out. Hetepheres stared at it, stared and stared at Sennefer's palette, stared at it. Her mind refused to accept the implications of what she saw, what she knew, its horror draining the blood from her heart and making her teeth chatter. She noticed Sneferu's anxious move toward her and shuddered. She stretched out her arms, palms out, to ward him off, and backed away from him. Her voice was the voice of death, hoarse and unrecognizable even to her ears.

"Where—where did you get this from?"

Sneferu's eyes were dark slits in his strained face. "Where indeed? From the man you left it with inadvertently—or gave it to—for who knows what purpose? From the body of your lover!" He spat at her contemptuously.

Nothing, nothing that had ever happened to her was as horrible as this. Nothing ever again could be. Her devastation was more complete than Sneferu could ever have planned or she ever have imagined. Death, oh, death was infinitely to be preferred! She heard her own voice—was it her voice—as she was holding on to the last vestiges of self-control.

"Keep away from me! I swear by Sekhmet the Destroyer, if you so much as touch me ever again, I shall kill myself!"

*****

But then, in the end, she did forgive him, after all.

That was almost thirteen years later, when Sneferu lay dying. For those intervening years, she lived in her own private purgatory, though with the ever-increasing realization that Sneferu too had his own private hell to bear. She lived in outward quiet, a retired and withdrawn woman, rarely seen outside her own apartments, only emerging to do those things which were expected of her as Pharaoh's sister-wife and daughter of Isis.

Into her bedchamber she had the servants carry a life-sized polished black basalt statue of lion-headed Sekhmet and stood her at the foot of her golden bed, in symbol of her oath. Daughter of Ra, wife of Ptah, earth-destroyer and protectress of the divine order, embodiment of the death-dealing, scorching power of the sun, she stood guard over Hetepheres's empty bed and sleepless nights.

She watched her children grow: her son Khufu turning into an efficient, ruthless, and secretive young man; her daughters, Henutsen and Meritites, growing into womanhood, becoming Khufu's consorts. She especially watched over her youngest son, Rahotep, ready to do battle, should he ever become threatened by Sneferu. But that never happened, even though the youngster bore a striking resemblance to a certain young commander in Pharaoh's army, long dead now. If Sneferu noticed, he locked the knowledge into his heart, along with so many things that needed saying but never were, just as she had locked her heart to him. Between them the silence grew into a wall through which no sound could reach.

Yet in the end, she did forgive him.

He and Khufu had gone hunting for lion and hippopotamus upriver, some distance from the city. Sneferu liked hunting; at forty-four he was still vigorous and active, albeit grown somewhat portly with good living. With peace established throughout the Two Kingdoms, he craved action and physical release for his pent-up energies.

He went hunting, and the next day, the messenger arrived, barely able to hold himself erect with exhaustion and grief. Pharaoh had been bitten by a charging male hippo—she must go immediately if she wanted to see him alive.

Hetepheres dropped what she was doing, reached for a cloak to wrap around her against the desert sun and dust, and gave orders to have her things brought after her. She was on her way without another word to waste, embarking in one of the swift, albeit less-than luxurious, boats which were used to carry messages to the various parts of the country. Swift racing camels awaited her and her escorts at the landing, which was only a short distance from the hunting camp. Khufu waited there for her, pale and serious but collected. Her eyes were on his face.

"Does he live?"

"Barely, Mother. You must hurry."

She did not waste time to ask how or what happened. She was a daughter of the Nile; she knew perfectly that an enraged bull hippopotamus, intent to defend his harem and territory, will attack. She knew about hippo bites, the enormous maw with the huge bone-crunching dagger-sharp teeth was considered the deadliest weapon capable to inflict a wound. Those who were bitten were not expected to survive. Still she was unprepared what she saw.

Sneferu lay in his tent on a cot, blanketed with leopard skin covers so that only his face showed. A face marked by death, so pale and sunken as though he were dead already, his eyes closed, and his lips drawn tight against his teeth. On his left side, where his leg and hip should have been, the covers lay empty and flat across the pallet. She paled, then looked around her, gesturing to the three physicians present.

"Show me," she commanded. Such was the force of her presence that they obeyed, although at first, they wanted to protest. They drew back the panther pelts.

Even though she had steeled herself, Hetepheres fell back a step, staring in mute horror. In place of the leg and thigh, there was nothing. Nothing, also but empty space, where the thigh would have connected with the body. The horrendous tear extended from the groin diagonally to part of the hip, all shielded by carefully wrapped bandages. The bandages were initially soaked in honey, but now they were saturated with blood still seeping from the cauterized wound. Another bandage encased the blunt stump of the left arm, which now ended halfway above the wrist.

Hetepheres staggered and sank down on a low stool which Khufu had pushed under her. She covered her face with her hands. The silence was so complete that only the rasping breaths of the dying man could be heard. Finally one of the physicians, their leader, took courage and commenced to speak in a low voice.

"For a very long time, we could not halt the bleeding, Great Consort. The hand and part of the arm we had to amputate, for all the bones had been crushed. But the arm, in itself, would heal with time. There was nothing we could do for the leg, for it had—it had been torn off. To staunch the bleeding, we finally sealed the wound with many applications of hot metal, but the animal had also bitten into vital parts…Now it is only a question of which will arrive sooner—death by the loss of so much blood or by fever, but we believe it will be the former. There is not so much blood in the human body to last very much longer…"

Hetepheres removed her hand from her face and looked at the physicians one by one. "How much time?"

The chief physician only shook his head. "It is in the hands of Divine Ra, our gracious lord's father, daughter of Isis. We know not exactly. Perhaps a little. Perhaps one and one-half of a water clock's measure, daughter of Isis, not much more."

"Is he in great pain?"

"Earlier he was, Divine Consort, when he was first brought here. But not now. We had given him draughts to kill the pain when we had to take the hand. He is in shock. He is not aware."

Suddenly Hetepheres rose and made an imperious gesture of the hand. "Leave me," she commanded, "all of you. You too, my son. I wish to be alone with him."

She waited until everyone had bowed themselves out of her presence. Khufu hesitated, touching her elbow.

"Mother, won't you take some food and wine? You need to strengthen yourself. The road ahead of you will be arduous and sad."

Without looking at him, she shook her head.

"I am stronger than you think, my son." She talked calmly, not taking her eyes off her husband's face. "Now leave us, you too. Go!"

When she was left alone, she pulled the stool closer to Sneferu and sat down again, reaching for the hand that was still left to him. It was cold and clammy. Quietly she sat so, not knowing the passage of time. *How often we had walked like this, hand in hand, under tall palms, in the shadowy corridors of the palaces at Memphis, at Tinis, at Thebes! First as children, then as man and wife. How often had we lain side by side, holding each other's hand! I had been your wife for two and twenty years, and your sister for nine and thirty. I had borne your children and laughed with you, quarreled with you, worried for you, desired you and then hated you, pursued you and then shut you out of my life. All the emotions of a lifetime...and when we arrive to this point, it becomes all the same in the sight of your travel to the Western Lands, the Land of the Setting Sun, the Land of Osiris and Anubis, the Land of Eternity...*

How pitiful you look, strong and whole that you were once, and now only a part of a man. I did not wish for this to happen! I wish I could go where you are going for all those I love are there—my father, my mother, Merneptah...But I cannot. Like so many stones shackled to me, my children hold me back yet. It should not be so because they are young and only belonged to you and me for a little while, and then they belong to their own families. There will be no pleasure in my living, and I shall count the days to the hour of my death.

She glanced at Sneferu and saw that his eyes were open and that he was staring with vacant gaze at the posts of the tent. She leaned over him and gently brushed her fingertip across his brow, over his eyes. The heavy gold and turquoise bangles on her wrists clinked. Whether it was that sound in the silence or the touch of her fingers, she did not know, but the eyes vaguely followed her hand and came to rest on her. There was a glimmer of recognition in the dark eyes as they slowly focused, while the parched lips moved weakly. Hetepheres dipped her fingers into a bowl of watered wine and moistened his lips with them. Very softly, still cradling his one hand, she began to speak to him.

"Do not try to speak, my brother, or to move, for it will only accelerate your weakening." Even now, she could not bring herself to call him husband again. "It is the will of the gods that you should die, though I wish that I would die in your stead. I have been sitting here and wishing with all my heart to take your place, for you are the center and the heart of this realm, while I am useful to no one anymore, least of all to myself." She felt the dark eyes hang on her face, drinking in each of her words. There was sadness in the eyes, and pain, and a question burning in their depths. She understood about that question too as much as the pain and sadness of parting. She drew a deep shuddering breath and continued.

"I have never brought you happiness, Sneferu. Perhaps it is not in your nature to enjoy such true happiness, as I think it was not in mine either. But I did...once, so I must believe that we all can! Maybe you would have been happy with Sennefer, for you two were so much alike in so many ways—willful, charming and gay, generous and selfish, petulant and thoughtless all at once. Except that she did not have your dedication to duty, your will to succeed and even to excel. But she could have made you happy, Sneferu, as long as you pleased her, and she was so very easy to please, for she had no self-doubts or envy, as I did."

She sighed, and again she moistened his lips with wine. She went on. "I was not a good wife for you, Sneferu, my brother. For you could not understand me. How could you? I do not even understand myself! I gave you children but was not happy with them as I should have been. For they are good, loving, and healthy children. You spoiled me, and I walked past your gifts, thinking that they were my due, even though in my heart, I knew that they were Sennefer's, not mine…never mine…So it was, my dearest brother, that I shortchanged you, for I cheated you out of the simple happiness you could have had with my twin sister, who, in so many ways, was your mirror image, though she should have been mine…"

Hetepheres felt unbelievably old any weary. She passed a hand across her eyes and bowed her head in silence. Sensing the dark eyes on her in mute petition, she straightened her shoulders and continued, "I think that was what drove you from me to Merit. For in her bed, you found what I had never given you—could not give you—simple and unquestioning love, admiration, and submission. I understood that, but even so, I was jealous, that odious weapon of all those who are insecure.

"Sneferu, I did indeed not understand the reason for my behavior and actions until I loved Merneptah. Never before had I said his name to you, but now at this hour of truth, let him be named! I loved Merneptah more than I can ever love anyone else. For a brief span of time, he filled the whole of my being. I did not want it to happen thus, and to hurt you, but when it happened, I was unable to prevent it. I gave you sorrow and pain and humiliated you, yet I am not sorry. He was a good and decent man, a man of great sensitivity, compassion, and honor. Never, never will I be able to perceive dishonor in what was the best and purest of feelings in my life.

"When you had him slain, thinking that Merneptah was only a passing fancy who would be forgotten once gotten out of the way, I swore never to forgive you. I was wrong, for more than anyone else, I learned that there is forgiveness for great sins, and it was Merneptah who taught me. I could not have forgiven you, even now, except that the hour of parting is upon us, my brother, and I want you to know that I understand. Now I understand. I understand your hurt pride and anger, understand that to look at Rahotep must have been a constant goad to you. Yet you never acted as though he were not yours, although you knew…I am sure you know, for he looks so very much like his father did…

"For this I am grateful to you, my brother. Never shall he suspect that his sire is not the great, the gracious and omnipotent Pharaoh, slayer of the Two Kingdom's enemies. I promise you that…" She had to stop for a moment. Two tears rolled down her cheeks but she did not wipe them away.

"When you stand before Osiris, the Great Lord of the Nether Life, and there Anubis weighs your soul on his scales against the weight of a feather, you must remind him—remind him how much greater were your merits than your sins! For you were a great and just ruler, a true father to your people, and made your kingdoms prosper and your enemies tremble. You exerted yourself and toiled ceaselessly on behalf of your people instead of coddling yourself as some would have. You must remind him that your only sin was against me and that I had hurt you long before you hurt me. You have only sinned against me, and I am but only one person, not the whole of a realm, and I forgive you, as I pray you forgive me."

Her voice softened, and she lifted his hand and, with both of hers, pressed it against her bosom.

"We have both hurt each other, my dearest. Perhaps that is always the way of two people who live together, especially if that togetherness begins with their earliest memories. Whatever guilt you may feel now, I release you from it…and I beg you to also release me from my guilt toward you…husband…"

Hetepheres felt a weak pressure of the cold fingers she was holding. Or perhaps, she thought, she was only imagining it? She raised his hand to her lips and kissed it gently, then laid her cheek against it. Tears were coursing down her face; she felt them drop onto her lap. So she remained for a few seconds, or for an hour, she did not know. Finally she became aware of the weight of the hand she was holding and laid it slowly back upon the covers. She lifted her gaze and looked at Sneferu's face and saw that the sightless eyes were staring blindly and unblinkingly into space.

*****

The news of Pharaoh's death overran the land like wildfire. Great were the sadness and lamentations, for Sneferu was genuinely well liked by most, and the manner of his death filled everyone who heard it with pity and horror. In the capital, as in Sais, Thanis, Buto, and Heliopolis in the Lower Kingdom, in Dahshur, Maydum, Lisht, and the Fayyoum in Upper Egypt, as well as farther south in Nubia and in Abydos, Koptos, Meir, Thebes, and Edfu, in all the cities and hamlets of the realm, the seventy days of prescribed mourning commenced. The wine shops and pleasure houses closed, there were no feasts nor marriages, no dancing or singing, and from the temples rose the deep sounding moans of the death horns, the murmuring chants of priests and priestesses, and the smokes of sacrificial fires.

The dead Pharaoh, whose name now, by ancient custom, was prefaced with Osiris, was borne in state to the Great House of Purification in Memphis, to undergo the required seventy days of ritual preparation, which made his body corruption-proof and assured him of everlasting life. For seventy days, all work on any of the dead other than him ceased. For seventy days, the priestesses from the temples of Isis and Nephthys, Divine Consort and daughter of Osiris, kept watch over the royal body, while their lamentations rent the air.

Not Hetepheres herself, not her children, not even the newly ascended Eye of Ra, the Horus Falcon Pharaoh Khufu were allowed to attend any the embalming ceremonies, led by the high priest of the temple of Ptah, wearing a head mask representing jackal-headed Anubis, he who judges human souls. All the sacred materials used for the embalmment were the property of the priests, and it was said that they had grown out of the tears shed by the gods at the death of Osiris.

Carefully the body was washed with sacred Nile water; thereafter, the brain was withdrawn through the nostrils, while the lungs, liver, stomach, and intestines were removed through an incision on the left side to be placed, after preservation, into four alabaster canopic jars. Only the heart alone, the seat of intelligence and of the soul, was left intact to aid Pharaoh in his perilous journey through the waters of the Underworld to the Western Lands. There the heart would assist him when, in the Great Hall of Judgment, Pharaoh would stand before Lord Osiris, ruler of eternity, who would pronounce sentence upon the deceased according to his merit.

Finally the royal body, to dry it out completely, was packed with natron and desert sand. Eventually the dried body cavity and skull were packed with strips of royal linen soaked in aromatic resins, herbs, oils, and precious spices. Gold-embossed amulets were distributed upon it, chief among them a scarab carved out of chalcedony, which, when placed upon the heart, awakened it to rebirth in the Land of the Setting Sun. Finally, and with meticulous care, layer upon layer of the finest linen bandages were wrapped about every part of Pharaoh's divine body, and he was lowered into an open casket.

The day of the funeral was cool and windy, and a brief rain swept the streets of the capital. People bowed their heads in prayer and raised their arms in lament, for even the gods wept for their fallen brother. The boats of the funeral procession had been loaded for many days before and lay now at anchor, riding low with the heavy load of a thousand precious items and everyday household goods, with food and drink, clothing and furniture, games, weapons, scrolls, tablets, musical instruments, jewelry, cups, goblets, and plates. Along with these lay untold ushabti figures: miniature models of servants, concubines, soldiers, and peasants, all to accompany Pharaoh on his journey to serve him though his eternity.

The funerary barge, made of fragrant cedarwood and bearing the emblems of Horus and the Eye of Ra, received the casket and, with it, the four canopic jars, the Pharaoh's cartouche showing his earthly name, the red and white crowns of the Two Kingdoms, the uraeus diadem with its rattlesnake crest, the crook and the flail, all symbols of Pharaoh's rule and might. Then Hetepheres, bareheaded and dressed in the red of mourning, and the young Pharaoh Khufu, together with his two sister-consorts, Meritites and Henutsen, his concubines, his brothers, and sisters, entered the barge. There followed a long processions of barges bearing the royal household and mourners, such as delegations of government personages, priests, and the military, who were accorded this honor. The last barge carried scrolls copied out of the Book of the Dead containing instructions for the soul of the deceased and a life-size statue of Osiris-Sneferu, representing his spirit and his life force, his ka.

Little of all this pomp and ceremony remained in Hetepheres's memory, for she, who had been dry-eyed at the deaths of her father, her mother, sister, son, and lover, shed bitter tears at this entombment and spent the voyage aboard the funeral barge secluded in the royal tent, shielded from all eyes. Later she could vaguely recall the groups of praise singers, musicians, and dancers who awaited the barges on the western shore of the Nile at Dahshur. In front of her, the just-recently-completed new House of Eternity for her husband, the third one he had built, glowed rose red. Taller and more imposing than Sneferu's earlier two structures had been, its rose color was embellished with gleaming white limestone and a huge and impressive temple connecting the causeway to the place of burial. She recalled how the wrapped body of her husband was held upright for Khufu to perform the Ceremony of Opening of the Mouth, and how, subsequently, the body was placed into its coffin of cedarwood, then into one of carved alabaster, and finally into the outer sarcophagus of polished black basalt. For days, her ears echoed with the groan and clang of the huge copper-studded bronze doors thudding closed upon the entrance to the burial chamber, and the thin wailing of her youngest grandchild crying and hiding his face on her lap.

******

Thus were the gates of her life closed upon Hetepheres too.

Thereafter, she was rarely seen in public, even on official functions. Attendance at those functions was now the domain of the current ruler's two consorts. She was rarely seen even in the palace, except in her own garden, her own apartment. She lived quietly and withdrawn, by choice and not by necessity. After the torrent of weeping and grief with which she buried her brother-husband, her soul quieted and became equally closed to sadness and joy. Events passed her as shadows; she felt herself a bystander at the marriages, births, illnesses, and deaths within her family. If she was cleansed of torment, she was also devoid of happiness and vaguely disinterested, even in those most crucial preparations for her eventual death and entombment.

Harvests came and went, good ones mixed with bad, the floods of the Nile arrived and reached the measuring steps of the Great Temple of Ptah at varying levels, then receded again, leaving the land fertile and green with young growth. She cared not for the scorching heat of the summer nor for the green of rebirth or the chill of winter nights.

In the city, in the stalls of the vendors by the docks, the places of worship, the shops of craftsmen, and the homes of the populace, the word had spread that the Queen Mother had been stricken down, that the words she spoke were senseless and her movements aimless. Occasionally they saw her, robed in red, mourning, being carried in her chair to the royal barge to do homage at the tomb of her divine spouse. At such times, she appeared almost like a graven image herself, looking neither left nor right but staring ahead over the heads of the crowd. She did seem purposeful enough at these occasions, but cool and haughty, as though all people were dust under her feet.

So it came as no great shock when it was heard that Hetepheres was dying. A whole new generation had grown up and matured to whom she was only a shadowy name. She was old and had long ago outlived her usefulness. Only her son Khufu had sought her advice and approval on occasion and planned her House of Eternity for her since she had no inclination or interest in doing it herself. Her daughters, Henutsen and Meritites, were long married, both Divine Consorts of her son Khufu, the Divine Pharaoh. All of them were more concerned with their own lives and families than with an aged and uncommunicative mother.

Khufu's visits were more the results of duty than genuine affection. But with him, it was questionable if he was, in fact, capable of true affection and devotion. Rahotep, her favorite, although a dutiful son, also grew up knowing her as distant and unapproachable and had early gone his own way. He now lived in the Nile Delta, at Heliopolis, with his beloved first wife Nofret, "the beautiful one." In Heliopolis, he was the high priest of Ra, greatest of seers and master of expeditions and supervisor of works. However, the title of this special child of hers, which pleased Hetepheres more than any other, was the appellation "son of the king, begotten of his body." In this she felt she had at least, to a small part, repaid to Sneferu for his acceptance of this particular child. Rahotep's wife, Nofret, became greatly devoted to Hetepheres and turned out to be one of those few people in Hetepheres's family with whom she always felt a special kinship.

Those three wondrous works on which, for almost three decades, a whole nation had labored during the annual flood tide, each breathtaking in the gleaming symmetry of their individual shapes, awesome in their dimensions, monumental like no other structures on earth made by men until then, Sneferu's three Houses of Eternity, the first at Maidum and the next two at Dahshur, dominated the country like three huge mountains. They rose out of the desert sand on the west bank of the Nile, and with them, a new age began, an age which did not include Hetepheres and which she no longer wished to understand.

Customs became looser and life more indolent. Memphis teemed with foreigners, peoples from the islands in the Northern Sea, especially traders and merchants from a great island called Keftiu, from Lagash and Uruk, between the two rivers far to the east, and with Amorites and Canaanites from Syria. Now Hetepheres was truly like a dried-up empty shell leftover from an earlier harvest, so thin and weak that she could have been blown away like chaff on the desert wind.

*****

In the death chamber of the Queen Mother, Hetepheres, who was addressed officially as Mother of the Dual King, attendant of Horus, and God's daughter of his body, in her capacity as the Pharaoh Khufu's mother, the members of the royal family were filing out one by one. The royal physicians closed their black boxes containing the implements of their science. They stood in a small group in the corner, discussing in low voices the case they had just attended, waiting for one of Pharaoh's attendants to pay their purses. The high priest of the temple of Ptah, who had also attended the deathbed, motioned to the servants from the House of Purification to bring in the bier on which the body would be carried away. The servants had been waiting interminably; they squatted on their heels and gossiped, chewing on dried sunflower seeds and spitting the shells all about themselves. The mistress of the Queen Mother's household, a tall spare woman named—or rather sadly misnamed—Nofret, the beautiful one, frowned when she saw the shells and thought that tomorrow the whole apartment would have to be scrubbed, cleaned, and aired. The priestesses, whose assignments it was to mourn for the dead, raised their hands above their heads, in the ritual posture of mourning, and commenced their keening laments.

*****

In Pharaoh's throne room, a delegation of ambassadors from the Land between the Two Rivers across the Eastern Sea, waited in the early morning to do homage to the lord of the Two Kingdoms. They were told to wait with patience, for Pharaoh was involved in family problems, there having been a death in his family. Outside the merchants in the market were beginning to spread out their wares in the various stalls. The servants from the butcheries were driving lowing cattle to the slaughtering houses. Women assembled at the wells to collect water for what was the first of many such trips for them during the day. Fishermen were bringing the night's catch to the wharves, and long columns of donkeys and camels milled about outside the city gates to bring the goods and produce of the known world into the city of the gods.

The Bull Dancers
ca. 1600 BCE Crete

Introduction

Far to the north, well away from the shores limiting the Great Sea, around which most of the lands of the known world are clustered, toward the rising sun, a lovely island rises from the waves—beautiful to behold, blessed with great riches, and an artistic and alert, inventive people. Their home and their culture had existed far, far back into the mists of their past. From generation to generation, the people of the wonderful island of Crete increased the knowledge, the wealth, the culture, and the commerce of their nation.

The various arts prospered. Great palaces, the beauty and harmony of which were unrivaled anywhere, rose up in the cities. Their wall paintings and colorful decorations became famous throughout the known world. The country's sea power and commerce enriched the nation with each passing year.

There were great inequalities in the lives of the citizenry, to be sure, but less so than most other places where humanity had prospered through the ages. These inequalities certainly were not so severe that they would force some to sell themselves into servitude or slavery. Those were customs practiced by other less-enlightened nations. Rather they were inequalities of great wealth and the power it bestowed, and also of abject poverty and its helplessness, and these did split the population. A ladder for advancement was almost nonexistent, except for highly prized artisans, artists, and architects, in the world of commerce or the maritime power of the nation. In the field of physical achievements, the top acrobats of the island's favorite sport, bull dancing or bull jumping, became the darlings of the population, at least for the brief time while they were able to perform—before being maimed or gored by the bulls.

As true of almost all civilizations, gold was the most prized metal, used extensively for special household utensils and for personal adornment. Those who were able to transform melted-down gold into the exquisite cups, rhytons, goblets, and bowls, those who were able to shape the beautiful hair, neck, and arm ornaments for the ladies of Knossos, of Malia, Gournia, Zakros, and Phaistos were revered and lionized for their skills and their sense and eye for beauty and style. Beyond such artists, a very few, very gifted ones, working both as goldsmiths and sculptors, produced exquisitely made small gold figurines of both male and female bull dancers, which have forever remained treasures of the world.

Great merchant ships commuted regularly between the northern shore of Egypt, along the many inlets of the river Nile, only to return laden with the gold bullion which flowed from the Nubian Desert, northward to Crete and farther north to Mycenae, and the small but wealthy colonies of Athens and Thebes, or eastward to Troy and the developing cities of Tyre, Sidon, and Byblos. There was no shortage of gold, the shortage existed only in the limited number of those with sufficient talent to perform the miracle of its transformation. But those who existed knew the secret of gold—how it could be worked and reworked again, to be transmuted from one item to the next without danger to its integrity, its glorious rich color and glow, or its exquisite malleability.

And so it was that the famous goldworker Patinos, favored by the king and his queen, received a large Egyptian shipment of various gold items, rescued by the master of the palace at Thebes, out of storage where it had been covered by the dust of centuries and the sheltering sand of the Sahara Desert. Many of the items showed their age; they were marred, badly scratched, their state and appearance making them no less valuable to the man who lived to reshape them and to make them come glowingly alive again.

If there is any one form of art which lives on forever, it is the goldwork created by such men as Patinos—inspired, inventive, imaginative. Long after their bodies are dust, their memories have faded, they live on in the glowing splendor of their creations.

It may have been the irony of fate, or pure happenstance, that the most beautiful of the gold ornaments which had originated on the island of Crete were created by the ugliest, most deformed of men—deformed in body but not in his mind and spirit. In no way seemed the degree of such ugliness to inhibit the wondrous creativity of the human spirit.

Prologue

The deep growling came up from the bowels of the earth through the cracks in the mountain. It persisted for almost two passes of the sun and moon. Of course, the population was quite accustomed to such noises and to the suddenly orange and blood-red-streaked sky over the neighboring island of Thera. It was, they knew, caused by the divine light emanating from inside the neighboring mountain of the Great Earth Mother. It was a frightening and wondrous event, which would lead to much trembling and shaking of the earth that would eventually subside.

But this time, the earth suddenly began to shake with great violence, and then the top of the mountain exploded with the shattering sound of a thousand bullhorns. Arching sparks winged through the dark of the night sky in every direction, falling into the water to sizzle and hiss with frustrated fury that they were being conquered and extinguished by the sea. Others that chanced to fall on the summer-dry land ignited the sedge and desiccated shrubs of the hillsides. Within seconds, screaming flames reached toward the sky. The choking smell of sulfur lay heavily over the ocean, over that blessed island called Crete and its beautiful city of Knossos. The ground began to shake so violently that people had to crawl on their hands and knees to move or not move at all.

Then the ocean, living beast that it was, rose up with an unearthly roar, like a wounded animal wanting to free itself from its prison, pushing, pushing from below, against the surface of the water. The surface rose and rose and rose even more until it almost reached the peak of Ida, the mountain of the great goddess. Then the wall of hungry water finally crested and broke, one wave on top of the other, in a desperate effort to catch one another on their way to the nearest shore.

The nearest shore was that of the blessed island of Crete.

Again and again, it was told, this had happened in the distant past, starting long before even the most ancients' memories. That this should happen now, in this moment of recognition between two long-separated lovers, knowing that these days were the end of the lives of so many they loved, the end of hope for living for so many; maybe their final days—but also the hope for living for however short a time—in happy togetherness; that this should happen now was the final irony, sadness, and joy of their lives, this seemed momentous to them.

Yet life went on, always, always, whether wished for or not, through endless devastation and then the short periods of joy. And going on, forward, but together they found that the struggles to stay alive were made so much sweeter by doing them together. And each of them thought and said to one another, marveling how unimaginably unpredictable and wonderful were the twists of their lives. The twists of anyone's lives.

Down by the wharf, the buzz of early morning activity slowly gave way to noonday quiet. The city lay shimmering and simmering in the heat. As the ships lying at anchor were off-loaded, they began riding higher and higher in the water, rolling more and more freely with the swell of the tide. Small knots of people were still congealed here and there. Around a trireme from the mainland, which had brought gold bullion, a row of soldiers stood guard, lances bristling and glinting in the sunlight. To the extreme right, a slow-moving line of half-naked slaves still carried bales of hemp off a Phoenician merchant ship. A few well-to-do citizens, merchants, or government agents perhaps, stood irresolutely in front of one of the waterfront wine shops, engrossed in discussion of some sort. The shrugs of their shoulders and broad gestures of their arms were clearly visible from her vantage point at the top of the cliff overlooking the harbor.

It must be noonday, Naïs thought, casting a glance at the sun overhead. The heat was oppressive. There was not a cloud in the sky, and hardly a breeze stirred the dusty leaves of the ancient olive trees around her. The air smelled of thyme, and fat bumblebees droned around the parched shrubs of the thyme-and-heather-covered hillside.

She sat at her favorite spot under the lone juniper at the top of the cliff, to the left of the harbor below. Behind her a row of rounded hills stretched down to the flat plain, which was almost totally occupied by the city. The seemingly endless rows of two and three-story apartment houses of Knossos outlined the winding alleys, which were barely visible from this distance. The more elegant residences of the rich winked through the green foliage of the hills to either side of the city. At the edge of the plain nearest to her, on a small elevation, stood the palace, perfectly centered under the dome of sacred Mount Ida, the shapes of its buildings indistinct in the haze. A mirage toy of white and red and black, she thought, its colors and detail diffused by the distance and the vegetation surrounding it.

Naïs shifted her position, for one of her legs—the one she had tucked under her—had fallen asleep. Making a grimace, she rubbed her tingling calf and ankle, then wiped her moist brow with her arm. She ought to go home, she thought again—god knows how often—to start cooking the family meal. Well, she would stay just a little while longer, just until the sun had moved past its highest point. Ido was bound to come this way on his return from the morning's practice; he should have come already. The morning sessions usually did not last this long to stretch into the heat of midday. Never mind that it would exhaust the people to jump and tumble in this heat, but the heat was also hard on the bulls, and that factor was really what mattered most.

The great spectacle of bull dancing, she thought, and the great business of commerce, those were the only two activities where, in general, the comfort of people did not take precedence. Not the comfort of the common folk, of course, for who cared if a servant or a workman was discomfited by the heat or by the wind or rain or cold, but the comfort of Those-Who-Mattered: the famous and celebrated bull dancers, the rich merchants, shipbuilders and shipowners, the great artists and the revered officials of the state, the servants of the gods, and the king and his family.

Those-Who-Mattered did not live in the city, in the squalor and stench of the narrow crooked lanes, with their houses side by side, the apartments up and down narrow flights of creaking wooden stairs, the stairwells reeking of rotting fish and urine. Their homes were spacious and richly appointed; their water flowed from taps and fountains and did not have to be brought up from the wells. Their walls were painted with flowers and animals of the land and sea and not with soiled whitewash, and when they lounged outside, ancient trees shaded them under wide doorways and canopied terraces.

One day, she mused, I will be among Those-Who-Mattered... *I'll wear ruffled skirts, show my naked bosoms for all the world to see and admire their beauty...wear high headdresses, and have my hair curled into the tightest little curls in long strands all about my face...I'll have servants prepare the meals and make my bed and wash my clothes...I'll wear gold snake armbands and gold hairpins made to look like honeybees and butterflies.*

She sighed with frustration. Well, she thought, for any of that to happen, one needed to take stock of what one could offer the goddess so that she would even consider giving her invaluable assistance! Having learned to be brutally honest with herself, there was precious little of real value or excitement; she was very pretty, attractive even, but no great beauty. Little pots of cream and paint and kohl, those could certainly remedy that. Her hair was truly her crowning glory—heavy, black as a raven's wings and as shiny, falling in cascades of carefully trained ringlets and curls almost to her waist. Her bosoms now were like two perfect small round melons. Once lifted and uncovered above the high waist of her dress, they would be just waiting to be shown to the world—with a little rouge on the nipples for emphasis. Actually, she corrected herself mentally, the dress she did not yet have but would wear eventually with the help of the goddess. The rest of her body was as athletic and lithe as that of Athenis, who was currently the most famous among the female bull dancers. But as everyone knew, fame was transient, as fleeting as a sudden storm over the waters of the sea. And in contrast, she was young—much younger than Athenis—and time was at her side, at least for a longer time than for Athenis. More than anything else, she had a mind that could plan, project, and adapt, something which, she had found out, was rare among women, perhaps among men as well?

What she did not have, to any degree, was wealth. Even the home she lived in was her father's and overcrowded to the point of bursting. Actually it was not even her father's but paid for by him each turn of the season from the coins he earned. She had no objects, goods, produce, or live animals to barter, nothing to take to the market to sell; the only thing she had was herself, her brain, her youth, and her body. Well, she knew fully that that field was already crowded; others were as endowed with physical attributes and willing to turn them into coins, but most of them did not have her brain, her capacity for planning and then to persevere once the planning was done.

She needed to face the fact that to sit here under a tree and observe the passing of another day's life in town, however entertaining, did not bring her any closer to her goals. Except perhaps if she would run into Ido, but Ido was evidently delayed, and she could sit here no longer because the dinner for her family had to be cooked, or else there would be hell to pay. And, she thought sourly, let's face it, Ido was mostly interested in himself and in advancing his fame and glory. It would take all her persuasive powers to make him look at her in a way other than that of a childhood friend.

With another sigh, she rose to be on her way down the precipitous hillside, to one of those narrow curving little wynd where her father's house was located. Well, actually not her father's house, but the house in which one of the apartments belonged to her and to her family. More to the point, the apartment did not even belong to them but had to be paid for at each passage of the moon with her father's and her precious hard-earned coins.

Halfway down the hillside, she heard the sound of loose gravel rolling by and footsteps behind her. The path was too treacherous for her to turn around to see who was coming, until she came to a scrawny shrub that she could grasp and hold on to while she turned her head. Much to her surprise, she saw Ido struggling, slipping, and sliding along the path, finding it more difficult to negotiate than she did because he was so much heavier than her. He was concentrating on the path ahead of him, and when he finally looked up and saw her, he flashed a smile at her and waved tentatively, not daring to move about too abruptly for fear of sliding down the rocky slope.

"Well," he said gaily, "finally! I thought I would never catch up with you! I figured you were looking for me?"

Naïs, meanwhile, had settled herself so that the bush was in front of her and protected her from sliding. Ido was standing above her, holding on to a withered branch at the very top of the same bush. She lifted one eyebrow and shrugged her shoulder. "Why on earth should I have been looking for you?" she asked nonchalantly.

She reached down, pulled up a short thyme sprig, and started chewing on it.

"What else would bring you up here day after day at this hour with the sun high above? You probably knew that this is the shortcut from the bullring I usually take?"

She shrugged again. "I like coming up here before I buy the food for dinner. It's a pretty view, don't you agree? And I can see all the ships that come and go."

Ido smiled at her with the gentle affection he had retained since they were childhood playmates. Back then she was a daring little girl, five—almost six—years his junior, always tagging after him, her short legs pumping hard not to fall behind. In her eagerness, she would climb up, jump down, leap across any obstacle to keep up with him.

"You, child," he said grandiosely, "were always a bad liar! Even then you could never quite deceive me, and now you still cannot. You are just a silly girl. What is it you want?"

Naïs looked him up and down with what she hoped was forbidding disdain mixed with trusting appeal. "First off, I do not want to hear you call me child ever again. It is insulting. I am no younger than most of those women you parade around you, or whatever else you do with them! Second, I want you to win me a place in the Sacred School!" She took a deep breath, hoping that the second want just imperceptibly slid into the conversation. There, she thought, now it was out and said, and she could no more pull it back or deny it. She had no intention to pull it back!

Ido was not just surprised, he was nonplussed. How could she say something like that so casually? How could she be even thinking about something like that? It was not fitting for her to try to push herself into a group that she did not belong to! Who did she think she was? Just because they had been friends as children did not give her the right—well, the whole thing was just too ridiculous! It was entirely unthinkable!

"Naïs, Naïs, please understand, I have no special influence with the judges! I cannot say to them, 'Yes, do this,' or 'No, refrain from doing that!' I am just a former student and one of their performers. All right, perhaps better than most of the other performers, but understand this, I have no special privileges! You cannot ask me to do something which I am not capable of doing." He tried to use his most reasonable voice, but obviously she did not listen to his points.

"Why do you assume that I am still a stupid child who believes every kind of silliness told to her? I know how much you are in favor at the Sacred School! I know how everyone bows to you because they believe that you will be the next master of the dance teachers. You are already almost a Revered Teacher! If you have no influence, then I would not know who has? It is more likely that you do not want to squander the goodwill of those in power on such an insignificant request as one made by insignificant me!" And as she finished her tirade, she half-twisted her body to be able to look Ido into his eyes while still maintaining some contact with the bush for safety.

She had wedged one of her feet and the other knee against the rough bare branches, and her calf-length skirt twisted up around her hips to expose most of her strong slender legs and most of one thigh as well. She barely paid any attention. The customs of her people did not attach great significance to exposure of parts of the body. Being supreme aesthetes, the only requirement was that the exposed body be young, well conditioned, and pleasing to the eye. Despite this, Ido could not help but notice. The look he gave her, although unnoticed by her, became decidedly warmer than it was before. She was more concerned with marshaling her thoughts into a logical argument, and quickly too before he decided to turn and walk away from her, down to his family's house, to eat his dinner.

"To be sure, if it were Athenis making a request to you, however onerous, you would strive to comply with all your power! But then, what you would receive in return would far outweigh anything that you could expect from me, for what could I possibly offer that would appeal to you?"

There, she thought, now it was out, spelled out as clear and plain as anyone could. The next move was entirely up to him. He could either pretend to ignore her or else, well, that would remain to be seen, wouldn't it?

Eager not to overplay her hand and not to have him believe that she was desperate, she rose, and smoothing down her skirt and adjusting the short tight little vest she wore, flicked her fingers at him as she blew him a kiss. Then she turned, cautious not to slip along with the small shards of shale and gravel rolling down where her foot had been, and flounced down the hill toward the city with as much dignity as the sloping terrain would allow her.

*****

They did not run into each other over the next weeks. Naïs was occupied with her family's needs, which seemed to only increase and close in on her since her mother's death a year ago. Her father was increasingly ill as well, his deep dry cough worse with each passing day, his rattling breathing more and more strenuous. Her two sisters and three brothers, all younger than her, were driving her crazy with their wants, their nagging and whining. She knew that at the root of her irritation was one truth—unavoidable, undeniable, and unchanging—she could not alter their circumstances nor provide for their needs in an adequate manner. To be poor and needy was hell, she thought, for the hundredth time. Like a sparrow caught in a cage, fluttering this way and that but unable to escape its prison, her thoughts went round and round on the mental treadmill imposed upon her by her thirst to get out of this trap of poverty and squalor which surrounded her.

When they met again, it was entirely unexpected and unplanned. She was just turning the corner from the fishmonger's shop, with the day's dinner wrapped in a piece of seaweed, and she was really not looking left or right but had her mind focused only on how to stretch one smallish fish into a meal for seven. She literally bumped into him, and the fish, with its wrapping, went flying, the wrapping opening and discharging its content into the sand and dust of the road. Ido grinned at her and helped her collect the dropped fish, as she stood there irresolute, not quite knowing what to do with the sand which now covered it. Ido laughed, flashing beautiful white teeth at her, took the fish from her hands, and carried it over to the well in the center of the square. Still shaking his head, he dunked the poor mauled fish, scraped off the dirt and dust, and, rewrapping it as best he could, gave it back to her with a flourish.

Naïs was watching him with a frown. Something, somehow must have lifted him up so much that he almost floated. She needed to know what it was and if it was something that she could use to her own benefit? Could she approach him again about admission to the Sacred School? Would he actually listen to her and—finally—treat her as an adult with adult needs and desires and not like the adoring little girl she had been once, tagging behind him wherever he went? And then, without prodding and most unexpectedly, it was Ido who approached the subject preying on her mind.

"Well, ho there! Look out, little girl! Continue not to watch were you are stepping and see just exactly what suspiciously shady persons you will run into! What are you doing in this part of town? Trying to wrap the poor old fishmonger around your little finger to sell you his day-old fish at half price, aye? Still playing the servant to your family, neh?" He shook his head in disapproval, cocked an eyebrow at her, and looked her up and down with a slightly lopsided and lecherous grin. "If you are on the warpath to seduce anyone, or practicing for it, at least pick yourself a worthier subject than that old guy with his half-rotted teeth and jiggly paunch! You, little one, are much too beautiful and delectable to be wasting yourself on someone like him. I thought your taste in men was better than that!"

Suddenly Naïs, never before acting impetuously but now encouraged by his compliments, smiled and gave Ido an unambiguous look of coyness.

"By worthwhile subject, do you mean someone like yourself?" She almost felt her knees buckle when he shrugged, tossed back his head, and laughed.

"That could be arranged, don't you think? You did ask me for a favor not that long ago and offered what sounded like a possibly interesting payment…As it happens, I have now been appointed the next master of dance teachers, so possibly—just possibly—it could be arranged…" And he let the suggestion float in the air between them.

Naïs's breathing hitched, and for a moment, she stared at Ido with eyes rounded and mouth parted in surprise. Ido laughed again and, bending down, tickled her chin, something he used to do when she was a child. He knew she had hated it even then, and his laughter only intensified when he saw the dark look she gave him as she swatted his finger away.

Lifting the heavy curled black hair from her ear, he put his lips next to it and whispered, "If you have serious plans of seduction, my dear, maybe you will need someone to practice on first, neh? Remember, one can only become a master through relentless practice, or isn't that what your, ah, admired 'friend,' the great Athenis, always says to the new recruits for the bullring? Well, if it would interest you, and assuredly in the spirit of our old friendship, I am willing to offer myself as practice object!"

And still laughing when he saw that the fish which she had been clutching was ready to slip from her suddenly slack fingers once again, he pulled the package from her hands and slipped it into the fold of the shawl she wore, like all Cretan women when they went about outside their homes. Just to make sure that the package was secure, he tucked the edges of the shawl around it, patting her breasts in the process with studious care, until once again, she slapped his hand away.

Naïs could barely mask the excitement she felt at the open offer. She was well past the age when most young girls lost their innocence and started acquiring lovers. She had so single-mindedly focused all her attention, all her admiration, all her desires on Ido that she literally ignored the other young men she knew or grew up with. She was aware that she was pretty and desirable, but then so were most of the young girls in her circle of friends. Altogether in a group of giggling, chattering, nubile young women, she was much the same as most, except that she stood out for her drive, her thirst to become better, richer, more famous, more admired, more desired: altogether more. And in her life, limited by her family's poverty, bounded by the few alleys and their inhabitants within which she moved, more was what Ido offered. He represented the bullring's glamour of wealth and fame. For her, he represented importance, connections, status, and the admiration of a whole nation—things that young girls who lack all of those privileges dream about. In addition, he was handsome and, in an entirely nonsexual way, already her friend.

She swallowed and desperately tried to arrange her expression into one of pleased surprise. She leaned toward him and let her fingers run up and down his arm, her palm finally resting on his well-muscled chest.

"You know that I am not free to roam, you know how difficult it is for me to get away from my family," she whispered with a coy look. "It would be hard for me to accommodate myself to your off hours…but…" And she gazed away, anxiously chewing on her lower lip.

Ido smiled and, once again, bent his head to her ear. "Well, then you should consider this as one of many future challenges you will encounter before long! I am quite certain that you know exactly the hour when I leave the Sacred School each day. You also know which path I travel from there to the city…Surprise me, child!" And he slid his fingers under her chin, lifted her head, and brushed a kiss like butterfly wings over her lips. Before she could answer, he had already turned and was disappearing in the noontime crowds of the bazaar.

Naïs could barely calm her excitement. As much as she wanted to immediately act upon Ido's invitation, she could not see herself free to search him out during the next day or the day after that. Her father, demanding attention from her at the best of times, had a fever and the shakes and lay on his cot, alternately shivering and sweating in the oppressive heat of midsummer. Naïs tried to cool him with extra water she carried home from the cistern around the corner from their apartment building. She soaked one of her father's old work cloaks in the wat and, wringing it out, wrapped it around her father's writhing, squirming body. Then in no time at all, the man began to shiver with cold, and Naïs tried desperately to quickly dry him and then stack several faded and ragged blankets on top of him. It seemed to be an effort without end and with no letup, which did not even leave her time to cook their daily supper. Finally she summoned Emeris, the older one of her sisters, showed her what to do, and bid her to keep calming their father while she went about to gather some cold cheese, curdled milk, a small bowl of olives and another of figs, and flat rounds of the bread she had just made the day before and laid them out on the much-scrubbed trestle table.

It turned out to be actually the third day when Naïs, filled with anxious anticipation, made her way to a little abandoned temple, built generations ago to the Great Mother of all animals. The goddess's worship had declined during recent generations. The little round structure with a simple stone altar, its roof already fallen into disrepair, its painting of bounding mountain goats almost entirely obliterated by the decades of rain and searing sun, silently crumbled back into the mountainside from whence it had once been erected. The path which Ido trod almost every day led by the temple, and she had often seen him pause there and have a drink from the hip flask of pig bladder he always carried.

Naïs made herself as comfortable as she could, leaning her shoulders against the stone wall. She had selected her prettiest skirt, usually only worn on feast days, because she knew the bright colors she had laboriously embroidered into the border of the bottom flounce suited her coloring and black hair. The little blouse was the only one she owned actually cut like those worn by the fashionable women—a short-sleeved little vest not quite reaching the midriff, the material extending from the neckline carefully looped underneath her breasts, leaving them bare. To follow current fashion even more, she had added a small daub of red paint to embellish her nipples.

She sighed, feeling entirely inadequate to the requirements of the assignation. Before, when she was more or less toying with the idea of Ido's seduction to exploit his hoped-for ardor for her aspirations, well, back then things looked simple. Now, however, she had to face her own lack of finesse—expertise? Oh, whom was she kidding? In practice she knew nothing of lovemaking, which was truly embarrassing because all of her girl friends had already had several lovers. She felt left behind. A totally inept loser. Tied to the needs of her family and without freedom to devote herself to the time-consuming experimentations of the mysteries of love, she had pretended in conversations, laughed along with her friends with a knowledgeably suggestive smile, a little wink when appropriate, while cringing inside with embarrassment. Now the truth would come out, and she could only hope that despite of her innocence, her virginity, Ido would either be understanding and discreet or so enchanted with her that no shameful gossip would be spread about her ineptness.

I'll simply kill him if he shames me or belittles me! she thought, and almost as soon as her anger blossomed, she heard the familiar footsteps. *Such strong footsteps taken so lightly, a well-trained bull dancer indeed*, she thought for a moment, then looked up, smiling at him as he stopped in front of her.

He smiled. "Well, finally. As much as that surprises me, I almost came to the conclusion that you were uninterested. In truth, I must say, I would have been disappointed. I have watched you grow up into a rather promising young woman and wondered why you have never approached me, until that day on the hillside. You wanted to use me to get into the Sacred School. Remember? You, my dear, are a lousy flirt. But now that is neither here nor there!"

He half turned away from her, dropped the pig bladder hip flask on the stone floor of the temple, then took off the wolf-hide cloak he had wrapped around his waist in preparation of wearing it later, when the day would cool off, and dropped that as well. Finally he sank to the ground with the athletic grace which had made him so much admired around Knossos, in fact, throughout the northern half of the island, and even beyond. He extended his hands to her.

"Well, now that you are here finally, let's not waste our time. There are many lovelier things to occupy us than just staring at each other, neh?" And he lifted his flask to offer the sweet Cyprus wine to her. She wrinkled her nose and shook her head.

"Oh, Ido, I am not accustomed to wine, but it is sweet of you to offer, anyway."

"Well, that's even more reason to get acquainted with it, neh? If you wish to move in more exalted circles, you should become familiar with the many finer things which now are not yet known to you!" And he caught her hand as she was reaching for the flask. Not letting go, he pulled her closer, nuzzling her knuckle, and then her neck as he pulled her closer still.

"We," he murmured softly into her ear, his breath sending shivers down her back, his lips moving down the side of her neck to her shoulders, "are wasting precious time chattering. Come, let's get rid of this skirt. However pretty it is and however much you wanted to show me how nicely you can embroider, right now it is surely in our way, neh?" He stood up, pulling her up as well, and hooked his fingers into the waistband of her skirt. She started for a moment but, anxious not to show any reluctance, shed the skirt as quickly as she was able to and, bending down, stepped out of it, tossing it to the side. As all women, she wore nothing under the skirts, except in the cold days of midwinter. Her legs, lovely and long, shimmered golden in the setting sun. Somewhat embarrassed, she knelt down onto the wolfskin and averted her face.

Ido followed her down to the cloak, his fingers busy with the ties of her little vest. His fingers purposefully brushed the soft skin of the swell of her breasts, then dipped between them.

"You must tell me what it is that you particularly enjoy, child. I need your guidance since we have never loved each other before."

Naïs bit her lip and, looking at him hesitantly, buried her face in the crook of his neck while she lifted her shoulder.

"I don't know," she stammered, "it doesn't matter to me... Whatever you wish..."

"Of course it matters! When we make love, it is my duty to pleasure you, just as it will be yours to satisfy me! Surely you know that—you must have been told such things?" He gave her a half-dubious, half-worried look that made Naïs smile, even though she felt more and more anxious with each passing moment. When she remained silent to his question, he grabbed her shoulders and shook her gently. "Tell me, honey, who taught you? Who explained things to you? Who did you make love to? Who made love to you? Or do you even have an idea?" And when she remained silent, he shook her shoulders again, more vehemently in his worry. "Well? No one? Neh? Please do not tell me that you had never—that you never had any lovers? Gods be merciful! You little bitch! You want me to get rid of your virginity and be your teacher? Like I don't have anything better to do? And you never told me so? And you pretended...pretended to flirt with me? Gods be merciful! I should just get up and walk away! What do I need a silly little clueless virgin to waste my time on? You devious sly little bitch!"

The muscles of his arms bunched as he commenced to push himself away from her and to get up. She grasped at his arm and clung to him with desperation. There were tears in her eyes as she looked at him. Her chin trembled. The corners of her mouth turned down.

"Please," she whispered, "please, don't! I am so sorry! Please, please don't go! Please don't be angry with me! I—I couldn't, I just couldn't get away from my family. Twice I wanted to meet a boy"—she quickly sucked in her breath and hurried on—"no one you would know, just someone from my building…when my father found out that I was planning to leave before the dinner was cooked, he beat me, and he told me never to dare do that again. And never to think of leaving during the night either, when he could need me…or he would really hurt me…The next time I went to meet the boy, I was so scared I ran away from him and ran home before I was found out…" She was sobbing now, great big heaving sobs, while the tears were streaming from her eyes. She reached for her discarded skirt and mopped her face with it. Any illusion she had before that she could appear pretty and desirable to him vanished with her tears and distress.

Like men always, everywhere, Ido became increasingly uncertain with each falling tear. She was, after all, an old childhood friend, a former playmate, and he knew the oppressive home she lived in, at least ever since the death of her mother, who, at least, had attempted to mediate daily strife. Although he considered any assignation with an untried innocent a waste of his time, and certainly no feather in his cap, should it get out and become known, he could not refuse the naked crying girl sitting on his cloak on the leaf-littered floor of the crumbling little temple.

He sighed, turned to her. "Stop that!" he ordered. "I guess it will be no harm if we try to enjoy each other and spend some time together. Here, honey. Let me just make you more comfortable. Stop that crying! Who has ever heard of making love to a sobbing woman!

This is not a drama in the theater, for the love of the goddess!" And he tweaked her nipples to make her laugh, even though Naïs only managed to give him a rather watery smile.

She watched him as he unwrapped his loincloth and kicked off his soft leather boots. She could see his sex, like a soft little furry animal curled up and asleep between his thighs. She watched him as he bent closer and closer to her until his lips were caressing her wet face, her brows, her temples, the bridge of her nose. His tongue circled the shell of her ear. He began to nibble on an earlobe. Gently the nibbling teeth tugged, then he drew the earlobe between his teeth. She moaned softly and saw his sex awaken, just like a little animal stretches from sleep, with a twitch, then another, and then unfold with unexpected suddenness until it rose up to become threateningly big and glistening against his belly.

She sighed, wanting to turn her head away, but Ido wouldn't let her. Two hands cupping her face, he started to kiss her mouth, soft gentle kisses at first. When she began to move with impatience and brushed the arches of her feet against his legs, he became more insistent, deepened his kisses, pushing his tongue into her mouth to play with her tongue, until her breathing and heartbeat became faster and more irregular. When he finally liberated her mouth from his, he rocked back on his heels to look at her, taking time and care to let his eyes roam over her. He shook his head and sighed.

"Lovey, you know—or maybe not—how many women's bodies I have looked at? None of them compare quite with yours! And you are right, the Great Goddess may have made you for success in her Sacred School. Long of limb, your arms and legs could be trained for strength, resilience, and flexibility more easily than most, your hips and torso as well. Maybe your wish to be a part of the school is not just a foolish young girl's foolish dream? You could actually have some success at it, I am thinking! But that is for another day, not for now. Now we should only have thoughts for each other and how we please each other, neh?"

Naïs, her heart racing with the excitement caused by what he had just said, and her body aching with an unexpected desire, clutched at Ido's arm and whispered with almost desperate urgency, "Is there anything you want me to do now? Anything to help you?"

Ido, continuing his critical examination of her body, lazily trailed his fingers down between her breasts to her navel. Fingers circling her navel, he frowned to concentrate on her question, raised his eyebrow, and nodded.

"Oh, aye, there is little one. Just lie down and find yourself as comfortable as you can. Then part your legs. No, not just your feet, silly dilly! Your legs, all the way up…ah, yes, like that."

She turned away. For a moment, her heart squeezed with a sense of longing for the days when she was much younger and so much more innocent of the world, of life. He used to call her silly dilly when she was a little, little girl, but she no longer was that, and she would better heed what he was saying.

"Now bend your knees! Oh, for the love of the goddess, raise your knees as you bend them! It may look silly at first and feel ridiculous, but trust me and just follow my lead. Aye, little one, brace yourself, here I come!" And with a laugh, he let his body settle upon hers.

Naïs's eyes widened in sudden surprise. He was so—naked. So warm. So hard and knotted with muscles. She closed her eyes in an effort to hide how startled she felt. She heard his murmur, telling her to put her hands around his neck. She did. Without looking, she knew he was kissing her breasts, gently pulling on her nipples, kissing her navel, belly. Beyond that, as his mouth moved farther to her hips, the length of her long thighs, she lost all her concentration. In truth she lost all ability to think. All she could do was feel. And the feelings which assaulted her were so exquisite, so incredibly wonderful that they shook her whole body. When she felt him touch and stroke places which she couldn't even name and had barely paid attention to in the past, her breathing stopped. She began to raise her body to him and moan with the agony of wishing to escape from the assault of his touches and the conflicting desire to be closer and closer to him, to the incredible exquisite sensations he forced on her. She felt her body spiraling out of control, falling apart, twisting, rising toward him, flying with him to some unknown place, ignoring the sudden short burst of pain that invaded her because the pain was so trivial in the greatness, the body-shaking incredible magnitude of all her other sensations.

When she descended back to the floor of the little broken-down temple, she heard herself whisper, "Oh, Great Goddess, I thought I was dying!"

Ido was propped up on his arm, watching her with a quizzical smile. His chest was heaving as he was gulping for air. It was only then that Naïs noticed how her heart was racing as well. He groaned and pulled her hip closer to himself, slinging his muscular thigh across her legs. "That wasn't dying, darlin', but taking your pleasure from me and giving me pleasure in return. That's what we call making love…and so now you know." He sighed sleepily and gently rocked her as he cuddled her in his arms.

Shaking his head as though in disbelief, he continued, "Well, darlin', here we are…all grown-up now, aren't you? You, little one, are just so full of surprises! Who would have thought that you would catch on so fast and participate with just so much enthusiasm? That is my second discovery about you today, you know! And I thought I knew you so well. Just goes to show one. My dear, in my opinion, you are a natural for love just as you are, I believe, a natural for the bullring. Mark my words, those two talents could make you famous and rich. And I," he whispered as he moved his head closer to her to nuzzle her neck, "I will be only too happy to assist you in your education and your quest, neh?"

*****

That day became the defining day for Naïs. Her life, as it had been before. And now her newly awakened life. It felt like in the before days, she really hadn't lived at all. She had just existed on the margins of existence, a guest in the activities of others. Only a guest, never a true participant.

The world suddenly opened for her. She felt free and liberated, a sensation totally novel to her. Even her family's dire circumstances appeared peripheral to what had become the real core of her existence—the hours she was able to spend with Ido and the Sacred

School, the Great Goddess's great bullring. All her thoughts, all her striving—everything. It was everything!

By rote she performed the required duties around her home, taking care of the father, the sisters, and brothers. Her father was too ill to notice the change in her, but her siblings did. Being younger and less astute, they drew their feelings mostly from a greater sense of unease, a tension which surrounded Naïs, and attributed that to their father's illness. The oldest brother, Tomo, five years Naïs's junior, was the only one who observed her silently, wordlessly until the day when he, like a little shadow, followed her to the crumbling temple. He found her there. There she was—his sister and Ido. Together. Gods, did he ever observe them! Their writhing, groaning, moaning, straining lovemaking mesmerized him as much as it shocked him. Then he ran home, hiding in the stairwell before ascending the four floors to their apartment. He could not, would not talk about it, only think about it in secret. But one part of him understood, understood that Naïs was searching, searching for a doorway which could—which would—open to her. And maybe through her, it would then allow all of them to escape their endless poverty, the relentless grinding squalor which surrounded and stifled them.

Two weeks and two days after Ido opened a new world to her, another change arrived for Naïs. She awoke one morning and, as she did each morning, first walked over to her father's pallet to see to his needs, only to see that the man had died during the night. His knees drawn up to his body, as though in a paroxysm of pain, his hands balled into fists and pressed against his chest; he had finally died after weeks and weeks of illness, suffering, alternate shaking and sweating, wheezing, and coughing. He must have died hours ago because his body had begun to stiffen into his death position.

Naïs was saddened by his death but unable to truly mourn the man who—other than giving her life—had never done anything to add to her comfort, her security or happiness, never given her one laughter, one moment of joy, or even just one hug or caress, other than his hand raised in anger. She went through the expected motions of mourning: preparing his body for burial, washing him, rubbing oil into his skin, and then wrapping him in the linen shroud which she had purchased, and which, because it was not a newly woven piece of material, she had painstakingly mended, washed, and bleached in the sun. She could not afford the aromatic oils used by the wealthier folk, only the cheapest kind of oil people used for oil lamps. But she sprinkled some leaves of the thyme growing wild on the hillsides in it and told herself that it was the gesture, the effort that counted.

She had not enough coins even for anything but their daily necessities. At least while her father had lived, he was able to work and earn during those periods when his health was just a little better. He was a very able painter who, in his younger years, had contributed to the beautiful wall paintings which adorned many important government and commerce building in the city of Knossos. In those days, his name was known, and Naïs had reason to be proud of him. *Long-ago days*, she thought with a sigh, too long ago for any of those coins earned back then to be of any use to her now. Now there was nothing, no matter how carefully she looked into the bottom of every wicker basket, every pottery jug, every wooden bowl.

As much as she was reluctant to do so, he talked to Tomo and Emeris, the two oldest of her siblings. A while back, Emeris had started to take in laundry from several of the wealthier houses in the vicinity. Tomo already worked as delivery boy for the corner butcher who cooked stews and roasted spitted meats to sell to those who lived in homes without cooking facilities. Tomo promised to talk as well to the baker of breads and little honey-sweetened pastries, and offer his services to deliver those products. No one objected. Children of the poor everywhere grew up quickly and learned to help earn coin to whatever extent they could, to add to the family living. Childhood was short and hard, and adults were too consumed by the problems of daily living to coddle their children. As much as Naïs felt constrained to make such a request of them, since she was not their parent, nevertheless, she was the head of the family now, and Tomo and Emeris understood without question.

The single rays of sunshine in Naïs's life were her assignations with Ido. They were no longer secret; nothing ever remained totally secret in Knossos. But honestly, nobody cared one way or another. Sex outside of marriage was shrugged off, and it was expected that young unmarried adults would not remain chaste nor refrain from promiscuity. Adultery among married couples was not necessarily applauded but also not frowned upon, except that custom demanded that these couples not produce any offspring. Illegitimate children did not fare well in Minoan society. In the poor and needy underbelly of Knossos, and the other large cities like Zakros, Phaistos, and Malia, too many children became a heavy burden for a poor family. And there was abundant assistance to terminate pregnancies; women who specialized in this were readily available.

Living was harsh and individual lives of little value, except those of the rich and the powerful. Those people lived, like the stars at night in the unlit sky, so much above all others that the manner of their lives became unimaginable to all lesser folk. Well, Naïs had no intention to just disappear in the morass of poverty and to spend her life there. No intention! And now that her and Ido's relationship became more and more intense, she was more than ever convinced that he was her road to salvation.

Many of the avenues to power, which existed in other nations, did not exist here at home. Even their next neighbors—Sparta, Argos, and Pylos to the north, Miletus and Troy to the east, and Egypt to the south—revered the strength of their arms, their military, and reveled in showing off that strength by putting their heels on the necks of the weaker. She had seen plenty of galleys filled with soldiers and bristling with weaponry sheltering in their bay, the soldiers strutting and displaying their skills with weapons to impress anyone willing to watch, especially the very lovely, very available young women of Knossos. She had heard that military success leads to exalted position, power, and wealth.

But Knossos was not inclined to warfare and the exploits of their small military. Long ago, her forefathers had accepted that their location—a center of commerce in the Great Sea—was both a blessing and a curse. Easily accessible harbors assured a steady influx of money and goods. Trade and commerce boomed, and always had, as long back as memory served. If they were threatened, they dug into their reserves of coins to hire mercenary galleys and foot soldiers, wisely accepting that their island was neither trained nor equipped for self-defense.

All these considerations aside, she loved Ido. Or at least lusted after him. Thoughts of him haunted her, pursued her. He had awakened her passions, taught her body how to feel, to love, and now she often felt that she could not have enough of that passion, of the feeling that only a man could give her. Among many handsome athletic young men, he stood out as exceptional, his prowess in the bullring and his beauty were both legendary. He was the feather in her cap, the source of her burgeoning pride and self-assurance as more and more of her friends became aware of the relationship blossoming between them.

Once again, she was sitting on the floor of the tumble-down little temple, her back leaning against one of the few remaining columns which still supported the partial roof. Once again, she was waiting for Ido. She sat. She waited. After a while, she jumped up and started to circle the floor of the temple, trying to control her impatience as she chewed on a twig of thyme. When Ido finally appeared, as always smiling his devil-may-care smile, she flung herself at him, wondering if she should hug him or scream at him for making her wait. Passion won out; she kissed him greedily and rubbed her breasts against his chest. He threw back his head and loudly laughed at her.

"Whoa, little one! Don't damage me even before the bulls have a chance to!" He grabbed her elbows and pulled her away from his body.

"Now not a loud word! Not one angry sound! Today you should treat me with adoration, little one! I have done the almost impossible! An almost miracle! Seven days from now, on the day of first examinations, report to the Revered Mistress of the teachers at the Sacred School. Early in the morning, mind you. And after what all I told them about your skills, you better do me right, or else no one there will believe anything I say ever again, you hear!"

Naïs gasped, pressing both her hands to her mouth, then squealed as loudly as her lungs would allow and threw her arms about his neck, pulling his head to her. Her lips fell on any part of his face she could reach, and when he still laughingly protested and finally caught her elbows again to push her away from him, she started to dance around him, singing a popular bawdy little ditty about love's varied but always enticing rewards.

Shaking his head and still grinning, Ido finally picked her up and, caught up in her dance, swung her around. After settling her on the ground and pushing against her shoulders to settle above her, he began to kiss her mouth. Between his kisses, he laughingly tried to admonish her.

"Remember, little one, how you were planning to seduce me? Hah! What a hoot that turned out to be! You are damn lucky that I am such a forgiving and understanding lover! But if your plans to wow the lady teachers at the school are based on such flimsy accomplishments as the ones you presented to me, then I would urge you to abandon your plans! I don't want to be shamed by promoting the talents of a talentless little squirt. Yeah, I have my reputation to consider, neh, little one?"

Naïs was not about to be put off. Nor did she allow him to diminish her excitement. Her happiness. Her gratitude. She kissed him again and again, nuzzled his neck and licked his ear, until she saw him rise to tear off the wide belt adorning his slim waist. Impatiently he yanked at the ties of his elaborately embroidered codpiece to release his awakening sex. When he fell upon her, his body entirely naked, she wrapped her arms and legs about him and raised her body to him. As always, their coupling was filled with the lustful eagerness, urgency, and impatience of the very young.

*****

The night before the examination by the mistress of the Sacred School, Naïs did not sleep. She tried, though, tossing and turning from side to side because she desperately wanted to be as sharp as she possibly could be. She wished she would know what to expect, but her best efforts to squeeze the information from Ido had failed. He tried to explain to her, patiently and repeatedly, the he did not know because the teachers, in order to be entirely impartial, varied the requirements they placed upon the new contestants. Other than the obvious need to be as limber, agile, and resilient as a yet untrained human body could be, their questions and requests varied from contestant to contestant and from occasion to occasion. Besides, he explained to her that the mistresses who selected future students were only involved with the girls they examined, whereas he was a master and thereby in charge of the selection of young men.

"You must understand, little one that we are forbidden to spread the knowledge of what is required for entry into the school. Otherwise how would there be impartiality in the decision to accept someone? Admission would no longer depend on great talent shown before the judges, and on innate ability, but on skill acquired by assiduous prior practice to satisfy the judges' requirements, neh?"

She grudgingly pretended to accept his explanation but stuck her tongue out at him, as soon as he had turned his back, and flounced away in a huff.

Finally she gave up on sleep and rose to the day, her heart squeezing with anxiety. She felt horribly alone, lost, and abandoned. Not only had Ido closed himself to her, but her own sisters and brothers seemed unable to comprehend the implications which hinged on what would happen on this day, or maybe did not have the imagination to do so? Both Emeris and Tomo, though closest to her in age and slowly growing up to become more adult in their emotions, watched her getting ready and came to hug her and squeezed her hands in a silent gesture of allegiance and affection.

Now she was forced to face the day. Naïs knew that, without a doubt, this would become the most important day of her life. And so the night before, she bathed herself in the public bathhouse, spending some of the coins she had squirreled away earlier. She washed her hair and wove it into tight little braids while still dripping wet and, once it dried, fashioning the necessary curls and waves to frame her face and cascade down her back. She wrapped a loincloth, bordered by bright weaving, about her hips and thighs, covering it with a flounced overskirt, and topped with her tiny vest, which left most of her upper body bare. She wove a thin leather band into her hair to keep its black mass out of her face, her eyes. Around her arms, she wound the two precious copper snake armbands, which had once been her mother's. Finally she took a deep breath, squared her shoulders, and took one more look at the squalid little room which served as their kitchen and living quarters, wrapped a shawl about her against the cool of the early morning, and slipped out of the apartment.

She ran down the creaking wooden stairs filled with the stench of rotting garbage, then along the almost-deserted alley toward the hill at one end of the city, the hill glistening in the rising sun with the incomparable opulence and beauty of the royal palace.

The guards at the palace entrance were well aware that this was the day of examination for candidates to the Academy of Playing with the Sacred Bulls. They moved their lances out of her way and nodded their heads to her, muttering good wishes. Bull dancers and bull leapers were much admired members of the community, and it was unthinkable to wish them ill in their efforts. The taller one of the two guards shrugged his shoulder toward the left and jutted his protruding chin in the same direction, then shifting his lance from his right hand to his left, he waved her along a long corridor, still in the semidarkness of early morning.

"You'll find the mistresses of the school on the terrace at the end of the hallway. May the gods give you strong limbs and good luck!" he mumbled, bobbing his head.

His few words immediately raised Naïs's spirits. By nature, she was lighthearted and, in the depth of her soul, somehow unshakably convinced of her destiny. She would not have been able to express it so succinctly, but etched into the recesses of her brain was the conviction that surrender was not an option. Nay, to surrender to poverty, to squalor, to a life condemned to just being, to just existing day-to-day, without any hope of something better was less tolerable than curling up and dying!

By the time evening approached, and Naïs was allowed to leave, she was beyond exhaustion. Hungry and literally shaking with fatigue, her nerves frayed to the point of rupture, she did not even remember walking home. At the entrance to the crumbling apartment house where they lived, she felt someone touch her arm. She almost shrieked but then vaguely recognized Ido's touch, Ido's voice.

When he took her into his arms, she groaned and dropped her head on his shoulder. Like a dam breaking, she began to cry until shuddering sobs wracked her body. She felt his palms move up and down her back, heard his murmured soothing words, sensed his kiss upon her neck and her sweat-soaked hair. Eventually she quieted, her sobs diminished and turned into occasional hiccups. She gave Ido a watery smile more suited to defeat than victory and listened to his steps as he left her to disappear into the evening crowd jostling to return to their homes for their evening meals, his lighthearted laughter lingering in her ears. At the time, it did not occur to Naïs that he never asked her; he already knew the decision made by the mistresses.

Yet Naïs was barely able to remember what had transpired during the fateful day. Words, comments, images all became a jumbled blur. The rest of her family attacked her with questions, but all she could do was shake her head and raise her shoulders. When they pressed her to tell them how well she did, she had to honestly confess that she was not certain but that Ido was convinced of her success.

She ate some flatbread and cheese, nibbled on a few dates, then literally collapsed onto her straw pallet. She slept like a dead person and awoke in the morning with a groan, much later than she usually did. Unable to face the chores awaiting her, she escaped to her favorite place on the hillside above the city to attempt to sort out the events of the past day still circling around in her head.

Slowly it finally began to sink into her consciousness that she had made it—she had been accepted. Of course, as with all new students, acceptance to the Sacred School was, at first, only provisional for the first five courses of the moon. If her progress was as expected, if she gave sufficient promise to be taught further, then she would finally be officially inducted into the elite group of those who were allowed to call themselves Praised Students of the Sacred School. Ah! She could not even think of that without heat flooding her body and her heart slamming into her chest.

Oh, Great Goddess, she prayed, *how can I ever express my gratitude? For ultimately it was you and your benevolence that guided me, illuminated Ido's mind to help me. How can I ever repay your service? I have nothing. How can I ever be worthy of you? You know, Great*

Mother, that I am nothing. I swear to you with my most solemn oath that I am dedicating myself to you. All I will achieve, I will achieve for you since I know that you were my help. All I will possess, if you allow me to possess anything, will be yours.

She knelt on the ground, not on the broken tiles of the little temple but on the scrubby soil below the temple's steps, placed both of her palms on the parched dusty earth, literally feeling the contact between her body, her thoughts, and the Great Goddess, Mother of All, who was present in all the plants, animals, and humans of the earth. She sensed that she could not have made a more solemn oath than the one she just swore, and finally, finally her anxious agitated spirit eased and lifted her up to a feeling of joy such as she had never experienced before. She was finally calm. She was finally self-assured. And she was oh so very, very happy!

*****

The whirlwind of the next weeks carried through each of Naïs's days from daybreak to the next daybreak without letup, without giving her a chance to think of anything but her rigorous schedule of training and exercise. From daybreak to the next daybreak, rest only came when she collapsed upon her pallet, long after sundown, to sleep like a dead person until shortly before sunrise. Then she staggered to rise, wash the sleep from her eyes, clean her mouth and teeth, wrap the scant clothing she wore for the training sessions around her body, run a comb through her hair before wrapping the thick strands with a leather thong, eat a sparse breakfast on the run, and jog her way to the royal palace. Jogging was a requirement as it would strengthen her legs, loosen her joints, and make her waist and hips more limber.

As Naïs jogged, her eyes were raised to the wondrous great palace on the hill opposite to the city of Knossos, shining in the rays of the rising sun. Its beauty and grandeur caught the breath in her throat, as it had always done ever since she had been old enough to notice her surroundings. Incredibly, Naïs thought, now she was becoming a part of it, however tiny and insignificant. She frowned over the thought, but then it came to her that everyone was insignificant at one time, when they were infants. Even the children of the king were insignificant at first, not really even counted among the population for the first ten passages of the moon. Only after that time had elapsed, once they were believed to survive the dangers of early newborns, were babies acknowledged as citizens of the community, were they rich or poor, highborn or low.

Significance hinged only to a small degree upon who your parents were, who your lineage was, but much more so on how rich and influential they were within the community. This very thought suddenly shook her to the bones. Never before did Naïs have such a revolutionary idea. She stopped jogging and stared at the dusty path ahead in stunned silence. Somehow she sensed that her thought was important, important to her and how she should arrange her future life. She sensed that contrary to what most people thought, one's destiny was, at least to a large extent, given into everyone's hands. Only a curse from the gods would destroy it by drought, flood, or fire, landslide or the trembling of the ground, which arose from the depth of the earth. But then those things were the affairs of the gods, beyond human help or human effort.

Naïs took a deep breath as this knowledge descended into her soul and settled there. *What is to happen to me will be guided by me! As long as I keep the gods pleased, give them reverence and sacrifice, and do them homage by my artistry in the bullring, they, led by the Great Goddess, will help me, and none of what I achieve will wither away like a blighted plant... Oh, Great Goddess, thank you for advising me. I pray to you to keep me in the palm of your holy hands!*

As she relentlessly forced her body to perform the same repetitive motions, hour upon hour, she did not realize how tightly wound she was and how inexorably the desire to excel drove her. Ido found her one day in the great bull dance practice yard, the only person there, late after everyone else had departed. He opened the gate to the arena and stood there, leaning on the gate, watching her, watching the grace of her body, the limbs that stretched to reach the sky, the twist of her slim body in midair as she flew over the stuffed practice figure of a bull, her hands barely touching the two enormous horns.

He had not been with Naïs, not even seen her since she had started her training over the passage of two moons ago. Contact of teachers or other officials with the new students was forbidden during their initiation training period, which lasted another four turns of the moon. Then the students, who were, at this point, only provisionally accepted, would be tested again, their progress assessed, promise for their future evaluated, and finally, finally they were either accepted or rejected. Those who were accepted faced endless hours of further training until they were—maybe—deemed to be good enough to continue their training facing a living bull. There only one out of a hundred survived or, even though living, survived unmaimed. This was the moment when they were allowed to enter the arena, one bull and one, two, or three young men or women; by that point in time, no distinction was made as to the contestants' gender as they attempted to shape their future, to become adored and famous, or injured for life or died an agonizing death, gored by those huge horns.

Mesmerized, Ido stood clutching the gate latch. He did not want to call out to her; he did not even want to move. His total attention was centered on her. The last thing he wanted to do was to distract her. She had wrapped up her vaulting exercises and started on the various prescribed dance moves. Ido could not take his eyes off her, marveling at the grace and strength of her slim body, a body that he surely was well acquainted with! But now Naïs seemed to be a young butterfly emerged from her chrysalis, transfigured into a woman with all the grace and charm that, until now, had been deeply hidden within her.

Ido watched and felt his heart, his lungs, all the muscles of his body clench with sudden wrenching desire. He had never felt real desire for her before; she had been a part of his life, of his youth, and in that way, he had always liked her. He had deeply enjoyed making love to her because she was so responsive and passionate, but now all of a sudden, he wanted her, fiercely and jealously. The latter was much to his surprise. He had loved many young women and had always delighted in their mutual passion, but fierce jealousy was an emotion unknown to him, and he found it puzzling and unsettling; he thought it a sensation which he disliked rather quite a lot.

Fear struck him so suddenly and unexpectedly that he had to clutch the gatepost for support. What if others saw her as he did and desired her as much as he did? Of course others would see her; she was here to learn to perform, for the sake of the gods, wasn't she? How could he alone claim her? What right did he have to claim her? He was not her father, her brother, or her husband. He was her lover—considering her future, doubtless one of her lovers—and that did not allow him any rights whatsoever. Loving between young unattached adults was entirely accepted; no one would question two unmarried young adults who wished to have sex, but it also disallowed any claim of one for the other. If he would suddenly raise any rights over her, he would only become ridiculed and, even worse, laughable in her eyes.

He literally gritted his teeth as he forced a gay smile on his face. Eventually Ido decided he could no longer just stand there without speaking to her and touching her. He began to move the gate back and forth until it squeaked, then waited until Naïs stopped her pirouettes and, squinting into the sun, noticed him. She scowled briefly but then shrugged her shoulders and, bending, picked up a drying towel, walked the distance to the gate.

"What you just did there, the leaps and then those dance moves, I have to tell you, darling child, I have never ever seen done better. They were spectacular…the gods know I believe they could not be done any better! You, my love, are by far the best, the most awesome newcomer to this court! If you progress with this speed, you will be the queen of the game and the darling of the city! Ah…and to think that I knew her when…"

Naïs looked at him with eyes slanted, and her brow arched. "Really?" She shrugged. "I think, though, that if I give it two or three moon's passage of really serious practice, I could be a good deal better and could possibly try a double twist of my body with a backward kick when I do the vault. Who knows?" Impulsively she turned her body toward him as her eyes became serious, searching his face.

"I feel—I feel that I could stretch myself a lot more, but I need to know exactly how to go about it, you know? I—I feel like a whole lot is bottled up inside me, but I don't have the skill yet to bring it out." And smiling wryly, she shrugged again. "Oh, I don't know how to say it, it's just a feeling, you know...and you should not listen to me because then you will think that I am crazy!"

But Ido just shook his head, bent to pick up the towel she had dropped, and reached over to drape it over her sweat-glistening shoulder.

"What you need is some food to give you the strength you just lost during the last few hours, a good jug of wine, and a nice rest under a shade tree. And after you have eaten and drunk, you need some loving under that shade tree as well. Come!" She grinned at him and, raising herself on tiptoe, hooked her arms around his thick neck. When he lowered his head to her, she kissed him, nibbling on his lower lip, and rubbed her body against him.

"You sound just about right, love! What are we waiting for then?" And with a giggle, she sprinted ahead of him up the hillside to their favorite little tree-shaded temple.

*****

Odaro shifted on his chaise, one arm carelessly slung over the headrest, one leg dangling, almost touching the floor. He leaned forward, stretching to reach the bowl sitting on the low table to his left. His beringed fingers rooted among the piled-high figs and clusters of grapes; he chose a ripe fig and bit into it, noisily sucking the soft flesh and tiny seeds into his mouth before discarding the skin. With a satisfied sigh, he raised his leg and allowed his body to slide down the length of the chaise. For a moment, he closed his eyes, then lifted his heavy eyelids and his beautifully plucked and kohled eyebrows. He slanted a look at the man standing deferentially in front of him.

"How is it that this woman never appears in public in between her performances? Is this what I hear just gossip or the truth? Does she have a constant lover? Or is she planning to become a priestess of the Great Goddess? Is she a man-hater or even a woman-lover? Who and where is her family? Is she married? I want to know whatever is to be known about her. I want to meet her. I want to engage her interest. Arrange it. As speedily as you can. Go."

Ninno, Odaro's secretary, bowed. Yet this time, he was reluctant to do his master's bidding. Revered Dancers of the Sacred Bulls were above almost all others in status, they were mostly unapproachable, even if the person wishing to approach them had lots and lots of riches. His master had very few reservations. For much too long, he had been accustomed to doing whatever he wanted without restraint. And what he most wanted to do was relegated to the activities of his luxurious bedchamber. At any other time, with any other request, Ninno would not have hesitated; he did so now, even though just for a brief time. Then he bowed and backed out of his master's presence. He knew he would do what was required of him. He always did. That was why Odaro paid him so well. And so he sighed, bowed again, and went silently on his way, letting the translucent hangings of the doorway slither softly into place.

Odaro was restless, impatient. He had spent the last two days at the bull arena, watching and enjoying the various acrobats, the tumblers, the sword-swallowers, and snake charmers and erotic dancers from the Land of the Pharaohs. He wanted to reward himself after this last exceedingly successful trading voyage into the islands to the east. Most especially his dealings with the Greeks of the island of Cypros and the Phoenicians on the mainland, to the east of Cypros, had proven to be blessedly fruitful. All in all, Odaro was quite pleased. The entertainment of the bull arena, however, began to pall and lose its appeal by the afternoon of the second day. He was tempted to leave and only stayed because the best, the most artistic and enticing of the events, the bull dancing and leaping, was to close the festivities devoted to the Great Goddess. He also heard that there was a new performer, a woman of great skill and grace of movements who had started to make a name for herself. And so he did not leave. Somewhat skeptically, he slouched into his pillow-studded seat, chewing roasted pine nuts sweetened with the fragrant honey of thyme, which grew in such abundance on all the hillsides.

Finally—finally—with only a brief inevitable delay, the bull, decorated and garlanded, was cautiously led into the arena. Carefully the keepers removed the shackles, which bound the animal's front legs together to restrict his gait, then ran out of the arena as quickly as they could. The bull snorted, shook his head, and then tried his front legs. When he perceived that he was no longer restrained, he attempted a quick run diagonally across the expanse, then lowered his head, dug his horns into the loose sandy soil, and threw dirt over his shoulders. His hide, gleaming with careful oiling and tending, allowed much of the sand to adhere, making him look the more wild-looking and menacing. In the middle of the arena, breathing deeply, he stood still and stared at the ground. Irritated by the hordes of flies, the skin of his neck and over his flanks flickered. His tail swished.

When the three bull dancers made their appearance, entering the arena from the side opposite to where the bull had been led in, the audience rose as one. The cheering, whistling, and applause were almost deafening and certainly not destined to improve the bull's disposition. While he shook his huge curved horns in tandem with short snorts, he began to raise the dust by pawing the ground. The three dancers, two men and one woman, used this brief period of the bull's inattention to run into the center of the arena. The two men approached from left and right, while the woman slowly walked up close to the aroused animal, who did not know if he should confront his frontal enemy or the ones to either side.

And then, in an instantaneous move so fast that it blurred the outline of outstretched, extended arms and legs, streaking straight toward the bull's head, his huge horns, the woman, mostly naked except for bright-blue pants, flew between the horns and across the massive back. As high as a flying bird, her arms reaching for the sky, she somersaulted over the curved rump to come to stand several feet behind the bull.

After that, bedlam erupted. The bull turned in a tight circle, trying to pinpoint his enemy, while the two male dancers attempted to capture his attention. The woman, calmly walking away, finally turned, smiled at the audience, and, raising both arms, waved her hands back and forth. Then the hands dropped, and she ran around the side of the bull with an incredible speed to gather momentum, grasped the horn closest to her. With a twist of her wrist and her body, she flew diagonally across the back of the animal, almost grazing the opposite horn.

To Odaro, the rest of the afternoon was a blur. When he finally departed and allowed himself to be carried home in his litter, he was bathed in sweat. He had thought himself to be a jaded middle-aged rich man, but he now knew, with not one doubt at all, what it was he wanted. What he wanted was this woman. Her willingness was inconsequential, her price immaterial. He wanted. He wanted her not just physically; he wanted her because no one else possessed anyone like her. She was the most audacious, most incredible status symbol to be paraded to the public—to his public—the richest, the most influential, the most powerful for the moment. He knew well enough that power, influence, wealth were fleeting commodities; if he did not seize the present, he would lose the future.

He could hardly wait for Ninno's return, his report on how the transactions were progressing. The outcome was never in doubt. Odaro always achieved what he wanted sooner or later. In most of his dealings, he practiced great patience until he had achieved his goal; this time, as far as he was concerned, not only sooner but *soonest* became the operating word.

Ninno had served his master for many years; never had he seen Odaro be so eager to achieve any of his desired goals. At the same time, Ninno heard the comments dropped here and there about her, the newest star of the sacred bullring and her accomplishment of such incredible feats as never had been seen before in the hallowed arena. Around the ale and mead sellers' taverns, the cheap cooking kitchens, and the bordellos, everywhere in town the townsfolk were talking of the marvelous skill and grace of the newest and youngest of the bull dancers. Her name, he heard, was Naïs, and she had grown up here in the teeming city of Knossos. She had, it was said, a large family but no parents; all the rest of her family were younger siblings. She lived in poverty—doubtless for not much longer—and thus seemed ripe for the plucking.

All he needed to do was to approach her with his proposition, be as honey-tongued as only he knew how to be, and be the first in line of would-be applicants for her of late so highly prized favors. Would that the gods allow him not to falter in his quest! Master Odaro had highly volatile emotions. Having been at the receiving end of those eruptions several times in the past, he had no wish to be in that precarious position again.

It took him the better part of two weeks to persuade the lady to agree to meet with Odaro. When Ninno and his charge arrived at Odaro's palace, the host was waiting for them, albeit eager to appear entirely uneager. He was newly bathed, massaged, pummeled, oiled, curled, hennaed, kohled, and ultimately clothed in shining silks of the bright colors so dearly loved by the population of the Land of Minos for both their clothing as well as their home decorations.

Before long, Ninno was dismissed, to walk up and down the flagged courtyard, listening to the gurgle of the waterfall, which had been led down from a little spring on the mountainside. He was agitated; no soothing murmur of the waterfall could calm him.

During his earlier contacts with Naïs, he had learned not to underestimate her. She was a driven shrewd young woman who had already learned to understand the value and also the worth of her fame. She also understood well enough that her fame depended on her physical abilities and that those abilities depended on the strength and health of her limbs. Literally. Since she had no support—not from family or through any underpinning of money—she could only rely on herself and what she could gather for herself. One way or another. Preferably both ways. Through her performance in the bull arena. Through her performance in the bedroom of a rich man. He could almost sense the shrug of her shoulder; while she loved the one and gloried in it, she was willing to put up with the other. An inconvenience to be tolerated, a task to be taken on to assure her future when the activity she loved could no longer support her and her family of siblings who seemed to have settled in to depending on her.

Ninno would gladly have spent some of his hard-earned coins to be able to hear, let alone to see what went on inside Odaro's luxurious reception room. Where he was, outside, the sounds of the waterfall obscured most of the sounds from indoors, except for the occasional tinkle of a woman's laughter. Two servants with trays of food and drink traversed the courtyard, lifted the curtains, and, on noiseless feet, disappeared inside. When they reappeared, Ninno was sorely tempted to intercept them and press them for information. Only the still remaining shreds of his now tattered dignity, abused for so many years since the days when he was the promising young son of an influential family, prevented him from doing so.

During the last years, reduced to peddling his contacts and limited influence to make a living for himself and his family, Ninno had learned many things. Most importantly how to accept his quasi-servile status, how to bow, keep his mouth shut, bury useful information until he could trade it in for coin, all because he had no other choice.

His family once had been wealthy and powerful shipping merchants. Like so many others, they were forced to learn that the sea is the most unreliable of mistresses. One or two heavy storms, howling winds with mountainous waves were sufficient to ruin the survival and future of a happy and hopeful family. His family. His father's family. His father, whom he had loved so much, who, one beautiful day, walked into the shimmering blue water, sank into the gentle embrace of the soft waves, and disappeared forever.

Those were things that Ninno chose not to remember. Ever. If only he could control his thoughts.

*****

Naïs was well satisfied with the course of recent events, with the way her future was developing. Why then was it that she did not feel happier? Her life was moving in the best possible direction, wasn't it? This was what she had been dreaming about when she was a young girl, wasn't it? She still delighted in her performances, the applause and admiration of the audience, the bowing and waving, and the throwing of kisses and flowers in her direction. Wherever she appeared in public, the shouting of her name—all of the outward indications of her fame. At the same time, she saw how fast fame faded, how short the public's memory was; she saw how Athenis slowly faded into the background, as she was getting older, and so she trembled whenever a promising new apprentice appeared among the new students.

Soaring through the air, the sudden rush of fear and the release of joy through her body, ah, these were wonderful feelings, and she felt that she would die before giving up what she was doing—what she was now able to do. But for how long? She was becoming wealthy, but it felt that she was only exchanging one kind of insecurity of her past with a different insecurity of her current life. She yearned for an anchor, for something—for someone—to lean on, not for just a few weeks but for the rest of her life. She wanted solidity, security. For the first time in her life, she wanted to feel that not everything was up to her, not all eyes were immediately turned to her to find assistance and assurance.

Odaro? He was a middle-aged man with a tendency to put on flab from overindulgence. He had no sense of self-control, no need to drive his body to any physical achievements; he was boorish, self-indulgent, and overindulged. That much was quite obvious. His drives—if he even had any—lay in different directions, directions which, however, strangely coincided with her interests as well. Her desires for wealth had always simmered on the surface, needing no awakening. At the same time, however much Odaro was lacking in pleasing physical attributes, his offer satisfied her needs. Since Ido had awakened her hidden sexual desires, she was anxious for more, for different.

According to their agreement, recorded by Odaro's scribe—she had insisted on that—she was to have her own household and servants, but she was to be at his request at any time other than when she was performing or practicing in the bull arena. He was not to call her to accompany him on one of his voyages, except if her services were not needed at the bull arena for the length of the voyage. She was not to entertain—or even see—any men other than Odaro. She was not allowed to befriend any of the male performers of the bull-ring, except if so needed for the performance or for training.

And so it went.

Naïs sighed. She had wrangled a nod from Odaro when she requested permission to say farewell to Ido. Well, she knew that was to be a difficult meeting. Even the thought of it squeezed her heart. After all, Ido, if anyone, had in a way been her mainstay, her support, the companion of her childhood, the replacement for missing parents. He was responsible for her career—if not for her success—and his belief in her abilities had touched her deeply.

With no doubt at all, Naïs knew that life was not designed for laughter and sunshine. What sunshine and smiles there were, were provided by the beautiful wall paintings dotting the walls of buildings here and there, paintings of lovely ladies with apparently not a care in the world, laughing together at something beyond the view of the viewer, of equally appealing young men, strolling with a cocky and carefree gait, of gorgeously iridescent birds and butterflies in flight, and of golden bees and the colorful flowers they visited.

While her new house was furnished, Naïs felt free enough to search out the recently appointed young Master of the Dance Teachers. Ido was not so easy to find these days, weighed down with the new responsibilities he was still learning. Finally on the third day, one which was free from both practice and performance, she found him at the little temple to the goddess, the place she thought of as "their place."

He stood there, leaning against one of the pillars still intact, which served as partial support for the roof. He faced down toward the city, deeply in thought, his brows knitted, his eyes staring without seeing. So engrossed was he in his thoughts that he literally started when he heard her light step. In amazement, Naïs noticed, for the first time, how the sunny carefree smile, that smile she had always associated with him, was forced to appear on his somber face. She was vastly surprised. This, after all, was his inherent smile, the sparkle in his eyes was something he owned. Wasn't it? Didn't he? Did he not wear them all the time? And for what reason would he not? She stepped up to him and hugged his shoulders, while she brought her cheeks to his lips. He kissed her and smiled, but somehow the smile of his mouth did not reach his eyes. He wrapped his arms around her. Without moving, he just pressed her to his body.

After a long-stretched silent moment, Ido sighed, slid his back down the length of the column to settle on the floor. He reached his hands up to hers to pull her down to his lap. He caught her chin and turned her face to his. He dark eyes searched Naïs's face with total seriousness and—she caught her breath—sadness?

"Is Odaro worth all that you are giving him?"

Naïs bristled. She yanked her chin out of his fingers to turn her face away. She shrugged her shoulders and raised her brows.

"Why do you ask me silly questions? Oh, Ido, of course he is! He is very, very rich, and he is willing to give me everything I want. Everything! He is absolutely enamored! How many such opportunities do you think I shall have? How big a fool do you believe me to be to ignore such an opportunity to advance myself? For sure this is a gift of the goddess!"

Then her face crumpled, she threw herself against him, sagging into his chest when he closed his arms about her. Wordlessly he let her weep and soak his tunic, only to lift her chin to his eyes when he heard her noisy hiccups.

"What is it, little one? Did he hurt you? Did he force you? You just explained to me how lucky you feel, neh? *So*...what is amiss, sweetheart?"

Naïs opened her mouth on a little sob, wiping her wet eyes with the back of her hands.

"He-he forbade me to-to see you at all after today! And today only to say farewell to each other. I explained to him that we cannot help but-but see each other at the bull court, and he said that he had eyes everywhere in town and that he would know immediately if there was more to our meetings than was neh-necessary...and that his punishment would be swift...And so—and so—" She sniffed, and then the tears began flowing again. Ido pressed her body closer to his and, like a child, gently rocked her back and forth.

"I know not how I can do this? How can I not talk to you when I see you? How can I turn away from you as though you were unknown to me? How can I just mouth words needed for our work together and then turn my back to you? When I run into you or you into me on this path going and coming from the arena, am I to look away or to look at you with eyes that don't see? You have been my brother, my friend, my lover, and now—nothing? Nothing? I do not believe I can do that, in all seriousness. This—this is the hardest part of the bargain. No, it is the only hard part of the bargain. I can put up with the garlic smell on his breath, the stale sweat masked by rose water, and the flab of his belly, but this…this is too much, Ido! Too difficult! How am I to bear it? How am I to go on living without you in my life but only present in the distance? To only look at you from afar…oh, Ido, I cannot, I cannot!" And she started sobbing again, in her distress, selfishly unaware of his distress, his unshed tears.

Ido did not have any idea how to console her, other than pressing her closer to himself. His fist rubbed her shoulders, her back, his other hand stroked her hair. He almost blurted out that this distress was of her own making, by her own choice, but then held his tongue. This, he felt, was not the time to play I told you so. He was her friend, and friends stood by each other in times of sadness.

"Somehow, little one, we will manage to find a way…You are a resourceful, determined woman, and I am no slouch either—as I am sure you know already. Do not carry on so, love! This is just the beginning of the beginning of your arrangement with Odaro. Is he not known to like to go sailing back and forth on this great water at our doorstep? He never quite trusts his ship's captains. He likes to strike his own deals, make his own arrangements, do his own haggling. Honestly, I think he believes that he can argue and fight for each additional coin better than anyone else. Can't think why he employs all those hordes of people when he thinks they are all out to cheat him. You had better tread lightly, though, sweetheart, or he will have your hide for some imagined wrong you did to him! Let's thank the goddess that your fame and popularity protect you from such spiteful harm!"

In time, as he managed to calm her sobs and to keep her attention focused away from what gave them both such misery, he began to fondle and kiss her. They wound up making love to each other, with such intensity of desperation as they have never experienced before. The sun finished what remained of its course, and the moon rose, almost fully rounded, floating with gentle grace above the pinnacle of the mountain called Ida, named for the Great Goddess. The soft breeze blowing in from the sea dissolved the heat of the day, and the air carried by the breeze was filled with the tang of salt water and seaweed. Occasional bird chirpings floated from the treetops as birds of the day settled themselves for the night.

The two lovers rested, entwined in each other's arms. Ido pulled Naïs closer to his chest, cuddling her to himself by curling his legs around her body. Eventually both of them dozed, exhausted by their emotional outbursts as much as by their lovemaking. Ido's last thought was that none of their present problems could be solved this day. Let the day die into the night; let tomorrow then make them both more clearheaded and less emotional to deal with things that needed a clearer head and lack of emotions.

The next day was a performance day for Naïs. When she woke with the early morning, still curled into Ido's arms, covered against the cold wet mist by his long woolen scarf, she sighed against his chest, smiling as she watched him slowly, lazily lift his eyebrows and smile at her in turns. She kissed his chest with all her passion and then his eyelids too, while she whispered her thank you, then slipped out of his arms, carefully folding his scarf before handing it to him.

"Thank you," she whispered again, the corners of her mouth wobbling, "thank you, my dearest, and may the goddess always keep you in her hands! You are my once, now and forever, only true friend." Swiftly she turned and ran away from him on silent fleet feet.

By afternoon, the Arena of the Sacred Bulls was filled and all but overflowing. All the powerful, influential, and rich citizens of Knossos were assembled. The king sat in the royal enclosure; most of his family had accompanied him. At the foot of the royal enclosure, the long row of seats, all equally gorgeous in their elegantly carved gold-covered gaily painted and silk-pillowed splendor were fully occupied by the priestesses and priests of the goddess.

The sun had not yet begun to set, but everyone was familiar with the view that it would present when later, she would slowly sink between the sculpture of the two horns representing the Sacred Bull. The horns had been carved into the gleaming white sandstone at a position where they perfectly framed the cone of holy Mount Ida. The sun would finally set and disappear behind the pinnacle of

Mount Ida and not appear again until she rose the next morning to awaken the world.

Naïs felt more than inspired that afternoon. She felt as light as a bird winging through the air. Her body was weightless. It felt wonderful to stretch her body and her arms and reach for the back of the bull. To then push herself off in a somersault gave her a physical delight that she had never felt before, except by the touch of Ido's body. She felt no exhaustion, no weakness; she did not notice the passage of time until the last bull, snorting with exhaustion, his sides heaving, was led off the arena. The crowd went wild then; Naïs thought she would never hear the end of the applause, the screaming. The king asked for her, and when she, in a fog, knelt before him, he leaned forward and gave her a thin gold band for her hair. It was embellished by tiny delicate flying bees attached to the band by barely visible gold wires to make the bees shimmer and dance with each motion of her head, as though they were ready to fly away. As he placed the circlet on her head, Naïs, in a sudden flashback to years ago, recalled sitting on the hillside above the palace and dreaming of, yearning for fame and wealth, and just such a gold band with flying bees to adorn her head.

Finally exhaustion caught up with her, and she felt her legs shake and buckle. Lightheaded, she noticed that someone lifted her and dodged and wove his way through the crowds. Once again, it was Ido who was close by, who knew her need and helped her. She closed her eyes against the fog which threatened to overtake her, held on tightly against her dizziness, and let herself be carried wherever he might take her.

*****

The day Naïs moved into her new home turned to be a blustery, squally fall day. Looking down from her terrace, through the tall pines, she could see the angry gray-green white-capped sea churning against the rocks of the shore, breaking on them, and, in its anger, spewing great spumes of water high into the air. Seagulls circled over the water, looking for dead or dying fish or other sea creatures to swoop down and catch. At this time of the year, their nestlings were almost old enough to leave their nests, and they were endlessly hungry, forcing the exhausted parents to hunt for food without letup.

She walked the house from room to room, Odaro by her side; he if only to point out the expenses incurred in making each room more beautiful to the eye, more comfortable to the body than the one before. She said yes, yes whenever she felt it was necessary to comment, she nodded her head, and each time she felt his eyes on her, she smiled engagingly. She also was, she believed, coming to terms with Odaro's intrusion into her life. After all, it was her decision to allow it. It was the only logical, reasonable thing to do, wasn't it? It would be of great benefit to her and her whole family, wouldn't it? Of course, of course.

She was becoming accustomed to Odaro; he was not so bad after all. He actually was thoughtful and accommodating to her. God only knew how unaccustomed she was to both of those behaviors! That actually won her willingness more than any gifts of his ever could. More than anything else, she appreciated receiving a home from him. A home! Dear god, not just a corner of a hovel, a cot pushed against the wall so that the rest of her family could walk by on their way to the piss pot—a chipped urn actually—the emptying of which was the cause of endless friction and squabble among the siblings. A hovel smelling of decaying fish and cabbage, with only one window to the outside and that window no more than a square hole-in-the-wall looking out into the equally fish-and-garbage-smelling courtyard shared by three similar five-story-high ramshackle buildings in a rectangle around that courtyard.

This, this unaccustomed, unexpected elegance, this light and airy graciousness (and she was yet too untutored to distinguish the lovely and elegant in her new home from the flashy and ostentatious), well, it delighted her and went a long way to lead her to find delight in the creator of this largess. She sincerely endeavored to ignore the rolls of fat around his middle, the slight whiff of stale sweat overlaid by his ointments and perfumes, the smell of onions and garlic on his breath. *I wonder*, she thought, *why Ido's breath had always been so sweet-smelling?* At that errant thought, she shrugged her shoulder and smiled at her own fanciful thoughts. She walked by Odaro's side, threading her arm through his, and when they entered the long terrace, which hugged the house on three sides except for the side leaning onto the hill, she leaned her head against his shoulder, very conscious of the gesture she made. For a short while, they stood there, appearing to anyone to be a devoted couple, admiring the breathtaking view of the angrily roiling sea, and a long line of white storks winging toward parts farther behind the setting sun. Maybe, she considered, they were flying to the fabled Mount Parnassus?

For a short while, Naïs was truly flooded by a feeling of gratitude. When she turned to Odaro and kissed him, there were tears in her eyes, and he, also for a moment, was truly touched by her kiss and her tears. But then the moment passed, and they settled back to the roles they were most comfortable with—that of the rich middle-aged merchant and his beautiful mistress, she, the star of the city, currently riding the waves of popularity. They both found relief in stepping back into their true characters. He bent and whispered something into her ear, and she laughed with apparent sincerity. After a while, they disappeared behind the billowing sheer curtains separating the bedchamber from the terrace to shed their clothing and continue their appointed roles.

Once she was assured that Odaro slept, Naïs cautiously slipped out of bed. In a country where nudity or partial nudity were unblinkingly accepted, she found herself shying away from being nude in her lover's presence. Somehow she felt that offering him her nudity would mar the thoughts, the feelings which tied her to Ido. The memory of when she and Ido had loved now unexpectedly intruded upon her each time she and Odaro made love. She had begun to hate those feelings and, with them, the emerging sense of guilt. She had no obligation to Ido, did she? They were childhood friends who had outgrown each other.

Why then was this sense of turmoil deep within her? Why then did she avoid the paths from the bull arena to her new home, which she used to tread once in fervent hopes of meeting with Ido? Why then did she turn and run in the opposite direction like a frightened rabbit whenever she encountered Ido at the bull arena? She knew that he was there all the time and not in order to accost her, but because he was the Revered Master of the Teachers for all students and had to be there. Why was she so stupid that she could not remember that? Besides that phase of her life was now over; she was no longer the downtrodden little girl with a crush, trying to lift herself out of the mire, and she should give thanks for all that each day of her current life—well, shouldn't she?

She heard stirring. Rustlings to tear her away from her dreaming thoughts. Odaro was waking. She had noticed that he became more and more exhausted from their lovemaking; it took him a long time to catch his breath and recover, and after, he usually fell asleep. Today he was actually recovering faster than she had expected. Naïs turned away from the archway to the terrace and slowly walked over to Odaro. She sat on the bed, then bent forward and gently lifted Odaro's hands to place them on her breasts. He smiled at her and, freeing one of his hands, slid it behind her neck. Grunting, he pulled her down on top of him and noisily began to nuzzle her neck. Then he rolled her and lowered his heavy body on top of her until she squirmed and asked him to lift some of his weight because she could barely breathe. He laughed, happily mistaking her meaning.

"Ah, my dove, I see I am too much for you, eh? My ardor takes your breath away? That will never do for I want you to be full of vitality and brimming with energy for me, especially since sadly, you will have to have the energy for both of us! I seem to have overworked myself in my negotiations with the delegation of merchants I have been hosting from Achaea. Ah, my sweet, bull dancing is not the only activity requiring an abundance of energy! But now, they have left at sunup, may we be thankful to the goddess, and so I have reserved a period for blissful rest and love play, my dove. I hope that will please you, my sweet, for I do not wish to make you think that I am neglecting you." And he commenced to laugh, his rolls of fat jiggling and his mouth breathing garlic into her nose.

His hands, white and pudgy, greedy and grasping, traveled her body, his mouth latching on to her breasts. Naïs shut her eyes and tried to convince herself that the man touching her so intimately was a generous, giving, warmhearted person deserving her gratitude and, at the very least, her affection. But she found the persuading heavy going.

Any further noises emanating from the bedchamber were drowned out in the screams of the seagulls fighting with each other for scraps of food and territory.

It was two days later that Odaro informed Naïs of his most immediately upcoming plans. One of his merchant ships was due to depart on a lengthier voyage toward the rising sun, to the land called Phoenicia, and inhabited by the people called by the Mycenaeans the *ponikoi* or "woodcutters." Those tribes, he explained, were fabled for their aromatic cedarwoods which were not available anywhere else in the known world and which the ponikoi sold to the highest bidder at exorbitant prices.

Softly giggling, almost like a child who hides his favorite toy from all others, Odaro lectured her, as Naïs schooled her face to pay him breathless attention.

"These are the opportunities to latch on to and turn into a large—and I mean really large—profit, my little flower." Oh, how she hated it when he called her his little flower or little blossom, or especially his little dove!

"I plan to be there before all others, to bid on the best lots of cedarwood before any of those other slackers. The Egyptians, hah! They are masters at building and most especially at painting their faces and fashioning their wigs. Commerce between competing nations? No, my little blossom, they are totally befuddled by such complexities! The Athenians and all other Achaean are somewhat better at it, but they enjoy their own comforts too much and arrive too late, when the best has been bought up already—by none other than me!" And he burst into a loud throaty laughter which literally jiggled not only every ounce of his body but his cushions as well.

Naïs sighed. She sat next to Odaro on a couch lined with striped silk cushions, placed so that it would catch the light cooling breezes coming in from the sea. She had been holding his fingers but now released his hand and slid down from the cushions to the floor so that she did not have to look into his eyes. The relief she felt over her sudden unexpected "freedom" would surely shine in her eyes, wouldn't it? With her eyes closed, just to be safe, she listened to the drone of Odaro's voice.

"This, my sweetheart, this will be the most important business trip of mine for the last several years. I have waited for this opportunity most anxiously, I can assure you! The locals do not want to flood the market nor to deplete their stock. For this reason, the wood of those indigenous cedars, you should know, will be harvested only every second or third year. This, this should be the year for buying up most of their supply cheaply, if I only get to be there earlier than the competition!" He sighed and shifted his body while he reached for his shallow goblet. He swirled the dark-red wine and stared into the goblet as though it held some hidden secret instead of wine. Then he shook his head almost imperceptibly as he raised his eyes. His hands reached her chin. Turning her face toward his, he gave her an almost shy smile. "Will you behave yourself while I am not here, little flower? I could not bear it—well, you know!" And he shrugged his shoulder.

Naïs was charmed by the unexpectedly sweet shyness in an otherwise so brash a man. Suddenly anxious to reassure him, she stretched herself toward him, her arms twining about his thick bull's neck. She brushed her lips over his. "Of course, my love!" She smiled. "How could you think otherwise? How often have I told you that I love you, my dearest? Only you! Do not let yourself be led by your earlier experiences with other women! And do not judge me by their standards! Besides I will be busier than usual. We will have the annual evaluation and judging of the new student candidates. Exhausting all around. Also I remind you that I have a number of siblings, and I need to check on them. All of them are younger than I am and need to be supervised occasionally. I aim to keep busy, to make the time fly by so that I do not start becoming anxious and worried about being without you!"

Odaro lifted her hand and, turning it over, kissed her touch-sensitive palm.

"I shall be no less anxious to rejoin you, my little blossom." He sighed. "Sadly tonight will have to be our farewell time together. I have too many other business arrangements to meet before my departure. How I wish that this night of love could last forever! But like all things, they say that nothing, not even the pleasures of love can last forever. All we can do is to make it as joyous as we can, right, my little dove?" he murmured.

Suppressing a sigh, Naïs slowly rose, using the time to draw her defenses about her, then turned limpid round eyes to Odaro. Her earlier moment of weakness was fast evaporating, but she had fortunately acquired great skill in masking her thoughts and feelings from him. Her mask firmly in place, she raised the palms he had just kissed to frame Odaro's face. She kissed his mouth with as much passion as she could muster, not only to deceive him but also to whip herself into a mood for passion. Inside her brain, she heard the refrain of Odaro's voice, *Our farewell time together…our farewell time together.*

*****

Ido was in a black mood. He had been in a black mood most of the time recently. Everything upset him or displeased him, and he was heartily sick of it, but quite especially of himself. God only knew what kind of an evil spirit had taken possession of him! Nothing would please him. He found no pleasure in even those daily things which, in the past, had given him joy: the sleepy chirping of birds roosting in the trees when the sun was setting behind the mountain of the goddess, the buzz and drone of bees collecting pollen from the thyme bushes covering the slopes of the mountain, the shimmering, quivering silver line, like a glistening path thrust across the surface of the dark sea by the shine of the full moon upon its calm surface. Just to be young and healthy and alive used to delight him. But no more; he was irritated and irritating as well, he knew, but felt too impatient to examine his own heart. Impatient? Why would he have to be impatient? Why would black thought and anger intrude into his life? His life was becoming more and more fulfilled. He was now the Revered Teacher of new students, one of the highest assignments, with time, sure to lead to even higher or to the highest positions!

And then on a hot blistering day, at the bullring, he ran into Naïs. She was running, ducking into the little enclosure shaded by a gaily striped awning stretched out over it, running to slip into the round tiled bath, which had been built years ago to serve the comfort of those who wanted to cool their overheated bodies in its cool water. She wore nothing but a pair of training pants, tied at the ankles, and a long strip of linen tightly wrapped around her breasts so that they would not be in her way when she approached the bulls. Just before turning into the enclosure, her eyes fell on him. She stopped herself and, sucking in her breath, leaned against one of the supporting columns, in the Minoan fashion painted black with bands of red and yellow decorating the narrow bottom and much wider top. For a brief eternity, she stared at him, her eyes wide and unblinking. Then he saw her lick her trembling lower lip and drop her eyes to the ground. Wordlessly she turned and disappeared from Ido's view.

He was shaking so violently that he could barely support himself. Forcing calm upon himself, he slowly walked away, his eyes watching his sandals and how each of his steps caused little puffs of dust to rise from the ground. Without a conscious thought, he eventually found himself slowly walking toward the half-destroyed little temple—their temple, as he still called it in his mind. He leaned against one of the remaining pillars and stared ahead to the ground, which, in places, was still covered with much-scuffed delicate mosaics depicting fragments of animals: gazelles, birds, butterflies, and fish. He did not see them. To his surprise, he found that tears, unbidden, unexpected, welled from his eyes. He was not crying. He was not sobbing. The tears flowed from his eyes, flowing down his cheeks, his neck, soaking his sweaty linen shirt, splashing to the dusty mosaics. His body slid down the pillar which had supported his back, and slowly he gave in to his grief, finally sobbing great heaving sobs, folding his arms over his drawn-up knees and resting his forehead on them.

Oh, Naïs, dearest companion of my youth! The little waif who tagged along behind me with determined relentlessness, or walked next to me, holding my hand, chattering and asking endlessly exuberant questions! The reckless abandon with which you threw yourself into everything you did, the fervor of your loving as we loved each other, the fearlessness of your dance with the bulls, light as the dance of a butterfly! Where are you now, so far from me? How did we separate? How did we grow apart with such breathless speed? I should never have…I should have…

Slowly his soundless weeping stopped. Exhausted by his emotional turmoil, he rose, turned to start to his way home. Athenis was waiting for him, he guessed, although no firm commitment had been made for the night, but she did usually wait for him and expected him to visit her at least a few times during the week. The last thing he needed, he thought, was Athenis. He smiled an ironic smile to himself. She would question him about his tear-reddened eyes, and then, then he would have to fabricate some sort of a story, a lie.

But surely Athenis knew. She was an intelligent, warm, placidly loving woman and would understand. He felt certain that he needed not explain, and suddenly realized that she must have known for a while. Seen his efforts to hide his heartache even from himself. Yes, Athenis would be the balm for his soul! Why on earth did he not realize that before? Surely she—she was what he needed to help him mend!

That was when he heard the crunch of soft footfall behind him. The light had been almost entirely leached out of the sky, but he could see a slight form slowly walk toward the little temple. A slight form he could immediately recognize.

When Naïs stepped up to the broken mosaic-clad platform, she stopped. Stopped and let the scarf which covered her head and face slide down to the ground. Her wide eyes were on Ido. She said no words, made no move for what seemed an eternity. Then they both moved toward each other in unison. Neither knew which of them first reached for the other nor who said the first word. Finally he was holding her tenderly, his knuckle rubbing her back, while she was blotting the tears from his face with her scarf.

"Do not cry, my love, do not. It kills me to see you cry because of me…" she whispered. There was a fervency but also a maturity to her voice which he had not heard before. "Please understand, that I had to do what I did. I could not turn my back on my family. I am their only hope. They have no one but me to turn to."

Ido bit his lip to keep silent. *And who could you have turned to, my love, when you so bravely struck out to conquer the world?* he thought, but of course he did not say so. Why hurt her, why, why dredge up things which could not ever be changed anymore? The past was impossible to change. But the future? Possible? He took a deep shaky breath and reached for her hand, toying with her fingers. He felt very insecure both about what he wanted to say and how to best express himself.

"Sweetheart, I beg you to consider that your family is either grown-up or growing up rapidly. Emeris is as old as you were when your father died and you applied to the Sacred School. You took your life into your hands, and look what you have produced, what you have achieved since! Perhaps Emeris may not have your sharpness of focus on your goals as you did, but she is your sister, and if you see her faltering, then maybe you can teach her, neh? And Tomo is only a little more than a year younger than Emeris. He is a resourceful young adult, full of drive, who did not shirk any kind of work he could get in your poorer days. Do you not think that perhaps letting them…well, cutting the strings that tie them to you—well, that may be of benefit to them, teach them responsibilities, help them grow up? Let them fly on their own, just like you learned to fly all by yourself, my love! If anyone, you, you should know how wonderful it is to achieve something all on your own! Sweetheart, allow them to find that wonderful experience all on their own!"

For the first time since Ido could remember, that certain look of childish adoration, which he had always seen in Naïs's eyes when she looked at him, disappeared from her eyes. The look he received instead was one of absolute anger. Her lip flattened mutinously. Her hands curled into fists. Her brows furrowing, she jumped up, grabbing the wrap which had slipped off her shoulders.

"Don't you understand what duty is? Duty to one's family? Perhaps you do not have feelings like that, but I do! By the goddess I do! My parents will not rest until I discharge the duty they expected of me! Do you think I strove and pushed myself just for my own glory? Well, let me tell you, not all of us are so carefree and irresponsible as you obviously are! No—do not talk to me—I will not listen to you! I will not!"

And when he reached for her to calm her and to explain, she shrugged his hands off and looked at him with true anger in her eyes. "I thought," she whispered, "I thought you understood me, that you were a true friend. But you are just like all the others who envy my good fortune and envy my family for having a share in it!" When he again reached for her, she jerked her arm away. "Leave me alone, just—leave me alone." She hissed, turned, and, on her silent fleet feet, ran down the track, not the one leading into the heart of the city but across the dip of the mountainside to the next rise, where here and there, the homes of the rich peeked out among the verdant green of well-tended trees and shrubs.

That was the last time he talked to Naïs for a long, long while. He did see her, encounter her, sometimes in the city, but most frequently in the bull arena. But their different assignments there prevented rubbing elbows, and the brief moments, the brief glimpse were the most that their current lives afforded them. Naïs was the adulated adored star of the bull arena. Ido did a yeoman's work to supervise the teachers of the newcomers, to instill in them all he could to prepare them for the deadly dangers of their chosen careers. He was the one who molded the young green recruits to become good, some even to become great, with the secret hope that maybe, just maybe, one of them would develop into a body in flight, arms stretched out like wings of a bird, flying in the air a finger's breadth above the horns of a bull.

Once, during a bull dancing contest held to honor the Great Goddess's feast day, Ido chanced to look up into the rows reserved for the great, the wealthy, and powerful of the state, with its focus on the king's seat and that of his wives, and doing so, he noted another, more screamingly opulent loge, not too far from the royal seats. The man lounging there, served by several offering him food and drink, was none other than Odaro. The wave of blistering hatred running through him, like a searing flame, surprised and frightened Ido, for he was not basically a hating angry man, and such emotions were foreign to him.

As he was watching Odaro, he watched how he caught the wrist of one of the serving girls and roughly yanked her so that she landed half in his lap, scattering the pomegranates she had been carrying in a shallow bowl. They were too far away to hear either her or his voices, but Ido saw the *O* her mouth formed and saw Odaro throw his head back and laugh uproariously. Then his hand caught the thick braid hanging down the girls back and yanked her head so that he could mouth and maul her more comfortably.

Ido, no innocent he, nor one who had eschewed to live life to the fullest of his abilities, felt like retching. He turned away, walked to the shaded arcade leading into the bath and changing rooms for the performers. In the corner, a fountain bubbled fresh water, led down to the city all the way from the heights of the mountains through conduits dug into the soil. An earthenware bowl on a pedestal caught the water, the overflow running away to feed the flower beds all around the arena. He held his hands under the bubbling water and, when both his palms were filled, bowed his head to take the water into his mouth. Carefully he rinsed his mouth and then, with a shudder, spit out the water onto the sand beyond the confines of the arcade. With a deep sigh, he leaned his forehead against the wall, waiting until his nausea slowly subsided.

Suddenly he felt a hesitant hand touch his shoulder. Bleary-eyed, Ido lifted his head to look at Saphero, one of his teacher colleagues and a good friend. Saphero, considered by all to be the handsomest man in Knossos—much to Ido's chagrin, even handsomer than he—looked at him, concern furrowing his brow, and a look of worry and commiseration in his eyes.

"Buck up, old boy, the world is full of beautiful women willing to relieve your misery!" He smiled. But his smile was forced and disappeared almost immediately. With a sigh, he continued, "Oh, I saw the pig as well as you! And believe me, he nauseates me almost as much as he does you, and I do not even have a love who is sharing the pig's bed!" His hand tightened on Ido's shoulder. "Come, let's sit in the shade and share a flask of wine that I just happen to have hanging from my shoulder bag. Actually have you ever, ever run into me without a flask, except when I am teaching or training?"

They slowly walked along the arcade which had a fine view of the palace itself, to which the bull arena was attached. The arcade curved onto a well-tended grassed clearing shaded by ancient trees. Tall palms, evergreen maples, pines, and cypresses shaded the area and continued to flank a beautiful winding road leading gently toward the more private areas of the royal palace and beyond its sprawling complex, rising higher still to the terraced mountainside of the rich homes of merchants and dignitaries. Under the trees, both sides of the road were lined with tall crocus shrubs and ebony bushes, under which aromatic sage and thyme flourished, spilling their perfume into the air. Long benches with low tables between them dotted the clearing, inviting those who wanted to rest and linger in this lovely well-shaded place.

Saphero pulled Ido to one of the benches and waited until he, reluctantly accepting the comfort the environment offered, had settled there. Taking a few deep breaths, Ido turned to his friend. Eyes full of tormented anger and anxiety in equal measure, he clutched Saphero's arm and shook his head.

"I am the greatest fool there ever lived, and don't you contradict me there! She will have nothing to do with me, and only because I have nothing to offer her to keep her in comfort and her damned sisters and brothers as well…never have I heard of a woman feeling responsible for her grown family. Can they not fend for themselves like everyone does and is expected to do?" He took a shaky breath before continuing. "She loved me once, she looked up to me then, now she behaves like I am dirt under her feet. The goddess is my witness, I was her first lover, I taught her how to love, I helped her to get into the Sacred School, I talked her up to the teachers so that she should be accepted. I grant you, she exhibited enormous talent, great skill, and a total lack of fear for her well-being, but…but without me, I swear to you, Saphero, she would be no one, she would be nowhere…Oh gods, it hurts, it hurts so much—and what hurts me even more is the knowledge that I had been a fool once, but am a greater fool still…"

He laughed bitterly and shook his head, then wiped his face on the edge of the heavy fringed wool scarf he wore against the cold and dew of the morning and evening hours. There was silence for a short while, and they could hear the song of the lark ascending from the meadows beyond the path. Ido took another deep shaky breath, then continued in a much calmer voice.

"I do believe that I make too much of this. I know I do. It used to be a lark, you know, my friend. She was a little girl who tagged after me, always at my heels and looking adoringly at me. Then she grew, and I knew she wanted me to help her, maybe she wanted me as well? And I taught her how to love, and without wanting to, without even being aware of it, I learned to love her. And to admire her, you know, she is so graceful and fearless and strong...the goddess help me, but each time I watch her working the bulls, my heart is in my throat, and I can barely catch my breath, though I should be accustomed to each move, each danger. This is my life as well, this is all I know, after all, neh? And now, now that I lost her, only now do I realize that she is my forever love—if there is even such a thing? Do you believe that there are permanent things like that, Saphero? Or are there just the fleeting short times of togetherness and love and tenderness and care, however priceless they are, which flicker through our lives?

"Aye, if you have an answer to that, my friend, let me know, tell me the truth. And do forgive me for prattling on like this, you must be wondering because I never used to be like this...See what love can do to one? Make him stupid and useless, just one whimpering lump! But I tell you true, what hurts me most, what churns my stomach and twists my gut is that she could lie with such a...such a...such a gross lumpy piece of disgusting human dung!"

Once again there was silence. Saphero raised his hand and laid it on Ido's shoulder. "Hear me, my friend. It's getting late, the sun will disappear soon. Please hear me, come to my place, I'll open an amphora of Cyprus wine, and we will get quietly drunk. Or maybe not so quietly? It'll do you good, and for me—even if it will not be of benefit to me, I shall enjoy it, I swear! Hear me, now come! At least for tonight, you shall forget your woes. Come!"

*****

Once Odaro left to sail to the eastern shores of the sea, the pattern of Naïs's daily life acquired a boring regularity. She had happily anticipated her freedom, but now that freedom was hers, she was at a loss as to what to do with it. She tried to enjoy the luxury of her home, the comfort of servants tending her wishes, but uncalled, Odaro's visage appeared before her, his loud voice and even louder laughter, his jiggling belly, the breasts almost as fleshy as a woman's, and she heard his shrieks of pleasure during the moments of their union. She visited with Emeris, thinking that she would also see Tomo and Milo there, only to find out that the boys—young men now, actually—were absent, gone to a championship cockfight held in the center of the city.

Greatly dismayed, Naïs held her tongue so that she would not appear to be shrewish, meddling, or judgmental. But she was well aware of the fact that heavy betting was conducted at these top-of-the-line fights. With effort she bit back a sharp comment about such an aimless, reckless life, when she realized that the person most to be blamed for these disturbing developments was no one else but her. Slowly she turned and walked out of the house, the house that she, her body, had provided to her family. Wordlessly she walked down the graveled path from the door closing behind her and those who lived inside that house to the waiting litter to take her to the arena of the Sacred Bulls to do her daily exercises.

Blindly, sightlessly, she watched the well-known scenery flow by her. Seagulls were wheeling and circling over the deep bay of the harbor, shrieking at each other in their eagerness for castoff pieces of fish from the fishing boats. The merchant vessels bobbed in the gentle swell of the incoming tide. The city of Knossos lay quiet, barely breathing in the torpor of the day. Naïs closed her eyes and sighed. This, she considered, was not how she envisioned success to be nor its concomitant degree of wealth and influence. Nothing, she thought, nothing is ever as lovely as anticipation. When she was anticipating all of those things which she now had, which she now even took for granted, how much sweeter was that breathless waiting than the reality of achievement? Bah, she thought, trying to chase away her somber thoughts, it's just the visit—such a disappointing visit—to her family's home which had soured her thoughts. Only a child with childishly unreasonable expectations lived in a dream-world such as she did!

She sailed through her daily exercises without giving them any thought; they had become so routine for her that she paid very little attention to them. Somewhere deep inside her brain, she knew that what she did was wrong, that ultimately she would pay in bodily damage and pain for her inattention, but she was too wrought up to force her thoughts into a channel away from her current distress. Eventually the session of acrobatics and body stretches was over, and she was slowly sauntering to the bathhouse to wash off her sweating body and cool it at the same time, when she almost ran head-on into Athenis, who was going in the same direction as well. Literally nose to nose, Athenis laughingly grabbed Naïs's shoulders and then stepped one small step aside.

"Whoa, watch out, sweetheart, watch out! Do pay care to where you step!" she called out with a laugh.

"So deep in thought? To my mind, nothing in life is worth taxing our hearts so much! Or if you listen to the great minds coming to us from the oh-so-very-smart Athenians, maybe it is not our hearts but our brains hiding up there in our heads, which get taxed. But, my dear, you truly look stricken, won't you take a few minutes to sit with me and talk about it, or just talk? I find that even just to converse with someone other than myself does help. When I am distressed, it will always help me to sort my thoughts and bring some degree of quiet and acceptance to my emotions."

Smiling with unexpected encouragement and warmth, she patted the bench under the spreading branches of an ancient acacia tree. "Come, and"—looking cautiously left and right, she leaned closer to Naïs—"if you can keep quiet about this to the powers to be that run this place, we can even share the contents of an unopened bladder of wine from the island of Sicilia that I carry. Come!"

Naïs was flabbergasted. The last thing she expected from Athenis, whom, in the past, she had envied, and for that reason instinctively disliked and distrusted, was this gesture of friendship and openness. She could not help but return the smile and lower herself onto the seat of the bench with a little groan of tiredness. There was a moment's pause in the conversation. Naïs felt her tears too close to spilling over and her throat closed as she choked for a moment. She shook her head, putting her hand on Athenis's arm. When she looked at Athenis, the tears came. Almost angrily, she wiped at them, then, between a sob and a laugh, reached for the wine skin which Athenis offered. She took a large gulp, then sighed and smiled at Athenis.

"Thank you, thank you for your kindness, thank you for your friendship. I am ashamed to confess to you that I never had expected anything such as these from you." She turned her body so as to face Athenis entirely and whispered, her eyes lowered because she felt ashamed, "Forgive me for having misunderstood or hurt you!"

Athenis shook her head with a smile, her smile growing bigger and bigger as she spoke.

"Oh, nay, I am indeed not so sensitive! I had watched you over the last years since I am older than you, my dear. And I must confess to you, I disliked you as well, I thought you to be a precocious little upstart. But you know, I believe you no longer need to consider me a threat to your success, as I no longer will do the same. I believe my days of bull dancing are over—or almost over—for I expect a little one, and soon you and everyone else will see it growing inside me… Do not wrinkle your brow and look at me with regret, for believe me, I am happy. No mistake, I loved the applause and the fame, but what all one sacrifices for it—well, I do not have to explain to you. The fatigue, the pain screaming in every muscle, every joint…then the serious injuries, which leave their mark on your body forever…No, I am not really cut out for that. I will be a happy mother and homebody. Embrace me and kiss me, if I may call you little sister? But then I feel we are almost related for you were always like Ido's little sister, were you not? I am surprised he has not told you yet?"

Naïs caught her breath and sucked some air into her lungs. Ido? Ido and Athenis? Oh, she knew that Ido had an on-again-off-again relationship with the lovely tall woman but not in a year of days would she have imagined that their relationship would turn into something more permanent—a family, a child?

With the greatest possible effort, she extended her arms and hugged Athenis. It was not a real fierce hug of joy—she just could not manage that—but a hug, nevertheless.

"A baby? Oh, Athenis, I am so very happy for the two of you!" She just could not say "the three of you!" Ido? Ido? His name hummed in her brain, and her stomach literally twisted with pain. But whether she wanted or not, there was that little voice—already—which whispered to her, *You see what you have done, serves you right!* She had taken Ido so much for granted; and now, and now he was lost to her, really, really, certainly, totally lost as a lover and probably also lost as a friend. Their relationship had become so very tenuous lately, and now—oh, gods! She groaned inwardly while she arranged her face into lines of intense interest as Athenis embellished on their plans to go to the priestesses of the Great Goddess to ask for her blessing upon their union and its fruit.

So it was to be not just living together, Naïs thought, but an actual official marriage. And Ido—Ido was then irrevocably gone out of her life forever. Except as sort of a big brother, whom she could go to occasionally visit. Of course, only after she apologized to him and the two of them reconciled. Yes, so that she could go and visit him and his wife occasionally and coo over the baby and watch it grow, how wonderful, and then to dissemble to Athenis. She had to do at least that much to please Athenis. Athenis had been so kind to her and did not deserve her jealousy. God bless her, she was so very, very, so totally trusting, so unsuspecting!

Or was she? Was she really unsuspecting or just very, very understanding and kind? So laid back she knew that ultimately she had won and now did not care to rub her nose into the dust. Really?

Naïs was clearheaded and honest with herself, if nothing else. She had never learned to romanticize. Except for Ido. Ido was her Achilles' heel. She had never been able to shed a little girl's adoration of her then-almost-grown-up friend, certainly grown-up enough to protect her every once in a while when needed. He would be the one to rescue her from the dangerously shaky limb of a tree she had climbed. He would pull her out of the sea when she went too far into the water to chase an elusive wave, which had licked at her ankles but then quickly drew back from her reach, only to disappear as she had waded in after it. To make matters worse, once she was a grown woman, he was the one to teach her about pleasure and passion—the first, and in her mind, the only one. Nothing could have made a more potent combination of a man! A man, moreover, who was also handsome, warmhearted, and generous!

And so, what was she to do in the future? Live her life with this never-to-be-fulfilled yearning for the rest of her days? Accept a future life with Odaro, even if he made her skin crawl? Or make Ido magically disappear from her mind? And how, in the name of the Great Goddess, could she do that? For the moment, she clearly was unable to put some sense into her muddled thoughts and yielded to what was the obviously expected behavior—inquire about when Athenis and Ido expected the birth of the "blessed little one," was Ido happy like a newly minted father should be, where they would be settling to live, would Athenis give up her activities at the bullring for good or only temporarily, and such inanities, on and on.

*****

The message from the office of the High Commissioner for Maritime Affairs reached her at her home on one of the rare days off from either practice or performance at the Arena of the Bulls. Because of the importance of both persons involved, Odaro and herself as well, a delegate of the high commissioner himself had been dispatched to bring the news. At first Naïs could not imagine the purpose of the visit. Dictated by polite custom, she bid the gentleman be seated in the airy verandah where the shades had earlier been drawn against the direct sun, thus permitting only the slight breeze from the sea to ruffle the delicately translucent draperies. She had, at some earlier time, installed tanks of colorful small fish to be attached to the wall of the building. These fish were caught in great numbers around the coral reefs where they abounded. She had also hung cages of small yellow songbirds caught on several of the smaller islands toward the setting sun, short-beaked and fleet on the wing. Their chatter and chirping filled the air.

At her behest, her maids brought sweet-spiced red wine from the island of the Sicani and, with it, served fresh fruit to the guest of the house. After these formalities, Naïs looked with curiosity to her guest who rose and, as on cue, pulled a facecloth out of the folds of his loosely wrapped leggings, as he started to dab his eyes and to wail and sob copiously. Finally he walked over to her seat and, taking her hands, lifted her up and pressed her against the equally copious folds of his chest. Finally he released her and, with muffled tones of appropriate sadness, informed her that the Office of Maritime Affairs had been visited by fishermen with irrefutable information of the tragic demise of the *Sail Fish*, Odaro's merchant vessel. The ship had run into a squall and subsequent heavy winds and had sadly run aground on a reef, where it literally shattered to pieces and sank very quickly with all hands onboard.

The loss of such an important and influential financial and mercantile personage as Odaro was a tragic and irreplaceable loss to the kingdom and, of course, a great and tragic loss to such a one as the great and revered Lady Naïs, he continued. Should the Lady Naïs need anything—anything at all—she need only appeal to the high commissioner who will do everything in his power, etc., especially in light of the fact that His Majesty himself, etc., etc.

Naïs let the words wash over her. Much to her surprise, she felt nothing, no sadness, no regret for the passing of a life which had become so intimately known to her. Rather a wave of irritation flowed through her. The fool, she thought, could he not have ended his worthless life a little sooner? Maybe then she could have clung on to Ido? And while such thoughts passed through her brain, she instantly felt ashamed of them, of herself for feeling no sadness, only selfishness at the thought of Odaro's passing.

She barely remembered saying her farewells to the delegate or even slowly walking back to her bedroom. There she continued to walk, rather aimlessly back and forth, from the doorway to the windows, open to the air and overlooking the sea. The sea! She felt a strange pull to go down to the beach, to look at the water and the endlessly eternal waves, and somehow there, maybe she would finally feel a sense of loss.

And so she did and continued to walk up and down the sand, over the scattered sand dunes overgrown with scraggly seagrass and scrub. Finally she sat down on top of one of the dunes, legs crossed under her body, her chin leaning into her palm, and her elbow supported by her knee. Sightlessly her eyes stared in front of her, her ears attuned to the slap of each arriving wave, to the sizzle and fizz of the foam as the wave broke on the sand and the foam, then withdrew, to be welcomed back into the mysterious depth of the waters. She looked up and down the beach, obviously the squall that took the *Sail Fish* and Odaro was far away from these shores, for the water's surface here was smooth and calm and the beach clean of the litter spewed out by the sea after a storm. She had lived her entire life at the water's edge, swam freely in its salty wet, yet to her, and even to those who spent their lives and earned their livelihoods from the sea, it continued to remain forever a mysterious and threatening unknown.

Is that, she wondered, how Odaro thought of the sea? Was he afraid of it? At the moment when he knew the water would take him, was he frightened? With surprise, Naïs hoped devoutly that he was not. It was her first feeling of sadness, of loss, the first sense of identity with Odaro. *Great Goddess,* Naïs prayed, *please let him not have died in fear, in terror! Please, almighty Goddess, let him be at peace and reconciled to his death! At that moment before death, let him have embraced the embrace of the waters! Would such have even been possible?*

Predictably she was unable to mourn at length. The void created by Odaro's death was no void at all; she had been too loosely, too tenuously attached to him in the first place, the attachment too brief and self-serving on both of their parts. Whatever impact he had made on her life, it was almost purely on an economic level.

The real impact—and truly on an entirely economic level—occurred two days later, when the same delegate from the Office of Maritime Affairs visited her again. This time, the visit was decidedly less congenial compared to the initial one.

Master Odaro, it seemed, had accumulated a large amount of debt owed to the Office of Maritime Affairs and indirectly to the state of Crete, most directly represented by His Majesty, the king. This debt had been increasing for years, partly because the very nature of seafaring trade, and the export/import of commodities, which dictated great outlays of coin and relied on trust in the structuring of debt. Debt, however, is dangerous, he explained. Just like a tower not sufficiently anchored into the ground, so does excessive debt no longer have enough support to carry it—it will collapse and topple of its own weight. The most unfortunate and untimely death of Master Odaro had suddenly pulled the support, the props, away from the great mountain of Master Odaro's, or rather his business's debt. Unfortunately Master Odaro had not designated anyone to act on his behalf during an absence, illness, or death. This, regrettably, was assumed to be mainly due to his suspicious nature. However, at this time, it was already a moot point.

Since creditors were anxious to clear up these outstanding debts, the Office of Maritime Affairs had decided to liquidate Master Odaro's assets and turn the proceeds to satisfy anxious creditors. Master Odaro, without any doubt, out of a sense of commitment and love to his new lady mistress, belatedly, only days before his last departure, visited the Office of Maritime Affairs. He explained that in order to show his great affection toward the Lady Naïs, he wanted documents of all of his properties to show her name as well. Thus with the demise of Master Odaro, all of his properties were owned by the Lady Naïs. Unfortunately that meant that Master Odaro's debts were also possessed by the Lady Naïs. And indeed, those debts were heavy and quite outweighed to proceeds she could acquire were she to sell any of her suddenly acquired properties.

Sadly time was of an essence, and it was imminent that creditors would be beating down the door to Naïs's home. She needed to have ready cash available to satisfy these creditors, and since she could not sell any of her heavily encumbered assets quickly enough, then she needed to procure ready cash very soon, or severe punishments would await her, which might probably include incarceration in the famously infamous underground prisons under the city of Knossos.

His voice droned on, but Naïs was beyond the point of being capable to absorb anything said. She stared at her hands clasped together on her lap, the fingers laced together. She stared at her fingernails, which used to be raggedly uneven and broken from needing to grasp the bulls' front lock of hair or one or both of his horns. Nowadays, since Odaro disliked to have the whole arena watch the woman he considered to be his exclusive property, her fingernails had grown out and were carefully trimmed, buffed and stained with the juice of pomegranates. The prisons, she thought, the prisons.

The prisons were actually deep caves carved eons in the past by the sea into the soft rocky soil of the island. They could only be accessed at low tide and, even then, with great care. Ventilation was only available through air shafts. Often some of these shafts became clogged by the soft soil and silt deposited by the waves assaulting the shore. At such times, the trapped air inside the tunnels tried to escape and emitted a horrifying, bloodcurdling sound like the bellowing of a wounded animal. The horrible sound could be heard all through the island and terrified the population, giving rise to stories of dread of trapped animals screaming for release. At other times, tides were higher than average and flooded parts of the prison cells. Life expectancy was short at best, and most prisoners were happy to be released by death from the unspeakable life they were forced to live there.

By this time, Naïs, her anger goaded by the apparently exaggerated hopelessness of the situation painted to her by the delegate named Master Itaio, as she recalled, rose and walked to the window to turn her back to the man and gather her wits. She knew that with her back against a wall, her reaction was always a drive to confront and fight rather than the opposite. Several times in her life, she had observed how this unexpected behavior would surprise and confuse her adversaries and so seemed to serve a positive purpose. Fisting her two hands at her side and then turning abruptly and confronting Master Itaio, she nodded her head coolly.

"My revered Master Itaio, please, I beg you to desist from your attempts to frighten me unnecessarily. I assure you that I have sufficient wit to comprehend the seriousness of my current situation. I also assure you that scaring me will not force me to act in a frenzy. I shall consider all that you have said and will give you a response in due time. However, hear me, sir, and understand this, I am not without great and powerful friends and well-wishers, including members of the court of His Majesty, in fact, His Majesty himself and numerous members in the High Council of the Sacred School of Bull Dancers and the Arena of the Sacred Bulls. But now, sir, I crave—nay indeed I insist—on solitude to consider all that has been said here. You will hear from me shortly, probably through the mouth of Ninno, who has been Master Odaro's secretary and counselor and now serves me in that same capacity."

She inclined her head, and then, with as much determination as she could muster, she turned her back on Itaio to continue staring out the window. "A good day to you, sir."

After that, she simply forced herself not to move at all, not to turn back toward Master Itaio but to continue motionless, to stare out the window toward the sea. She had never before noticed how difficult it was to keep one's body absolutely still when every muscle screamed for action. She wanted to smash something against the wall, to scream and stomp her feet, and to kick some piece of furniture. She was literally shaking with impotent fury, her breath coming in short quick gasps, her fingernails digging into the palms of her hands, her teeth grinding against one another.

Eventually, however, she calmed sufficiently to be able to gather her wits and dispatch one of her servants to summon Ninno. Ninno—not her own cluelessly self-serving family—would be able to give her counsel, suggestions, a tenuous path to follow to wiggle herself out of this—this totally disastrous mess which she had gotten herself into. Ay, yes, this was a horrendous calamity, one which she would never have envisioned when she had entered into her relationship with Odaro. Ninno—Ninno was to be her salvation; well, maybe not a salvation but some sort of solution to extricate herself—oh, goddess, oh, Great God of the Seas, she was so confused and still too heart-poundingly upset to be able to think and reason.

And her family? Without ever noticing it, she shrugged her shoulder and waved her hand in a gesture of dismissal. She had not energy, not patience, not any inclination now to concern herself with them. Bitterly she came to the conclusion that they, as well, would not concern themselves with her. All their focus should be on their own survival. That was actually good; it relieved her once and for all of responsibility for them. They were all adults by now, let them shift for themselves, just as she had to—for better or for worse. The only obligation to them was a brief visit, as soon as she was able to manage. She would have to inform them that they were on their own; the home they had been provided for would be forfeit within days. They better gather all the necessary coins to purchase a humbler place of residence for their future, and yes, better also start looking for paying employment for all of them. For they needed to understand that no help would be flowing to them from her any longer! Oh yes, Ido had been so right! And she had been such a fool! A blind, blind damned fool!

And Ido? Ah, Ido was no longer hers, he was lost to her. Too late! Too late! He was building his own future, his own home and family and career, no longer could she expect help from him or lean on him. She swallowed and her heart twisted. And yes, this, this was the bitterest loss, the bitterest poison to swallow.

Thus Ninno was summoned and stood in front of her, his eyes darting here and there, his Adam's apple bobbing frantically up and down with his repeated swallowing. His hands moved unceasingly, clasping and unclasping one the other, then occasionally diving into a small pouch dangling from the belt of his long embroidered shirt to retrieve a large piece of cloth, with which he alternately wiped his eyes and his face. He had apparently been apprised of Odaro's and, consequently, his very own fate, and looked more like a frightened field mouse than any other creature Naïs could think of. Finally she took pity on him and, with a wave of her hand, invited him from the courtyard into the house, away from the searing sun of midday. She directed him to a stool next to her own chaise and ordered a cooling glass of wine, mixed with fresh spring water for both of them. In her mind, she had no doubt that she had great need of Ninno. Her kindness to him was more needful than any gestures of elegance she would normally be reluctant to offer the man.

Briefly and with utter truthfulness and straightforward honesty, she summarized her problems. She had unexpectedly, and by default, become Odaro's heir—heir of all of his commitments and debts. She had become responsible, for the goddess's sake. She was responsible! Almighty goddess, how could that be? How had that happened? And how could it possibly be dealt with? She was utterly out of her depth when such matters of finance were discussed. Forcing herself not to break down and not to throw herself in front of quavering little Ninno, not to beg his aid to do something, anything, anything at all.

She drew a deep shaky breath and, much to her surprise, found that Ninno understood, actually understood her without having to explain to him how desperate she was. He seemed to relax and grow, like a plant starved for rain will stretch branches and unroll its leaves to open itself, he grew under the weight of his self-importance, for once in his life, real and not just imagined or wished for. Here he was needed, needed to do something serious and something that probably no one else would be able to do. He nodded his birdlike head repeatedly, the big nose reminding Naïs of a bird's beak. He narrowed his eyes in thought and finally opened his mouth to speak, while lifting both hands as in supplication to be heard.

"My revered lady, pray you take a deep breath at this point in your life and look to list all those things which you do have, not only those that you have regrettably lost. What is lost is lost. It is in the past, and the past will not awaken, it will lie in the bosom of the goddess to slumber there for all time to come. There are things—many things—lady, which I and my family had lost once, but what I had learned from those losses is this—that life flows on, and things slowly repair themselves. Maybe not to return to the glories of the past, but repair themselves, nonetheless. We—you—must marshal all that you still possess and catalogue them and then act accordingly.

"You are young and strong, famous and greatly revered for your incomparable accomplishments in the Sacred Bull Arena. You are admired for your beauty and your desirability. Why else, pray tell, did Odaro pursue you and spend a fortune to please and possess you and, by your possession, impress all who live in Knossos? That, dear lady, is your wealth, and that you must guard to use as your coinage!

"We need to look for someone who is rich enough to rise above your debts and who desires you more than what he would have to pay to obtain you. There are many those here in Knossos who have the coinage to influence others and who would be willing to do so for your sake, lady. Allow me to depart now and put out my *feelers* to search out such men. Give me a good faith amount to start my search. It need not be coin if you are currently lacking such, give me some item of value which I can then convert to coin for my and my family's use. I shall return in two or three days and give you a report of what has been achieved. Until then, lady, do not act other than to smile graciously and with mystery, as though you had a secret. In fact, you have one—me, if I may be bold enough to say."

*****

Ninno's promise was as good as gold. He came in two turns of the sun, bowed to her, and was most grateful when she offered him a seat and some refreshments. Once he had satisfied his thirst, he launched into the narrative of what he had accomplished during the last days.

"Most revered lady, I shall immediately tell you to relieve your anxiety, that I believe to have found a good—well, to say the least, an acceptable solution to your problem! As you may remember, I assured you that your accomplishments, fame, and beauty are a beacon to call you to many wealthy persons' attention. I have received several offers which might interest you, but alas most were offers which included only limited financial rescue, and thus I believe that they might not be of serious consideration by you, lady. However, I did receive one exceptional and outstanding offer. Like anything offered to us by life, it is not perfect, but I trust will be acceptable to you. Allow me then to elaborate.

"This offer was made by one Master Patinos, of whose fame you may or may not have heard. He is a goldsmith and goldworker frequently employed by the royal palace to the pleasure of His Majesty, the king, as well as his royal household. His workmanship is so exceptional as to be impossible to duplicate by anyone, it is claimed. Master Patinos has great influence, great power and great wealth. In fact, he is assuredly one of the ten wealthiest men in Knossos and wherever this city's influence sphere reaches, in fact, I believe not to exaggerate when I maintain, throughout our island.

"Master Patinos is enchanted. He has become a great admirer of you, and immediately as soon as he heard the financial misfortune which innocently befell you, he offered his assistance. I have no doubt that it would be easy for him to altogether extricate you out of your current financial straits. Moreover, his desire and admiration for you is such that he wishes to establish a more solid bond between the two of you. Should you be willing, revered lady, he offers marriage to you, which of course will guarantee you total financial security. You must understand that this man's wealth is such—"

Ninno shut his mouth at this point because Naïs had jumped up from her seat and, grasping her wine goblet, began to stalk quickly up and down the length of the reception room where they were sitting. Almost fiercely, she turned to him.

"Master Ninno," she whispered, her eyes pinning him, "I understand what you are saying. But allow me to interject. This offer is too generous by far, there must be a fault, a hidden defect somewhere. I have, of late, become very suspicious and, well, jaded and cautious with my opinions of human nature. In short, something must be wrong with such an offer! Please be so kind and acquaint me immediately of all aspects of the arrangement!"

As she watched Ninno shift uncomfortably, her heart began to hammer with the premonition of a litany of ugly things to come. Ninno rose, his eyes fixed on his feet and the inlaid floor. The shrug of his shoulders was almost imperceptible, but his hesitant stammer was most obvious.

"My dearest, most revered lady," he whispered into his chin, "you are, above all, I have found, a realist. What we are talking about is a business arrangement predicated—if you will permit me to say—upon financial need—yours—and emotional and bodily desire, his. Master Patinos, just as you, is also a realist. As I said, he will face and satisfy all of your creditors. What he wishes is to enter into a marriage with you with all aspirations of making that marriage a pleasing one to both of you. He assures me that his greatest pleasure will be your presence in the household. As you, lady, have pointed out, there must be something wrong with this offer. My answer, lady, is a question—have you ever met Master Patinos?"

And when Naïs just shook her head, he continued, again returning his gaze to a contemplation of his feet.

"Madam, lady, Patinos is not...well-formed. He is—well, he was born with a defective body. His back is twisted so that he is forced to limp, which limp is aggravated by one leg being shorter than the other. His neck has almost grown into his shoulders. His arms, though, are complete, totally well formed with beautiful skilled hands, which allow him to be the most brilliantly accomplished and widely famed artist of goldwork of our age. He has a pleasing face with beautiful black eyes which perceive beauty everywhere and in all things...His brain is equally agile, as well as his sight, his hearing, and all his other faculties, if you understand my meaning."

After that, there was silence. In the silence, the harsh screams of the gulls flying over the dunes and shallows could be heard, almost drowning out the excited chattering chirpings of the little yellow birds flitting in and out of the creeping ivy which covered the north wall and pillars of the house. Some of the birds were still courting, but most had already mated and were building their nests. The lacy leaves rustled as the birds flew through the protective screen of leaves to do their nest-building in secrecy behind the veil of ivy against the wall of the building.

Ninno shifted uncomfortably and then continued, "Howbeit, my gracious revered lady, please keep in mind that Master Patinos had repeatedly avowed to me his great admiration and respect for your person, which, coupled with his desire for you and the guarantees I made a list of to you before—which I may stress, he is ready to put on document for your assurance—all of these bode well for your future, lady. You will be the legal mistress of a large and very elegant household and the legal wife of a highly regarded citizen, several times honored by His Majesty, the king, for his service, not just to the royal household but to our country far and wide."

When Naïs, with a sigh, opened her mouth, but before she could even voice her request for a few days to think over this offer, Ninno raised his arm in anticipation of what she was going to say.

"When Patinos made his offer, he stressed most vigorously, dear Lady, that he is not blessed with a great deal of patience. You must take his offer or not—now and not in some future time. He wants to know yea or nay within twenty-four hours. I regret this, lady, and know that it only adds to your stress, but I assure you, could I have swayed him, I would have done so for your sake. I can allow you overnight, lady, but then I must return tomorrow for your answer. So should you have any questions to me before I leave you, please voice them now. Possibly you have questions to me which will make your decision easier. Allow me to listen to you now. After all, you have listened to me long enough!"

Naïs's thoughts were almost frozen; she felt like her brain was paralyzed. There were a thousand ideas, questions buzzing around in her head, but she was unable to sort through them and prioritize the most urgent ones. In puzzlement, she shook her head.

"Is this man—this Patinos—is he...well, what age is he, do you think? Has he been married before? Has he a family? Is he from Knossos?" She had to shake her head, considering the foolishness and triviality of such questions.

Ninno spread his hands. "Probably yes, my lady, yes, I think he may be about ten years older than you are or perhaps less than that, and closer to your age? He has been well established in his profession and recognized by the court for a number of years. He is not old by any means, no. I do not believe I have seen any gray hairs on his head, no...And he has beautiful long shining black hair! Family? Well, I do not believe he has a family, that is to say children. Hmm...I do not believe he had a wife before, that is, I do not believe he is widowed. He—he has had women, though, several, I understand, but none of those developed into lasting relationships, my lady...On the other hand, he is not known to be a womanizer and keeps to himself most of the time. But then he is also so very busy, even though he employs many—well, numerous apprentices. But they only do the preparatory work for him, as well as some of the routine finishing ornamentations, wherever necessary.

"He is not known to be parsimonious. No, no one have I heard to complain that he exploits them or does not pay well for good work. I hear he has a wicked temper, though, but rarely exhibited. Mostly he is just quiet, keeps to himself, as I have said before...My most revered lady, I do wish I could give you more details, but unfortunately I cannot. The man does not socialize, even with neighbors or with his fellow artists, goldworkers. I cannot believe that this is because of his reticence due to his—his defective body. He seems mostly to be reconciled or else unaware if it...you understand?"

There was a hesitant pause after this, Ninno had evidently exhausted his fund of information he deemed pertinent to her questions. The silence dragged on, until Naïs shifted her body on the pillows she was sitting on. She sighed, then rose and, in a gesture of gratitude, laid her hand on Ninno's shoulder. Ninno colored, then jumped in surprise and rose quickly, evidently assuming that Naïs's gesture indicated his dismissal. He turned his body toward her, bowed, and murmured softly that he would return, at the latest, on the afternoon of the next day.

"Revered lady, I cannot give you longer to deliberate. Would that I could, but I fear to lose the momentum of the negotiations, lady, and we—you—have too much at stake to allow that to happen! I bid you the blessings of the goddess. Until tomorrow then." And he bowed again, and then again by the doorway as he let himself out.

*****

One week later, the couple knelt before the priestesses to receive the blessing of the Great Goddess upon their union. Well, kneeling was not an option for the groom, but he did make the effort, with the assistance of his helper, Somiro, to bend his one unaffected knee.

Naïs tried hard not to be obviously staring at her new husband. From the corner of her eye, shielded by lowered lashes, her eyes repeatedly darted to him. Patinos was indeed not an old man, albeit not a young one either. His deformities, the twisted backbone and hip, the humped neck, the one shortened leg and clubbed foot, and the halting gait caused by them, prevented a correct assessment of his age. His face was unlined and surprisingly attractive, with glowing dark eyes, his voice strong, and so was the hand which held hers in an almost painful grip. He looked at her while making his oath to the goddess and his obsidian eyes revealed nothing of his emotions.

She wished she could do the same, but no effort of will prevented her look of shock and trepidation. She told herself that her hesitation was due to her surprise. Hidden emotions were infrequent in Crete; people were demonstrative and noisy, often too vocal in expressing their feelings, hiding fairly nothing of their joy, anger, hesitation, or grief. People laughed, hugged, flirted openly, just as they screamed their anger and sobbed their grief in public. This was not a society of people with unrevealing obsidian eyes, and they frightened her. She took a deep breath and smiled at her husband, after all, this was her wedding day!

Patinos, aware of what was expected of a happy groom, had come for his bride in a carriage drawn by two gray horses. The carriage had been decorated with garlands of mimosa and small climbing roses interwoven with laurel leaves. On the way home—his home, which now was to become hers as well—he periodically dipped his fingers into a satchel containing small copper coins and scattered them among the population, followed by their cheers and applause. During the whole ride from the temple of the Great Goddess to his house, situating somewhat isolated from other wealthy homes climbing the hillside behind the city of Knossos, he had not once addressed his new wife or even offered her a smile. His hooded eyes shielded any expression, his handsome face closed forbiddingly. His hand held hers in a hard grip.

There was no wedding celebration, no guest invited for a nuptial feast. The house waited for them silently, the few servants she saw walked on silent feet and bowed to them wordlessly. Patinos released her hand and leaned on a cane Somiro held out to him, then dismissed him with a wave of his hand.

He threw his words over his shoulder without turning, while commencing to shuffle slowly along toward the inner part of the house.

"Come," he urged Naïs, "you need to be shown around to get your bearings of your new surroundings."

Naïs followed him, trying desperately to slow her usual long loping steps to her husband's painfully slow gait. The house was literally cavernous, most of the rooms silently dark, the hallways lit by oil lamps kept in place by beautifully worked bronze brackets. In the semidarkness, she could discern wall paintings of birds in flight, gazelles bounding over bushes, bees buzzing around delicate flowers, scenes of ocean waves with fish of all shapes abounding in them. She could barely believe the beauty which she expected to be revealed with the next sunrise. To the right, they passed a heavy wooden door reinforced by bronze studs and bronze hinges; here Patinos halted his painful progress and, turning, looked at her sternly.

"Beyond this door are my workrooms, wife. Under no circumstances are you ever to enter. When I work, I wish to be undisturbed, except by Somiro on occasion, and even he, only when I summon him. He knows the times at which I need him, and the sound of my summons, beyond those times he, as well, is forbidden to enter.

"You will find our bedroom and the round bath beyond it as you walk straight along the hallway. The hallway ends in our bedroom. In a while, I shall join you there. A servant will bring you food and drink, as I believe you must be hungry and thirsty by now. Your personal servant is waiting for you to comply with your orders. For a while yet, I will be in my workrooms. Await my arrival, wife."

And with that he turned, painfully pulling his body along as he shuffled through the door.

*****

Naïs found her new husband to be a coldly manipulative, secretive, and demanding man and an equally hard and demanding lover, who had a bent to become brutal when he had more than his share of the wine Somiro supplied to his workrooms. What upset her more than any other aspect of their marriage was that she felt Patinos enjoyed his brutality, most times verbal but very rarely physical abuse. She kept trying to convince herself that his solitary isolated life, forced upon him by his deformity, had embittered him.

He had been born deformed, he explained to her; his father had disavowed him, and he only stayed alive due to the devoted attention of his mother. When she died, he was, in fact, totally abandoned, and only the astonishing skill of his hands, both—just as his face—

intact, whole, and appealing, had ensured his survival and his eventual miraculous rise to great fame.

On the other hand, Naïs had to admit, he had immediately and with great precision paid all her debts, liquidated her house and that of her sisters and brothers, and given her a monthly allowance above her actual monetary needs. At the same time and in the harshest of terms, he forbade her to ever have her family set foot into his house. With cruel frankness, he told her not to ever dare see her family or former friends again; from now on in, he was to be her only concern, her only family.

Naïs found this distressing but also mystifying. It was not that Patinos needed her companionship, for long tracts of the day, he was involved with his work so that she barely ever saw him, except in their shared bed. He moved about as though still single, never giving her an account of where he went when he went out or for what reason. Occasionally from Somiro, she heard when his master went to see the king or any of the members of the royal family, received commissions from them, or delivered finished work to them.

Like all other aspects of her married life, their behavior in their bedroom was strictly under Patinos's control and his unbending rules. Whenever he was at home, he expected her to join him for dinner. Like most of their lives together, dinner was also consumed in silence, except that occasionally he would acknowledge some dish which had especially pleased him. After the meal, Patinos would retire for a few more hours of work, then join her in their bedroom. She was expected to be there waiting for him. In the silence of the great dark house, with no one to talk to, she had a hard time to keep awake while awaiting her husband. In bed, he had his explicit instructions for her. He was a vigorous lover and, because of his physical limitations, obviously expected his partner to facilitate their sexual activities. He was in awe of her limber body, and several times, Naïs attempted to point out to her husband that such a limber body depended on daily workout and exercise, only to be turned away from such topics in anger. Eventually, though, Patinos did relent and did allow for her to go and continue her daily exercises in the bullring; but she remained strictly forbidden to enter into any of the public performances.

More distressing than any to her was this—her husband's attitude toward the Arena of the Sacred Bulls. It seemed that he nurtured an inexplicable jealousy, not only toward her profession but any other activity which she pursued outside of their household. Before long, she noticed one or another of the household servants trailing her or loitering around wherever she went. This surveillance somehow disturbed Naïs almost more than any other of her husband's unwelcome activities. Since childhood, she had been accustomed to freedom of movement. Like all Cretan children, except those of the very rich, she was self-reliant from an early age. Later her professional life was certainly well regimented but also offered her free association with colleagues, teachers, and students alike.

The first time she became aware of the reality of her restricted life came on a day she unexpectedly ran into Athenis. Athenis no longer performed. For that, she was too well advanced in her pregnancy. Like so many women carrying a child, she positively bloomed, radiating contentment and happiness. When she saw Naïs, her eyes lit up, a genuinely joyous smile curving her mouth. She extended her hands and embraced Naïs, in the custom of her people kissing first her right, then her left, and then again her right cheek.

"My dearest," she murmured, "how happy I am to run into you! I have heard about your recent marriage—and to such an illustrious personage no less, a favorite of Their Majesties—but have not yet been able to wish you great happiness! Maybe you and your husband will soon be as blessed as Ido and I are, to expect a little one, neh?" Then she stepped back to look at Naïs, and her eyes clouded as her brows drew together. "But what has happened? Have you been ill, love?"

Naïs drew a deep breath. Of late, she had not once peeked into her polished crystal mirror to look, so she was totally unprepared to give an account or an excuse for her appearance. She knew that she was suffering from the shock of events before and ensuing her marriage. She could barely eat and slept poorly, in addition to stress due also to her husband's demands. She had an emotional turmoil to carry even before her marriage. Much to her surprise, some of it was not only caused by her suddenly looming financial problems but actually by grieving for Odaro. That took her totally by surprise. The last thing she had expected was any emotional attachment to him. He was but a self-indulgent, petulant, demanding, overfed, overindulged adult child with incredible skills of managing wealth and acquiring more of it. Like children everywhere, he was insatiable in his need for more wealth as well as more physical pleasure. Like a child, he reached and grasped, but also like a child, he had a disarming openness and ingenuity with those he professed to love, in his own way.

She awakened from her reverie by Athenis touching her, gently stroking her face with the back of his fingers. "Naïs, my dear, is something wrong? Are you not feeling well? Please do not make me worry about you! Tell me!" She shifted uncomfortably, then placed her hands on Naïs's arms, and shook her gently. "Come, love, walk with me and let us talk, if there is something worrying you, please understand that you can share it me without my tattling about it!"

Her husband's severe instructions suddenly came to Naïs's mind. She shook her head as she disengaged herself from strolling along with Athenis. Utterly flustered, she mumbled some excuse about already being late and literally fled down the path they started to take, her feet barely touching the ground in her haste. Her heart thumped loudly enough that she believed Athenis would hear it. With flaming cheeks, she ran back toward the arena, shame flooding every pore of her body. Ah, goddess, had she already become so cowed, so cowardly, that she would not dare open her mouth to a friend? Was this going to be her new existence? If that was true, then may the next bull gore her to death, for she could not endure it, could not!

When she arrived home, she fled into their bedroom, knowing that Patinos was closeted in his workrooms for the length of the day, and he and she would not run into each other until dinner. She sat on a low cushion-covered stool in front a large window and stared out without seeing. She pulled her feet up under herself and folded her hands in her lap. To all outward appearances, she presented the picture of serenity. Only her eyes, normally a warm chestnut brown, and now a bottomless black, gave away her stormy emotions.

*****

Over the next few months, slowly the relationship between Naïs and Patinos moved to some sort of balance. While he was still a man often filled with insecurity, malice, and secretiveness, he also slowly and hesitantly began to reach toward her. His lovemaking became less aggressive, less harsh, and at rare times, Naïs sensed him to watch her almost with kindness, if not quite with tenderness, seeing her as a person, not just a someone to be fled from, except in the bedroom. On those rare occasions, he began to talk to her, haltingly, hesitantly, as though communicating with another was an unaccustomed exercise. Then one evening, some kind of a crack appeared in the wall Patinos had erected about them.

Naïs lay, observing her husband turn toward her with a torturous groan and watch her with his blacker-than-black obsidian eyes. He seemed in pain, with a heavy furrow between his eyes, and Naïs felt a flood of pity open her heart to him. Aware that he disliked conversation, she hesitantly reached her hand to touch his shoulder and began to talk to him in a barely audible voice.

"Husband, you are in pain. Understand that I am well aware of bodily pain, pain caused by the body's injuries. At the Sacred Arena of the Bulls, we have been taught how to deal with them. I beg you, please allow me to help you! Why suffer so much if some of the suffering could be lessened?"

Startled, Patinos looked at her with utter surprise, for a moment, at a loss for a response.

"Please," Naïs begged, "please hear me, I am your wife and wish to help you!"

"There is no help for this pain, wife." He finally answered with another groan. "I have borne it for many years. It exists. It is a part of my life."

Naïs lifted herself upon her elbow and shook her head. "Nay, husband, there is some relief to be gained if one is only responsive to the pain! But you have endured yours because of years of neglect and lack of knowledge—and you have been enduring it unnecessarily, forgive me…" she stammered, not wishing to offend him or those who were charged to care for him. "I beg you, please allow me to minister to your need!"

Ultimately she convinced him. She ordered hot water in a large urn, some soft towels, and oil of aloe which she had in her pain-relief arsenal. Dismissing the servant, she gently assisted Patinos to roll to his stomach, and carefully laying the warmed towels on his back, shoulders, and thighs, she let the heat seep into his joints and muscles. Then as carefully as she could, she massaged his muscles with the oil, repeating this whole treatment several times. She was surprised and very pleased when she noticed that her husband had fallen asleep and was breathing softly, and even eventually stretched himself freely in his sleep.

Each of these events became watershed occasions. Each opened one more little crack in Patinos's carefully constructed protective walls. After the first few such openings, it seemed to Naïs that the cracks were barely noticed any longer. And then one day, somehow a decision was made in his tortured brain to grant her entry into his workrooms. Naïs was allowed to see the wonders of his handwork, the elaborate amphorae, rhytons, cups and bowls of hammered gold, ornamented with delicate figurines, here a long parade of men and women bringing gifts to the goddess, there prancing bulls or flying birds and bees. The beauty of these things took her breath away.

Watching her watching and openly admiring his treasures gentled, softened, shifted something in Patinos. When she turned to him, asking endless breathless eager questions about how it was possible to make such beauty, how his mind conceived what his hands eventually wrought, at first Patinos was left wordless. Slowly, in his need to express himself quickly, stammering to form his answer correctly, while not accustomed to do so, he began to explain.

His hands commenced to draw lines and circles in the air, and then he began to lift one or another of his works. His fingers lovingly glided over the lines, the gentle curves of the decorative figures. He talked of sitting at night by the window and looking at the sky, the stars, the endlessly moving ocean. He talked of dragging himself to walk on the beach until an idea would take hold behind his eyes. Of dragging himself back to his workrooms as fast as his body would let him.

Eventually he realized what he was doing—that he was talking intimately to another human being, not just muttering to himself. With some confusion, he closed his eyes and, once again, reverted to a hesitant stammer, licking his lips and closing his mouth. Heavy silence once again pervaded the workroom. Naïs was speechless, awed, and confused. In confusion, she shook her head, feeling like awakening from some dream. Reluctantly she rose from the stool she had been sitting on. Her hand on the door, ready to push it open but hesitant to do so, her questioning eyes looked into her husband's gleaming obsidian ones. She saw how the joy of talking about his work, the joy of expressing his creativity had briefly transformed him, put a faint blush of color on his face, the hint of a smile of his lips, and freedom of movement to his arms. She sighed.

"I thank you, husband, for your courtesy in allowing me to—to invade your workroom, to look at these wondrous things. Truly the gods have given you a great blessing to compensate you for…I beg you to forgive my bluntness…for the disabilities of your body! A great and miraculous blessing, indeed." She bowed to him slightly and then retreated to those parts of the house which were habitually open to her.

That night, when Patinos came to her bed, she discovered a never-before-experienced hesitant gentleness in him. Now instead of almost attacking her, he actually kissed her with what, for him, could be counted as tenderness. She was totally taken by such unexpected behavior, and her body responded to it. It had been a long, long time since she had experienced tenderness, not since the now-gone days of Ido, and her response to her husband was more surprising to her than to him. After the passion passed, he lay next to her, panting, his chest heaving, until after a while, he rolled away from her and pushed himself upright. For a while, he sat at the end of the bed, his head bowed into his palms, his twisted elbows resting on his thighs. Then he heaved himself upright and slowly, painfully shuffled to the door.

Before walking through the door, he turned. His blacker-than-night eyes pinned her. He bent his head slightly. In a voice as slight and soft as a sibilant breeze from the ocean, he muttered, "Thank you…for tonight," and then was gone.

Naïs sensed that somehow, they both had crossed another new watershed. The house servants sensed it as well. Things were still tense, the servants still walked carefully and without looking to left or right, but the cloud shrouding the home of the famous gold-worker became ever so slightly lighter. Naïs herself became imperceptibly more relaxed, which exhibited itself in her performance at the bull arena. Grudgingly Patinos had allowed her to perform on occasion, albeit only infrequently, claiming that he and the house needed her presence; this claim in itself astounded his wife. The unfortunate by-product of her successes in the arena was the flare up of Patinos's jealousy. To Naïs, since she truly did not have any desire to fraternize with colleagues, the single reason for jealousy was her husband's deeply ingrained insecurity. She could understand that, to some extent. He was so disfigured, so horribly deformed, that he had condemned himself to spend his life believing that his talent was not enough to counterbalance his appearance. In a land where beauty of the body, litheness of gait, prowess of swimming in the sea, grace in dancing, running, and athletics were much treasured attributes of the successful ones, Patinos had none of them.

He was ugly, and so to many people, he was evil and to be feared. But Naïs realized that her husband was not ugly, his deformity was. He had a handsome face and actually beautiful hands with delicate long fingers. The only thing making him appear ugly was his deformity. She also knew that for him, it would be difficult to view himself in such terms. Once he would be able to do so, he would be able to fight his feelings of degradation. Maybe then he would be able to form attachments he was afraid of now for fear of revulsion or, at best, of rejection. His aggression was a form of self-defense against just that. He must have grown up with this belief, surviving a doubtless miserable childhood and adolescence.

Suddenly she wondered about her husband's parents, his childhood, his adolescence, whoever his teachers were to teach him such miraculous skills. She wanted to know all of it. They were married, tied together for the rest of their lives, she suddenly wanted to not just endure it but to—could it be possible—be happy. If fate gave her this man, this vindictive, malicious, angry, brutal, gifted, suffering, contorted, tortured outcast of a man, could she ever get to know him, like him, and he to know her and like her? To be at ease, at peace, content in each other's company?

She sighed, rose from her seat on the terrace, and slowly walked to the forbidden door, the door to her husband's workrooms. She raised her hand hesitantly to gently scratch the door, the customary request to ask for admission. She waited, her heart drumming in her chest. Then she raised her hand again, but before she could repeat her scratching, the door tore open, revealing Patinos's head and torso in the light of the oil burners. His look of anger changed when he saw her, his eyes enlarging and boring into hers.

"Is there any…what is wrong? What is going on?" He rasped, his voice rough from disuse. "Are you unwell? Are you ill, wife?" Naïs was surprised that he would be concerned with her at all. She swallowed, trying to mask her fear and lowering her eyes, stammering.

"I beg you to forgive me for my intrusion, husband. I know that you have forbidden it, but you have awakened such a desire, nay, a thirst in me to see how you create the miracles you make here, that I have come to beg you, if I could, if you would, to…to…please permit me…" She was stammering pitifully now, in a quandary how to express herself so as not to raise his ire. Then she noticed that Patinos eyes had stopped boring into hers but were moving up and down her body, as though he would need assurance that she was not an apparition.

For the longest time, he eyed her, as though weighing something in his mind, his eyes repeatedly roaming over her. Finally, in silence, he nodded and stepped aside, holding on to the door while also holding it open. Without a word, a slight movement of his hand indicated that she should enter. He turned his back, letting the door close, and began to shuffle to the other end of the room where a long line of oil lamps had been laid out on a worktable. Half turning to her, he jutted his chin toward a wobble-legged settee.

"Sit there," he muttered. She obeyed silently, folding her hands on her lap, and in silence, she watched her husband. He went back to what he had apparently worked on before. It was a double-handled large gold kylix, such as were usually carried by priests, or the king himself, to bring offerings to the goddess. Its smooth surface glinted in the light of the oil lamps. Patinos picked up a small piece of soft charcoal, a thin short piece of wood burned black at one end only. Carefully he rolled it against a flat piece of pumice, probably to sharpen the blackened end, she thought. Then lifting the kylix in one hand, and the sharpened length of blackened wood in the other, he brought both close to his squinting eyes. With infinite care and delicacy, he began to draw lines and curves upon the gold surface. Naïs comprehended that delicacy was important to keep the gold surface from being scratched, only marked by the charcoal yet to force the charcoal to leave the outline of a design onto the gold.

After what seemed an endless silence, he began to speak. His voice was so soft as to be almost inaudible, as she strained to understand.

"This is a piece commissioned by the chief priest of the goddess Ida. It is to be used in the next harvest festival for him to carry the best of the oil harvested from the royal olive grove. It must be handled with the greatest care so that the gold surface remains without blemish until I solder the figures I will design onto the surface, you understand? The figures I will design will be three dimensional copies of what I am now drawing onto the surface of the chalice."

Squinting, he fell silent. Naïs had to smile, seeing how he licked his lips and how the tip of his tongue followed the motion of his hand, just like a little child's. The ensuing silence stretched out endlessly. The only noises were Patinos's heavy breathing as he turned the kylix this way and that and, from the distance, the crash of waves below the house. Naïs was so absorbed by what she was watching that she was totally unaware of the passage of time. Eventually Patinos moved away from the workbench upon which the kylix rested and dragged himself to a corner of the room where a shielded brazier held the glowing remains of the earlier vigorously burning fire. After peering into a brass bowl, he shook his head, his forehead creased.

"Not yet, not ready yet, the gold is not ready for me yet," he muttered, sighed, then sat down on the settee next to her and, pulling his short legs under his body, bent his head into his palms. His straight dark hair, which he kept immaculate and cut to shoulder-length, flopped forward to fall over his hands. Suddenly he looked almost young, giving Naïs an idea of how he would have looked as an undamaged young man. Then slowly Patinos lifted his head to look at her, surprise and wariness reflected in his eyes.

"Oh," he mumbled, "I had forgotten altogether." Then he squared his twisted shoulders, one sloping and the other perpetually drawn up so that it almost touched his ear. "Forgive me, wife, for I cannot show anything more to you tonight. The gold for the inlay is not yet ready, not until tomorrow. Leave now."

But Naïs was loath to rise and walk out. She felt like she was in an enchanted world. She wanted to see more. She wanted to know more. Gently she laid her fingers on his shoulder.

"Please forgive me, husband. I do not wish to make myself difficult, especially since you have been so forthcoming in showing me…showing me what you do. But I beg you, could you talk to me about—well, about anything that connects you to your work? How you learned? Who taught you? How do ideas come into your mind? Does that happen suddenly or over a period of trial and then adjustment, correction of that initial vision?" Without conscious thought she let her hand slide down from his shoulder along his twisted back. He shuddered and started briefly at her touch. He turned his head, his depthless black eyes again pinning her. Then his lips tightened, and he shook his head.

"Nay, not tonight, wife. I am tired. Go."

Later that night, she awoke to her husband climbing into bed. It was a cold night, and he was struggling, scrabbling to pull the covers over himself. Naïs lifted the edge of the bed cover for him, and with a groan, he slid under it. There was a long silence, and then Patinos sighed. His voice was low and slow, and she could hear the reluctance in it.

"I have been honored by your interest, wife. I find it flattering and inspiring at the same time. No one had ever asked me questions such as you directed to me. They surprised and confused me at the same time, and when you asked, I did not know how to answer. Still I find it difficult to do so…Please give me more time to be equal to give you answers. Please do not think that I do not value your kindness, Naïs, for I do, indeed I do. It is—well, it is just too new to me." And his voice quavered and broke before becoming even softer than a whisper. "It is too new to me…"

When Naïs turned her head to look at him, he was asleep.

*****

Two months after this ice-breaking event for both Patinos and her, Naïs found that she was pregnant. She had suspected it for some time, but a visit to the healing priestess of the Goddess of Serpents, the Great Goddess of Fertility, Prosperity, and the Harvest confirmed it for her. The priestess encouraged her to continue for a while to do her accustomed bull dancing, with no more than two events for each week. She was to come back, if everything was going well, and she was feeling well in two months' time. Should something be going wrong, she was to return immediately, seeing that she was such an important personage in society! But by that time, Naïs would need to prepare herself that her kind of dangerous and strenuous activity would be out of question for the rest of her pregnancy. The priestess smiled and, dipping her hand into a large shallow woven basket at her side, sprinkled a handful of white petals of the olive flowers upon her head.

"Be as fruitful as the olive tree," she whispered, "as tenacious to survive, to live, and prosper. May the Goddess of Serpents shelter you and protect your womb!"

All the way homeward in the litter, which Patinos insisted to have ready at her disposal, Naïs rehearsed what she was going to say to her husband. While he continued to be occasionally, unexpectedly volatile, much of the time, he was calm, devoted to his work as ever but more forthcoming with her. She would spend long hours sitting in his workshop, in silence, watching him, observing how he molded the gold to his will, to his imagination.

They did, finally, achieve a balance, a relationship based upon mutual regard and respect and a slowly growing affection. When she married, Naïs could not have even imagined any kind of affection coming from Patinos. Yet in their relationship, he had mellowed, quieted, and had shown her a degree of love she would never had expected before. And now, now he was to become a father. Naïs had no idea how he would receive her announcement, but she had to inform him and soon, before her appearance would begin to change. Since he shared her bed almost every night, surely he would notice right away!

As it happened, she could not restrain her excitement. Her news slipped out that same evening. As Naïs was able to understand more and more the gift, the miraculously exceptional genius of her husband, her regard, admiration, and yes, her affection for him grew. Their custom had become to spend the hours after dinner together in his workroom. Patinos still did not allow the servants to enter, and so Naïs would bring in some fruit and wine to be consumed at leisure while her husband worked. The last few days, he had been working on the figure of a beautiful nymph lifting her two arms to the sky in the gesture of a gentle dance, attached to an onyx base. As he was turning the base this way and that, he glanced at her. Then he held it up to make the gold glint and glow softly in the light of the candles, and muttered, partly to her and mostly to himself, "This, this is the piece I made which will never ever be sold. I shall guard it jealously and keep it so that it can be placed by my side onto the pallet on which they will bear us both to be made into ashes—into ashes, yes, but this statue will never be destroyed because after its completion, I will completely encase it in the heavy rock which is spewed out of our mountains when they commence to glow! This statue will live on forever, long, long after I am gone…

"Does she remind you of someone, wife?" he asked, and when she shook her head smilingly, he nodded slowly and gravely. "Aye, wife, she is modeled after you. You have a beautiful body! Indeed, you have a beautiful face. But of all the beauty your person holds, nothing is as beautiful as your soul and your spirit, my wife!"

Naïs rose and walked to the window, her heart thudding as she heard her voice. "Husband, I must tell you my news. I am pleased that you think my body beautiful, but you have to understand that it will not remain so for long. Husband, I must tell you that I am—we are going to have a child."

Patinos stared at her for a long time, his expression stunned, his mouth slack. Then he wobbled to a little stool which had been placed for him to use next to the worktable. He literally collapsed on it, burying his face in his hands. Silence wrapped itself about him, but as she looked, she watched his shoulders shaking. She hesitated to talk to him until she realized that her husband was crying. Then she went to him and gently forced his hands away to look at his face. His mouth contorted; silent tears streamed from his closed eyes. Slowly the tears ceased, he opened his eyes and looked at her.

"I have never," he stammered, "the goddess help me, I have never thought, never believed that I could—oh—" And as his tears started flowing again, he buried his head once more into his hands. "How is it possible that I am to be a father—that I have fathered a child?" And he reached out his fingers to hesitantly touch hers. "That you would give me a child?" The palm of his other hand wiped at his eyes. "Are you certain, wife? Are you really certain?"

Naïs smiled and nodded her head. "As far as I can tell, my husband. Also I did go to the priestess of the Goddess of Serpents, and she examined me as well. She is quite convinced that I am carrying a child".

He wiped at his eyes again with his sleeve. "Goddess, help me," he muttered, "as much as I want this"—and he shook his head—"it would kill me if that child were born as malformed as I am!" He pivoted on his stool to look Naïs in the eye. His face was contorted, and tears were still coursing down his cheeks. Something shifted in Naïs, accustomed to seeing his face handsome, the only pleasing part of his body, and his magnetic eyes, blacker than the blackest night. She had seen him in anger, in hate, and in passion, but never had she seen him look as vulnerable as at this moment. She rose, walked over to his workbench, and slid down to kneel beside him. She laced both arms around his misshapen neck, twisted shoulders, and hugged him with all her strength. Her head bent to him, and she kissed his soft black hair which always smelled of the wild heather growing around their home. She kissed his eye, one and then the other, tasting the salt of his tears. Slowly she began to rock him gently, as she once did her brothers and sisters when they fell or bruised themselves, or when they were bested in a children's street brawl.

"The priestess assured me that any child you would beget would not bear the taint of your deformities. She said that those deformities were formed in your mother's womb, due to too little space for your growing body or due to some other such constriction. But hear me, husband."

Naïs straightened herself and rose but held on to both of her husband's beautiful hands, with their beautiful long slim fingers.

"I tell you, my husband, if such a calamity would happen, then we both would continue to love and shelter and nurture this infant, this growing person, and love it. The maturing child would receive all the care, attention, teaching, and wisdom from you, Patinos, my husband, and anything that I can impart to the child as well. This child would not be cast off or abandoned and disowned, but treasured and cherished by both of its parents. This I promise—nay, this I swear to you!"

*****

For weeks Patinos anxiously hovered about her. If he could have, he would have locked her up in their bedroom and forced her to rest all day long. Finally Naïs summoned an old priestess of the Goddess of Serpents to their house, hoping against hope that under the guise of examining her again, she would explain to her husband that lying about was unhealthy for both mother and child this early along her pregnancy. After that, Patinos reluctantly allowed her to continue her exercises at the bull arena. The stress was on exercises only. She was to keep herself far away from the bulls and most especially not to participate in any performances. About that, both of them were in complete agreement.

And that was exactly how things went for the next several weeks. She felt well, wonderfully well, in fact. She had none of the side effects of pregnancy she heard other women complain of. The only sign seemed to be a greater tiredness. While she was literally never fatigued before, now she craved rest during the midday heat. This established a new semiroutine; she used the cooler early hours for exercise, then slowly walked her way home. Even though Patinos wanted to send a litter to transport her back and forth, she refused to use it, arguing that she enjoyed the slow leisurely walks to and from the arena, along a mostly shaded walkway, the walkway winding along the undulating crest of the hill above the city of Knossos to the suburb of the wealthy.

She thought of her sisters and brothers, and her breath caught as fear invaded her body. Were they well? Were they alive? Were they healthy or suffering from some illness or from deprivation? She had been forbidden to have contact with them or even to see them. Maybe, she thought, maybe as Patinos mellowed, maybe she could approach him? Just to see them from afar. Just to know—oh, dear Goddess, what am I thinking? But if it were possible, help me, and forgive them their childish shallowness and greed, and me my misguided permissiveness toward them!

Naïs's pregnancy proceeded entirely uneventfully. The child was born after, for a first-time mother, a relatively short confinement. Already days before, Patinos had been incapable to concentrate on work. He would lock himself into his workrooms, not talking to anyone, not accepting any food. Then again he would order a rhyton of Cyprus wine, get his coat, grab his walking staff, and drag himself down to the beach to squat on his favorite stone and, with blank eyes, stare out over the water.

As soon as she noticed, Naïs carefully wound her way down from the steeply terraced house to the beach. Patiently she waited for her husband to move, shift his position or sigh deeply, signaling to her that he was slowly awakening to the here from wherever his spirit had taken him before. Then she bent to gently touch his arm, his misshapen shoulder, or his soft shining black hair whipping around in the wind like a silken banner. He would sigh again and then turn to her, never once surprised by her presence. He just nodded to her and slowly rose, struggling laboriously but not allowing her to assist him.

Bobbing his head solemnly, almost shamefacedly, he explained to her that he had been praying for the health of the child and the child's mother. Often Naïs was so touched that she felt she needed to bend to kiss his hand or his hair. Over the course of her marriage, she had learned that Patinos, as much as he fought against her touches, her tenderness, as much as he pretended to shoo her away, ultimately was softened by her gestures of affection.

In their bedchamber, in the silence of the night, he stammered out his thanks, trying hesitantly to explain how tongue-tied he always felt whenever it became needful to express his feelings, his emotions. A lifetime of bitterly lived past had taught him to shield himself from people, from their viciousness, ridicule, and scorn. Those, he said, were the only responses he had ever expected. His work, his arm, and hand were the only exceptions. A nation inherently revering beauty in any form of expression admired the products of his hand but, by the very same reason, scorned the person who had produced such beauty. All this he understood, but understanding did not lessen the hurt of decades.

At the same time, Naïs wondered about how the course of her life had changed with the changes in her husband. Was it possible that just a little crumb of attention to, interest in Patinos, the person, the human being, her husband, not the ruler of her married life, could so change him, could change him in the very center of his being? At his core, was he capable of warmth, of love, and of happiness and joy? She began to understand that even if expressed occasionally, these hesitant bursts of affection, coming from a man who had led such a repressed, reclusive, secretive life, were a testament to the resilience of the human soul.

That night, for the first time, husband and wife lay side by side on their bed, their bodies touching, her head on his shoulder and his arm rested protectively on her belly, sensing the movement of the child who was the product of his fatherhood. For perhaps the first time in his life, Patinos fell asleep with a small smile on his lips.

And so after a remarkably easy birth, the babe, a little girl, made her appearance into this complex difficult family. She announced her presence with a lusty screaming which reverberated throughout the silent house, normally until then quietly going about its accustomed business. Perhaps the cry was intended to announce loudly that life would now start moving with a different rhythm.

Her parents named her Helia, "light," and she truly was a gracious gift of light and sunshine given to them by the Goddess Ida, Mistress of Fertility, and of the god Poseidon, ruler of the waves.

The child's presence changed the parents and the whole household as well. In a land where young mothers languished abed sometimes for weeks, Naïs recovered from the birth unexpectedly quickly. She was back at the Arena of the Bulls in a matter of weeks, this time with no interdiction, only a muttering of displeasure by her husband. A wet nurse was hired, and she spent her days not only feeding Helia but watching over her with great care. Naïs as well spent most of her time with the child; she had explained to Patinos that she only wanted to go back to the Sacred School to regain the limberness of her body after months of pregnancy-enforced inactivity. More strenuous activity in preparation for working performing with the bulls would come much, much later. Patinos continued to grumble and was only appeased with great reluctance.

*****

It was during one of these work sessions at the arena that Naïs unexpectedly ran into Ido. They literally ran into each other; Naïs was slowly walking down one of the walkways from the practice grounds to the mountain-stream-fed little pool where the performers cooled themselves off and washed the sweat and sand off their bodies. It was her habit to wipe her face with the little square of linen she always inserted into her belt for that very purpose. Striding along with her long gait, she collided with Ido, the collision almost a repeat of her running into Athenis, ah, so long ago!

She dropped the kerchief and stared, stared at him like staring at a stranger or a dead body. She took a tiny step back before whispering his name, her eyes never leaving his face. He looked taller, more muscular, older, or perhaps just more mature?

His eyes, with a serious glance, raked her body. Where, Naïs thought, where was the gay smile, laughter which used to greet her? Then Ido shook his head, his old youthful smile on his mouth, in his eyes, crinkling the corners of his eyes. He removed his two hands from her forearms where he had grabbed her when she ran into him. He shook his head in amazement.

"Ah, my dearest! This is a miracle! What, pray tell, are you doing here? I heard that you were forced—well, required—to retire from the arena and devote your life to your husband and household? Like most gossips, this is also not true, neh? Talk to me! It's been so long. Athenis told me that she had seen you, and you looked, well, suffice it to say that she was worried about you! But then you just disappeared from the earth! Come! Sit with me for a little while at least so that we become reacquainted again. Come!" And he gently pushed her to the nearest bench, only a few steps away.

Once they were seated, Ido let out a big sigh. Shaking his head, he looked her over carefully. His eyes seemed not to miss anything during his inspection. Slowly the smile left his face, and his eyes became serious.

"Oh, my dearest! You have no idea—no idea! I have missed you so desperately! I have worried about you, my dear...my dear friend... and I have heard such horrible—such worrisome stories. But despite all the gossip stories, you do look well, you are thriving. So maybe the gossip stories are just that—gossip. But tell me, how is your life? Are you happy, little one?" And he shook his head. "Nay, no longer a little one, are you? All grown-up and an adult. So how is adult life treating you, darling? Tell me!"

Naïs just gently wagged her head at him. "All in its good time, my dear, just be patient a little while.

"First of all, you—just as everybody else on the island must have heard about Odaro's demise and the mountain of debt he left me with. It is of no consequence at this time to contemplate if he did it deliberately—I do doubt that—or out of sheer negligence or simply out of that very human conviction that we are invincible, that harm will reach others but never us. I engaged Ninno to help me, he had been Odaro's right-hand man. And Ninno did come through and found me a wealthy, indeed, a very wealthy man who was willing to pay all my debts outright for the price of marriage. The fact that the man was severely deformed and very, very unpleasant, albeit famous and rich for his beautiful goldwork, was mentioned as an aside. We met at the wedding ceremony upon which he insisted. I suppose without the law of marriage binding me, he was worried that upon seeing him, I would run away shrieking. And I tell you true, I almost did so.

"Secondly we all must admit that truly the twists of life are wondrous. My husband was all that was ugly, mean-spirited, jealous, suspicious, demanding, and malicious. His ugliness is mitigated by a beautiful face and beautiful arms and hands. And those hands are capable to form things of such great beauty...beauty beyond anything I am able to describe. After a time of living together—and sleeping together—I became accustomed to his deformity, and I suppose he became accustomed to have a woman around the house. He allowed me entrance to his workrooms, and I marveled, oh, gods, how I marveled! I believe it must have been the first time someone admired his works with no ulterior motive. Eventually I asked him to show me how the ideas for design are born in his head and then translated to molted gold. We—we became accustomed to each other and grew to appreciate each other.

"He told me about his horrible childhood, rejected by his family, his mother even, ridiculed by everyone—he...he only told me snippets, but even that was truly devastating, inhuman.

"And now thirdly, I became pregnant and, two months ago, gave birth to a little girl who is her father's little treasure and joy. He named her Helia—'sunshine,' and truly that's what she is for him. She is perfectly formed, a beautiful, beautiful babe.

"But now tell me, I do know that Athenis was expecting when we last met. Do you have more than one? Please tell me all!"

Ido shifted and, leaning forward, clasped her hands and kissed both of them.

"Oh, my dear little girl! You did have your ups and downs, didn't you, neh? But so do all of us. Life ruffles our feathers, to say the least. At my home, there is little to tell. We are content, I suppose, well suited to each other. There is no great passion, no conflagration. It is not—well, it is not like it could have been." And he stopped with some hesitation. "It is not like the grand passion or the coming together of two people who have known each other so well that they seemed made for each other..." He stopped himself, stuttering, casting a quick glance at Naïs, and then looking down at his sandal-clad feet.

"Athenis is a sweet warmhearted motherly person. She is one of those who just wraps her arms about you and gives you her love. Even with you, even knowing which she must have known without ever being told...she accepted that my feelings for her could be no more than a pale shadow of..." And he sighed again. "Anyway that is all behind us, neh?

"But we are very compatible and have a happy little family, one little boy, Novoro, and then another one who we called Miro, and then, just last year, two little girls, Naïs and Taïs, and I tell you that Athenis wanted to name her...to name her for you! The two are so alike that only Athenis can tell them apart! I tell you truly, I certainly can't! Our household is topsy-turvy with those four!"

Much to Naïs's pleasure, when Ido raised his eyes to her, he was again smiling with delight, the shadows gone from his eyes and the tightness from his lips. She rose, smoothing down the towel she had used to wipe down her face. She put her hands on Ido's two shoulders but then appeared to reconsider and hugged him to herself. She kissed him and then stroked his—as always—carefully shaved face, and he kissed her back. Kisses were insignificant signs of greeting and friendship, and no one would have construed any greater meaning to them.

"I must run, my dearest, I have a family to look after now, just as do you. I send my loving kisses to Athenis and to your darling little ones. See now you have your own true 'little ones' as well. May the goddess keep you and those you love close to her bosom!"

As was her custom, after her dip in the pool to clean and refresh herself, she started to lightly jog homeward along the shaded path that led there from the royal palace compound, which also housed the arena. She was halfway to home when the ground under her feet began to move gently. It was a soft rocking motion at first, which increased in strength, shuddered to make the bushes shake and the tops of the trees sway to and fro. Having experienced the same several times before, Naïs threw herself to the ground, flattening her body and hanging on to the trunk of the tree closest to her in order not to be rolled down from the path to the hillside. In no longer than a minute, the ground steadied, then the shrubs, and then the crowns of the tree ceased swaying.

She—all of the island—had experience with this shaking of the ground under their feet. It was something caused by Poseidon, the Great God of the Waves, whenever, for some reason, he was displeased or angry. She knew that in the coming days, many sacrificial fires would be lit on the great god's altars and songs, dances, and prayers performed along with gifts offered from the sea and earth. She had seen such scenes engraved upon rhytons and labryses in her husband's workrooms, of famers offering sheaves of wheat, large clusters of grapes and branches laden with olives, along with newborn lambs, feet tied together, received by priestesses clad only in skirts of animal furs.

Once she felt she could stand without difficulty, she started jogging again, this time a little faster, anxious to get to her child, her home. In a few minutes, she turned the corner to their gate. Softly panting, she hung on to the gatepost for a moment, then took a big gulp of air and, plastering a relaxed smile on her face, sauntered to the courtyard.

It was recommended and customary for island residents to leave their homes, any buildings, or structures there were when the earth movements started at any time. Thus she was not surprised to see Helia's cradle outdoors under a large spreading mulberry tree. Her husband was squatting on a low stool next to the cradle, offering his little finger to the cooing child. When he heard her footsteps, he looked up, his forehead creased, his black eyes boring into her. He stood up with effort and slowly shuffled toward her.

"Wife. I am glad you have safely arrived home. Have you been hurt anywhere at all? You should not have been away at a time like this. See that the next quaking finds you here at home." But then he realized the ridiculousness of his comment and shrugged his good shoulder.

"Actually," he said with a smirk, "that was a statement sillier than most." Naïs was so pleased with his good humor and the willingness to actually exhibit it in public that she walked over to him, bent down, and kissed his cheek and then his soft black hair.

"I will most earnestly strive to do just that," she whispered to him with a small smile. "But actually I believe I was safer on the hillside than closer to the sea or especially inside a house. Has it not been shown that houses are dangerous, especially the larger stone-built structures since stones can be dislodged here and thereby lead to collapse of the roof and so the whole house? And also, the roiling sea can overtake the shore and destroy structures close by. Of course," she added, "mercifully our home is situated far enough and high enough from the sea!"

"Well, then I have expressed myself incorrectly. What I meant to say is that I wish you to be here, in my eyesight, whenever there is a calamity. I want...I do not want you to be away from me..." He stopped, searching for words and shaking his head. "I want you near me. I want to know that you are safe and in my presence and the child's. It is bad for a child to be anxious, and its mother's absence would certainly make Helia anxious."

Naïs bent down to pick up another one of those little stools scattered about everywhere outside for Patinos's convenience ever since he ceased to shut himself away in his workrooms. She sat down next to him and looked at him with all the seriousness which his somewhat-ridiculous request deserved.

"Husband. I promise to be here by your side and with our child during all of my sleeping hours and most of the waking ones. Please do not ask me to abandon my career at the Sacred School, though. In my own specialty, I am almost as well regarded and known as are you. The great, the everlasting difference, of course, is that what I produce is fleeting, and the moment of my achievement cannot be immersed in amber and kept for the future, but yours can, in a manner of speaking, much to the joy of future generations. Nevertheless, that what I produce in a special way gives me as much happiness as that which you produce does to you. I beg you, do not deprive me of this—this great pleasure!"

Patinos stared at her, his black eyes bottomless and showing no emotion. His look seemed endless to her, until finally, she dropped her eyes to her soft leather slippers. Finally she heard his sigh as he arose. For a moment, he just stood there, looking at her with thoughtful attention, then turned and started to shuffle back to his workroom. He turned his head back toward her and threw his words over his shoulder.

"As much as I would wish to, I no longer can shout and scream at you anymore, wife. You have grown on me, wife. I am too tired to fight you, or maybe just too confused in my head. I no longer know if I would ever want to...Do as you wish, wife, and consider I also rather see you happy than unhappy."

No more than a minute later, she heard her husband's loud explosive curse through the open window of his workroom. She was on the run to him before she even noticed that three of the house women, who had been sweeping up the debris of leaves, branches, and pottery shards from the terrace, were also running toward the work room. Her full skirt billowing, she stopped at the entrance, catching herself at the doorframe. Her eyes roamed the large gloomy normally cluttered room. With a sudden indrawn gasp, her hands flew to her mouth to stifle her cry. She looked, saw, and knew not if she should cry or laugh.

It seemed that each available piece which had not that long ago sat in some alcove, some recess, or on some tabletop was now lying scattered on the floor. Much of what was there was shattered or at least cracked, but mercifully, the tile floor had been strewn with a thick layer of dried grasses. The grasses had always been there, she was told, because Master Patinos had a tendency to stumble, especially when occupied with the design or execution of his art pieces.

Master Patinos also fell much more easily than others. The dry grasses undoubtedly constituted a fire hazard, but the master of the house had ruled that his health and safety was more important than the safety of the workroom. Besides there were huge pottery casks along the walls, filled with water and ladles hooked onto their openings, to prevent an actual fire.

Embedded or cradled in the web of dried grass were all the countless intact items housed in the workroom, or those which were broken, as well as those just minimally damaged and thus, obviously, not beyond expert repair by Master Patinos' magical hands.

Naïs struggled to hide her laughter, but evidently her eyes mirrored her mirth. Patinos, enraged by the inconvenience, to say the least, and the potential financial loss—obviously he had yet to double-check all that was littering the floor—took one look at his wife. Somehow the ridiculousness of the whole situation that he saw clearly on Naïs's face began to seep into his enraged brain as well. The vehemence of his anger and curses slowly tapered off and then stopped altogether. His eyes locked with his wife's, and a smile, ever-so slow and hesitant, tugged at the corners of his handsome mouth. Naïs watched in amazement, realizing for the first time how truly beautifully shaped his mouth, his whole face, was when it bore not a scowl but was lit up by a smile.

Without thinking what she was doing, she followed her natural inclination to be forthright and openly demonstrative, bent, and hugged her husband. Her laughter, no longer suppressed, bubbled up as she kissed Patinos's smiling lips. Shocked by the unexpectedness of her behavior, Patinos took a step back and peered at his wife with surprise mixed with pleasure. Then an unexpected sound—unexpected especially in the wake of a frightening calamity—and not heard before floated in the air. The master of the house was laughing. The women working to right the household, fallen and shattered objects in their hands, stopped in midwork. The mistress of the house looked at her husband with an expression of utter confusion, but then clasped his hands into hers, sagged down onto a stool to be closer at eye level with him, then threw her head back and laughed. Laughed full-throated, happy, without self-consciousness.

It was a moment which became another turning point in their lives.

That evening, when they retired to their bedroom, they made love with pleasure equally shared between the two of them. In the silence of the night, Patinos began to talk to Naïs, hesitantly reaching for her hand and guiding it down to the folds, the angles of his contorted body. Hesitantly, with a stammer, he began to speak to her, so softly at first, that she could barely understand him. It was a raw confession, a raw description of how his life had been. Only after he drew a ragged breath did Naïs become aware that he was crying, his tears flowing soundlessly down his cheeks onto the pillows. She heard fleeting images, descriptions of his childhood's cruel rejection, his growing up learning to shore up all his defenses against ridicule, the slow difficult learning of his trade during a brutal apprenticeship. He confessed how he had found great pleasure in the shaping of objects out of the clay he had found in small pockets of the seashore, how he became inspired by the idea to do this kind of work for a living, how he—after a great deal of searching—finally found a master goldsmith who was willing to teach him. The man's brutality aside, Patinos still felt a sense of gratitude to the master, now long dead, because without him, he would never have been able to continue his own self-improvement, which, in turn, led him to where he was now.

He released her hands to search for a kerchief to wipe his tear before turning to her.

"And then," he whispered, "then your man—your representative—came to speak to me one day. He had a request, nay, a proposition to make to me on your behalf. I had, of course, heard of you. Everyone in Knossos and beyond had, by then, heard of you. But I had never seen you until we met each other in front of the priestesses, and you as well had never seen me before. I am certain that had you seen me before our marriage, you would have turned away in horror."

"I cannot tell you what prompted me to accept your man's proposal? It was something inside me pushing me to say yes. It was as though I had reached a border, a bridge which needed to be crossed for me to continue on, unless I truly were to go mad…mad from the silence of this house, mad from the echo of my shuffle through the empty rooms, mad from loneliness. I cannot tell you why I believed that this person—this woman I did not know—could, would help me? Aye, truly, wife, I tell you, it was as though the gods would have reached down. Reached into my soul." He stopped for a moment, and Naïs hear a little snicker.

"A soul I did not even believe I possessed. Yes, yes, it was a most remarkable moment of my life, indeed."

He turned to her then and gathered her into his two hale healthy arms.

"Naïs, wife, words cannot express how I feared your response! Your response to my hideous ugliness. Your turning away from me with a shudder and running away from me, from this house forever…your running away from my bedroom, from my bed. The only thought that calmed me was that I had bought you, bought you like all the other women who came to this house to service me. Indeed, bought you at a higher price than any of the others but also expected more from you in my bed.

"How then have things changed so much? How has life itself then fallen into a totally different path? How then has it become so… so wonderfully sunny and full of light? Only because you, my wife, have entered my life? To share the road with me which the gods have marked for me to tread? And why have you done so? Why have you been willing to look at me…to look at me and see a human being, nay, a valuable gifted human being instead of a monstrous gnome of a man, an abomination? I will never forget how you touched me the first time, maybe with hesitation but without shudder and cringing. I think that that first night together, the first heavy band which had constricted my soul fell off, my dearest wife.

"And look now, wife, you have taught me to laugh. What a wonderful feeling, indeed! How then, tell me, wife, how can I thank you for your gifts? I do not know what love is, wife, not love between man and woman, not any kind of love, really! But I am learning to love the child you gifted me with. I want to learn to love you, Naïs, and I believe that I already am learning, and ask you to teach me more! And then more! I believe I am the greedy man who has never tasted honey but now wants to taste it all the time! And when you have taught me all you can, wife, I believe I shall be the happiest person on the face of this earth!"

*****

For the first time in her life, Naïs experienced contentment and peace. Her days flowed quietly, one into the next. Helia prospered and grew into a curious energetic toddler. She had to assign one of the household's maid servants to oversee the little girl, for curiosity constantly drove her into her father's workrooms. She became so fascinated with all the shiny things she found there that she learned to be amazingly fleet and adept to propel her chubby little body through the magic forbidden door before anybody caught her.

The following year, Naïs gave birth to a little boy who, by agreement of both parents, was named Athinos. His father literally floated on air, but as much as he was thrilled to have a male child, and as much as he was disinclined to show any favoritism, little Helia, his firstborn, was the one embedded deepest in his heart.

The road Patinos had traveled toward change was literally immeasurable. Much of the time, he was good-natured, well balanced, and calm. He could not overcome his basic withdrawn, silent, suspicious behavior, basic to his personality, nor the occasional outbursts of anger; but the periods of deep dark depression, malice, and outright fury were things of the past.

He loved his children—and his work—but the delight of his life was his wife. She was his pride, his focus, his support, and his love. Ah, yes, she did teach him warmth, devotion, and love true to his request. He did understand not to expect return of his love with passion, fervency equal to his. Yet he did not feel wanting; what she gave him, had given him, and continued to give day by day was such an unexpected and boundless gift that he could never have asked her for more. What he had now far exceeded any of his expectations. It was simply above any desires or hopes he would have had in the past.

With his approval, Naïs attempted to track down her brothers and sisters. She was pursued by the sinking feeling of too little, too late but, at the same time, told herself that she was, for the last years, not in a position nor even allowed to do anything on their behalf. Now she summoned Ninno and charged him to do all that he could.

As it turned out, all that Ninno could uncover was insufficient. Like petals of flowers, once shed, were swept away by even a small breeze, nothing could be traced at this time of Emeris and Kyana. Both Naïs and Patinos had a good idea what their fate had become. Ninno had, however, been able to trace Tomo and Milo. According to his best information, the two had signed on with one of the larger merchant groups, whose vessels routinely brought assorted goods from the south and the east to Cyprus and departed with luxury items produced in their major cities, to be sold abroad. Patinos accused himself of being the guilty one, the one who was too self-involved, too hating, when he once forbade Naïs any contact with her family.

The birth of little Athinos was not one to breeze through for his mother. The child presented a breech birth, and Naïs, the priestess of the Serpent Goddess, and her acolytes struggled for almost three days until the babe—himself weakened from the long process—made his weakly protesting appearance. The priestess pronounced both mother and child well, though weakened and needing much rest. She also added that Naïs only survived the ordeal because of her supremely strong and conditioned body. Once she had recovered, Naïs held this pronouncement over Patinos's head to force him to agree with her. She had announced that she fully intended to return to the Sacred Arena. She needed the physical exercise to keep fit but moreover to feel well balanced and happy. Although she loved her children, she was only too happy to pass the daily chore of caring for them to a wet nurse and one of the household women. Much against his better judgment, Patinos agreed reluctantly, both of them knowing full well that he could not deny anything to his wife.

Thus Naïs returned to the bull dancers amid the ecstatic applause, screams, and waving of banners, the flower petals showering her thrown by her innumerable admirers. To her, at least, it seemed like the ovation would never end. For the longest time, she stood there in the center of the arena, the bull handlers waiting for the signal to open the gate to the bull selected for today's performance.

Finally Naïs moved. She turned slowly round the whole arena, waving her arms, while she raised her eyes to the great glowing palace, seemingly sheltering the arena on the one side. Then she looked in the opposite direction, toward the cone of Mount Ida, blue green in the haze of the afternoon sunlight, the mountain framed precisely by the two horns of the Sacred Bull, carved out of limestone and placed to the left and right of the arena. Overcome by the reception she received after a long absence during her pregnancy, she buried her face in both hands. Only the shaking of her shoulders indicated her emotional upheaval.

The crowd, silent for a moment, erupted into a truly deafening cheering. The sound flowed toward her, surrounded and embraced her, seemingly unending. Finally in a gesture of homage to the Sacred Bulls and the sacred mountain shimmering in the background, she bent to touch the ground, then walked to touch each of the carved horns marking the perimeter of the arena, and finally placed her palms together to bow to sacred Mount Ida. The crowds fell silent, and Naïs signaled to the guards to summon her two assistants and then to open the gate to the chosen bull.

To the extent that she thrived on the crowds, the life on the edge, which epitomized her existence as a bull dancer, Patinos hated it with equal vehemence. Every evening, before arriving home, he paced the courtyard, the terrace, the whole house until he heard the latch of the gate lifted and recognized her footsteps. No one, he thought with a smile—a very small smile, and even that one he was eager to hide from her—no one walked like his wife, so easily with such lightness, as though her soles hardly touched the ground, while he slogged, shuffled, dragged himself, grunting toward her as quickly as he possibly could. When he beheld her, his heart melted, his eyes glistened, and he could hardly find the words to greet her. He held the greeting, short and stern, not having the heart to contradict her but still wanting to convey his displeasure in playing with life-or-death danger with such facility.

But only he knew how much her avowed profession sapped her. Only in the darkness of the night did he see her toss and turn after performance days, too full of the euphoria which lifted her up during her performance did he see her bandage her arms, her wrists, her ankles, swollen from the strain of her performance. Only then did he watch her sink with a groan into the big wooden tub he had made for her so that she could soak her weary wounded body. Immeasurably these things upset him, but he bit his lips, bided his time, and, for the first time in his life, learned patience and diplomacy.

And then it happened, one morning, when, maybe the third or fourth day in a row, Patinos woke before it was even morning to hear Naïs, head buried deep in the slop bucket, shuddering and retching. He knew the signs well enough; this was now her third pregnancy. He knew that she had suffered greatly from morning sickness during her last pregnancy, at least for several weeks, almost into the middle of her pregnancy.

When she finally was able to lift her head, she slowly dragged herself back to bed and lay there, with her breast heaving, staring at the painted wood ceiling. Patinos turned to ring the cord hanging by his side of the bed and pulled, in the silence of the early morning, hearing the tinkle of a bell in the far reaches of the house. When the servant arrived, he ordered her to bring an empty slop bucket and empty out the one that lady Naïs had just used. Also to bring fresh water for drinking and some wine to mix into the water. Also a stack of clean cloths and a large bowl of hot water, where lady Naïs could freshen herself.

When the servant disappeared, Naïs turned to her husband, the track of tears still visible on her stricken face.

"So you saw?" she whispered, her voice still a little hoarse from her earlier effort. "Then you know, neh?"

Patinos caught both of his wife's hands, turned them over and kissed her palms, then laid them to his cheeks. Wordlessly he nodded, eyes shining, all malice gone for now.

"And you are not displeased, husband?"

Patinos's eyebrows drew together. The look he gave her was puzzled.

"Wife, how is it that you can even ask me such silliness? Have I not happily welcomed the first two children we produced together? Children are the blessings of the Great Goddess of Fertility, the Great

Goddess of Serpents. Are you not as well pleased as I am, my dear?" He sighed, then gave her a sideways look.

"But I must tell you, wife, and I charge you to listen well, I will no longer allow you to go to the Arena of the Bulls. Your bull-leaping days are over, wife. I have watched you struggle to get home, to get over the pain, the hurt, the injuries. I have watched and bided my time, guarded my tongue. The gods only know how difficult that is for me—and you know it as well, Naïs. I will not forbid you freedom of coming and going, but if I so much as hear a whisper that you are near the Sacred Arena, I will put a guard on you, and you will be staying in this house and only go out with my explicit permission. I hope that I have made myself entirely clear, nay?"

Naïs continued to look at her husband, the hand holding the towel she had used to wipe her face dropping to her lap. Her expression was forlorn. Slowly then, she nodded to him.

"Aye, husband mine, you are right. I no longer can pretend to myself that I am the same age as I was when I first danced with the bulls. Years have passed since then. I bore two children and am carrying a third one and will bear this one as well, if the gods be willing to grant us the boon! I have struggled—as you saw only too well—struggled and maybe pretended to myself. But with each turn of the moon, with each week even, it becomes more difficult to ignore the pain, the exhaustion.

"I will not argue with you, husband. Not this time," she added with a little smile, "for aye, you are indeed right. I will abide by your wishes, husband, and give up my career. You know, Patinos." She turned to him, shaking her head. "The hardest part to give up is the applause, the clapping, the screaming, the flowers thrown at my feet..."

There was a silence. The maidservant came with the items Patinos had ordered. When she left, Naïs slowly rose and walked over to the tray with two glasses and a jug filled with water. She poured herself and drank it down in big thirsty eager gulps. Then she dipped one of the cloths into the hot water and buried her face in the welcoming steaming folds. She continued to hold the cloth to her face for a long time, then, with a sigh, dropped her hands and dropped the wet cloth to the tile floor. She gave a brief mirthless laugh.

"You know, Patinos, it is said by those much wiser than I, and perhaps even wiser than you, my husband, there is a season, a special time for everything. For growing and learning, for being young and filled with boundless energy, for loving and being in love, for the begetting of children and growing a family."

Another mirthless laugh followed. She shook her head, walked around the bed to her husband's side, bent down, and kissed his forehead.

"I am truly sorry that I disturbed your sleep, my dear. As you know, this is only the beginning. If I am lucky, it will not last as long as it did with Athinos, but it may. As in the past, I suggest that you let me move to some other room where I can retch to my heart's content without robbing you of sleep. Do not forget, from now on in, you shall be the only one earning coins in this household!"

Patinos did not even deign to answer her, he knew that she knew. He would not leave their bed, nor would he let her do so. This had been an argument now resurrected from the past, and each time in the past, Naïs had lost the argument.

*****

Thus the era of the great Naïs's triumphs at the Sacred Arena passed. New faces, new names, new talents rose, but for generations to come, no one was called the equal of the great, the incomparable Naïs. After many years only did her fame wane. After she retired, she was rarely seen about town, except occasionally at the king's court. The king had been in the habit of frequently inviting Patinos, whom he valued, indeed treasured so much, that he had willed himself to overlook the man's quirky manners and atrocious appearance. That his manners had noticeably changed since he married was marked with delight by the court officials. Invitations not only to the official unveiling of one of the master's new works but also to more intimate court events had increased as a consequence. The couple—so dissimilar, one so lovely with such perfectly honed and toned body, the other truly the expression of atrocious deformity, painful even to look at—became popular. The king and queen appreciated the Lady Naïs's pleasing manner and entertaining little stories, while Patinos—who would have ever predicted—exhibited a streak of wicked and somewhat salacious sense of humor.

As the years rolled by, the Patinos household filled with noise, the running of small feet, the laughter of children—surely the least expected development for that particular house. There were now five little ones, and may the gods be merciful! Patinos became a devoted and affectionate father—almost! He allowed the little ones to clamber all over him, as long as they were careful not to hurt him. To compensate for the deficiencies of other parts of his body, his arms and hands were enormously powerful. He would lift the squealing little ones and swing them around and around; he knew that it was the biggest thrill he could give his children.

He also began to allow Helia and Athinos occasional access into his workroom, slowly, carefully, and methodically explaining and teaching. Naïs was amazed when she first heard her husband. He had an amazing sense of how to put his son at ease and how to bring complex concepts to him, like the handling of gold, the realization of designs onto a roll of papyrus, onto a piece of bark, or even scratched into sand. Athinos, only eight birth years old, had obviously inherited his father's sense of style, his feeling for beauty and harmony. With a hesitant smile on his face, his father would mention that most fortunately, that was all the child inherited; his appearance was entirely that of his beautiful mother.

Naïs settled down into motherhood and domesticity, as much as it was possible for her to do. She was a lovely woman, more beautiful now with maturity than she was in her eager years of wishing to mold the world to her needs and wants. She radiated strength, health, contentment, and well-being. Ah, yes, she was content. Not a doting mother, she enjoyed supervising their growth under the eyes of two nannies and a tutor. Master Oneyo, a highly regarded tutor avidly pursued and eagerly engaged by several high-class families in Knossos, had just recently been employed out of the needs of the two older children who—so Patinos decreed—needed a firmer hand and the beginning of a structured teaching, in addition of what he could show them of his artistry.

Naïs did not interfere, how could she? She had hardly any education at all, most certainly not anything remotely approaching a structured teaching program. Patinos, born into and later abandoned by a wealthy well-respected family, did initially. This then remained her husband's responsibility. Every once in a while, she sat in on a lecture given by Master Oneyo, a happy smile on her face. Always direct and without pretense, she had no qualm at all showing her ignorance.

In many ways, she thrived. If not happy, she was content. She did not love her husband passionately but had a great deal of admiration, respect, and affection for him. She had learned to avoid or to ignore his occasional rages, black moods, and the very rare suspicions. Naïs knew that her husband loved her, with an increasing desperate possessiveness, as the years went by.

One day, after they had made love, and the house was as still as though no one lived there, he turned to her with a sigh. "Every time such total silence wraps itself around me, I become fearful, nay, totally frightened"—and when he saw that Naïs cocked a brow at him, continued—"I feel like death is surrounding me, like everyone I learned to love, to depend on or to cherish, has disappeared from my life. I feel as alone as I did before—before you, wife. Nay, worse, because now I have learned that there can be life, sounds, laughter, joy around me. Not just the silence of death…" And he shook his head so vehemently that his silky blacker-than-black hair, now gently laced with silver, slid from one side of his face to the other.

It was no more than a handful of days after that night. The house awoke to deep rumbling, accompanied by a slight and slow movement, as though a giant beast, who slept underground, would be breathing slowly, in and out, up and down, then, with excruciating slowness, stretching his limbs. They both woke up at the same moment. Naïs was out of the bed a split second later, leaving her husband to slowly struggle to rise and find his wrapper to put around his body.

She flew down the few shallow steps which led from the private apartments to the enclosed courtyard and turned toward the children's bedroom, the soles of her feet slapping against the stone pavement. As she turned the corner to the door she wanted to reach, a deep shudder ran along the ground and threw her to the doorframe. She held on as another more violent, deeper rumble growled under her feet, and the door flew open hitting her head-on in the face. She jumped backward and ran the back of her hand across her nose, sensing the warm wetness of blood running down her face.

By then the children were awake, she could hear them screaming and the two nannies who slept with them as well. Naïs let her eyes run along the room, saw that all four of the older children were on the floor, shrieking and looking at her with wild eyes. The baby, probably awakened by the noise, added his loud cry to the noise. She took a deep breath, then pointed to the two terrified women.

"Annina, you take the two girls! Tannis, you take the boys. Take them out from the building into the yard by the brook. I'll take the baby. We'll all meet there. Go!" Fortunately there was a little pause in the tremors. She was exceedingly grateful for that as she glanced up to the roof and saw two long cracks running along in each direction from the roof gable. By this time, she could hear her husband's slow shuffle, as he was dragging himself along, out of breath by his exertion. She glanced around her and saw the two men who were employed to carry Patinos around in a low palanquin running toward him, settling the empty litter in front of Patinos and lifting him into it.

She leaned into the crib and lifted out little Ilyo, crying just as loudly as he could and angrily waving his chubby little fists in the air. She pressed his warm little body to her breast, swiped one of the blankets which the infant had been wrapped into, off the crib, and ran as fast as she could, hearing the ominous cracking of the rafters. Without wishing to look back, she ran as fast as she was able. At the designated little brook, there were some stone benches; she saw the two nannies attending to calm the young ones. Barely pausing and without thinking, she almost threw the baby into Tannis's hands, then turned to sprint and assist her husband.

Eventually the whole family, indeed the whole household, assembled under the spreading trees by the little brook. The brook was actually to the side, almost in back of the house. A large door from the kitchen led out to it; the practice of the kitchen staff was to lower anything needed to be kept cold into the frigid waters. The waters flowed underground from high above, from the peak of Mount Ida, only to burst above ground right by the location where Patinos had determined his house to be built. Perhaps, Naïs thought in one of those strange moments of digression from the reality of life, perhaps it was premonition or the guidance of the gods then, as it was now, when the brook served to center them all?

For a while, there was silence, the calm before the storm, Naïs thought. This was not the first time the ground had shaken and groaned under them, and invariably, there were periods of calm interspersed with frightening quakes and quivers. For many generations, their island country was accustomed to such frightening events when the Great God Poseidon would shake the seas and the earth in anger. But then these events always passed rather quickly and left the population and their dwelling, more or less, unscathed.

Then with frightening suddenness, an enormous clap filled the air, as a barely breathable stench filled their nostrils. The stench invaded their lungs and forced them to cough and gasp for air, the little ones more so than the adults. With heartbreaking fear reflected in their wide open staring eyes, they gasped and coughed. But then so did the rest of them as well.

Naïs turned her head toward Mount Thera, sensing more than knowing that it was the source of the vile air. Visible most any day, rising out of the shimmering waters of the Great Sea toward the rising sun, what she saw now was so atrociously incredible, so unbelievable, so altogether frightful, that her brain simply refused to process it. As though pulled up by and invisible giant hand, the whole top of Thera Island's Mountain of the Great Earth Mother rose, illuminated from beneath it by a fiery red glow. The top of the great mountain shattered with a sound unlike any that had been heard by any human before, spewing great arcs of glowing, blazing shards in every direction. The shards were slowly sinking down into the water, onto the land.

The water responded by vicious sizzles, the land by instant ignition. Steam from the sea and heat and smoke from the dry sedge and grass filled the air, while the sulfur stench emanating from the wounded mountain increased. Glowing particles of stone, fragments of rock rained down, pelting every living body, and then, even more horribly, molten parts of the mountain began to fall. Wherever they landed, on the ground or on a living body, they clung and remained glued to the surface. The substance could not be removed, scraped, or pulled off, causing excruciating pain. The searing heat was so horrible that people and animals alike shrieked with the pain and rolled on the ground in agony. The odor of burning flesh was added into the air. Birds, dead or dying, fell out of the sky. The air was filled with the laments, screams, shrieks of the humans and the shrieking, bellowing, bawling, lowing howls of the animals.

Patinos, having clambered out of his palanquin, dragged himself to Naïs's side, who was trying to shelter her children with her arms, with her hands from the hot missiles raining down on them. Panting, gasping for air, like all of them, and using his cane to point with, Patinos indicated a narrow gravel and stone path leading up from their house to the heights of Mount Ida.

"We are safer higher up the mountainside." He gasped. "I recall some old person telling me that long ago, there was a great eruption like this, and that the sea rose up and flooded the lower parts of the land. We would be drowned or swept away! Go!" And when he saw Naïs's hesitation, he shoved her ahead of him. "You must go and take the children, wife. I will follow as best I can!"

Naïs looked around her, and her eyes widened. "Husband, where are the litter-bearers?" And then she whispered, hands against her mouth to prevent a scream. "They left us! Oh, gods! They left us!" Before hysteria would possess her, she shook her head vehemently. "No, no, no! The two women each will then have two of the children. I'll take the baby and help you…I'll help you, yes!" And she stomped her foot.

Patinos grabbed his wife's shoulders and shook her. His eyes glowed with anger like blackest onyxes. "You will do what I order, you will obey me." Then he continued, much softer, "You, my love, matter and the children. I order you—I beg you to go and take care of them! I'll—I'll meet you at the mountaintop. May the gods be with you," he said, reaching up to her face, stretching himself upward to kiss her. "Yes. Yes. I thank you for my life, Naïs, precious wife." A moment later, the decision was taken out of their hands. All of a sudden, total silence reigned. Both Patinos and Naïs glanced back and then turned toward the sea in mute horror. What Patinos had just described was enfolding right to their eyes, only much, much more horrifying.

In total silence, the waters drew back and emptied out of the harbor below their feet. The well-known shores, cliffs, bays became bare of water—empty. As far out as the eye could see, they could see nothing but sand, sea bottom, and seaweed now spread out against the sea bottom. Normally unseen little animals—small fish, crabs, cones—were flattened, flopping, gasping for air, reaching for water, which no longer sheltered them. The utter silence lasted for minutes, more ear-shattering than all the noise that went before.

And then, as though an unseen hand had released the lever to a dam, out there where the water stopped to shrink away from the shore, in total silence it began to rise. Suddenly a horrifying new voice filled the air. A shrill shrieking, roaring, hissing rising from the sea so frightening that it obliterated any other fear that went before. A sheer wall of angry foamy green water, carrying dirt, rocks, dead animals, and dead humans began to rise. Straight up toward the sky, the dirty dark wall of water rose and rose, as though there were no limit to its power to rise to new heights. The sound emanating from this wall of water was unlike anything else heard before; it was like the desperate shrieking, roaring of thousands of voices. With unbelievable speed, the wall of water advanced, reaching for the shore with watery claws.

"Run, go, run!" Patinos screamed at Naïs, and she looked at him, her eyes showing her total shock. She only nodded. Then pressing their baby, Ilyo, to her bosom, she began to spring straight up the hill. She did not dare to stop, it seemed to her, for minutes. Finally she no longer could bear not to look. She stopped, looping the one shaking arm that was not holding the baby around the twisted limb of an ancient olive tree. She looked and looked, but beneath her, all she could see was the muddy, dirty, foam-ridden waters swirling around no more than ten paces beneath her feet. There were no houses, no roads, no people, no trees—nothing, nothing at all but the swirls of black water twirling broken remnants of vegetation, human and animal bodies, and houses in its maw.

She wanted to open her mouth and scream for Patinos, but no sound came out. Transfixed by the inconceivable sight, she stared until somehow, her brain began to function again, and she looked around for her four older children with their nannies. The last she saw them, they were several steps ahead of her, clambering up the mountainside to her left. She turned to her left to look for them and saw nothing. That entire side of great Mount Ida seemed to have disappeared. She could still see remnants of boulders, smaller rocks, gravel, and all sorts of vegetation slowly sliding down toward the muddy waters just below her feet. She fell to her knees and carefully, on her belly, inched herself toward the big gap. Once again, she saw only the angry waters swirling beneath her gaze as they received the disappearing mountainside and all its detritus into its hungry, angry arms. Vacantly, without a single thought left in her head, by force of habit, she extended her arm and pulled her one remaining child tight to her body, then sat down. Squatted and stared tearlessly with unseeing eyes into space, feeling that she would, at any moment, shatter into a million tiny fragments.

Until the hungry squalling of her infant son woke her to an unfathomable reality. Until after an unaccountable length of time, she noticed that the noise of the sea had decreased, and that indeed, the waters receded and settled into their accustomed level. The surface of the sea was not visible, so filled was it with broken bits of flotsam and floating and dead human and animal bodies. The level of noise also decreased. Many, she noticed, sat, just like her, and stared vacantly into space. Others were beyond hysteria, their screams and shrieks vibrating the air. They were tearing at their clothes, at their hair, clutching dead or dying children, or clinging to dead and dying adults, shaking them to awaken them with the deep anger born of desperation. Several women, staring at the bodies of their dead children floating in the waters, flung themselves down the rocks to reach them, perishing as they drowned or, instead of reaching the water, smashed onto the jagged freshly exposed rocks.

It was truly something out of the most unimaginable nightmare conceivable. Much of it the brain refused to process all at the same time. But then, the newest torment was that the Mountain of the Great Earth Mother opened its maw again. The earth shook with more fury than before; it felt like the whole of the island would be split apart. Then the now-truncated mountain of what used to be Thera Island, having blown off its peak, started to eject hot glowing rocks, small, large and gigantic, as though now that it had such a wide mouth, it was eager to vomit out all the contents of its bowels.

The distance from the mountaintop to the blessed island of Crete was no great barrier to the missiles, great and small; they rained down on everything and everyone, everywhere, indiscriminately. They burned the fur of animals, the skin of humans, the still-remaining grass, the roofs of the remnants of, once upon a time, gorgeously decorated, painted, lovingly designed buildings as well as the hovels of the poor, the remnants of trees which caught the sparks, which then heated and lit up like torches within seconds. The darkness of the day—or was it already night, who knew—was illuminated by flashes of light with each landing missile, only to show the pain-distorted faces, the writhing bodies.

It was too much. It was unendurable. It was all that hell, the great dreaded underworld would be. Nay, it was much, much worse, it was not just the end of life but the destruction of everything, everyone, *everything*! Naïs sat on the ground, the ground which trembled and shook beneath her body, she sat cross-legged so that she could shield little Ilyo beneath her thighs; she sat and began to shriek, endlessly, in terrible wailing ululations, rocking her body back and forth while her two arms wrapped themselves around her waist. She shrieked and rocked, rocked and shrieked endlessly, until she had no voice left and no strength to rock any more. Then she slowly slid down and laid herself on the ground, cradling her infant under her belly. The ground still continued to tremble on and off, like a great beast in its death throes.

*****

For two more days, the mountain continued to erupt and shower glowing, burning sparks and rocks down upon those who were still left living on the island. Twice again, the sea retreated, only to rear up and roar upon the land with renewed fury and frustration because most of that which could be swept away had already been swept away. Vacant-eyed people walked about, in search of water and especially for food. Small amounts of water could be scooped up from the springs which used to bubble up on the mountainside, what was left of it. Food was to be found nowhere, unless someone was lucky enough to snare a hare or a grouse. There were no fish in the water—they had been killed during the churning of the seawater. Those who were lucky found an occasional dead bird killed in flight during the bombardment by burning matter from the mountain, not yet decomposed and so partially edible. Naïs was one of the lucky, after starving for almost two days. The bird had been roasted—unbelievably—while in flight and thus was still palatable enough. She tore it apart in seconds and devoured it almost as quickly. She was more than grateful for the food; her milk had started to dry up, and now at least, for a while, she could suckle her child. When she had finished eating, she heaved herself up and settled Ilyo into a sling she had fashioned out of some pieces of cloth she had found lying on the ground in front of her feet. Then she started walking, wandering about, with no specific aim and the same vacant stare that all those wore whom she encountered.

She had no awareness of the passage of time, knew not how many days had passed or if, in fact, any. At night, she did not have to fear any wild animals; it seemed that almost all animals, those domesticated or those that would have roamed about wild, had either died in the great conflagration or were killed by other starving, who came upon them before her. To find any would have been useless; she had no weapons or even any implement that could have been used as a weapon. Her best resource were small birds, as before, which had dropped from the skies, already roasted. But she found that even that resource slowly dwindled into scarcity.

She could ignore her hunger but was concerned about her child. The baby became more and more silent, and while it cried lustily in the beginning, now lay listless in his little sling and often did not even have the energy to suckle. Vaguely Naïs remembered the teaching of the priestess who had prepared her—oh gods, how long ago was that—for the first birth. She had stressed that a pregnant or nursing mother needed to mind what she put into her mouth. She needed to drink a lot of water and milk from healthy goats, she needed to eat fish as well as fowl, and occasionally the meat of a lamb or goat, or even one of the more-or-less tamed cattle, roaming the hillsides. But Naïs, in all her misery, had to smile as she clearly recalled the priestess's raised finger; but the mother needed, more than anything else, to eat much fruit and greens of any sort as they became seasonal.

As these thoughts came to her, Naïs felt reinvigorated and, despite her weariness, forced herself to search the ground, the bushes, the almost-burnt barren trees for anything edible. She was not only rewarded but greatly surprised by the riches at her feet. Using the sturdy stick she found much earlier to help her in walking, she dug up roots of all sorts, then collected handfuls of berries, which she hungrily stuffed into her mouth. The roots she cleaned as best she could by scraping them against a sharp stone. Of course, nothing could be cooked; most wood was too wet to ignite and besides, flint was not available. Thank the gods that she possessed a good healthy set of teeth—she had always been assiduous in cleaning them in those once-upon-a-time incredible days of her luxury—so she bit down chunks and chewed them into a pulp. Much to her surprise, the taste was actually delicious, so fresh and flavorful. She stuffed little bits, just big enough to fit between two of her fingertips, into Ilyo's mouth, watching carefully that he swallowed it down without coughing or gagging, and felt the first excitement of achievement since she had lost all that she had held close and dear.

The next morning, she found her little boy more animated and smiled—actually smiled—when he anxiously attacked the nipple she offered him. He suckled hungrily, until her milk flowed down his little chin, and he could not swallow any more. She then laid him down onto her lap, cleaned his little bottom, red and chafed, with a large leaf she had found earlier and had kept with her just for that purpose. When the baby emitted a sound somewhere between a gurgle and a chuckle, she scooped him up into her arms and pressed him to her chest. Her heart swelled with love for this tiny morsel of human life that remained, that still belonged to her. She pressed her cheek against his downy head and let hear tears flow. These were cleansing tears, though, Naïs felt, for instead of searing a path of torture through her soul, they seemed to refresh her. Pressing her child to her body, she lay down on the earth and slept. Slept peacefully, without horrific nightmares, for the first time since—since she had lost her husband, four of her five children, her home, her existence.

She awoke in the afternoon, feeling refreshed. But the refreshment was only one of the spirit, and as the next lower level of discomfort, she now craved her body's refreshment as well. Over the past days, she had slowly descended from the top of the mountain, where vegetation and any hope for food was sparse, to be now close to sea level. She looked down and, much to her surprise, found that even though the shore was littered by debris, in places pushed into veritable mountains by the waves, the water was calm, and if not clean, certainly no longer murky. Naïs felt a desperate need to let the water wash her body and that of little Ilyo.

The water felt wonderfully cleansing. When she returned to the shore, the baby draped over her shoulder to shield him from the splashes of seawater, she just stood there, her eyes closed, gently swaying her body and humming a little children's melody.

The sound of her name invaded the edge of her somnolence. The last sound she expected to hear was that of her name. At first she barely reacted, then she felt a soft touch upon her arm. It roused her, and she turned, more than anything, with utter surprise. What she saw in front of her buckled her knees, and she would have sunk into the sand but for the pair of hands keeping her upright. She had no idea if she was dreaming or facing the reality of Ido standing in front of her. With her mouth suddenly dry, she gazed up at him, still feeling ready to collapse except for his assistance. She had no words, no sound would escape her mouth; she just looked at him, looked and looked.

Finally he smiled and, shaking his head, wrapped his arms around her and the baby. His one hand pressed her face into his shoulder, into his chest. She felt his chest heave and his body shake as he held her endlessly, embracing her with such fervor, as though he were afraid of ever losing her again. Then finally, he released her and, holding her face tenderly in both his hands, kissed her, her eyes, her nose, her lips. Time did not exist as they stood there, touching and looking, as though still not quite convinced of the reality of what was happening to them.

Eventually Ido released her and helped her settle on the sandy beach. It had gotten dark, and a beautifully big almost-full moon shone down upon a calm sea. It almost seemed as though everything was totally normal and what had happened had not, but they knew better. They looked into each other's wounded eyes and tried to fathom the loss that each had suffered, afraid to ask. Then Ido quietly asked her, and in fits and spurts, the memories of loss, of sadness and tragedy and horror emerged out of her mouth, from her brain. Finally exhausted, she looked up at him, her fingers cupping his face.

"And you, my love, what has happened to you?" She lifted her fingers to his short-cropped hair, now peppered with gray. "What of your family, my dearest?" Ido looked down into his lap and slowly shook his head.

"Athenis was killed by one of the flaming missiles from the sky. The children as well. The missile fell onto the roof of our house, and it ignited with such a speed that I could not rescue them." A great sob escaped him. "I was outside, somehow before things happened, I felt disturbed and could not sleep. I tried, I tried to go inside but could not"—he sobbed—"the gods forgive me, but I could not. Everything was engulfed with such speed! I could not do anything to save my wife, my children! Oh, gods!" He heaved one more time, then quieted.

After a moment, he turned to her with a wistful little smile.

"I had a little boy, you know, our oldest. His name was Novoro. He was born not too long after you and Athenis talked…at the bull arena…He-he had just turned eight years. He was so in love with bull dancing. That was all he wanted. Bull dancing…We also had twin little girls, you know, and Athenis insisted that one of them be named Naïs. She did love you dearly, you know, and wanted to befriend you, even though you didn't stay in contact. And she understood your reasons. She so greatly admired you and always said that talent like yours would appear on our land like a shining comet, only once in two to three generations. She was right, you know…Well, the other little girl we named Taïs. Yes, Naïs and Taïs…And they—they all burned inside of that damned house because I couldn't—I couldn't…" Another great sob escaped him, and he bent his face into his hands so that only his heaving shoulders would witness his agony.

Naïs grabbed Ido's hand, looking at it as intently as though it were a foreign object to her. Slowly she entwined her fingers with his. The hint of a smile, the first in a long while, appeared on her face.

"Athenis and you named one of your girls Naïs. How lovely! I'm truly honored. Thank you, Ido. We shall always remember them, with great sadness and great love, Ido. And mine as well. Won't we?"

"And you had four, did you not, love," Ido muttered. "Other than this dear little fellow you now have placed on your lap. Four little innocents…and what of Patinos? Did he—was he—was he decent to you? While he lived, I mean?"

"He loved me. He loved me deeply, I think. He had had such a horrible life before—before I entered his life. It was not easy. Yes, I had to force myself…but you know, that all slowly changed. I learned to value and admire him and have—well, great affection for him. Before he died, he told me that I had given him life. Yes, and he thanked me for that."

Suddenly with great vehemence, she turned to Ido, shaking their entwined hands.

"I promise you, and you must promise me that we will keep them in our minds, pray to the gods for them, remember to talk about each of them every day so their memory, their spirit continues to live on through us, while we live and breathe! Promise, yes?"

And Ido nodded, his tears falling to the ground, seeping into the sandy soil of their incomparable land, beautiful then and still so today. But his eyes were on Naïs's face.

Nest of Eagles
704–705 BCE Assyria

Introduction

There had never been a time, a life, without the great rivers, flowing with grace and majesty from the breathtaking snowcapped mountains down toward the arid desert. The desert eventually softened into an endless-seeming expanse of grass, reedbeds, and marshes; and even these would give way to huge mudflats alternating with shimmering blue lagoons, in which great flocks of wading birds watched their mirror images.

Between the mudflats and lagoons, uncounted waterways divided and connected the land, giving its population almost unlimited ability to commute and to do what they did best—to buy what they needed, to sell what they produced, to bargain, and, whenever possible, to increase their wealth and, most importantly, their status. During all daylight hours, reed barges moved to and fro, shouts of greetings or farewells of adults and the high-pitched laughter of children vibrating in the air.

Anything available to the residents of the little villages, with their round wattle-and-daub houses, was avidly gathered and taken to the nearest market. The surrounding little gardens, which grew onions, peas, lentils, sesame, and turnips under rows of grapevines, pomegranate bushes, and spreading pistachio, apple, olive, citrus, and fig trees, and farther away from the homes, the flax grown in long rows, the wheat, barley, and millet of the fields, as well as the dates of the statuesque tall date palms, all were available and sold up and down the Euphrates and Tigris Rivers. Anyone lucky enough to have sold his wares so that extra coins remained to buy something of true value above and beyond the necessities, invariably turned to buy decorative items.

The rich bought decorations for their homes, the less affluent bought things to decorate their bodies and enrich their appearance. Colored stones, beautiful corals taken from the Great Bay into which their glorious rivers drained, and from the adjacent Narrow Sea, were avidly collected as well, but more than anything at all, the most admired, most valued, most prized item was gold.

Gold was expensive because it had to be brought in from great distances, and so it also was not readily available. But it was needed—needed not only for personal embellishment, or family wealth, nor even just to decorate rich dwellings. Lately the eagerness of rulers to enhance their prestige by the construction of new cities, one greater, more elegant, more opulent than the one before, predicated the lavish use of gold to enhance the exteriors of important buildings. What was used were thin layers of gold leaf carefully and sparingly layered onto outside walls, doors, and columns. Artisans who worked on such assignments were highly valued because in addition to an eye for beauty, they also needed a hand which could translate the beauty their eyes saw into painted designs. More than anything else, they needed to be trustworthy, to be entrusted with the possession and use of the precious gold.

Understandably punishment for any transgression or lapse of trust was immediate and harsh. Those the Great God Ashur singled out with graciousness and giving were also expected to give more in return, by whatever means Ashur asked. Transgression of any kind was severely punishable, and the punishment to be meted out to unfortunate victims were most imaginative. Not that the government would have been considered more repressive than others. Life everywhere was harsh and demanding, especially for the poor and lowborn laborer. But the rich, the powerful, also had severe restrictions handed down by both the priests and the ruler. Overarching the population's inborn joy of living, there was a lifelong sense of fear, of doom. Everyone trod lightly and assured themselves that for each of them, their fate, assigned by the all-powerful gods, was indeed unavoidable.

Prologue

In the twelfth year of his glorious rule, one of the caravans sent out by the great King Sargon, ruler of the Known World, arrived into his newly rising city of Dur-Sharrukin. The city, still under construction, was buzzing with all sort of activity. The caravan leader had never been in this particular city, and his eyes immediately went to the enormous structure in front of him; indeed, no one entering through the southern gate would have been able to miss the sight. Gleaming in the sunlight, the walls encased in white plaster with gilt embellishments, the massive gates a sparkling deep ocean blue, with more gold designs of the Goddess Ishtar and her husband, the great God Ashur, the structure dominated the city. This domination was not only visual. Noticeably most of the traffic back and forth through the city's streets seemed to eventually pass through those great gates.

The leader's instruction had been precise, he was to enter from the city gate directly to the palace and search out one or another of the gold merchants whose shops were scattered about the great square. The load of gold which this particular caravan carried was not just singularly valuable—it was exceptional. It was said that the gold had been dug out from under layers of dirt, stones, and lava covering a ravine, and most of the whole mountainside on one of those mythical mist-shrouded islands, in the middle of the sea, at the center of the earth, far to the setting sun.

Much of the island had disappeared under the sea when their neighboring mountain erupted in flames and caused massive devastation. Prospectors had invaded the island again and again, and some of them became very lucky, indeed. Many of the items in this lot were miraculously undamaged and of great beauty. The leader had not seen any of this since the intact items had been carefully wrapped in many layers of straw and then strips of cloth. Nonetheless, he was anticipating to become a rich man.

Once through the gates, the leader led his caravan to the biggest richest-looking booth. The owner lounged in front of his tent, fanned by a little black boy's huge palm fronds. He was chewing some kind of kernels and spitting out the shells with relish. When he perceived that the caravan was weaving its way to his display, he rose, adjusting his robes and the belt holding those robes with great dignity, and indicated to his servants to start off-loading the wares strapped to the sides of the bleating camels.

As the bales were brought in front of him, and he carefully inspected each and when all were seen, a lengthy discussion ensued between him and the leader of the caravan. Finally he paid with a flourish so that all could see his wealth. Then he dismissed all and had a few selected chests carted inside his tent for his private inspection.

Inspection of the newly received wares must have been satisfactory. Already the next day, a messenger wove his way to the royal palace, where the merchant had several contacts who negotiated for him in front of His Exalted Majesty, the great king. What transpired remained unknown for a number of years until the king had acquired his new queen and, it was said, learned to treasure her above all others.

To please the king, the betrothal was to be celebrated on the earliest most propitious day the seers could designate. He, of course, was anxious for the ceremony to take place as soon as possible, now that the gods had deigned to take the life of his queen. Not that her death in itself caused him undue grief; it was nothing. Long ago, he had ceased to have the same feelings for Neghanna that he had when he first bedded her and made her queen. Her only real value to him was her royal birth, which would have assured the king of a royal lineage to carry on his name. But the male heir was not to be, not one of royal lineage, at any rate, and not from this queen. Birthing four girl infants who each died within a week of being released from their mother's body had taken the bloom from Neghanna and left her sickly, brittle, and bitter. For many months now, he had stayed away from her bedchamber. He knew that this added to her grief, but he preferred to nurture his own bitterness to salving hers.

The alliance with King Mita of Phrygia had been discussed by the council for months and months without coming to fruition. Mita had introduced the prospect of future kinship by giving his firstborn daughter, Himene; she was said to be young, a virgin, and beautiful. Also the Phrygians were well known for their culture and gracious mode of living, all of which were great inducements for the Lord Sargon, Great Ruler of the Known World. Above all, now that his conquests had been accomplished according to his desires and plans, he wished for nothing more than to introduce culture and gracious living to his capital. In his heart of hearts, of course, and not ever to be mentioned or even thought of by any of his subjects, was the matter of his own questionable royal descent. But like so many before him, and ever since, he trusted the short memories of people. In this matter, the official word was that the lord king was the younger brother of the previous king, the Great Shalmaneser, and, as such, a younger son of the great King Tiglath-Pileser. As it always happens with information too often repeated, by this time, in Sargon's reign—undisputedly a very successful reign of a popular ruler—fact and fiction were blurred so much as to make the one indistinguishable from the other.

The Princess Himene, Mita's daughter, could not have entered the king's palace other than as his official bride and queen-to-be, and the king already had one of those in his House of Women, however inadequate to his needs and her purpose. When she died, the road was suddenly open to achieve this much-needed, much-desired alliance. The day after the late Queen Neghanna's funeral pyre was lit, Sargon sent his emissary to Mita's court, to attend to the bargaining, the dowry, the bride-price, and all the necessary arrangements with every possible speed.

Once the bride-price had been agreed upon and paid, the dowry and the bride, with her attendants and a detachment of palace guards, embarked upon the long trek across inhospitable, dangerous, and barren mountains to reach Dur-Sharrukin, the princess's new home and her husband's. The main detachment of mounted soldiers dispatched to guard the princess was well behind and in front of the column of pack animals carrying the enormous amount of dowry goods as well as the belongings of the princess and her noble attendants. With the beat of drums to ward away evil mountain spirits and wild animals, the long column wound its weary way along the steep foot pass. Each pack animal had to be as sure-footed as a mountain goat here, and only the occasional desperate screams of a mule, a horse, or a human slipping on the loose rocks and tumbling down into the precipice caused a temporary stop. To retrieve the unfortunate victim was futile but an account of lost life and lost goods had to be made to Mita. The scribes, therefore, quickly attended to these details so that the caravan would be able to continue with little delay on its slow, noisy, drum-beating progress.

When the first scouts reported the procession's approach to the great king, he stopped his regular daily activities, dismissed all those who were in his Hall of Audiences, ordered his horse, and rode out with his royal palace guards to meet the new bride. He did this with anticipation, for he was yet far from being an old man and, what his polished bronze mirrors told him, not unhandsome. He was tall for a man of the Land of Ashur, well built and well weathered from many campaigns and hunts, scarred but not disfigured in face or body. His long hair and long square-cut beard, which showed sparse strands of gray, were oiled and carefully curled. He had heavy bushy eyebrows sitting like two black slashes over unblinking black eyes, a sensuous mouth under a large hooked nose, much like a bird of prey's beak, thick neck, powerful hands and arms, and a long torso, with short muscular thighs. He was also an active, authoritative, combative, cunning, willful, virile man who could show great cruelty and occasional tenderness, mostly toward his younger children, the offsprings of his minor wives and concubines.

The Princess Himene was purported to be a great beauty, but then Sargon knew that in such circumstances, words carried little weight. Presumably every princess yet born had been described to be beautiful by those anxious enough to marry her off at the best bride-price. Nonetheless, he was curious and anxious about his new queen's appearance and comportment, not to mention the promise of her future fertility. Always a frugal and provident ruler, he had already begun to wonder whether he had paid the bride-price prematurely before any concrete proof of his new bride's fertility, or else if he had asked for too little in the way of her dowry. When he was informed of the wedding caravan's approach, he wisely decided to abandon such gloomier thoughts for a while on a day which should be filled with anticipation and joy.

The transfer of the bride from the guardianship of her father to the authority of her intended husband was to proceed according to prescribed ceremony which had been agreed upon after many jointly held consultations between the masters of ceremony of the two royal households. Both the great Lord Sargon and the Princess Himene had been instructed well in advance of what to do. The princess was too heavily veiled to guess either her appearance or her feelings, but Lord Sargon made well known both his impatience and annoyance with what he considered an unnecessary delay, dismissed the courtiers of both camps, turned his horse's head, and gave terse orders to follow him back with all possible speed to Dur-Sharrukin and his palace. When the princess's master of ceremonies actually had the temerity to address the Great Ruler of the Known World and remind him that the bride was, in all likelihood, probably exhausted and that an overnight camp should be struck at this place of meeting, Sargon glared at the man so fiercely that he visibly shriveled and took himself away.

Several hours later, the procession, with drumbeat and the unceasing sound of trumpets, entered the gates of Dur-Sharrukin. At the royal palace, the princess alighted and, as prescribed by protocol, threw handfuls of coins and flower petals to the assembled crowds. When she reached the heavy metal-studded doors, both wings flung open to her, and Sargon drove his horse to her side and, bending down from the saddle, lifted her up and seated her in from of him. At this the crowd went wild, screaming and ululating, dancing with their arms upraised in joy. Sargon, with a wolfish grin on his face, looked left and right, nodded to the left and right, and then rode his warhorse through the gate. With satisfaction, he heard the two wings of the portal clang shut, as he had ordered at his departure, before all of the wedding retinue could squeeze themselves through.

The betrothal feast, like all banqueting affairs at the Assyrian court, was noisy with loud laughter and hearty bellowing of the assembled male guests. Custom demanded that no women should be present other than those who had no rank and served the dishes of food, the bowls of wine and ale, and then scampered out of the way as fast as they could before the hands eagerly reaching for them could grab the edge of their skirts. The women of status sat on the heavily shuttered balconies and had no other entertainment than that of observing the feasting men below. Himene sat in the center of a circle of the noblest women of the land, all of who had been introduced to her but the names of all of whom she had already forgotten. She was dizzily tired, hot to the point of fainting from the many layers of gorgeous clothes she was obliged to wear, and hungry and thirsty while her stomach rebelled at the unaccustomed fare offered to her. She was also slightly repelled by the coarseness of manners she saw before her, the noise, the fumes of fermented drinks, the smells of sweat and horses overlaid with the vain attempt at covering them with the aroma of sandalwood and orange blossoms assaulting her senses.

Most of all, she was anxious and fearful in the midst of this strange and bewildering setting in a strange and bewildering land, which she now had to call her own. More than anything else, she was terrified of the silent man with his black hair and beard peppered with gray, who had so effortlessly lifted her up on his horse and who had, before that, been introduced to her as her husband-to-be, the Lord Sargon, Great Ruler of the Known World.

Eventually her hunger conquered her revulsion, and she did eat and drink sparingly, mostly because of the kind prompting of a thin elderly lady who sat next to her and was presented to her as the first wife of the king's chief minister and turtanu, who was also named Sargon but usually called Lord Shutur-Nahhunte. That lady, Simirrah, looked at her with kind eyes full of wordless understanding. She even had the temerity to reach for Himene's hands and, squeezing them, whispered that everything would be easier and better with the passage of time. Should the Lady Himene wish or need help with anything at all that now bewildered her, she should send a runner to the Lord Shutur-Nahhunte's house and summon his first wife.

The ladies departed much before the feasting was over, and Himene was escorted into the most elegantly and lavishly furnished chamber she had ever beheld. Gold and bronze gleamed everywhere; on the doors, the most delicate hangings of translucent wool wafted in the slight breeze from the mountains, while alabaster, jasper, malachite, onyx, marble, precious ivory, and fragrant sandalwood were used for furniture and decorations. Her servant girls were waiting and ready to divest Himene of her hot and heavy clothes, wash away the dust and sweat of the road, rub her body with fragrant oils, and offer her some fruits and sweets. She allowed all these ministrations to wash over her, too tired to consent or protest, and when the women withdrew, she sank down onto a cushioned chair, staring down at the tips of her slippers, not knowing what to do or what was expected of her next, her feelings swinging from heart-pounding terror to feeling too exhausted to care.

It was a long while later that the hangings over the open doorway to the gardens moved, letting in more of the welcome cooling breeze from outside. Himene was half-asleep by then, and her body wrenched itself into awareness as she looked toward the source of the breeze. A shadow was standing there, in the guttering flicker of the flames from the oil lamps. She knew immediately, without a doubt, that it was the Great Ruler of the Known World, the king himself, who had come to—do what? Say a private welcome to his betrothed? Bid her a good night? Spend the night with her? But surely not; they were only yet betrothed, the marriage would take place in several months! She knew not what the customs of this new land were but, as all women, was raised to understand her duty to obey her husband, comply with whatever his wishes were, and bear his children. She rose and bowed deeply to the king, unsure what kind of greeting was considered to be appropriate in this, her new home.

Sargon walked slowly into the room and stood in the center of it, his two hands clasped behind his back, staring ahead, almost unaware of her presence. Then he raised his eyes, looking at her bowed head, nodded a greeting, and, with a sigh, lowered himself into the same cushioned chair that Himene had just vacated. He waved to her to come closer and, when she was close enough to him, reached out and caught one of her wrists. She did not flinch or shrink away, nor did she move closer either. She just stood there, like a deer cornered by hunting dogs, their eyes locked together by the force of his will.

Then he released her with a sigh and asked, "Have you been well attended to by my court, my lady, according to your wishes? Have you any complaints or desires? If so, you must register them with me. From now on, I shall be the source of all your comforts."

Himene bowed her head. "My lord," she whispered, "I have no complaints, only thanks to give to you for the graciousness of your welcome. You honor me greatly."

The king nodded absently, then rose with a sigh. "Yes," he said, frowning. "That is as it should. It is late, my lady. We both must be tired. I hope not to detain you longer than necessary. You now have been my betrothed and the future mother of my heir-to-be for several passes of the moon, even before we met. In two more, if the gods so will, you shall be elevated to queen and mother of the heir according to the agreements drawn up. I emphasize this last part of what I am saying because it is all-important. It was the reason for our betrothal and for all that has happened since and will happen by the time of our marriage. But what will happen now is the consummation of our betrothal. I would ask you to shed your clothing and to lie down on the bed, lady."

Himene shrank away, as though he would have struck her. She raised her hand to her mouth and stared incredulously at the king. "What, my lord?" she stammered. "What?"

Sargon stood up to face her, rocking back and forth on his heels, his two fists on his hips. "I have been told that you were instructed in our Akkadian language as well as in Aramaic and Greek and can communicate with equal facility in each. If that is untrue, please tell me now so that I can summon one of the many interpreters at my court to facilitate our converse. But I believe you heard me well. However innocent you may be—or pretend to be—about the affairs of men and women together, it could not have escaped your attention that this is the way by which children are produced. I have bought you dearly with a lavish bride-price. Do you believe that the reason for our intended marriage is only to keep your father at my side as an ally and relative? You, my dear, will not only be first among my wives but also the chosen mother of the future master of the Known World, who will succeed me. Do you believe that I would do all that I am doing without assuring myself that you are an appropriate choice and fertile? Before our marriage, I must know that you are not barren, lady. And should you prove to be barren, then this marriage will not take place."

Himene was still so stunned that she could barely speak. "And would you shame me thus, my lord, to send me home?"

Sargon's laugh sounded like the brief bark of a dog. "Lady, shaming you or not does not enter into the calculation. It is not my intent. Should it happen that way, very few shall know about it. Your bride-price has been paid and received. You will remain here in my House of Women and be given all the deference you may expect, except the anticipated title. That will go to another one who will prove to be a better breeder than you." And when no answer came, he continued, "Lady, you may know or not how these things are done. If you wish, pretend to be innocent of all such knowledge, or perhaps in truth, you are innocent. It does not much matter. In two more passes of the moon, this marriage would be consummated anyway. All we are doing is advancing the timing ahead a bit. Come, it isn't like you did not anticipate this occurring to you at some time soon. Pray remain calm. I will be as gentle as possible, or not, if you resist me. But I am no rapist, lady, and would vastly prefer the former. I can arrange this to be quick but not very pleasant, or if you consent, it can be our first encounter at becoming better acquainted with each other. The choice is yours, lady."

He looked at Himene, who still stood before him as though frozen to the ground. "And now pray, lady, do as I ask, lie upon that bed. Obey me."

Slowly and still as in a dream, Himene turned away and walked to the bed. For a moment only she hesitated, then bent down to unlace and remove her sandals. When that was done, she proceeded to remove her headdress and the veil attached to it. Finally and with agonizing slowness, while the king watched her, she sat down onto the cushions, lifted her legs, and stretched out on top of the bed. Her arms lay by her side, fists clenched, her eyes looking unblinkingly at the king, until she broke her gaze and turned her head into the pillows. He, however, steadfastly continued to watch her. For what seemed an endless time, silence pervaded the room. Then he heard her whisper in a small voice, muffled by the pillow.

"You will wish to make love with me, my lord?"

He was so aghast by her question that he hardly knew how to respond. "Of course," he answered in a voice of surprise, and then asked her out of his innate sense of courtesy, "and that displeases you, lady?"

Evidently tonight was the night of surprises, for when she answered, it was hesitant. "I cannot say, my lord."

"Cannot say? How so, lady?"

Again the hesitation from her. "I do not know, my lord King."

"Do not know if something pleases or displeases you?" And now there was irritation in his voice. "How so, lady?"

And again a long silence, followed by the same small voice. "My lord, forgive me. I know neither of it would please nor displease me."

"What are you saying, lady? Is it that you do not know—you were not taught—what man and woman do when they are together?"

There it was again, the barely audible whisper of yes, and then, "It is not our custom, my lord."

This, Sargon thought, was foolishness beyond comprehension. Everywhere, not only in Assyria, but in the ancient land of Akkad, in Babylon, in Egypt, in Scythia, in Samaria, in the land of the Cimmerians, in Colchis, Urartu, in Judah—everywhere women were taught these matters and most especially how to please their husbands. But to allow young girls to grow up—it was not to be believed! For the moment, he did not know if he should be angry, laugh, or just shake his head. Finally he decided on the last; after all, this lack was not Himene's fault but of the place where she grew up. There was no reason to be either angry with her or to laugh at her; there was no reason at all to affront or shame her.

"Himene, lady, for your sake I am sad to hear this. Whoever instructed you, or rather did not instruct you, however it was the custom of your land, it was a grave injustice done to you. But there is no help for it now. What needs to pass will pass. Please do not be fearful or even disquieted, for I am not your enemy."

And when no response was forthcoming, he continued with a sigh, "Well, my love, what shall we do next? Shall we quickly come to the end of this now, or shall we take it in slow stages? Is your fear still so very great within you? Or can you look at me and see just an ordinary man? Tell me, in earlier days, did you have a brother at home who was dear to you? Who is a ruler-to-be in the eyes of the people but who was just a friend to you? Can you not look at me the same way? If you can't, tell me so now, quickly, and we shall behave as two strangers who have come together in lust. But you know nothing of lust, do you, my dear? And so when we are together, we can also try to be friends to each other. Look here, I do not expect you to swoon with love and passion when you see me. Do therefore not also expect me to be more than attentive to you.

"But the truth is usually hidden somewhere in the middle between two extremes. It is like water, which is hurtful when it is frozen into ice or when it steams and bubbles with heat but is pleasant to the body when between those two extremes. If you can look at me as the man who has the right of ownership over you, but who has no wish to hurt or harm you, ever, then your feelings for me would perhaps be more trusting. Can you not begin to do that?" Mostly he was just stringing words together because he thought that a calm and steady voice would calm and steady her too.

Observing her, the king walked to the bed, shook his head with a sigh, and sat down heavily next to her. "Lady," he said quietly, "Himene. This is not how it should be. If you can bring yourself to abandon your fears, and to believe that I truly do not wish to harm you, if you could but begin to trust me in this matter, it would be much more pleasing for both of us. I said before that I have no taste for rape, my dear, unless I must. Let us do things together, shall we? Help me to remove your clothing, or if you won't, I assure you I will remove them without your help."

Himene finally stirred, turned her head, and sat up, while her hands hesitantly reached for the laces which held her embroidered and fringed gown together. The laces were in the back, and she could only reach the top row, however much she struggled and fumbled with them. With some irritation, Sargon brushed her hands away and, holding her shoulders, turned her so that her back faced him, one by one loosened the laces until the gown fell away from her body. He bent and, lifting her slightly, pulled on the obstructing material. When it fell to the ground, he kicked it away with his sandaled foot. He turned her then, his heavy hands still on her shoulders, his eyebrows two straight lines in a creased forehead, his eyes boring into her. His nostrils flared to breathe in her flower-petal scent. Himene cringed to evade his gaze upon her but found it to be impossible.

After a moment's silence, Sargon, still inhaling her scent, murmured barely audibly, "Ah, my lady, how beautiful the gods consented to make you! Beautiful and created for love, Himene. Shall we then not proceed?"

He moved slightly, rose, and divested himself of his garments and heavy jewelry, the latter clattering to his feet. Moments later, he stood by the bedside, naked and obviously already aroused. Himene closed her eyes, shivers of fear and shame raking her body. Her heart thundered so hard that she thought the king would hear it. But he heard nothing, and all he saw was her lovely face, framed by waves of black hair, her dark lashes lying softy upon her cheeks. He stretched out the length of his body next to her and, leaning on his elbow, raised up his head and torso. With unwavering eyes, he looked at her, every inch of her; no sounds now other than his heavy breathing. Tentatively his free hand reached out, fingers touching her nipples, dark against her creamy skin, dark head bending to kiss them until he heard her sigh, as gentle and soft a sound as that of the night breeze. At that he raised his head and, for the first time allowing a smile, looked into her face.

"Slowly," he murmured. To her? To himself? "Let us take this slowly now, my dear. If you so want too, there can be pleasure ahead for both of us." The dark head bent down again, finding her mouth. She started once again when his tongue forced her lips apart and pushed itself into the cavity of her mouth, and she felt the top of his heavy body pressing down on her. His tightly curled beard tickled her face, and now that his mouth had released her nipples, both of his hands, roughened and hard by many years of using sword, battle-ax, arrow, and javelin, were hurtful upon her breasts, squeezing and massaging, then caressing and stroking, before moving farther down her body. His breath smelled of the rind of oranges which he must have chewed to obliterate the smell of ale and the banquet's spicy food. His curled hair and beard smelled of sandalwood oil. He lifted himself on his elbow again, his expressive eyebrows now raised questioningly, his mouth smiling briefly.

Slowly he shook his head from side to side. "You are so delicate and lovely, truly like a delicate bird in a snare. I do not wish to crush you. But if we do this now in haste, that is what would happen. Brutality and cruelty are for one's enemies on the battlefield or for a city after its siege is broken. They do not belong in the bed shared by man and woman."

There was silence in the room for a while until Sargon sensed that her heartbeat had slowed and her breathing become quieter. Satisfied, he nodded and kissed her again, this time lingering quietly over her face and neck, kissing her eyes and the corners of her mouth, burying his face in her dark hair and inhaling its fragrance. When he felt her arms, until now lying immobile by her side, move slightly, he caught both of her wrists in one of his big hands and twisted them above her head, slowly and carefully lowering the length of his body onto her. He heard her gasp but, at the same time, felt her thighs move apart ever-so slightly, surely without her awareness. A mixture of sweetness, tenderness, and desperate fierceness shot though him. "Good," he murmured and good again as he let his body slowly slide down to allow him to touch her between her thighs. She moaned softly, and he felt her body stir involuntarily to meet him while, at the same time, trying to twist away from him, not able to do so, pinned down by his weight.

The impatience of his desire flooded through him now, and he barely recognized his own voice, harsh and hoarse. "Come, do what I want, open your legs to receive your lord!" Putting his hands beneath her buttocks to raise her and pushing into her slowly and deliberately until he heard her moan and cry out in surprise. But by then, it was impossible for her to struggle, impossible to want to struggle. She was panting from exertion, fear, pain, and something else also, something as yet unexplainable, foreign and hidden deep within her. Slowly her body began to rock and move in rhythm with his movements, and slowly the pain and distress gave way to an indescribably delicate sensation; it spiraled from delicate all the way to a desperately needful explosion which was beyond any feeling she had ever known and which left her elated, destroyed, and curiously content all at the same time so that when she felt him draw away from her, she wanted to cry out and beg him not to leave her.

There was nothing but silence in the room for a long while. Noises from the outside, man-made or made by nature, filtered through the curtains and even more slowly into Himene's brain. She struggled dizzily to sit up but gave up the effort. Her head swimming, she felt exhausted beyond exhaustion, utterly spent and weak as a rag doll. With effort, she turned her head and was shocked to see her lord's face only a hand's width from her. He was leaning on his elbow, as before, and looking down at her, as before, his brow raised, a barely perceptible smile on his face.

"So," he said. "So and now it is done." After a moment, he continued, less severely. "Ah, my lady, I am happy to see that you have survived the horrors that were so heavily preying on your mind lately!" There was now no mistaking the hidden laughter in his voice, Himene thought. She did not answer, for she did not know what to say, nor was she yet able to organize her thoughts.

"Tell me, lady, did it please you what had just passed between us in the night? Did any of it please you at all? You can answer me without fear, for it will not impact me. I will do what I will do. But I wish to have your answer. Tell me!" It quite pleased him when the answer came with a hesitant nod of her head. The great king seemed to be enjoying the moment. "Ah, yes, that is a good first step, lady. We may yet become friends, might we not then? My dear, most of our fears are much worse when they consume our thoughts than when we act upon them. You must believe me when I tell you this, and it is something I had learned facing many enemies in many battles. And yet, lady, I am not your enemy and, with the passing of time, hope to become not only your lord but also your friend. And then, perhaps on that day, you, lady, will know how to kiss me as well as I did kiss you, maybe? Eh?" And when he saw the doubting, stricken look Himene gave him, he threw back his head, and his booming laugh floated through the chamber and out into the sleeping garden.

He bent down to her and gently kissed her moist forehead, then, with a quick movement, left the bed and rose. "And now, my dear, as I know you have given the last grain of your energy to me, I shall leave you to rest and sleep."

Putting on his clothing but not bothering to retrieve his jewelry, he looked at her speculatively and added, "You have pleased me beyond my expectations. I will find it hard to resist but will not come to your bed tonight. After my invasion, you will need to mend your body. My servants have unguents and ointments which will help ease any of your discomfort. Do not be shy, let them minister to you. But mark it well, I shall come to your bed the night after the one that is to come and every night thereafter. I must have an answer to the question of your fertility or barrenness before the day of our intended marriage."

He was already at the door, ready to leave, but looking back at Himene, he saw something in her face which prompted him to turn and, with quick steps, stride back to the bed. He picked up her hand closer to him, lifted it, and laid it against his cheek so that it was buried in his curled, scented, graying beard. His eyes looked into hers with unrelentingly steady gaze. There was no smile now on his face or in his voice. "Rest well, Himene. Much of your future will depend on the next few weeks," he said softly, turned, and was gone from the chamber before Himene was able to answer him.

*****

The city of Dur-Sharrukin, Sargon's capital, was growing. Most of it was still under construction by the hordes of laborers, some paid but the majority conscripted from the populace, given the promise of debt forgiveness in the king's name, or slaves acquired during the king's almost unending wars. Communication among these people speaking in many languages and even more dialects was difficult. The architects, the foremen, and those who did the heavy lifting communicated by the two most predominant languages of the area, Aramaic or Akkadian, or else when those failed, in the lingua franca of any nation—sign language. The air reverberated with noise—draft animals bellowed, workers yelled at one another in fifteen different tongues, the sound of hammering and sawing vibrated in the air, along with thick clouds of dust and smoke. The city was situated in a valley and surrounded by rocky hills alternating with thick woods on three sides and rolling fields to the south, all the way to the river Tigris, with its great reedbeds stretching even farther to the south, where the cultivation of vegetables, grapes, and much-needed olive trees was promising. The hills to the north and east rose in tiers to increasingly high mountains with treacherous roads and deep gorges, the bottom of most filled with sparkles of water. Best of all, the revered old city of Nineveh was little less than a day's riding away to the south and connected Dur-Sharrukin by a well-maintained road.

Bagtu-Shar, the stonecutter's, house lay about halfway between the royal palace and the outskirts of the city, bordering the growing fields of olive trees. He was one of those relatively few city dwellers who were neither wealthy nor miserably poor either. He had a good trade; much of his handwork was well known and valued in a land where all manner of stone carving, for decoration and for documentation, were highly prized and much in demand. His house was more spacious and comfortable than most in his section of town, certainly the most prestigious home on his street. It was solidly built, with a sturdy flat roof for sleep in the summer heat, and in back of the house, a walled garden with a few trees, a goat, a vegetable patch, as well as a private well and enclosed privy, both almost unheard of luxuries for a family home. There was a front room for cooking and visiting by the men of the neighborhood, and behind it, a women's room used for sleeping and, alternately, for a living area for the womenfolk and children.

There were only two children, and both being girl children, they were of little account. The gods had evidently seen fit to punish the household for some transgression of the past. Thus two little boys, no older than three and five years of age, had died within two passes of the summer moon of the shaking swamp fever, which periodically rose from the reedbeds to the south. Bagtu-Shar had only two wives, one of whom he had been betrothed to as a very young man, rather a boy than a man. She had been a friend of his mother and a widow. She was much older than he, and at any stage of their marriage, she was more a mother to him than a wife. She had done her wifely duty by him, though, but he had never loved her, albeit he respected her judgment and appreciated her wisdom. She was the mother of his two little girls and the two little dead boys, but was now an old woman beyond the age of bearing another child.

Bagtu-Shar's second wife, Ahnaputta, was a bond woman, sold to him by her family for the money he could give them to keep them from starvation. She was young and pretty, but her family and connections were low. Bagtu-Shar was fond of her, and she was a strong worker, but after four years of living under his roof, she had never shown any signs of being able to conceive a child. Often Bagtu-Shar felt greatly tempted to put her away from him, but then he reconsidered; she was, after all, a good worker and suited him well at night.

But there was no denying the fact that Bagtu-Shar felt the passing of his days. The need for a family, at least for one male child, weighed heavily on his mind. The only thing keeping him back from acquiring another wife was the lack of space in the women's room. With two women, two children, and all the household furnishings, the weaving frame, the meat-drying rack, the yarn-dying wat, there was barely any room left for the sleeping mats. And although Bagtu-Shar preferred to spend his nights on the roof with Ahnaputta, there were many winter days when the wind screamed off the mountains down into the city so that rooftop-sleeping became impossible.

Then sadly, but also most fortuitously, one morning, Bagtu-Shar found his first wife curled up on her mat in the women's room. He—as he was accustomed—had spent the night on the roof with his second wife who, in the morning, had clambered down the ladder leaning against the side of the building to start the fire in the kitchen room. Bagtu-Shar had descended to the sleeping room to wash his face, clean his teeth and nostrils, and trim his beard before facing the day. That was when he noticed that his first wife did not seem to move or breathe. When he bent to wake her, he saw with much alarm that she had vomited during the night, and then after that, at some time, must have stopped breathing.

Bagtu-Shar was truly saddened by her death and arranged for a fitting funeral for her, paid for two mourning women to be in attendance and accompany her body to the funeral pyre, paid for expensive unguents to anoint her body, and paid for two priests to say the blessings over her burning body. Her two little daughters, wide-eyed with fright and wonder, stood shyly by the pyre, clutching Ahnaputta's skirts with their fingers in their mouths. The loss of their mother was much beyond their understanding, but because they heard the women wail and saw the tears on Ahnaputta's face, they started sobbing too so that Ahnaputta was fully occupied with comforting the little ones.

After the expected length of mourning, Bagtu-Shar went out in search of a woman who would be an appropriate choice for him to marry. By that he meant firstly that she should be from a house of good standing, for he had his own status to uphold in the city. Secondly, he thought that she should, if possible, be pretty and young, and—even more desirably—a virgin, albeit this was difficult without having to pay an exorbitant bride-price. Actually here was the rub, if a man wanted a virgin—and who didn't—then how did he know if she would be fertile? On the other hand, the knowledge of certain fertility precluded the demand for virginity—well, he thought with a sigh, life certainly did have its ways of presenting problems!

Once he had gotten this far in his contemplations, and also made same mental calculations about the extent to which he might wish to go with the bride-price and how much of a dowry to demand in turns, he set his mind to the task at hand. He contacted one of the neighborhood marriage brokers and laid out his case to her. After much enjoyable and stimulating haggling over costs and demands, in addition to the extent of the broker's fees, an agreement was struck, contingent upon the broker's services being delivered within the next three turns of the moon. Actually the marriage broker rather disliked those terms, finding them too confining. She kept insisting that to find real quality in a bride, as Bagtu-Shar seemed to demand, was a difficult and delicate assignment demanding more time. But Bagtu-Shar could not be dissuaded, and eventually the marriage broker, fearing that she might lose his business altogether, relented.

Following an anxious wait of several weeks, the marriage broker came and made her triumphant announcement. She had indeed found a worthy maiden, beautiful beyond imagination, virtuous, young, smiling, and from a first-class family, her father being a very minor functionary at the king, ruler of the Known World's, court. Very minor was emphasized repeatedly so as not to create false hopes or impressions, but nevertheless, the royal court, indeed! She was one of many sisters, her father's house was filled with children, and he himself was anxious to get several of his female children situated quickly. The young lady had an impeccable reputation, had hardly even been glimpsed by any man other than her father and her uncles. She was skilled in housework, dyed and wove exquisite cloth, had gracious and compliant manners, good teeth, and a sweet breath. Bagtu-Shar, hearing all this, was already enchanted, at least until he was told the bride-price.

Thereafter, a new round of discussion and haggling commenced with daily new offers and counteroffers. All this took weeks, until finally a hard-won agreement, more advantageous to Bagtu-Shar than the original one, won the day. Bagtu-Shar was pleased with his success, paid off the marriage broker, and made plans for bringing his future wife into the household. Ahnaputta quietly went about her work, tried as much as she could to clean the house and especially to embellish the women's room. Unfortunately it was the time of changeable weather, with occasional fiercely blowing icy gusts swooping down upon the city from the western mountains, only to die far to the south in the waves of the great river Tigris. Thus she decided to put up a pretty curtain, which she had woven especially for this occasion, to separate off a corner of the women's room for the privacy of the new couple. Bagtu-Shar was greatly pleased with Ahnaputta's inventiveness and, being already in a generous mood, added to his expenses by buying her a pretty hammered copper bracelet, similar to the ones which he was planning to give to his new wife.

Finally the great day of the marriage arrived and the transfer of the bride to her new home. Thanks mostly to Ahnaputta's labor, the house was spotless, there were even newly woven coverlets on the straw sleeping mats, the children wore freshly washed clothes and had their hair braided with pretty-colored yarn woven into the braids, and fragrant laurel branches and thyme leaves had been strewn everywhere upon the floors.

Bagtu-Shar was considered to be a handsome man. Like most of the men of the Land of Ashur, he was broad-shouldered and stocky in built, with muscular arms and thighs, flowing black hair, and a well-trimmed black beard of which he was very proud. He had a handsome open face with a ready smile, the gleaming white teeth of youth, a sensuous mouth, and limpid black eyes under long lashes and bushy brows. On this morning, he spent a long time washing his body and his hair and tried as best he could to rub all the grime of work from his hands. When all that he could had been done, he put on his best coat, which Ahnaputta had carefully rubbed with the fragrant petals of lemon and orange flowers dried during the last summer. He laced up his best pair of boots; it was also the only pair other than his daily work boots for winter. The ceremony of tying the bride's mantle to his wrist and the exchanging of bride-price and dowry were to occur when the sun was at its highest. After that, family and invited guests would stay at the bride's house where mats had been laid out for everyone's comfort, and a great cauldron of mutton—traditionally a gift from the groom—had been cooking on the fire all morning.

The groom, of course, in addition to Ahnaputta and his two little daughters, brought his family of brothers, uncles, cousins, nephews, and all the womenfolk who belonged to these. There had been much worrying on the part of the bride's family about how to accommodate even a small part of such a crowd of people. The bride's father had gone to a priest of Ashur to ask for a small sacrifice and some prayers, all that he could afford, to be performed with the request for good weather. Much to his joy and the surprise of the priest, who judged the payment for the request to be too niggardly to be worthy of Ashur's attention, the day began and ended with weak sunshine, a lovely breeze, and a beautiful cloudless blue sky.

The feast, laid out the whole length of the alley in front of the bride's house, did not break up until sunset. By that time, most of the men were drunk and staggering. However, this only increased the value of the event, signifying that no amount of beer had been spared from the revelers. All the guests who could still walk accompanied the groom, and all the women scurried to form a circle about the bride. Thus with the beating of drums and much singing and dancing, the bride and her belongings, strapped to a donkey's back, were brought to the home of her new husband. There everyone threw flower petals in their direction and implored the gods for the young wife's fertility.

As the festive group arrived at Bagtu-Shar's house, the groom, glowing with beer and pride, grabbed his wife and lifted her high up while she shrieked and laughed and, kicking the air, hung on to his thick neck for dear life. Amid hooting and yelling from everyone, he swung her around twice and then ran into the house, most likely afraid that if he delayed his exit, someone would surely play a joke on him. Along with all others of his culture, he was endlessly conscious of the need to save face in public and was not inclined to take any chances in that respect. By then, Bagtu-Shar was laughing and yelling as well and did not stop running until he reached the women's room and dropped his prized new wife onto the sleeping mat. As quickly as he could, he pulled Ahnaputta's new curtains across the doorway.

*****

Sargon, Great Ruler of the Known World, was watching his elite troops practice war games on the Field of Heroes, a huge levelled area south of the city proper, designed for just this purpose. The field was large enough to accommodate many soldiers all at one time, along with chariots, warhorses, and war camels. He wore his beautifully worked engraved breastplate of small pieces of ivory and polished metal fastened together with chain links decorated in precious stones over a cream-colored wool tunic, with an intricately knotted fringe. The armor was designed mostly for effect rather than protection, and the king would never have dreamt of wearing it into battle. His shield lay at his sandaled feet and his sword across his knees. He was watching the exercises intently and with apparent enjoyment, occasionally stretching out his arm so that his cupbearer could freshly refill his bowl with wine.

The king was in a mellow mood. The land, for the time being, was quiet, and no new campaigns loomed in the immediate future, which allowed his army to become better honed by exercises such as these conducted today. His days were mostly filled with audiences and legal matters, or in consultation with his architects concerning further plans for Dur-Sharrukin, his beloved city. His nights were filled with pleasure. He could not have dreamt that the addition of one small person to his House of Women could add such passion to his life. The thought of Himene put a tentative smile on his face, and he shifted his weight on his chair to hide his body's sudden response to the thought of her.

He was not a man of great introspection or sensitivity, and certainly to analyze the nature of a woman—any woman—would hardly have crossed his mind. All the same, he had to admit that she was a puzzle to him. As promised, he went to her bed every night, and every night she quietly awaited him, deferential and submissive, but without ever showing either joy or displeasure at his approach. He did not think that she feared him any longer, but he sensed that she feared his lovemaking or, at least, shied away from it. What excited him each night was to observe this reticent passive young woman slowly respond to him and then watch the escalation of her response into full-blown passion.

That night, when he arrived at the House of Women later than usual, he found Himene in her chamber, sitting on the edge of the bed, looking more forlorn and dejected than he had ever seen her before. When he entered, she rose in greeting and tried to put on a smile as she furtively wiped her eyes, but Sargon, never a man to favor evasiveness or delicacy about any matter that needed his attention, strode to her side with a few quick steps, grasped her elbows, and pulled her down next to him on the couch. He felt puzzled, worried, and displeased all at the same time. It had been a long and active day; he was tired, and the last thing he was prepared for was to deal with a woman's tears.

"Himene," he said with some irritation, "what is this? What has made you so unhappy today?"

She tried to hide her face with its telltale sign of tears from him, but he caught her chin into his big hand and forced her to face him. Her eyes were closed, and her mouth trembled. "It is nothing, lord," she murmured. "Pray be not concerned about me."

He creased his forehead, the dark eyebrows two thick lines above stormy eyes. "Himene, listen," he said. "No one cries without reason, except maybe a fool. Now I know that you are no fool. Often I have observed that you appear to be unhappy. Your unhappiness can stem from homesickness, but thousands of women confront that and conquer their feelings, or else it comes from revulsion to me. I know that that is not so. Although your welcome of me is not happy, when we make love you do respond to me with such abandon, as I believe cannot be acting. But there is something to make you languish, and I must know what it is. No one would dare to mistreat you or even to treat you with less than great courtesy. I trust I have not mistreated you. But there is this, I have never seen you be joyful, to laugh, or even to smile with genuine pleasure. You control your tears, except for tonight, but in everything you do, happiness is lacking. What ails you, lady, what complaint do you have? Remember how I told you on the day you arrived here that from that day on, I shall be the source of all your comfort. Tell me, I will know."

Himene tuned her head away from him and said in a barely audible voice, her two clasped hands pressed between her knees, "Oh, my lord, forgive me, but I am so ashamed! Forgive me! My behavior must seem shameful to you. Before I left home, my father came to talk to me most seriously about my duties to you and to my new country. At home, you see, my lord, women live much freer than here. We do not have a separate house for women or eunuchs, and we often talk openly with the men of our family and even express opinions occasionally. But my father instructed me that in the Land of Ashur, women are expected to be subservient to all the men and most especially their husbands. But above that, women should be quiet and unassuming so as not to call attention to them. Most particularly he told me—and those were the only instructions he ever gave me—that when my husband would—wished—is—visiting me, I should at all times accept this—honor—quietly and chastely, and…and…I was…I am…I have not been able to do that. I beg you, my lord, to forgive me"—and at that, her lower lip began to tremble perilously again while tears started coursing down her cheeks—"and…" She gave a great sob without being able to finish her sentence.

Himene wanted nothing as much as to rise and run somewhere where she could hide and cry to her heart's content, but Sargon's two hands were upon her arms and forced her to remain seated. He was not sure if what he heard should anger or amaze him; this was, in fact, a confession of such unexpected nature that at the end, he found it only laughable. How in the name of all the gods, he thought, could anyone give such a foolish advice to an unsuspecting young woman and such an account of his country? Was there any country that would think this way? What kind of a fool did she have for a father?

He sighed and, still holding her hands in his, said as patiently as he could, "My child"—he had never called her that before, but now he somehow felt older than her by generations—"how could you—how would you want to believe that I—that any man—enjoys a silent and motionless woman to lie beneath him like a lumpen mat filled with straw? Love is designed by the Lord Ashur for the delight of the husband, certainly, but, if possible, also for the delight of the woman who is loved. The gods, in fact, charge us with the responsibility to satisfy the wishes of our spouses, to receive and give love with equal generosity. I cannot imagine that such misleading ideas about my land and my people could exist anywhere! Your father has indeed done me wrong and, my dear, you as well. When you respond to me, to my loving you, surely that is a glorious thing! It pleases me, and when it pleases you also, it flatters me by pleasing you. Do you understand what I am saying, Himene? Please abandon your foolish guilt planted into your heart and brain by a foolish man, be he your father. Why he did this, I do not know, nor do I care, but I do care, my dear, that your life here should be as pleasing to you as possible. The people of my land may say about me that I am demanding, hard, and willful. So it may be, but always remember that I am not lacking in understanding where deserved. Since the day I met you, lady, I have found no reason to fault you or to be displeased with you. Let that be enough to calm you. Go and wash your face, and when you come back to me, we shall commence with what should have begun when I arrived. Go!"

After that, there was an almost immediate transformation in Himene's behavior. She became visibly more at ease, the tense hunted look she wore before, and which Sargon had thought was an expression natural to her, disappeared slowly, and when he made her a gift of a pair of small caged songbirds, she laughed with pleasure, hugged him spontaneously and then, mortified by her own bravery, begged his pardon. This astonished him to no small degree and gave him great satisfaction. It was the first time he had seen her not just to smile but to actually laugh.

A few nights later, for the first time, she surprised him once again. That morning he had exercised his throwing arm with his javelin at targets set up at various distances, and when he missed the closest target, a small stone flew up high through the air to hit his forehead. The damage and pain were minimal, but the small cut bled copiously—as head wounds will always do—and looked more menacing than the danger it presented to him. When he entered her chamber, she of course immediately noticed the wound and inquired with concern whether it hurt a great deal. He just laughed and shook his head but saw her eyes straying to his face again and again, as she followed his motions of undressing. When he came and stretched himself out next to her, she reached hesitantly toward the wound and stroked it with great gentleness. It was the first intimate physical contact that she initiated, and Sargon was curiously moved by it. After making love to her, he held her gently for a long time and talked to her of this and that, little events in his day's flow, and asked her about how her day had passed. None of what was said by either of them was of any great consequence, but he sensed her relax as he had not sensed before and was pleased by their mutual closeness.

In the House of Women, a place of constant watchfulness and idle gossip, it had been said for a good while that the Great Ruler of the Known World had, at least for the moment, a passion for his recently acquired queen-to-be. Those who had lived there for a long time attached no great significance to this, having, on occasion, seen the great king's passions flare and wane with equal speed. The Lady Himene was generally liked, for she was thoughtful and courteous but too uncommunicative and remote for any of the women to form a closer friendship with her. Perhaps the fact that she was probably destined to become queen and the mother of the next heir also inhibited real closeness with her.

Then unexpectedly, one day, it was as though a door opened to her soul. She began to talk to the others, first haltingly, then with more animation. She remained reserved as before, but there was an unmistakable change in her comportment and a newfound animation in her manner. The ladies began to realize that she was making great efforts to fit in and become a part of the community. Those ladies, who had born sons to the king but who were not entitled to be called lady of the house and wife of the king, by virtue of the fact that they were not royal-born women, had most reason to dislike the new arrival, for they also had the most to lose. They had great vested interests in the persons of their sons. Foremost among them was the Lady Atalyā. Her eldest son, Sennacherib, firstborn of the king's sons, just growing out of boyhood, had been shown favors by his father and had good reason to expect to be named his heir.

The Lady Atalyā had been brought into the House of Women as a gift from Marduk-apla-iddina of Babylon as part of the peace treaty between the two nations. She became well favored by King Sargon and had already produced two male children by the time of Himene's arrival. She had hoped in the past to be chosen mother of the heir. But albeit she had been selected by the King Marduk-apla-iddina personally as his gift to Sargon, she was not of royal lineage, and in no uncertain terms, the Great King had told her to abandon her hopes unless no future royal heir could be produced by another lady of the court, who had a more exalted lineage. Brought up in the harem at the court of Babylon, it was second nature to her to submit to her lord's wish. Never for a moment did she demur, as much as she was disappointed when Himene arrived and was pointed out to her as the king's chosen future lady of the house and wife of the king. Her acceptance opened a path for a tentative friendship between the two women. In many small ways, Lady Atalyā helped Himene to become settled and more familiar with the customs of the House of Women, not a gesture appreciated by her son Sennacherib. He, in fact, started to nurture a deep-rooted mistrust of Himene. The reason for the king's choice of another woman to become first wife had, of course, never been made known to him, even though he suspected; but he fully understood that the king was law unto himself and not accountable to anyone.

At this same time of blossoming and ebbing allegiances in the House of Women, with each passing day, a cloud of uneasiness descended more and more persistently upon Himene. There was no one she could talk to about this, certainly not to any of the women; and even more so, she shied away to talk to the king. She knew well that he was aware and, without saying a word, was counting the days and looking at her with a question in his eyes each time they met. They were approaching the end of the two-month period he had allotted to her to become pregnant. She really did not know if that was a generous length of time or not. There were, at this time, no recent pregnancies in the House of Women; actually no one had seen the king come and visit any of the women there since Himene's arrival, and so she felt that she could not ask any questions without arousing curiosity or laughter about her obvious ignorance.

She needed not to have worried because the king, always direct, not knowing or caring who he upset by his directness, brought up this very subject the next night when he strode into her chamber. He looked irritated and out of sorts, his brows lowered, and his eyelids half-closed so that nobody should discern his mood by looking into his eyes. When Himene rose and bowed to him, he nodded to her briefly, then sat down onto his favorite cushioned chair with a groan. It was just before he sat that Himene noticed the slight limp caused by favoring his left leg. She ran to him quickly and squatted in front of him. She looked up at him with concern and begged him to tell her what happened. But the king just waved his hand, as though waving away a pesky fly. "Nothing worth mentioning, lady," he muttered and threw his head back against the cushions, closing his eyes with a sigh. "I am tired," he added as an afterthought. "This is not your concern, lady," he added again for good measure.

It was to the Lady Himene's credit that she stood her ground, although her inclinations would have made her retreat. But she swallowed her fear and wordlessly reached up for the king's hand. She could only manage to hold one of his large hands in two of hers, but it was enough. She raised it to her face and, as he had done to her, laid his palm against her cheek.

Taking the final grain of courage, she whispered, "My dearest lord, you cannot ask me not to feel when you are hurt, not to worry about your health or your pain! I beg you, please tell me so that I can be of aid to you. If you must walk, lean on me, if you wish for anything, tell me!"

This finally elicited a snort and a chuckle. He pulled his hand away from hers and took her face between his palms. "Himene, my dear, you would collapse if I ever leaned my weight on you!" The thought must have amused him because he chuckled again, ruffling the hair on top of her head. "It is really nothing. I just stepped the wrong way and twisted my foot. It will heal in two or three days. But it distresses me to notice that my body is betraying me more and more frequently." He looked away into the distance, into the darkness of the night showing between the curtains. "I am becoming old, Himene," he said simply. "My allotted length of time is beginning to run out." The words fell like heavy drops into the silence, and when they vanished, the silence continued. "I need a son, Himene. I need a son most urgently. I don't want him to be anyone else's but yours, Himene. I have sons by other women, but I want a son of mine of your royal blood to follow me when I die. Understand?" He clutched her shoulders and almost shook her. "A son, Himene, give me a son!"

Then his desperate mood passed, and he released her shoulders, pulling her close to his body and rocking her like a child.

"Well, well! Never mind, lady, never mind! It is early days. It will happen soon. I will breed many children upon you, my dear, wait any see…many! And they will be beautiful, like their mother, and strong and shrewd, like their father, you'll see!" He waited for a minute in silence, then rose and stretched himself, bent down and lifted her as though she weighed nothing. He walked over to the bed and dropped her onto the cushions. In two short motions, he rid himself of his coat and kicked off his sandals, then sat down by her side. He placed his large warm hand upon her belly, spreading his fingers. "Soon, you hear, soon!" he murmured, bending to kiss her mouth.

*****

Five bowshots from the palace, Bagtu-Shar, stonecutter in the king's employ, felt like walking on air. He wore an almost-new coat and brand-new boots made of the soft leather of the mouflon, the sure-footed sheep of the mountains. These treasures came to him through his wife's dowry, of which he had used just a little bit to improve his own lot. And look! After wantonly spending good coins on himself and causing a good deal of guilt for himself, just two days later, he received a new commission from the architect in charge of designing the inlay plaques for the new Hall of Ambassadors, right next to the palace itself. So much good fortune worried him; he felt that he was unworthy of it and that the gods were, in some way, testing his piety. Piety equated money; he made a reluctant mental note to visit the temple and make a small donation for the Lord God Ashur. This decision somehow took the edge off his unease so that he could contemplate the other great fortune which had just been revealed to him. His new wife, Enheduanna, who had now shared his sleeping mat for no more than three months, had just told him that she was with child. She also assured him that the child, without doubt, was a male child; she could feel it in her insides with certainty.

Such a sudden shower of good fortune was enough to intimidate anyone. Bagtu-Shar hardly knew what to do next. His first inclination was to go to the temple and drop a small bag of coins into the priests' waiting hands. Then again, he felt that one should be more practical and go to seek out the honorable architect through whose intercession his latest assignment had come, not just to seek him out and thank him but to inquire more specifically as to what exactly was expected of him. But because he was so elated, he finally decided that this day warranted a celebration, and so his feet took him first to the modest tavern just around the corner from the alley on which his house was situated.

Fortunately Bagtu-Shar had still enough common sense left to resist any inducements to stay even after drinking a large pitcher of beer. He rose and remembered that he needed to talk to the architect of the building project in order to be able to start his work in the morning. As it turned out, it was a major commission—the largest and probably most important one of Bagtu-Shar's life so far. Given the general outlines of the assignment, he was free to make designs as it appeared to his mind's eye, and only before the design was to be chiseled permanently into the stone was he required to obtain final permission to proceed. Such trust from higher-ups was unprecedented and documented to Bagtu-Shar that the work he had done so far was valued. He knew if he did well, it would cement his standing, not just as a stonecutter but, most importantly, as a design artist.

It was well known that the Lord Sargon, Great Ruler of the Known World, had an appreciation for finer things and a great desire to mold his city of Dur-Sharrukin into a center of culture, architecture, literature, and art to equal or outshine any other place of magnificence, including the fabled cities of Nineveh and Babylon. To become a designer of decorations on an important building was enough to make Bagtu-Shar's heart race and his head spin. After his conversation with Adad-Nirani, the architect who was proposing and would be overseeing his work, Bagtu-Shar felt quite dizzy and had to squat down on his haunches for a while before the racing of his heart and the spinning of his head subsided.

Eventually he recovered and wanted—as anyone would have—to tell his good fortune to those willing to listen. At first his feet took him toward his house, but then he reconsidered; there were only women and children there, no one who would really appreciate or even understand the significance of what had just happened to him today. Thus he retraced his steps to the same tavern he had visited earlier in the morning, installed himself onto the best seat between two open windows, where the breeze would cool his sweating body, and where he had the attention of all who were present, as well as those who were just entering. He spent the rest of the day in pleasant discussions of what his artistic prowess would yet produce for all the world to admire.

When Bagtu-Shar finally wove his way home, he found that rather than expect him with joy and praise, Enheduanna felt ill and, according to his two little daughters, had been unable to eat all day long. Of course, he knew that he had no reason to expect a welcome other than what he received on any day of his life; none of his family knew as yet of his fortunate assignment. The children had already had their meal, and obviously Enheduanna was not anxious to eat anything. Ahnaputta went quietly about ladling gruel into a bowl for him, adding some small pungent roasted greens to it and serving it to her husband, along with some crumbled goat cheese. The latter she regularly prepared from the milk of the goat housed in a lean-to in the corner of their walled garden.

By this time, Bagtu-Shar was properly famished and exhausted from all the day's events. He took the food gratefully from Ahnaputta's hands and, leaning his head against one of the posts that helped to support the roof, ate his food with relish. When he was done, he rose, went out to the well in the back to wash the food from his fingers, and, to refresh, wash his face as well. Finally he went to the corner of the garden to relieve himself. After all that, he was truly ready for sleep when it occurred to him that one more action was missing from this day's celebrations. So he looked about himself, and finally his eyes found Ahnaputta in the front room, putting all the dishes away on a shelf built into the wall. He gestured to her, and she nodded wordlessly, finished what she was doing, and climbed up the ladder to the roof after her husband.

When he had settled himself on his sleeping mat and pulled the second sleeping mat close, Ahnaputta knelt down on it and, while kneeling, looked at her husband with a prolonged silent searching look. "There is something on your mind, husband, which has put your emotions in disarray. Forgive me, and silence me if you wish, but I ask you humbly, are you unhappy? Are you happy? I cannot tell. If you wish, please unburden yourself!" That having been said, she cowered down on her mat, with her face turned to Bagtu-Shar, her two hands supporting her head, and waited in silence.

Bagtu-Shar was reminded that he had always appreciated her quiet nature which, he found now with the surprise of a revelation, had never failed to soothe his emotions. He turned to her and slowly, because he was not accustomed to speak to an inferior person about his own affairs, gave her an account of the events of his day. The more he talked, the bigger Ahnaputta's eyes and her smile became, until finally, very much against accepted custom, she threw her arms about him and pulled his head close to her.

She did not dare to kiss his mouth without his permission, but she kissed his cheeks and his forehead and then his hands, one by one, and murmured joyously, "Oh, my master, my husband! How happy this makes me! Seeing you come home looking quite not your usual self, I worried that there was bad news, neh? And then this wonderful event! You are truly a master of your art, and this is much deserved. At the same time, many a person never receives what they justly should! This is such wonderful news, indeed, and if you allow, I shall prepare a special meal of goat meat for you and all the family tomorrow. I have saved some little money from my daily shopping, thinking that the children may need new sandals, but that certainly can wait, the summer is upon us..."

She finally ran out of breath so that she had to stop. But she continued to look at him with brightly shining eyes. Bagtu-Shar thought that he had never heard her string this many words together, and that had made him laugh. He grabbed her hands while laughing, and then she had to laugh also, and he hugged and kissed her and made love to her with more affection and tenderness than he had ever done in the past.

During the next few months, Bagtu-Shar's affection for his second wife grew gradually and imperceptibly. All his life, he was conditioned to accept certain tenets of life—at least the kind of life he and his friends led—on the borderline of trading marginal living for the beginnings of affluence. They were the young new generation who took advantage of the great king's enthusiasm for culture, opulence, and grandiose building, worked in the trades or commerce, and could afford the luxury of a larger home and a larger family. They were the dwellers in the big cities that had more than one wife, even though the second wife was little more than a servant woman. But the unchanging tenet of this arrangement was that the first wife, the lady of the house, was the mother of the legitimate heir and first in the husband's regard. By this very arrangement, she had to be of higher birth, more refinement and wealth than any other women in the house.

Bagtu-Shar was not a pioneer in social behavior. For him to first realize, and then to accept the fact that Ahnaputta was a great deal more likeable, useful, and diligent person, in fact the first woman in his house, except in name only, took many days and weeks. The first realization occurred when he saw Enheduanna's response to the tale of his great good fortune. She was still not feeling well enough and suffering all the adverse effects of early pregnancy, but still. She had just looked at him with her lovely limpid black eyes, sighed, and nodded wordlessly, and then turned to Ahnaputta, requesting to give her some fresh fruit. Bagtu-Shar, until then, had lived on a cloud of enchantment by anything his first wife did. Suddenly he found it irritating that Enheduanna should importune Ahnaputta, who was cooking the family supper, when the bowl of figs sat within an arm's reach of her.

Other events of the same nature followed in quick succession. Bagtu-Shar tried his level best to ignore them, especially since he knew from earlier experience about the mood swings of pregnant ladies. His main pleasure after a long and invariably stressful and tiring day of work was to relinquish the sleeping chamber to Enheduanna and the children and take refuge on the rooftop, whenever the weather permitted, where Ahnaputta would join him after finishing her chores. Often he was too tired for sex and suspected that she was too. On such occasions, they would just companionably lie next to each other, enjoying the warmth of each other's bodies, and quietly discuss all the events of the day, both his at work and hers at the house, and make plans for the next day or week. He discovered that she very much loved to study the night sky and actually knew a great deal about the great clusters of stars above their heads, many of which she could readily identify by name. When he showed amazement at this talent, she explained that her father, a very poor man, was well educated, having been in the service of one of the palace library scribes as a child, and that he, in turn, had taught her as a little girl.

It was a revelation to Bagtu-Shar that one could spend time in conversation with a mere woman and that such a one would be of use in ways other than those for which the gods had created them. As the days and weeks of Enheduanna's pregnancy progressed and limited his physical intimacy with her, he learned to value Ahnaputta's company more and more. He was not a stupid man, and slowly it became abundantly clear to him that however enticing the attributes of beauty and playful sexuality might be in a woman, they were not the true source of a man's and his family's welfare and contentment.

This was a happy time for Bagtu-Shar. His family was increasing, and by ignoring Enheduanna's acid tongue and almost constant complaining, they had achieved a fair degree of domestic tranquility. His work gave him much satisfaction. To stress the importance of his work, he would not stop to complain, to anyone willing to listen, about his newly acquired grave responsibility. At the same time, he loved to repeat the praises coming from his superiors. He felt healthy, young, and vigorous. Life was wonderful and full of promise.

*****

The third course of the moon through the heavens had passed since the arrival of the new bride for the Great Ruler of the Known World. Summer was in full swing and the heat almost unbearable throughout the city. The only relief was to be found outdoors in the gardens where the great king had caused pools, waterfalls, and fountains to be laid. He had seen these in Babylon after he had laid siege to that city and forced King Marduk-apla-iddina to flee into the great swamps to the south. Sargon was much taken by the beauty of the conquered city. After he had himself declared the new king of Babylonia, he actually remained there for a length of several years. Ever the observant and shrewd ruler, with an avid taste for beauty and comfort, he ordered the designers of his new city of Dur-Sharrukin to have many gardens with great shade trees everywhere and, in those, to have many flowing waters and pools with waterfalls.

Himene, who had felt sluggish and unwell for the last few days, spent most of her days outdoors, under the shade of the big trees on the north side of the House of Women. In a kind of semitorpor, she dozed or listened to the splashing of the water and watched the fishes flit by, as though they were streaks of silver. The cool breeze from the mountains occasionally ruffled her veil or the hem of her dress. Birds screeched raucously from the treetops, and everywhere the persistent high-pitched chirps of nestlings eager to be fed could be heard. From far, far away, at the other side of the palace complex, she could hear the weak sound of horses neighing. Sargon had told her that the new young stallions of the royal stables were to be taught to carry riders or to draw war chariots. This, he explained to her, was a most important, crucial, and difficult training, which often lasted many weeks and where the occasional loss of human life had to be expected.

She had looked at him with genuine fear, for she had, by degrees, learned to care for him and was most grateful for his kindnesses to her. She also felt closer to him because he talked to her about events of his daily life and explained many things to her, which she otherwise would not have known. On this particular day, though, Sargon had just laughed at her fears, that somewhat superior laugh of a male who feels called upon to appease the worries of his women.

"Dear lady, this body has felt more bones broken, backside kicked by horses' hooves, nose bloodied, and ribs fractured than you would ever be able to count. It is a part of what I am. It is part of who I am. My army respects me because I do not pull back from danger and participate with the best of them. There is no need to worry. But if you wish, say a prayer to the gods that your husband will not approach your bed tonight with a limp." And he turned and walked away from her, still laughing.

In the evening, Himene ordered a lukewarm cooling bath for herself in hopes that the bath would alleviate her sluggishness and bodily discomforts. While her servants were drying her, she allowed her mind to wander. Since she had arrived in the Land of Ashur, she had never felt homesickness and was grateful for that. Numerous ladies at her father's palace were given to him from foreign countries, and she knew that many of them suffered from homesickness for years. That she had not encountered the same fate was, she thought, due to her lord's concern and affection for her. She had to confess to herself, that the dread which had almost overcome her in the beginning, whenever she saw Sargon or whenever he touched her, had disappeared. She looked forward to his late visits, not just to their intimacy but to the slowly blossoming companionship between them. At one time, he had told her that this was something new and not altogether unpleasant for him, and that—as he said—unburdening his thoughts and emotions to her before the sleep of night had made him sleep better.

Occupied with such contemplations, she dawdled so long over her bath that she had barely put on her lightweight wool shift of soft green, the color of jade, before she heard the familiar quick footsteps outside the half-open door. Her ladies were just able to gather up their pots of scents and creams and scamper out the back-door, which led to the other areas of the House of Women, when the lord king entered. She bowed to him but then could not resist giving him a quick glance, followed by a joyous smile. "No limping for you tonight, I see, my lord. All the horses must have been well behaved!"

"That is so, lady," he agreed. "Either your prayers were very effective, or all the horses of my stables have become lambs. Whatever is the cause, the result is such that I am anxious to prove to you how the daylong sun has not sapped all my strength. But I am mightily thirsty. Join me in a cup of wine, my dear." And with that, he walked to a low table on which several jugs of wine were kept embedded in snow brought down from the mountains to the king's table by relay runners. He poured two cups, took a long draught from one, and gave the other to Himene. She usually enjoyed sharing some wine with him, but today, as soon as the smell of fermented grape juice struck her nostrils, she shuddered and turned her head away.

"Not today, please," she whispered weakly and swallowed the saliva which unexpectedly filled her mouth. "I have no desire for it," she added in an even lower whisper. Since she had turned her head, she did not notice Sargon's expression. With eyebrows raised and eyes that seemed able to look through flesh and bone, he scrutinized her carefully. When he talked again, it was not a conversational request but a command.

"Himene, sit down." She had learned that tone of voice and, in some alarm, sat on the edge of the large bed. The king stood before her, frowning, then sat down as well next to her, trying to look less severe.

"Lady," he asked, as always choosing directness above courtesy, "when did you bleed last?"

Himene almost dropped the wine-filled goblet she still held and looked at him fearfully.

"How…how do you know such things?" she stammered, her eyes wide open with anxiety. "What are you saying? What do you mean?"

Sargon was greatly amused.

"Oh, you little lamb, you!" He laughed, throwing his head back. "Over three times a hundred women in my house, and you are amazed that I know? How so, lady? Think of it! And now answer my question, truly and quickly, because I am overcome with the need to know!"

Himene obediently started counting on her fingers. "I think about three changes of the moon from fat to thin or thin to fat, my lord, maybe a little more," she said shyly, still not quite sure what this was all about. Sargon watched her intently.

"And tell me, lady, have you eaten well lately?" To this she just made a grimace.

"Oh, no, my lord. I would best like to just turn and run away from food." She felt somehow guilty, as though her lack of appetite would displease her husband. Much to her surprise, it did just the opposite. He chuckled again and, standing up, looked down on her with a sparkle in his eyes.

"Truly," he said, still greatly amused, "you are a little lamb! Or sillier even than a little lamb. Do you not know that you are with child? You are carrying the next royal infant and," he added with mock severity, "woe be to you if it turns out to be less than a princeling!" And, without letting her form an answer, picked her up, as though she were indeed nothing more than a lambkin, and deposited her upon their great bed. In seconds, he had shrugged off his wrap and, kneeling over her, commenced to kiss her with as much tenderness as he had ever exhibited to her before.

"Ah, yes." He breathed softly into her ear. "A princeling from my Phrygian princess. Imagine! Finally!" His kisses continued until she had to beg him to stop because she was becoming breathless and dizzy.

*****

The young prince Sennacherib, firstborn son and presumed heir to the throne of the Great Ruler of the Known World, was, at this time, growing up in the House of War, attached to the main palace building by a long columned covered walkway. He was learning the art of being a soldier and a leader of the army. His days, from early dawn to night, were full and fatiguing and his sleep short. He was quite aware that his august father, whom he saw only on rare occasions, had acquired a new wife who, after their marriage, was to become the first lady of the House of Women. This did not disturb him too much because both he and his mother had known that that position, which had once belonged to the Lady Neghanna before her death, by the king's decree, was reserved for a lady of royal birth. This fact, he trusted, was unconnected to his own status as first son and heir. He reassured himself that he was, after all, the oldest of the king's sons, and while the king paid no close attention at all to any of his other sons, he did occasionally summon Sennacherib to ask him about his progress in the House of War. He had no particular dislike for Himene, only a sense of latent distrust. He had only seen her briefly on the day of her arrival in Dur-Sharrukin, and he judged her, even in his childish way, to be most beautiful, indeed.

This particular day was destined to become one deeply etched into his mind. It had started like all the other days since he had entered the House of War—with training exercises which quickly became exhausting in the searing heat of the summer. There was a short break from the toil when all the young men were allowed to rest for a while in the shade of some old trees and to eat and drink from the food and the fresh water offered up for their noonday meal. Sennacherib, who had a more exalted position than any of the others, was allowed to have a personal slave, whose main occupation was to give the young master lengthy and very expert massages in the evenings before going to sleep. The slave, named Empyades, who had been born on the island of Cyprus, was evidently expert in his work, and for this, he was much treasured by the young prince. Today Empyades had gone abroad in search of a special leaf found in shady and boggy areas which, cooked to soften them, pounded and ground to a paste and then mixed with the oil secreted by the fruit of certain palm trees, had the power to ease his master's sore muscles. Empyades had just returned from his search and squatted on the dusty ground, intermittently casting such glances at Sennacherib, which he instantly recognized as meaningful. Empyades had found out something which he thought important enough to impart to his master before the evening hour.

Sennacherib rose and sauntered over to the cooking fire to refill his bowl. On the way, he looked toward Empyades and, with a slight gesture of his head, indicated that he wanted his slave to attend to him. Empyades scuttled over to his master and, squatting down on his heels, proceeded to impart his just-acquired daily dose of palace gossip to Sennacherib. It seemed that the House of Women had been thrown into an uproar over the news that the future queen, the Lady Himene, had conceived a child by the Lord Sargon. It was, of course, well known that the king desired to be assured of the fertility of the lady before the royal marriage would take place. In the minds of many, there was, of course, no doubt that this would happen, especially considering the passion which the Great Ruler of the Known World had for this latest woman in his house. The opposing camp, however, maintained that a man's passion and virility were still no guarantee for conception.

"Of course, of course, Master, at this time, only the gods would know if the Lady Himene's pregnancy will result in a birth and if that birth will be a male child or not? But still, but still, one must consider, my master, that all that may happen. Of course, of course, by the time that male child would grow up, many things can and will undoubtedly occur, my master. Also consider, Master, that by then, you will be a fully grown adult warrior, the leader of the army, and probably the leader of this nation as well. Still if you would permit me to speak my mind, kindest and greatest of all young masters, you should, as much as possible, strengthen your ties to your august father, who is lord and ruler over all of us…"

And when he noticed that Sennacherib wanted to interject some thought of his own into this unending flow of words, he just raised his voice and his hands for emphasis. "Your father is accustomed to be the provider of all good things to his sons, for in truth, where would young men receive everything that makes their lives pleasant but from their father? It would probably cause great pleasure to your august father if you could give him something in return, some work of your own hands that he could look at and say, 'Ah, this came from my grateful son, it is the labor of his hands and, as such, a labor of his heart, showing love and gratitude.' Something to be cherished by him, because it would remind him of his beloved firstborn son…" And with that, Empyades allowed his voice to trail off for better effect.

Thus were the first seeds of jealousy and dislike sown into the heart of young Sennacherib. During his following short time of growing from boy to young adult, these feelings, well-watered and fertilized by Empyades, would grow and blossom with abandon. He became obsessed with the new queen-to-be and tortured himself with imagining varied events, which would rob him of the current status he held, as well as his father's regard. He did, however, agree with Empyades that in some way, he needed to ingratiate himself to Sargon and call his presence more emphatically to his father's attention.

And then luck—should it even be called that—provided him a way to achieve his goal, albeit not exactly in the fashion he had envisioned.

Ever since entering the House of War, he had become one of the best chariot drivers among the young students. By inclination, he had already been a horseman before he started his actual training. As a child growing up in the House of Women, he had spent as much of his time as he could, and was allowed, hanging around the paddocks and horse stables. To be finally permitted to deal with horses, both for riding and for driving, the chariot was, for him, a glorious continuation of this interest.

On this particular morning, Sennacherib, together with a smallish group of his classmates, were taken to the large oval training area for chariot races. The area had a hard-beaten earthen track which allowed for two chariots to either run in one direction side by side, or in opposing directions. Since the students had already mastered control of the horses abreast at full gallop, on this morning, for the first time, they were to run one each in opposite direction against one another. This was a crucial exercise since it taught the fundamentals of what would occur in battle with two facing chariots.

When the lots were drawn the crown prince was matched with a young man a year older than Sennacherib but not nearly as adept at handling horses, let alone at full gallop. At the crucial moment, when the two chariots had to pass each other, coming from opposing directions at thundering speed, Sennacherib's opponent allowed the near wheel of his chariot to catch that of Sennacherib's. The two sets of warhorses suddenly pulled to an unexpected stop, screamed, and reared, and Sennacherib, who realized what was going to happen and tried to balance precariously to prevent his chariot from toppling over, was tumbled to the ground, his foot entangled in the lead line by which he guided his horse team. In a panic, his two horses surged ahead, pulling him along on the ground, and eventually smashing him against the roots and gnarled trunk of one of the trees which edged the oval of the training area. There he lay with a big gaping gash in his forehead and one leg broken, the ragged edge of the large leg bone sticking out through muscle and skin.

The uproar that this accident caused was endless, not for that one day only but for a whole sequence of days. The master of the House of War pronounced a sentence of death or castration upon the youth who had caused the accident. However, since the Lord Sargon was supreme commander of all troops, and also father of the injured, his permission had to be asked. The Great Ruler of the Known World once again showed his bent for kindness and clemency by allowing the young man to live and only sentencing him to castration.

At first no one knew if the crown prince would ever awaken from the deep faint which his head wound had caused. While he was borne back to the House of War, a runner was sent to his father. With great trepidation, the runner gave the grave news to the king, expecting the king's wrath to reach him before anyone else. But he escaped with no worse punishment than a black look and vicious kick. The king, who was conducting an audience with the turtanu, his second-in-command, immediately broke off the discussion, turned on his heel, and gave orders to summon his personal healer. In the healing powers of this man, a gift from the Pharaoh Sethos, Sargon had infinite trust. The knowledge of Egyptian healers was well known in general, but this particular one, named Akh-Merami, had proven his worth again and again whenever the great king suffered an injury.

As fast as he could walk, and without waiting for his bearers to carry him there, the king strode to the House of War to inspect his son's injuries for himself. Although he expressed no opinion or showed any emotion, it was obvious from his severe expression that he was gravely concerned. He knew better than to be in the healer's way, and thus once he had ascertained for himself how things were, he withdrew, giving strict orders that he was to be informed four times during the course of each day and night and, additionally, every time that there was a significant change in his son's condition.

For three days and two nights, the crown prince hovered at the edge of consciousness while Akh-Merami forced obscure concoctions into his mouth for him to swallow. Akh-Merami was especially concerned with the leg wound and fracture. He stressed to the king that extreme steps needed to be taken as soon as the king would allow because otherwise, the leg would begin to rot from the inside, and then only the act of cutting off the limb would save the prince's life. After a short hesitation, Sargon gave permission, mostly because he knew that the loss of a limb would permanently close the door to his son's progress as a soldier and to any likelihood of becoming the next ruler.

Thus the surgery was scheduled and proceeded to the greatest amazement of all those who watched. Akh-Merami needed to enlarge the wound caused by the fractured bone in order to cleanse it and cut away some of the tissue around the bone. Then the bone needed to be pushed back in place while two ropes were tied to Sennacherib's ankle and hip to stretch the injured leg sufficiently in order to fit the bone back to where it belonged. Finally the ends of the two bones were firmly bound together with strong ties made out of the clean-scraped and boiled intestines of hogs. No one had ever witnessed such a remarkable healing act before in all the Land of Ashur. Everyone, however, agreed that it was fortuitous that the young prince was not yet conscious and spared the awareness of such agony. The whole procedure was so greatly admired and magical that upon hearing of it, Sargon summoned Akh-Merami into his presence and not only amply rewarded the healer but also gave him his freedom, while retaining him attached to his person and his court.

When Sennacherib wakened, however, it was to a world of pain. Slowly the initial pain caused by the wounds to his head and leg abated, but when he cautiously tried to move his injured leg, he had to grind his teeth together so hard to bear the pain in silence that he lost one tooth in the process. It took many months for him to be able to hobble around with the aid of two crutches. The first time he mounted a horse, with the assistance of two others who helped to hoist him aloft, almost a year had passed since the day of his injury. But thereafter, he progressed with amazing speed, spurred by boredom, determination, and pride in equal measure. The pronounced limp he first exhibited became less and less noticeable and eventually disappeared altogether, except on those days when he was particularly tired. Akh-Merami had prescribed a long sequence of boring wearisome exercises which the young prince hated to do but did anyway, and assiduously after he saw how much they helped him. His father, the Lord Sargon, was quite proud of him, and the whole miserable accident largely served the purpose of bringing father and son closer together.

Actually, although he would never have admitted it, Sargon was at a loss and bored. Throughout the months of Himene's pregnancy, his visits to her were curtailed to mostly those of courtesy. By ancient custom, any intimacy between a man and his wife or concubine was disapproved as a bringer of bad omens while the woman was carrying a child. To his surprise, it was not just the physical intimacy with Himene he missed but also their intimate often-bantering conversations. No one before, most assuredly no woman, had the temerity to banter with the Great Ruler of the Known World, and again much to his surprise, Sargon missed the kind of lightheartedness this had created. Lightheartedness, as a matter of fact, had been an emotion unknown to him, and in small doses, he rather liked it. It helped him unwind at the end of a long day usually filled with face-saving ostentation, swagger, bluster, or outright anger.

It was in this fashion that what the slave Empyades had recommended to his master actually came to pass. Once Sennacherib was able to hobble to the stables and mount his favorite horse, with the assistance of two slaves, he was invited by the king to ride to the main palace building in the evenings. After the business of the nation no longer employed him, Sargon and his eldest son would sit companionably together and drink goblets of strong wine poured by the king's steward. Often no words were spoken for great lengths of time, other than an inquiry made by Sargon to know how his son was progressing to make up for all the time lost during his recovery.

The king learned that his firstborn son was not exceedingly gifted or well learned but had a quick and clever mind and was a shrewd and observant strategist, attributes which he altogether valued more than an educated mind, especially since he found that in his son, they were coupled with a quick and inventive way of thinking. He also found that his son was obstinately determined, vengeful, and unforgiving, quick to judge and to anger. These latter were faults only in the lowborn, he decided, which anyway would be tempered with age. All in all, he could not find them detrimental in a mighty and powerful lord.

As much as these observations pleased him, they also complicated his decision with respect to the succession after his death. He had planned to choose a son of royal blood and thought that he was right in this. But even if Himene did give birth to a son, it was far from secure that this son would be blessed by the gods with health and vigor; and the intervening years from infant to adult were many and perilous. His final decision—at least final for the moment—was to assign to his firstborn an acting leadership, under the guidance of his turtanu, during the next campaign that the king would embark upon; and then—well, to see how that would play out.

It was in this sense that Sargon took the extraordinary step to allow his firstborn son to sit by and listen in on the proceedings of royal audiences. For a while now he had toyed with the idea of allowing his wife to attend such audiences, of course unseen by those in the audience hall and sitting behind a curtained screen. He did not deny that his decision was motivated by vanity—he simply wanted

Himene to witness the majesty and power of his person. Himene was awed and thrilled in equal degrees. She did thereafter understand a great deal more of many problems and decisions made by her husband, and when he visited her, in the quiet hours of their evenings together, she could now actually comment on some of these events with sense and intelligence. This was quite a surprise to Sargon, who had never expected a woman's intellect to be comparable to that of any man. She found it exciting to see the way in which the king enforced his will, never using more than the quietly spoken words, "It is my word. Obey." Once uttered, there was no appeal to that, and even the turtanu, as Sargon's half brother, greatest of the nobles of the land and closer in friendship to Sargon than any other, had to bow to that invincible decree.

Once the queen was allowed into the audiences, even though unseen by others, the next logical step was to admit the Prince Sennacherib into the Hall of Audiences as a silent observer. The king hoped that this gesture would teach his firstborn son the fundamentals of making decisions with wisdom and temperance and—at least most of the time—devoid of anger or passion. Sennacherib, on his part, felt greatly complimented by this obvious gesture of trust by his father, and for many years to come, the lessons imparted to him on these occasions lingered in his memory.

*****

Himene had heard a great many things about childbirth from the women at her father's palace and also after she arrived in Dur-Sharrukin, from the women she resided with in Sargon's palace. None of the pieces of information or gossip imparted to her were reassuring, and she had steeled herself to the horrors that awaited her on her confinement. As her pregnancy wore on, its daily discomforts increasingly occupied her mind, and as they did, the thoughts of the impending birth facing her receded into the background. By nature, she was a compliant and accepting person who also possessed a steely strength and resolve, passed on to her by her ancestors, which she could rely on in extreme situations of her life. Just as she had accepted the separation from all that had surrounded her in her childhood, and the truly frightening prospect of becoming the wife of the very man most feared by all in the world, she had also now accepted her imminent confinement; there was, after all, nothing that she could change in all of these, her life's most fearful events.

During these days and weeks of waiting, the king, with a solicitousness which took all in the House of Women by surprise, came to visit Himene whenever he could spare time from the obligations of statecraft or military planning. Himene was happy with his visits. In his own way, the king was the one person who had alleviated her loneliness after arriving in the Land of Ashur. Not renowned for kindness, Sargon had nevertheless been thoughtful and vigilant of her welfare, more than what she had ever received from her father. When he came to her, he brought her little gifts of a small piece of jewelry or other finery, some exotic flower or fruit, or some special sweets which he judged she would enjoy. Most days she protested laughingly, saying that she was already getting too fat without eating more. At such times, he would pat her belly and was thrilled to be present and actually feel when the infant was turning somersaults in one of its more active moments.

There was a sweet domesticity developing between husband and wife, which became further cemented when the royal marriage was celebrated. Sargon was anxious to have this done as quickly as could be arranged, for Himene was big with their child and would go into labor not too many weeks hence. Confinements were perilous events in a woman's life. This was a first pregnancy, which made it even more dangerous. Sargon did not wish to take any chances and wanted to have the whole of the realm know this child's royal ancestry, if indeed it turned out to be a male child.

As much as her pregnancy was a cross to bear for the Lady Himene, the birth of her son was miraculously easy. Her labors began early in the night and progressed so quickly that by the time the king awakened in the morning, the squalling infant was born, had been attended to, the umbilical cord cut and cauterized, and, after its first suck, was—just as his mother—quietly sleeping in his basket. Sargon, upon hearing the news, immediately strode to see both child and mother before he even had his first meal of the day. This was entirely against custom and etiquette. A mother who had just given birth was to be avoided by any male for one full cycle of the moon. But Sargon, unconcerned about such palace or temple rules and superstitions when they did not suit him, just waved away the chief eunuch who was fluttering about him. By the gods, he wanted to see for himself if the child was indeed a male and whole in his body. He also wanted to see the child's mother, to see how she was faring, and if she was attended to properly.

Such behavior as this was only too well designed to spread the immediate verdict throughout the palace that the Lady Himene had—as many had suspected before—used witchcraft to trap and beguile the Great Ruler of the Known World. And if that was so, then this newborn boy child would possess extraordinary powers, even now within his small body. What kind of a masterful person he would grow up to be, only the gods could determine. All this caused in many a great reverence toward both Himene and her son.

Echoing the same sentiments which had recently taken root in Himene, the king found that his initial fondness for his wife had grown into a genuine attachment and affection which was only partly fueled by what took place in bedding her. The gods only knew the number of bed partners that his House of Women had offered him over the years of his reign. Beyond those women—if he so wished—there was really no woman who could or would be permitted to say no to his desires. When he had been a young man, he had found this power exciting. With the passage of the years, he found that ardor and desire were not sufficient to fill a void in his soul. To his amazement, he found that in the midst of all the riches, all the power which his position provided, surrounded by personages who all desired nothing more than to serve and please him, he was alone.

Then totally unexpectedly, this young woman, half his age and half his size, was dropped into his life. He had not solicited her presence; she was a diplomatic offering to serve a dynastic purpose. Because the diplomacy she was destined to cement was in Assyria's interest, she was accepted and integrated into his life. His expectations from this arrangement were purely practical—beget a male child, or preferably several, of royal lineage, out of this union to be groomed as his successor. Times were changing; whereas in the past, it was sufficient for a ruler to be strong and ruthless, a powerful conqueror who also knew how to rule with wisdom and foresight, nowadays to keep the throne and the power, it was also helpful to claim a strong royal line.

Then unexpectedly, he found that he had acquired someone who could participate in his thoughts and his emotions and, without any self-interest, could be his companion every day for a short time. After a while, these short periods became the most calming, fulfilling moments of his days. Many times, while Himene slept after their lovemaking, he would stand at the open door leading out to the terrace. As he observed her even breathing, he found a peace descend upon him, such as before he had never experienced.

To be sure, in all fairness, he did not allow his feelings for Himene to cloud his judgment about the decision to be made regarding the succession. He had a clear-enough understanding that the royal baby in its basket was, except for his lineage, an unknown brain, an unknown heart, an unknown body, with an unknown future. Would he grow up? Grow up well and think and act in the way he needed to continue his father's heritage? Or would any one of the jealous gods claim his life in infancy? Or while growing up? Or grow up to be incompetent, vicious, and brooding? All of these questions were unanswerable, yet all his planning depended on their outcome.

A compromise solution, at first just in flashes, had by now fully matured in the king's mind—let Sennacherib temporarily take the controls in his father's place the very next time that Sargon set out on his next warfare campaign. Of course, this would be done under subtle supervision by a very trusted servant such as the turtanu himself. Sargon would very well be able to spare him when he was with his army; the turtanu's strength was diplomacy, not warfare. In an unobtrusive way, he would be able to oversee and, also when necessary, advise and assist Sennacherib in his first tentative foray into statecraft.

Once the king got this far in his planning and was reassured by the solid reasoning behind it, he set about to summon his son. By this time, Sennacherib no longer resided in the House of War but had been allowed to set up his own establishment. Considering the splendor that his august father lived in, Sennacherib's household was certainly meager; it consisted of his slave, Empyades, who had procured two elderly women charged with managing the cleaning and cooking, and a young girl who had already been known to the prince from the days when he was still a child living with his mother in the House of Women. The girl, a sweet and pretty young Babylonian, who had accompanied one of the ladies given by King Marduk-apla-iddina of Babylon to the King Sargon of Assyria, had become a playmate and friend of the young prince. Thus when asked if he wished to take a woman from the House of Women into his household, he had chosen her. Her name was Maleanna, and she was just a few years older than Sennacherib. Her presence, because it elevated the prince to adulthood, added status to the fledgling household.

The cordial relationship which had been established between father and son during Himene's pregnancy and Sennacherib's recovery certainly facilitated the plans for any temporary transfer of responsibility—for Sargon was careful not to name it a transfer of any real power—in the event of an approaching war. Once the ground rules were established, the turtanu was requested to join the planning. He was already known to Sennacherib, and the reverse was even truer. Unbeknownst to the prince and by request of the king, Shutur-Nahhunte had long been quietly observing Prince Sennacherib. This was not unusual and certainly not a sign of distrust. Sargon, as much as he wished to have eyes everywhere, knew how to delegate, especially to those who had won his trust. To the greatest degree, Shutur-Nahhunte, companion of the king since his youth, companion of many battles and many diplomatic plans, was one of these few privileged persons. His predominantly positive reports had a lot to do with Sargon's decision in favor of his firstborn—for the time being.

In the midst of all this future planning, plans for the future, but of a different nature, were underway as well. Following many consultations with the court astrologers, the most propitious date was established for the naming and presentation of the recently born royal child. The presentation to the Great God Ashur was of paramount importance for any male child, most especially for the crown prince of the realm. No naming ceremony could occur, except with the assent of the Great God who would not accept a weak or defective child. Ashur, in contrast to any mortal, could look into the future and see the special future of each child presented to him. His acceptance, therefore, made certain the success of the infant for the course of his life.

At this same time, documents would be prepared for the royal archives. They informed the world of the Lady Himene's elevation to First Wife and Queen Mother. Copies of these documents would be dispatched to the more important neighboring countries, primarily to document the royal lineage of the little princeling. Sargon, who showed the extraordinary courtesy of consulting his wife on this matter, had selected the child's name to be Tiglath-Pileser, which had been the name of his own revered father.

Only a few days after these ceremonies, the Ruler of the Known World made an unexpected visit to his queen. She had recently—probably to alleviate the boredom of her pregnancy—taken into her head that she wished to learn the art of the scribes, the runes which they knew how to etch into soft clay and also how to read these etched messages. Not only was this unheard of as an aspiration for a woman but, in fact, extremely difficult to learn, as it was repeatedly pointed out to her. All this notwithstanding, the lady insisted and assured everyone that she did not wish to become a master of the art, only a fledgling practitioner.

When Sargon heard these reports, he was greatly amused. By then he knew enough of his wife to understand that as compliant and obedient as she was to his wishes, she also had a strong mind of her own and an almost unbending willpower when she wanted to accomplish something. Thus he was not overly surprised to see her bending over a clay tablet, chewing contemplatively on the etching reed, while two of the half-man court scribes squatted in front of her, their hands and fingers flying with their eager explanations.

Himene looked up and pleasure flooded her face. The eunuch scribes hastened to gather up the paraphernalia of their trade and scurried out the door, while the king, shaking his head, strode to his wife and bent to kiss the top of her head.

"You are too overjoyed to see me, lady mine!" he murmured." I believe that your expression of happiness is only partly caused by my appearance, but mostly because it gave you reason to get rid of those ghastly little fleshpot men. And how are your studies going, my dear? Can we make ourselves ready to engage your services in the royal archives? And while his mother seems to abandon him, how is my son Tiglath faring? Well, well, don't look so stricken with guilt, lady. I daresay there are enough women here to care for the child when his mother is occupied, eh? Actually I am here to occupy your time as well, my dear, and require that you pay close attention to me."

He sat down comfortably, then waved to the slave who was hovering at the door. Even at those times when Sargon made a private visit to his wife, a personal servant was in attendance at all times to see to his comfort and execute his wishes. Now the king indicated that he desired some wine, and while it was poured, he politely turned to Himene to find out if she wished to have some too. After they were both served, he again turned to Himene, reaching out to hold her hands.

"My dearest wife," he said to her gravely, "not only custom but my wish as well as decree that we should acknowledge your elevation to be my wife and queen, and not just by words but in actuality. That, my dear, has been accomplished. What remains and need yet to be said and done is the gratitude that I and our country owe you for giving us what I and this country most desired—a healthy vigorous male child. If I would never have felt any affection for you before, I would so now. But I tell you truly that I now know how, from the very first day of our life together, you have pleased me and made me happy as no other woman ever had. I know now, my dear, that there is, there never had been anyone who I hold as close to my heart as you. What I wish to give you then is only a meager expression of my feelings. I hope that you accept it as such and cherish it as I cherish you."

And with that, he again gestured to the slave who scurried to his master with a magnificent ivory and gold inlaid box. Sargon opened it, extracted its contents, rose, and clasped it around Himene's neck. It was a heavy gold neck chain, the gold links carved into the most elegant filigree designs interlaced with enameled ones, all the links encrusted with precious stones. The center of the chain was a large round sun disk, lavishly carved, which flashed with each rise and fall of Himene's bosom. She gave a little cry and raised her hand to touch the disk, then looked at the king, speechless for the longest time. But eventually, she recovered from her consternations and—in her way, being as direct as her husband—without any court ceremony, threw herself into his arms. She forced herself as best she could not to cry; nevertheless, silent tears were rolling down her cheeks as she raised her husband's hands and kissed them.

"Oh, my lord husband, there was no need—truly it is you who has given me all my happiness, and…oh, my dearest, don't you know that I love you so very, very dearly anyway, without gifts…" she stammered, hardly knowing what she said until Sargon stopped her words with a kiss, and rose, laughing and shaking his head again, muttered something about not ever having encountered a woman like this one before.

Once again, the king made a gesture with his head to summon the slave who was still carrying a large box. This he laid on the ground at Sargon's feet, then proceeded to open the box and unwrap its contents. The king's hands were still held by his wife, and so he sat down onto his favorite chair and pulled his wife onto his lap.

"My dearest heart," he whispered after he had kissed the shell of her ear. "This other gift I give you is one only to be viewed by one or another of us. It shall be our own glorious secret. Let me explain to you that it is a wondrous treasure. It had lain covered by a whole mountainside on a mysterious and mythical mist-shrouded island named Crete, supposedly lying in the very middle of the Sea at the Center of the Earth. Many think that the island is only a legend, but this statue I give you is mute testimony that people did and do live there.

"It appears that this place had gifted artists who worked in gold and produced things of such beauty…depicting their life, their people, their beautiful women…this island is closer to your home country than it ever can be to us; its art may be more to your liking than what you live with here? Be it as it may, this blessed island had artists with blessed abilities, but maybe the people they tried to portray were also blessed with great beauty and grace…" And Sargon's voice trailed off. "We shall never know because of the crushing number of years that separate them from us, long dead they are, indeed…long dead…

"Well, somehow one of these monumental works of art—actually the nude statue of a beautiful young woman—had been buried by the eruption, eons ago, of one of their mountains. Recently half-hearted searches were made for just such buried treasures, and among many shards, fragments, and such, one lucky man found an intact box. What was in it amazed him and everyone since who had the good fortune to behold it…

"When I saw the piece, I immediately purchased it. It was irresistible to me because—well, because, my love, it was a model of you, your slim body, your long limbs, your elegantly lifted arms, your smile, your eyes, even the way the statue of the woman lifts and turns her head. It is all you, my lovely beautiful wife. And so it is yours now—and also, of course, mine! The nude statue of my beloved exquisitely made in gold. It shall be our secret, neh? For no one else will ever lay eyes upon it, but you and I!"

At the door, he stopped himself and turned back to Himene. "I want for you and the child to be situated in a private apartment, larger than the rooms you now occupy, lady. It shall be a place of peace and privacy for you, and for me as well when I am here. I have already discussed the details with the architects at my court. They understand what I desire, both in the way of the indoor space as well as the attached gardens. I wish it so. But as it will be built, you must tell me if there is aught that displeases you. That is my wish as well." With that, he nodded to her, turned again, and was gone.

When these ceremonies were over, the baby Tiglath-Pileser continued to grow, devoting himself at first to his three chief occupations: sleeping, nursing, and chewing on his fists. Later on, he started to give out little gurgles of laughter as well and then an eager desire to crawl as fast and as far as he could. He was a happy child, thriving in the sunshine of the devotion of his great father and beautiful mother; truly a parentage which could not be equaled, except in one or another of the ancient fairy tales. The clouds, which were gathering on the horizon, were vaguely ominous, but no more so than those which would gather with almost yearly regularity before the beginning of the summer. The time from spring to fall was campaign season. All of Assyria knew this well enough, and even the queen, who, as a child, grew up at her father's court in isolation, incomprehensible to most, was vaguely aware of it.

Still it was like a stab in her heart when one lovely early spring evening, playing with the baby Tiglath under the shade of the striped awnings, outside her newly completed apartment, Sargon, as was his custom, came to visit her and turned to her with the news that he and the army would, in a month or two, be embarking on a new campaign. She quickly placed the infant into the care of his nurse and turned to look at the king with a frightened and questioning glance.

"My dearest lord, why? What has happened? Who is disquieting your days?" she stammered, greatly surprised.

Sargon tried to reassure her, resorting to the superior manner of males everywhere, meant to calm worries, diffuse problems, and reassure doubts of their women. "Himene, my dear, do not be troubled! It shall be but a smallish campaign that needs to be executed against the Cimmerians. Again they have grown bolder with each passing month, and their incursions inside our borders have given us cause for much grief. They destroy villages and crops, drive away our cattle, and kill our people if they do not drive them away as well. They must be stopped, once and for all, and be taught a lesson."

"Must you be there yourself, my lord? And is there no one else you could send since this—as you say—is a minor matter?"

Sargon rose from his chair with a sigh and slowly walked over to her. He placed his large hand on her head and then bent down to kiss her mouth. "Yes, I fear I must, lady mine. When I just said that this will be a smallish campaign, I did not imply that it is of small importance. Rather than that, it should be of short duration. I shall return before you will begin to miss my presence."

"And you, my dear lord, will miss your son's growing!" Sighed Himene to which the king shrugged his shoulder.

"That, my lady, is the fate of warriors everywhere. It can't be helped, I am afraid. So let us enjoy the time we still have together. It will be a while yet before I and the army will be ready to leave."

That night, when they made love, Himene clung to her husband with such desperation, as though it would be her last chance to touch him, to be close to him. He laughed and, gathering her into his arms, cradled her and rocked her like a small child, until she finally quieted and fell asleep. For a long while, the king sat and watched her sleep, her bosom rising and falling gently with each breath she took, her lovely face framed by her dark hair, the gentlest hint of a smile lurking in the corners of her mouth. He wondered how such a creature of loving sweetness and graceful gentleness could ever have been given into his care by the gods and felt gratitude as he never had felt before. All the gods' gifts he had taken for granted and without questioning, but now Himene's possession took his breath away and moved him as nothing in his past life ever had. Finally he rose and walked heavily out of their sleeping chamber into his own bedroom, cluttered with maps, plans, and charts of all sorts.

*****

Bagtu-Shar was a happy man, in as much as happiness depends to a great degree upon one's satisfaction with work achieved. In less than a year's time, he had completed more than half of the decorative engravings which had been assigned to him as a first test of his capabilities. His immediate supervisor, a sharp-faced earnest young architect named Adad-Nirani, was well pleased and recommended that his wages be increased in proportion to the quality of his work. Adad-Nirani had, long ago, learned that his own success very much depended on the success of those beneath him, and nothing stimulated success as much as proper rewards. About the increase in his wages, no decision had as yet been made, but Bagtu-Shar was hopeful of the outcome.

In all truth, he needed more money. His household had increased by the addition of a servant girl. He told himself that this was necessary because of his new child, whom they had named Shammuramat, born two moons ago to his wife Enheduanna. Unfortunately the child was just a girl, but even so—of course, he had high hopes that the next one would be a man-child to carry on his name and craft, and so he speculated that sooner or later, more help around the household was necessary. Enheduanna showed little inclination to share the workload and claimed that she was still suffering from the ill effects of pregnancy and childbirth. And who could prove her otherwise? However, if he wanted to be honest with himself, he had to admit that what he actually wanted was to lighten Ahnaputta's workload and make her daily life easier.

He had become greatly attached to his second wife. His first wife insisted on referring to her as her husband's concubine, but such subtle distinctions in status really depended upon the final decision of the master of the household; and in his eyes, Ahnaputta was, without a doubt, his second wife. During many conversations with her—in itself almost unheard of in the contacts between men and women—he found that she was intelligent, had a quick inquisitive mind, and, even more unheard of, an interest outside of those matters concerning the household, which were a woman's domain. She was also devoted to her family and tireless in performing her endless duties of caring for them. Her devotion even included Enheduanna who, as first lady of the house, many times sorely tested her patience but who was mostly forgiven because Ahnaputta thought being obedient to her was also one of her duties.

Shammuramat, the baby girl, much smaller than the length of Bagtu-Shar's arm, from wrist to elbow, was a weak and sickly child. She lay in her basket, barely moving or crying, only occasionally emitting a soft little mewling sound like a sick baby kitten. When on rare occasions her cries became louder and more vigorous, her face, instead of turning red, took on a bluish-gray pallor, and her little chest began to heave so violently that either her mother or Ahnaputta had to pick her up to soothe her.

Bagtu-Shar was concerned with what he could no longer deny to himself—that this new child of his was not thriving. His concern was genuine albeit certainly not as serious as it would have been if the baby were a man-child. He did not examine the justification for this reasoning because, after all, females had their own value, especially if they were pretty and well trained in obedience. In those circumstances, they could bring the family a good bride-price, and if the father was a skilled bargainer, he could easily succeed in lowering the dowry. But male children were different; their value did not only reside in how many coins they were worth. Firstly, there was the sheer status of having many—or at least several—boys in the family. It attested to the virility of the father. A male child could also help his father in his labors or, if the father was in a higher position, learn his trade. All in all, for reasons practical, as well as emotional, the gift of a male child from the gods was indeed a gift of much greater value. Since Bagtu-Shar already had two little girls romping about his house, he thought with certainty that the arrival of this infant would satisfy whatever quota of girls the gods had assigned to him.

On this particular day, he was, like all the citizens of the Land of Ashur, exempt from work. It was a very special day of celebration, for the divine lord, Great Ruler of the Known World, had a new son who was to be presented to the Great God Ashur and receive his name. To receive one's name from the Lord God Ashur was actually not really true because everyone knew that royal children were already named before that day. Doubtless, Ashur, on this day, gave his consent to the chosen name when he was pleased to be presented with the next person who would be his representative here in the land that was named for him.

Other than the prescribed feast days of the various gods, these events of a royal wedding, a royal birth, or—may the gods not allow it to happen for many, many years—the death of the king were the much welcome breaks in the drudgery of daily labor. Bagtu-Shar, like everyone else, welcomed the holiday with pleasure, dawdling over the freshly cooked gruel which Ahnaputta, in honor of the holiday, had studded with leathery-skinned dried dates. Earlier in the morning, she had milked the family goat and given a big mugful to her master, who had just finished drinking it and was wiping the white foam from his upper lip. He sat in shaded comfort in their back garden, leaned his head against the doorframe, and settled himself to be able to enjoy his leisure in greater comfort. For the moment, life was good, and he even forgot the pangs of intermittent envy, which he experienced whenever he thought that the Great Lord Sargon, who, after all, had already bedded hundreds of women and had untold numbers of children and probably many sons, now had another one, while he—

Later in the day, long after the sun had passed overhead, he announced it to no one in particular that he would go to spend some time in his favorite tavern, only two turns away on the same alley where they lived. There he could see his friends and soak up as much gossip as he wanted, and more. Ahnaputta did not respond because she did not think it was seemly to inquire into what the master of the household decided, or why. Enheduanna, occupied with some ailment of her own, just shrugged her shoulder and told him not to stay out too late because of the dangers lurking for anyone after darkness and without an oil lamp or torch, and of course, they did not have the money to waste on torches for the outdoors; they were not rich folks like some. After this, Bagtu-Shar was only too glad to duck his head under the low lintel and be on his way.

At the tavern, much of the conversation revolved around the supposed campaign plans of the king. Somehow nobody quite knew who did it, but this kind of information invariably leaked out of the palace. No one was ever supposed to know whenever such plans were discussed by the king and his turtanu or the Prince Sennacherib and other such august beings. Despite this, in less than one day's time, the taverns, the market stalls, the barracks, the parade grounds, all were buzzing with the supposed secret news. The Great Ruler of the Known World was once again girding his sword and collecting his soldiers, warhorses, and war camels to do battle for the benefit of the Land of Ashur.

Secretly, as he listened to the conversation and the glowing reports of bravery given by the lame, one-eyed, or otherwise battle-scarred veterans of earlier wars, as much as he envied the prestige which their scars gave them, he was also happy that he would, in all probability, not be conscripted. Customarily only men with families of no more than two children were called into service and only men whose occupations at home were not considered important to the country. In Bagtu-Shar's judgment, to complete decorations for the Hall of Ambassadors was doubtless of greater importance than acquiring one more soldier for the army.

At this time, no one knew when or where the army would be dispatched to. The when was greatly influenced by the seasons and the weather. Battles could not be fought in the winter, for the mountains were snowy and often barely passable and the flatlands and huge reedbeds to the south along the two rivers inundated by the rains and meltwater coming down from the mountains. Much of the in-between seasons, on the other hand, were often capricious, given to late snows, early heat, and draught or raging torrents of rain. Except for all-out war, campaigns had to be selected and designed judiciously, either to take these problems into account or to limit the military forays to shorter durations.

The second guess was who the army was going to be arrayed against. Babylon, the eternal problem for Assyria, was one possibility, but since Marduk-apla-iddina's subjugation, his land became a vassal of King Sargon's; it was hoped not just in name only. Urartu and the Cimmerians, to the north expanding in a semicircle from west to east, were potentially constant threats and periodically rose up with vigor against their Assyrian overlords. They presented endless problems with their almost annual incursions and raids into the Land of Ashur, threatening the lives and safety of the inhabitants and their possessions alike. Guesswork was cheap and plentiful, and by the time Bagtu-Shar thought it time to go home, his head was fairly swimming with all of the various suppositions.

He had not realized how long he had stayed at the tavern. His house was altogether dark with everyone asleep. Without waking anyone, he pulled up some water from the well in his back garden to drink and, then as quietly as he could, clambered up the ladder leaning against the side of the house to the roof. Normally the last action he took before sleeping was to pull up the ladder and lay it flat on the roof so that, with the front entrance barred, no one could enter the house. He was thankful that Ahnaputta had the wit not to do so today, and so he was able to bed down on his sleeping mat and fall asleep almost instantly.

Next morning, Bagtu-Shar awoke with a headache big enough to make him feel like his head was ready to explode and take his shoulders as well. Ahnaputta coaxed some extra food into him because she was convinced that his aching head was due to not having had enough to eat the night before. She massaged his thick neck and his shoulders, wrapped a cool cloth across his forehead, and tried every trick she could think of to make him feel better. Finally just to reassure her, he agreed solemnly that he was feeling a lot better, mostly in order to get out of the house and to get to work. There he was at a critical point and the supreme overseer, a delegate of the great king, was to come any day now to check the progress and quality of the work done on the construction so far. It was important for him to show off his work in the best possible light. Headache or no, he had to be there as early as he could and be bright and ingratiating, in case that today would turn out to be the day of the visit.

His calculations were absolutely correct; just past the time when the sun reached its highest point in the sky, and every human and animal had only one desire—to loll under the shade of some tree where the ground was a little cooler than the sun-exposed hard-baked soil elsewhere—the king's supervisor of works arrived in a curtained litter. His bearers must have been suffering the punishment of hell, and as soon as the litter was allowed to stop, they literally collapsed on the ground, not even being able to drag themselves under the branches of the nearest tree. They just squatted down where they were allowed to stop and, with tongues lolling and chests heaving, stared ahead like dumb animals.

Nor could it have been any more comfortable within the confines of the small curtained cubicle of the litter at this midday hour, yet the man who alighted seemed as fresh and unaffected, as though he had just risen from his bath. He was an unusually tall thin and stately gentleman of middle years and certainly seemed to be a slave to fashion: his shoulder-long shiningly oiled and curled hair, his luxurious and equally well-curled and well-oiled beard, his elegantly embroidered, richly befringed coat, be-ringed fingers, the heavy hammered copper bangles on his arms, the elegantly turned slippers with their narrow upturned toes, the high conical mitra on his head, in fact every inch of the man breathed wealth, class, and power.

The gentleman, whose name turned out to be Borsuk-annam, was evidently oblivious to and unaffected by the heat, for he immediately summoned the architect of the construction and several of his underlings and demanded to be shown forthwith all that had been built so far. Bagtu-Shar tried not even to look in their direction and to melt into the background as much as possible. It was more than an hour later when the group finally reached his station. He had been laboring for the last months on a representation of great Sargon's victory over Marduk-apla-iddina and the subjugation of Babylon. Some of the tablets adjacent to one another had been completed, others next to them were waiting to be painted or gilded, and the last few had only rough sketches etched into their surfaces, preliminary to carving the designs into the stone.

Lord Borsuk-annam carefully examined each of the tablets, and every particular aspect of each design. All in all, he was well pleased with what young master Bagtu-Shar had accomplished, had some specific suggestions which he wanted to have done by the time of his next visit, and, as a sign of his general approval, gave a small box of precious gold leaf to Adad-Nirani, Bagtu-Shar's immediate supervisor. Adad-Nirani was to issue the gold leaf to Bagtu-Shar in small portions, just enough for one day's work, and with the admonishment to keep a strict account of how each sheet of gold leaf had been used.

With a sense of too much, too soon, Bagtu-Shar prostrated himself and gave his profuse thanks in a stammering voice that he could barely control. He was staggered that he should be presented with the opportunity to not only apply the gold decorations but also be given—even if in a limited way—access to the gold leaf. In his eyes, this was not only an almost incomprehensible honor but also a grave and worrisome responsibility. If he wanted to be honest with himself, he would, even though the honor was flattering, have rather dispensed with the assignment. But then he remembered that elevation of one's status went hand in hand with a rise in responsibility. This, he told himself, is how the gods and one's superiors tested those whose position they wished to further.

*****

Some weeks after Sargon told his wife about the campaign into the north, he intended to mount shortly, the plans were discussed in the Hall of Private Audiences. This was a Spartan smallish room, consisting of little more than a long table against one of the walls, some exquisitely woven wool wall hangings on the opposite wall, and an assortment of chairs and cushions laid out in a rather haphazard fashion in between those two walls. There was no throne, for in this room, and surrounded only by the closest of his friends and advisers, both they and the king liked to move about, mingle, and, if necessary, argue without ceremony. The king, who at any time radiated self-confidence and assurance, was not plagued by the need to constantly assert his domination. At such times, when plans were laid which would gravely impact the future of his rule and his realm, he preferred to dispense with ceremony and to listen intently before making his decisions.

All those present, not just the king and his turtanu, Shutur-Nahhunte, were in agreement that the kingdom of Urartu, expanding along the north and east of Assyria, was more and more becoming a threat. At the same time, the Cimmerians, sitting right on top of the northernmost territories of Assyria, had made friendly overtures toward Urartu and had become a continuous irritant to the Assyrian Kingdom. Under no circumstances could an alliance between the two be allowed. Both of these nations once again needed to be set back on their heels and contained, preferably eliminated forever. They also had repeatedly threatened and even invaded vassals of Assyria, such as the Phrygians and Colchis. If they were not eliminated or, at the very least, taught a lesson now, they would undoubtedly grow bolder and, within a year, become a real threat to the land.

Equally it was agreed by all that such a campaign should be initiated, furnished, and provisioned with all speed. The weather, as always, was to be a factor. Since the campaign planned was to proceed to the north, the deadly heat of midsummer would probably not impact the army at all, but in contrast, an early snowfall or, at least, frost on the ground had to be calculated into the plans, unless those plans were executed with all speed. Sargon entirely agreed and sent his commands with all haste to the garrison commanders of the gathering army. After this crucial decision was made, he rose to leave the meeting, which was charged with hammering out all the details, and then report back to him tomorrow when the council would reconvene here, in the Hall of Private Audiences. Receiving their obeisance, he nodded and left the gathering with his usual manner of speed.

But unlike his usual habit of visiting his wife and child only after all other work and concerns were laid to rest at the end of the day, with the desire to unwind in their company, this time he straightaway proceeded to Himene's apartment and entered with a small smile of anticipation, which he was no longer even willing to hide. He knew that his happiness in his wife was common knowledge and could find no reason to conceal it. The days of concealment, accepted custom where a large number of women had no other interests or concerns than to devote their thoughts to the moods and desires of their master, were no longer pertinent. He knew full well that his affection for Himene could not be hidden; but he had at least tried to abate gossip by the creation of a separate apartment for both himself and the queen. His wishes were clear to all—to set aside an area of privacy within the structures of the House of Women; and since it was his wish, there was no appeal to it. All of a sudden and very unexpectedly, considering his age, the king had acquired a family, something that was totally alien to his way of life and that of his fathers. He was charmed by this unexpected gift, found it restful and pleasing, much to his surprise, above and beyond the satisfaction of his desire for his wife.

Deep in his secret heart, he had to admit that he was—probably for the first time in his life—reluctant to give up this family idyll to join his army. Always, always before he had relished the thought of being with a group of his tried-and-proven comrades in arms. He enjoyed the easy camaraderie of men, the depth of friendships and loyalties—or hatreds—formed and forged on the battlefield. He enjoyed the physicality of weapons, horses, chariots, arrow, and javelin, the pleasure to be gained from a well-aimed throw of a spear or a well-placed cut of a sword, the tumbling down of his enemy, the screaming of horses and camels, the shouts of men, some in agony, others in triumph—all of these were second nature to him and long ago had become part of his life.

As he entered the large and airy chamber, open on two sides to the breeze blowing gently down from the distant mountains, where Himene usually spent most of her days, he thought to himself, with a tinge of sadness, that his reluctance must be a result of his aging. Then Himene looked up, saw him, and, with a little shout of joy, rose and ran to him in welcome, and Sargon knew that aging had little to do with his reluctance. When he thought back to that day of Himene's arrival, and seeing her on what was to be their wedding night, sitting and then looking up in fear and dread upon his arrival, and compared that recollection with the smiling young woman looking into his face with shining eyes, and then impetuously throwing her arms around him—old fool that he was, he told himself—he was moved as he was only moved when he had looked at the child of theirs for the first time.

With a smile, he extricated himself from her embrace and, as was sometimes his habit, lifted her off her feet and swung her around, before placing her back into the comfortable cushioned chair which she had occupied on his arrival. All that while he was trying to keep a forbidding and serious expression, chiding her for behaving unbecoming a matronly woman. She was evidently unimpressed and, looking at him with a challenge in the corner of her eyes, demanded to know how he thought her to be matronly, when a few months ago he had called her "my child."

The king raised an eyebrow before commenting that truthfully, he did not remember, to which his wife asserted sweetly that she did, very much so, because she did not wish to ever forget anything he had told her.

"Anything, lady?" Sargon asked, "that does not please me too much."

"Why so, my dearest lord?" Himene asked, genuinely surprised.

"Because, my dear, there were things said between us, which I would express differently now, if I had the chance to repeat them."

Himene laughed. "Ah, yes, my lord, but this way, they can always be used to create guilt in your heart when you are angry with me." And then she continued, after a little reflection, "If that should ever happen to me. And may the Great God Ashur prevent that that would come to pass."

Sargon had stepped to the doorway, open to the north toward the mountains. He was looking intently into the distance. His hands, clenched into two fists, were clasped behind his back. As she looked at him from the back, Himene noticed how his hair was now generously shot through with silvery strands. She rose and went to him, putting her arms around him and laying her face against his back. He sighed, turned around, and lifted his hands, fingers uncurled now, until he caught hold of her face, and then looked solemnly into her eyes.

"Himene, my wife," he said quietly, "we will be parting. I shall leave as soon as we have finished all the preparations. That will probably be in a few days."

She withdrew her arms and stood facing him, now looking into his face, his eyes. Her face, otherwise immobile, had grown pale. She was silent, and then when he released her, turned silently, walking first to Tiglath-Pileser's basket, and looked at him intently, without seeing him. Then she slowly walked back to her chair and sat in silence, until he came to stand beside her, taking both of her hands in one of his. Both of them seemed reluctant to break the silence.

"It will be a short campaign, be sure of that," he said, continuing his earlier thoughts. "A few days' hard ride, a difficult climb up the mountains, if the enemy be holed up there, then after a good rest for men and horses, a hard charge, hitting them, I hope unexpectedly, at dawn. If that does not finish the business, I should be greatly surprised. If Great Ashur allows, I shall be back in Dur-Sharrukin before the end of two passages of the moon." When Himene continued her silence, he raised her hands and kissed them gently. "I would not wish to miss too many hours of your company nor that of my son." And then he added with some hesitation because he was not accustomed to saying such things, "You are both too precious to me."

His surprising words floated in the silence of the room. Finally Himene gently freed her hands and moved slightly to make room for him next to her. He looked at the chair doubtingly and shook his head, then lifted her and, sitting down, put her on his knee. "Now," he murmured, "at least now there is room for both of us."

As she had done before, Himene laid her head on his shoulder. "So too are you precious to me, my lord," she continued what he had said. Then hesitantly, she asked, "May I tell you a fairy tale, my dearest lord?" Not quite knowing want to expect, Sargon smiled and nodded.

Himene settled herself more comfortably and continued, "This, my lord, is a tale about a young woman, a very scared young woman. She was told by her father that he had given her as wife to the most powerful, most ruthless, most feared ruler in the whole wide world. Needless to say, this terrified her beyond anything that could have happened, but there was no recourse for her. Thus her father paid her dowry, gathered up all the soldiers, servants, slaves, dignitaries, all the officials, and women to accompany her in sufficient opulence to her new home. Once there, her new master came to receive her. Without a word, he lifted her—as custom demanded—in front of him, onto the saddle of his horse, and rode with her into his city, which now was to be her city, her home.

"When all the feasting and celebrating was done, she was led into her bridal chamber, and there she sat, exhausted by the day, in fear and trepidation, with pounding heart, until she heard her husband, her new master, arrive at the door. Although the words he spoke were more terrifying than anything she could have imagined, she did understand the truth behind the words and also vaguely comprehended how, at each point of our lives, our needs and necessities drive our actions. This man, her master now, although demanding, was patient and soft-spoken, gentle and tender even, and did everything that he could to ease her fears and make her acceptance of him easier for her to endure, if possible, to take pleasure in it.

"Later when she was guilt-ridden to have experienced pleasure in his loving, he explained to her with kindness how love and pleasure are special gifts from the Lord Ashur and not something to be ashamed of. He taught her how to express love and how to accept love. He taught her to be trusting and generous in loving. He taught her that the greatest happiness in life was to make the one you love happy.

"Since their union, he had, in a hundred different ways, shown his regard and preference for her, valuing not only their nights but the quiet talks they had when they spent time together, teaching and explaining and also listening to her when he thought that what she said was worth listening to. He showed her in a hundred ways that he thought of her as a partner of his life, not just of his bed."

She took a deep shuddering breath and then continued, "To lose him now, to lose him ever, is something that cannot happen. I cannot contemplate it. I could not endure it. Death is a thousand times preferred to life without him…Oh, yes, oh, yes! A thousand times…" And then there was again silence in the room, until Sargon stirred.

He put his heavy hands on her shoulders and shook her gently. "Himene, my wife, you are not to say this—ever! It is unworthy of you, unworthy of the queen, unworthy of Sargon's wife! Should you lose me, you will bear it with dignity, with pride and grace and without a complaint. You will rejoice in our son! But this will not happen. In a few short months, I shall be back, and all things shall be again as they are now." Then just as he had done so often before, he wrapped his arms about her and rocked her back and forth as one would rock a child. "Oh, my dearest," he whispered, "my one and only dearest beloved wife!"

*****

Sennacherib, in a fever of eager anticipation, awaited his father, the king's pleasure to summon him and tell him what his decision was. To be allowed to go with him to war or to remain at Dur-

Sharrukin and learn how to administer the needs of the realm, at least in a limited way, were both heady enticing prospects for a young man just grown out of his school years. Honestly he could not decide which of these two fates he wished for more, and each day, his desires switched from one prospect to the other. He could not remain at home, had his horse saddled, and rode out or walked out with the excuse to inspect some construction work or road building underway. At the end of each day, he returned to his house only to find that no messenger had arrived from his august father. Both Maleanna and Empyades tried to reassure him with one excuse or another, but evidently to no avail. He could not sleep, spent his nights walking around in the woods surrounding his house, at the northern perimeter of the palace complex, or in the stable to sleep with his horses.

Finally on the fifth day, a messenger arrived and told him that the Great Ruler of the Known World desired to have his company for dinner in the king's private chambers, just before sundown. For a while, Sennacherib hesitated as to what to wear, and although he would have preferred a plain soldier's uniform, he decided against it, thinking that it would be too forward to make an assumption what the king's wishes were. He put on an unadorned fringed cream-colored light wool robe, a heavy golden neck collar—a gift from the king—some copper bracelets, red boots, and a fringed red wool shawl about his shoulder against the chill of the evening to come.

When he arrived, he was much surprised to find no one else in the dining chamber but his lord father and the Lord Shutur-Nahhunte. It was from these two men, the two most powerful individuals of the land, that Sennacherib found out what his role was to be during the king's absence. As much as he wished to be involved in a glorious war accompanying the mighty Sargon, he could not quarrel with the decisions made by these two men on his behalf. This, said Sargon, was a great opportunity for his son to spread his wings and to learn something about managing the affairs of a nation. He would not be alone, for the Lord Turtanu would remain behind and advise the prince. Sennacherib had enough intelligence to read between the words and to understand that in this case, to advise meant to supervise. That was only to be expected, and all in all, the decision of these two men of power flattered him greatly. When dinner was finished, fortified with several goblets of strong Cyprus wine, he was almost floating on his way home.

His father had charged him to be at his side early the next morning, when he, in the presence of the nobles and the scribes, would temporarily transfer much of the information and many tablets of documents and instructions into the hands of Prince Sennacherib and the turtanu. It was to be understood that the duration of this authority was only while the great king was away on a military expedition. Strict accounting of all activities undertaken, as well as those which were declined to be undertaken, was expected by the great king on his return and not one day later. Therefore, Sennacherib was charged to employ as many scribes as were necessary to record all these various events and to make them available to the great king immediately on his return.

When the king concluded his orders and dismissed all, everyone prostrated themselves and then backed out of the august presence, except the turtanu and the crown prince, to whom the king indicated that he desired their presence for longer. It was for a short time only; the king wished to say his farewells to both privately. Obviously in a generous and gracious mood, he embraced the turtanu, which was not so unusual since he had been seen to do that before. His son Sennacherib, however, had not received such distinction since the days when he had to hobble around on two crutches. Much surprised, he bent down, touched his forehead to the ground, then lifted his father's hand, laid it on his heart, then on his forehead, and finally bowed over it and kissed it. Lord Sargon appeared to be pleased with his son's reverence and nodded to him several times. Then in his customary brusque and brisk manner, he turned and quickly walked out of the room.

That night, when Sargon entered his wife's sleeping chamber, he found it unchanged from the picture he had seen so many times before. He stopped in the doorway, trying to fix the scene in his mind. Himene sat, as she did almost every night, on a low stool by the open door, looking out into the dark, her hands serenely resting on her lap, her long dark hair loosely bound with sky-blue ribbons to match the color of her night shift. He had not told her about the hour of his departure, but preparation and anticipation were in the air like thick smoke. She gave no sign of sensing anything, and after his last reprimand to her, he was unsure if her serene demeanor was genuine or an act to please him.

When she saw him enter, her face lit up, and as always, she rose and bowed deeply, formally, but then as soon as she straightened, she turned and ran to him with the eagerness of a child. His solemn mood of the day vanished, and with a smile, he held out his arms so that she could, straining herself on her tiptoes, rise to kiss his mouth. He sat down heavily into his favorite armchair and pulled her down onto his lap. This was how their evenings and nights together almost always started, sharing a goblet of her favorite wine, talking about little Tiglath's exploits of the day, what she always found fascinating, and he pretended to find them too, mostly so as not to disappoint her. The daily events in the life of a growing infant were not near to his understanding, and he could not elicit much interest for them in his heart of hearts. He told her about his day, carefully explaining the temporary transfer of administrative power to his eldest son, to act with the advice and under the supervision of the turtanu. In all of these explanations, the day of departure was carefully avoided, and Himene asked no further questions.

Eventually and inevitably, their bodies expressed their desire for each other. With more than her usual passion, she responded to him, but eventually she quieted and fell asleep under his watching eyes.

In the middle of the night, she awoke and found her husband looking silently, intently down into her face. The moon, full at that time of the month, illuminated the room, the outlines of her body glinted back at her from the depths of his eyes' unfathomable blackness. He reached out and gently brushed her hair from her forehead.

"My wife, I will leave this morning at sunrise," he said softly. She remained silent, but he could sense her body shudder, as though he would have struck her. Then silently, slowly, she reached both her arms up to embrace him and pull him down on her. Thus they remained locked together in silence until he felt, almost without his will, his body enter her. It was the gentlest of invasions until finally, neither of them knew where one body ended and the other began—a union so perfect in its simplicity that neither of them would experience such again.

Eventually, slowly, and gently, he drew away from her and left their bed. She did not move, nor did she say a word, only her eyes followed him in the darkness. He bent to gather his robe and slippers and, without looking back, quietly walked out of the room, out of her life.

The departure of the army proceeded in its usual noisy manner—the air, thick with the dust of uncounted soldiers' and camels' feet and horses' hooves, reverberated with the bellowing of the camels, the neighing of the horses, all of them overarched by the marching music of the cymbals, trumpets, tambourines, and drums, which customarily lead the soldiers into battle. All the generals rode on magnificent horses, selected from the king's stables and trained with great care. Wheels of long lines of war chariots threw even more dust and small stones into the air. As many of the population as could be spared from working that morning were given permission by their masters to go and see off the king's army. Cheering, ululating with joy, and dancing with their arms upraised to Ashur and to the morning sun, they followed the slowly receding soldiers, who wound their serpentine way up the slight slopes of the hills, which rose layer by layer into the mountains of the shimmering distance.

The king, although taller than most others, could be glimpsed only occasionally and then with difficulty. He rode a great black horse, one of a number raised and kept just for his royal person. He was surrounded by his court of nobles and generals. As was his usual habit, he looked neither left nor right but stared gravely at the dusty road ahead which led him away from Dur-Sharrukin. His eldest son, Sennacherib, as well as the turtanu had accompanied him a good distance. This was probably a show of good will and solidarity, a demonstration that the transfer of power, which was occurring at the moment, happened with the consent of the king. Eventually they parted ways with no further ceremony, at a point where the road branched into two, and one branch curved almost upon itself to lead back to the city. As the turtanu, Shutur-Nahhunte, and the prince silently rode homeward, Sennacherib turned his face to the back several times. No longer could he even make out the figure of his august father, and then the whole column disappeared in the receding dust. The din of music still filled the morning air for a while, and finally even that abated until eventually, the wooded hill-side returned to its usual quiet, the quiet only interrupted by the gentle splashing of a nearby brook and the chirping of birds working eagerly on their nests.

Himene, after finally forcing herself to rise, did it partly for her child, but mostly because her husband's words still rang in her ear. Not ever did she want to be unworthy of him, and so she bit her lip and forced her usual gentle expression on her face. She ordered a bath and some food for the sake of the appearance of normalcy. The bath did revive her somewhat, but the food was almost impossible to swallow. She toyed with the fruits a little, had half of one of those small fragrant oranges she loved so much, and a few grapes, and even forced down a few bites of goat cheese, but then she rose and had all the remaining food taken away.

She walked out into her walled garden, shaded by the lightest woven wool awnings in a pattern of bright sky blue and cream stripes. This was the place where she and her son usually spent their mornings. Normally she loved the serenity of this secret place, where caged songbirds where preening their feathers under the shades of ancient trees, and a pool glistened in the middle of the place. Before she had started to use the garden, the pool was designed just for splashing or wading. When Sargon saw how much she loved the privacy of her garden, he had summoned some of his architects, those who were best among builders of waterworks, and charged them with the design of an enlarged pool.

The result was a large glistening expanse of water, almost a small lake, with steps leading down to it, should the royal occupant wish to refresh herself there. The steps were marble, and the bottom of the pool was laid out with an embellishment of small colored stones showing trellises of fruiting trees. Golden fishes were stocked in the pool and flitted around unceasingly, occasionally one or another breaking through the surface, much to Himene's delight. She loved to swim, which she had learned as a small child from one of her father's concubines who had been born by the Sea at the Center of the World. The lady had suffered greatly from homesickness, and King Mita had allowed her to visit the ocean occasionally. Under protective guard to accompany them, the lady took little Himene's hand and led her into the warm salt water. Since little Himene had never been told that such a thing, as salty water, existed and in such endless quantity, as far as the eye could see, the little girl was endlessly surprised and delighted. Kindhearted and patient, the lady—whose name Himene had long forgotten—had taught Himene the act of swimming.

Now that she had her very own pool, Himene had renewed her efforts at swimming, at first floundering—literally—but then finding her sea legs so that she could strike out and swim about freely, round and round her pool, occasionally laughing out loudly when one of her golden fishes swam close to her with interest, nipping gently at her skin.

Today she sat listlessly, an inexplicable dread constricting her heart. Pushing away emotion from her thoughts and trying to be calmly reasonable, she had to confess that she was excessively overwrought without any reason at all. Battles and campaigns were facts of life for royal personages; she was exposed to this since childhood, living at her father's court. Of course, she was young then, and there were many things she did not comprehend. Of course, her emotions had no part then in what passed in front of her eyes. But she did not remember any of his father's wives or favorites in a state of hysteria, as she now was. Granted her father was a harsh and vain man, difficult to please or to love, and granted also, what she recollected now was based on observations made with a child's eyes.

She finally roused herself from these contemplations, sternly admonished herself not to be overwrought, for Sargon would either have been displeased or laughed at her. She rose and went to watch little Tiglath crawling around on the ground. As soon as he learned to crawl, he did it with amazing speed, and watching him, she had to smile because she thought that he must have inherited his urge for speed from his father. At that, she felt anxiety stab her again, and hastily, to overcome her anxiety, she scooped up the protesting and squirming child and pressed him to her bosom with both her arms.

*****

Prince Sennacherib arrived at his house in a state of high agitation, anxiety, expectation, and elation in equal portions. What he had dreamed of for so long, in his most secret thoughts, had finally come to fruition! Well, perhaps not quite to fruition but to the first step toward fruition! His revered father had demonstrated that he had chosen him—Sennacherib, his eldest son—for his successor. All the worry of the past two years, ever since the arrival of the royal bride, was unnecessary! When she had been brought to Dur-Sharrukin, it had stabbed him in his heart because it showed him, like nothing else would have, that the king wished to have a son of royal descent to succeed him after his death. What else could it have been? Sargon already had many sons, some of them with qualities that could have recommended them to their father, but that same father was casting a net to acquire a royal bride—for what other purpose than to breed an heir of more elevated descent?

As much as he thought that it was unworthy of him, he hated—no, perhaps not hated because he had only met her once or twice—but surely suspected and disliked the woman who had now become his father's first wife and queen. He hated the fact that she was so accommodatingly fertile, that she was said to be kind and generous, and therefore well-liked, and most of all, he hated that his own mother had become a friend of hers. In the past, he had tried to subdue these thoughts and ascribe them to unwarranted jealousy. Now it was with relief that he realized that after all—after all—the king, his father, valued him sufficiently to put his trust in him. He tried to mitigate his elation with the thought that this was to be only a trial period, a test so to say, but this thought only spurred him on to become worthy of his great father's trust. He thought back to those painful dismal days after his accident and his worry about never to be able to ride a horse, drive a war chariot, or even to be agile enough for swordplay, and how his dear father befriended him. He thought back on the talks they had and how Sargon taught him about the use of power both for one's subjects and one's enemies, about friendship and its limits when one was a ruler, and how the ruler always stood alone at the final moment of decision.

Then he stepped into his house and was immediately engulfed by turmoil. A dozen servants were carrying his furniture, his personal belongings, his carpets and bedding and clothing, and all sorts of other knickknacks out of the house and up onto waiting oxcarts, like so many ants carrying little pellets of food down into their nests. As most men, at any time in any country, he was immediately put into a state of panic and would have withdrawn if Maleanna would not have seen him approach and run to him with the news that a palace official had arrived only an hour ago, had confronted her in the absence of the master, and told her that the great king left orders for the transfer of all of Lord Sennacherib's household to a wing of the royal palace. This, the great king desired not only for the Lord Sennacherib's greater comfort but also because in this fashion, the Lord Sennacherib was more accessible to the various dignitaries and ambassadors, the generals from the field, and the couriers dispatched by the king. Already, Maleanna told him, most of his personal belongings and much of those items that belonged to the kitchen and the women's quarters were packed and transferred. She invited the Lord Sennacherib to proceed posthaste to the palace, where he would find greater comfort in his new quarters than here, where everything was topsy-turvy. In the fashion of women everywhere, she asked him to get out of the way of those who were working, lifting, carrying, sorting, and organizing, and Sennacherib, in the fashion of men everywhere, was only too glad to comply.

The new home turned out to be a spacious and airy building, connected to the main palace by the same covered walkway which also connected the palace with the House of War and, at the other end, with the House of Women. His building stood about halfway between these two pivotal structures. It also had a beautifully maintained walled garden with a pool and two attractive waterfalls, which nourished the pool. Water was then led off from the pool by a meandering channel well stocked with golden carp, which were free to follow the channel and swim away but preferred to collect in groups below the waterfall, where there was ample shade. Altogether the garden was a delightful place, inviting the residents to linger and enjoy the shade provided by the many large trees with spreading canopies.

Once all of the furniture and household furnishings were installed, the house looked spacious, luxurious, and elegant beyond anything that Sennacherib had ever occupied. Granted when he lived with his mother in the House of Women, he lived in great elegance and luxury, but the House of Women was also a noise-filled place occupied by many women, their children of all ages, and their servants, where privacy, even for one of the king's favorite wives, was nonexistent.

Young Sennacherib could barely believe his good fortune. For all purposes, he was the master of the realm, even though for a short time, lord over all he beheld, with almost absolute power over life and death of the land's inhabitants. This was no less than an intoxicating power for a young person who was as yet not accustomed to power. To top it all, Maleanna had just announced to him that it was indeed high time to have acquired a more spacious home, for she was expecting their first child. This was wonderful news, and they were as happy as two little children, walking hand in hand in their wonderful new garden, where Maleanna, much to her delight, found in one corner, and hidden by tree branches, a brand-new swing installed. She was convinced that it had been installed just for her, and Sennacherib was only too happy to support her belief.

The next morning, and each morning thereafter, or at the latest by midmorning, a mounted courier arrived from the king's camp with details of how the Lord Sargon was well satisfied with the speed of their progress and hoped to reach the high mountains, which separated Urartu from Assyria, within a week or less. So far all seemed well, and evidently the mountain guards of Urartu who policed the mountain passes had not become aware of the advancing army.

Also starting with the day after the army's departure, Sennacherib, after consulting with the turtanu, just to be sure that he was acting correctly, convened a meeting of the various magistrates and judges to address the problems that invariably arose during the passage of each day. These issues could be the result of the feverish construction going on in Dur-Sharrukin or some kind of crime committed in the outlying districts of the farmlands. Many of the problems were trivial, but still they had to be dealt with. Many others were referred to the capital city by magistrates of other cities or regions because of the magnitude of the problem or crime. Both the prince and the turtanu knew that Sargon, who was very much a hands-on ruler, expected to get a daily report, just as he sent them a daily report as well.

Ten days into this newly established routine, a local case of theft was brought to the attention of Sennacherib and the attending judges. Since it was a local case, it only merited attention by the august body assembled because it involved a major crime—the theft by one of the workers laboring on some phase or another of the city's construction of a sizeable amount of gold kept for the decoration of the buildings under construction. The accuser was a man named Adad-Nirani, one of the many architects working on the construction of the new Hall of Ambassadors. His report was supported by the overseer of building works for the king, a man named Lord Borsuk-annam.

In cases of theft, Sargon's law was exceedingly harsh and unforgiving, except if theft was committed by a child so young that it was unaware of its actions, an orphan, or a homeless widow. In all other cases, the king did not believe in giving in to clemency, maintaining that if it were practiced at all, it would set a dangerous precedent for the future.

Upon Sennacherib's order, the accused was brought in to face his accusers and give his own account. The law demanded this so that no one accused of a crime should be sentenced without first seeing his accusers and his judges. After a short recess, the accused shuffled in with difficulty because of the heavy shackles wound around his ankles and his wrists, which were connected to each other, limiting his movements even more. He was a good-looking young man, brown-skinned not only by his heritage but also from continuously working in the sun, with a well-cared for beard and hair, soft black eyes, and gleaming white teeth in a well-drawn mouth. He claimed that he was born in Nineveh but raised here and indeed worked on etching the decorative tablets affixed to the colonnades of the Hall of Ambassadors. And yes, his name indeed was Bagtu-Shar.

Bagtu-Shar stood in front of his judges and the golden-robed Prince Sennacherib, who sat on a raised shaded throne in the center of the assembly. He was frightened beyond anything he had ever felt in his life, as his eyes darted left and right, until one of the guards who brought him in pushed him in the small of his back, whereupon he fell to his knees and prostrated himself as best as his shackles would allow. The senior judge then addressed him.

"Bagtu-Shar, you stand accused of theft of the most gracious lord, our king's, property. Rise to your knees and face your accusers and the most gracious Lord Sennacherib, our lord king's delegated master of our land. Give an account of how and why you stole the gold you are accused of stealing."

With some straining against his shackles, Bagtu-Shar rose to his knees. He was more dead than alive with fright and, at first, just stared ahead. Then finally he roused himself and, in a quavering voice, began to explain as best he could.

"May the Great God Ashur strike me dead right away here and now, my lords! May he destroy me at this moment if I do not speak the truth, Great Masters! I—I know nothing of theft or being a thief! All my life, Great Masters, I have—" At this he got interrupted by one of the judges who growled at him to be brief and to the point. However, poor Bagtu-Shar knew nothing of what the point was or how to stick to it.

He swallowed hard, and then stammered on. "Gracious lords, every day, Master Adad-Nirani gives me a small amount of gold leaf, not more than what I will need for the next few days' work. This he does because in the mornings, he is not always there where I am to start my work, he may be some other place and so that I should not waste time in waiting for him—" And again, he was silenced by the same judge, crashing his fist down on the arm of his chair, to make his tale short. By this time, Bagtu-Shar had visibly withered under the wrathful eyes of this judge and was barely able to control the shaking of his body or the urgency of his bladder.

"Pardon me, great lord, I am only trying to explain why Master Adad-Nirani would give me more than one day's allotment of the... of the...gold...you see..." And his voice trailed off. He swallowed again and then continued, "When he gave me this week's allotment, great lords, it was already late in the day. I had finished... finished..."—he stammered—"my work for the day and started to gather up my basket, which my second wife always fills with food for me in the mornings so that I can...I can—" From the corner of his eye, he saw the same judge make a gesture of impatience, and hurried on as best he could. "I started to walk home, and by the time, I got half the way to home, two men, two godless bandits jumped at me and tore the little packet with the gold, which I was carrying along with my food basket...tore it...tore it...My lords, they tore it right out of my hand. And it was so dark that I could not...could not see to follow them, my gracious lords, and they were two, and I was only one..." Bagtu-Shar's voice finally trailed away into hopelessness, and then he was silent.

Master Adad-Nirani, who sat to one side of the grouping of dignitaries, felt compelled to stir now and rose from the low stool he was sitting on up to now. Since he had made the accusation to the judges, he needed no introduction to them. He raised his right arm and pointed to Bagtu-Shar. "As you see for yourselves, gracious lord judges, this impudent man has the temerity to confess his grave sins without hesitation! I most humbly beg you to pronounce me innocent and deal with this criminal as the law prescribes!"

In response to this request, the same judge who had reprimanded Bagtu-Shar several times now shifted his weight in his chair, glared at Master Adad-Nirani, and admonished him with rising anger.

"The accuser has nothing to say until asked. And most certainly, he shall not have an opinion to give to or demands to set for this august body here assembled!" And for emphasis, he rapped the heavy ring which adorned the first finger of his right hand on the armrest of his chair. "The accuser should sit silently and await the deliberations of this august body, and certainly not voice an opinion until or if he is required to add to his earlier testimony."

Master Adad-Nirani bowed deeply and quietly subsided onto the stool he had previously occupied. After this unwelcome interruption by Master Adad-Nirani, the presiding judge, spokesman for the assemblage, looked around and, in a loud voice, asked if indeed there were anyone present who would be willing or could put in a word against the accusations of, or in defense of, the accused. He waited for a brief period, and when nothing but silence filled the court, the judges put their head together, conferred for a few minutes, intermittently shaking their heads or nodding in unison. Bagtu-Shar, kneeling on the ground, ready to prostrate himself any moment, watched surreptitiously, his heart beating so hard that he thought it would fly out of his chest. He was not so stupid as not to understand that his life—and very likely that of his whole family—would be decided within the next few minutes.

Finally the judges returned to their seats and made one final request in this hearing. They asked for the appearance of Lord Borsuk-annam, only to hear him repeat his initial account of finding the work of Bagtu-Shar appealing and competent and, basing his decision on that observation, giving permission to Master Adad-Nirani. Master Adad-Nirani had by then proven his dependability well enough to be allowed access to gold leaf in larger quantities and always had good accounts for each sheet of gold, until the disappearance of several sheets given to the accused. After that the Lord Borsuk-annam bowed to the judges and bowed to the ground to Prince Sennacherib, turned, and returned to his seat.

Thereafter, it took the court less than a minute to pronounce judgment. The accused, as the law dictated for major cases of theft, would have both his hands cut off so as not to be able to commit theft again. Because the case also involved the theft of greatly valuable items, namely gold, the beauty of which was admired by all, the accused also would have both his eyes put out so as never again to be able to look at anything of beauty. His house would be levelled to the ground, and his family, consisting of women and girl children, would be sold on the Dur-Sharrukin slave market. After that the accused would be taken to the reedbeds of the Great Mother River, Tigris, there to be left to his fate. Prince Sennacherib then rose, reached out for the dried reed stick lying in readiness on a plate next to a brazier of glowing embers. Grasping the stick with both hands, he broke it in half and threw the two halves into the fire. The immutable sentence had been pronounced.

When Bagtu-Shar heard his sentence, it took him a long moment to comprehend. Then he threw his head back and let out such a howl of *no* that it sounded more like the bellowing of a wounded ox. He tried to rise from the ground, using both his hands to push himself up, but then he crumbled into the dust and had to finally be carried out by the soldiers of the court. His howling echoed from the distance for a long while, until one of the court soldiers kicked him in the face, after which he was silent.

*****

For Himene, the days dragged by with excruciating slowness. She floated along day by day, trying to motivate herself to do something enjoyable or at least productive, but all of her good resolve wilted with the oppressive heat of the day. Even baby Tiglath became cranky during the hottest part of the day and cried or slept in his basket, hung up to swing between two branches under a tree's shade. He had outgrown the first one that he had occupied as an infant and was on the verge of outgrowing this one as well.

A hundred times during each day, Himene, on impulse, would think of something that the child did which she thought would amuse her husband, only to remember that he was not going to be with her in the evening to listen to her accounts. She missed him terribly and had to admit to herself that much of the aimlessness of her days was that she simply was without his company or at least the promise of his company later in her day. In a hundred ways, she missed him. She missed their nights together but even more the intimacy of their conversations—sometimes serious, sometimes bantering, but always stimulating—because those were the times she could spend with him. For a long time now, she knew that she loved him, but only now did she come to realize how her husband had filled her whole existence and had done so before she ever became aware of it.

This much feared, often cruel and vindictive, demanding, impatient, imperious man, twice her own age, was her tender, thoughtful lover and husband. In her mind, at first, he was only a feared stranger, a despot, a tyrant. Her love slowly blossomed under his patiently nurturing tutelage, but now it filled her whole world until even the thought of living without him was inconceivably offensive. Somewhere in the back of her mind, she wondered how other women, in love with their husbands, bore the pain of eventually losing that love to another more favored woman. This was common occurrence in houses of women; she had seen it happen again and again, and even then, she had marveled at the forbearance—or was it self-control—of those who bore it with so much greater grace than she ever could. Of course, she had to admit to herself, for each woman in any House of Women, who devotedly loved her lord, there were ten who hated, feared, or detested him and were relieved to be rid of his unwanted attentions.

Each day, she received a brief private message sent to her by Sargon. It was separate from the dispositions and information sent daily to Prince Sennacherib and the turtanu, and it came etched into a clay tablet, not by words memorized by the courier. She was flattered that the king, in the midst of a campaign, would take time to have a message etched and sent, but most of all, she was flattered by the implicit acknowledgment by her husband that she was able to read the engraved runes and symbols. As an equally implicit answer to him, she etched her own tablets, sometimes spending most of her day on the labor. The tablets' messages were crudely written, but after all, she was no scribe. They, however, were readable enough to whoever the trusted person was, authorized by Sargon to read these most private messages to him.

Slowly, want it or not, the days began to assume an established rhythm of their own. Himene was mindful of a saying which she had heard many times as a child in the House of Women of her father, especially after the death of her mother, "A human being can slowly get adapted to any condition, good or horrible, given enough length of time." At that time, she was too young to fully grasp the concept, but now it came back to her again and again to haunt her. The only change in her life was the inexorable growth of her son and the pleasure she took in his company, if indeed the presence of a toddler could be called that. If she felt alone, she never showed it and perhaps did not even admit it herself.

Of course, she had access to every part and every occupant of the women's house. She knew that she would never really know whether her welcome there was genuine or not. But she never actually considered moving back into the mainstream of that life. Since she first arrived in Assyria, the open preference that the master of the House of Women demonstrated toward this newest wife of his did not endear her to the other wives. Later when Sargon had a separate apartment built for her—and for himself—Himene had understood that it was a declaration from the king. He wanted to establish a private little island for his family. To move back to the hustle and bustle of living with over three hundred wives and concubines and all their children, servants, and slaves was repellent. Moreover, it would have felt like betrayal of a life which her husband had designed and desired for her. If that life occasionally proved to be lonely, well, she just had to cope with it as best she could.

She did occasionally invite the Lady Simirrah, the turtanu's first wife, for a visit, or the Lady Atalyā, Prince Sennacherib's mother. She did not wish to expand her list with additional women from Sargon's House of Women, for she was unwilling to instigate jealousies. Lady Atalyā was the exception, but then she had befriended the young Himene first on her arrival and had shown her affection for the young woman almost from the first day. Also Himene realized that Prince Sennacherib's mother was at an age where jealousy would not play a part in her sentiments toward her.

After no more than two months of living almost in limbo, a change happened in Himene's daily routine; all of a sudden, the tablets, which came with such regularity until now, ceased to arrive. The first two days, she suppressed her worry and disappointment, but then decided to act indirectly. She sent one of her attendants to the Lady Simirrah to invite her to spend their afternoon together. It was then that she requested the lady to inquire from her husband, the turtanu, what news there was and why she had suddenly stopped receiving messages. With no other words said, Lady Simirrah immediately understood Himene's unspoken distress and promised to let her know as soon as she could. Before leaving and on a sudden impulse, Simirrah leaned over and warmly embraced the queen, who in age could have been her daughter. This was not a gesture approved by protocol, but Himene not only appreciated it but returned the embrace with all the warmth and appreciation she felt toward her friend.

Simirrah's promise turned out to be as good as done. By the evening of the same day, Himene received information directly from the turtanu, saying that he most sincerely regretted this omission. The reason for it was that he thought the Lord Sennacherib would inform Her Majesty. Shutur-Nahhunte promised that a better protocol would be strictly enforced from now on. He was grievously saddened to have caused any distress to Her Majesty. However, to reassure Her Majesty, he wanted her to know that the delay in messages was due to a skirmish between the forces of Assyria and of Urartu. Presumably the first messenger was intercepted and killed but lookouts sent from Dur-Sharrukin just reported that they had spotted a new courier proceeding with all speed to the city, carrying a certain flag which would immediately indicate that all was well.

Within a very short time, two more messages came, delivered to Himene posthaste, informing the Prince Sennacherib, the turtanu, and the council of difficult battles. The first of these was made difficult by the extremely hazardous terrain, filled with rocky outcrops and abysses and very dense vegetation which aided the enemy who, after all, lived in this region and had better knowledge of it than Sargon's army. The second battle had been made unexpectedly difficult in that the Cimmerians, a ragged wild-eyed reckless bunch of mountain dwellers, apparently joined the Urartian forces. But may the Great God Ashur be praised forever! The Assyrians remained victorious in both incidents, albeit with great loss of blood and life. Himene was happy and reassured, and after receiving a personal tablet from her husband assuring her of his most tender love, she literally floated on air.

And then again, after less than a week, there was nothing but silence. Not the prince, not the turtanu, not the council, or Himene received one word for days. While Himene suffered agonies of nightmares, walked circles in her garden for half the night, could barely force herself to eat, the council and its two leaders, Sennacherib and Shutur-Nahhunte, in private, were gravely concerned as well. Not only had they not heard from the king's couriers, but none of the posts deployed in the mountains to follow the army had returned with any information.

For all concerned, the waiting grew more intolerable with each passing day. And then finally a messenger arrived. He was near-death from his wounds and from exhaustion and lack of food and water and almost collapsed while he gave his report to the council. He had to walk, as best he could, the final leg of his journey to Dur-Sharrukin because his horse had perished from a fatal arrow. The spare horse, which all couriers were given was led on a line and riderless; thus he had no one to calm and to control him when he shied away from some forest animal, reared, and plunged to his death into a gorge.

The news the messenger brought could not have been worse—it was catastrophic. Actually he was acting on his own, and the words he carried were his own as well. Few remained from Sargon's army, but those who did sent him. In the middle of the night, three days ago, when everyone except the sentries lay in their tent sleeping, a Cimmerian war party threaded their way silently up the hill, one by one, treading so carefully that not even the rustle of a leaf could be heard. This was their home territory, and they were totally at home in these forbidding and dark woods. In silence, they assembled on top of the hill, encircling the sleeping Assyrian Army. Individual Cimmerian soldiers crawled on their bellies to the Assyrian sentries and, still in total silence and almost total darkness, garroted each before they even had an idea of what was upon them.

When this was accomplished, the Cimmerians, in a frenzy of war cries and screams, fell upon the tents, the whole of the Assyrian camp. Most of those who were there did not even have a chance to wipe the sleep from their eyes or to reach for their weapons. Truly it was an unprecedented bloodbath unleashed upon Sargon and his army. When the enemy withdrew, it became obvious that they had no desire to take prisoners or slaves, for literally every soldier was put to death where he stood.

At this point, the courier stopped and swallowed hard while tears were streaming down his pale dusty cheeks. It was, he said, easy to find the royal tent with the king's emblem still fluttering by the entrance. When they entered, what confronted them was more horrible, more grisly than anything they could have imagined. The floors, the carpets, the floor pillows were sodden with blood. All those in the tent had been hacked to death—the king's two personal slaves and his bodyguards. The king's body was virtually unrecognizable; he must have died from at least fifty stab wounds. But then the dead body had been mutilated and hacked to small pieces so that the courier was only able to find and bring with him one finger of the Great Ruler of the Known World. And that finger was only recognized as the king's by the heavy gold ring carrying the royal seal.

When he had finished, the frozen silence in the council chamber was complete. The messenger slowly dragged himself to Prince Sennacherib's chair, and reaching into his shoulder bag, in which he regularly carried his written tablets, he took out a small blood-soaked wrapping and, unwrapping it, put it into the prince's hand. Sennacherib only cast a short glimpse at it, covered his eyes, rose, and, turning away from the other council members, tore his cloak in two and let out a heavy sob. Since for the other council members there was no need to pose a question, one by one they rose as well and followed the prince's action, the universally accepted sign of mourning. The Lord Shutur-Nahhunte was the only one who remained seated, visibly so overcome that for the moment, he did not have the strength to rise.

Within minutes, the well-oiled protocol of the court started to function and took the first step in heralding the death of a king and the process of mourning. On all the major street corners of Dur-Sharrukin, trumpets, one by one, began to sound, and then the sacred horns of Ashur added their mournfully wailing notes from all the temples. Runners were dispatched almost immediately to the other cities, to villages and farms, announcing to all that Sargon, the Great Ruler of the Known World, was dead.

It was greatly in the interest of the country that continuity be preserved in governing the land. The turtanu, as soon as he could rouse himself from his grief, took the precious little packet with his friend and master's finger, with utmost care and reverence, removed the ring from the dead finger, and, holding it in his own two fingers, raised his hand and turned all around the council chamber so that everyone there assembled could see it.

"Charged so by our now-dead master to uphold rule in the Great God Almighty Ashur's Land, I am passing this ring as the sign of rule to Lord Sargon's firstborn son and heir, the Lord Prince Sennacherib." With that he walked over to the prince, prostrated himself to the ground, and kissed Sennacherib's feet and, upon rising, both his hands as well. Then he took his new lord's right hand and slipped the blood-splattered ring onto it.

Sennacherib was literally shaken to the core of his being. He could think of nothing but the mangled body of his revered father. The fact that for years now, the succession to his throne was the thought foremost in his mind paled when weighed in the scales of life and death of someone who had become dearly valued by him. Next to the personal grief, something he experienced for the first time in his young life, there were a daunting multitude of actions to initiate right away. Immediately after the council meeting dissolved, he summoned Shutur-Nahhunte to his house, requested the presence of two scribes, and, walking up and down in his workroom, tried as much as he was able to marshal his thoughts to initiate actions that he deemed most urgent. When he started to tick these off, the turtanu raised his hand and begged Sennacherib to dismiss everyone else for a short while. When Sennacherib looked into his serious face, he understood immediately that the turtanu had something to say to him in private. The prince nodded and, with a wave of his hand, sent everyone else out of the room. Then he turned to Shutur-Nahhunte.

"What is it, my lord?" he asked quietly and with as much composure as he could muster.

The turtanu walked over to the prince and put his hands on Sennacherib's shoulder. "My Master Sennacherib, please allow me to call you that, and please, I beg you to forgive my audacity in touching your august body without your permission, but I am an old man, and old habits are hard to break. I love and cherish you as I would a son…"

He looked away with tear-filled eyes into the distance, then he rallied and continued, "My lord Sennacherib, it seems to me that there are certain things to be considered before all else. Please keep in mind that your august father had at no point made public an absolute decision about his succession. You and I are both aware of the child that was so recently born to him and his wife, the former princess and now-queen Himene. We both know what the reasons were for arranging that marriage, but the fact remains that despite your august father's assumed desire, circumstances have suddenly developed which, it seems to me, have taken away any claim on the part of Lady Himene and her child to any possible succession. For consider, the child is less than a year old. This land needs a ruler and needs him now, today! And in that now, there is no one else but you, my lord.

"Also consider that not only does the land need you, there is no other in the remotest sense who would be qualified. You know, my lord, that your father had begun to train and nurture you for just such an event. Neither he nor I had expected anything that just happened to happen. But it did, and we have to face it." Here he broke off, wiped his tear-wet eyes, sighed, and then went on, rubbing his forehead.

"I know that you are willing to take the mantle of power, the crown, the ring, and the sword and to step into your father's seat. Make no mistake, my lord, even if every fiber of your body desires it now, the day will come when your only wish will be to shed the same…But I am getting ahead of myself. At this moment, you must secure your inheritance. It is a rightful inheritance, but not everyone will see it thus. I beg you, my lord, to believe when I assert that my love and loyalty to Queen Himene is in no way affected by what I must express. She, of course, has no say in such state matters, except—if she so wishes—as spokesperson for her infant son. However, if there were any faction in this Land of Ashur which would question your right of inheritance, they may invoke the name of the queen and of the infant Tiglath-Pileser. Believe me, my lord, that would end in bloody upheavals, war, misery, destruction, and famine for the whole realm. You, my lord, must act now and place the crown on your head at the same time when the funeral fires will burn for your father." After all this, he fell silent to give Sennacherib time to digest all he had said.

Sennacherib stirred, walked from one window to the other, then to the door, in an effort to compose himself and gather his own thoughts. Absently he stared out the window, then turned abruptly and asked, "And the queen? Should I send a message to her or go myself with this dreadful news? What role will she have in the future? Will she have any role at all? To return her to her father's palace is impossible. To relegate her to a subordinate role in the House of Women is difficult. How should I behave toward her? And the child, what privileges should he retain?"

Shutur-Nahhunte looked his new master square into the eye. "My lord, I best not advise you there. My affection for the queen and the child may cloud my judgment. But I do believe that since you now rule—in effect, if not in fact—neither the queen nor the crown prince can retain their titles and positions. The future queen should be a lady you choose for yourself and the crown prince an offspring of your own body. However"—and here he hesitated so long that Sennacherib finally looked at him with curiosity—"however, my lord, keep in mind, past history tells us stories similar to this one, how the new ruler of the land took the pervious king's spouse by the hand and made her his wife to underscore the legitimacy of his claim to the throne." Here the turtanu bowed and begged to be dismissed from the royal presence.

"You, my young master, have a great many things to mull over. Do not take much time with your decisions, as time now is of essence. I have many dispatches to send throughout the land and certain legalities and questions for the magistrates. I beg to be allowed to withdraw. Of course, I stand at readiness the moment you call for me." And bowing again, he turned and, with dragging steps and bowed head, walked out of Sennacherib's house.

*****

Later in the day, shortly before sundown, Prince Sennacherib's presence was announced to Queen Himene. She had heard the wailing sound of the trumpets and the horns, and although she was a newcomer to the land, and uncertain what those mournful sounds meant, she certainly assumed that they meant some disaster. She had given little Tiglath into the care of his nurses and withdrew into her workroom. The room was generously littered with the activities she had abandoned earlier in the day, with untouched and half-finished clay tablets lying everywhere, along with some chipped, cracked, or broken ones; wet animal hides were heaped on a table, which also held a bowl of water, all to keep the clay tablets soft enough to accept the etching quill without breaking. Here she sat patiently, her hands folded on her lap, until she gave in to her anxiety and impatience and started circling the room, walking untold times from one end of it to the other.

Eventually, just before dusk, the doorkeeper eunuch, in a great flutter, announced the Prince Sennacherib, who desired to speak to her. Before the eunuch had even withdrawn or the queen given her consent, Sennacherib was at the door. He bowed his head but just, Himene noted, and then came directly to face her. His eyes were red-rimmed and his face haggard, all of which Himene noted as well. He stood in front of her, irresolute and obviously agitated. Finally Himene took pity on him, rose, and, with a gesture, offered him the chair next to the one she was sitting on. "Prince," she said softly, "something has greatly distressed you! I hear the mourning sounds of horn and trumpet outside. We both seem to be most anxious. I beg you to tell me the bad news if that is what you have for me. I promise you, I will bear the news, whatever it is."

Sennacherib looked down at his feet. The lady's grace and composure had affected him deeply. Brought up in the House of Women among women who usually exhibited varying degrees of volatility and hysteria, but a lesser degree of self-control than what he now witnessed, he began to grasp part of the reasons for his father's attachment and regard for this woman. He swallowed hard, then looked Himene in the eyes because he thought that he owed her that much.

"My gracious lady, Himene, I am the bringer of most grievous news. The council, the lord turtanu and I have this morning finally received news of the army. It had been"—he hesitated in an effort to choose his words properly—"attacked by marauding Cimmerians during the night of three day ago. Our army was unsuspecting and asleep. The Cimmerians massacred almost everybody, and those who did not die immediately, or were unable to run away, were put to the sword. The great king, my father, your husband, is dead, lady, and the little what is left of the army is on the run."

In the ensuing silence, only the splashing of the fountains in the garden could be heard and the breathing of the two people in the room. Himene gripped her two hands together so hard that her nails dug into her palms. She felt a sudden weakness, a roaring in her ears, while the room spun around her with dizzying speed. She forced herself to take a shuddering breath and waited until the hammering of her heart subsided somewhat. Still dizzy, she rose with difficulty, almost stumbled, and addressed Sennacherib, who was totally surprised by her words and amazed by her calmness.

"I wish to thank Your Gracious Majesty for the courtesy and kindness you have shown me in this hour. You now are faced with many duties which await you. May the Great God Ashur give you guidance. I am much indebted to you for having found time to personally inform me. I am your obedient servant, Majesty." And with that, she bowed to him, a little unsteadily.

Sennacherib noticed, saw her white face, and reached for her elbow to steady her. When she was seated again, he nodded his head to her and, turning, walked out of the room. *It had been some of the most difficult moments of my life*, he thought, *and I hardly knew my father. How much harder must it have been for her, who loved him!*

Himene did not know how long she sat there. There were no thoughts in her mind, no sense of sadness or grief, only a heavy band constricting her chest so that she could barely breathe. *Oh, gods*, she thought, *let me just get over this sense of illness, and then I shall have the rest of my life to grieve!* She repeated the same thought again and again, in hopes that the awareness of her loss would bring the tears which were burning in the back of her eyes. *Oh, gods*, she prayed, *allow me to die, for I have no more business here.* Then her son's face appeared to her mind's eye, and she knew that because of him, she could not even allow herself the luxury of death. The household was quiet around her; the servants must have heard by now what had transpired, or maybe they knew before she ever did and could not bring themselves to tell her? Someone brought in some oil lamps, and a tray of food was laid in front of her. She just shook her head and waved the food away.

Poor Prince Sennacherib, she thought. No, no, she reconsidered, at least in his grief and distress, he was lucky to have things, chores that he needed to do, that pushed him on but also took his mind away from this unspeakable, this horrible grief! Anything, anything to do rather than to sit here by the light of the oil lamp, stricken, paralyzed, crushed by the weight of grief. She tried to think of her husband and could not, each time her mind's eye stumbling at the point of seeing Sargon's body, now torn, mauled, desecrated, to never, never breathe again, talk again, laugh his booming laugh again, kiss her again, to wrap his arms about her again. Only one more day, one more hour with him, she thought, and that thought somehow eased the constriction of her chest by bringing the first tears to her eyes.

After that, she did cry. She sat in the almost-dark of the room for the gods only knew how long, the tears welling endlessly, silently from her eyes and coursing down her cheeks, dropping onto her lap, upon her clenched hands on her lap. She had no recollection what happened later, when to her surprise, she found herself in her bed, lying exhausted from crying and staring out into the dark night. Out there, somewhere, her husband's dead body lay—or what was left of that body—and she would never, never again be able to see him, to hear his voice, to touch him.

Obedient to her obligations to the living, and her promise to her husband, she followed her daily morning routine as best she could the next day. Delegations of women and court individuals were waiting outside to greet her, to assure her that they shared her grief, but at this point, she did not yet feel capable of facing them and still retain her composure. That would come later, and so she charged the doorkeeper eunuch to turn them away as politely as possible.

Then sometime in the afternoon—it had turned pleasantly cooler after ominous black clouds had descended from the distant mountains and brought with them an unexpected downpour—it was announced to Himene that Crown Prince Sennacherib requested to see her. She was sitting in her garden, this time by the pool, her one hand trailing into the water because drops of rain were still falling from the trees' foliage, where she was accustomed to sit. When Sennacherib entered, he was shocked by her pale drawn face, the heavy dark circles under her eyes, the hollow cheeks, all accentuated by the stark whiteness of her mourning tunic and veil. In all of this unadorned white, the gloriously beautiful neck collar, which had so recently been the gift of her husband, shone and glinted in the late-day sunlight, reflecting its rays with each rise and fall of her bosom. She attempted to rise, but the prince hurried to her with a quick gesture, asking her to remain seated.

After that, he seated himself on a cushion opposite her, looking exceedingly uncomfortable, and when asked by her if he would require any refreshments, he just shook his head. During the ensuing pause, he looked left and right, remarking to no one in particular what a delightful place this garden was.

Himene nodded with great seriousness and said by way of explanation, "Yes, Majesty, I do think so too. Your gracious father, my husband, had it built for me during the days after our child was born." With that, the pause returned until finally, Sennacherib jumped up and, walking to and fro to hide his agitation, finally turned to her.

"My lady Himene, what I have to say to you is important and serious, and I would like for you to follow my thoughts all the way to their end before you respond to me. What I have to say to you, lady, may also seem to you to be premature. However, you will understand that under the circumstances that exist, speed is a requirement. I do believe that I need not go into the reasons why my father desired to marry you, my lady. These days, the proof of royal descent carries equal weight to a strong arm or a bold mind. In many countries, those who have been maligned as usurpers of the throne have not found allegiance from the people they wished to govern, while a weak ruler of royal descent has been welcomed. You, my lady, may also be aware of certain totally fallacious rumors with regard to my father's and, through him, now of my claim for, and right to, the throne of this land. Simply put, Lady Himene, I am now confronting the same necessity as did my revered father—to add royal blood to my line and my posterity." Here he stopped for a moment and took a deep breath, as a swimmer does who prepares to dive underwater.

"My lady, you and I have now known each other for two years. We are of the same age. I have now and have ever had a sincere admiration for your intelligence, kindness, grace, graciousness, and beauty. I pray and trust that you also do not have reason to think ill of me. What could be a simpler, more straightforward, yet, at the same time, beneficial gesture to the whole of this land, signifying the ruling family's unity in thought, but that this unity should become the union of their new king and the queen of his father? I have no wife and not one lady in our House of Women who is close to my heart. I have not looked to select a first wife for myself, having indeed thought that step to be premature. I beg you to forgive my bluntness, lady, but you no longer have a husband, and your position as the queen of Assyria is under challenge. Your only course of action would be to return to the House of Women and live out your life there."

Here Sennacherib stopped, took another deep breath, and then plunged along.

"On the other hand, Himene, your marriage to me would assure your position and, through you, also strengthen mine. I am well aware that in your heart, no one can replace my august father. But you are young, and life will carry both of us on for many years to come. I ask you to think on all these things and to hear your consent when I return here tomorrow. I believe that you are a sensible woman who understands that you are in a position where your answer will unavoidably have to be yes."

And with that last sentence, Sennacherib nodded, turned, and walked out of Himene's garden. As she watched his receding figure, she noticed, for the first time, the almost-imperceptible limp which tended to afflict him at moments of fatigue or stress and was the only residue of the disastrous injury he had suffered almost two years ago.

For a long, long eternity, Himene sat frozen, her heart beating so furiously that she thought it would leap out of her chest. Last night, she had thought that nothing worse could ever happen to her. She was mistaken. This, this was worse than anything else that she was expected to bear. It was an offense and an insult to her, to her child, and most of all, to her now-dead husband, who was not yet dead for the stretch of even one week! It was a slap in her face, a trivialization of all her and her husband's most intimate feelings for each other, for the act of love which bound them, for their marriage, which had been blessed by the priests of Ashur! How could he—how would anyone dare to assume that they could take the place of her husband in her bed, in her heart? It was monstrous, it was inconceivable, not to be borne!

Then the affront implied in the threat of Sennacherib's last words flashed through her head, *I believe that you are a sensible woman who understands that you are in a position where your answer will unavoidably have to be yes.* She caught her breath and jumped up from her seat, finally mobilized by fear. Was that really true? Was she so powerless? Was she this much at the mercy of events as they were unrolling in front of her mind's eye? Did she truly not have an alternative but to submit to Sennacherib's wishes? The answer to each of these, it seemed, was yes, yes, and yes.

She thought it peculiar that submission to a man was so onerous to her now. This is—was—what she was taught, raised to believe and to accept. For her, for thousands upon thousands of women, submission was the only way of life; and most of them, including she in her past life, accepted it as such. Did the love of her husband teach her this much self-assurance? About being her own person? *Yes, yes, a thousand times yes*, she thought! *To honor him, not only to pursue my own wishes, I cannot, I will not give in to this atrocious request.* With this resolution, absolute calmness returned. For the first time since the moment that she heard of her husband's death, she felt hunger and thirst, ordered some fruit and honey cakes to eat, some wine to drink, and then withdrew to her and Sargon's sleeping chamber to sleep a long, peaceful, uninterrupted sleep.

When she awoke the next morning, she was instantly mindful of Sennacherib's promise—or was it a threat—to return during the day for her answer. She tried to keep as calm and composed as she could manage and follow her usual daily routine as much as possible. To receive some of the delegations waiting to be seen now became unavoidable. Naturally these groups were women from Sargon's own House of Women and senior wives from important dignitaries of the land, as well as from the ambassadors of foreign countries who had established households in Dur-Sharrukin. Though these formal events were very brief, still she found them draining, probably because of the effort she had to extend to keep her emotions in check. Afterward she ate sparingly and played a little with her son, Tiglath. It was then that the arrival of King Sennacherib was announced to her. She noted that he no longer was addressed as Prince Sennacherib or even as Crown Prince Sennacherib, though no official coronation had yet taken place. That she could readily understand; if his position was—as he had claimed—precarious, then it was important to consolidate that claim as soon as possible.

Himene rose slowly, with great deliberation, smoothed her tunic, gave her child into the care of his nannies, and then waited by the open doorway for Sennacherib. When she saw him, she bowed deeply, giving him all the courtesy of his station, if not his person, and murmured the prescribed words of welcome. He nodded to her and then, indicating for her to sit, seated himself on one of cushions next to a low table with a bowl of fruit on it. He reached for a fig but, instead of putting it in his mouth, began toying with it in an obvious attempt to calm his nervousness.

Marginally Himene felt sorry for him, understanding that he was seesawing between too much obsequiousness and too much haughtiness, too inexperienced to be able to establish the appropriate balance of each. Fortunately, she thought, politeness dictated that a woman should never directly look at any male present or speak first to him, and thus looking down at her hands folded on her lap, she patiently waited for Sennacherib to break the silence. He finally did so while still playing with the fruit in his hand.

"My lady." He commenced. "I ask you to forgive me for making my visit with you of necessity a brief one. Many duties and decisions await me in addition to this one." Himene noted with detached amusement that he referred to this visit as a duty. Sennacherib plowed on.

"As I had indicated to you when we talked yesterday, my lady, I cannot delay my actions too long, nor is it in this case, I find, necessary to delay. Yesterday I did you the honor of laying out to you my thoughts and reasons which led me to my decision rather than acting peremptorily without explanation. Our marriage, which will need to take place soon, unfortunately without the traditional time allotted for mourning, will strengthen my position greatly and thereby undercut any unrest which would arise otherwise. It is a most logical and wise step to take, and my father would fully understand and approve. As the gods have seen fit to make you the mother of many children, our royal line would be assured. Happiness and love—if they follow our union—will be an additional blessing of the gods. As soon as I leave your presence, I shall instruct the appropriate persons at my court to take the steps necessary to arrange this union. My lady, I can assure you that in our future together, I will always treat you with the care and respect you deserve. Also I am fully cognizant of the sacrifice you are making for this land and for me."

He rose, bowed his head to her in preparation to leave, and then turned back with surprise when he heard Himene's quiet voice.

"Majesty, my lord Sennacherib, with your kind permission, I would like to point out that I have as yet not agreed to the arrangements you are alluding to and call to your attention the promise you made yesterday, when you left here, to return and hear my consent." And almost subconsciously, she raised her voice on those last three words.

The surprise on Sennacherib's face was obvious. His face turned a shade darker as he retraced his steps to the cushion which he had just vacated.

"Lady, it seems to me that you are hardly in a position to bargain," he said with suppressed anger.

Himene shook her head. After two days of turmoil and distress, she felt an absolutely icy calm and purpose. "On the contrary, Majesty. The explanation of your request, made to me yesterday, and the eagerness to proceed with your plan with all possible haste only underscore that I do have a position and, in fact, a very important one. I understand very well that by way of my position as the mother of the only male child of royal descent—and possibly the only legitimate heir to Assyria's throne—by my husband, the Lord King Sargon, my assent to become your wife, Majesty, would greatly strengthen your position. At the same time, Majesty, it would, without a doubt, nullify any claims that my child would have to the throne. Himene quickly continued as she noted Sennacherib's small gesture of interruption.

"However, these are considerations that reach too far into the future. The present also, Majesty, dictates to me. I was the lawful wife of your father, the now-dead king. Much more than that, he and I loved each other with steadfast devotion, not for just today or tomorrow but for all the rest of our lives. He is dead, but I am alive, feeling the same sentiments I felt two days ago and bound by my oath to Sargon until I die. To belong to another would be a desecration of my feelings, my body, all my emotions, and an affront to my dead husband. I cannot allow it to happen, on my behalf but also out of reverence to your father, my dead husband. It is entirely, altogether, for now and forever, out of the question.

"Majesty, I am and shall always be mindful of the great honor of your offer. As long as I live, I shall be your obedient subject and servant. I am prepared to outlive the rest of my days wherever your command would send me, except in your household, in your sleeping chamber, in your bed." She stopped and drew a long quivering breath, only now realizing the wild hammering of her heart.

Sennacherib watched her and listened to her with increasing incredulity and anger. Still somewhere in the back on his mind, he admired this magnificently fearless woman who stood up to him with such well-chosen words and such fire in her heart. He rose, adjusted the richly edged fringed robe which every fashionable man wore, draped over his tunic, and, scowling at her, made a dismissive gesture.

"It appears to me, dear lady, that you are in no position to argue and only one path that you can—or shall I say, will be allowed—to take. You have been outmaneuvered and encircled, so to say. It would be wise for your own and your son's comfort and future to accede to my wishes."

"Indeed, Majesty, I do have choices and friends who will stand by me. Please understand that I do not aspire the power either for myself or my son. I will repeat what I said earlier, that at any time, I shall be Your Majesty's most obedient subject in everything else, but I will not relinquish my power of choice."

Sennacherib gave her the courtesy of a brief bow. "Lady Himene," he murmured in farewell, "I regret that you do not wish to be more…ah…accommodating! But no matter, you would not be the first person to relinquish a position, or…shall we say a mindset, one way or another, in favor of a more reasonable one. Rest assured that this plan will not be dropped and that you will not be allowed to thwart my wishes…And now, lady, I bid you farewell—for today."

*****

Master Adad-Nirani was worried. Ever since the incident involving one of the artisans assigned to his section of designing and carving the wall decorations, a fellow named Bagtu-Shar, he had been unable to find a capable replacement for him. In addition, every time he was reminded of Bagtu-Shar, he had a vague sense of unease and irritation. Why, he thought for the hundredth time, why did that dumb ox of a man have to get himself involved in theft? And theft of gold, no less! Did he really think that a major offense like that would go unnoticed and unpunished? And what could he do when the two accounts, that of what he gave out and that what was reportedly used, turned out not to match; what could he do but report the man? He really felt sorry about it, knowing that the fellow had a family, and besides that, the man could have had a peaceful, successful life because he was truly good at what he was doing!

So much so, Adad-Nirani thought, that now he had a real problem to find a replacement. Twice he had hired people who had been hotly recommended to him by an acquaintance or relative, obviously someone who had to pay off a debt for a favor, and both times he had to let the worker go for either lack of talent, know-how, or just sheer laziness. Dammit, Adad-Nirani thought, he really missed Bagtu-Shar, not only for his skill but because he was an obliging man, pleasant to work with.

In that sense, Adad-Nirani finally decided, one day after work hours, to saunter down the alley where Bagtu-Shar's house was located and see what he could find out about the unfortunate man, if anything at all. He had never before been in that part of the city, but after receiving directions several times from passersby whom he asked, finally he entered the little winding alley. He was lucky because an elderly woman, who was sweeping away some dead leaves and dog droppings from in front of her house into the shallow gutter, was only too glad to take a break from her chores for a well-deserved gossip. She invited Adad-Nirani to sit on a low stool she brought out from her house, then invited him not only to sit for a while but to drink some freshly milked goat milk. Adad-Nirani, overheated from the walk he had just undertaken, was grateful for both offers and more than happy to listen.

Since the woman had no idea that she was talking to poor Bagtu-Shar's former supervisor who had been his chief accuser, she had no reservations about talking and giving her opinion freely.

"May Great Ashur have mercy on him," she muttered, flashing the few teeth still left in her mouth, "but I think he must have perished by now. Few people survive long in the swamps, they say, even if they are able-bodied. But what chance does a blind man have with no hands to defend himself or just to pluck a fruit off a tree, even if he could see enough to find it? They say that when he was sentenced, one of the guards kicked him in the head so hard that after that, he lost almost all of his hearing as well. And besides that, he was no longer able to walk straight but in circles round and round, maybe from the kick, or maybe from not seeing? Ashur would be kind in allowing him to die as soon as possible." She sighed and looked thoughtfully into the distance, nodding her head.

"You understand, young master, that everyone around here liked him very much. Everyone believes that he was set up by some enemy, maybe, or else just could not prove that the gold was stolen off him and that he was innocent. But how can a poor man prove that? And being a poor man, how would anyone have thought that he was carrying treasures of gold? In that case, sir, think of it! Why would anyone think of robbing him? Maybe he bragged about it before, and someone overheard and, in the dark of the night, grabbed the gold? Well, no one will know for sure. But it is certain that he liked to talk, and to brag, about his work and his good fortune for being blessed by the gods with such talent."

Finally Adad-Nirani put up his hand and was able to stem the flow of words. He reached into a small purse, which hung on a chain attached to his waist, concealed by the robe he wore draped over his work tunic. He pulled out a small coin and put it into her palm. Then he prompted her with as much calm as he could muster to conceal his curiosity.

"Well, go on, old mother, but do not go here and there with your story, just stay with what you know, not what you think." Easier said than done, he thought wryly, as he nodded to her to continue.

"As I said, young master, he was a person well liked. Had a big wedding celebration when he took a lady for his first wife, after his earlier first wife died. Anyway I think that was a bad deal, though she bore him a child, a sickly girl who died recently. Which is a blessing, for when the soldiers of the court came and drove everyone else to the slave market to be sold, surely they would have put to the sword a babe who still sucked from her mother's breast, neh?

"But all the others in the household, young master, had been condemned by the king's court to be sold on the slave market and the proceeds from their sale to be paid by the magistrates for, what they called, restitution…restitution for the gold stolen by Bagtu-Shar.

"I tell you, young master, that was a shame! Such pity! Those little girls, they did not understand anything, they just stood there with their mouths open and their eyes wide, crying, screaming for their Ahnaputta, who was the good one, Bagtu-Shar's second wife, and really she was the one who raised them and ran the house and did all the chores and…" Here she had to catch her breath.

Again, Adad-Nirani quickly asked the woman to go on. "Old mother, which did you say was their house?"

And the old woman just shook her head and said with genuine sadness. "No need to go there, there is no one but bats and scorpions living there and an old goat which they had and which keeps foraging in their garden, and I go occasionally to milk her when I hear her complain too loudly about the pain of her full udder. I wonder why no one would take the goat because she still gives good milk and needs little to keep her alive, but I think most folk living here feel that the house is cursed and fear to go near it…"

This momentary silence was Adad-Nirani's signal to get up and, thanking the woman again, walk back in the same direction he came from as quickly as he could. He had heard enough and more about this sad story and understood that not he, not anyone, could help; there was nobody left to be helped.

*****

The new king, Sennacherib, whose rule at this time extended back in time for less than a week, and the turtanu, who had also been turtanu and trusted friend of the former king, sat together in a small room of the king's palace in earnest conversation and planning. The king was exhausted, with noticeable circles under sleepless eyes. Every once in a while, he would rise precipitously from his seat and walk about the room, from one window to another and window to door, in an obvious effort to curb his tension and agitation. The turtanu, Shutur-Nahhunte's, calm voice was the only sound to be heard. He was expounding upon a subject which they had been discussing now for a while.

"Majesty," said Shutur-Nahhunte as his eyes followed Sennacherib's movements. "I beg of you to believe that with all my heart, I do understand the Lady Himene's arguments and feelings. Please keep in mind that I had a close friendship with your deceased father. Please keep in mind that I am a half brother of his, that we grew up in amicability and had forged a strong bond of friendship over many years…" He had to stop for a moment to wipe his eyes. "Your father, Majesty, knew little that he did not bring to my attention. Repeatedly he talked to me about the strong bond of love that had developed in his heart for his new queen and about his joy on finding that the Lady Himene returned those feelings. They delighted in each other's love, and I was delighted in their happiness. Nothing, therefore, would be farther from my mind than to doubt the sincerity, the seriousness of Lady Himene's objections. Unfortunately a ruler, or even the adviser to that ruler, cannot afford the luxury of emotions. Like it or not, we must therefore look at the necessary facts which drive this problem. And, Majesty, I beg you to believe that whatever personal feelings I may harbor, I am and shall always be a loyal servant of Your Majesty and of this land. My private affections or allegiances will never be allowed to enter into my arguments or cloud my judgment…Let me therefore marshal my thoughts.

"One, so far, there have been no objections to your assumption of rule, my lord. But have no doubt, these are still early days, the country is reeling from the loss of a beloved king and also from many personal losses, given the number of the dead. Between now and the intended coronation, there will be objections, softly spoken or loud.

"Two, your revered father was quite right in assuming that the claim of royal birth would strengthen both his reign and those of his successors. This is where Queen Himene comes in, although in a different way from what your revered father's plans were. However, for you, Majesty, marriage to a princess of the blood would also strengthen your claim to rule, especially if a royal heir would be born out of that union.

"Three, we have to face the totally negative mindset of the Lady Himene. Unless she relents—and I have little hope that she would—you, Majesty, would have to acquire a royal bride from another ruler, another country, and do so soon. But this will present a problem. We already have a royal lady who, in this case, cannot just be set to the side. She is, moreover, the mother of a son whom many will regard as the legitimate heir over you, Majesty. The power she holds is—if I may say so—being the mother of her royal offspring. She cannot just be shunted over to the House of Women as a dowager queen because for many, she is—she has the status of being—the legitimate Queen Mother, mother to the legitimate heir.

"Four, as a direct consequence of this, your future—shall we say presumed future—royal bride would have no status or position other than first wife of the king. Frankly, sire, I do not believe that any of the current rulers would be willing to enter into such a relationship with you on behalf of any of their daughters, unless they were coerced. And at that point, sire, we enter another, even more uncertain, territory, and this I would very vigorously advise against."

Here the turtanu took a deep breath and then plowed on. "My fear, sire, is that the Lady Himene's presence may yet become a huge problem. She may be compliant and promise you to withdraw in silence into the House of Women, but as much as she would do that—and I believe that her word is good and honest—there are factions in this land who harbor ill will to you and would exploit the lady or rather, through her, the son's legitimacy. She would in fact become a rallying point for many dissenters. She cannot just be made to disappear, and as she now belongs to Assyria, not to her native land, she also cannot be sent home."

Sennacherib was listening to all this with great concentration, and when Shutur-Nahhunte finished, he turned and, with a sudden dismissive gesture, retorted, "My lord Turtanu, there is one thing missing from your equations. If necessary, I promise you, I will be capable to apply sufficient pressure on the lady, one way or another, to have her as my wife. Be sure of that! You may think it to be the impetuousness of youth. Be it as it may, I will not be thwarted in this, and I have said the same to the lady herself. I will be happy to welcome a gentler solution and, in that sense, give the lady one more week to reconsider. Should you come up with another, as I say, 'gentler' solution, I will welcome it.

"And now, my lord, let me assure you of my deepest gratitude for your good advice. I know how much my august father loved you and depended on you. As a younger man much in need of the same good advice, not just as your king, I welcome your guidance and the sharing of your vast store of knowledge with me. May the Great Lord Ashur preserve you from harm for my and our land's benefit."

Shutur-Nahhunte understood that this was a gracious way for the king to end further discussion, bowed deeply over the hand that was extended to him, touched his heart and his forehead, and withdrew. His two scribes, who always accompanied him, and the bearers who carried him in his palanquin were waiting for him outside the door to the king's chamber. In the sudden melee of bodies all rising and preparing to leave, the turtanu noticed only vaguely that the favorite slave of the king, the first one he owned in his earlier days as prince, was also loitering in front of the door. In the past, he had frequently made himself indispensable to his master in many ways, had the king's ear about many things, and, in general, had turned out to be a very resourceful Greek fellow. When the slave, by the name of Empyades, fell to his knees for the turtanu, he nodded to the Greek with kindness, murmured something that it was unnecessary for him to do so, and was carried on with his retinue.

Empyades, on the other hand, who made it his business to listen to everything, walked away from the doorway deep in thought. His agile mind was occupied with all that he had overheard. There were many things that he knew already, even before today's discussion between his master and Shutur-Nahhunte. What he had just heard either filled in gaps in his knowledge or underscored certain parts of it. By nature, an inquisitive and acquisitive man who was convinced that information equated wealth, he knew that this was the only kind of wealth he had as a bargaining chip. He also understood that any welfare or improvement in his current status could come only from his master. Actually he liked his master who now, almost by miracle, turned out to be the most powerful man in the land. The position, however, which was the source of his power, was in jeopardy, perhaps not today but at some future time. This much he understood from overhearing the two men's conversation.

If this were so, Empyades thought, and the threat came from a mere woman, then the danger should and must be eliminated. Dealing with a woman who lived within minutes from where he now stood could certainly make things easier? Better? He would have to think about it and see. The important fact was that this woman threatened his master's oh so promising future, and he thus believed that of his very own as well. Empyades was not afraid of action as long as the desired effect could be achieved. And so, thoughtfully contemplating what needed and what could be done during the next few days, he settled down on the rush matting in front of his master's sleeping chamber, where he spent his nights in case his master needed him.

*****

Queen Himene and her infant son played together on her shaded verandah. It was midmorning, before the heat of the day acquired its full force. Both had a peaceful night. In fact, Himene woke early, walked to the door open to the outside to enjoy the sight of the rising sun and the sleepy chirping of her caged songbirds, then went back to her bed and, much to her surprise, slumbered on until the sun was fully up and her serving girls were bringing in a tray with food and drink for her.

Almost with desperation, she clung to her established daily routine, subconsciously trying to maintain some normalcy in her life. This routine and her son were the two anchors in her current life. Two days had passed since her last contentious conversation with her stepson Sennacherib. The day after that, she did receive a message from him, carried by his Greek slave, telling her that he gave her a week, and no more, to become "reasonable." She sent back her answer that same day, letting him know that the passing of time will not alter her decision. There was no further communication between them since.

Himene tried not to guess whether Sennacherib gave up on his plan or if he was planning some way to coerce her into submission. Since the news about her husband's death, she had felt like a swimmer who has submerged underwater. Every sound, every movement reached her distorted and as in a dream. Sometimes she could hardly differentiate between outside reality and her own thoughts. The sharp-edged logic, which allowed her to argue her case against Sennacherib, deserted her as she floated through the hours of each day. Many groups of women still came to pay their respects to her; she spent the time allotted by courtesy with them, and no more, and, except for the daily visits by Lady Simirrah, spent her days alone with her child. When the days imperceptibly merged one into the other, that was just fine with her.

Eventually, however, the day arrived on which King Sennacherib announced that he would pay her a late-afternoon visit after most of his work was done. Himene acknowledged the message with a wordless nod, then set about to dress herself in a fresh white shift and the white veil of a widow. Again her only decoration was the gold neck chain which had been a gift of her husband. She ate an early meal, sent her son to be with his nannies, and then found her way to her verandah, where she sat in quiet waiting, her two hands resting calmly on her lap. If she wanted to be honest with herself, she had to admit that she was perfectly calm. This admission drew a slight smile when she remembered her heart-pounding anxiety when her husband first approached her on their wedding night.

Sennacherib arrived just before sundown, alone other than the accompaniment of his Greek slave. Himene wondered if the man was his master's shadow or guard dog. She rose and silently bowed to the king. Again, as before, while wondering about her detachment, she noticed how haggard he looked in his plain woolen tunic, the earthy tones of which only accentuated the paleness of his face. He was a stocky young man with bulging muscles and a handsome face, but now, even though he still looked powerfully built, he also looked vulnerable and deathly tired. So much so that with a sudden sense of compassion, she inquired of him if he had his evening meal yet or if she could invite him to share a supper with her. He looked up at her in genuine surprise, and the shadow of a smile flitted across his mouth.

"You are most gracious, my lady," he murmured, "no, indeed I have not yet had time to eat." And then he continued with a broader smile, "Actually I seem to recall that I have not eaten a midday meal either."

Himene shook her head. "Sire," she said in disapproval, "that is a certain way to become ill. Forgive my forwardness, but this country can now ill afford a sick ruler. I beg you to allow me to order a light meal for you, it would take no time at all." And before he could even answer, she clapped her hands and gave brief orders to the woman who appeared in the doorway.

If Sennacherib wanted to object, he did not. He closed his eyes for a moment, enjoying the sense of being pampered, not to be served by a slave or servant but of being a guest. Suddenly he realized that he had never been a guest, never had moments like this in his young life. But then the moment passed, and more urgent problems pressed on his mind. He roused himself from his reverie when he saw Himene rise and offer him some wine that she had just poured from an earthenware pitcher. Gratefully he accepted it and, realizing how thirsty and hungry he was, drank the goblet full down in one draught.

For a while, there was silence between them, and Himene noticed that the stern line of frown between his eyebrows had smoothed a bit. The silence was only broken when several serving maids arrived with trays of cold venison and lamb, a platter of flatbreads baked in hot ashes, a heaping bowl of curds, some fresh cheese, some small honey cakes and fruit. The king ate hungrily and with relish while Himene picked at a bit of cheese with a segment of flatbread, and a honey cake, her favorites. The silence between them became almost companionable, both of them, in their own ways, sensing the easing of tension between them.

When the king had finished and had washed his fingers in a bowl of rose-petal water, he sighed with contentment and leaned back on his cushions. His eyes went to Himene with a gaze that felt like stabbing her into her very bones.

"My Lady Himene," he said slowly, carefully measuring each of his words. "Let me first express my gratitude for your hospitality. You have entertained me graciously, treated me with kind hospitality, and I must confess that I was hungry and thirsty without even recognizing it, I suppose because I had been too involved in too many problems, all of which need to be faced at the same time. This need then brings me to the next point. I do not believe that there is a necessity to restate the various reasons—both mine and yours—which we had been discussing the week past. The deadline, lady, is here and now.

I need your answer, Himene, and I would prefer that it was freely given and not coerced, if that could be avoided."

There was no doubt as to the meaning of those last words, and Himene was immediately alerted to it. At the same time, it did not come as a surprise. She wanted to rise, but then did not because it would then have placed her in the position of a supplicant rather than an equal sitting opposite to him at eye level. So she just pulled her shawl closer to her body, involuntarily searching for some protection.

"Majesty, Sennacherib, my lord and king. I had thought that I gave you my decision in no uncertain words the last time we met. At that time, I also assured Your Majesty that I shall freely, gladly, and immediately comply with any other wish of yours without questioning your reason for it. But to this request of matrimony, to you or to anyone, my answer was, still is, and will evermore be no."

Still looking at her unwaveringly with eyes of icy coldness, Sennacherib finally smiled, shrugged his shoulder, and, picking up a pomegranate from the bowl, began to toy with it in a gesture which Himene now recognized was his habit whenever he needed to calm himself. He leaned back more comfortably on his cushions.

"Well, Himene, no matter…You have voiced your opinion because I had the courtesy to allow you to do so. I hope you do understand that it was a gesture of courtesy only, nothing else. I have noted your opinion, the reasons and objections are immaterial, coming from a woman, they do not signify. We shall therefore proceed as I wish with planning this marriage. I and my court will see to the details. Your role in it will begin on the day of the wedding and… thereafter. Again I thank you for your hospitality and bid you good night."

With that he rose swiftly, letting Himene realize that this swiftness, this impatient speed of movement was an inheritance from his father. Her eyes suddenly filled with tears, and she lowered her head in farewell, not wanting to have Sennacherib see any tears or weakness in her.

*****

Two days after Sennacherib's last visit, he and his turtanu were conferring with each other on a multitude of pressing subjects, some of them highly secret. For this reason, they did not stay indoors but, taking advantage of a mild morning breeze, walked about in the palace garden. They were alone, except for the inevitable presence of Sennacherib's Greek slave, Empyades, who followed them, as always, a few deferential steps behind.

The turtanu was talking, every once in a while, gesturing in emphasis. It appeared to be a somewhat-heated discussion, and Sennacherib listened with obvious annoyance. He stopped and interjected while shaking his head vehemently, "My lord, as I have told you before, I will not start my reign showing weakness. If weakness is perceived, it will set up a precedent for the future. You of all people should know how adamant my revered father was on that point. And most especially, I will not be dictated to by a mere woman, be she my father's chosen queen."

Since the king had stopped walking, Shutur-Nahhunte had no choice but to do the same. "Majesty, I certainly remember your father, my half brother's, opinions on many things. I also remember that he had often voiced to me his conviction of the value of compromise between serious thinking mature men."

Sennacherib rounded on him almost triumphantly. "Ah, yes, but here is the difference, we are not dealing with two serious thinking mature men. One of the two is an ignorant, obstinate, capricious bitch!"

The turtanu had opened his mouth for an answer but then thought better of it and remained silent. Obviously Sennacherib interpreted this as a sign of assent and went on. "Just before, you had mentioned your concern about ill treatment, my lord. I am afraid I do not understand where your concerns originated? I trust you will not hold me capable of cruelty to anyone, even an obstreperous woman! She will be well treated, sir, rest assured, but damn her, she will understand that I shall wed her and bed her!" And he let out a great huff of breath, which he had suppressed during this diatribe.

Shutur-Nahhunte bowed in surrender but could not help adding a quiet comment, "Sire, however you wish to handle this situation from now on in, please keep in mind that you are not dealing with an unknown wench, who can be hidden from sight, but a woman who, by virtue of not only her birth but her grace and accomplishments as well, has earned the admiration and respect of many, not only of your father. The eyes of our allies and of our enemies are on us—on you, Majesty, especially. Everyone is eager to find out how you will handle problems during this difficult time of transition."

The king, with the easy overconfidence of the young, laughed at him. "Handle, my lord? I will give you my assurance that I will handle the bitch only too well for her own good. It is obvious to me now that my father had an old man's besotted love for her and spoiled her shamelessly. That, rest assured, sir, will come to a fast halt! She must understand the reasons. She thinks that I want to marry her because of her royal blood? She is mistaken! She does not understand that that is only a half truth. I must have a wife of royal descent. I will have it so. If not her, then it must be someone else. What the bitch does not comprehend is that in that case, she will be in the way, and I cannot just make her disappear. I will not do that!" And again he let out his breath with a loud huff.

Shutur-Nahhunte bowed. "Majesty, your counselors are at your side to advise you. But you, sire, are the law of the land. As always, your will shall rule supreme. It shall be done. And, if I may be so bold as to say, I am glad to hear you will not make her 'just disappear,' that would never do." He bowed his farewell, the subtle irony of his words obviously escaping Sennacherib's notice. With a smile of self-satisfaction lurking in the corners of his mouth, he gazed after the receding back of the turtanu.

Through years of practice, Empyades had gauged his distance from the two lords just so that, while appearing to be obsequiously following them, he was still able to overhear their conversation. This was crucial to him; the information he could gather in this way was the only coinage that he owned and could put to use to ensure his safety and his future. He was not a man trained in statecraft, but he was shrewd and had a quick wit and a mind that absorbed bits of information readily and, even more readily, was able to combine the bits into a whole, not necessarily correctly but usefully.

Today's little walk, he thought, proved to be most illuminating. If he would not have sensed that his master's rule was under threat, today gave him the proof. And whatever threatened his master also threatened him. Moreover, it was threatened by the triviality of a woman's presence. Born on a Greek island and infused with Greek values in childhood, his position was that women were inconsequential, except to run their husband's households, serve their wishes in bed, and bear their children. Period. No exception, regardless what title that woman bore. His master had expressed his reasons for wanting to acquire this particular woman. She did not want to comply with his wishes. This would endanger his master's future to rule, but at the same time, his own future welfare as well. His master had said that he was not going to go to—what Empyades thought—any extreme measures. It followed that he, Empyades would need to. At this point, his agile brain began to work on a plan, examining and accepting or rejecting variations to its execution. It was one of the few occasions that he did not accompany his master back to the palace but, deep in thought, lagged behind, walking to and fro among the trees.

At this same time, Himene was getting out of her bath to face a new day. It was inconceivable how slowly the days dragged on and on, each appearing like an endless succession of meaningless actions, motions, interrupted only by periods of sleep. That was the best part of each day because it either gave her oblivion or dreams of her husband.

Last night's sleep was filled with dreams of Sargon, as were all those prior nights which followed the encounters with his son Sennacherib. She realized what was happening; son and father were so much alike that just seeing him reminded her painfully of what she had lost. Not that they looked physically alike; Sennacherib had softer features and was much stockier, with a thicker neck and a less muscular body than his father. What hypnotized her was the similarity of certain gestures, the way both of them seemed to rush and stride with suppressed impatience, as though life would not be long enough for them, their impatient hand gestures, the way they raised their eyebrows when amused or lowered them in irritation, the way they both cocked their heads to the left while listening intently.

She sighed. That was where the resemblance began and ended. Sargon, with his booming laughter, was brash, arrogant, self-assured, impatient, demanding, driven, and often ruthless. He was, at the same time, also gentle, gracious, loving, tender, courteous, and thoughtful. Evidently maturity had taught him self-control, grace, and wisdom. His son, unfortunately, only inherited the father's drive, willfulness, arrogance, and impatience but none of the more gracious, gentler attributes. Well, she sighed, it was of no concern to her; and after all, he was young and had immense responsibilities suddenly thrust on his shoulders. Perhaps with time, he would mature, and the rough edges would be smoothed? Ultimately none of this was her particular concern, as she expected to quietly retire to live out the rest of her days as the widowed dowager queen in the palace's House of Women. It was not a life that she looked forward to and secretly longed that, once her child was sufficiently grown not to need a mother's hand, she could join her husband under the guarding wings of the Great God Ashur. She firmly believed that at that point, there were no further duties to hold her back from that eagerly anticipated meeting with her lord husband.

Empyades long ago had become familiar with the layout of the House of Women. Not for nothing had he loitered about, offering assistance, when King Sargon commanded the addition to be built for Queen Himene and her little boy, Tiglath. He was genuinely intrigued by the construction of the pool—actually a small lake—the water channels, and waterfalls, which fed it and led any excess water away from it. He had heard how Babylonian engineers were able to work miracles of water engineering and how the results of their plans now dotted the great cities of Babylon to the south. He had also heard that Sargon, after the subjugation of King Marduk-apla-iddina by the Assyrian Army, had imported many of these engineers and treated them well in exchange for their knowledge.

It was well known that sooner or later, Empyades would turn up at any corner of the palace complex almost each day, and since it was also known that he was a trusted slave of his master, the king, no one would have questioned his whereabouts. When they saw him, most of the palace workers just waved a cheerful greeting, which he not only returned but usually stopped for a little chat. He was not only well known but well liked as well.

In the past, he had been sent to the queen's apartments on numerous occasions with messages from his master, the king, and when he turned up that evening, no one questioned his presence there. He found out, much to his surprise, that Himene was still in her garden without little Tiglath, who had already been put to sleep. She had dismissed her serving ladies after requesting some cooled goat milk, to refresh her if she needed, and some honey cakes should she become hungry. Otherwise, she claimed, she was in no need of anyone's services. Should she need anything, before morning, she reassured them, she would clap her hands to summon someone.

Empyades stayed well in the background covered by the luxurious well-tended shrubbery for a long time, patiently waiting for the noises to quieten as one by one, residents of the household went to bed. The lights of oil lamps were extinguished one by one, and slowly his eyes became accustomed to the dark. Then he heard the cry of a child, maybe little Tiglath's or the child of a servant, he was not certain. It did not matter. He heard the voice of a woman in answer, and then the voice continued in a soft little song, evidently so as not to awaken others. Finally even the woman and the child settled down to sleep, and silence wrapped itself around him.

He dropped onto his knees and, with absolute concentration on silence, inched his way forward. Himene could easily be discerned in the dark, the white of her widow's shift and veil lighting up the dark whenever the moon shone through the foliage. The progress of no more than ten paces from shrubs to the open area around the pool took Empyades, what seemed to him, forever. Finally he was crouched just behind Himene's couch. She had drunk about half of the milk and ate one cake, the remainder was resting on the low table next to her. She must have dozed off in the soft quiet of the night, Empyades thought, which made his plan easier. Without a sound, he reached into the bosom of his short slave's shift and pulled out a length of thin hemp cording, such as farmers used to tie together bales of barley at harvesttime.

Himene sighed and stirred without waking up. Even from where he was crouching, Empyades could see the gentle smile about her lips. Licking his own dry lips, he waited another minute to make sure that the queen was indeed asleep and then, slowly and silently, rose from his crouch. For a moment, the shadow cast by his body bent over her darkened the whiteness of her clothing. He wound the two ends of the cord about the fingers of both hands and dropped the length in between around her neck. With one jerk the rope tightened about her throat, and as Himene awoke, her hands flew to her neck to rid herself of what was choking her. But already it was too late, and she had too little strength or breath left. For a long second, the eyes of both met. Empyades understood that she knew what was happening. Before her gaze clouded over, he could clearly see the happy little smile playing about her lips.

*****

The next morning, at first light, one of the eunuchs in charge of the House of Women arrived at a run at the main palace building, requesting to see the king. When told that the king had not yet awakened, he insisted that he needed to talk to him immediately. Finally the king's chamberlain complied with some trepidation. When Sennacherib appeared, hastily wrapping a robe around his body, the eunuch threw himself on the ground and kissed the king's feet in a desperate attempt to appease him. As Sennacherib gestured to him to speak, he cast a wary look at those present and begged His Majesty to be allowed to speak to him alone. At a signal from Sennacherib, everyone else withdrew.

What was discussed thereafter remained forever a secret, but the king immediately called for his turtanu and then quickly, accompanied only by the eunuch, walked over to the House of Women. No one but he and the turtanu saw what needed to be seen—Himene's body, still clothed in her white mourning clothes and the golden neck collar, which had been a gift of her late husband her only adornment, floating facedown in the lake. Her collar must have caught on the clumps of papyri in one corner of the lake so that the weight of the collar was unable to drag her body down to the bottom of the pool. The dead body moved gently to and fro with the current. It was only released by its papyrus prison when two of the eunuchs swam to that side of the lake and worked her collar loose from the fronds.

Throughout this, Sennacherib, Great Ruler of the Known World, stood aside, immobile, stone-faced, still clutching his robe about him. The turtanu had arrived, and one glance was enough for him to understand much, although not all. He turned away and covered his eyes so that no one should see him weeping.

Once again, so soon again, mourning was prescribed throughout the land. Everyone who heard the story of Queen Himene mourned, for it was the story of fairy tales, of the beautiful young queen who loved her dead husband so much that she longed to be reunited with him in the arms of the Great God Ashur, and so drowned herself. Himene's body was prepared for the funeral pyre. When removing her clothes and her gorgeous gold necklace, gift of her now-dead husband, from her body, no one seemed to notice the thin purple line running all around the queen's neck. If someone did, he kept it to himself; to know too much could be a dangerous thing.

Wind from the East
AD 895 Hungary

Introduction

Every civilization, every culture which has yet existed has valued gold for its beauty, its color, luster, malleability, and above all, its immutable durability. The value of gold increased greatly as cultures understood and appreciated, most especially, this last of its characteristics. Gold objects became highly prized. The beauty, the artistry and elegance of their forms, the infinite and infinitely varied details which their creators were able to give these objects astounded and amazed. Quite often the designs appeared unusual, especially on objects which were labeled to have an ancient heritage. Their value increased, for it opened a glimpse into that, which generations long past and dead admired, considered to be elegant, graceful, desirable. Simply put, the wealthy vied with one another to own something which had been touched or worn by someone all those many hundreds, or even thousands, of years in the past.

During its flowering, the East Roman Byzantine Empire was more powerful than any other outside of the Chinese Empire. Byzantium was later overshadowed by the Holy Roman Empire of Germany, by the power of the Catholic Church, and the growing and strengthening Ottoman Empire. But Byzantium had wealth. Wealth flowing into its coffers from all its vassal nations and all the various marauding tribes from whom they extracted tribute in the name of "protection." Ah, yes, it is a true saying that "nothing is new under the sun!"

Byzantium, along with its twin, the West Roman Empire, overseen by slowly crumbling Rome, were the first nations to show an interest and a desire in the collection of antiquities. Exquisite jewelry, statues small and large, mosaics, portraits, engravings, any and all items of beauty were valued higher if they had a past history, what today would be called a cachet, a provenance.

Considering the above, it would be no surprise, when time traveling into the past, to walk into the shop of one of the numerous jewelries and gold dealers along Constantinople's *Arcadianae* and its many bazaars, and find exquisitely designed and wrought gold pieces from many long-gone places, along with gorgeous oriental silks. These were, in fact, the first daily meeting and mingling of new and old civilizations. Exquisite ancient Persian, Celtic, Scythian, Mycenean, and Minoan gold art lay side by side with silks from the cities of Cathay and from Samarkand. From its one end to the other, the known world was opening up, and gold and silk were the keys to this opening.

Prologue

Over centuries, push from the east exerted a relentless force upon the loosely allied tribes and nations living toward their western borders. These wide and sparsely populated spaces, stretching from the high plateau of Tibet to the shores of the Black Sea, responded with seething unrest, tribal warfare, and repeated resettlements of their populations, encroaching farther and farther to the west. Like waters of stormy seas, roiling and then rising into enormous waves, so also moved wave after wave of warring tribes and nations, pushed by the next wave against their backs, and pushing those ahead of them in the only direction available—to the west.

Arsonists of homes, buildings, cities, killers of children and their mothers, entire villages and cities, of opposing armies and opposing governments, these tribes appear and disappear, causing damage, destruction, and death. But after a time, the heat and fervor of conquest wanes, conquering monsters and their subjects both adapt and accept. Over time the invaders submerge into the mass of those they conquered. Today we would say that they become "absorbed."

One single entity emerges out of these centuries of turmoil. It is the one single conqueror who conquered with the deliberate desire to live just there and move on no farther. The single group composed of tribes, nations, indeed, which after settling, not only preserved their unique blend of customs, traditions, and language, shedding only their pagan religion to fervently adopt Christianity, were the Magyar tribes. Out of these tribes blossomed a homogeneous nation with distinct borders known as the Christian Kingdom of Hungary. In Anno Domini 1000, it received the Holy Crown from the Holy See in Rome, thereafter forever the symbol of the nation. Now, for longer than a thousand years, it struggled to maintain their nation and nationality. The odds were enormous: invasion by Genghis Khan's armies, occupation by Sultan Suleiman's Turks for close to two hundred years, annexation by the kingdom of Austria for seemingly endless centuries, most recently the yokes of national socialism and communism.

But—and this is the paradox—one exception is just that, an exception. The Alans, the Avars, Cumans, Khazars, the Goths, Sarmatians, Scythians, Lombards, the Petchenegs, and Huns, and so many others came, destroyed, and then were absorbed into the mass of those they conquered. And not unlike in a forest fire, mindless destruction will be followed by renewal. The lives of nations are nothing but renewal and decay following one another in a perpetual cycle. Do not either censure or delight with pride in the successes of the conqueror, but also do not applaud the rule of the great and revered or feared nation, for they all will follow a pattern no less predetermined than that of each living person, whoever was or ever will be.

In the early morning, with the first rays of the sun to their backs, they finally came upon the river. It lay at their feet, not more than two bowshots away, like some immense glistening animal, stretching itself across the broad plain which had lain hidden from them by the sparsely wooded westward-rolling copse and groves. From the copse, behind which they had camped, they looked down the bank, the morning sun warming their backs. The river seemed endless to the left and right and across to its yonder shore, still shrouded in the mists of dawn.

All the night before, they had heard the sound of great masses of water flowing in the distance. Around the fires, the dogs would sometimes lift their muzzles and sniff the night air when the smell of the water floated along with the breeze. Then the horses would lift their heads too, stop grazing and listen, the torn-off grass hanging from the corners of their lips. When the breeze died, they would snort softly and shake their heavy manes before bending their heads toward the earth again. Even the thud of their hooves upon the soft grass was impatient.

Their advance guard had left well before dawn, horses and men covered up to their necks by the thick fog, which heralded the nearness of a great river, so that the men and horses appeared to be swimming in the fog, the horses' heads swinging rhythmically to the left and right. Shortly after they had left, the wind started to blow, making the bottom of the sky glow blue red, like embers. There was no sleeping after that, and long before the camp would come alive on other days, one heard the noises of feet padding upon the turf, of hushed voices talking to horse and dog, and of leather creaking and metal clanging as gear were strapped upon the packhorses.

Since dawn, even before the main camp had extinguished the last fires, the seven chieftains, the chiefs and elders, led by the grand prince, had driven themselves onward with the impatience borne of long waiting. The stars flickered with cold blue light in a graying sky and the chill of the hour before sunrise sat in their bones. Somewhere behind them, in the heart of the prairie, an elk bellowed. And then they heard the dull thunder of hooves, first far away, then approaching, as the advance guard was returning. Finally they heard the long drawn-out *ay-ee* of their cry. Árpád himself had stopped his horse, commanding a halt, and now his chieftains were clustered around him, the servants and arm-bearers behind their masters. All watched the dark figures of the advance guard as they first dotted the horizon, then got bigger, swiftly swooping down on them. They drove their horses around and around in a circle, while one figure separated from the rest. Marót, who had command of the advance guard, rode over to his master, horse and rider steaming alike with the heat of the chase. He stopped short of Árpád's horse.

"As you can see from here already, the river lies just beyond those mounds, lord," he said and pointed westward. His voice was as flat and even as ever, but his eyes, below the heavy eyebrows, one black and one white, when he raised them to the lord of lords, betrayed his excitement. A light was dancing in those eyes as he jutted his chin toward the line of shallow shrub-crested mounds forming the riverbank below the western sky.

For a moment, the Lord Árpád did not reply. Then he nodded and gently nudged his horse forward. He did not signal to the others, and so they let him go alone, watching wordlessly as the lone horseman put his mount to a slow canter. They watched his figure diminish in the distance and finally disappear behind the line of birch trees.

When Árpád finally arrived at the rise above the water's edge, he stopped. He was alone, but he was not aware of being lonesome. He gazed at the river, thinking to himself how it was that the river's presence was no surprise to him, yet was it a surprise to see its greatness, the might of its eternally moving and eternally present power, wealth and life hidden beneath the silver surface. *Oh,* he thought, *how well I know this river, not ever yet met before, except in my dreams.*

River of legends, river of dreams! he thought. All the plans, the desires, and strivings of his past—of their past—had been flowing toward it. He owned the river as much, he thought, as the beating of his heart or the feel of his horse, Szárnyas, between his thighs. He belonged to this river, just as he belonged to his people, and the river was his and his people's, a legacy of his ancestors and his people's ancestors.

The wind gently lifted his long hair lying on his shoulders. Árpád was unaware of it. He had folded his hands across his horse's neck and squinted against the brilliance of the rising sun's glare over the water's vibrant surface. *You are mine*, his heart sang, *mine to take and to have forever, river of prophecy, river of destiny, oh, Danubius, river of Great Attila.*

*****

By noon, the scouts and divers had found a shallow underwater ridge to the south, and the cautious work of fording the river began. It was more than customary caution; it was common instinct that made them put the river between them and what lay behind. What lay behind were screaming hordes of Petcheneg warriors, incited by the Bulgarian Armies of King Simeon, intent on killing. Once across, the tribes began to erect their summer tents on the grassy shore, no great distance from the river. These were, after all, to be temporary lodgings until more study homes could be built, designed mostly to add to the dubious comfort afforded by their transport wagons. Then, of course, there were also the stories of the great Roman city of Aquincum, home to Roman emperors and also—so the story was told—of Great Attila. But the stories contradicted one another, and the seven tribes had learned not to depend too much on hearsay but much more on the labor of their own hands.

For almost a week to follow, the air vibrated with the shouts of men, the baying of dogs, and the lowing of cattle, the pack-horses struggling for foothold under their weights and slipping in the upchurned thick slimy mire, the scrawny little cows wild-eyed with terror, their calves torn from them by the swift undertow in the stream's center, getting trampled underfoot, the creaking high-wheeled oxcarts drawn by long-horned white oxen, bogged down in the oozing black mud, the priests, the seers lifting their heavy bronze gongs and sacrificial axes overhead. At the end of this caravan, finally the women and children rode their horses across from shore to shore, the women carrying their infants in slings across their breasts and their very youngest ones in front of them in the saddle or across their backs, slung in sling seats. But any child past the age of three, male or female, was expected to ride their own horses without assistance.

On the west bank of the river, a great tent city began to grow far up and down along the water. At first, there appeared to be no planning, no single-minded organization, as tent rose up after tent. Then slowly, an internal order began to define and shape the assortment of hundreds upon hundreds of dwellings for man and beast. The tents grouped themselves around their chieftain's tents, and overhead tribal standards and animal insignia began to arise everywhere. And everywhere among the tents, there was activity. Young and old, always in clusters, were talking and laughing, moving, carrying, bending and lifting, unpacking, hammering, tying down, or just loafing. The women, released from the drudgery of the daily loading and unloading of their households—an unavoidable chore unless their household were rich enough to have lower-class concubines, servants, or slaves—descended upon the river's edge to do their washing. The rhythmic *slap*, *slap* of cloth against stone became a staccato accompaniment to their shrill voices and raucous squeals of laughter. Children shrieking with playful glee ran between the tents over the muddy tracks, among the snoozing dogs and the few horses that were not pastured but tethered close to their masters' homes.

Most of the horses, including all of the pack animals, had been released at the outskirts of the tent city for grazing. They were guarded by indolent-looking young men, lazily stretched out upon their mounts' backs for extended naps or interminable rounds of gossip. The cattle were out to pasture too, but they were herded together every evening into corrals hastily erected from cut-down birches still wearing their green crowns. They were tended by servant girls, moving among them with gaily painted large earthenware crocks in which the milk was collected. From the corrals and the grazing ground of the horses, the eye could move over the long rows of tents, all alike, made of skin or some of roughly made felt, except for those of the noble households.

Their homes, even though only summering tents, were decorated with painted flowers and colorful designs of animals: horses, bears, wisents, panthers and wolves, and especially of hawks and falcons. Displayed by the entrance, on the top of tall poles, were the arms of the owners and the emblems of the tribes they each represented. The chiefs' tents ruled over each of the tribal sections, large tents with spacious overhangs to shield against rain or sun. These tents shimmered with priceless colorful silk draperies and costly embroidered awnings. The huge bronze animal heads, emblems of their tribes, which decorated their supporting pillars, gleamed in the sunlight. There was always more activity at these tents, with large groups of men coming and going. In the shade of the awnings, barefooted little slave boys guarded the mounts of the illustrious visitors.

Árpád's tent was not amid this hubbub. It stood by itself a bowshot away from the huge tent, which the servants of the priests and seers had erected to hold the most precious of the sacrificial vessels, the God of War's Great Sword of War and the holy emblem of Árpád's own tribe, the turul-hawk. Árpád disliked noise, and he also disdained ostentation; his tent was larger but simpler in look and decoration than most of the others. In reality it consisted of two tents connected by a passage shielded by awnings. Behind these two, a smallish round tent for his personal use housed only quarters for himself, his pages and body servants, and the two scribes who alternated in readiness to serve their master. Of the two main tents, the larger and simpler one contained the council chamber, also a small waiting room, and the huge dining hall, with its flaps now opened to the breeze. The smaller but more amply decorated tent was the House of Women. In the back, where it was opened to the grass as well, it was closed off by a high fence of birch branches, their green boughs left intact to festoon the top of the enclosure.

Noise forever emanated from the House of Women, but now there was noise coming from the council chamber and its waiting room as well. The standards of most of the chieftains and many of the elder nobles were struck into the ground in front of the tent's entrance to indicate that their owners were inside. The Grand Prince Árpád's emissary, a man named Vazul, whom Árpád had sent ahead to the south with gifts to the great emperor, master of Byzantium and of all of the Eastern Roman Empire, had returned and was giving his report to the council.

The emissary now stood in front of the assembled groups seated around Árpád. Vazul was a short stocky man with long tumbling brown hair turning gray, tied at the nape of his neck with a leather thong, his traveling clothes stained with sweat and dust. Servilius, his Roman interpreter, much more resplendent-looking than his master, with the curled short hair, beardless face, and flowing robes of Rome, held an armful of documents. One by one he was giving these to Árpád's scribe who squatted to the side, just a short distance from his master's feet. He was reading the last parts of a longish letter. The scribe held the scroll close to his eyes, its many seals and gold-and-purple tassels swinging to and fro with each movement of the reader's head.

"Thus it is with all the love and fondness of a father for his errant children—"

"I'll be damned to call him my father, that little weasel." Growled a grizzled old chief to Árpád's left, whose face was hideously marred by a long and poorly healed cut from his left earlobe almost to the corner of his mouth. "I was siring my young when he wasn't out of his swaddles yet. Although I doubt if he is out of them altogether!"

There was a low general laugher after his words, and several called out, "Yeah, Tas," to show their approval, but it quickly ebbed away when the men saw that Árpád did not join in.

"That I shall clasp you, my brother, oh most wise and noble, Grand Prince Árpád, and all of your people, to my bosom." The scribe continued, "After your spirit has been cleansed by baptism through the grace of the Almighty, the One True God, and you have come to see as I see the errors of your ways and beliefs—"

"He should be damned together with his One True God!" Screeched a little shriveled-up chieftain, who sat on the corner closest to the entrance. "We have seen the almightiness of his god and his fatherly kindness too. Must we have to listen forever—" He clamped his toothless mouth together abruptly, as Árpád turned to him with a slight gesture.

"Let him finish first, Huba," he said and the room grew quiet again.

"Of your ways and beliefs," the scribe went on, "you shall be to me as my very own. Faithful to the One True Belief, you and your people shall prosper in the shade of my mantle and under of succor of my might—"

"By god, before the first frost he shall be running for succor from our might, dragging his shadeless mantle in the dust!" Stormed the man to Árpád's right as he jumped up and slammed his fist into the palm of his other hand. "He will run as the Bulgarians ran last year. Does he truly think we send our women into battle to do men's work?"

A rising murmur of consent followed his words as heads all around began to nod and to lean toward one another in dispute. "Although that seems to be the deceptive custom of his household," the man continued and looked around himself to gauge the effect of his words. Here and there, a bubble of laughter rose. "Perhaps"—he grumbled, seating himself again—"that would behoove him better, for they might frighten us more than he does." At his last words, the laughter finally erupted, and even the servants in the back of the room were grinning and slapping their thighs. Everyone knew tales of the power of the Empress Teophano.

The speaker, a handsome man named Zalán, a leader of the nation of Nyék, unusually tall for his race and powerfully built, had a shock of straight chestnut-brown hair, a short well-combed mustache and a pleasing face. Now he looked around him again in obvious pleasure and then pulled on his mustache to hide his own pleased smile. Even Árpád looked cheered for a moment as he shifted his weight on his chair.

The scribe waited for the laughter to die down. Then with a sidelong glance at Árpád and a nod from him, he continued, "May these sentiments of mine illuminate your souls and endow your spirits with the harmony and grace which comes from the service of the

All Eternal and All Mighty God and from his only rightful ruler on this earth. In the name of Kristos Pancreator, marked by my own hand on the fifth day after the Feast of Pentecost—"

The murmur which rose again during these last sentences drowned out the reader's voice with the remainder of the salutation. For a short while, Árpád waited, then raised his hand for silence. The obedience to his gesture was immediate. In this silence, he confronted his emissary. His face was composed, and for the moment, neither cheerfulness nor grimness could be read from his features.

"Did you personally receive this letter from the emperor?" he asked.

Vazul shifted the weight of the leather pouch hanging from his left shoulder and nodded.

"I saw him twice while I was in Byzantium, Árpád. The first time, I gave him the message and your gifts. He seemed well pleased with both. That may have been for show only. Everything there is for show, my lord, and one man may not gauge another's words sufficiently. Everyone is afraid of the other and looks more to his back than forward. It is said, lord, that the emperor locks himself into a vault at night, that he fears even his wife and trusts only those of his guards who have proven their loyalty to him. It is said that all night long, he shivers and kneels in prayer to his god to deliver him from the assassins. These stories I find an exaggeration and do not believe them. I think the emperor not brave but shrewd in a bookish way. I think that when he locks himself away a night, it is not in fear but to work on his books of law, which he has called the *basilika* and which are of the ultimate importance to him. I was told that the term means actually 'imperial laws.'" Then taking a deep breath and shaking his head, he commented, his mouth pulled into a small lopsided smile, "I also think that this letter was produced by one of his sycophants who write these standard sentences in beautiful calligraphy!

"After I gave him your message, Árpád, I waited in vain for many days but was not allowed into his presence. Finally when I threatened to leave and to take his silence as his message back to you, I was allowed to be received again. When the emperor enters the throne room, everyone falls to the ground and pretends to tremble with fear and to shield their eyes from the brilliance of his person. The first is laughable and the second unnecessary. I did not kneel to him, Árpád, because I believed that you would not have wanted me to do so, but I bowed and told him that I was still awaiting words to take back to you. He acted surprised by this, but then his scribes immediately produced a completed documentum, which he had them read in my presence so that I also should know its meaning. Before leaving, he waved me to his side and allowed me to kiss the ring on his right hand. That was a very great honor, I was told later, especially so since I did not kneel to his person as before. Most are only permitted to kiss his slippers or to touch the hem of his robes."

Vazul hesitated for a moment, as though unsure if he should continue, then went on. "It was the same honor, I was told, which he bestowed, two years before, upon the emissary of Tsar Vladimir. That, if you recall, was when Vladimir's Bulgarians laid down their arms to Byzantium after your son Levente's and chieftain Tas's armies overran them." Vazul nodded to the scar-faced old chieftain who had spoken earlier. "The emperor then invited the tsar to the court himself, in the sign of peace and love between the two nations. When the tsar arrived, he found his father, crazy old Boris, there too, whom the emperor sent for from his monastery. Before the whole court, the emperor and Boris both embraced Vladimir, kissing him, and the emperor gave him a ring. Before the court, this was the sign of peace and love between the two nations.

"After Tsar Vladimir had left to return to his camp, still in the sign of peace and love between the two nations, his father, Boris's, armed riders were sent after him, with the explicit approval of Leo. The riders caught up with the Bulgarian camp, four days' ride from the city, toward the setting sun. They took Vladimir back to Byzantium, this time in chains. Emperor Leo would have nothing more to do with him. Then orders were received to have the tsar's eyes put out and he to be locked away in a dungeon, presumably on the island of Samothrace. Although the court says those orders came from Vladimir's own father, yet everyone knows that Boris would not have acted on his own behalf, and that at court, not even a pin is dropped without imperial consent. I ask you, my lord, are any orders given in Byzantium without Leo's or his wife's will? And so Vladimir's son Simeon now sits on Vladimir's throne, and that is probably a very good thing. Most believe that Vladimir has perished long ago, but then there are those who say that he still wears the emperor's ring of friendship and that he now is just as lunatic as his father is supposed to be."

The speaker stopped. The room was suddenly enveloped in total silence. Outside a horse neighed, and from somewhere, the sound of a woman's laughter drifted in. A slanting bar of the afternoon's sun threw a pool of light upon the carpet in front of the scribe. Golden particles of dust danced in the beam of light.

Árpád had sat motionless for the past minutes, his eyes looking down into that pool of sunlight. Now he raised his head and let his eyes sweep over the chamber. Slowly, with care, he looked at each of his seated councilors. Then he let his eyes rest upon the patch of sky showing at the tent's entrance. His face was closed; except for a sharp pinch between his brows, it appeared to be devoid of emotion.

He was not a handsome man, by any standard of male beauty, but possessed an arresting and commanding presence. Taller than most, he had a neck too thick, a nose too large, dented at the bridge by a long-ago fracture, and a mouth too wide to be entirely pleasing. His cheekbones were broad and high, the eyebrows like two slanting straight lines of black above almond-shaped eyes, shaded by long black lashes. Like most of his family, he inherited those long lashes as protection for his eyes against the brightness of the sun and the grit of the occasional sandstorms of the steppes. Like most of his family, he also inherited a cleft chin, full sensual lips, and rather heavy lids, which shielded the expression of his gray eyes, sharp and piercing, like the eyes of a bird of prey. His brown hair, the color of the shining soft-brown skin of chestnuts, and his darker mustache were carefully trimmed. His battle-worn heavily calloused hands were large, bony, and strong. Except for the gray streaks to the left and right by his temple, he looked surprisingly youthful for his age of five and forty and his position of leader of the Seven Nations and the additionally assimilated three Kabar tribes. On the rare occasions when he smiled, a light shone in his eyes, his face lost its brooding expression and became transfigured to make it appear close to one beautiful and tender.

The silence dragged on, and nobody dared to break it. Árpád finally moved; he shifted his weight again, uncrossing and recrossing his legs in a visible effort to shake off thoughts known only to himself. With his inward-looking gaze becoming animated and direct once again, he looked to his right and left to gather everyone's attention. Then he looked at Vazul.

"Was anything said about my terms for cessation of tribute to them?" he asked.

Vazul shook his head. "No words were said to me, no, except at first, my lord. Also there have been no words written about it. I told them your message, lord, that we consider our aid in subduing the Bulgars sufficient tribute payment for the past and our promise of further help against any of their enemies, tribute enough for the future. Yet behind my back, carefully arranged for me to overhear, it was said that the state coffers were dependent on the vassals' tribute."

Árpád's shoulders twitched at the word *vassal.* If he felt displeasure, he showed no other indication of it. Rather he leaned forward, resting his face in the palm of his hand and his elbow upon his thigh. In silence, he waited for the man to continue. Vazul looked uneasy, his glance sliding off his master's face, dropping to the ground. After some hesitation and an almost imperceptible nod from Árpád, he went on.

"In the same manner, it was whispered behind my back—with your pardon, my lord—that Byzantium would regret the day it started to relinquish tribute money from every roaming band of barbarians that wander through the fringes of its territory." Vazul shifted again uneasily. "If I may, lord, I do wish to add to that how I also overheard it said that such opinion of divisiveness could only come from the Bureau of Barbarians, which forever wishes to sow discontent and strife and which the emperor even cannot control."

This time the ensuing silence had the quality of shock. One could hear the sharply drawn breaths of the listeners. A few of them stirred uncomfortably, and the tension, the effort of exclamations withheld became almost palpable. Árpád continued to glare into the emissary's face. Then he raised an eyebrow and permitted the shadow of a smile to cross his face.

"They would do well to take care not to regret the day when they refused to deal with this roaming band of barbarians." He spoke slowly and softly, as though trying to marshal and organize his thoughts while talking, but his voice carried to every corner of the quiet room. "Unless they wish the fate of Svatopluk's Moravia visited upon them. My next messenger will not go asking for relief of tribute any longer. If Byzantium will not heed the language of friendship, it will learn to listen to the voice of force. Should my next letter not reach more willing ears, then before the next snow comes, their tribute shall enrich our nations." He lifted his right hand to stem the rising clamor of voices. With his other hand, he waved his own two scribes, standing behind the grand prince's chair, to his side. The men must have expected the gesture, for in a moment's time, they were at their master's side, tablet held ready, as Árpád began to dictate rapidly.

"Messengers are to ride to the tribes of Keszi and Tarján. Tarján is to swing immediately to the south and start moving toward the closest of the Bulgarian fortresses. Those held by Byzantine mercenaries are to be surrounded but not attacked. If any of them wish to ride with us, I want them not, they may prove to be treacherous. I want none of our blood spilled nor any prisoners taken to slow down my riders, should bloodshed be needful. Keszi shall follow them from their present encampment in the mountains"—he stopped and shut his eyes to reconstruct an imaginary map in his mind—"and ride along the Tisza River to join with Tarján toward the midday sun. Tell old Chief Töhötöm, should he object, that I am cashing in my due as his son-in-law...he'll not be able to refuse...They will likely meet and join before reaching Bulgarian land. If any of Simeon's people wish to join, let them. They shall be given horses for speed. They shall be permitted to ride with our warriors but never allowed to remain together in groups. Separated from one another, they may turn out to be worthwhile fighters for us." He was speaking to himself now. Then he sighed, and in an effort to shake off some hidden thoughts, he moved his shoulders one by one and again directed his dark gaze upon the scribes.

"Both the tribes must take as many men into the south as they can spare, also at least four horses for each rider. Only the fewest number of men necessary should stay to accompany the womenfolk, children, and their belongings until they reach us here. They can then remain here in safety, the perimeter can easily be enlarged. Now that there are no Moravian raids expected, they can—if they wish—safely settle to the north of us along the riverbank. Send special message to Lord Töhötöm to select a worthy second to himself, should he wish to remain at their main camp in the mountains." Lost in thought, he remained silent for a long moment, then continued with a little smile lurking around his mouth, "Write this last with care so he does not take offense. But I am concerned about his health and want him to retire in slow stages." He stopped again and, with a gesture at once thoughtful and tired, raised his hand to his eyes.

The room was enveloped in silence until Árpád resumed dictating.

"I want the nation of Kér to break camp and to move from the far side of the Tisza to a place where fording of the river can be done quickly. They are now too far behind us and too much exposed. It makes me uneasy. There is no merit in leaving our rear-hanging tribe exposed to the peril of Pecheneg marauders. Even if the rear-guarding Kabar Army engages any Pechenegs, I doubt that they would have the strength to annihilate them. If Kér encamps by the Tisza, they could follow the river's course south in easy rides, and after joining at the confluence of the Danube, they could strengthen Tarján or Keszi as needed." Árpád stopped and cast a searching look around.

"Servilius?" he asked. "Where is Servilius?" But Vazul's Roman interpreter had left the chamber after the reading of the letter. When no response came to his question, Árpád twisted his body with sudden impatience toward a sallow-looking beardless young man seated at the far left. Throughout the meeting, the young man had sat entranced, chin upon his hand, leaning forward to peer at Árpád, his eyes bright with interest, and his pale lank hair tumbling forward by his cheeks and gently swinging to and fro.

"You, Jenö! Find Megyeri and send him in search of Servilius at once! He is to tell Servilius to saddle and prepare to leave for Rome on the morning with my message. He shall accompany Lord Szilárd and give counsel whenever the lord seems lacking in the saintly behavior expected by His Holiness which he should have, but probably did not, learn in his Moravian prison. Find him, wherever he is, and tell him to report to me. Go."

There was a general laughter about the reference to Szilárd's recent Christian captivity. Despite himself, Árpád smiled, but his smile vanished before reaching his lips. So did Szilárd, sitting further down the table to Árpád's left, next to his father, Chieftain Előd. Árpád's face turned toward father and son and nodded to Szilárd. "You, as well as Servilius, will receive my letter and instruction on the morrow.

"Arnulf of Carinthia is in Rome now," the grand prince continued, "courting the pope's sanction to wear the German crown. Arnulf is our friend, or so we shall remind him. By going to Rome in support of our Arnulf, we shall have good cause to expect his support of us with the Romans. Pope Formosus is old and his throne shaky. He will not wish harm to come to him either from us or from the German, though if he fears Arnulf, he is more fool than old. Keep this in mind, if we wish to strike to the south, we must be assured of friends to the west."

Again Árpád stopped abruptly. Slapping the arms of his chair with his palms, he pushed himself to his feet. There was a rustling and shuffling from all the others seated as they arose too. The scribes and the dogs scurried out of the way. Servants commenced to raise the tent flaps, and the pungent odor of horse dung, along with swarms of flies, invaded the chamber. Árpád reached for the sword his bearer extended to him. Still holding it in midair, the grand prince looked about himself.

"And now I crave solitude, my lords. We shall all have to think on those things which have been said here today. It occurs to me that only a fool would hasten into calamity without due deliberation. The initial steps I have outlined today can be replanned, for our armies are light and easily rearranged. I need for each of you to address to me any points which you question or disagree with. I stand open to consultation and advice. But it also occurs to me, we show ourselves weak whenever we do not show force. We can only be one or the other. Once we have settled in this place of our desire, then we can keep to the middle road, to remain independent. That is the way of the world. But what we cannot be, and should never be, is hesitant. For the forceful are feared and the weak ignored, but hesitation breeds in itself the seeds of disdain and destruction. Think on all this, my lords, and do not advise me today. Tomorrow, in council, I shall await your words. Tomorrow, in council, you shall also hear my answer to Leo of Byzantium."

Without farewell, the grand prince turned and, with quickening steps, strode out of the council chamber. He was gone before the ascending babble of voices could reach his ears.

*****

The sun was setting, taking with it the warmth and light of the day. Virág shivered and tucked her legs up closer under her skirts. The garbled sounds of the camp's life were muted as they drifted to her from the distance. Then all of a sudden, there was the burst of men's voices nearby, announcing the end of the high council's meeting. The chiefs and elders were dispersing.

Most of the afternoon, she had spent sitting in the shade of a small clump of beeches by the river's edge, not resting really, for she was too tense to rest. She had come here in anger and curiosity, selecting a spot well hidden from the other women's eyes and one from which she could observe the comings and goings at the council tent without herself being observed. From her position, only the top and one side of the women's tent was visible, nestled behind Árpád's main tent. She knew that all the other women would be within the tent enclosure. She should have been there herself, spinning, weaving, embroidering, or busying herself with one or another of the endless meaningless tasks amid their meaningless incessant chatter. She knew that when she returned, none of them would really dare to scold her. But they would chide and nag and whisper behind upraised hands.

She twisted the corner of her mouth in defiance. Well, why not? They thought it unseemly and unthinkable that one of Árpád's wives should roam around unattended. Yet when she was a girl, had she not been allowed as much freedom of movement as any man? Árpád must have been well aware of this, knowing the customs of her people and the ways of life in her father's household. If Árpád accepted it—well, more or less—then it was not his other women's place to gainsay him or to raise questioning eyebrows.

Perhaps that was the reason the others disliked her, Virág thought. Did they envy her because Árpád indulged her and permitted her to behave as he would not have permitted any of them? It was, she decided, not her fault that they were all too timid to explore the limits of their confined lives! Were they angry with her for making them realize that their compliance only enhanced this confinement? Were they jealous because Árpád preferred her to any of his other wives ever since she had entered his household? Certainly she knew that the Lady Alán was, but then she loved Árpád.

Poor woman, Virág thought, she was forever fluttering about him when he visited the women's tent, calling for her younger children, as though to press upon him a reminder of what she had once produced for him. But in Virág's eyes, the Lady Alán was old. When she first entered his tent, she must have been years older already than Árpád, and for a long time now, Árpád had looked upon her only as the mistress of his household and the mother of his firstborn.

Virág sighed and moved a little, trying to find a more comfortable position on the sparse grass. She did feel sorry for the Lady Alán, she told herself, for the mistress had been kind to her when she first arrived as Árpád's new wife. Virág had never bothered to search for the reasons of this kindness but had accepted it as natural, coming from her father's tent, an only girl child amid many boys, and coddled by all. The boys, her brothers, she thought with a sigh, had all been destroyed by the constant warfare; only she was left now.

She could not know that the Lady Alán had appraised the new arrival with shrewd eyes and found the child wife a coltish young thing, wanting in knowledge to please a husband, bewildered by the strangeness of her new surroundings, her new duties, awkward and shy and tongue-tied.

From the time that a young widowed Alán had first entered Árpád's house, she had seen many new women enter there. Long ago, she had learned to recognize which of them would find the prince's pleasure. There seemed nothing about this child to set her apart, to make her stand out to anyone, and Alán had felt generous enough to show her some affection and care.

No one, certainly not the Lady Alán, could have foreseen Árpád's response to his new wife. The chieftain was at an age at which he no longer thought of himself as youthful. In loving his young wife, he relived his own days of youth. Her very awkwardness beguiled him and aroused his fatherly instincts. He indulged her and relished her ebullience and sense of adventure, her uncaring boldness mingled with sudden bouts of shyness. Virág was so unconcerned by his position of power as to make him believe that in him, she saw only his person. Her sudden childish enthusiasms and affections, the equally sudden moods of reticence and sullen defiance, bewildered him and, at the same time, enchanted him more than all the artful seductiveness of other women. Her initial unresponsiveness, just as her inexperience, only served to fan his passion. He was behaving, Lady Alán thought sadly, as she had heard so many other middle-aged men behave when confronted with a young mistress. She felt a sense of betrayal at such thoughts, and that made her sadder still.

Virág was not given to introspection. She would not have found in herself patience or caring enough to understand the currents of turmoil around her. She was aware of the effects of her presence upon the household, to the extent to which they upset, inhibited, or inconvenienced her. She did not like women very much; she had never learned to get along with them. She could not remember her own mother. Her childhood had been spent in the rough-and-ready atmosphere of her father's compound, surrounded by brothers, uncles, her father's friends, horses, dogs, and campfire talks of hunt and battle. Her nurse was an old woman and her father's servant, so were all the other women around her. Surely it would never have crossed her mind to regard any of them in a manner other than one regards servants. No wives were living anymore in the women's tent. As she grew up, she neither questioned nor wondered about her father's way of life.

Sitting now by the river, such thoughts were far from Virág. She was weighing in her mind how and when she would best return home. It was getting chill and most unpleasantly damp. The warmth of an early summer afternoon and her own impetuous impulse had made her forget to bring a coat. Now she regretted it. The prospect of embers glowing in their finely hammered braziers, scattered throughout the women's tent to ward off the cool of the evening, was becoming more and more alluring. Yet she wished to remain a little longer. Through the latticework of tree branches, she had spied Árpád emerge from the council chamber and swing himself into his saddle. She knew that it was his habit in the evenings to ride down to the river to allow his horse to drink and wade in it. Ever since they had set camp here, she thought, Árpád had become strangely drawn to this river. He would remain there on top of the sloping embankment, sitting on his horse, immobile, looking toward the heart of the prairie they had so recently crossed. *Waiting, thinking—waiting for whom? Thinking of what?* she wondered.

Only when all the light had been leached from the sky would he return to his tent to resume work, aided by one of his scribes and an occasional adviser or visitor, making plans, sending and receiving messengers and messages deep into the night. He usually partook only of a frugal solitary meal. Sometimes he would summon her then to serve his food or to sing one of his favorite ballads. Rarely did he banquet with the other chiefs and nobles. Rarely did he cross the compound to the women's enclosure. When he did so, he grew quickly weary of the noise of women and children. Did he not wish to spend the night at work or alone in his chamber, then long after nightfall, he would send a manservant for her or one of his other wives.

It should be safest to return after dark, Virág reasoned, after Árpád withdrew again to work. At all costs, she wished to avoid running into him. Yet if she delayed much longer, she would truly become chilled to the bone. She sighed, gathered her skirts about her, and pushed herself up from the grass. Something rustled nearby, and a frog, startled by her sudden movement, plopped into the water. Moodily Virág stared after it, hugging herself against the chill and the silent misery of her indecision.

A dog's angry barking called her back to reality. The dog stood on top of the embankment, by the edge of the trees, a big yellow animal with an iron-studded collar around his neck. He was looking down at her, legs spread apart, tail fanning back and forth, barking half in anger, half in curiosity. She turned and smiled at him, for contrary to most women, dogs were creatures she knew well and could deal with. She made a low clicking noise with her tongue. The dog stopped barking, backed up slightly on stiff legs, cocked his head, and regarded her with frowning deliberation. Gingerly Virág picked her way closer to the edge of the copse, through the slowly rising evening mist. She raised herself upon her toes and peered out over the tops of some young willow bushes. The dog backed up again and growled, but his tail continued to wave; evidently he was on the verge of choosing amicability or aggressiveness.

Her eyes leaving the dog and moving up the grassy slope, Virág became aware of the figure of the man coming toward her. He was obviously the dog's master, coming to see what his animal was making such a fuss about. In the descending darkness, it was hard to see his face, but Virág recognized his walk, the set of his shoulders, and the slant of his head. She felt a giant fist suddenly push itself into her chest as her heart began to thud furiously. It had been over two years ago that she had last seen the man. She had never expected to see him again, for he was her father's close friend but not of his tribe and infrequently at Árpád's court. Yet their last meeting seemed to her like yesterday. She saw him sitting in her father's tent, like on so many other evenings before, lazily stretching his long-booted legs toward the brazier, his face lost in the shadow above the glowing embers. Her father's voice droned in her ears. They were discussing some problems concerning horses, grazing rights, and slaves.

She had arisen to pour them some wine. After the evening meal, her father liked to have her nearby to serve him and the closest of his friends who happened to visit, and on those occasions, he usually dismissed the servants. As politeness decreed, she first offered the wine to the guest and only then to her father. She could still see the man's outstretched arm to accept the goblet from her, see his twinkling eyes as he lifted his face to look at her, and the smile lurking behind his mustache.

"Well, my friend's daughter," he said, "no more shall you serve me your father's wine, I hear. But tonight, I shall drink to you and your future. You are much honored by our Lord Árpád, and you have reason to be proud. You are indeed lucky to enter his tent instead of mine, for mine is but a bachelor's abode and haphazardly appointed. Doubtless it would have pleased you in small measure."

Oh, Zalán! Virág thought, not realizing that her thoughts were the same as they had been on that evening two years ago. *Everything about you would have pleased me greatly! In your household, I would have been mistress, your first wife, and mother of your sons. In your household, there would be gaiety and laughter. In your household, there would be freedom, and I could have ridden by your side into the hunt, and you would not have thought it strange or condemned me for it. Who else should have suited me better for a husband than you, friend of my father, companion of my childhood?*

She felt herself engulfed by anxiety that he might turn and walk away without ever seeing her. The thought of never talking to him again became so unbearable that Virág acted without hesitation or deliberation. She squeezed herself through the branches of the willows, heedless that her dress caught in them, and her boots sank into the mud. Tugging at her skirts in desperation and struggling for release from the wet sucking loam, she finally freed herself and began, as best as she could, to run up to the top of the slope. The dog, invited to a game of chase, threw his head up and wheeled, barking joyously, and, in great jumps, raced ahead of her.

Zalán stared at them in amazement. He had expected a rabbit, or perhaps a deer, to dart out of the bushes, but not a young woman. He stepped closer, uncertain if the woman was running to him for assistance, or if she and the dog were engaged in some private play of their own. Only when the woman was a few paces away from him did he begin to smile in disbelieving recognition.

Now they stood facing each other, he still smiling and Virág panting, pressing her hands to her side. The dog, pink tongue lolling out of his mouth, looked expectantly from one to the other. Then he gave a short bark, impatient with the delay in his game, his front legs crouching down to the ground and then jumped up on Virág, paws leaving muddy splotches on the white of her tunic. She staggered with the unexpected assault, struggled for foothold, and suddenly sat down upon the wet grass. Virág began to laugh at the look of incredulity on Zalán's face. At that he began to laugh as well. Then his laughter was swept away by a look of concern, and Virág, looking at him, knew that he remembered.

He bent down to her and pulled her up. "Virág, lady," he stammered, "what has happened? How is it that you are here? Are you lost? Why are you not—" He glanced over his shoulder to the chieftain's compound, then back to her again. "But you cannot be lost!" he concluded. He backed away from her, and his expression changed to disapproval. "Just look at you," he chided her gently. "It is merciful that others are not around! What would they think! What would Árpád say is he knew! You are truly behaving very badly! A lady of your position—"

"My position is of no concern to you anymore." Virág stormed at him angrily. She was bitterly disappointed and hardly knew why. She had expected surprise, pleasure, and yes, happiness from Zalán, the same feelings she had on seeing him. They were friends, weren't they? After all, they had grown up together, she thought. She was to become his wife; she had been promised to him as a little girl. Did everyone always have to see her as the grand prince's wife? Did even Zalán have to think of Árpád when he saw her?

She caught her breath, reached for the hand he had extended to help her rise, and clutched it, desperate that he would go away and leave her. "I wanted to see you!" All of a sudden, her words became the truth. Why, she wondered, it was the truth. The words tumbled out before she could consider them. "I wished to see you so badly, and then I heard there was to be a meeting of the High Council. I thought that perhaps you might be there, and that perhaps, if I hid myself, I might be able to see you again..." Her eyes searched for a response in his face. Then she looked down and continued, still breathlessly intent to keep talking, to keep him standing there and listening to her, to stretch out the minutes with the bitter awareness that what she meant to say could not be said.

"I—I wanted to hear of my father. I wanted to hear of home, from my people. All these long months I have not heard a word… not one word of him or of anyone! I hardly know if he still lives! The corners of her mouth trembled. "I don't even know if my old mare is still living!" All her pent-up homesickness somehow became embodied in the yearning for her favorite horse. She gave one heavy sob and then bit her lip to hold back the tears as she turned her face away, unable to continue.

Gently, Zalán pulled his hands from her grasp. He was still smiling at her, half a male's helpless pity in the face of tears, half embarrassed disapproval, just as one will smile at a likeable but unreasonable child.

"Pray calm yourself, my lady," he begged her, "or you will arrive at home not just raggedly disheveled but red-eyed to boot. You are upsetting yourself over nightmares. Your father and all his household are well and think of you often and lovingly. You must not disappoint their pride in you. You must behave with dignity, Virág, as your father would expect from his daughter. I shall send information to him with the request to send you messages regularly to ease your mind on his behalf. As for your mare, lady"—his smile broadened—"I cannot tell. Would I have but known that I shall see you, I would indeed have tried to find out for you."

He stopped talking, and his intent gaze examined her with mounting concern. "Why this sudden distress and agitation, Virág? Why the tears and the frown on your face?" He waited for her answer and, when none came, went on more urgently. "Are you not happy with your new life? Truly you cannot have reason for unhappiness! Your exalted position alone makes you the envy of women throughout the seven nations. Were your husband ugly, deformed, or cruel, you might still console yourself with your station and with the knowledge that you have helped forge a stronger bond between Árpád's nation and your own. Yet Árpád is known to be a kind and generous husband. It is said that he cherishes you above all his other wives and that, however stern and demanding he might be with others, he is unable to deny you any request. You should be happy in the assurance that you please him. You should be proud to become known as the woman who has eased many years of tribal strife. Your father and all there think so and are proud of you, does that not add to your pleasure?"

"I want to go home. I want to visit…see my father again." Valiantly Virág struggled with the words. Her chin quivered. "I just want to see him for a little. I miss him so," she added in a small voice.

"Of course you do, lady." Zalán's voice was kindlier than before. "But you know your place is here now, and your home is here at your husband's side. You also know that you are asking for the impossible. Your father's camp is a distance of many days' ride from here, and it leads over treacherous ground. Some of the fords are still under high water with the spring thaw, and if you veer off to the south, you would likely meet up with Pechenegs and Bulgarians too. This is no time or place for a lady to travel. But soon, maybe, we will move closer to the main army, and then you father will surely come to pay his respects to Árpád and to see his daughter again."

A sudden gust of wind swept over them, and Zalán continued anxiously, seeing her shiver. "Come, lady, you must get home! Look down at yourself! Forgive me, but you do look disgraceful and you a child no longer! Your robe is wet with the evening dew, muddy, and full of grass stains, and your hair has become undone. I tell you, you will get ill. You know they say how the swamp air breeds illness."

But Virág still stood with her face averted from him. "And you?" Her voice was so muffled that he had to lean down to her to understand. "Are you well yourself?"

Zalán straightened with a chuckle. "Better than well, my friend's daughter!" He used the teasing name he had once called her by, unaware how it twisted her heart. "I have a fine young son, nearly a year old now."

Virág bit her lip again and swung around to face him. In the shadow, he could not see the cold look she gave him. "You have taken a wife, then?" she demanded, her voice as hostile as her eyes.

"Why, yes," he said, taken back a little by her tone. "But you would not know her," he added swiftly, thinking that she was angered because she had been left uninformed. "She is from Moravia, Virág. Her father is the chief of one of the Kabar tribes and had fought with us against Svatopluk. He and his family had advisedly remained under Árpád's shelter. I took her for my wife the winter after you left your father."

"Is she beautiful? Do you love her?"

"Beautiful?" Zalán repeated with amazement. "No. I don't think she is, but she is a kindhearted and gentle woman. And she is strong and healthy, just as our son." Then he added slowly, with a shrug, almost as an afterthought to her second question and because he felt such matters were not for discussing, "she is my wife, lady."

After that, they both remained silent. The dog had settled down by his master's feet and dozed, occasionally flicking his ears against the mosquitoes. The darkness was now almost complete and the shadows lost themselves in it. The rushing of the great river carried through the evening air, its water a pale gleaming streak of silver through the willows. Thousands of campfires glimmered throughout the tent city, the closer ones flickers of reddish orange, those farther away pinpoints of starlight in the distance. A bat flitted by on velvety wings, darting and swerving them noiselessly. It was Zalán who spoke first.

"Please, Virág," he implored her. "You must go now, I beg of you, lady. You must not remain any longer. Let me call my horse, and I will ride you back to your tent.

Virág shook her head. "No," she said, "no, I shall go alone as I came. If they knew that I saw you, they would talk and talk... besides," she continued lightly in an effort to reassure him, and perhaps herself too, "I can find my way about very well. I come down to the river all the time. You must not worry about me." She turned to go, quickly whirled around, her hands tugging at his arm. "I must see you again, Zalán," she begged. "Will you come down to the river every evening while you are still in camp? Oh, please! Please, will you? Promise that you will!"

She backed away from him and released his arm. For a second only, she waited, on the verge of saying more, then changed her mind and, picking up her skirts, ran quickly up the hill away from him, leaving him to stare after her with his answer unsaid upon his lips.

*****

Árpád had left the council chamber in turmoil greater than he wished his councilors to perceive. It cost him much in self-control to temper his final words and to give an appearance of calm deliberation. He felt himself stifled by anger and disappointment and more so by his inability to express his true emotions. Only those who knew him best, his sword bearer and his squire, were able to interpret the curtness of his movements, the frown on his brow, and they both scuttled eagerly out of his way. Outside the tent, he threw himself upon his horse, wishing nothing better than to be alone. Impatiently he waved off the squire readying to follow him. Szárnyas, his horse, sensitive to the master's moods, turned a circle and skittered under him, then, bunching his muscles, jumped ahead, his hooves throwing up clumps of sod in his wake.

By the time they reached the outskirts of the camp, both horse and rider had calmed somewhat. Árpád reined in his mount and let him descend to the river at an easy canter. The horse knew his master's habits; once reaching the edge of the river, he stopped altogether, then descended to the rocky riverbed in careful mincing steps. There he halted again and snorted softly, shaking his head and extending his neck down toward the water, his flanks still rising and falling to the rapid rhythm of his labored breathing.

Árpád dismounted, letting the reins slip through his fingers. He sighed, crossed his arms over his chest, and leaned against the trunk of a young birch. Cautiously, the horse waded fetlock-deep into the water and began to drink. Árpád paid no attention to him. His eyes wandered over the steely gray glinting waves, the flat treeless expanse of the opposite shore, slowly becoming obscured by the rising mists, and finally came to rest upon the pebbles at his feet, which the river had washed to the water's edge. Bending down, he picked one up and, holding it gently in his hand, let his thumb slide over its smoothness. Then he sighed again and pitched the stone into the water, watching how the expanding circle of wavelets chased one another from the point of impact.

His anger had fled, leaving him drained and depressed. He was struggling, now not so much for composure as for an understanding of his mood. For more years now than he cared to remember, the one driving force of his life was directed forward, culminating in reaching this river, this land. Now that the goal was in his reach, he felt bereft and deprived. Somehow, oh, how foolishly, he had made himself believe in the secret places of his heart, that once he held this land, it would provide him with haven and security for his people. Now he saw how he had misled himself, and the bitterness of disappointment rose in his gorge like gall.

Had he really believed that subduing the Moravians would gain him peace forever from the north? Germans would come and harass him from there. Did he think that Bulgarians were the only threat from the south? Greater yet loomed the menace of Byzantium. From the east, the Pechenegs would soon be nipping at his heels like a pack of hound dogs, and not far behind them was the much more ominous shadow of the Cumanian Empire. Would he then forever have to keep one step ahead and one eye to his back? How much farther? But there was no place to go! The land ahead was settled land, not by the kind of tribes the likes of his, to be either destroyed or, if they were willing, pulled into the churning vortex of his army, but by homes of stones and brick and mortar, towns and cities, solid and unyielding, housing peoples whose speech and thoughts and prayers none of them could understand. Other nations, no more valiant but bigger and stronger than his, had tried to breach those strongholds. Like floodwater against rocks, they pounded against those gates, spilling over the land and carrying off the weaknesses and wastes of its humanity, but then they had exhausted themselves in the effort and were destroyed in turns.

He raised his head and looked into the sky. No, he thought, not that fate for my people! Let them prosper here, if they can, where they can remain true to themselves or else be destroyed in the trying.

But to become like the docile sheep of the western world, bleating behind the closed gates of stinking and decaying cities, servile shopkeepers and ragged peasants with their back bent for foreign masters, no, he would not be the one to bring that fate upon his people.

This is the land we have dreamt of, he thought, his eyes sweeping the distance. *We have reached it. Here we have come to rest. So be it then. Here we will remain. This land is good and rich and full of promise. It will sustain us. It was willed to us by our long-ago ancestors, and they and the turul hawk they sent were our guides ever since. It is indeed a land worthy of our possession, to retain it shall be worthy of our battles.*

The distant horizon had cleaved the sun into a narrow band. Sundown had turned to dusk. As brilliance and color drained out of the landscape, so Árpád felt the tumult of his emotions seep away. In their stead, he was invaded by weariness, as leaden and lightless as the country around him. The decisions were his to make, the disappointments his to shoulder. Not the council, not his advisers, nor even his few chosen friends could stand by him at these final moments. So it had always been. In his younger years, he had hoped to get accustomed to it, now he knew that like the birth of each child, each decision was an agony unto itself. Since that long-past day when the chieftains of the other six nations had chosen him, lifted him upon their shields, and swore allegiance to him, named him grand prince, and then cut their wrists to mingle their blood with his as symbol of their oath, their fealty, he had been alone. He was tired, he thought, tired of carrying the burden and oh, so longed for a simple, thoughtless life, which the lowliest of his slaves seemed more deserving of than he.

Árpád made to leave, and in turning, his gaze fell upon a small waterbird still busy scrambling up and down the length of the shore. On impossibly spindly legs, it darted about in search of its food. Mindful of ever-present dangers, its restless and purposeful concentration was only broken by quick left-right glances before continuing its ceaseless search. As he watched the bird, Árpád smiled, but his smile turned sour on his lips. *Aye,* he thought bitterly, *none of us are better off than that bird. We run and chase and tug and find no rest in the getting. At first we exhaust ourselves in the getting, then when gotten, we are compelled to stand constant fearful guard over that which is ours.* He is a fool indeed who hopes for peace after whatever it is that he achieved.

Árpád whistled softly to his horse and began to walk back toward the camp. The horse had been cropping the new grass nearby. Now he lifted his head, trotted after his master, and rubbed his ears against his shoulder. Árpád caught the reins. He stepped up into the stirrups and eased himself into the saddle.

Horse and rider had reached the great empty circle leading to the grand prince's compound, beyond which lay the main encampment, when in the gathering darkness, Árpád became aware of the man and woman. They were standing alone on the grassy slope which slanted down to the riverbank. So intent were they upon each other that they did not even notice the solitary rider looking down on them. At first, Árpád's eyes had only grazed them in idle curiosity. Men and women were often seen together, especially young unmarried ones, on secret trysts. But now something familiar about them caught his attention. The man he could recognize almost immediately, for he was taller and more powerfully built than most others. The figure of the woman was hidden from his view. She looked very slight and small, more so because she stood on lower ground than her companion. Then the woman moved, her movement bringing a flash of near recognition to Árpád. She appeared to hesitate for a moment, or perhaps to say something, then she whirled and fled with a flutter of garments, to be swallowed up by the darkness.

Árpád had reined in his horse to observe them. Now he gazed after her, a deepening frown between his brows, a sudden pang of foreboding constricting his heart. He tried to shake off his unease and rode on. By the time he had reached his tent and dismounted, he believed that he had dismissed the incident. But he could not entirely rid himself of a sense of premonition, and the frown remained on his face.

In somber mood, he threw himself into his work. He labored until very late, drafting and redesigning his messages to Constantinople and to the Holy See. While his scribes bent their backs to the task, he tasted some of the cold venison and cheese, which had been laid out for his meal. The wine he hardly touched at all, only lifting the golden goblet to stare into its amber depths, as though hidden there lay the answer to his questions. Shortly after midnight, he finally dismissed the scribes, called for a servant, and sent him to the women's tent to fetch Virág.

She came almost immediately, bringing her *koboz*. While the servant deferentially bowed himself out of the chieftain's presence, she stood at the entrance to Árpád's bedchamber, her head bent, her fingers playing with the silk ribbons of her instrument. Árpád could not see her face, only the top of her head, the shining honey-streaked light-brown hair parted in the middle. He motioned her to a low stool in front of the brazier and watched as she sat down, focusing all her attention on studiously arranging the folds of her skirts. Still her eyes stubbornly avoided to meet his. Finally Árpád turned from her and stared moodily into the glowing embers of the brazier. Then with one of his abrupt gestures, he lifted his head, walked over to her, and dropped a heavy hand upon her shoulder.

"Well, little one." He kept his voice even. "And how did you spend your day today? What mischief did you get into?" This was a recurring teasing question whenever she was in his chamber, and usually her answers, gay or petulant, brought a smile of amusement to his lips. Today he saw with surprise that she reddened, the flush suffusing her face and creeping down to her neck. Swiftly and uncertainly, she raised her eyes to his, and then just as swiftly, she dropped them again.

"Nay, my lord, no mischief at all. I—I haven't... Why do you ask me?"

Árpád's hand was still on her shoulder. He was thinking that this was the first time he had heard her stammer.

"Did you not go out at all then?"

An imperceptible hesitation there, and she looked up to him again. Her blush was gone, and this time, there was neither hesitation in her voice nor furtiveness in her eyes.

"No—no, I meant to, but I was too busy all day. Before I knew it, most of the day was gone." She quickly went on in answer to Árpád's unasked question. "I am working on some embroidery for my Lady Alán, my lord. It is to surprise her, and I have to hide myself when I am working on it, or else someone would see it for sure and spoil my surprise. But, oh dear, it's hard work for me! I'd sooner clean a mucked-up saddle than do this. You know how I am with a needle and thread…" And she giggled.

Árpád pulled his hands away and then clasped them behind his back. His knuckles were white. "Yes," he murmured, hardly audible to himself, "I think I know how you are…" He threw himself onto the heavy armchair next to the writing table and stretched out his booted legs. The table was littered with scrolls and splotches of dark-red sealing wax. "Come." He nodded to her, forcing a tone of lightness. "I am weary of this day. I want to forget it. Sing something to me."

Árpád always liked her singing. She had a small voice, but a warm and young one with a slight edge of huskiness. He listened and watched her finger move over the strings, her long carefully plaited hair drop onto her lap. Her boots extended from beneath the hem of her skirts. He watched the thick dried crust of caked-on mud on their soles and heels. He was barely aware of what she sang, could hardly hear her for the roaring in his ears, the hammering of the blood at his temples.

After a while, Virág stopped, searching her mind for a new melody, a new ballad. She glanced over to her husband and thought that he had fallen asleep. Quietly she rose and began to tiptoe out of the room. She did not notice the hard darkened eyes under lowered lids pinning her. His voice was like the crack of a whip in the stillness. "Stay!"

She twitched, as though the voice would have struck her, and whirled around, flattening herself against a tent post. Never before had he used such tone on her. Never before had she seen his face look so closed and stormy—his mouth a thin line, the eyes dark and menacing. He walked over to her, his eyes on her boots. When he reached her, he leaned against her, propping his hands against the post on either side of her face. "I fear," he said slowly, "that you are all too eager to be gone from me so soon."

She opened her mouth to answer but dared not speak. She was much shorter than he, the top of her head barely reaching his shoulder. For an interminable moment, he kept her imprisoned against the post, not touching her except with his eyes. Then he leaned closer and, bending his head, kissed her, still not touching her, his mouth like that of a stranger, foreign and hurtful. Fear made her knees buckle under her. When he lifted his mouth and released her, she was hardly able to stand. She did not notice the sudden expression of contempt on his face, and something else too—a look of surprise. When he spoke, it sounded muffled.

"Get you to bed," he said, "it is very late."

*****

It was still dark when Árpád awoke to some slight noise from the outside, maybe the rustling of a night animal brushing against the tent or the snorting of a horse. He lay still for a while, then quietly slid from under the covers and got up. The pale shine of a moonlit night outlined the room in grayness. He walked over to the entrance, where the tent flap had been raised a little, and stared out into the sleeping encampment. In the distance, the ring of the guards' campfires flickered. A servant lay in front of the entrance, rolled into wolfskin coverings, snoring. His task was to serve the master whenever Árpád was awake at night and demanded food or drink or the presence of one of his wives. Now he was oblivious to his master's feet close enough to his body to nudge him.

Silently Árpád withdrew into the chamber and, on quiet feet, went over to the bed. Virág was sleeping. She slept soundlessly, only the gentle rise and fall of the covers betraying her breathing. Over the animal furs, which now replaced the heavy felt covers of winter, she had flung one arm over her face. The roundness of her childlike chin protruded between her arm and the cover's edge. Her faint breathing stirred the surface of the fur. Her naked shoulder gleamed pale in the night-light.

I could crush her head between the palms of my hands, Árpád thought. *If only she would not have lied to me! Calmly looked me into the eye and lied...I would have understood. I do understand. It was never a part of the marriage contract that she should love me or that I should love her. She was to be the price of curtailed animosities between our tribes, between her family and mine, her father and me. That only and nothing more. She never swore to love me. She never asked me to love her. My love must be more burden than pleasure for her. One so young and lonesome is also vulnerable at heart. Before I took her, she was betrothed to Zalán. The handsome, the young, the childhood companion. Oh, I would have understood! But not the lies, the smoothly and unblushingly told lies. Her lies shame her—they shame me as well. No wife of the grand prince should lower herself to lie. Peasant girls lie to their lovers. But the grand prince's wife... How can I forgive the loss of my faith in her which she had sworn to uphold. That I cannot understand. That I will not understand. That I cannot forgive—will not forgive!*

Árpád sank down by the bedstead. His large hands fastened around her slender neck. In long-gone days, wives died for less, it flashed through his mind.

At his touch, Virág stirred faintly. Her eyes flew open. For the length of a heartbeat, she smiled, then the smile slowly drained from her face. Their eyes locked together, his searching her eyes, searching for something in her soul, for something he knew was not there—perhaps never been there; she, her pupils wide with the fear of a cornered little animal. Árpád saw a shadow pass over her face. It took him a moment to realize that it was the shadow of his body over her, blocking out the moonlight. Almost of their own volition, his hands slid down to her shoulders, to her breasts. He buried his face in the warm hollow of her neck. His hands, clutching her hips, tightened. Not wanting to yet wanting, he felt himself slide into the warm inviting secret depths of her being. *May all the gods forgive me,* was his last rational thought, *for I cannot forgive her, yet I will!*

*****

As soon as it became light enough to see, Szabolcs gathered up the horses and took them down to the river to swim. He was convinced that the coolness of the water and the exercise of wading in it offered far greater healing powers for the overstrained legs of the animals than all the incantations and nose-wrenching salves of the priests and shamans. Ever since their return to the main camp, he had been concerned about the horses. They had an arduous journey behind them, traveling at great speed, with stops and rests for only as long as was necessary. The terrain over most of the Balkan Peninsula was rough, even in good weather, and they had covered most of the road from Constantinople during the spring thaw. Many of the mountains were still blanketed by snow and the lower regions covered with thin layers of ice. The rivers they had to ford were swollen with meltwater and running treacherously fast. In addition, they also were iced, and the horses had suffered from innumerable cuts whenever the ice broke through under their hooves. And now, they were to turn right around to go back to that hellhole of a golden den of thieves and cutthroats!

He had fervently hoped that this time, their stay at the main camp could be a longer one. Man and beast alike needed the rest. It was not right that the Lord Árpád should constantly send the selfsame man on these errands, crisscrossing the land from east to west, from north to south. Secretly, of course, he was quite proud of his master, and he knew that Árpád sent Vazul on these missions because he deemed him most suited to the task. Nobody, Szabolcs felt, was Vazul's equal when called upon to represent the grand prince, nobody as skilled at acting with proper refinement at court or at bargaining with as much shrewdness in an audience hall. Being at his side all the time, and also being his friend, Szabolcs had learned much and was proud of his learning.

Yet enough was enough! Last summer, it had been to the Holy Roman court, to the Rhine River, to marshal the bastard king Arnulf's signature, then in the fall to Moravia to accept their terms of surrender of the northern territories. Even before the winter broke, back to the Bosporus, may the gods smite all those who live there! Well, in a way, he did not mind; how many of his friends could discuss kings and courtesans, foreign cities and imperial courts? No, indeed all they could talk of were raids, their horses, and their women!

He sighed, scratched his round bald-shaved head, and slid off the lead horse, Vazul's great bay stallion. He slapped him on the rump to make him lead the others into the fast-flowing current. With loving pride, he watched the horses cavort in the water, swishing their tails and snorting at each other in gay challenge when they raised their dripping muzzles out of the water. Once in a while, he cast an eye to the east to watch the sun's progress over the water's edge. When it finally separated from the horizon and floated freely like a golden disk among the cloud streaks, he commenced to whistle his charges back to shore. Árpád had called an early meeting of the High Council, and his own and Vazul's mounts had to be taken in hand by the stable boys to be curried and shined and saddled, their manes braided, and their hooves polished.

The council took an inordinately long time, Szabolcs thought much later. Together with the other nobles' senior attendants, the head grooms and arms bearers, he lounged in the shade of a protruding awning, which had been raised by the council tent's side, more for the comfort and protection of the mounts than its people. The lesser servants had no claim to such comforts, and the sight of them sweltering in the bright sunshine gave Szabolcs a pleasing pang of importance. He settled himself more comfortably against the tent's side. Half dozing, he attempted to keep his ear cocked to the currents of gossip around him. The council meeting had dragged on into the noonday meal, and Árpád had hosted the nobles in his banqueting room. He had also passed orders to have food and wine offered to those waiting outside. The grand prince had never been a niggardly host, even though his own eating and drinking habits were said to be sparse, Szabolcs admitted with ample satisfaction.

This was the drowsy hour at camp. Bellies were full, eyelids heavy, and movements and speech slow. The lazy droning of the hundreds of flies added to the torpor. The only activity issued from the priests' enclave across the large circle from the chieftain's compound. There servants were dragging out the requisites for a sacrifice, the huge well-scrubbed flat-topped stone which Zombor, the high priest, used to stand upon so that he should be seen by all, the knives and sacred vessels wrapped in silk cloth and the drums, along with the stringed and wind instruments of the musicians.

Marót, who for years now had been the lieutenant of Árpád's advance guard, was among the gawkers watching the elaborate preparations. Now he sauntered over to the group gathered around Szabolcs. With eyebrow cocked and a nod toward the sanctuary, he commented, addressing himself to no one in particular, "Whenever those fellows get busy, it bodes no good for ordinary folk. They perform their rituals, rake in the coins, and divine to carry about the bloodstained sword as a signal for us all to start yet another campaign. Well, they know that their coffers would quickly become emptier than their heads are should they ever counsel peace! Who would be fool enough to pay good money for sacrifice in times of prosperity? To give worthless advice to the sick and to sing over the dying, to make potions for lovesick women and hoof-sore mounts would hardly keep them as well as they are living now!"

Marót's long-standing feud with the shamans was well known. For years he had poured money and gifts into their hands in the futile hope of his wife's recovery. But she had suffered greatly and finally died anyway, and not one of their repeated prayers or sacrifices was able even to reduce the agonies of her illness or ease her dying. He had loved her, and his anger and bitterness toward the priests had mounted in the same measure that he mourned her.

He bent down to tear off a blade of grass and began to chew on it. "The servants are full of news that the grand prince has ordered a great ceremony. He wants to assemble all able-bodied men tonight at sundown. He wants Zombor, that old fake, to perform the Great Sacrifice. They told me that Árpád has already selected one of his own favorite mounts to be sacrificed." Contemptuously he spit out the grass. "As though those peddlers in miracles could see any more in the guts and gore of a battle horse than those of a nag!" He growled.

Szabolcs rose to the bait. In many countries, he had observed many kinds of worship, and although they were conducted to the great sad-faced god of the west, invariably he had found them to be resplendent with pomp and filled with reverence. He had little faith in the god they addressed, though. It seemed unlikely to him that a deity who permitted himself to be manhandled and, finally, killed in the most disgraceful manner could have power enough to come to anyone's assistance. Yet time and again, he had been impressed by how even the mightiest and richest at those courts were willing to arrange their lives by the dictums of this meek god. He considered the ceremonies to that god to be of greater refinement and superior import than the primitive bloodlettings and slaughters practiced by his own people. *How powerful,* he thought, *would our sacrifices become, if only those wondrous magical words and motions could be transferred to the service of our own Great God of War! Surely whatever misfortunes plague us could be eliminated, would our own gods be worshipped in such a fittingly opulent manner.*

"Marót is right," Szabolcs concurred. He was elated to become the center of attention for the little group. "Our sacrifices are crude. How do we dare to believe that they are pleasing to the gods? We dig around in the insides of dead animals and look for a sign placed there by fate—or by the gods. Isn't it stupid to believe that the Lord of War would send us messages in bits of gut and chunks of liver and lung? Or even in the color of an animal's fur or feathers? If the mess and smell turn our stomachs, why should we expect that it does not displease the gods?"

A youth, who had been loitering at the periphery of the group, leaned forward in eagerness. He was the eldest son of Törs, Árpád's arms bearer, known throughout the seven nations as one of their best swordsmen. It was this distinction of his family which perhaps made the youth bold enough to speak up.

"But the signs! How would we ever receive the Lord God's signs? Where else could we read them?"

Szabolcs scoffed. "What signs, boy? If the cadaver's stomach is empty, it points to a lean year. Do we need priests to tell us that? If there is a bloody lump on the lung, it is a bad sign of the gods' displeasure. Bad for whom? Surely bad for the animal, but why bad for us?"

Törs, himself a graying stocky man with a chest like a barrel and disproportionately short legs, for which behind his back he had earned himself the nickname "Sitting Dog," shook his head earnestly.

"Through all the known ages, we have been led by these signs. They led us true as they had led our fathers. Why doubt them now and invoke the Great God of War's displeasure? Without these signs, we are like children lost in a strange land!"

"Look around you, Old Father!" Szabolcs cried out. "If it's signs you want, look around. They are all about us! The trees and the clouds and the flight of the birds, they all tell us messages, give us signs if we would only watch and listen properly."

"If you ask me, it is not signs from the gods that I trust in but the strength of my arm, the true flight of my arrow, and the fleetness of my horse," Marót answered with a resounding slap of his palm against the hilt of his sword. "Women, and children perhaps, they may be reassured by those imagined messages the shamans read from their sacrifices. But in the heat of a fight, I stake my life upon my sword's sharpness and my horse's response to my thighs. Anyone who feels differently has yet to face his enemy in battle!"

Heads all around nodded in murmured assent. Törs, who was of an earlier generation and had lived his life in accordance with the ancient laws and rituals, unexposed to the eroding effects of western culture, looked vaguely disturbed.

"I perceive great danger to us in such thinking. Are the peoples of the west better guarded or better guided by their gods than we have been? Through the years, we have become stronger and more powerful until even the forces of Byzantium and the Holy Roman Empire tremble before our armies. Was it not our aid that the Germans sought against the Moravians? Was it not our army which smashed the Bulgarians and secured peace for Constantinople? What reason would we have to change our ways or our beliefs when it has been clearly shown to us to that they are superior?"

Before anyone could answer Törs's challenge, the attention of the group became riveted to a small caravan slowly weaving its way through the narrow passageways between the tents and purposefully approaching the gate to the enclosure housing the ladies of the grand prince's family. Perhaps half a dozen gaily harnessed and bedecked mules carried heavily inlaid boxes of sandalwood and ivory, as well as fat rolls of cloth and carpets. The tinkling of the mules' bells attached to their harnesses filled the hot lazy air. Each animal was led by a turbaned black slave, barefooted and wearing only a loosely flowing robe of black-and-white-striped cotton. Their master, proud owner of men, beasts, and goods, sat upon a large white camel. With haughty arrogance, he stared ahead, disdaining to turn his face left or right, except to cast swift furtive glances at his belongings. At the gate, he alighted, gathered his voluminous orange djellaba around his short fat body, and began a quick exchange of words and gestures with the guards.

The group watched the proceedings with wordless contempt. It was not for the first time that a foreign merchant had come to peddle his wares to the wives of the rich. They found nothing objectionable about that. What they found distasteful was that any man should parade around clothed in such garish garb and speak and move with such jarring noisy manner in an environment other than his own home. That he made his living by haggling with women just fanned the fires of their disdain. Törs grunted, scrambled to his feet with a groan, and walked over to his horse tethered to a post a short distance away. As he patted his horse's neck, his gesture had something hesitant and forlorn about it, like a child touching his mother's skirts for reassurance. Marót raised his heavy eyebrows again and spat on the ground. Silently he and the others watched the merchant gain entrance to the inner courtyard and carefully herd his possessions inside.

"Shit," Marót mumbled in disgust. "Goddam' clowns running around everywhere you look nowadays. If you ask me, our women have become too spoiled anyway! Give them work, and straightaway they demand two servant girls for help. Let them sit on a horse for two days' ride, and they whine and need an oxcart lined with pillows to cool their arses upon. Have them bear you a child—a son no less—and they act like that's their special favor to you. Silks and perfumes and feathered fans! That is all they want, and if my good wife were alive today, she would laugh at them and teach each a thing or two about hard work and economy and the place a woman should keep to honor her husband!"

Szabolcs could barely endure the loss of his audience. "Well, and who is to say but that we will yet have to swallow these new ways and digest them too? For as soon as Árpád takes to himself a wife from the west, it's a sure bet that all the rich and mighty will follow her example. Then we will have silk merchants and goldsmiths coming and going all day long, for can you expect such fine ladies to be content with the crude life of our camp?"

The others looked at him in shocked disbelief. The raucous old Chief Huba's groom, Uruk, a tall bony man with an enormous beak of a nose, at odd variance with his gentle blue eyes, was the first to find his tongue.

"What kind of nonsense talk is this, man? Why would Árpád take to himself a wife from the west? Are you telling us that our own women are not good enough to warm his bed anymore?"

Szabolcs shrugged. "Good enough or not, that is not what matters. Such things are done," he added importantly, "because of affairs of state. When we were in Constantinople, my master and I, we saw ladies of the court married off all the time because of such affairs of state. I can bet that they have already picked a lady to be escorted here to become Árpád's"—Szabolcs stumbled over the unaccustomed new word—"*consort.*"

"Bullshit!" Marót roared. "No Byzantine lady in her right mind would ever dare set food on this side of the mountains. I hear they believe we run around naked in animal furs and drink the blood of our enemies."

"It is not a question of what they want or don't want," Szabolcs explained patiently. "In the first place, women there are not asked who they feel like marrying, anyway. The ladies of the court, the princesses, and such, they all have to abide by what the empress tells the emperor to tell them. If she bids one of them marry Árpád, then marry him she will. That's what is called statecraft or a part of that, at least, and all the princesses are expected to be married for affairs of state. They are important for that and as valuable as good currency."

Triumphantly he looked around himself. "Is there one of us who doubts that Árpád is worthy of any Byzantine princess?" he challenged. "Of course not," he concluded when no answer was forthcoming. Then he added, relishing the shock his words were bound to create, "And mark my words, once such a lady arrives here, she'll bring servants and attendants, and then in no time at all, our other nobles will follow suit, and before long"—he shrugged his shoulders and spread his hands apart—"our settlements will be overrun by ladies in gold-brocaded gowns tripping across silken carpets, with perfumed eunuchs following them around to carry their fans and turtledoves and spangled prayer books."

There was a good dose of mischievous malice in Szabolcs's delight as he anticipated the effect of his words. He was quite certain that most of the others were unacquainted either with eunuchs, spangled prayer books, or turtledoves. Inwardly he grinned as he settled his back more comfortably against the tent's side to await their startled questions. But his enjoyment proved short-lived. With a sudden surge of raised voices, the gentlemen of the council signaled the end of their meeting. Some of the voices drifting out appeared to be angry, others only puzzled. A moment later, Vazul appeared at the entrance. He looked flushed and displeased. Waving an angry arm toward Szabolcs, he walked across the clearing toward his mount. Even before Szabolcs could scramble to his feet, Vazul was already in the saddle. He looked down upon his friend and shield bearer and spit out the words from the corner of his mouth.

"Get the horses ready and the gear together before nightfall. At daybreak, we leave for Constantinople. And get also changes of horses for Alaricus. He is coming with us as an interpreter. A scribe is not coming, so Alaricus will be our scribe as well. We take as many horses with us as will allow us to travel fast and light, and take no gifts, only small tokens with us, this time."

He calmed his horse by walking him off a few paces, then guided him back. He continued his instructions.

"Servilius is going to Rome today, so make sure you take all the letters, if he still carries any, from his last trip to Byzantium. Give them all to Alaricus who will carry them with us to use for additional leverage, as needed. Also give any letters which Alaricus may have to Servilius for the same purpose. Do I wish it were Servilius coming with us? Aye, I do, but he speaks the language of Rome, in words and thought, so is too important to Lord Szilárd on his mission." For a moment, he hesitated, contemplating if anything has been left unplanned, then continued with an afterthought, "And get together with the Lord Zalán's servants to tell them what to pack for their master. He, and his second and arms bearer are coming along too, goddam." Turning his mount away from Szabolcs, he murmured his displeasure barely audibly. "We will travel with a veritable caravan, not a very discreet way to surprise the court at Byzantium, is it?"

*****

The merchant of the caravan stood in the middle of the room. The women surrounded him in curious clusters. While he conversed with the Lady Alán and bowed to her as frequently as he remembered to, he kept casting disquiet glances to the work of his slaves. They busied themselves with opening boxes, unwrapping and unrolling his wares, and spreading them out for inspection. The slaves were North African Moors, purchased specifically for this trip at the slave market in Tripoli on the Barbary Coast. Now they were sweating profusely in the tent's oppressive midafternoon heat and more so with the effort to do well by their master.

The merchant, whose exact name nobody knew but who styled himself as Sidi Ben Moussa, had purposefully left his best wares at home, to be taken later in the year to Adrianople and Constantinople. Most of the stuff he had brought along were of inferior substance and workmanship. For the current expedition, he had found them to be quite good enough. What his display lacked in true quality of design and workmanship, he compensated for by his swaggering manner and the ostentation of his retinue. He felt assured that these women, even Lady Alán, unskilled in judging such subtleties, would be suitably impressed, nevertheless.

Sidi Ben Moussa had been born in the city of Córdoba on the Iberian Peninsula, but now made his home in the southern part of Macedonia, a much more propitious place for trading. In his lifetime, he had had occasion to acquaint himself with many languages. Now he was speaking a fractured combination of Turkish, Arabic, Greek, and Latin, even Parthian, with as much Hungarian thrown in as he had been able to master. Hearing him, some of the younger women giggled softly behind their hands.

Behind the Lady Alán's chair, Virág stared at the Moors with open-mouthed amazement. This was the first time she had seen Moors face-to-face. She could hardly take her eyes off their dark complexions, the prominent noses and lips, the beautifully gleaming black eyes, and short curly black hairs. Her rapt attention was disarmingly childlike. She leaned against the first wife's chair and propped both of her elbows upon the broad backrest. Her soft round chin cupped into her palms, she let her eyes, alive with curiosity, follow each motion without turning her head. An unconscious smile played about her lips. She looked pretty, young, and vulnerable. Her shiny golden-brown hair, parted in the middle, plaited down her back, then tied with a red ribbon, the high-necked white tunic with its hem of colorful embroidered flowers and birds, the gold spangles on her round arms, all emphasized her youthfulness.

The Lady Alán was feeling poorly, and at such times, she liked to keep Virág by her side. Perhaps having someone nearby, so obviously young and healthy, buoyed her spirits. Or perhaps she expected a more compassionate nature from someone who appeared so artless and unspoiled? There were shadows upon the lady's face and a furrow between her eyes. She leaned back against the cushions of her chair. Her hands, trembling almost imperceptibly, toyed listlessly with a length of brocade spread across her lap. Alán had lately begun to suffer increasingly from headaches; when they came, they numbed her fingers, blurred her vision, and produced a sensation of dizziness and nausea.

Though the lady herself remained silent, the other wives and concubines of the great prince were oohing and aahing over the wares spread out by Sidi Ben Moussa's slaves in the center of a circle at the first wife's feet. Gorgeous bright silks with designs woven in gold or silver thread, brightly patterned tribal rugs from Turkey, Syria, and even from Parthia, as well as from Tunis, Meknès, and Tripoli on the coast of Africa were spread out, one after the other, until the spectators' eyes could barely follow their succession. Then one of the more splendidly dressed Moors, seemingly the overseer of the others, had two men drag in a large lacquered and ivory-inlaid box. The man looked at his master with a questioning gaze and, upon a nod from

Sidi Ben Moussa, unlocked the box so skillfully that the box tipped ever so slightly to spill out part of its contents.

The sound of indrawn breaths ran around the tent, and most women, as though in a trance, moved closer to the box. Even the Lady Alán leaned forward with a small tired smile. Strands of pearls, wide filigreed or embossed gold bangles and anklets hung full of tinkling gold bells, circlets inlaid with gemstones designed to hold the translucent veils of the women, untold array of rings set with precious stones, all tumbled out from the depths of the lacquered box onto the white silk cloth spread out to display Sidi Ben Moussa's wares.

Lady Alán made a barely perceptible gesture to Sidi Ben Moussa who could not move fast enough to come to her side, dragging his interpreter along. The interpreter, an Iberian by birth, from a village in Andaluz, whose native language was Arabic, had, through all the travels with his master, certainly appropriated at least a smattering of a dozen or so languages. But as much as he listened with furrowed brow to the softly whispered words of the lady, it became obvious that he had no idea what the lady requested. Alán turned her head to Virág who, in turn, bent to whisper to her mistress. She then straightened, shaking her head and lifting both of her shoulders, but seemed to reconsider and addressed Sidi Ben Moussa with hesitation. It was obvious that she was searching for words, filling in blanks with gestures. Warming to her task, she took a step away from behind Alán's chair and came forward with mincing steps, acting out a sort of pantomime. She put her palm to her forehead, then to her heart, and took a few hesitant staggering steps forward while she extended both her open palms toward her mistress.

The black slaves stared at her in a kind of horrified fascination, not knowing if the young woman was trying to convey some meaning or parodying her august mistress. When they noticed that the other assembled ladies all began to discreetly giggle behind her hands, they assumed that what was enacted before them was some kind of a play. When they noticed that the Lady Alán also offered a thin watery smile, the slaves started laughing in earnest, joyfully slapping one another's shoulders. Within moments, the tent resounded to sounds of happiness.

The only person not participating in the merriment was Sidi Ben Moussa, who kept casting uncertain questioning looks alternately to Lady Alán and Virág. Finally he prostrated himself to the great lady, and upon rising, using mostly sign language as well, he indicated that he had many wonderful remedies for ailing parts of a body, from the head to the heart and every other part in between. He also assured the ladies that he had in his employ a most eminent gentleman who, also born in Andaluz, had studied the methods of healing in the great city of Córdoba. If he were permitted to do so, he would instantly send for the wise man and bring him here to look at the most august mistress and, if allowed, to examine her.

The examination conducted by Sidi Ben Moussa's healer was a great excitement and an equally great success. Just by virtue of his intervention, the Lady Alán felt reassured to an extent, which the tribal shamans were unable to do, proving the old wisdom that distance casts a special magic of its own upon things and people. Even Lord Árpád, hearing about the excitement in the women's house, smiled and nodded in pleased approval when the news was brought to him during his busy day.

Árpád's relationship with the Lady Alán had begun long ago. When he married her, he was a young warrior, oldest son of Chieftain Álmos, the fabled leader of the populous and important Federation of Hungarian tribes. It was during Árpád's childhood that his father had invited three Kabar tribes, splintered off from the Khazar Federation, to instead join his Hungarian tribes. Together they defeated the Rus of Kiev, then continued to move westward toward the Danube River. The Khazars, in order to cement a closer connection with the Hungarian tribes, offered a family alliance—a marriage.

Thus it had been arranged that Prince Álmos's young son Árpád be offered a Khazar bride, daughter of the senior Khazar chieftain. Her name was Alán, and she was the beautiful blond-haired young widow of a slain Khazar warrior. She was also several years Árpád's senior. As often happens, this particular political arrangement turned into a love match. Alán bore her husband five sons, of whom Levente, Tarhos, and Üllö grew into adulthood. After her last birthing—a stillborn girl child during which Alán almost bled to death as well—she no longer was the beautiful blond wife but a spent and sickly shadow of her old self; alas, the fate of so many wives. Árpád, while emotionally still devoted to his senior wife, mother of his sons, avoided her bed altogether. He believed that this was in Alán's best interest but was also honest enough to acknowledge that his physical desires lay elsewhere, most especially recently with his young newest wife.

In his middle forties, he was in every sense a vital man in the prime of his life. His innate fastidiousness prevented him from being promiscuous, and he thought he had his passions well under control. He had his choice of women, junior wives and concubines, in his household. Some he considered attractive, even desirable, some had become companions during nights he would otherwise have spent alone and lonely. Most were given to him for political reasons, either from tribes wishing for closer relationship with him or from other nations desiring, more or less, the same. Although in all of these arrangements love was not considered or required, he had grown fond of some of these women, and some others he learned to value for one or another of their particular traits. Passion was easily aroused but love rarely entered, as it had when he first bedded Alán and as it did now, when the Lady Virág was given to him by her father, the old chieftain of the tribe of Tarján.

Virág had become both the passion and the love of his maturity. She was so lacking in subterfuge, so innocent and transparent—all of those things his other bed partners lacked. Although he would have wished that she came to love him, it had become sadly evident that she did not. She accepted him with calm equanimity and even showed pleasure in their mutual loving, but he came to realize that there was no depth there, no real emotion. He kept assuring himself that she was too young, that she grew up without a mother or any other female to guide her growing and maturing, that eventually she would; and while thinking those thoughts, he smiled at his capacity for self-delusion.

Now he was standing at the open door of his private chamber, bracing his arms against the two posts holding back the drape over the entrance, allowing two of his pages to put on his ceremonial robes. He was preparing to participate in this evening's sunset sacrifice. The sacrifice was to be a thanksgiving homage to the sacred bird Turul, messenger of the Great God of Creation, who had guided the tribes westward to lead them to the land of their ancestors, which once had been the land of Great Attila. At the same time, the God of War's sword was to be exhibited and shown to the four corners of world so that each of those directions should learn to fear the power and might of the Magyars.

*****

For the first time in their history, since the seven chieftains of the tribal federation had raised the young Árpád upon his shield and swore fealty to him unto death, he would be confirming his dual roles. In one person, he would be not only the sacred spiritual head, or *kende*, of his people but also their *gyula*, or military leader. It was in this dual role that he now was called upon to participate in the ceremony and to raise the Great Sword. The sword, kept in the sanctuary tent, was first to be used at the sacrifice. For this, the most beautiful white stallion was chosen, and it was his blood upon the sword which would be raised in symbol of the nation's pride and power.

The great square between Árpád's tent complex and that of the priests was the result of the trampling of untold hooves over the course of the past month or so. A much larger area had been designed on the other side of the priests' tent. It had been carefully tended by the temple servants. The center of the square was slightly elevated and topped by a stone altar, with a stone ramp leading up to it. In a great circle around this altar, the population had started to gather before sundown already, men and women alike.

The distinction between the sexes was delineated vaguely, if at all. In most tribes, women, on occasion, were expected to be warriors, wielding sword and arrow. Superb horsemen, just as their men, they were equally lethal in sending a shower of arrows from the backs of galloping horses, as cutting down enemy foot soldiers with their curved *kilij* sabers, lighter in weight than their men's swords.

As the sun sunk below the horizon, the gathering grew increasingly silent. When the procession of priests exited their tent, the younger ones blowing horns, there was an expectant shuffling of feet and clearing of throats. Finally Árpád appeared at the entrance to his tent, the heavily embroidered ceremonial cape around his shoulders, the gold-encrusted helmet on his head. He stood in silence, his eyes slowly moving over the populace. Then he walked to the side and lifted the sword lying on a table in his path. There was a collective softly sighed *aah* from thousands of mouths, even those belonging to people too far away to see what was happening. But Árpád seemed not to notice the crowd or the servants of the Great God and his emblem, the turul, nor the horse, which was rolling frightened eyes toward the man leading him to the stone ramp. Totally absorbed in his thoughts or prayers, Árpád mounted the few steps which led to his throne to the left of the altar stone. He sat, laying the sword across his knees, and nodded to the ancient chief shaman who had led these ceremonials for many years. The sacrifice could begin.

Meanwhile, unseen and unobserved, a great deal more shadowy events were taking place at the enormous compound's perimeter. Sidi Ben Moussa's caravan had settled there, amid the bellowing of camels, the loud laughing of the men enhanced by the high-pitched shrieks of the camp whores who, immediately and unbidden, had flocked to the merchant's camp. There was another one, his gray cloak blending into the near darkness, only illuminated by the campfire, who stood somewhat apart from the rest of the group at the edge of the camp. Leaning against an acacia tree, his tall body almost melted into the shadow of the tree. He was patient; he knew that tonight, while everyone was mesmerized by the ceremony taking place at the center of the compound, time was on his side.

And in truth, before long, his patience was rewarded. The short rotund figure of Sidi Ben Moussa separated from his noisy servants and their even noisier women. He was cautiously striding toward the acacia tree, looking left and right in his search for the man he was expecting. When he saw the form leaning against the tree, a big grin split his face. He made a perfunctory bow, touching his forehead, lips, and heart and, without hesitation, extended his hand. He spoke in fluent albeit slightly accented Latin.

"Master Alaricus. I have been expecting you. It is good to see you again. I hope Allah has been kind to you, and you are well?"

Alaricus inclined his head. His answer was also in Latin. "As well as one can be in this accursed land of god-cursed heathen. I got your message. What is it that you want?"

Sidi Ben Moussa spread his hands and wagged his head at the same time. "What is it that I want?" he repeated Alaricus's question. He made a motion with his hand, and the two men seated themselves upon the coarse grass. "You know very well what I want. And those who are above me and for whom I speak want the same thing. Unobstructed trade routes for the riches of Africa and the Orient to flow freely to here and to the north of the Barbarians. We, and those for whom I speak, want linkage with the Norse ships so that trade can indeed flow freely, all the way to the land of the midnight sun. This is where the greatest demand exists, and moreover the greatest acceptance of goods with shallow criticism, and will exist for a long, long time."

There was a brief silence during which the sound of the bells hung around the sacrificial horse's neck could be heard from the distance. Then he picked up the conversation to continue in answer to Alaricus's question.

"I know there is a delegation leaving for Constantinople at daybreak. You are to be a member of the delegation. The delegation also has two other members, both must be replaced. Future delegations to the golden throne, as well as the Holy See in Rome, and the Frankish court need to learn from the fate of this delegation, be more reasonable, more—eh—compliant...Afterward and with the assistance of well-meaning—eh—friends, you should easily be able to advance your diplomatic career, once there will be an—eh—opening."

Alaricus shifted his body, unaware that he was even doing so and thereby indicating his discomfort with what he heard. Sidi Ben Moussa delicately raised a hand to intercept what Alaricus was going to say.

"Nay, do not disquiet yourself, my friend. It is clear that the future of your career is of vastly greater importance than one or two condemnable acts. Let's leave the accomplishment of those rash acts to one who is more—eh—adept at their executions and also—eh—expendable. That one will see that the advancement of your career and all that that implies will occur smoothly. And afterward...Well, you are a literate man, quite capable to document events—eh—shall we say the way you see it? I note we see eye to eye on these things and understand each other well. Your rewards will not come to you immediately, you understand, for that would—or at least could—become obvious and thereby maybe condemning, aye? But be sure it will arrive after a prudent delay, and shall we say, its largesse will be, of course, commensurate with the success of your undertaking and the risks which you will be willing to take in the process."

Once again, Alaricus shifted his body to indicate his unease and impatience at the same time. He looked at Sidi Ben Moussa with narrowed eyes.

"And who are the ones who desire all of this? Who initiates these events? Who will give me my rewards and when? You understand that I need to know more than what you are willing to tell me? Where is my guarantee? Who stands behind me?"

Sidi Ben Moussa shrugged. He rubbed his hands together to get rid of the gritty soil clinging to his palms. Then he rose, smoothing down and arranging his robes. He continued to embroider the theme he had been talking about before, without directly answering Alaricus. "You will be given the—well, the instrument, so to say for the required acts. I will transfer him and his property papers to you before you leave. I can assure you he is very efficient, capable, and well trained in what he has to—eh—accomplish. He has his instructions. If asked, you can claim that now, as you are a freed man and—well, not as young as you were once—you desired to travel in greater comfort and want to have a slave to ease the discomforts of your travel. This man is an excellent horseman and swordsman. If your group is ever attacked, he will acquit himself to everyone's best satisfaction. If there is grumbling about the unplanned increase by one additional person, you can assure you traveling companions that this man will not be a nuisance nor a useless extra mouth to feed. He can hunt, is good at fishing, and can serve as the cook for the delegation. Any grumbling should be short-lived. Besides you are irreplaceable by virtue of your language skills and your reading and writing as well. They will put up with this 'salve' to your comfort, just to appease you."

He sighed briefly, then continued in an effort to address Alaricus's question. "Of course, you must understand that those directing me do not wish to reveal themselves. Nor would you if you stood in their place. I am their spokesperson in this venture. I gave the instructions to Beni Mellal, the slave you have just acquired. Beni Mellal also knows whom to contact in Constantinople. Should a misfortune befall him on the way there, his Constantinople contact will seek you out. You understand that the fewer persons there are and the less they know, the safer everyone will be."

He stopped, silent now, and then gave a low whistle. There was some rustling behind the acacia trees, as a tall thin black man appeared. Alaricus had difficulty in making out his features but could clearly see his smiling lips, the gleam of his white teeth, and the brilliance of his eyes. Beni Mellal salaamed deeply, touching his new master's feet, then walked the short distance to stand behind him. Alaricus turned to say something to Sidi Ben Moussa, only to find him showing his back to them, walking away. From the distance, Beni Mellal again bowed to Alaricus, then extended his thin arm to indicate the direction toward the center of the Hungarian compound.

*****

Next morning at sunup, Szabolcs led the horses, saddled and provisioned, to the shaded sundown-side of Árpád's council tent. He had chosen three spare horses for each rider. They had been corralled in an enclosure two stone throws from the council tent and the sacrificial altar on which rivulets of the white stallion's rust-red dried blood were still visible. He had not provided spare horses for the Lord Zalán, assuming that that was done by the lord's master of the horse.

Szabolcs had also overseen the loading of provisions onto the packhorses and a change of clothing for all, including a ceremonial outfit, except two for his lord, Vazul. For him he added an extremely expensive and ornate ceremonial outfit, cut in the same fashion of the everyday riding outfits but heavy with gold and gemstone-encrusted decorations, and a voluminous gold and silver woven cloak, lined with sable and sweeping the ground. Not for nothing had he spent many months at court in Byzantium. He knew that lack of elegance would diminish the status of the Hungarian delegation. At the same time, long ago, Árpád had decreed that he would not tolerate western clothing on his nobles or even their servants. He had learned that the barbarian riding outfits of long trousers, chausses, and padded cotuns worn by the tribes added the right threatening aura to their appearance, and when dealing with the West, he was sufficiently a statesman as well as warrior to exploit even such trivialities as their clothing.

When Vazul arrived, he nodded toward Szabolcs and, with one motion of his head, indicated his second to join him to receive their last instruction from Árpád. Entering the council room, they found Zalán already present. A table had been set up by the servants to seat Árpád, with Zalán to his left and Vazul to the grand prince's right. Szabolcs and Zalán's second, a handsome young man named Ügyek, owner of two seductive dimples, a short-trimmed mustache, and curly golden-brown hair, were invited to sit opposite their leaders at the narrow table. Árpád, Zalán, and Ügyek were eating their morning meal when Vazul and Szabolcs were invited to do the same.

It was no more than an hour later that Árpád dismissed the delegation members, wishing them a safe and successful travel. There was no need to remind any of them one more time of all the expected pitfalls and caution them about all the unexpected ones that would await them upon their arrival in Constantinople. Should they—even if for a moment—forget this one overriding reality, then the one who was to be their living, breathing reminder, Alaricus, was already cooling his heels, walking up and down in front of the grand prince's council tent. The bulging saddlebags showing to the left and right on his saddle contained copies of each of the documents carried by the leader of the delegation, Lord Vazul and, by Árpád's special envoy, Lord Zalán as well. All was ready for departure, and the men were swinging themselves into the saddles when a woman's sweet high voice floated to them on the fresh early-morning air.

"Zalán, Lord Zalán, if you please! Before you leave, I beg you for the courtesy to stop at the gate to the ladies' garden! Please!"

Zalán, already sitting in the saddle, turned his startled face toward the source of the voice. With an apologetic glance toward his traveling companions, he urged his horse toward the women's enclosure. He was even more startled when he saw who the servant girl ushered forward. Clutching a long veil reaching down to the tips of her shoes, head bowed to hide her face, only her fingers clutching the veil showing, it still only took him a few seconds to recognize Virág.

Zalán made a tentative gesture to dismount but then stopped himself when he saw the almost imperceptible shake of her head. Frowning, he bent forward, leaning upon his horse's neck. His brow furrowed; he gave her a confused glance.

"Lady, is aught amiss?" he muttered.

"Is it true that you are leaving? Is it? To go away from this compound into deadly danger? How will I be able to…to…each day… Did my husband cause you to go? Is it true? Was he angered? Is this his—his revenge? Tell me!" And for emphasis, she stamped her foot impatiently.

Zalán, embarrassed, shook his head with a slight smile. "Nay, my lady, you misunderstand. And I surely do not understand the meaning of your questions. I serve at my lord Árpád's pleasure. I am his emissary. This is what I have been aspiring to since I was a boy. To do this. Not only to be the leader of our tribe. To stand in front of great nations and be proud of what I represent—who I represent. I go because not only my lord but I as well want to…want this…In time I shall return, to my people and my family. I am only sorry to miss so much of my son's growing…" He was silent and pensive for a moment. Then he tilted his head slightly, and under lowered lids, his eyes were suddenly filled with an awakening look of puzzled suspicion.

"May the gods watch over you, my lady, and give you contentment and happiness. We all do our duty, each of us in our own way.

Watch over our lord, your husband, for he is, for all of us, our hope and our treasure. Cherish him and support him…for the sake of all of us who serve him. Farewell, my lady." With that he turned his horse's head and followed his companions. Virág, her fingers white from clasping the willow branches that fenced the garden of the women's house, silently stared after him until the riders' figures became too small to see in the distance.

*****

It was one day short of two weeks following their departure that the little group bound for Byzantium camped in a tree-sheltered glade by the river Nišava, within eyesight of the small trading town of Naissus. Vazul planned to spend at least a day here, resting the men, but most especially the horses, and replenishing their travel supplies. The woods surrounding the glade stretched deep to the south and east, offering the promise of good hunting. Far in the distance, great mountain ranges were visible in the shimmering haze. To the west lay the town and, beyond that, rolling flatlands, giving way to gently rising ridges in the distance. Fish was plentiful in the little river.

Vazul planned to send Beni Mellal into town to do the shopping and haggling tomorrow. Such things were not within the realm of a Hungarian warrior's capabilities, and without a doubt, to do so would be considered greatly insulting. At the moment, Vazul reclined with his broad back supported by the gnarled trunk of a tree, wiping his mouth after chugging down a flask of the mead which he greatly preferred to the red wine customarily served by Hungarian households. Zalán, sitting opposite him, hid his smile; evidently the old boy had a sweet tooth. Ashamed of his thoughts, he quickly corrected them. Vazul was only ten years his senior, vital and strong like a bull. In no way should he be thought of as an "old boy." He rose and, to atone for his errant thoughts, offered to replenish Vazul's flask.

Vazul, however, shook his head and lifted himself. He walked to the river's edge, turning his head left and right, and, with his fists on his hips, sniffed the evening air. "I smell rain," he announced. "Probably before the morning."

Szabolcs, who was never far from his master, added, "Maybe we should go to the town for night shelter?"

Vazul shook his head. "Nay, remember I sent Alaricus's slave ahead, and he told us that the town is filled with Syrian merchants. I'll be damned if I bunk with those peddling and piddling dogs. A little rain never hurt. It will beat down the dust and the flies that have plagued us these last few days."

By the time darkness became absolute, the thin curve of the moon and every glimmer of a star were hidden by lowering clouds. It was close to midnight. The horses were becoming unsettled by the long jagged streaks of lightning in the distance, which were so continuous that they fired up the bottom of the northern sky. By then none of the men could sleep either. Huddled in their heavy fur-lined oiled-skin-to-the-outside traveling cloaks, they sat in a semicircle facing toward the north to watch the play of the unceasing lightning.

Then the heavy warm drops of summer rain began to fall, first in a slow measured cadence, making little indentations into the parched sand. Within minutes, the drops increased, and in no time at all, the rain became a deluge. In misery, the men pulled their cloaks over their heads and now turned their backs to the north, whence the rain was coming in impenetrable sheets. Their backs to the little river, and the wind now howling into their ears, the endless claps of thunder almost deafening them, none of them heard the changed sound of the flowing water.

It was the screaming bucking horses who alerted them to the river. By the time they turned around, the horses were standing up to their fetlocks in the raging river overflowing its banks. Szabolcs and Vazul moved almost in unison, untying the animals' leads from the branches of the trees they had been tethered to, trees which no longer formed the river's edge but stood deep in the swirling water. Szabolcs looked to his right and saw Zalán do the same to some of the remaining horses, and then noted that the tall thin form of Beni Mellal stood next to Vazul, bending, evidently to pick up one of the horse's leads which had gotten entangled in a tree. The tree was shaking, pulled along by the river's strength, and finally snapped, most of its crown smashing into Vazul. Vazul screamed and fell facedown into the river, Beni Mellal bending until his face touched the water, apparently struggling to pull Vazul free from the tree.

Szabolcs struggled against the current, leads of four horses in his hands, and saw Zalán try desperately to reach the two men, saw him extend a hand to Beni Mellal and try to pull him and Vazul away from the tree. He saw Alaricus wading toward them, dragging himself against the current, unable to make any headway, saw Beni Mellal, for endless heartbeats, bent over the motionless Vazul and evidently still trying to lift the tree's crown from him, watched the agonizing slowness of his effort, saw Zalán reach Vazul, and finally—finally—saw the two men slowly pull themselves and the inert body to the river's edge.

They laid Vazul on his face and chest onto the sodden ground. Szabolcs joined them and gently turned his master's face to the side, then straddled him and, putting his hands to both sides of Vazul's chest, began to squeeze. Although his body did not move, a stream of fluid flowed out of his mouth and nose, then the body sagged, however. Szabolcs continued to repeat the same motions, again and again, endlessly until the rain slowly subsided. Sweat poured off his face and neck, his arms trembled with the strain of exhaustion, and still he could not stop himself. Ügyek and Zalán finally pulled him away from the body despite his screams and his fists now pummeling the two. His agonizing screams of *no* echoed back from the edges of the little clearing. Finally Zalán bent down, detaining the flailing fists and shaking his head at him. His dripping hair scattered water left and right about his ears.

"Enough, enough!" he yelled. "No more! Let him go, man, let him go. He is done for. He is dead. Give it up, Szabolcs, there is nothing more any of us can do." He lifted his face to the sky, not sure if the wetness was from the residue of rain or his streaming tears. The others stood around the body, forlorn, speechless, thunderstruck, shifting from foot to foot, irresolute as to what to do next. Vazul was their leader, the leader of the delegation, Árpád's spokesman, and who could replace him? The mission was done for, in shambles, wasn't it? None of them could ever replace him, could they? Were they to turn back now? But how could they? Wouldn't that be unacceptable to Árpád then? He was counting on them and their success, wasn't he? And who could lead them now?

Slowly, one by one, their eyes focused on Zalán. Beni Mellal, who had collapsed at the river's edge after pulling Vazul's body out of the water, his chest heaving, slowly crawled to Zalán and lowered his forehead to the wet ground. "He needs to be cremated before we leave here, Master." He panted. "We are awaiting your word, lord. The Lord Vazul cannot just..." He did not complete his sentence, shuddered, and bowed his head again.

Zalán stirred, like someone awakening from a dream. He passed his hand across his eyes, glanced hesitantly at the men who stood, stunned and ashen-faced, around the body on the ground. He felt the gaze of each person slowly turn in his direction. The looks felt like daggers piercing his body. With the weariness of an old man, he bent and removed a key which hung from the dead man's sword belt. His eyes wandered to Szabolcs and Ügyek. Not really counting the freed slave, Alaricus, those two suddenly had become, after him, the two most senior persons in the group. He nodded to them and, with a sigh of obvious reluctance, hung the key onto his own sword belt.

As early as the dark outlines of the trees became visible, the servants and Beni Mellal, Alaricus's black slave, gathered as much wood as they could for the funeral pyre. Wood was now more than plentiful after the devastation of the storm, but all of it was sodden from the heavy rain. Then Beni Mellal found that by digging down deep enough into the roots, they could access as much wood as necessary for a—albeit meager—funeral pyre. The servants washed the body, rinsing off the layers of silt and sand that had become lodged in the folds and crevices of his skin, then redressed him in his cleaned traveling clothes. Szabolcs spent what seemed to be endless time to polish his master's sword, clean his hunting bow and arrows, and, finally, gently combed Vazul's graying chestnut hair. He disappeared then into the thicket and returned a short while later with a young goshawk he had snared. The hawk, angry yellow eyes glaring at his captor, was tied securely so that his talons and beak could do no damage to anyone.

Finally the body was raised and gently laid upon the funeral pyre, his sword placed into his stiff hand, his bow and arrow into the crook of his arm, and his horse led to stand by his side. It was Zalán who was asked to plunge his sword into the horse's neck, and the struggling breast, screaming in his death throes, was dragged to lie next to his master, his blood soaking Vazul's body. Zalán, assisted by Beni Mellal, struggled for a minute to light the fire of the pyre, but eventually they succeeded, and the flame took on a life of its own, blazing toward the morning sky.

As the flames began to assume the dead man's body, Szabolcs cut the ties restricting the goshawk and let him soar. With an angry shriek, the animal lifted his body and rose so fast that in less than three heartbeats, he was barely visible behind the still-lowering clouds. The dead man's soul, freed by the act of cremation, rode on the bird's wings to heaven, to meet Old Father God of War, the most powerful one in the pantheon of gods, so powerful indeed that he was able to cause the creation of the worlds by ordering the lesser gods to obey his will.

*****

The great basileus of the Byzantine Empire, Leo Porphyrogenitus, the to-the-purple-born ruler of all, was still sleepless. Valiantly he struggled to contain his ire and forced calmness upon himself. Also known as "The Wise" because of his large collection of books and wide range of learned writings, he felt it unseemly to be so caught up in emotions. Was he not a calm and detached person guided by cool and logical assessment? And for that very reason, he studiously kept his distance from the ebb and flow of family affairs at all times, didn't he? Even though he sometimes wished to take a pillow and stifle his wife's mouth to stop her never-ending complaining, plotting, planning, her never-ending push to get her family more importance, more wealth, greater advancements, anything, everything to make them shine more at the imperial court. As though the Martinike family would not already be enormously influential! Sometimes he actually felt like he was swallowed up by her family. And sadly, she was blessed and he, at the same time, cursed with such a very, very large family.

The sun was rising above the narrow strait of the Bosporus to the left of the palace window, where he had now stood for a long, long time. Still he could not feel sleep approaching him and drawing him to his bed. The bed, which had become the symbol of his misery.

Sighing, the basileus gathered his night-robes about him as he decided to forgo sleep and most especially his—their—bed, and instead spend some hours in his favorite place. His private reading room and study, actually his bibliotheca, although he disliked calling it that, feeling that it put a stamp of consent upon his bookish reputation. Be it as it may, he favored this room because it was well known that entry was granted by special, and often prior arranged, permission by the emperor. Here he could think, contemplate his own writings and those of his father, Basil, the first Byzantine emperor by that name. He could codify the existing Byzantine laws, called the Basilica, and write additions to them, which he called the Novels, or New Laws. It was this latter that he exceptionally enjoyed working on; it gave an avenue to his plans for his country's future and the future of his family, of which, he had to admit wryly, there were, to this day, exactly none.

If only, he thought, his wife was as fertile as his recently acquired mistress, Zoe Zaoutzaina, who was already pregnant with their first child! Zoe was the daughter of his adviser Stylianos Zaoutzes. She was also lovely, very ambitious, and so very, very giving!

His musing having run full circle, he now came back to his marriage and his wife's family, now his own family by marriage. His father-in-law had been a great friend of his own father, Basil, and that alone would have prevented any closeness between in-laws. Leo's dislike—to put it mildly—of his father was well known. Probably it was a mutual dislike. Probably, so Leo speculated, it was his father's not-so-subtle revenge to foist the young Lady Theophano upon his son. For young Leo, it was truly a marriage from hell, for Theophano unfortunately was demanding, self-centered, loud-mouthed, coarse, ill-mannered, and as frigid as they came. Leo's infrequent attempts at continuation of the erstwhile consummation of their marriage met with less-than-lukewarm reception. He still thought back with a shudder at that consummation. Having found his bride in their marital bed fully clothed from neck to ankle and trying to divest her of all that material, he first met with angry resistance, which then faded to eventual resignation, culminating in shrieks of "Lord Jesus and Mother of God, save me!" at the crucial moment.

Needless to say, such welcome put a serious damper upon the young groom's ardor. After more than three years, their marriage was still childless. Whether this was due to his frequent straying from their marriage bed or to Theophano's barrenness could not be determined. The emperor had produced offsprings, "on the left side of the bed," as the saying went, and so the royal couple's childlessness could be squarely laid to the empress's debit.

Leo forced his mind to consider matters of greater importance than his wife's foibles. He was informed that he could expect the unexpected—a smallish delegation of Hungarians was seen traveling south, traveling the main road from the river Nišava southward, presumably toward Constantinople. Where else would they be going if not to Constantinople? Everything south of it was immaterial, inconsequential. But he was puzzled. All of the informants, all of his dignitaries occupied with analyzing Hungarian affairs, all information from the Bureau of Barbarians as well, steadfastly informed him that no such delegation was expected, in fact, that there was no reason for sending such a delegation.

The small size of the delegation was another puzzlement. Who in their right mind would let loose a group of less than ten people—and that included servants and slaves as well—to approach the golden throne and its emperor? Atrocious! Ludicrous! Another example of the total disregard of protocol and etiquette by these shuffling hordes!

Leo, much quieter and more introspective than most of his advisers put together, had an ill feeling. He still remembered the leader of the last delegation by the name of—what was it again—Vassal, no, Vazzel—ah, Vazul! Well, he recalled that this individual, without falling to his knees in front of him, only bowed his head and then had the audacity to look him in the eyes! His eyes, indeed! How incredible! How unacceptable! In the solitude of his bibliotheca, the emperor smiled. The first person who was not intimidated by the great basileus, Leo Porphyrogenitus! Under different circumstances in different lives, he thought that he would have liked to chat with that barbarian, just one on one, stroll through the park by the Bosporus and maybe share a flask of cheap red wine from a street seller.

Leo also remembered that this Vazul raised—dared to *raise*—an eyebrow when one of his royal underlings reminded him that tribute was still due to the empire. He also made the court understand that intervention on behalf of the empire in the Bulgarian wars was considered by their grand prince as equalizing the books, so to say, with reference to the past. Any future assistance given to the empire should be considered to be in place of future tribute. Leo remembered the shocked silence that followed and the farewell response of the delegation, collectively inclining their heads and then turning on their heels and marching out of the audience room without being dismissed by him.

The emperor smiled. Those men, that audacity was admirable. It lacked refinement—thank God—it lacked polish, but it showed raw power and self-confidence in its place; perhaps misplaced and foolhardy, but oh, so exciting! Other than in his books, he hardly ever encountered excitement, and indeed, who at the age short of thirty would not crave excitement? He vaguely felt it stirring his blood and, at the same time, thinking, *Do not let them find out that I secretly envy them!*

It was no more than one week later that the current Hungarian delegation arrived at the golden throne. Their arrival, especially since it was not one previously planned, arranged, and fostered by the appropriate dignitaries, caused barely a ripple in the concerns of the court; more so since the one person who carried any weight, who had actually already negotiated on Grand Prince Árpád's behalf, was absent. Apparently he had been replaced by a handsome young barbarian-chieftain-turned-diplomat, for whom this was the first trip to a civilized city.

The emperor occasionally liked to inform himself personally, without input from his many advisers and ministers. Whenever he did so, he found his own curiosity actually amusing. Wearing a monk's brown robes and pulling the hood over his head, ostensibly as protection against the wind blowing in from the northeast along the Bosporus, he was free to roam through the large palace gardens, a favorite place for meetings of all sorts, mostly of the sort which desired to be unobserved. It also afforded him unlimited access to information, important and trivial, which otherwise would have eluded his attention.

And right now, his attention was drawn to two seated on a bench almost directly below him. The walkway he was strolling along was one of several serpentines leading from the palace to the high fence separating the rocky beach from the lush parks above. Ornately uniformed guards patrolled the fence; entrance for anyone by scaling the fence would be punished by immediate death. No one but those very select personages, whose admission to the august basileus's palace was granted by His Majesty's edict, were allowed to enter the ground, let alone to wander there. For the enjoyment of those few distinguished ones, benches were placed along the walkways, some shaded by canopies of gaily colored silk shot with gold or silver thread.

It was one of those canopy-shaded benches that momentarily drew the basileus's attention. Immediately he recognized both figures and watched them with a small indulgent smile as they slowly settled themselves on the bench, arranging their heavy embroidered tunics and the translucent undertunics just so. One of the two ladies was his wife, Theophano, the inveterate meddler who assuredly did not merit an indulgent smile from Leo; but the other was his sister-in-law Julia, Theophano's little sister. She, on the other hand, very much elicited such a smile from her brother-in-law.

She was young, just awakening to her womanhood and its potent powers, no doubt under the expert coaching of the *basileia* herself. She was pretty, delicately built, graceful, and elegant. She obviously had recently discovered men and the role they could take in a young woman's life, especially one who was the empress's sister. Leo was certain that such discovery went hand in hand with the shedding of her virginity which, after all, would not be a trophy but rather a hindrance for someone of her status and appeal.

The two women were chatting so intently, they were so preoccupied that much to Leo's pleasure, they paid no attention whatsoever to their surroundings. Leo was fairly certain that they would not have noticed him either, would he have approached them more closely. While he stood there, absorbed in the little scene played out in front of him, he heard the gravel of the serpentine walk crunch with footsteps. A tall thin man, of an undetermined age, his sandy-blondish hair cut straight at just below his earlobes, slightly stooped, as were so many tall persons, strode purposefully along the walk, only to stop in front of the two women. He bowed deeply, bending from his waist, and then continued to stand before the two women. They were idly fanning themselves with their curly ostrich feather fans, which all the women at court preferred because "one could hide one's smiles and whisper with ease" using them.

The arrival of the stranger, by Leo's estimate, a member of one of the Germanic tribes, judging by the color of his hair and by his height alone, piqued the emperor's curiosity. His eyes, which usually barely hid his boredom, now brightly alert, scanned the environment. Much to his surprise, he found no one else near the august ladies and their solitary companion. He assumed that his empress would have insisted on accompaniment, at least of some soldiers, not to speak of a court lady or two. Theophano has been exceedingly fearful even of short forays like this—a little walk through the gardens. Ever since a minor functionary had been found in this very garden with his throat expertly cut, she saw threat behind every door and every bush outdoor. However, interestingly today, she had ventured out without protection, unless, for some strange reason, she counted Julia, half her size and heft, as protection. Thus one had to assume that the presence of this lanky stranger accounted for the lack of guards present.

Quickly losing interest in what he saw, Leo was ready to leave when he noted that the conversation, at least on the tall man's side, decidedly picked up steam. The man pulled some rolled-up papers out of one of the folds of his robe and proceeded to unroll them and read from the opened page. Whatever he was reading began to excite him, and he emphasized his words by expansive gestures. Surprisingly the ladies were listening with interest, the idle to-and-fro move of their fans picking up speed, while their heads nodded in unison.

Shortly the man must have run out of breath or topic because, while bowing to both women, he rerolled the page and replaced it into his bosom, along with the others. Obsequiously he bowed to them again and then disappeared into the bushes. With a slight frown, Leo the Wise turned and slowly ambled up the serpentine to his private office, where he had left the door open to accommodate a brief afternoon stroll. He was not sure if he should ascribe importance to the brief meeting of the unknown man and the two women of his family. But one thing he had learned from almost the day of his birth was that at the golden palace of the emperor of Byzantium, there were no insignificant events.

It was less than a week—five days exactly—after the chance observation in the park that Leo Porphyrogenitus, the basileus, had, at last, a continuation of the story he had observed in the park. With the master of imperial audiences gracefully skipping around him while whispering into his ear the name of the next group on the list for his gracious attention, the master of ceremonies was already shepherding them into his August Majesty's line of vision. At first Leo only noticed the outrageous clothing worn by the delegation. Over homespun tight chausses bleached to a sparkling white and tightly fitting soft high boots, with their tops gently turned under, and over brightly embroidered homespun shirts, they wore the most outrageously beautiful capes, ermine or sable-lined, and embellished richly with intricate embroidery of flying birds and stags running wild in some magic forest. They were thrown over one shoulder only and held in place by heavy gold chains, secured by even more massive gold and gemstone clasps. The whole group consisted of only five men and one black slave. Out of the five men, one was obviously the leader of the group, while two others, no less conspicuously and richly clothed, flanked the first man.

But what caught the emperor's attention was the tall thin man with lank dark-blond hair, standing to the side and slightly behind the group's leader. He had a satchel slung over his shoulder, obviously for the purpose of carrying documents, and was apparently ready to remove one or another of these documents or else to assist his master as an interpreter.

His master, whose alert brown eyes were scouring the audience hall with unabashed interest, was nothing if not impressive. Almost as tall as his scribe but with broad shoulders and chest, a thick neck, and heavily muscled arms, he stood quite obviously disinclined to genuflect to the emperor, ignoring the desperate prompting and urging of the master of ceremonies. Instead he gave him a brief look, as one would to an annoyingly yapping puppy. In response, he shifted the off-shoulder cape and positioned his legs further apart in a stance indicating a hint of defiance. Leo leaned forward with curiosity. Surely the man was an exceptionally handsome specimen of his race, even though the heavy mustache he wore disfigured his strong face. Or perhaps not, was it just that Constantinople was unaccustomed to unshaven upper lips?

The master of ceremonies, a certain Alexander Ingerinus, continued to flutter his hands in desperation, until Leo motioned him to cease and to advance the Hungarian envoy to his presence. Magister Alexander made the presentation, his tongue stumbling over the Magyar names. The Hungarians advanced and stopped at the place indicated, where their leader spread his two legs again, then inclined his head. Leo noticed that the inclined head did not involve any part of his body, other than his neck and head, and smiled faintly, turned to Magister Ingerinus, and asked for the envoy's name again, including its correct pronunciation. Ingerinus floundered until the Hungarian pushed him out of his way with obvious irritation and took one more step toward the throne.

A collective gasp could be heard throughout the audience hall, forcing the Hungarian to look around in puzzlement and raise one of his eyebrows. His eyes returned to rest on the emperor's face, and the two men, each with a slight smile, eyed each other silently. Then the envoy once again bowed his head and slowly enounced, all the while looking into the emperor's face, "Zalán, of tribe Nyék," and then repeated, "Zalán, of Nyék."

Leo almost laughed with delight. Suddenly he was overwhelmed with the desire to learn, the same urgency he always felt when entering his bibliotheca. His hands on the two lion-headed armrests of his throne, he leaned forward eagerly, his brows knitted with concentration as he attempted to mouth the strange-sounding words. The Hungarian smiled and nodded encouragement, then repeated his name. The gesture of his hand, palms up and fingers beckoning was the universal gesture for *repeat please*. Leo threw back his head and laughed—actually laughed—casting the assembled court into stunned silence.

*****

The news reached Árpád's tent city one week after the departure of the delegation bound for Constantinople. He was still seated at the small table in his private tent, eating his customary sparse breakfast, when the messenger was announced to him. He knew the man; he had been the regular go-between for messages concerning Árpád or Virág and Töhötöm, Virág's father, the tribal chief of Tarján. Töhötöm, the truculent chief in a forever-adversarial love-hate relationship with Árpád, had given his much treasured, much coddled only daughter in order to bring a degree of mellowness to his position toward his chief of chiefs, the great prince. And now, the terrible news was that Töhötöm had been shot by a stray arrow during a boar hunt. For two long days and nights, he had floated between life and death, but now he showed signs of a slight improvement.

The chief shaman and the healer who had always attended Töhötöm and all members of his family held out some marginal hope for his survival. He had been asking for the man who was to succeed him. Sadly there were no men in direct line of succession. All three of Virág's brothers had died in battle. Zalán, not only a close friend of the old chieftain but also a trusted dignitary of the closely allied nation of Nyék, had long ago been chosen by the tribe's council to succeed him. Now the old man was eager to see him, talk with him at such a critical junction of his life. He was eager as well to see his daughter and hoped that she could safely undertake the dangerous and long travel under Zalán's protection?

As soon as Árpád had dismissed the exhausted courier and sent him to his kitchen tent for food and wine, he rose and summoned Virág to his presence. When she arrived, her fingers were still busy plaiting the single thick braid which usually hung down her back to past her waist. She wore her nightshift with a heavy woolen wrap reaching to her ankles, her bare toes curling against the cold dew-moistened grass in front of the tent's entrance. It was early morning, everywhere the mists were still sitting on the grass like steam above a kettle. Árpád, known to be an early riser, was not surprised that she had just awakened. When she stopped at the entrance, holding on to the tent flap, and looked at him with a smile and gathering worry in her eyes, she reminded him of a wary young doe. Speechlessly, he extended his hand and pointed to the low stool by his side.

Unable nor even desiring to hide his unease, he reached for her hand, letting his thumb gently caress her palm. Sighing and, with unaccustomed hesitancy, searching for the correct words, he turned his eyes to his youngest wife.

"I have just received a courier from your father's headquarters, little one," he said, his voice low and as calming as he could manage. "There is worrisome news of your father, my dearest. He has been wounded by a misguided arrow while on a boar hunt." He stopped when Virág's body twitched, and she began to rise from her stool. Holding her hand so that she was forced to sit and to listen to him, Árpád continued, "But be of good hope, child. I have also been informed that he has passed the crisis of wound fever and is expected to slowly improve. Of course, while he is as strong as an ox," Árpád added with a small nod, "he is also no longer young. You understand, little one, his age works against his recovery. We shall all offer sacrifices and prayers to further that recovery.

"Meanwhile, my love"—he turned toward his wife more fully and allowed himself a wintry smile—"it is both his and my wish that you should go to see him. It would be the most powerful boost toward his health, and I believe strongly that it is what I owe an old and faithful—howbeit difficult—ally. I shall miss your presence greatly, but that is unimportant when considering your father's health and happiness. I am taking steps to send you on your way as soon as you can pack up, my dear, with some of your serving women and a large detachment of my most trusted guards.

"Thus, my little one, I wish you safe travels and send with you all my prayers and wishes for your beloved father's health. May he thrive yet for many a day. May you, wife, be safe and be returned to me as well and as beautiful"—and here he allowed himself a gentle smile and a tender look—"as you are now sitting in front of my presence." And with that, he pulled her shoulders close and let his arms move around her. He kissed her, gently at first, but then with increasing passion until, with a sigh, he released her reluctantly.

Virág hardly remembered getting back to the women's tent. Tears were running down her cheeks, and when several of the ladies inquired, she gave a sobbing account of her conversation with Árpád. She began to pull items out of the heavy carved wooden trunks housing her belongings and let them drop in an ever-increasing pile on the floor. Finally the Lady Alán was alerted and requested Virág's presence. Virág was close to the first lady's heart, probably more so than any of the other wives. She had such a disarming and engaging youthfulness and innocence about her, which had captivated the first lady from the day on which she had become the grand prince's youngest wife. Lady Alán had long ago given up her jealousies and had learned that whatever loving emotions still remained between her husband and her, they were those of long years of affection, care, and devotion between the two of them.

Eventually the last satchel was stuffed to bursting, the last box and trunk strapped to the sides of the packhorses, and Virág gave her final hugs to the other wives. She went to kneel in front of the first lady, in a gracious gesture of farewell and obeisance, and kissed her hands. At that point, not only she but all the ladies were crying. The lady bent, embraced the young woman, and kissed her forehead, stroking her flushed cheeks in a motherly gesture.

Virág had spent the last hours since Árpád talked to her with feverish packing. She needed this; she had to take that. Much of what she had her women pack, in all fairness, was not serving her needs or comfort but were little gifts to practically everyone she could remember. For her father, she could not think of anything that would please him. Then just before their departure, Prince Árpád's stablemaster led a beautiful young stallion on a lead to the other horses impatiently waiting under the shade of a tree. She was told that the animal, one of the prized stud stallions from Árpád's stable, was to be a gift to her father. Virág, who was familiar with horses and their conformations, had rarely seen such a beauty. A delicate-appearing but strong-boned black animal, his coat gleaming in the sunlight, his large eyes flashing equal parts of defiance and intelligence, he was truly spectacular. Virág could not think of anything more appropriate.

She was ready to burst into tears and storm into Árpád's tent when the stablemaster appeared again, this time leading one of the elegant deceptively delicate-looking mares, again from the grand prince's stable. She was a love, her light-chestnut color shining golden in the sunlight. Her mane and tail were most unusually lighter than her coat, and altogether she presented elegance with wiry strength. The stablemaster smiled at her and transferred the mare's lead into her fingers. In response to her puzzled expression, he waggled his eyebrows.

"Your husband's gift to you, my lady. She has an exceptionally soft gait and a heritage of great endurance despite her delicate appearance. She should serve you well on your long trip, my lady!"

And so finally, the group of riders departed: Virág, five serving women, one of them a healer to assess her father, the courier, and a large detachment of soldiers. They were facing a five or six-day-long travel, with endless hours in the saddle each day, the last two days over rocky and increasingly treacherous mountain terrain. There was danger not only in the land traveled but even more so in marauding gangs ready to attack anyone for profit, as long as they were deemed to be weaker. There were also larger groups of wandering Pechenegs, interconnected by a mighty tribal support group, who potentially were a truly lethal danger and the main reason why Árpád insisted on such a large group of warriors for accompaniment.

Virág, not usually a weepy person, could barely stop herself from tearing up during the most unexpected times of the first two days of travel. Each time she thought of her father, or her husband, her tears would begin to fall. She imagined her father suffering, maybe close to death. Arrow wounds were invariably very dangerous, prone to infection, fever, and then the—end! When she pushed those horrible thoughts away, her husband's face, his serious eyes smiling at her, his sensuous mouth moving over hers, oh, and his lovingly thoughtful gift to give her some happiness on the somber day of departure, well, at that her tears began to fall in earnest.

And that was not the only reason this trip turned out to be sheer torture for her. She had always so much loved traveling, riding, just having the wind blow through her long hair, left loose for more comfort during the long days in the saddle, but this travel, there was something wrong! For days she and her ladies fretted that she must have eaten something which upset her stomach, even though no one else complained about bad food. The convoy was forced to stop repeatedly each day as she ducked behind the closest bush or tree, heaving endlessly, while the ladies pressed cooling wet kerchiefs to her sweat-soaked forehead. By afternoon, her distress usually subsided, but by then she was almost too exhausted to continue so that the convoy was forced to set up camp much earlier than planned.

Virág just wished to have the travel over with as soon as possible and yearned to arrive at her father's settlement. With each passing day, the older ladies accompanying her looked to each other with more and more meaningful gazes, raising knowing eyebrows. They were united in their opinion and as well in feeling that Virág should not be alerted to her pregnancy until the troupe was safely ensconced at their destination.

Her first meeting with her father affected her deeply. She had been warned that in the close to three years of intervening time, she would need to expect her father to have aged, even without his accident and illness. Several of the women in the women's house had cautioned her before her departure, even the first lady herself.

"If you find your father changed, aged, do not show your shock to him, my dear. You must understand that as one ages, beyond a certain age, the unraveling, the decline is so much more rapid and noticeable than it would be in an adult of middle years. Smile and tell him how

well you think he looks, considering that he is just recovering. That will assure him greatly."

Saddened, she now remembered those words. Instead of the vigorous older chieftain, she encountered a shuffling, bent old man, leaning on two canes to drag himself around. He refused to be assisted and angrily shrugged willing hands away from his body. He was rail-thin, and with each breath taken, his breathing whistled in his chest. He was impatient, had lost his appetite, and, more than anything else, his zest for living. He had been an active person since, as a growing boy, he was sent to squire for Grand Prince Árpád's father, Prince Álmos, oh, so many years ago! Now he seemed content and even happy to slowly walk himself out into the garden where he could sink into the deep cushions his servants had prepared for him under the spreading branches of an old chestnut tree.

Sitting there, he raised his bushy eyebrows to his daughter. She had finally been advised of her condition and had told her news to the old chieftain. Töhötöm understandably glowed, at the same time fretting over Virág's travel back to her husband while carrying his child. As was his habit, he became querulous to cover his anxiety.

"You have been married now for close to three years, and this is all you have to show for it? The first child in your belly—eh—what? Does he avoid you much of the time? Sleeping with his other women more to his liking, hmm? Or does he dislike you so much? Enough to hardly go near you, eh? I must confess that I would be surprised if it were so! Or else you, daughter, have still not learned how to entice a man—what?"

Virág just smiled and rocked in the ancient rocking chair she had always enjoyed as a child. She tilted her head and looked at him with the forbearing affectionate smile of a mother, then caught herself. My god, she was behaving as the parent of a somewhat precocious and petulant child, she thought. She thought of answering him but then thought better. As it turned out, she was right. Within moments, her father had closed his eyes with a sigh and burrowed himself deeper in his cushions. He gave another sigh, close to a groan, but then he fell asleep, his head lolling to the left so that his chin rested on his shoulder.

Virág also closed her eyes and continued to rock, enjoying the silence enveloping her. Silence was at a premium at Árpád's women's house, and the great silence of the mountains and the woods was so profound that she could hear the whisper of the brook in back of her father's great house. Somnolence surrounded her, invaded her brain, and she slept, a little girl's smile on her face.

She awoke, with a start, to whispers, followed by increasingly loud voices and then a woman's keening wail. Opening her eyes, she saw two of her father's serving women kneeling by his side, their hands covering their eyes, rocking their bodies back and forth. A terrible sense of foreboding invaded her so that she almost fell out of the rocking chair. Without asking, she knew immediately. The great chieftain Töhötöm, her father, feared by everyone except his one coddled, sheltered daughter, was no more. The knowledge tore into her like the shaft of an arrow, so painful that she doubled over, unable to take a breath. Gasping laboriously, she dragged herself to where her father lay and, picking up one of his hands, still warm and feeling just as it did only a short nap time before, brought the hand to her face and gently cradled it against her cheek.

Life, not just for Virág but for the whole tribe, came to a standstill. Between the sacrificial fires, the beating of the drums and gongs, the blowing of the horns and the trumpets, the murmurings of prayers by the shamans, everyone knew that life would never be as it had been. The man who had led them and ruled them for over forty years was dead—gone—no longer to lead them again. They may not have loved him, but they respected and trusted him for his strong dependable rule, for he had been the one to bring them to Árpád and then to the so-desired and plentiful land between the great Danubius and Tisza Rivers.

What frightened everyone more than just the death of one great leader was the absence, at such a time, of the man who had been chosen to succeed him. Sent to Árpád's court to learn statecraft, an art sorely needed now that the seven tribes had finally found their home, and that home greedily contested by Byzantium, Rome, Bulgaria, Moravia, and the Holy Roman Empire. Unease pervaded the air. Virág, absent now for years, unknown and forgotten by most of them, could not offer calm or words of assurance.

In all truthfulness, Virág was frightened herself. Beyond her grief, all she now desired was to be near her husband. He would give her strength and her people stability. But he and his court were many days' hard ride away. She was literally desperate to leave as soon as the burial ceremonies were completed. Pushing her women and Árpád's courier who had acted as liaison between her husband and father, she partly ordered, partly beguiled the detachment of soldiers sent by Árpád for her protection. Finally the day after the burial was agreed upon for departure. Mercifully she appeared to have passed the stage of her pregnancy demanding hours spent with her head mostly hidden within a bucket; god, how fervently she hoped never to have to revisit that condition!

Virág was ready before the sun even rose above the mountains to the east. Wrapped in coarsely woven gray hemp cloth, the sign of mourning, she stood impatiently, her hand on her horse's saddle, her head bowed. She had said her farewells—once again in the time span of less than four years—and felt certain that this was to be the final parting from her roots.

Never before had she been given to introspection. But now, with that great distance between her and her husband, suddenly she yearned for him with a new desperation never felt before. She felt incomplete, empty, and bereft. He, he was the center of her life. She had clung so long to the thought of her home, her father, her tribe, the accustomed things, people she grew up with, that she never realized that growing up was a thing of the past, that her life belonged to her husband, and she was suddenly desperate to see him, to be with him. So surprised was she by this sensation, by this new anticipation, which now far exceeded the distress of parting with her past, that it took her a while to understand. The sudden insight almost made her knees buckle. She knew, she knew absolutely, that her home and happiness were wherever Árpád was and only there. The sound of his voice in her ear when he loved her, the warmth of his body embracing, surrounding her, the tenderness of his big hands stroking her, that feeling of being a part of him as he became a part of her, especially now when she was the mother of his—of their—child was all—was everything—she wanted.

*****

Following that once-in-a-lifetime event at the imperial palace, talked over and repeated for days, of the basileus actually laughing—laughing, mind you—and not at the barbarian but with him, well, it was not a surprise that the handsome Magyar with the unpronounceable name became the most well known, most sought-after personage at court. Courtiers sought his favor, aspiring diplomats and men of the military suddenly bowed, or at least nodded, to him in recognition, and all the nubile—and the older and more voracious—ladies of the court flocked to his presence wherever he made his appearance.

At the same time, Lord Zalán moved about either pretending or else actually oblivious to all the waves his presence was causing in the accustomed flow of life at the august court. He was seen here and there, on the outskirts of power, not really aware where the various layers of powers existed around him. He openly enjoyed the simple pleasures: the smile from a beautiful young woman, the view from the serpentine walkway in the imperial garden on a sunny day, a ride from the harbor in one of the fleet imperial sailing boats offered to him by a high-ranking official of the Imperial Navy, a tasty meal brought to him by a servant from the imperial kitchen, he accepted it all as his due, never demanded more, talked to no one other than his delegation, and withdrew into his chamber for a chaste slumber. He was simply an enigma to everyone!

Then a short week after the Hungarian delegation was presented to Leo, his Imperial Majesty remembered the barbarian with the unpronounceable name, who gave him the gift of a genuine laugh, and instructed his chamberlain to have the delegation admitted to his presence for an audience within the next day. The chamberlain gasped—silently of course—made his obeisance, and hurried off to speak with the master of ceremonies and the master of audiences, each of whom also gasped, silently of course.

And so it was that with unheard of minimal delay, the delegation of Hungarian barbarians were able to deliver their master, the Grand Prince Árpád's, message to the golden throne. In turns, they were told to wait for an answer which would be given to them as expeditiously as possible. Again without bowing, behavior which was now becoming almost acceptable from them, the Magyar delegation turned on their heels and walked out of the vast Hall of Audiences. Not for one moment did the delegation give the impression that they were aware of the high honor accorded to them by the great basileus.

The inhabitants of the court, however, breathed the rarified air of their exalted environment. Emotional self-defense alone dictated that they disdain these offensive foreigners disdaining to thread their way through the intricacies of court procedure. The same self-defense also told them that anyone who looked, talked, or behaved differently from them was, well, frankly to be looked down upon. Zalán's sudden elevation lifted the stature of his whole delegation to a higher level, a vastly greater importance. The very possibility of something so unusual, so unpredictable happening, frankly disturbed the way of things. Charts were examined, maps unrolled, books opened, and codices, documents of treaties, and veiled threats of wars brought out and reread. The passing of staggering amounts of bribe gold or the blood and death of thousands became the leading motive in all of this. All in all, Zalán and his delegation raised more respect and regard than ten others put together which had gone before them.

And so it was as well that the very next day, one of the court underlings—Zalán was at a loss to account for the innumerable titles and positions occupied by them and just nodded his head to him—scratched on the wood of his door. Zalán had learned that this was the polite request for admission to the room of a higher-positioned person. He rose from sprawling on his bed and opened the door. Communication was too difficult to attempt, so he waved the messenger to wait and sent the servant detailed to his personal service to fetch Alaricus; he needed an interpreter. The servant squatted all day long in front of his door and snored, curled up all night long there, as well. Zalán had assumed that his work consisted of trying to anticipate his wishes as best as he could, given the vagaries of sign language and grunts.

When Alaricus arrived, after lengthy and occasionally halting conversation, he informed Zalán that her Exalted Highness, the Princess Julia, wished to make his acquaintance and, for that reason, desired to have dinner with him. In her apartments. Tomorrow at sunset. By now Zalán had been in residence long enough to know who Princess Julia was; he had even seen her and was—as all other young men who saw her—amazed at her appealing, graceful, and youthful presence. He was learning the ropes rapidly and immediately assumed that he could only gain by this association, but also that Julia had something to gain, probably something beyond the pleasures of a night together. He had also learned that there was no declining such an invitation, nor did he wish to do so; he was curious and aroused by the thought of possible things to come.

After the messenger had departed, Alaricus assured him that such assignations went hand in hand with a gift, and given the status of the "hostess," a gift of this nature was not to be trifling. He suggested that he would summon Beni Mellal who was friends with several expensive jewelers; Lord Zalán only had to go there to select something to his liking. Payment in cases of such well-known illustrious buyers could, of course, be not only negotiated but also deferred; Lord Zalán should leave all these details in Beni Mellal's hands.

Thus it was that Zalán found himself in the company of the endlessly chattering black slave in the elegantly appointed shop of a Greek by the name of Aristophanos Kouronos, sipping sweet wine and being treated to the most eye-poppingly gorgeous jewelry he could ever—or maybe never—imagine. After showing him some less-opulent pieces, Aristophanos raised his hand to gain more of his customer's attention.

"Your Grace, forgive me, but I now understand the importance of this single piece of jewelry to you! Allow me to show you the most breathtaking piece in this shop, nay, I venture to pronounce, the most breathtaking piece in all of our city." And with that he turned, gathering his flowing robes and snapping his fingers, nodded to his assistant. Zalán smiled, thinking the ploy to be quite obvious—

take the interest and expectation of your client higher and higher by first showing only lesser items. He had seen this same method employed by various horse traders, though in less comfort than this man afforded him.

The assistant returned with a package wrapped in heavy white silk shot with gold. Aristophanos, once again happily chattering, commenced to unwrap the package.

"Your Grace, I ask you to understand that something of this splendor only comes to my hands very occasionally. It is a rare piece and, at the same time, a relic of another age, which reeks of the patina of centuries. It came to my hands only about a month ago from some mysterious buried city of the Abbasid Empire. A wonderful and touching story is attached to it, of a beautiful young queen somewhere in Persia, much enamored of her husband, who no longer wished to live when she heard that her husband, the king, had been killed in war. It is said that she clasped the necklace, her husband's gift of love, about her neck one last time, and then drowned herself so that she no longer would need to remain separated from her love."

Slowly the merchant finished unwrapping the package and laid its contents onto his lap. He sucked in his breath, his large hands, lifting the necklace, more accustomed to lifting a sword, almost dropping it. Never in his life had he seen anything like this, this creation of beauty, this dream of glorious elegance, shimmering in the sunlight filtering through the windows, glinting with the sudden flash of brightly colorful jewels, embraced by the most exquisitely delicate filigree goldwork and enamel. He was at a loss for words and knew that the merchant knew how bowled over he was as well.

Slowly he allowed himself to breathe. He nodded, lifting questioning eyes to Aristophanos. The merchant was adept at such sign language. Delicately he lifted and shrugged his shoulders.

"Of course, great lord, such beauty most assuredly is not inexpensive. It comes at a high price. I am not certain…" At that point, he let his voice drift off with dramatic suggestivity. "I am unsure if your lordship would be willing to even consider…"

Zalán felt his honor questioned. During the weeks of his residence in this city of labyrinthine intrigues, he had felt his assurance erode. He was accustomed to being in charge, being admired, important, and obeyed. At home he was also considered to be very wealthy, very influential. Suddenly he felt angry and very much wanting, nay, in need of, well, of assuring himself that he was as good as the best, not only at home but in this puzzling nest of intrigue. He was a spoiled young man full of himself; suddenly all he wanted was to show off. He lifted his arm to stop Aristophanos's babbling and nodded his head to both Aristophanos and to Alaricus, his interpreter.

"Aye, Master Jeweler, I perceive the beauty and value of this piece. It is truly worthy of adorning the neck of the person for whom I purchase it. See to it that both the package and the bill are delivered to my room at the golden palace. Thank you." With that he rose, inclined his head, and exited the shop, Alaricus in tow, while Beni Mellal remained behind. Zalán also assumed negotiations from here on in would be of benefit not only to the merchant but to the slave as well. Under the circumstances, he thought the benefit to Beni Mellal should not be begrudged.

Later in the day and with assistance from Alaricus, Zalán was dressing for the evening's invitation. He had a prior soothing warm bath, which he greatly enjoyed, as always. It was a consternation to the court that these strange Magyar barbarians actually bathed and even enjoyed it! How was that, when all the varied Germanic delegations presented themselves with greasy hair, breath which reeked of garlic and ale, and an almost unendurable body odor overlaid by sweat-laden clothing? This observation, among several others, concerning the Magyars were profound mysteries indeed and cause for revision of earlier assumptions.

Alaricus suggested that he remain only for a while in the early part of the evening. He would then take his cue to disappear at a time when he could assume that verbal communication no longer was relevant. Right now, he only wanted to advise his master that the Princess Julia was Leo, His Imperial Majesty's, sister-in-law and sister to the Empress Theopano. In other words, she was as highly placed as anyone could be without sitting on the golden throne. He, Alaricus, would thus implore the lord to proceed with not only caution but also with an exceeding degree of delicacy. The necklace had already been wrapped in layers of brocaded silk by the merchant and delivered to Julia's apartment with a message from the sender, assuring Julia of his undying gratitude and admiration.

Everything was set, ready, and awaiting the final action.

*****

The great tent city that Árpád's army had initially erected, just a bowshot away from the west bank of the Danubius, was being dismantled. The grand prince had decreed that yet before the winter, he wished his people to withdraw from their summer camp city to the old partly fallen-down city of his ancestor, Great Attila. That city had actually existed long before the Huns had occupied it, had been a favored bathing and summering place of the Roman emperor Marcus Aurelius. He found the hot waters spewing from the cracks of the mountains, just to the west of the river, beneficial for his bodily pains. His well-being improved so much that he penned most of his Meditations there. In those days, the city had been called City of Waters, *Aquincum.*

Árpád had also directed that the usable stone buildings, many of them still showing their past glory and elegance, be restored and made habitable posthaste. No longer would dusty, muddy tent cities do. They had arrived. They were home. Reconstruction was already beginning. The noise everywhere was deafening, the dust choking. But nobody minded; they had arrived. This was to be their home, their country, their nation, their future!

Two days prior, a herald had arrived, dusty, on a lathered horse, giving account to the grand prince of the death of his father-in-law, the great Chief Töhötöm. Árpád was truly saddened by the news. Almost since the day he was first raised upon a shield by the other chiefs and elected to be their chieftain and grand prince, he had appreciated the querulous old man.

And now he had a final duty to the old man's tribe. He knew that about half of the fighting men of Tarján were, by now, riding to join forces with the tribe of Kér and proceed south toward Byzantium. This was not to be a war party, only a means to put pressure upon Leo of Byzantium, if needed. At the same time, it was dangerous to leave the home guard of Tarján without a leader. Zalán, albeit of the tribe of Nyék, had been duly elected to follow Töhötöm. He was also to assimilate the two tribes of Tarján and Nyék into one. This was planned to be the first such step of several such consolidations, hoped to bring about the future formation of a new nation. Well, anyway, he concluded his own runaway thoughts, Tarján needed a new leader to be sent eastward to act for Zalán until that one's return from Constantinople. As always, Árpád's agile mind was already weighing the contenders to be considered. Under the urgent circumstances, it would take him no longer than a day to present his proposals to the council. He gave instructions to Megyeri, his senior squire, to summon the council in meeting for the morrow.

Árpád sighed and ordered Szárnyas, his favored riding horse, brought about posthaste. He could always think best when in the saddle, alone and away from people. But lately, he was somehow disquiet, impatient, and uneasy perhaps? Much to his surprise, a familiar stirring assailed his body. He smiled somewhat grimly, thinking that it was lucky it happened when he felt, so to say, doubly protected; not only was he sitting in a saddle, his seat obscuring his condition, but also, he was alone. How so? Did he need a woman in his bed? He had been so involved with rebuilding a city, was that it?

Without guidance from him, his horse had found his way down to the bank of the river. The horse had obviously picked up on his daily habit to end his workday with a brief visit to the Great River. He swung down from his horse's back and let the stallion go into the water. He looked around, suddenly thinking of Virág. Just like he, she also liked to stand or sit by the river to watch the sun go down and the moon rise from the east. Just thinking of this most recently acquired wife, he felt his body stirring again. Shaking his head, he admitted that he missed her, her youth, spontaneity, gaiety, her naive trust. She was good for him, he thought, bringing lightness into an otherwise overburdened life. She neither understood nor was interested in all those things which occupied his days, and most of his nights as well. Did that mean that she lived on the surface? That she was flighty or uncaring? Once when he had first wed her, he used to think so. But no longer.

She had been raised to assist her father to run a large and complex household. He had never shared more serious concerns with her. Why then would he expect greater understanding, deeper introspection from her? Indeed, he did not expect it from any of his other ladies, except maybe Alán. But that had been a different relationship; she was older than him, and at the time of their marriage, she had amazed him with her insight, her clarity and wisdom, and he had depended on her opinion, absorbed it eagerly, and often assimilated it into his decision-making.

For a long while, he stood by the river's edge, letting his horse wade deeper, drink, and stamp around with obvious delight before splashing back to him, put his dripping muzzle on his master's shoulder, blew warm breath into his neck, and fixed liquid black eyes on his face, waited for their next move together. A small smile crossed Árpád face as he settled himself in the saddle. Why, he had now spent more time thinking on one small insignificant woman than on the plans for the settling and resurrection of the imperial city of Aquincum. Well, why, indeed? Obviously because she had become very much central to his existence, indeed his well-being. Yes, because he loved her? Did he? Well?

Aye, he sighed to himself, that he did. When she had first arrived to his tent, a wide-eyed young girl, well skilled in riding and the care of horses, the lifting and swinging of a sword with lethal precision, and the dispatching of arrows with aim no less deadly than any of his soldiers, she had been totally lost in the foreign world of a women's house, and she was unabashedly unhappy. He had asked the Lady Alán to take her under her wing and decided to allow her more time to settle in, to delay the ceremonies of the wedding and the ensuing bedding. As it had turned out, Virág had grown up devoid of contact with women, except her nursemaid and the servants who cared for her well-being. Her mother had died giving her birth, and there were no older sisters nor an aunt or any other relative in her father's household. Töhötöm, her father, had shown no inclination to remarry and claimed that the constant chatter, noise, and arguing from the women's house irritated him, and his needs were sufficiently met by several of his willing serving girls.

All in all, upon her arrival, Virág had felt totally out of place and desperately ill at ease with women of all ages and among his other wives and their female attendants. More than that, she was totally lacking in knowledge as to what a marriage entailed. Árpád still had to smile when he recalled their wedding night. Had he not, with great patience, explained and guided her into what was expected of her, the wedding night would have been a disaster in different ways for both of them. Virág understood and treasured this kindness. The first tenuous threads binding them together were Virág's gratitude and his burgeoning desire. A desire which now had grown into passion; and he no longer needed to question himself. *Love? Aye,* he sighed again, *do you never forgo honesty, especially to yourself! Indeed, indeed, 'tis love...Love and passion mixed up in an enormous sense of wanting and desire!*

He was impatient to see her again, to have her again. He was impatient to know that she was well, to know how to help her in her mourning. He was impatient to hear her play the koboz, hear her small beguiling voice once again, raised in song to relax him before he would take her koboz from her, lift her in his arms, and take her to his bed. He shook his head at his own folly for falling in love once again, and especially with such a child! Well, why not? He was no falling-down, shuffling old man! And she a child no longer! At two score and five years, he was remarkably youthful, both in appearance and all of his many activities. His aim with the arrow was still true, he could outride any of his men any day, his sword arm's prowess was feared by all, and his brain could devise plans as devious and successful as ever before. And, he thought with a mixture of truculence and self-flagellation, if this be the love of his aging, then so be it!

Through the hubbub of loading and unloading, of moving, shifting, hoisting and lowering, of scrubbing, hammering, repairing, yelling, and whistling, of the neighing, barking, and bellowing of animals, of all the dirt, dust, debris which swirled through the air, through it all, Árpád's familiar figure popped up here and there, mostly to advise, encourage, or help. His Aquincum was slowly re-emerging from the rubble, tree roots, and dead leaves, which had been inflicted upon it through the passage of time. But through it all, one worry he could not shake.

Where in the name of the Great God of War, where was she? She should have arrived already, surely! The messenger of her father's death told him that Virág had only arrived five days before her father's death, and that she had been adamant of leaving right after the funeral ceremonies. Even if delayed somewhat longer, she should by now have arrived. Did she sicken on the road? Were they attacked? Were they overwhelmed? But he had near fifty soldiers to protect her! It was unfathomable!

Looking around him, he motioned to Törs, his arms bearer, trailing behind his lord, carrying his sword and heavy curved shield at the ready. The heavyset stocky man moved with a speed quite unexpected of someone of his bulk. His eyes, brown and moving about forever to ensure that no threat to his master escaped his attention, were now fixed on the grand prince's face.

"Arrange for a group of light riders to go east beyond the Danubius, to scout for the whereabout of the Lady Virág's traveling party. I would have expected them to arrive already and wish to know if they have encountered any difficulty on the road. Have the group you send also take a few fast messengers to track back to me with any news, good or bad, before the main body returns."

Törs nodded and turned to go, but then turned back. "Do you wish me to lead the group or designate a leader, my lord?"

Árpád only hesitated momentarily, then nodded. "Aye, Törs, I want you be the leader. Summon Ugron to replace you here, then. Be off as soon as you can manage." Abruptly he turned away from Törs to hide his sigh. Truly he was greatly disquieted and wanted, once and for all, to receive information of Virág's whereabouts or herself. Ah, yes, very, very much herself, indeed! He promised himself that he would wait one more day, either for news or the actual arrival of his wife. After that he would send a massive detachment of his best to sweep the steppes east of the river, if needed, all the way to the foothills of the Carpathian Mountains. He was done with waiting and worrying.

Then suddenly and unexpectedly, fate stepped in to take the grand prince's mind off such musings. While instructing the masons what he wanted and how he wished the restored front of Marcus Aurelius's palace to look, he was interrupted, literally in midsentence, by a servant running along the roadway and calling for him. Evidently he was needed desperately. A herald, having ridden relays of horses from the south, was calling for him with most important news. Árpád turned immediately and loped after the servant, his long legs literally eating the distance, until he spied the herald. He was leaning against a tree, its broad trunk literally saving him from falling down with exhaustion. His chest was heaving as he held a mug filled with cider, the mug almost ready to slip through his shaking fingers. The grand prince only took one look at the man and ordered two chairs to be brought so that both of them could sit under the shade of the tree. Then he shook his head as he saw the messenger struggling to calm his breathing in order to be able to speak. One more gesture brought a large drinking bowl with wine diluted in water as he nodded to the messenger. He drank deeply and then took a few deep breaths. Finally he looked able to talk.

"Speak, man." He nodded. "What is your name?"

"Botond, my lord." He gasped, then nodded. "Botond. Árpád, my lord, it is very grave news I bring you. I have been sent by Lord Zalán. He encountered our encampment south of the river Nišava and, lacking anyone he could spare for this, charged me to come and bring you the news, exactly repeating his words to you, lord. His message—and I had learned it by heart—to you is"—and Botond closed his eyes in his effort to recite with precision—"Greetings to you, my Master. My soul bleeds and is in sorrow. Lord Vazul died when the Nišava River flooded us. Trying to rescue our horses out of the floodwater, a tree limb fell on him, and he drowned. We could not revive him. He was buried according to custom. I have taken command of our group. I have studied all papers Lord Vazul carried. I will act according to all your wishes. Greeting from me, Lord Zalán of Nyék, future lord of Nyék and Tarján."

Árpád did not respond. It was his nature to absorb good or bad news equally before reacting in body or thought. When he finally moved, his eyes searched those of the messenger, who was obviously drooping, having trouble to keep his eyes open. Árpád reached forward to touch the man's arm.

"And Zalán? Was he well when you left him?"

Botond nodded. "Aye, lord, he was but very aggrieved and sad. He told me to say to you, if you should ask as you just did, that he hopes to execute all of your commands to your satisfaction, my lord. But it is a day of sadness and mourning for all, he said, my lord."

Silence ensued after Botond's words. Finally Árpád nodded and, with a sigh, rose from his seat. He clapped both of his hands on Botond's shoulders.

"Well done, my son. Go to the kitchens to fill your empty belly and have a flask of wine. If they object, tell them it is my command. Then seek your pallet and sleep. You sore need both sustenance and sleep. When you feel rested and filled, come to me. Should you not wish to return to your settlement, I will see to it that you are trained as a member of my elite guard, for you have distinguished yourself greatly. One way or another, you shall be rewarded, my son. Go."

For a long while after, Árpád's eyes followed the messenger, watching as the man weaved his way among the various workers. He watched as the man stopped to obtain directions, then changed his own direction, and finally disappeared among the many people moving about. He frowned and then lifted his hand to his face to rub down his face with his palm, from forehead down both eyes, his nose to his chin, in the customary gesture of grief.

He had loved and trusted Vazul a great deal, watched him deal with people, problems, and dangers, face threats and joys with equal calm and composure. He had always valued men possessing that one something—calm and composure in the face of everything thrown in one's way by fate, by life? No anger, no fear, no emotion, which would carry a man toward irrational thinking or actions. He himself always strove for that calm and composure when confronted by events which could lead one toward the opposite direction. He greatly appreciated that same ability when he saw it in others.

On top of that, he personally had liked Vazul, indeed very much. They had survived battles in which one had protected the life of the other, they had gone through the tumultuous days of their youth together, lusted, loved, sorrowed together. Vazul had been a friend, a part of his life, their lives tightly woven together. That he was no longer was a sadness, a loss, not just for now but for all the future as well.

For a long time, Árpád just stood there, leaning against the thick tree trunk, staring at the ground in front of him, at the tips of his scuffed boots, his soul wracked by the pain of loss. He was well aware that the pain would lessen with time, oh, yes, how often had he now gone through the same progress of emotions? But he was reaching some kind of tipping point, he felt. A tipping point beyond which he no longer wished to face losses, battles, confrontation, the rise and the dashing of hope.

How many, Great God of War, how many more will be needed to go ahead of me? I am tired, God, now that I believe my work is becoming completed! Tired, God, of the battles, the deprivations, the mourning. I am ready, God, ready to go to wherever you will send me, I should or even deserve to reside after I also pass on to meet my dead relatives, my dead friends. Until then, God, do not make me mourn any more! Of that, God, I am tired more than anything else, so very tired.

*****

Both Alaricus and Beni Mellal, resplendently dressed for the occasion, were ceremoniously accompanying their master, the leader of the Magyar delegation, to the golden throne for the momentous invitation to dinner given by Her Highness, the Princess Julia. Alaricus was to serve as interpreter, and Beni Mellal was carrying the ornate box containing the gift from Lord Zalán to the lady. The two guards by the entrance to the princess's apartments must have received instruction because the little procession was admitted immediately.

Inside the apartment, they were greeted by the master of the princess's household, who conducted them through several ornately furnished rooms into the lady's more private rooms. Julia was expecting them. Dressed in a colorfully embroidered gold robe, the hem and wide sleeves of which were made of a material showing the reverse that of the robe, colorfully flowered background with embroidery of gold bees; her hair was loose and only covered with a short transparent veil, held in place by a thin gold and diamond circlet. She rose from the low stool she had been sitting on and, with one wave of her hand, dispensed with any ceremony, immediately sending the master of her household out of the room. She extended her hand to Zalán but gently withdrew it when she saw that instead of kissing her fragrant fingertips, as was the custom of the court, he only inclined his head to her.

She then directed him to the softly cushioned ottoman sitting under the window, open to the view of the gardens and the sea. There she joined him, sitting opposite him on a low-cushioned stool, shyly arranging the folds of her robe, and then lifted her eyes to him. Her eyes were a beautiful gray blue, large and glistening, rimmed with lines of kohl, fringed with long black lashes. Her mouth, delicately outlined with red paint, smiled at him, opening softly to reveal her teeth, and then the tip of her tongue, which she hesitantly ran along her lower lip before speaking. As she spoke, she lifted her eyes to Alaricus and inclined her head to give him permission to interpret for them.

At that gesture, universal in its intent, Zalán turned to Alaricus as well to ask him to offer his gift with the seemingly necessary flowery words, while he gestured to Beni Mellal and urged him to present the box to his beautiful hostess. When Beni Mellal did this with a flourish and then prostrated himself as he disappeared from the room, Julia hesitantly pushed open the clasp on top of the box. It sprang open immediately, revealing its glorious content nestled among folds of white silk.

Julia must have expected a gift, the obvious custom of the palace whenever invitations of a certain kind were issued. However, her expectations were evidently outstripped by what she saw, for her indrawn breath and largely rounded eyes were not in any way produced by the usual palace playacting. She could not prevent her eyes swiveling to Zalán's face, her cheeks pinkening with pleasure. He bowed toward her, and she shook her head.

Alaricus's interpretation was precise to the word. "My lord, the Lady Julia is truly overwhelmed by the beauty and generosity of your gift to her. She says that she did not believe such appreciation of delicate beauty was practiced in your land. It does, at the same time, warm her heart and gives her a desire to better get to know the man whose heart is filled with the admiration of things to be treasured and beautiful at the same time." Zalán, understanding the double entendre of what Julia was saying, smiled, looked into her eyes, and bowed his head again. Julia rose and carefully lifted the necklace from its nesting place to lay it around her neck. Pulling her hair and veil off to the side and to one shoulder, she presented the back of her neck to Zalán.

"The Lady Julia," Alaricus intoned, "would be much obliged if you, my lord, as the giver of such an opulent gift, would personally affix it to her neck." And then, as Zalán rose to obey the lady's wishes, Alaricus rose as well and murmured, audible only to Zalán, "With your permission, my lord, I think I best withdraw at this time. Although you will be on your own, I believe that many words will not be necessary from this point on. The language of courtship and love, my lord, are universal." And with that, Alaricus bowed and quietly backed himself out of the room.

Zalán stood in the middle of the room, for a moment, lost as to what he needed to do next. He applauded that Alaricus had withdrawn from the room but, at the same time, felt inhibited by his deplorable lack of communication with this beautiful woman who—he had no doubt of that whatsoever—was offering herself now, probably had already intentions of doing just that when she had invited him for an intimate twosome dinner in her private apartment. Certain things did not change whether they were done in a tent encampment on the steppes or in the palace of Constantinople. Why else would he have spent a veritable fortune on this blasted necklace, for the gods' sake? As recompense, he expected a pleasurable affair or, at least, a heated night in Julia's company, each scenario something which would advance his standing here and indirectly his status at home.

He was ambitious, why on earth would he not be so? He was a cocky young man. He was handsome of face and appealing of body.

He was well educated in the arts of war and the more complex arts of peacemaking. He was well born, well-mannered, and already well thought of by Árpád and his inner circle. He knew how to lead on the battlefield or a whole tribe. He had sincere aspirations to unite two tribes under his leadership, something which Árpád supported vigorously. Most importantly, at least at present, he knew how to make love and how to pleasure women—with a wealth of experience of women of all stations. He also had been brought up to be respectful of a woman's wishes, of women of all stations. His father, a strict taskmaker, made certain that this one lesson, more than most, sunk into his son's hard skull. Women were much respected, had indeed much status in Zalán's society. That particular lesson he had learned early in his life; not only his father but most especially his mother had seen to that!

And so, now he was at an important point in his life—to seize the opportunity with this delicious woman and, at the same time, to keep a certain distance from her body. A few kisses, well executed and well placed, a few caresses to keep Julia's interest burning, but then a quick pulling back, rather like a snail pulls back into its shell after a delicate exploration of his environment.

Slowly he walked to touch Julia's back, her shoulder, and lift the two ends of the necklace. For a few seconds, he examined the workings of the clasp, actually a very simple one. On the one side, there was a largish ring, and on the other side, an equally sturdy hook. Sturdiness was required to hold the weight of the jewelry. He hooked the one end to the other, gave a little sigh of satisfaction while he allowed his palms to brush down her shoulders, in order to make certain that the necklace rested properly over the heaving bosoms. Then his fingers tightened on her shoulders, and he gently urged her to turn toward him and take a step closer.

"Ah," he murmured, "Julia, my lady you cannot be made more beautiful by my gift than you are already. Beautiful and desirable, love! And I am certain you have heard all of this kind of drivel from many other men. The question is what they did thereafter, is it not, dearling." And he lowered his head slowly until his lips touched the hollow of her neck above the necklace. He let his tongue glide gently along the tender skin until he encountered her chin. With a little sigh, he then lifted his head and looked full into her eyes.

"We will go slowly here, and I, as I always am, will be guided by your wishes, beautiful." While he talked, he was quite aware that Julia could not understand him, except perhaps some of his gestures and the inflection of his voice. But as Alaricus said, this was the time when he needed to depend on "other things."

Julia raised her eyes as well. Without any apparent shyness, she looked at him, her big liquid sea gray-sea-blue eyes wandering over his face, then dropping farther down to take careful stock of his broad shoulders, his strong hard chest ending in slim hips, then further south. A soft smile appeared on her lips. The palms of her hands slid to his neck, then slowly down his shoulders, arms, to drop farther down, and gently stroke his burgeoning sex. She gave out a soft sigh, then lowered her head to rest it on his shoulder, coyly offering her lips to him. When he finally began to kiss her, her palm began to stroke his erect sex, delicately, ever so softly and tentatively. In response, he deepened his kiss.

So absorbed was he in what he was making to happen and Julia also made to happen that when she stepped back from him, he first raised his head in confusion. Her palm was touching his, and gently, she urged him to the opposite end of the room. She reached up and pulled a cord which ended in a heavy tassel. The curtain covering that end of the room parted and revealed a wide bed covered with the same silk as the curtain. Lush pillows lay scattered all over the bed's expanse. For a moment, Zalán resisted, but for a moment only. Julia's gentle urgency and the smiling promise of her eyes were irresistible. With one leg, she knelt upon the bed, then within one second, her face contorted, her hands grabbed the neck of her gown, and tugged viciously until he heard the material tear. Her hands sought her cheeks and her chin as her fingernails began to rake her skin until long red streaks appeared, starting to seep blood. Then she clutched the heavy necklace into both hands, viciously twisting the heavy gold links to dig into her neck, leaving immediate purple bruises.

To Zalán's utter horror and disorientation, she picked up a wooden club hidden among the pillows and began to swing it at him, catching his upper arm and his shoulder. In utter horror and disorientation, Zalán heard her repeated scream for help. When the door opened, and several guards poured into the room, in utter horror, he saw Julia collapse upon the bed, sobbing hysterically, screaming, "Oh god, oh god, oh god!" Again and again. Finally she raised her scratched and bloodied face from the bedcovers, and raising a shaking hand with a trembling finger to point at him, she groaned in a voice barely recognizable.

"Help me, oh god, please help me! This barbarian tried to rape me! Oh, my god, oh my god!"

Still totally horrified and disoriented by what was playing out in front of his eyes, Zalán turned to the soldiers.

"No, no," he screamed, shaking his head desperately, seeing several of the soldiers advance on him with their curved scimitars raised up. He lifted his two arms above his head in a futile attempt of protection, then felt one of the swords going through his body. Embraced by instant and total weakness, he dropped to his knees, watching in amazement as blood drained from his abdomen onto the silk carpet. "No-no," he whispered weakly, amazed by the sudden loss of his voice. "No-no," he whispered again, puzzled. "No-no, I did nothing, I did nothing." And after that, there was truly nothing but silence.

*****

Neither the Lord Szabolcs, second to the late Lord Vazul, or the Lord Ügyek, who was Lord Zalán's second, were distressed by the lateness of Zalán's arrival back to their quarters, assuming that his assignation with Princess Julia was a success. It did not occur to them to question his delay; in matters between a beautiful woman and a virile man, who knew? When the summons came, therefore, from the master of audiences, that their presence was requested immediately by the emperor in the Hall of Audiences, they tried to delay at first, to wait for Zalán's belated arrival, but the master was adamant, and really, a command from His Majesty the basileus himself had to be obeyed without deliberation.

Thus without even changing into their court clothing, the two looked at each other, lifting their shoulders, and followed the messenger through the winding hallways leading, finally, into the Hall of Audiences. They were worried. Their interpreter was missing, in fact, had mysteriously disappeared since the evening before. Without the ability to communicate correctly, any conversations between them and the court was problematic and open to misinterpretation. At the entrance to the Hall of Audiences, they looked at each other with a sigh and a shrug. This was not good; in fact, it was evidently turning out to be quite the opposite.

But things could not be changed. Accepting the inevitable, they walked in to the veritable lions' den, bowed their heads, and marched toward the throne, then bowed their heads again. Only when their heads were raised did they become aware that Alaricus, on whom they needed to depend so heavily, stepped out from behind the back of some guards. He looked thoroughly distraught and disheveled, his eyes darting this way and that. Slowly and with apparent reluctance, he walked toward Szabolcs and Ügyek. Beni Mellal, as it appeared, was shuffling right behind him, eyes firmly fixed to the ground.

The two emissaries, at the moment lacking a more senior delegate, fixed their eyes upon the emperor. Leo was angry and ill at ease at the moment. Eyes staring over the emissaries' heads, eyebrows drawn, he finally lowered his gaze. Hands clutching the two lions' heads decorating the armrests of his throne, he leaned forward, tapping his silk-slippered foot impatiently.

"There is a most grave matter which has been brought to my attention and which I must lay at the door of the Magyar delegation, indeed. Last night, my beloved sister by marriage, the Princess Julia, was attacked in her apartment by the leader of the Magyar delegation, Lord Zalán. He made a vicious attack to rape the princess. She only escaped bruised and scratched when the guards heard her cries for help and immediately entered her apartment. Seeing the dire danger she was in, they drew their weapons and slew the attacker. It is unknown how he was able to enter her apartment."

Leo made a brief rather stiff gesture, which was the only indication of his anger. The guards obeyed immediately and dragged in

Zalán's lifeless body, laid out on a piece of carpeting. The silence in the hall was deafening as everyone except Szabolcs and Ügyek shrank back, while those two, eyes rounded in total surprise, stepped up to the dead man. Then Szabolcs turned around, his eyes, aflame with anger, on Beni Mellal. He only needed to take one step to the cowering slave. In an instant, his saber flashed in the air, and the sickening sound of gurgling breath sounded followed by the dull thud of a head hitting the inlaid marble floor.

"Die like a cur, you duplicitous dog." He hissed, then turned when he saw the sudden movement, which Alaricus made toward the tall double doors. His arm shot out in command at his order. "Detain him and put him in shackles!" And when the guards hesitated, he bellowed, "I mean now!"

Then he turned back toward the throne, eyes flashing.

"And to you, Leo of Byzantium, I say, shame on you and all your servants, big and small! For having no honor! For assuming guilt without even a question! For butchering an innocent man without hesitation! No longer will we abide in this place of vileness and treachery. You will clean up my dead lord and make his body ready for us to take with us, for not for the blink of an eye would I leave him with you, dogs of Byzantium. We leave on the hour."

He took a deep breath and glanced toward Ügyek. Some kind of silent communication appeared to pass between them. Both of them stepped forward then, closer to the throne, while Leo seemed to shrink back against the headrest. Szabolcs adjusted the embroidered gazelle-skin bag hanging from his left shoulder, from which the tail and the legs of the animal were dangling, gently moving with each movement of the wearer.

"Beware, King, you called Leo of Byzantium! As we leave, so we will take all our goodwill with us. Do not think to detain us, for our followers and friends are many and whetting their knives and swords against you even now. Know this, oh King, this treachery will be made known to the Grand Prince Árpád and to all others in his council. The assassination of our Lord Zalán will not be forgotten nor go unavenged. This I swear to you by the power of the God of War!"

And as he turned away, Ügyek stepped up to the throne and, laying his hand on his chest above his heart, flashed his eyes and shook his head at Leo. "And this I swear to you as well, by the power of our God of War!"

Without even a nod toward the throne, the two men turned as one and marched out of the Hall of Audiences.

*****

It seemed to Virág that they had been traveling forever. Maybe, she thought, it was only her eagerness to again be home with Árpád which drove her, or perhaps the discomfort of her pregnancy. But she had been in greater discomfort on their trip out to her father's place, wasn't she? And the road did not seem to be so *never-ending*. Perhaps the heat of late summer, the sun's rays beating down on her were the cause? She was, after all, a daughter of the mountains, had spent much of her growing years there, where the air was cool and refreshing, and not on the flatland they were traversing now.

Whatever it was, she felt each day, each hour of each day, to be dragging along interminably. The saddle was rubbing her buttocks, which, she had to confess to herself, was ridiculous. She had spent her years, as far back as she could recall, sitting on horses. It felt as natural as walking. Oh, well, she told herself, it still must be her pregnancy more than likely! She was not familiar with the discomforts of pregnancy but decided that probably anything out of the ordinary in her life these days could very well be ascribed to that. Jenö, their guide and the commander of the guards, seeing his mistress's unease, had assured her repeatedly that no more than two days were left before reaching their destination. They had already been apprised by the patrols circulating about the wider perimeter of the headquarters, that those headquarters were now in the process of moving from the riverbanks to the old city of Aquincum. That, Jenö said, would add maybe half a day, but no more to their travel. Once they had forded the great river Danubius, there were well-defined roads leading to Aquincum.

After that reassurance, Jenö disappeared from Virág's side, as he was wont to do many times during each day, to scout in every direction around them. She now recalled him mentioning to her that marauding bands of Pecheneg warriors had been spotted several times during the past days. Virág nodded abstractedly and smiled at him, preoccupied with daydreams of her husband and the tiny miracle growing in her womb. She had been busily daydreaming over the past days, to alleviate the boredom of traversing the seemingly endless hot prairie between the Carpathian Mountains eastward, all the way to the river Danubius. Then suddenly she was roused by Jenö's voice literally shrieking at her.

"Quick, quick, my lady, my lady. Move it now! Pechenegs!" he screamed, waving his arm toward a little copse of tired-looking acacia trees. "Over there, now!"

Blinking, Virág looked around her, turning in her saddle as she looked for the little copse indicated by Jenö. It was then that she instantly saw what Jenö was screaming about. A large group of warriors, swiftly advancing toward them, ululating and hugging their horses' necks as they waved their sabers above their heads, were obviously engaged in running them down. It was not so hard to do; they were hampered by the women minding a large horse-drawn cart. Almost immediately, Virág noted that running for the little copse was futile; the warrior band would easily reach them before they reached their destination. Apparently Jenö also came to the same conclusion because he ordered his men to form a defensive circle around Virág, her women, and the wagon.

Without a second thought, an automatic reaction, Virág slid off her horse, placing her in front of herself and crouching under her belly, pulling her quiver close and pulling out an arrow. She nocked the arrow into the bow she always carried, slung over her shoulder, and waited calmly. She had often noted and her father had, in fact, complimented her on her calm in the face of danger. She counted down the seconds until she saw the eyes of the leader, literally gleaming with the lust of battle, then let her arrow fly, then a second and a third. She noted with satisfaction that each of them hit home, as three of the warriors fell off their horses. The others reined in, but then rode even closer and encircled them, whooping and screaming and continuing to swing their sabers above their heads.

Aye, they were indeed Pechenegs, she thought, and took a quick look around to assess their situation. Their numbers were about equal or somewhat more, but they had the advantage of no women, no baggage wagon, and also the element of surprise. Four of the Magyar soldiers were lying on the ground, not moving, as well as the Pechenegs she had shot and two others. Jenö was riding his horse and controlling him with difficulty, his one arm dangling down along his side and bleeding copiously. Virág shrank back to cower under her horse, who, being obviously superbly trained before Árpád gifted her the mare, did not even move a muscle, when a new shower of arrows hit them. She saw several more of their men hit.

Grabbing five arrows out of her quiver, she nocked each of them with calm precision, then let them fly. She did not need to look at the results, the dull thud and pursuing outcry told her that each of the arrows hit target. She glanced at her quiver and noted that there were only a handful of arrows left. She twisted her body to roll to the side and lifted her ankle-length skirt to pull out her short dirk stuck into the top of her riding boot. Laying its hilt close to her palm, she rearranged her skirt and continued to send the remaining arrows to the Pecheneg riders until her quiver emptied out. Then she allowed herself to look about again.

Shock took her breath away. Every single one of the warriors of her small army were down. The Pechenegs had dismounted and were going systematically from one body to the next, kicking them, and then slitting the throats of any who moved or groaned. Jenö was among them. Virág had to turn her head away, as she felt bile rise to her throat. Then she saw a pair of dusty boots by her horse's belly and a horseman's voice ordering her to come out. Leaving her now-empty quiver and the bow but palming the dirk so that the long loose arm of her tunic flowed over her wrist and hand, she slowly crawled out and rose to stand and face the owner of the voice.

The man, of medium height and thick built, with enormous muscular thighs and arms and malevolent eyes, looked at her, then smiled.

"Ah," he said conversationally in fractured Hungarian, "*so* here we have the little shooter of all those arrows? Very well done, girlie, too bad you working not for us! Well, I take you to other women. They will belong to all. But you are young and pretty, you will entertain me and very well, yes? Ah, yes, many times, very good!" And with that, he grabbed both her shoulders, his fingers viciously digging into her, and dragged her along, his legs eating the distance from her and her horse, to a little clump of horses and men forming a circle, surrounding something which appeared to be very entertaining. The men were clapping their hands and shouting encouragement, while she heard the shrieks of women.

Virág turned her head away so that she would not have to see what was happening. She clenched her teeth so hard she thought her jaw would crack. The Pecheneg who had caught her was walking so fast, she literally was on the run next to him, and even then he was half dragging her. By then she was aware that he did not want to join the rest of his group who were so intent on group rape; as he had said, she was to be his, and he wanted to assure that it would be so. He made for the small group of acacias which, at best, offered a minimal amount of shade or screen.

When they got there, he threw her to the ground and then began to kick her viciously. With each kick he grunted. "This is for an arrow," then, "This is for arrow," and again, "This is for next arrow." She tried to roll to the side and wrap her arms around her middle in a hopeless effort to shield her baby. Her attempts to escape his kicks must have angered him because he crouched down, straddling her, then, fisting one hand in her hair, began to slap her face. Hard. Putting all the force of his beefy arm in each swing. Each slap vibrated through her face, from her cheeks and nose to her jaw, slamming into her skull until she felt like her head was going to explode or separate from her neck.

Eventually though he tired of this and, for a moment, only glared at her with so much evil, so much anger, that it made her wish she was already dead. But she was committed; she was a mother, for the sake of the infant inside her, she could not give up. She was Töhötöm's daughter, she would not give up! She was Árpád's wife, she would be damned before she surrendered! She saw him loosen the ties of his trousers; with her face afire, a number of broken ribs making her barely able to breathe, she made a small gesture with her right arm and wrist, the small gesture in itself an agony, as she held the handle of her dirk so that the blade was pointing straight up. She shut her eyes and waited. She felt the man tear her skirt and grope her thighs, forcing them so far apart that she cried out. She felt his manhood push against her, hard, then felt him lower his heavy body onto her, his weight pressing down on her. She felt the pain of her chest, of her broken ribs, and his one arm coming up to press down upon her neck, obstructing the flow of air into her lungs.

She tried to move, but it felt like trying to move a mountain. There was a roar in her ears, and a film of mist in her vision. With a calm that surprised her, she thought, *So this is what it feels like to die.* Then the buzzing stopped, and there was only black silence.

When she awakened, she noticed that the shadows of the trees had lengthened, and the sun's rays were less searing. Objects were fuzzy and going in and out of her vision. Slowly her ears were becoming attuned again to the noise of screams and laughter to her left. With surprising detachment, her mind registered that, and she thought, *So the raping is still going on*, and with equal detachment, she wondered if she had been raped. The man lay upon her like a deadweight, unmoving and unmovable. She made a feeble move to dislodge him. Useless, she hurt too much nor did she have the strength. She lay under the heavy motionless body for several heartbeats, then gathering all her strength, digging her heels into the sandy soil in one enormous burst of effort, willing her brain to ignore the pain, slowly rolled the man off to the side.

For a moment Virág just lay there, heaving, desperately trying to push her mind through her pain, then willed herself to turn to the side and slowly get to her knees. Cautiously she crawled to her attacker, and even more cautiously, she touched his neck, moving her fingers to the point under his chin where the beat of the heart would be felt. Nothing. She felt nothing. With rising excitement, slowly her hand moved to his arm, to his wrist closer to her. Again, nothing! She sat back on her haunches and again gathered her strength, then pushed the man's shoulders with all her might. After an initial hesitation, his heavy body slowly rolled so that he now came to lie on his back, more or less. Her eyes ran down that body and then widened. Her dirk was embedded all the way to the hilt in his abdomen, where a thick stream of blood was still seeping out, slowly finding its way to the sand on which he lay.

She sucked in her breath and, for a moment, just squatted there, afraid to breathe. Her eyes darted to the left, to the group still clustered around the unfortunate women of her retinue. The men were—if possible—more boisterous than before, but she heard no more screams from the females. Maybe, she wondered, maybe they were dead already, and then mentally added, *If they are lucky.* Then her eyes moved back to the dead man by her side. She forced herself to think calmly, just as her father had always taught her to do in moments of danger. She needed a weapon, reached over, and, with a shudder hearing the sucking noise it created, pulled her dirk out of his belly. With a grimace of disgust, she wiped the weapon on his tunic, then struggled to reach her thigh to replace the dirk into its shaft.

A wave of horrible weakness enveloped her. She lay back onto the sand, gasping for air, trying to absorb the coolness of the breeze beginning to move over the prairie. She tried to figure out why on earth she felt so weak, struggled to sit up, and, when she eventually achieved that, looked down upon herself, with idle interest, contemplating the hem of her skirt. It was sodden with blood, some of it already dried and caked on, making the edge of the garment stiff. She must have been bleeding, indeed was still bleeding. Was she wounded? She felt around her body as best she could and realized that the blood must be leaking out of her, out of somewhere from her lower parts; and suddenly she felt a cold hand grip her chest in fear. Was she losing her child? Did that monstrous man rape her, wound her so that she was losing her baby in that flow of blood?

This, Virág felt, was the last straw to paralyze her. She felt totally defeated; all she wanted was to continue lying there on the ground, until all her blood would seep away, and she would be dead. She was so very tired!

Was it at that moment, was it later, that she felt a velvet-soft warm nose nudge her and blow a gust of warm air onto her face?

She lifted her arm—it must have weighed as much as her whole body—and heard a soft nicker, then felt another warm blast. Finally her brain began to function. Her horse. The horse that her husband gifted her and whom she had lovingly named Goldilocks. Almighty gods! How was that possible? Then she remembered that the well-bred best picked-out mounts of the nobility were trained even more rigorously than the everyday mounts of soldiers; they were trained to remain with their masters and assist them if they were wounded or incapacitated in any way.

Excitement began to course through her being. *Oh, Great God of Warfare*, she prayed, *only let me be able to get up, to get on this animal!* She will know enough to move with silence. She will see in the darkness of the night, and if I only point her nose toward the setting sun, she will follow that unless I give her another direction!

She groped one hand toward the stirrup and heard, more than saw in the dusk and with her cloudy vision, that the mare lowered herself, allowing her mistress to clamber upon her back with enormous effort. Virág gave a soft clicking sound with her tongue and, as the mare quietly rose, began to lope away, moving as softly and carefully as she could, she allowed her mistress to point her nose to the west and then to bend forward over her withers, draping her two arms about her neck.

This was how she was eventually found by the perimeter guards of Árpád's Aquincum. In the shimmering heat of midday, one of the young riders saw hesitant movement which turned out to be a dusty exhausted light-chestnut horse, almost the same color as the summer-dried prairie. To the amazement of both men, the initial one and his partner, there seemed to be a package attached to the back of the horse. As they came closer, the mare nickered and stood, her legs shaking with exhaustion, her head hanging. While one of the men busied himself to untie the package, the other gave the horse what probably was the first drink of water for at least two days. Sparingly too, not wanting to cause colic, especially to such a magnificent young animal. The first man let out a cry, as soon as he caught the package into his arms, he laid it on the ground. It was a woman, seemingly a young one.

She was barely breathing, and when she heard human voices, her eyelids twitched. The younger of the two men poured some water on a piece of cloth and gently wiped the woman's face. Her face was disfigured, bruised, and swollen, with great big discolored wheals, her eyes blackened with bruising, her lips split; indeed, she was a horrible sight to behold. After they poured water from their flask down her throat, she began to move her mouth. At first what she said was so faint that neither of them could hear it, then one of them placed his ear next to her lips.

"Árpád," she whispered as faintly as a spring day's breeze. She moved her head slightly. "Prince. The prince. Please!" After that, she fainted.

*****

The grand prince was in the newly restored Audience Hall, most of his nobles and advisers surrounding him. It was an emergency meeting; all those who could be reached were present. Árpád sat on his high chair—he had steadfastly refused to allow a throne to be installed. He also steadfastly refused to sit while all others stood. His high chair was bracketed in a semicircle by the seats for all his councilors. All, except for two, of the seats were occupied. One had been kept for the return of the Lord Zalán and the other for that of the Lord Levente, Árpád's eldest son, who was leading the delegation of mourners to the home of the dead Lord Töhötöm. Levente was supposed to stay there and see to matters until Lord Zalán, who was Töhötöm's duly elected successor, would return from his mission to Constantinople.

However, late the day before, a lathered rider—the second in less than a month, Árpád thought with his mouth set in a thin line of displeasure—had requested urgently to speak with him. He was named Dörge, he said, and lived in a small community of the tribe Megyer in the southern regions of the river Danubius. Two days past, he said, four men rode into their village, the Lords Szabolcs and Ügyek and their servants. They were on their way from Byzantium, where they had talked with the emperor himself. However, there were problems which ensued, and the two were most eager to speak to Árpád. They had hired him, since he was the breeder of fast horses, to select two of his fastest horses to ride to give this message to the grand prince, and also this, "Lord Zalán is no longer. His killing can be ascribed to the emperor's men. We beg you to await our report before listening to any fast riders from the emperor."

Now Dörge was brought to the Audience Hall, where the grand prince asked that he repeat the message, exactly as he said it the first time.

After that announcement, total silence reigned in the Audience Hall. Árpád wanted to jump up and scream at Dörge to tell him more, but immediately he controlled himself. Only those who knew him well or were watching him at the moment would have realized the degree of his self-control. His fingers turned white from the force with which his big hands gripped the armrests of his chair. Then he nodded, dismissing Dörge with admonishment to go and eat first and then seek his rest.

The nobles rose as soon as Árpád did and collected in small knots of men. They were shocked; they were silent. Those who spoke did it softly, aware that Árpád disliked loud and vehement discussion without the support of sufficient information. After a while, they were all dismissed until such time that Szabolcs and Ügyek, now evidently the only members of the small delegation left, would arrive. Árpád himself retired to his private quarters, walking up and down, back and forth in his workroom, his hands clasped behind his back. There was a heavy scowl on his face. A large ewer of his favorite wine had been placed on the small table by the window, also a cup next to it. Every once in a while, he stopped to pick up the cup to drink. Little meat cakes, made with smoked meat, flavored with onions and herbs, were also left for him to eat. He took one and slowly chewed, sighed after swallowing, then, glass in hand, continued his rounds. He was roused from his thoughts by a knock on the door.

Ugron, second to Törs, Árpád's senior arms bearer, walked into his room, remained standing by the door, waiting patiently for his master to address him. He knew from past events that Árpád disliked being disturbed when he was alone, mulling problems which had not yet matured sufficiently in his mind to be presented to his advisors. Eventually he stirred slightly, which jangled his sidearms. Árpád glanced up, his severe closed gaze easing as he nodded. Ugron was one of his favored retainers.

"Whatever it is, my friend, it must be important. You know my habit and would not be here if it weren't!"

Ugron ducked his head, trying to hide his pleasure hearing his lord address him so favorably, and stepped closer. "My lord, two of the perimeter guards intercepted a lone horse. The horse was lame, in need of food and drink. She is a sorrel mare who looks familiar to me, lord. She carried a woman, lord, a half-dead woman who was asking, nay, insisting to be brought to you, lord. The men fashioned a sling between their two horses and brought her in. She is in a bad way, Árpád, but I think—I think…" His voice trailed off. By then Árpád was already at the door, through the door, and walking down the hallway with his distance-eating long stride.

"Where?" he asked only half-turning to Ugron. But the doors were already opening to him, the two door guards stepping aside. Indeed, there was a sorrel mare standing there, her sides heaving, head lowered in exhaustion, as she was allowed to take slow gulps of water out of a large animal skin. The makeshift sling-litter had been lowered to the ground, and its occupant disappeared at the moment under the layers of animal skins covering her.

In a matter of seconds, Árpád was at the side of the woman, sinking down onto the dust of the ground, his strong fingers grasped the edge of the covers and lifted them with care. The men watched his fingers shake as he stared at the lump lying there. Árpád's face crumpled, and for a moment, he closed his eyes. When he opened them again, his face was white and haggard, his lips drawn back over his teeth.

"Get me a healer. Get me Emö. And be quick about it!" He growled, then his eyes fell again down to the motionless body of the woman. "Ooh, ooh, ooh…" He crooned softly. "Virág, Virág, my little flower, who did this to you?" He reached both arms toward her and, with infinite care, lifted her toward himself, cradling her body. She felt so terribly light, frail, and ill! Her breaths were so terribly shallow, chest barely rising and falling. Her face was so deformed from bruises and cuts that even he had trouble recognizing her. Her trousers and tunic were so heavily soaked with blood that they were literally stiff. He prayed that it was mostly not her blood, but he would not know until the healer looked at her.

The two men who brought her in shifted uneasily, seeing Árpád's distress over this woman who was evidently important to him. Their movement redirected the grand prince's attention. As gently as he could, he lowered her body, and then rose to look at the men. He was opening his mouth to talk to them when two women, their skirts flying in their rush, rounded the corner, and then skidded to a halt before running him down. The older of the two looked at Árpád, before kneeling down to the litter, her eyes large and anxious.

She wrung her hands, lifting her knuckles to her lips, and whispered, "Is she?"

At Árpád's barely perceptible shake of his head, she lowered her eyes and set her face to her task. All Árpád could hear was her quiet voice, whispering commands to her younger partner.

Árpád stepped back and lowered himself on a stool, which Ugron brought out for him. When he offered him the goblet of wine he had been drinking in his private chambers, Árpád just shook his head and waved Ugron away. He did not speak, not wanting to disturb the two women's concentration. The quiet was more stifling now than the heat.

Once the women removed all the covers from Virág's body, they rose, somewhat irresolute. Árpád guessed their problem and waved them into the building, leading the little convoy of the two men carrying her litter, followed by the two women. Árpád led them to his study and pointed to the pallet in the corner, which he occasionally used for short naps or periods of rest.

Forcing any emotion from his mind, Árpád watched the two women cut the blood-soaked stiff tunic, and then the pants, from Virág's body. He did not move except to wave the two men to him and whisper to them briefly, to instruct them to go, have some food and wine and, after that, to come to him; he wanted to speak to them at greater length. After that, he laid his two heavy callused hands on his thighs and sat, his eyes without blinking, to watch the two women's activities over his wife.

Once the clothing had been removed, the women gently washed Virág's battered body. It appeared that someone had beaten her severely, and as it was evident from the bruises to her chest, also kicked her and broke some of her ribs. One of her arms also appeared to be broken, the lower arm lying there at an unnatural twisted angle. Her chest and abdomen were caked with blood, but after repeatedly washing off the blood, it appeared that most of it was not hers. They also noticed the bloodied dirk strapped to her leg, and the younger woman rose to bring it over to Árpád.

Finally they moved to her lower body, washing and rinsing, washing and rinsing her thighs repeatedly. Then the older healer rose and walked over to the prince, murmuring, "My lord, maybe it would be best if you were not here when we examine her body for—for an invasion of one or more men, lord, for evidence of rape—"

But Árpád only shook his head and ordered, "Do it—do it now!"

So the older healer knelt by Virág, trying to shield her mangled body as much as she could from her husband's eyes. The moments ticked away; there was total silence. Then the healer raised her eyes to Árpád, amazement on her face, and murmured, shaking her head. "My lord, she is pregnant, perhaps four months, mayhap more! I do believe there was no rape, my lord." She closed her eyes for a moment, wiping at them with her elbow. "The blood on her lower parts is only partly hers. She must have been injured there. But I see no damage to her womb or the entry to it!"

She raised her eyes, brimming with unshed tears, to look directly into the lord's eyes. "Most of the blood is that of the man, or men, who attacked her, not that of rape. She has lost a great deal of blood, as is... and...and I do believe the child she carries is well, better than her, my lord, considering..." She shook her head so that her long graying plaits shifted from one side of her shoulder to another. She sighed deeply.

"My master, Lord Árpád, we will do all that is within our power to do, to keep her alive and so also that the child will live! Please allow us to remove her from here so that we can clean her more thoroughly. Also more than food, she needs to drink. I'll have one of the apprentice healers by her side at all times, charged to dribble fluid into her mouth carefully so we do not choke her. If she will only swallow half of that, she—and we—will do well. Then we can slowly attempt some broth and eventually some food. We will also pack her wounds with poultices of herbs which keep infection and fever away. We will—" She stopped, wiping her eyes again, then turned away. Árpád saw her shoulders shake.

He rose, suddenly, and walked over to her. Placing both his hands on her shoulders, he murmured as he shook her gently. "Emö, Emö, I have no doubts in you or what you do! I expect to be informed of her progress or the opposite!" He nodded to the head healer once more, and then slowly turned and walked out of the room.

*****

Just when Jenö, doing double duty now that Servilius had been sent to Rome, was toting a heavy stack of scrolls and other documents into the master's study, there was a loud commotion outside the window, opened against the heat of the day. The shouts of men, mingled with the jangle of horses' gear, was followed almost immediately by the sound of running feet. The feet skidded to a halt at the door, but then the doors were quickly opened, and one of the guards, against all decorum, almost ran into the room.

"My lord Árpád." He panted, almost shouting, quite unable to hide his excitement. "My lord, the delegation from Constantinople is here. Lords Szabolcs and Ügyek, and, my lord, they have a prisoner with them—Alaricus!"

Getting up from his seat, Árpád pushed his chair away so forcefully that the chair toppled over. He was halfway to the door, standing there as immobile as a statue, legs braced apart, two fists on his hips, glaring toward the entrance.

The two men entered together and quickly strode toward their master, then bowed their heads to him. In this land, at least, the thought flashed through both of their heads, no noble born genuflected or knelt to the ruler.

Árpád walked over to each, first to Szabolcs, as the more senior of the two, then to young Ügyek. He touched them each on their shoulders and nodded to them, his eyes scanning their faces, their bodies.

"You both look like hell! When was it that you last got off your mounts? That you had eaten or rested?" And without further questions, he ordered food and drink for them as well as for himself. He waved Jenö near to his side and ordered him to take down everything the delegates were going to say.

"I have been apprised of Vazul's death, but what happened thereafter? What happened at Leo's court? What happened to Zalán? What happened to Alaricus?"

Ügyek looked toward Szabolcs, expecting him to speak for both of them. Szabolcs lifted his shoulders and shook his head. Even though he had just sat down, he now jumped up and began to pace back and forth, trying to control his agitation.

"It was a trap, a setup, lord." He turned to Árpád, his anxiety and anger plain on his face. "We had been received after long waiting, but the audience went very favorably. Zalán had impressed the whole court by making Leo laugh. Would that he could have made him choke instead!" He stopped, grinding his teeth, then continued, more calmly, "Immediately Zalán and, through him, all of us, had become famous at court. Everyone wanted to meet us, to talk to us, to invite us. The fawning was truly revolting! And Zalán, good-looking that he is—was—was beset by all the women, young and old, and he did seem to like it...hell, what man would not have liked it?

"But we felt that, slowly as things move along at that cursed court, we were making headway, step by step. While other delegations languished, we were recognized, known, and the chamberlain as well as the master of audiences both had placed us on the list for the beginning of the coming week. They assured us that Leo was interested to hear us out now that he not only met us but was looking forward to conversing with us again.

"Then over that Sunday, coming out from their church, the Princess Julia, the empress's sister who, of course, is a Christian, sent a messenger to Zalán. She wished very much to have a private dinner with him in her private apartments. Well, more fools us. We, of course, thought we knew what that meant and were certes convinced this would further our cause even more at the throne. For this is surely how statecraft is practiced in Constantinople!

"Alaricus and Beni Mellal arranged everything, those two goddamned dogs. Beni Mellal assisted Zalán in the purchase of a gift. I did not see it, lord, but it was an extremely rich and beautiful gift of a gold necklace, so I was told. Zalán was duly marched to the princess's apartments and left there by Alaricus after he made the introductions, at least that was Alaricus's plan, he told us, Ügyek and me, lord. Then all we heard was—nothing, nothing all night long. By early morning, we did not know if we should be concerned or jubilant at the success of the meeting."

Szabolcs took a deep breath, then reached for the cup which held his wine. He drank eagerly and deeply, then continued.

"Suddenly, lord, we were summoned to the Hall of Audiences. Leo wanted to see us immediately. That, we worried, was not a good sign. We marched in there, with our weapons at our sides. The guards wanted to take those, but we did not allow it. Told Alaricus to tell them that without our weapons, we would not walk into that hall. The guards knew not what to make of that, for they had never before encountered such behavior. But by then, we were well known for our strange customs and odd behavior, so they just shrugged and allowed us to walk in like that.

"It was then that Leo, the faithless liar, had the guards drag in Zalán's dead body to lay him at our feet. Leo accused Zalán of trying to rape Julia. Without a doubt in our minds, as we knew Zalán would—could—never have done so, we knew that this was a play, the end of which we did not wish to see. Beni Mellal and Alaricus both were conspirators in this. By then both of us believed also that their hand was in the drowning of Lord Vazul. Out there in the river, they were not trying to help him but exactly the opposite. I slew Beni Mellal right there, at the feet of the emperor. Alaricus I had put in chains to bring him back to you, lord, so you should judge him and mete out his punishment.

"That, lord was seven, going on eight days ago. We sent ahead a messenger. I hope he has reached you so that some of this is already known to you, lord. Our mounts literally collapsed under us as we rode into Aquincum so that we walked the last half league to your palace."

There was a long, long silence in the room. The sounds of daily life flowed in through the open window. Finally as all expected, the Lord Árpád was the first to move. His face was carved of stone, his eyes black darts pinning the two men in front of him.

"Where now is this scum—this Alaricus?" he demanded in a voice entirely devoid of any emotion.

"Outside your palace, lord," Ügyek was the one who answered this time. "More dead than alive. The horse he rode collapsed under him before we forded the branch of the river we had to cross to get here. He had to swim or paddle across, mostly, as best he could to keep from drowning, then, being more like a drowning rat, had to run behind us, or was dragged, likely, until we arrived here."

"Get him in here." Árpád growled.

The sound of running feet was followed by more silence, then finally the clanking of metal chains and some shuffling. The guards pushed Alaricus into the room. He stood there, truly more dead than alive, frightened, bruised, exhausted, barely able to stand, unable to look up and at his former liberator, the grand prince of the Seven Tribes.

Slowly that person advanced on him, until he stood in front of him, toe to toe. He leaned forward, until his breath brushed Alaricus's face, his eyes, black and bottomless like a tar pit, looking at, looking through him.

"The true story and not one word altered from that," he said in a deadly voice. Waited no more than five beats of his heart. "Now!" the lord bellowed. And then with deadly softness—"Begin now."

Alaricus twitched with each sound of the dreaded voice. He fell to his knees, his head bowed, as though already expecting the ax. He swallowed with difficulty. Árpád gestured impatiently.

"Give him a drink. I want to hear him talk and tell me all."

And Alaricus did. He talked. Oh, how he talked. His words tripping one over the other, he told the story from its inception, starting with the day of the sacrifice of the white horse. About Sidi Ben Moussa talking to him, talking to Beni Mellal. About the plan. About Sidi Ben Moussa's offer of rewards. Great rewards. About the storm—a gift of God really, to help their plans along—south of the Nišava River. About the tree that fell and helped in the drowning of Vazul. That was the first of the obstacles eliminated. About how Zalán won the regard of the emperor. About the meeting with the empress and her sister. About Julia's eagerness to help, she did want to meet the lionized man of the hour; it would be a feather in her cap. How she agreed to help for the sake of possession of the necklace and the large purse Sidi Ben Moussa gave to Alaricus for bribe money. Julia was always short of money; she loved to gamble. About the dinner, how he withdrew but hung around until the shrieks from Julia's apartment were heard, and the guards broke in and slaughtered Zalán. How he and Beni Mellal dragged the body.

In a gesture which those who know him well enough were familiar with, Árpád raised his hand to bring his palm to his forehead, then brush it down his face. It was his only sign of mourning. The only gesture of sadness and loss.

"So two friends, two of the best this nation can offer…to die to serve the needs of this—this money-changing, self-serving, shop-keeping merchant, who is not even here any longer within my reach. But mark this, Sidi Ben Moussa, or whatever name you may wish to call yourself, who disappeared from me! Mark this well, you Arabic dog, my reach is wide and my arm long, and so is my memory and that of this whole nation. There will be nowhere for you to hide, this I promise you. Oh, yes, this I do promise!"

And with that, the prince turned away from the prisoner. He gestured with his head to the guards. "Take him away. I wish not to lay eyes on him any longer."

The guard hesitated. "My lord, what should happen to him?"

Árpád shrugged. "Get rid of him. I care not how. It is foolish to torture him, though, he told me all he knows. Deal with him as with any other traitor."

Weakened as he was, and shackled, Alaric fought wildly. It was, of course, of no use. The two guards dragged him out of the room, screaming, along the length of the hallway. His bleeding feet, long ago having lost his shoes, dragged along the inlaid marble of the floor, leaving bloody tracks. His screams of *no* could long be heard, even in the noise coming from the outside.

*****

Árpád had decreed that the Lord Zalán's funeral—actually the ceremonial burning of his ashes—should not take place until his wife, the Lady Virág had sufficiently recovered to be present. He did this out of an excess of courtesy; after all, Zalán had been his wife's first betrothed and a childhood friend and companion to her, to boot.

Virág, recovering from her injuries in painfully slow stages, was touched by her husband's thoughtfulness. The first days after she had been found and taken to Aquincum, she was unaware of herself or anything else. The healers tended her ceaselessly, washing her body with warm water, massaging her limbs, using healing salves, some to combat infection, others to alleviate pain. They constantly dribbled fluid into her mouth, while stroking her throat to make her swallow.

Árpád came to visit her every day, sometimes more than once. He would talk to her softly, even if she did not answer. He remembered that long, long ago, his younger brother had been injured about his head. For days he lay in a deathlike sleep, and their healer then advised to talk to such a person, even if they did not respond. Their spirit, she claimed, ready to flee the body, would often stop and look back and even return from whence it wanted to flee. And Árpád saw how right that had been, for one sunny afternoon, the sixth or seventh day after her arrival, when he removed the cool wet cloth from her forehead and eyes, she looked up, smiled at him, and whispered, her voice as frail as the rustle of a leaf falling off the tree, "Oh, husband! You are here. I heard your voice and feared I had gone blind!"

Thereafter, her recovery proceeded as quickly as her body allowed it to happen; she was no longer a passive puppet just lying there. Slowly she was able to give halting account of the events at her father's camp, of his death and burial, of their departure on the journey home, even of the attack by the Pechenegs. She knew she carried a child, was happy and basked in Árpád's delight. Her memory only shut down at the moment when she herself was attacked by the burly leader of the group. From that point on, she did not recall anything, not how she escaped, not how she—or rather her horse—found their way westward, how they were brought back to Aquincum at breakneck speed to save her life.

The chief healer, Emö, assured Árpád that this was a usual part of the healing process. The brain just shut away truly frightening events, like someone shutting the lid on a pot which had spoiled meat in it. Sometimes with the passage of time, slowly these events emerged, sometimes it was like the bursting of a dam, and occasionally this never happened. There was no purpose to forcing the memories, that did not help at all, only caused great anxiety in the patient.

There were little changes, yes, in Virág's outlook and attitude. Árpád was moved, yes, when for the first time, she had called *home* here, with him, not her father's place, and when she now no longer called him my lord but husband. He was also amazed that she looked forward to the birth of their child without worry and with total serenity. This was, after all, her first birthing, and Árpád knew from many past births that first-time mothers tended to be nothing if not uneasy.

All these things passed through Árpád's mind, as he made ready to leave his wife's side. She had been installed on a cot, piled high with pillows, placed under some old chestnut trees in the palace's overgrown forgotten garden. The garden had probably not seen the hand of a gardener for perhaps centuries but served as a lovely and secluded resting place for Virág, and the gentle autumn sun and breeze did indeed do wonders in bringing bloom to her face.

"Are you going to be gone a very long time?" she whispered. "Please don't leave me alone! Will you come back home, husband?" He smiled, nodded, and, bending, kissed her sun-warmed cheek.

"Of course," he assured her. "I am not going anywhere but to my study. Rest, my dear."

The mind, he thought, was a magical wondrous mystery. Once, he had always sensed that his wife was ill at ease in his presence. There was always a diffidence, a constraint. How was it that it had now disappeared? Why? Had she grown up? Had she matured from coltish young womanhood into—into being his wife, the mother of his child-to-be? Now that she had been restored to him, this wife of his had become a wondrous mystery, one that he would be absorbed in unlocking for a long time! If—if only—she would survive childbirth. She was young and obviously strong and healthy to have survived her recent ordeal. And the child appeared to be strongly embedded in her womb; it would live after having survived as well. Walking away from her, toward his workroom, he looked back and felt a shadow of unease twist his heart.

Jenö and Adair, the grand prince's chief scribe and assistant, were waiting for their lord with an impatience they were unable to hide. Adair, a most handsome young man from the faraway island of Alba, who had been bitten by wanderlust very early in his life, had eventually made his way as far as the mountains of Carpathia, where he had met Árpád. Surprisingly each was impressed by the other, young Adair by the grand prince's power, his ability to talk to, listen to, and motivate his people, his grasp of the complexities of the current political arena and power structure. Of course, he was too young to formulate his opinion in such a precise fashion, but his admiration nevertheless was based on his observations of a most exceptional man.

Árpád's opinion, based on more precise observations of a young man wise beyond his years, was a mixture of admiration and paternal instinct. At any rate, Adair was hired as a page, then became a copier of documents and letters, when he was taught reading and writing, at his request. In the course of all that, he learned how to utilize those several languages, including Latin, which he had acquired through his slow travels through Europe.

Jenö and Adair were literally hopping with excitement. Just a short time ago, a delegation, carrying the official imperial seal, brought a message from Leo, emperor of Byzantium. It was addressed to His Highness Lord Árpád, son of Álmos, Grand Prince of the

Magyar Nation, residing between the rivers Danubius and Tissus. "Greetings" and ended with "loving greetings and prayers for the continued health of Our Beloved Brother, the Grand Prince, etc. etc. etc." Jenö had seen to the comfort of the delegation, conducting them into the already refurbished audience room of Árpád's palace. He had invited them to be comfortably seated and ordered wine and some small sesame cakes for refreshments. The group consisted of the head, thus speaker of the delegation, and three others, whose function could not be determined immediately nor their names or titles. There was also a contingent of soldiers, bristling with various types of weapons attached to their bodies, which amused both Jenö and Adair.

It was obvious that the gentlemen were quite hesitant to demean themselves to speak any more than was necessary to a lowly scribe. They also were hesitant to sit, even after invited to do so repeatedly, let alone to accept any food or drink. Unfortunately Jenö was not acquainted with the finer aspects of Byzantine court etiquette or else he would had been quite mortified by his own forwardness. He was also unaware that these gentlemen expected their food to be tasted for them.

Once Árpád arrived, the delegation visibly relaxed, albeit they continued to be surprised when they were first assigned chambers, food and drink, and also heated baths, the waters sweetened with the fragrance of acacia tree blossoms.

They were told to relinquish the message they carried for the inspection and interpretation of Lord Árpád's staff, and thereafter, they would be able to speak to the grand prince; but that would be not before the morrow. When the leader of the delegation, a tall thin sour-looking gentleman by the name of Contantinos Baïana, commenced to object, Lord Törs, Árpád's senior weapons bearer and, by virtue of that fact, also Árpád's second, informed the man that unless they followed Árpád's wish, they were welcome to depart, with Magyar military assistance.

This, basically, then left the delegates no choice other than to obey or to depart. Fortunately accustomed to court practices in Constantinople, they did not take offense greatly, except perhaps by the fact that a barbarian prince would deal with them in such an offhanded fashion. Under any circumstance, they were too travel-weary to offer objections.

Before retiring, Árpád summoned Adair to his bedchamber and had him read Leo's letter, repeating the reading several times. After Adair had finished his task, Árpád suddenly, unexpectedly, turned to him.

"Adair, my son," he told the youngster, bringing a bright blush of pleasure to Adair's cheeks by calling him my son, "do you love what you are doing, boy?"

Adair flushed even brighter and stammered distractedly. "Aye, my lord, Highness, indeed I do quite like it." His eyes diligently examined the toes of his boots so that he did not have to look at the grand prince.

Árpád rounded on him almost vehemently. "But do you love what you do, really, really love being a scribe and a clerk? Are you satisfied of a life with that? Answer me truthfully, boy, and keep in mind that if you do well, you could rise to be a major domo or the seneschal in a big important house, maybe even mine? You are intelligent, traveled, speak languages, have a future, but, but there are limitations to that future. Unless you are a noble born, which you are not, or—*or*"—and raising his voice, he paused briefly—"unless you become a knight! Think you on these things, my son, and I will pose the same question to you tomorrow. Think carefully and answer truthfully, and keep in mind that there is no disgrace to choose a lesser choice as long as that is what pleases you."

Adair, still red-faced with embarrassment, ducked his head, gathered the documents as quick as he could, and literally fled from the study. Árpád looked after his disappearing feet with a small smile hovering about his lips. Growing up, he thought, is a difficult business, especially for a shy orphan boy. Deciding to spend a few minutes more in his study, he began to marshal his thoughts for the morrow's meeting with the other chieftains of the seven tribes, those who were, in fact, in the vicinity and his close counselors. He wanted to have all of them dissect and discuss his decision made in response to Leo's letter, the text of which he now knew from Adair's reading. Let them debate, and then he would make the final decision and dictate the letter to go back to Leo's Constantinople.

It was truly late. He was truly tired. Thinking about it, he was surprised—but not really surprised—that exhaustion overtook him more and more suddenly and frequently. He was getting older, he thought with a wry smile. Two score and six years. And they were not easy years. He almost laughed at the thought of how "not easy" they were. The years had abused his body and his mind and his emotions, and now he was tired, bone-tired, and weary. He thought of youth, was it his own aging that drew him to youth like Adair's? Like Virág's?

Oh, Virág, he sighed, no, no, that was an entirely different emotion. *Aye*, he thought, *admit it, old fellow, for what it is and accept it. Love*. Never before this same emotion, with any of his wives, or any of the others who had just briefly passed through his life. There had been desire, lust, passion even, but never this, this sense of need. To shelter, to protect, to possess, to understand, to simply be with. *Oh, Virág*, he sighed again, *may the gods be thanked that you have re-entered my life. More grown, more adult*. Could she become his partner, his companion, not just his bedmate, like Alán was once, so very long ago, only more so? *Stay with me, my young love, for indeed I cannot face the thought of your absence, your loss, your death!*

*****

Shortly after sunrise the next morning, the chieftains and all the lords were filing in through the iron-studded heavy double doors to the audience chamber. Each of them was trailed by their own scribes or right-hand men, the scribes armed with rolls of parchment, bottles of ink hanging on silk cords slung around their necks, quills and quill pens in slender cylindrical drawstring bags, swinging from their leather belts. Clothing for rich or poor eschewed ostentation; that was a practice of the degenerate courts of Rome, Constantinople, Aachen, Worms, Fulda, Spoleto, and others, but not here! Except in battle, they mostly wore homespun and leather, finely embroidered and velvet capes—or fur ones for winter—lined or trimmed with precious furs to shelter against the weather when needed.

Little knots of men were forming inside the chamber, "cubiculum," as it was inscribed above the doors by the long-gone Roman builders. The men conversed in low tones; somehow although each of them would have denied it, they felt the weight of majesty steeped into all the structures of Aquincum, when they were more at home in a large tent rather than all this marble and bronze. Well, it was all a part of having arrived, being at home. They understood that Árpád was intent on driving that point home. Impromptu conferences on horseback were invaluable when decisions had to be made quickly. In fact, this speed had been one of their winning strategies as far back as could be recorded, but now when documentation of certain decisions was needful, a place had to be provided for the scribes to do their work and to store rolls of documents as well.

When servants arrived, some with small tables which they placed in the center of each cluster of chairs, others with viands for breaking their fasts, the men easily settled into groups around the tables and the food without breaking the flow of their conversation. Some of them became so immersed in the talks that they did not even notice when the grand prince entered, except by the slow decrease in sound and then a final silence. They all rose, bowed their heads, and murmured a morning greeting.

Árpád seated himself at the table and armchair provided for him on a slightly raised dais, and summoned his two scribes to his side. Once each settled on a low stool on either side of their master, quill pen at the ready, their inkhorns, filled with freshly ground and dissolved charcoal, now uncorked and placed to their sides, Árpád nodded and let his hooded eyes wander around the room. As other eyes met his, he nodded slightly, his visage otherwise not giving away any of his thoughts or moods.

Finally he raised his hand for attention and then, nodding to Jenö, started speaking.

"My lords, my counselors, advisers, mainstays of the nation of Magyars. We have received a delegation yesterday with a letter from the Emperor Leo. You all have been apprised of what has been done to our last delegation to the emperor. Pray listen." Again he nodded to Jenö.

"My beloved Cousin, Our greatly Admired and Gracious Grand Prince, you will have to know that your delegate, the now-late and greatly lamented Lord Zalán was a most engaging and exceptional person. Not only as Your emissary, but on a deeper personal level, I had a great desire to become more closely acquainted with him. It is my grief and sorrow that I had been denied that pleasure. As You also have, without doubt, experienced in your life, opportunities such as that are rare and thus to be treasured. I tell you these things, in fact, am compelled by emotions to start with such an unceremonious beginning to this letter."

When Jenö then hesitated, unsure if he should continue, Árpád nodded.

"Read on," he commanded.

"His unexpected death—slaughter, really—touched me. What I now tell You is the absolute truth as it has been established by the Captain of the Palace Guards. Take it as it was given to me and as I now give to You, whom I consider with the sincerest of feelings as My Cousin. A merchant by the name of Sidi Ben Moussa, who travels hither and yon with his caravan of goods, had visited Your encampment by the river Danubius. His desire was to have secure trade routes through Your Nations and beyond because he considers them needful to be open for his trade. In these endeavors he, I believe, is also supported by others who give him money. He approached one Alaricus, a freed Visigoth prisoner used by Your Grace, an interpreter sent to us with Your much treasured guests. This man was bought off and thus induced to make any possible mischief as to achieve Sidi Ben Moussa's plans.

"Thus a certain slave named Beni Mellal accompanied Your group as instrument of Sidi Ben Moussa. Thus was the death of Lord Vazul also achieved by Alaricus and Beni Mellal in a flooded river, made to look like a rescue attempt. Thus also was Lord Zalán's life extinguished when he was on his way to accede to my sister by marriage, Julia's, invitation to a private dinner. Of a great and generous mind, Lord Zalán bought a most expensive jewelry gift for Julia. When my palace guards saw him with the jewel at Julia's door, the cry went up for a thief. Zalán, thus accused and condemned for thievery, was slain by the said guards. They have all paid the price for this haste and error of judgment, and the guard's captain as well, as I can assure You, Cousin.

"To all this, I wish to add the degree to which my young sister by marriage, Julia, may or may not have played a part. She is young, lacking wisdom, and easily influenced. Suffice it to say that I have placed her under severe restrictions and am diligently involved in the process, shall we say, of her learning wisdom and restraint.

"At the end, all I could do in this dreadfully lamentable event is to send back to You, my Dearest Cousin, Lord Zalán's gift, as You will see, a necklace. I would beg You to give it to Lord Zalán's family. I grieve, and thus in grief ask for Your Understanding and Absolution! I ask that You, my Gracious Cousin, consider this whole mournful loss, a loss certainly to You, My Lord, and—as I beg to be believed—also to me, by virtue of the inexplicable bond I felt that bound me to the Treasured Deceased. I ask that you allow me to be outside the Acts and words of Diplomacy with which we would address each other at less personally sorrowful days…Perhaps this sorrowful beginning can lead to a more fruit-bearing relationship, yea friendship…

"On the Day of the Lord etc., etc.

"Leo, Impertor, Basileus of etc., etc."

There was silence for a while. The chieftains and lords looked at one another, then at Árpád and the two returned emissaries, Szabolcs and Ügyek, who had made their appearance, albeit somewhat belatedly. Both were still pale with dark lines of exhaustion under their eyes. They had sat down together at one of the small tables. Now Ügyek stood up while Szabolcs was still working to swallow his last bite of food and wipe his fingers.

Chieftain Tas raised his eyes to the grand prince. "Do you believe him?"

Árpád shrugged and spread his hands. With a slight smile, he nodded. "Mostly, my lords". His eyes moved to the standing Ügyek, who now shrugged as well, then shook his head.

"My lords," he said with a slight hesitation. "Neither of us were witnesses. Maybe the details are wrong, either deliberately or due to Leo being misinformed as well. But at least in broad lines, yes, I do."

Szabolcs, who now had finished his meal, also stood. "My lords, Leo can be as devious as any of his ilk. But I was also a witness to a bond which had formed between him and my master Zalán. He was—for lack of another word—charmed and amused by him. There was something in what Zalán had said when the master of ceremonies introduced each of us, something which amused and captivated the emperor. He and Zalán actually laughed together about something! There was a long look from one to the other, a communication in silence. When we left the emperor's presence, he still looked bemused, and so did Zalán.

"The effect of this was that we were summoned to a second audience very much before the time we expected. I cannot believe that Leo carried ill will toward Zalán or even would have allowed such to exist in the mind of someone else, at least not knowingly!" He sat, shaking his head, spreading his knees and placing his two beefy hands on them.

"Actually, my lords," he added as a postscript, "actually I believe that there were evil actions done by Beni Mellal, supported by Alaricus, who was paid by Sidi Ben Moussa. Sidi Ben Moussa did not act alone but had backers financing all this."

"That," said Tas, "that makes things difficult...If we respond with an armed attack, which I would have recommended before I heard what I heard, but now, well, as things are, we need to—well, to consider—to consider that what Leo writes is mostly true. Such plots by outsiders for their nefarious purposes can, nay, they do happen. And so—"

Tas stopped his ruminations and turned his eyes to Árpád. Árpád nodded to his old friend and continued his musing.

"Aye, so it will behoove us to tread lightly. We are beset by potentially threatening neighbors. Not only Leo but also Arnulf of Carinthia, emperor of that sham nation of the Holy Roman Empire which is not holy, neither is it Roman, and most assuredly not an empire. Then there is Rome and the Holy See of the pope, whose earthly embodiment changes from year to year to make the head spin! And then, one is not even counting Moravia and Bulgaria! None of them threaten us at the moment.

"That is very meaningful, if we—as we do wish—will make this our land and remain on it. Should we arm ourselves now, when much of the summer is already gone, to ride into a winter campaign? If there is even a part of truth in Leo's writing—and I must say, never before did he write with such a contrite self-effacing tone—then we cannot destroy this thread of friendship, a request for friendship from him, can we? And if this is all sham, methinks there will be time enough to arm ourselves and stand before the gates of great Byzantium in the spring. But to now start to wage war because of a possibly imagined offense, a deliberately planned killing, or even killings, by agents outside the sphere of Leo's empire? Nay, methinks now when our best interest is to get us settled first and make this Land of Attila truly ours, that would be foolish, indeed. What think thee, my lords and friends?"

There was a nodding of heads and a murmur of ayes, increasing until every person present was agreeing. There was an audible sigh of relief. For better or for worse, they would have at least a respite from warfare, however short a time to build and prosper. Maybe if the God of War was kind to them, this would truly become home?

One day later, the Byzantine envoys, well-rested and carrying small gifts to the emperor, as well as the return of Julia's necklace, were sent back to Leo. The letter they carried assuring him of equal fraternal feeling as he had expressed. In addition, it was affirmed that the grand prince and the Magyar lords believed that Leo indeed had been duped.

Árpád felt a deep sense of relief. This, he knew, was just a temporary condition, a first attempt to transit from a constantly warring, constantly moving collection of tribes to become a true nation, a real sovereign nation. They were now slowly learning how to do that. Perhaps, perhaps now finally, the prophetic dreams of their ancestors, the prophesies of the gods would come true? In this land, the land of their honored ancestor, Attila, who died and was buried here, here they could settle and thrive forevermore?

*****

It was exactly three months later from the day Leo's delegation returned to Byzantium, carrying with them Árpád's congenial response. The grand prince was wrapping up his day's work in his study. His newest scribe, Jenö's youngest brother, Taksony, was sweeping the documents into one large pile, from which Jenö carefully pulled certain ones to be rolled up and added to an already bulging sack hanging from his shoulder.

Adair had left his service as scribe with Árpád's blessing, and he now served as squire to the Lord Kond, chieftain of the tribe of Keszi. He was learning horsemanship and swordsmanship, and should he do well, he would earn the right to become a leader of troops in due time, and possibly more later on. Árpád was pleased with this. Young Adair had always reminded him of his own firstborn, Levente, whom the West called Liüntika. He had not seen him since he sent him east to replace Lord Zalán after Lord Töhötöm's death and had not yet been able to return. He had been such an affecting little boy, and Árpád had loved him dearly. Perhaps he was in error to transfer those feelings to Adair, Árpád thought, but could not quite hide the small smile that lit up his stern face.

As was always his habit, after finishing the day's work with his two secretaries, the grand prince planned to ride down to the river's edge, and Fajsz, the stablemaster, was already holding the reins of his favorite mount in readiness. Once they had attained their destination, both he and his horse seemed disinclined to make a speedy return to their home and stable. Árpád watched his animal stamp his feet and then snort when the spray got in his nose. He was obviously enjoying the game, for he kept repeating it. When his master finally whistled for him, he shook his head but nevertheless returned to him, though with reluctant obedience. This was not the first time such a game had been played because Szárnyas blew out his lips gaily, nodded his head up and down, and then took off, splashing as much water onto his master as he was able to. Twice he jogged around Árpád, then stopped, directly facing him, reared and slammed both of his hooves into the water, looking happily at the great spray that tumbled down on Árpád's head and body. His master laughed, pulled the horse's head into the crook of his arm, and lovingly rubbed his black velvet nose.

It was as they were leisurely jogging back to the castle that he heard a voice urgently calling for him. It turned out to be Megyeri, Árpád's senior squire, running toward him, waving his arms. He was urgently needed in the women's quarters, and it was the Lady Virág. Beyond that he knew nothing. Árpád, without hesitation, threw his horse's reins to him and began to run. At the door to the women's wing, Emö was waiting impatiently. Her information came as she continued to run with Árpád toward Virág's room.

"Lord, she had some beginning birth pains. We came when we heard her cry out and comforted her and that was when we noted, lord, that she was bleeding, lord, copiously. We are unable to stop the bleeding, and she has gone into labor. As best we can account, she is close to eight months of her pregnancy now, maybe a little more or a little less. I have examined her, and the babe is strong and has rotated so that it is head down and ready to come...lord! I worry not about the child but about her. She has already lost so much blood!"

Árpád rounded on her as he was running. "Whatever it takes, do for her first! She can give me other births, but she has to live to do that!"

The child, a girl, came with an easy birth only a few hours later. The women marveled at this ease, especially for a first-time mother. The little girl, crying lustily, was given to her mother, but then she barely had the strength to hold her, and so they took her and gave her to the father. Stonily, Árpád looked at the infant, then returned her to Emö and the other women.

He had gone through this so many times! But now it seemed to him none of them were quite as painful as this. He walked the hallways, then the dark and silent gardens, finally he called for Fajsz and had him saddle Szárnyas. The horse seemed to feel his master's distress, whickered and rubbed his big head against Árpád's shoulder, then started toward the river as soon as Árpád swung himself into the saddle. Tonight, though, there was no cavorting in the water. Horse and rider stood silently at the bank, Árpád not moving at all, and the horse only snorting and shaking his head every once in a while.

When he heard a crunch in the sand, he turned around without surprise, nodded, and had his horse follow Fajsz back to the stables, while the reins slipped from his fingers.

He was shocked when he saw Virág. She was whiter than white, her cheeks sunken, her eyes huge in her small face. She smiled, though, when she saw Árpád and made an infinitesimal movement toward him. Her mouth moved, but he had to lean right to her mouth to hear.

"My husband, I remember, now I do, you know! Listen! I do remember—everything! Everything…they were…Pechenegs. They…killed everyone, and I…I shot all the arrows I had! They all went true, you know…all killed."

She became more and more invigorated as she talked, nodding her head and trying to raise herself upon her elbow. Árpád bent down to support her almost weightless body. She gave a little smile, and her eyes, the old alertly sparkling ones, flashed at him. As she pushed out the words, her head bobbed with each sentence, lips drawn back over her teeth. For the flashing length of seconds, she became the old mischievous woman.

"I killed every damn one of them, Árpád, each of my arrows…I am very good! My women…raped by them all…they were laughing and clapping their hands. One of them saw my attack…yes…I took—my dirk in my palm! Oh, gods! He kicked me, one kick for each arrow…then—then he slapped my face, one slap for—for each I killed! Became dizzy…but, but…I did want to kill him so badly! That kept me awake!" She became more animated, more forceful.

"He—he pushed my legs apart and pulled out his—his—you know…ready to rape me! He…he was so big and heavy. Then he groaned and groaned…and fell on me…like—like dead. Árpád, and he was dead! My dirk…in my hand! Ha! It went into his belly! Yes!" Her eyes began to sparkle, and she nodded her head vehemently. "And…and then Goldilocks's sweet nose touched my face, and… and…she lay down to—to help me…help me on her back. She saved me and brought me home. To you, husband! To you…"

Árpád, gathering her icy hands into his, interrupted her gently.

"My love, who is Goldilocks?"

Virág looked at him with surprise, wrinkling her forehead, looking as though awakening from a dream.

"Goldilocks," she mumbled, "Goldilocks is my horse—the horse you gifted me with, husband."

By that time, Árpád felt like his heart, his emotions had been shredded. No longer just able to sit and listen, he gathered her into his arms and pressed her thin body as close to him as he could. She pushed even closer and burrowed her head into the crook of his neck. He could feel her soft hesitant breaths on his skin. Her whisper was as soft as the lightest breeze in his ear.

"We had such short—short time! Remember me, please. I love you now…love you so very much. Husband. Only you! Oh yes… always…you…"

*****

It was the hour after sunrise. The work of restoring the great city of Attila was already in swing. A hundred different activities, a hundred different noises assailed the ears, the eyes, the nose. Árpád sat in the palace garden under his favorite chestnut tree. They had laid the newborn, heavily swaddled, into his big hands. He was looking at the little girl's tightly shut eyes, scrunched up little red face. With infinite tender care, he shifted the blanket to cover the baby's head.

"Yes, yes, little girl, little Virág," he whispered to her. "You shall grow up to look like your mother! Laughter and sunshine in your eyes! Your fingers playing the *koboz*, your voice singing to the music, will delight your husband, and your laughter will add joy to his life! You shall be the symbol of the new Magyar nation, my nation and yours, rising even now on the ruins of the past. The growth will be hard and dangerous, but if the gods allow, we shall not only grow but prosper! And survive despite enemies! And you, little one, will be the first over centuries and centuries to be born and live in this place and call it truly home."

To Repel the Dark
AD 1401–1510 Italy

Introduction

The flow of gold from one destination to the next changes with the passage of time. Its final destination is dictated by the constant fluctuations of wealth. Wealth, just like power, is ultimately just as ephemeral. One usually does not exist without the other, since the two rely upon and support each other.

Very, very rarely in human history, there will be a miraculous confluence of wealth, power with a monumental flowering of intellect on the part of a select few. It happens over a relatively short time. Just think, the time elapsed among the deaths of Francesco Petrarch, Nicolaus Copernicus, Leonardo da Vinci, and Johannnes Gutenberg was no more than one hundred years. The time elapsed among the deaths of Thomas Paine, Patrick Henry, Benjamin Franklin, George Washington, John Adams, Thomas Jefferson, and James Madison was less than fifty years! Like threads from the most disparate sources, ideas converged to form a multicolored tapestry, able to assimilate all those colors and form an exciting new pattern.

The name of this new movement was humanism. Within that time of a hundred years, the change in the thinking of men, however, was truly shattering.

But isn't it also true that nothing is new under the sun? This "new" humanism also was not truly new. It was based on the rediscovery of ancient cultures, forgotten under the influence and neglect of church doctrine, literally buried under the sands of time. The great discoveries of a da Vinci, of Copernicus and Gutenberg were based on theories of Plato, Socrates, and Archimedes. The glories produced by Botticelli, Titian, and Michelangelo had their roots in the art of ancient Greece and Rome. Humanity reveled and rejoiced in its resurrected glorious ancient past.

Thinking was no longer corralled into the narrow confines of church doctrine. Representations of humans and their interactions were no longer limited to religious figures and topics. Backgrounds of paintings shed their layers of gold leaf and exchanged it for exuberant landscapes. And those landscapes and backgrounds were no longer flat two-dimensional canvases but a visual representation of what the eye saw. Once landscapes abounded in art, immediately the need arose to represent faraway mountains and close-by trees in proportion, as the eye perceives them. Paintings began to be ruled by that wonderful new concept of perspective.

All that did not necessarily mean that gold consumption decreased. Church vessels, church decorations, interior decorations for the innumerable palaces of petty rulers in Italy, in France, in the German states all thirsted for greater and greater quantities of gold. In 1401, the Guild of the Cloth Importers of Firenze, the Arte di Calimala, announced a competition to design doors for the baptistery of the Duomo Santa Maria del Fiore. The church of Saint Mary of the Flowers was the most significant church in town, and when it was made known that the bas-relief bronze doors were to be embellished with gold, the veritable floodgates of gold importation into the city opened, once again revealing the versatility of gold, which, like no other metal, survives the demands of aging and still provides the greatest degree of beauty.

What other substance than gold could have been chosen, gloriously gleaming, malleable to the artist, unchanging and incorruptible over time, and, at the same time, exhibiting the wealth of the owner? Indeed, no other.

Prologue

Young Lorenzo Ghiberti, better known here in Pesaro as Lorenzo, the running youngster from Firenze, received the news of the competition on a Sunday. He had been climbing the backstairs to his room, the room he had been given for his work here at the castle, when one of Lord Malatesta's guards intercepted him. Lord Carlo wished to see him immediately. *Immediately?* Lorenzo thought. That was indeed out of the ordinary, for Sunday was the time for quietude, reflection, prayer, and good deeds. What good deed was in his master's mind or in his hands to give to him? Some new chunks of a mineral to grind into paint? Some gold leaf to adorn one of the works he was occupied with?

He turned and took the steps down two at a time, then traversed the inner courtyard to the main building at a lope. The guard at the door saw his rush and opened the small door cut into the left wing of the huge portal studded with metal for reinforcement and embellishment. The guard smiled and nodded at him. Lorenzo found that most people smiled or nodded when they saw him; some of them even took the trouble to wave from a distance. From childhood on, he had been a very gregarious little boy, and people seemed to just naturally respond to his friendly chatter. He had friends everywhere, in his hometown of Florence, in Rimini, where he had fled when the plague hit Firenze, and now here in Pesaro.

Without breaking his stride, his long legs pumping, he ran along the ground floor hallway, with door upon door on the one side and arched windows looking out to the courtyard on the other. At the end of the hallway, he put on brakes and skidded to a stop. Out of breath, he bent over to alleviate the pinch in his side. Once again, the guard at the door to the lord's study nodded to him and opened the door, but then quickly extended his arm to bar him entrance. Using the same hand to ruffle his own hair, he cautioned Lorenzo about the disarray of his. Lorenzo nodded quickly, muttered his thanks, and, with a deep breath, walked in, smoothing his hair and arranging his clothing as best he could.

His current master, the famous condottiere Lord Carlo Malatesta, recently named by Pope Urban VI to be his gonfalonier, his standard bearer, only ten years Lorenzo's senior, was sitting at his desk. Both his seneschal and his secretary were at his side. The lord motioned Lorenzo to advance, murmured a few words to the seneschal, and then nodded his dismissal. When his secretary made a move to leave as well, Malatesta detained him with a quick gesture. He lifted his eyes to Lorenzo, eyebrows raised high up on his forehead.

The gonfalonier was an exceedingly handsome young man with clear skin, a gentle oval face surrounded by waved dark hair, dark eyes under delicately shaped eyebrows, a well-drawn mouth, round chin. Altogether the face could have been the model for one of the biblical archangels, not for a condottiere famed for his valor. The contradiction amused Lorenzo each time he saw the lord.

"There you are!" Malatesta said amiably, "and I assure you, I did not disturb your Sunday devotions unnecessarily. What I have in my hand"—and he proceeded to wave a sheet of paper he held in his hand to the left and right—"well…it is, or could be, of utmost importance to you, my friend. You had, a while back, indicated that you received notice from several of your friends in Firenze about a competition to design the new doors of the cathedral's baptistery?"

When Lorenzo shifted, hardly able to hide his anxiety, Malatesta obligingly waved him to a seat across from his desk.

"Sit, sit," he murmured, scanning the document, then, with a little sigh, put it down on his desk. "At that time, I had promised you to make inquiries. To be honest, I had hoped that this whole thing would turn out to be fluke or an exaggeration, at least. But I must tell you, my young friend, it is neither, and being an egotist, I greatly dislike the telling to you. Knowing you, I would not be too surprised if you were to throw away your current very promising work here, something I know you enjoy because you have told me often enough how you enjoy painting. Even though I do feel that your heart belongs to sculpting and metalwork! Yet listen here, my friend, you are too gifted, and your gifts need to be expanded, not hidden here in Pesaro! Well, anyway this is what I found out." And he ran his eyes down the page to read aloud.

"The Cloth Importers' Guild has announced a competition for the design of doors to be placed to the east side of the baptistery, as a votive offering from the city of Firenze for escaping the Black Death. The topic is the sacrifice of Isaac. It should be in the shape and size of current door panels and made in brass. Four tables of brass will be given to each contestant to produce one panel. Judging will be within a year from the inception of work on the part of the contestants."

Malatesta studied Lorenzo's face and, sighing, laid the paper down, leaned both elbows on the desk, and made a steeple of his fingers.

"No matter what you decide, I will not allow it to influence the amicable nature of our relationship. You have great talent, my friend. If you decide to follow this siren's song, I will have great faith in your success, your future. If nothing else, I'll then be left with bragging rights to say, 'I knew him when,' and 'he worked for me when…' However, whatever your final decision will be, I insist—insist—that you take a full week to decide."

One month after this discussion, Lorenzo Ghiberti, twenty-three years of age, arrived in his hometown of Firenze and had himself installed in the home of his parents. He started working in his father, Bartolo di Michele's, gold workshop. The number of artists competing against him was large. Finally seven semifinalists remained to compete.

In 1402, the judges had to decide between Filippo Brunelleschi, the architect of Firenze's stunning cupola for the cathedral of Santa Maria del Fiore, and Lorenzo Ghiberti. The decision was in favor of the latter.

It took Ghiberti twenty-one years to complete twenty-eight panels of gilded bronze on topics from the New Testament. Thereafter, he was commissioned to make two doors with topics from the Old

Testament. These designs employed the most recent concepts of perspective and a method of working the figures in the foreground, in very low or shallow relief to have more ability for intimate spatial perspective. The results were precedent-shattering and are probably the greatest early examples of the depiction of depth and distance and also of the depictions of human bodies as they relate to the space they occupy and as the eye sees them.

The little girl ran down the hallway, her slippers sliding along the polished marble floor. Her extended arms gently swayed up and down to the rhythm of her torso and hip, which she also swung from side to side. She hummed a little tune, popular at the moment and often heard at court during the balls where grown-up ladies and their gentlemen danced. She almost ran into a richly dressed lady, slightly corpulent, her neck showing the very beginnings of a double chin. At the last minute, the little girl stopped herself from running head-on into her. Instead she instantly gathered her wits and her skirts and curtsied gracefully. Her eyes still sparkling with mischief, she slanted a look upward.

"I ask for your forgiveness, Your Grace," she whispered sweetly. "I confess that I was not looking at all where I was going. The beauty of this floor and the magnificence of the hallway have dazzled me, Your Grace." She gave the lady a radiant smile and then curtsied again.

The lady nodded with a kindly smile. "Aye, little girl, you are quite right, it is a magnificent inlay of marble, isn't it? And I would suppose that you also like to sing and dance, is that not so?"

The little girl curtsied again, but then she lifted her head without shyness and looked directly at the lady.

"Aye, Your Grace, you are quite right. I do so very much like to dance, to twirl and skip with the music, especially the galliard, like grown-up ladies do! And you, my Lady Bona, do you as well?"

The woman lifted her chin as her smile grew bigger. She raised an eyebrow. "And what is your name, child? Since you know who I am, it is only fair that I should know who you are?"

And again, the little girl executed a perfect curtsy. "My name is Caterina. Caterina Sforza, Your Grace. I am the daughter of your husband, His Grace Duke Galeazzo, and the Lady Lucrezia Landriani. I was told that it was your kindness, Lady Bona, which effected the invitation for me and my sister, Chiara, and my two brothers, Carlo and Alessandro, to live and study here in the Palazzo Ducale. I wish to thank you for your graciousness, Your Grace."

Duchess Bona inclined hear head and nodded quite seriously. "Now that I had the pleasure to meet you, Caterina, I am most happy to have done just that. Are all your siblings as obliging as you are, my dear?"

Caterina nodded in all seriousness, but then gave her another of her sidelong mischievous glances. "Oh, yes, Your Grace, of course. Not quite as much as I am, perhaps, but almost."

The duchess laughed loudly, and the ladies who were accompanying her, and now clustered behind her and the child, tittered with their hands in front of their mouths. She, either quite accustomed to that background noise or adept at ignoring it, bent down to Caterina.

"And tell me, what dance was that which I thoughtlessly interrupted?"

"Nay, Your Grace, actually I must confess, what I was doing was to imitate a bird flying with its wings, not even flapping but just soaring. The wind then lifts the wings, the young master Leonardo explained that to all of us yesterday in the courtyard!"

"Ah, Caterina, of course. I did not know that you were there as well. Is not young master Leonardo from Vinci a most fascinating person? Was it not a wonderful idea, to fly like a bird? I think that has been a secret desire of most of us, has it not? I see it most certainly has been for you! Tell me now, how old are you, Caterina?"

"Going on seven soon, Your Grace."

"Ah, seven soon, my dear…how is it that you are not in the schoolroom like your brothers?"

Caterina actually gave the Duchess of Milano a pitying look, wagging her head.

"Your Grace, I cannot—don't you know that girls are not supposed to be there?"

Duchess Bona raised her chin and her neck, like a militant hen. Without another word, she clasped the little girl's hand and rushed down the hallway in the direction she came from.

"Come with me!" she ordered. "We are going to that schoolroom right now. From now on, Caterina, you will be attending."

Little did the duchess know that seven years later, she would lose her husband. Despised by most of the population, the duke, an outrageously cruel and licentious individual, was stabbed to death the day after Christmas. He died almost instantly. Shortly thereafter, the duchess, even before she was asked to serve as regent during her son's minority, adopted all four of Lucrezia Landriani's illegitimate children.

Caterina's mind soaked up the knowledge of science, alchemy, languages, the arts, music, and most especially the art of politics. Her body loved to move, to dance, and to hunt, and she had a lifelong passion for it, inherited from her father, Galeazzo, himself a passionate hunter. From her paternal grandmother, the former Duchess of Milano, Bianca Angelina Visconti, she had also learned to be proud of her warrior ancestors and their skills in government. Later in her life, that pride did serve her quite well.

She loved her life at the Palazzo Ducale, under the wings of Duchess Bona. From a gawky little six-year-old—"six, going on seven"—she blossomed into a fast maturing ten-year-old. She was tall, slim, and already beginning to curve in all the right places. Being not only precocious but observant, she learned the art of flirting and seduction early on, neither of those being lost to the young and the not-so-young men at court.

All these mental and physical endowments, together with her adoption, now suddenly elevated her to be an important marriage asset.

*****

She was returning from a day's hunt, exhausted but exhilarated at the same time. Her quiver swung empty from her left shoulder, brushing her back. Her stable boy, appointed to his position just that morning, and for that reason unable to wipe the smile from his face, had four rabbits strung on a line and two gamecocks, their dead wings hesitantly extended and hanging down from the boy's shoulder. She smiled again, not even making an attempt to hide her pride. She saw her father, guiding his huge chestnut warhorse, move in her direction. The horse's earlier gleaming coat was now darkened with sweat, his hooves caked with dried mud.

Galeazzo, an avid hunter, had introduced all his children to the pleasures of the hunt, the bastard ones, by now living in the Palazzo Ducale, as well. Not much to his surprise, he found that it was his ten-year-old daughter, Caterina, who was the one to most enthusiastically embrace it. By then she had become an accomplished horsewoman and a very good archer. To the child, hunting seemed to be just an extension of those skills. She was always good with physical things, in addition to her mental abilities. Her interest in physical things brought along his next thought association.

Galeazzo pulled his warhorse level with Caterina's and, extending his gloved hand, laid it on hers, where she held her horse's bridle. His eyes looked her up and down, not just the glance of a proud father but the assessing look of a man looking at a girl turning into a very young woman. Recently he had received letters from His Holiness, Pope Sixtus IV, as well as from His Holiness's sister, Bianca Della Rovere, uncle and mother of Girolamo Riario. Girolamo was in the market for a wife. A well connected accomplished virgin bride, with a dowry of acceptable size. Thus the duke, following the dictates of his paternal duties, needed to talk to his daughter Caterina.

"You make me proud, daughter. Your riding and archery lessons were well placed, indeed."

Caterina inclined her head and looked up at her father, giving him a saucy sideway glance under her long lashes. It was a look that she had practiced at great length and had now perfected, or so she hoped.

"It is only through your loving concern, Father, that I had the opportunity to learn both. But I must confess to you that now, when I know what I am talking about, I truly enjoy hunting…"—and rewarded him with a gleaming smile—"quite extraordinarily!"

Her father nodded. "That is very pleasing for me to hear, Caterina. But attend to me, daughter. I have a mind for a serious discussion with you. Shall we separate ourselves from the others and talk, just you and me?" He took the lead to guide his horse off to the side of the road, waving all the others who gave him hesitant looks to precede them. Then he nudged his stallion closer to Caterina's mare.

"Well, now. Good, good! I have watched your progress, daughter, from child to accomplished young girl, now just at the cusp of womanhood. To a father, that time in his daughter's life bids him to start searching for an appropriately fitting husband. And an appropriately fitting marriage contract. And this is just what I wish to discuss with you. Before I could even begin to institute such a search, an offer was presented to me. A most unexpectedly excellent offer, daughter. So, attend to me!

"Girolamo Riario, nephew of His Holiness and son of Lord Paolo Riario and the Lady Bianca Della Rovere, who, as you need to know, is sister to His Holiness, is looking for a bride. In addition to—as you can appreciate—being exceedingly well connected, he is also wealthy, handsome, and was just recently been given the lordship of Imola by His Holiness. In every possible way, he would be a most excellent match for you, daughter. He is a score of years older than you are, but that may turn out to work in the favor of a happy future union. For I need not tell you, my dear, that you are willful, headstrong, and often impetuous by nature. Such traits are usually not pleasing to a husband. Most men yearn for a peaceful home to come to after the stresses of their days. They yearn for a quiet biddable wife. You, Caterina, will never be that!"

He saw the slight smile lurking at the corners of his daughter's lips, hear her slight chuckle, and, in return, smiled himself.

"Look me in the eye, daughter, and tell me if I am wrong in assessing your being!" And when she laughingly shook her head, he continued, "In this case, then I do believe that for the sake of the domestic bliss of this union, a husband who does understand and appreciate a wife with a mind of her own would be needful. From what I have heard about Girolamo, he is such a person. Not mean-spirited or cruel, but a man with a strong hand to guide a wayward girl into a fascinating wife."

Galeazzo looked thoughtfully ahead of himself to the ground and finally nodded. "Aye, I do believe that I will be proven right. Of course, daughter, I would never force you into a union which is objectionable to you! I advise you to think on this. You need to know that there was some talk of consummation of the marriage immediately after the wows are given. You need to know that initially, the feelers for a betrothal were directed to Costanza Fogliani, the illegitimate daughter of the Marquis Ludovico of Mantua, who is the same age as you. Costanza's mother did object to a consummation at the age of ten, understandably deeming it too young. Indeed, she was right. The negotiations then collapsed, and that was when they turned to me and to you. By now they understand that some restraint for the ensuing years will be called for, until the bride reaches the legal age of four and ten. So I hope that you will not find any objections in that regard."

Galeazzo took a deep breath and then, turning to Caterina, took both of her hands into his. He may be reviled by many of his subjects, as a matter of fact he was, very much so, but he thought with a sigh, nobody, nobody could accuse him of not loving his children and probably this little girl more than the others.

"As I have just said to you, daughter, I wish you to think on it. Remember, for the rest of your life, never ever make an instant decision. Good or bad, always defer your decision for a day. At least until the next morning. This rule will serve you well, especially since I know you are, by nature, impetuous!"

He smiled at her again, then pulled her close to him, and gently kissed her cheek.

Caterina did not need a day, not an overnight, not even an hour to think on the proposal. Was there ever a precocious young girl, self-assured of her beauty, brain, and her ability to manipulate men, who did not look forward to becoming an almost instant grown-up? If there was, she certainly was not that one. Her excitement prevented her from sleeping most of the night, as she was daydreaming of living in Rome, close to—nay, related—to the pope and all the shining dignitaries who formed his coterie. After all, she would be related to him! Rather than living in a remote town, one of the many, many centers of the many, many duchies of Italy, she would be living in Rome, rapidly becoming the center of Italy. She would be the wife of a man of import, with the status of wife rather than a green chit. And in Rome, she could meet so many of the greats of philosophy, writing, the arts, and most importantly, the art of statecraft. This latter avenue of mental exercise had just been opened to her, but she found it endlessly fascinating. Ah, yes, she, of course, did not even realize how, given her age, her thoughts were entirely outside the realm of the thoughts of other ten-year-old girls.

And being endlessly curious, she was most curious about that aspect of marriage that she really knew nothing about. She did hear whispers, of course, here and there, but they were only disjointed snippets, the end of sentences bitten off or altogether deleted and left to the imagination. She wanted facts, specifics, details, God knows she liked to be well informed about anything which interested her! Be it how to attach fletching to an arrow or dance the most recently fashionable la volta. Now that she was growing into marriageable age, how could she not be interested in that one thing more than any others? But she had no idea who to ask or even approach before outright asking.

Then it occurred to her like a flash—the bibliotheca! There it languished most days, unvisited except for a cleric or a magistrate here and there; hardly ever did anyone go to the library. Well, what else was such a place for but to read up on things, to gather information. Before turning in that evening, she made a mental note to visit the library at the earliest possibility!

The next day, waiting impatiently for the twenty-four hours to pass, she went to her father. She found him in the armory, examining the progress of the new pair of gauntlets, which were made for him by the master smithy. They were actually finished, except for the gold inlay embellishment on the high cuffs. There was a pinch between her father's eyes. Caterina could read the signs, her father was displeased. The smithy was babbling something; when he saw her enter, he turned his eyes to her with entreaty. Caterina intercepted his glimpse with a nearly imperceptible nod, then strode forward as though there were no storm clouds gathering overhead. Her steps speeded up so that she almost ran to her father, playacting the youthful eagerness perfectly.

"Oh, Father, Your Grace, please forgive me, I had been hunting for you and lo! Now I have hunted you down!" Galeazzo looked up, displeased by the interruption, his eyebrow rising on a question. He quickly glanced from the smithy to Caterina, and back, and she knew that he knew that he was being appeased. But for once, probably for the sake of this daughter he loved, he went along with the game. He turned from the smithy, throwing the gauntlets to him with the terse command, "Fix it!" Then he linked his daughter's hand on his arm and walked out. Only when they had walked a distance the length of the courtyard to the main stairs leading to the main floor of the castle did he turn to his daughter, a small smile lurking at the corner of his lips.

"You will do quite well in Rome, daughter, you have all the guile it takes to succeed. I hope your future husband will treasure you!"

Caterina slanted her head to look at him. "And how, pray tell, did you know my decision?"

Galeazzo threw his head back and laughed. "Caterina, Caterina, was there ever a doubt?" And she had the grace to blush as she smiled.

"Come with me into my study, daughter," Duke Galeazzo commanded. You can hear my response to both His Holiness and to Paolo and Bianca Riario, your future father and mother-in-law.

*****

It was at this time, that interim period following her betrothal and being, as she felt, in limbo, that she befriended Madeline, and Madeline befriended her. They were of the same age and going through the same experience in preparing for adulthood, becoming old enough for marriage, and that unavoidable mystery, the wedding night. Madeline was the daughter of the French envoy to the court of Milano and had grown up there since she was five. Her father, le Comte de Saint Salieu, was a short dapper man, with a shock of white hair and a prodigious mustache, old enough to have been Madeline's grandfather. Her mother had died when she birthed a son, two years past, and sadly the child died with her. There was, though, an older son, child of the first comtesse. The son, Etienne, lived at the Milanese court as well, doing absolutely no discernable activity other than wenching (after hearing her father utter that word in her presence, it became Caterina's favorite for a while) and playing chess. Just like her father, Madeline was petite, delicately boned, blond, and very lovely. It must have been true that opposites attract because Madeline was everything that Caterina was not, and the two girls became fast friends.

They knew that their friendship would be short-lived; both soon were going to places new to them to live their future lives with men unknown to them. Nothing about this seemed unusual to the two girls, it was how things were done, at least in their strata of society. That did not diminish the stress they felt; this stress was probably, more than anything else, the ribbon which bound them together. At least initially, until they discovered that they really, really liked each other. They spent endless hours guessing how their husbands would be, beyond those things that they had already found out. Caterina was most grateful to her father, for he had indeed given her some information upon which, for better or for worse, to build an image of the man who was to become her spouse and of the life she would face. By comparison, Madeline's information was very threadbare, indeed. His name was Jean-Luc, Marquis de Landes. With much effort, she also discovered that Landes was in the south of France and also that it was very pretty and had a long coastline on the Atlantic Ocean and rolling forested hills and low mountains to the east.

Frankly, she confessed to Caterina, geography did not mean a lot to her. She wanted to look into the books in the library to see just where France and, most particularly, the Atlantic Ocean were located. But she did not dare go there for fear that she would be caught in a place she did not belong and be reprimanded. Fortunately Caterina had no such compunctions, and so Madeline, with much trepidation, allowed herself to be led there. Once in the bibliotheca, which was and remained entirely empty of other humans, they spent a wonderful afternoon inhaling the dusty smell of old leather and glue, leafing through tome after tome showing them the most amazing and unexpected drawings and miniatures. They could not get enough. They also felt quite naughty, and the whole afternoon kept their ears cocked to the sound of other footsteps. After they found a much-thumbed decadent book—really, more than decadent—brought over from the mysterious Orient, well, the two little girls were unable to take their eyes off the paintings. Looking at the pictures of men and women engaged in explicitly drawn sex, Madeline lifted frightened round eyes to Caterina, whom she admired for her worldliness.

"They"—she swallowed nervously—"they don't really do those things, do they? It—it looks so—so revolting, don't you think? To think that maybe we—we would have to…"

She began to gnaw on her thumbnail, just like whenever she became nervous or frightened.

Caterina reveled in her status as the sophisticate. "Of course it is done. That is the way to please one's husband and also the way to have him beget children on you!" And she bent to Madeline and lowered her voice to a whisper. "And if you do it right and please your lord, as a reward, you will be pleased as well and am told that it is a pleasure unlike any other, such an exquisite experience it can be! So it behooves us to learn all this from our husbands and be always willing, and for such wives, the rewards can be great!"

She sighed and continued her lecture to the complete fascination of her friend.

"You see, we are always told that our reward of the marriage bed is the gift of a child. But I think maybe not. I do not believe that children are, at all times, such a blessing. But to receive great pleasure each time one couples with one's husband, that could be a great reward for us women. But I heard my ladies' maid talk to one of the housemaids that as much as she loved this coupling, she would only do it with one who was skilled at—at—well, at what she called—ah—arousal. Whatever that is, you know? It is supposed to make a woman receptive to this pleasure somehow, you know? I don't quite understand, but she also said that men can find their pleasure anytime, anywhere, with anyone…I kind of wonder about that, it seems to me to be an exaggeration, you know? That it should be such a precious thing for us women but so commonplace for them, no? That just does not sound right to me, you know?"

Madeline looked at her with wide rounded admiring eyes.

"Oh." She sighed. "I do so wish you would be with me when I have to leave here! I am so much afraid of my betrothed! He has been wedded and widowed three times already. Well, actually, the first one was his betrothed, and she died of an infection. Then one of the wives developed a lung disease, and the next one died in childbirth."

Caterina shrugged. "Having had wives before cannot be such a bad thing. He will have experience enough to teach you all you would need to know to please him. And also he would know how to please you. No?"

Madeline's eyes clouded, and she started to nibble on her thumbnail again.

"But, but, sweet friend, listen to what I have found out just last night. My father was having an evening of conversation with some of his gentlemen friends. They talked about this and that, and then the talk turned to my betrothed. One of my father's friends knew him rather well and mentioned that it was a good thing that I was such a nice biddable girl, for Jean-Luc was very demanding, easy to anger, and heavy-fisted." And she gave a little sob, then another, then fell sobbing around Caterina's neck.

Caterina shrugged.

"I overheard my father say once that he just absolutely loved women, all of them, but if they were young and pretty, then he really adored them! All they had to do is smile sweetly at him and be compliant! Well, if you are afraid, think this, you are young and not just pretty. Look into the polished mirror, and you will see how very beautiful you are! And you are certainly not like me, for you are compliant, and you can be even more compliant if needed! Just you think of this and act as needed when it serves its purpose!"

Aye, this truly had to be a most difficult stressful time for most young girls suddenly betrothed to an unknown man, often decades older and countries away!

Caterina, never one to have patience enough to offer gentle understanding for long, finally tried to redirect her friend's anxiety. Soon the two girls were chattering about gowns, shoes, and jeweled necklaces, lace garters with pink ribbons to be tied into bows to hold them tight on one's calves, embroidered gamurras with puffed slashed sleeves, the matching underdress material filling in the slashes.

Then quite unexpectedly, the day came which brought with it a letter from Jean-Luc to Madeline's father. Before the end of the day, the Comte de Saint Salieu summoned his daughter to his solar. Indicating by gesture for her to sit, this, she thought, was also an indication to her that he now considered her an adult. Madeline sat, filled with foreboding, her hands desperately clasping each other on her lap. As always in the past, when he had need to speak to her, her father rose and repeatedly circled about the room. It always made her think that he was impatient to be done with her.

Then her father stopped and, looking into her eyes, lifted his hand holding the letter. He held it as though it were a weight, then slowly lowered his arm.

"Daughter, there is sad severe news in this letter. You must listen with care and remain strong, child. Your betrothed has had a dreadful accident. There was a terrible forest fire which started to encroach upon the village which sits under the Chateau de Landes, his ancestral home. Of course he hastened to assist in the effort of firefighting, and while he was inside one of the wooden huts, the roof collapsed and fell on him. By the time they could bring his body out and lay upon the grass, everyone was convinced that their master was dead. A woman, their healer, supposedly very gifted, came and knelt by his side and looked and his horrendous wounds and pronounced that she thought she could heal him. This she did, and over many months of recovery, and enduring great pain during those months, he now exists in a recovered state. But, as he writes, 'I carry such repulsive scars not only on my face but throughout my body and am otherwise limited in my movements, albeit those are supposed to disappear within one or two years, and am often reclusive in my pain…etc., etc. Therefore, I would never condemn a woman to share her life with my bed and life. Thus I would willingly rescind the betrothal between your daughter, Madeline, and myself. To be honest with your daughter, however, I invite her and you, my lord, to make that long and arduous journey to travel to Chateau de Landes, to see my deplorable condition. Thereafter, the decisions should be—departing from custom—entirely in Madeline's hands.'

"The remainder of the letter," her father continued, "is the customary farewell greeting with hopes to see you—us—if we would be willing to take such a trip, in which case he also wishes you—us—a bon voyage." Her father concluded and then dropped the letter on his desk.

"These are," he concluded, "extraordinary circumstances and, as he says, an extraordinary suggestion to rescind a betrothal. As you know, Madeline, the betrothal is a commitment between two people almost as sacred as are the marriage vows. In any event, the breaking of the betrothal should be signed by both parties to the agreement. When the betrothal took place, I signed for you, daughter. But now I must follow Jean-Luc's request to leave the final decision to you. Since he considers you as an adult, I must do so as well. Thus we must travel to Landes and either nullify or reinstate the betrothal, the choice will depend on you! In all of this, it is understood that your impression of him, the degree of his infirmity, and the question whether you would be willing to undertake life with such a man…"

He gave her a partly surprised, partly kindhearted look, then took the extraordinary step to walk to her and stroke her hair.

"Sleep on all of this. Tomorrow is soon enough to take action. But if you do decide to go to Landres, would I be able to accompany you, daughter? That would depend upon my master, His Majesty Louis, the eleventh of that name, our ruler, king of France. Before leaving, it would be necessary to secure a permission to leave my post here in Milano."

Madeline lowered her head. A most unexpected sadness welled in her chest, and she suddenly felt mature beyond her years. Even though she made her decision right then, she abided by her father's wishes and only told him the next morning. Yes, she did want to travel to Chateau de Landes, did want to meet Jean-Luc de Landes. She also was well convinced to remain in the betrothal agreement, albeit did not want to talk about this with her father, lest he think her decision premature or romantically immature. But she was not immature, she was thirteen years old and felt absolutely grown-up. Somewhere, she thought, she had heard or read that adversity matures people. Well, if that was true, then here was her adversity, or rather Jean-Luc's, and she somehow felt connected to him. For the first time, she not only thought of him but was actually feeling for him, while until now her thoughts never even moved into his direction. How extraordinary!

And so the wheels of progress where induced to roll, the process of informing Jean-Luc, recruiting a suitable dowager to accompany the young woman, hiring the required detachment of guards with their captain, outfitting the traveling coach for the young bride-to-be and her chaperone and the luggage wagons, all the hundreds of such incidentals. They all made Madeline's head spin but also added to her suddenly growing maturity.

The two friends said their farewells the evening before the departure. Caterina wanted to remain strong and stoic, but when the sad moment arrived, she felt tears press against the back of her eyes, and she looked up to the sky so they wouldn't leak. They promised to keep in touch and to write—frequently! Considering the turmoil which their future lives were to be embroiled in, the two remained remarkably true to their childhood promises.

*****

The wedding, Caterina thought, was certainly not as impressive, nor as much fun, as the betrothal celebration had been, without the groom-to-be, of course, four years ago. And then, the thought of the mystery of an unavoidable wedding night had loomed, getting bigger and bigger with each day, which brought her closer and closer to the day. Unfortunately it did not help whatsoever that her father, being surprisingly considerate and understanding, suggested that she spend more time with the Duchess Bona, his wife. In many ways, Caterina felt very close to the older lady. When a young child, she took charge of her life and education and that of her siblings. Bona was immensely well read, well informed about the leading intellectual thoughts blowing like strong breezes through the land. She was a crafty stateswoman who had a hand in ruling Milano and was also one of the few who could actually control her husband, Galeazzo. In some ways, she was also an old-fashioned stogy lady, and her summary to her fourteen-year-old adopted daughter was to "close your eyes and lie there quietly while you say a prayer" and to "obey your husband in everything he demands, and think of your future children." Not a great help there indeed to an uneasy youngster.

Finally she was sent to stay at the home of her mother, Lucrezia. Mother and daughter had been always close, and Caterina's stay at the ducal palace did not interrupt that closeness. She quickly adapted herself to the Landrini household, even so far as to become friendly with her mother's husband, Gian Piero. She never could change her opinion, though, that he accommodated her presence as a courtesy to her father. Ever did Gian Piero strive to be a good friend with Duke Galeazzo.

The months spent at the Landrini household helped to stabilize Caterina and the emotional roller coaster she had been on. Lucrezia, a famous ethereal blond beauty, was not quite as ethereal in matters of the bed. She was an outspokenly bawdy lady, albeit she seemed to always know and never transgressed the limits between that and coarseness. In that regard, Caterina became almost a mirror image of her mother, with the addition of political savvy. By the time she was to marry, she had become her own person and a personality not to be trifled with.

Caterina had met her betrothed, Girolamo, on several occasions but only briefly. Albeit twenty years her senior, one score and fourteen years to her fourteen, he was a handsome, youthful, tall, well-muscled condottiere, the captain general of the church under his uncle's pontificate. Like most of his contemporary nobles, he also had a vicious streak, sometimes difficult to hide. When Caterina finally arrived in Rome for the marriage, he was charmed by her; she had grown and matured since he had last met her. Caterina, on the other hand, was much flattered by the courtly attention he accorded her. The marriage seemed to be off to a flying start!

The wedding night, as Girolamo had expected and Caterina had feared, proved to be awkward, mostly due to her efforts to prove to be a sophisticated siren. Her stumbling efforts to charm and arouse caused a chuckle in him. She took offense, he chuckled even more, and a dreadful vicious cycle was the result. In the end, Caterina's youthful sensitivity caused her to erupt in sobs, and his rarely noticed sensibility and a sense of male superiority—and perhaps a shot of innate good manners—kicked in to appease her. Then with one thing leading to another, before long, the appeasement led to hot kisses and more and more unexpected sensual caresses, and those to the removal, gently but unequivocally, of the bride's night rail. After that, the continued caresses did their magic, and except for Caterina's initial pain and discomfort, the act was accomplished in a most satisfying manner. Indeed, the groom was able to boast the next morning, when the bedding sheets were collected as proof of the bride's innocence, that he had given his bride proof of his passion for her three more times during the night.

Caterina and Rome were made for each other. She thrived in its air of power and intrigue. Soaked up its cultural fever, love of innovative ideas, and drive to effect renewal. Fortunately her uncle-by-marriage, His Holiness, was an eager scholar of the relatively new humanist movement. Caterina was as happy as a lark when she was allowed short periods of time to spend with him, helping to sort and catalogue the large number of books in his private possession, which the pope wished to donate in order to enlarge the disused and aging Vatican Library. While sorting dusty volumes, they conversed companionably on any and all the subjects which His Holiness assumed were close to a new wife's heart. In the process, he discovered, much to his surprise, that this young bride's vision and interests were vastly broader than what he had expected.

On rare occasions, His Holiness would also mention a desire to increase the number of participants to the chapel choir, to bring in works of such renowned newer composers as the masters Gaspar van Weerbeke and de Orto from the Low Counties. Caterina was enchanted. Finally! She no longer only learned of these master composers, she no longer listened to lectures on magically electrifying books but was allowed to hold them in her hand, turn their pages, and, after a kind permission from her uncle, to read them cover to cover!

Considering Sixtus's multitude of duties and obligations, Caterina was only too happy to volunteer her services to become a go-between the two composers and the Vatican, hesitantly at first, but with great enthusiasm and conviction of her abilities. Much to her amazement, her uncle took advantage of her offer, and she was allowed to handle this, the first of many diplomatic successes. Full of self-confidence now that she was a married matron, wife to a most important personage, she felt that there was no limit to the things she could tackle. After a brief and triumphal visit to Imola, the lordship of which was His Holiness's wedding present to Girolamo, she and her husband settled in into existence in Rome.

It was indeed a heady time for her! Her marriage had reached a state of cordiality; both partners enjoyed each other's company and attentions. Caterina, never a shy person, enthusiastically embraced the pleasures of sex which her husband introduced her to. Her adventuresome nature flattered Girolamo's vanity—was there a man not flattered by the task of teaching his young wife the pleasures of the shared bed? In addition, she immediately fell in love with Rome and almost immediately became popular among the Roman population.

In short order, Caterina decided to offer the Vatican her connections to the Milanese court. In slow stages, she became equally a significant influence in the Roman court. She often intermediated between the courts of the Vatican and that of Rome, or Milano, or even between the courts of Rome and Milano. Her voice was heard. It often was respected. This, after all, was the age of humanism, when the voices of gifted and powerful women were not only heard but actually respected. The d'Este sisters, Isabella and Beatrice, and her grandmother, Bianca Angelina Visconti, probably were, first and foremost, among them, and Caterina did not propose to be left behind in the dust!

These days, though, she mused sadly, communications between Rome and Milano no longer went to her father but to his second wife, Bona, the selfsame one who, once upon a time, had befriended her and brought her and her siblings to the ducal palace, eventually officially adopting them all.

When a lathered courier, wearing the Sforza tabard brought the news, she was sitting just where she was now, in this small room which she had furnished to be her study. As the soft breeze of a balmy winter day blew the silk window drapes into her face, she teared up again, just thinking of the shock the message caused. She had sat by the window, then open, just as now. Her husband was not home; he had been gone to make one of his periodic visits to Imola. He was to be gone no longer than a week, ten days at the most, but, oh, how she had needed him then!

Once again, as then, the breeze was playing with the curtains. Once again, she rose and tied back the errant curtains, then with a sigh, sat down again. Aye, Galeazzo, her father was gone. Slowly her tears began to course down her face and drop onto her lap. He had been murdered, murdered the day after Christmas last year, in the church of Santo Stefano. A church! Stabbed, his dead body dragged through the streets, and then the corpse beheaded and hung upside down. She felt her gorge rise again each time she thought of her father's death. She rose, poured herself a goblet of cool water from the silver carafe, then sat down and closed her eyes, taking great big gulps of air.

She put her hand on her belly; the baby, evidently not liking Mommy to be upset, kicked her vigorously, reminding her to behave. She was told that little boys were usually more vigorous than girls. She was convinced, though, for some reason, that the baby inside her was a girl and had already named her Bianca, for her much-beloved paternal grandmother and also for her Riario mother-in-law. As always, she made a face thinking of the appellation mother-in-law. She had never liked it. How much more kindhearted and endearing the French terms *belle-mère* or *beau-père* were! Beautiful mother and beautiful father—how sweet!

Ah, her father! She could not think of him as the world did, as a cruel despot, a lecherous womanizer, an occasional sadistic torturer. To her, he was always kind, well, maybe not loving but thoughtful of her welfare, of her interests, of her future.

When he had the time for it, he did like to do spur-of-the-moment things to please her. Her first memory of him was at a hunt, she probably was not much more than two or two and a half years old. Even then, she had already loved horses, horses and dogs, and tried to sneak into the stables as much as possible. That day, Galeazzo was riding out to a hunt and, seeing her in the stables, on a spur of the moment, asked her if she wanted to go along. Of course, she nodded vehemently, and with a permissive little paternal smile, Galeazzo had lifted her in front of him on his horse.

It was winter, snowy, cold, and windy, and her father had wrapped her into a big heavy fur to keep her warm. After a while, though, she started squirming, and eventually, putting her two pudgy little hands on his cheek, she whispered to him that she just had to get down, she had to go pee-pee. Then she looked into his eyes and shook her head, leaning her forehead to his. "Don't tell anyone! Yes?"

He nodded in all seriousness, commanding the group to stop but turn their horses in the opposite direction. The princess, he said, needed a little walk into the woods.

They did, and after he and she, together, managed to deal with the difficulties of various shifts, underskirts, and overskirts, he turned away. When she was done and dressed, she was so entranced with what she had produced, she caught his hand and pulled him to the scene of her product. Supposedly, according to her father, who had never tired to tell the story, much to her eternal embarrassment, she then pointed with pride and said to him, "Look, look, Papá! I painted the snow lellow—with my pee-pee." That, after his explosive laughter, she supposed was the last time she talked about colors until she learned to pronounce them correctly.

Such a small event, she thought, wiping her eyes and blowing her nose, yet so warm and loving a memory! How was this man the same one of whom they were telling stories of unspeakable cruelty? Is that what was, perhaps, her heritage too? Good god, she was impetuous, quick to anger, but this? This was totally frightening! May God keep her in his hands and prevent—oh, prevent such unthinkable behavior!

That day of retrospection and sorrowful mourning was not to end, however, with the same. Shortly before sundown, a messenger arrived from the Vatican, dressed in the papal colors. He brought a handwritten request from His Holiness, for his niece to be present at the newly established library of the pope. Unexpectedly three gentlemen had arrived in Rome and had requested audience from His Holiness. When Caterina read the names, she almost fell off her chair: Marsilio Ficino and his two students, Angelo Poliziano and Giovanni Pico della Mirandola. Together these three were the leaders of the humanist movement, which was gaining more and more acceptance, especially in Italy, but also everywhere else in Europe.

After that summon—invitation, really—she was not surprised at all that she tossed and turned most of the night. Girolamo finally got up from their bed in the middle of the night, shaking his head with a small smile.

"Wife, I understand when you suffer from sleeplessness because of our child doing somersaults inside you. But your tossing and turning is making me seasick, woman! It is indeed a sad day when the prospect of meeting some dusty stodgy old men will make you chase your handsome and loving husband out of our bed!"

With that comment, he swiped away his covers and pillows, bent to kiss his wife's cheek, and wandered out the door in search for one of the guest bedrooms where he could bunk down.

The next day, Caterina always thought, was one of those days, not ever to be forgotten, when intellectual, physical, and emotional pleasures meet in one glorious explosion. On arrival at her uncle's library, she had one more most delightful surprise. In addition to the three gentlemen announced to her before, there was a fourth one, introduced to her as Master Domenico Ghirlandaio. He turned out to be an exceedingly handsome tall young man with seductively glowing dark eyes and matching dark hair flowing in shining waves down to his shoulders, a half smile of mystery to complete his seductiveness. Of course, she had heard of Master Ghirlandaio, of his great talent, of his large, busy, and influential workshop which had taught so many of the greats! After meeting the man, who was probably younger than her husband, about one score and ten years perhaps, she told herself to remember to tell Girolamo that instead of being with "dusty stodgy old men," she enjoyed the company on four handsome men, only one of them older than he was! Hah!

It was an unforgettable day. Signore Ghirlandaio had actually surprised even their gracious host. He had just finished a commission to execute frescos of the life of Saint Fina in Firenze's church of San Gimignano and was—he expressed with such fervor—above all, desirous to travel to Rome and see its great marvels, even though his time here would be short. He had secured a commission for the Church of Ognissanti, and therefore soon needed to return to Firenze. But as he asserted, short was infinitely better than not at all, and his dear young friend Giovanni Pico encouraged him to seek an audience with His Holiness.

Never, he cried out, throwing his arms out dramatically, never would he have dreamt that His Holiness would honor him so greatly by inviting him to a private conversation, especially not, he shook his head while covering his eyes with his hands, and then extending them, palms up, since he earned his living with his hands, not his brain! Caterina watched him with ever-mounting fascination. Oh, this man could as well earn his living by enacting the famous ancient Greek dramas and comedies, which had become so fashionable during the last decades! Heavens!

After such impromptu theatrics, conversation settled down and became wide ranging, with someone throwing in the question as to what idea had led to greater and greater naturalism in art. Was it the concept of perspective, making distance, and thus the whole picture, more "real" in the two-dimensionality of paintings and frescos? Or was it the understanding that in the distance, objects become hazy? Both of these recently discovered concepts, when applied to canvas, wood tablet, or fresco lead to greater naturalism.

"Not necessarily," Master Ghirlandaio interjected, "because distance and thereby perspective could be realized in drawing or bas relief as well, and both techniques not relying on color! All these things we have seen all our lives, without really seeing. Our eyes," he explained earnestly, "have been accustomed to this and taken it for granted. But then for many generations, we became the servants of two-dimensional imagery. The imagery was jarring, yet the two-dimensionality of subjects and objects in all representation of real life were accepted as the only way to do things.

"Then suddenly, like a window's shutters thrown open"—once again the exuberant gesture to accompany his words—"we began to see—to really see. Thanks to Master Ghiberti and many others, we began to see differently! But then, to go beyond these great men, thanks to the remnants and excavations from ancient Greece and Rome! Then one thing led to another, lo, saintly individuals could be represented without a golden halo! It was, after all, not something that saints actually carried around with them! We began to represent what our eyes actually told us! A new naturalism, a new humanism had arrived! And it seems that the more we looked, the more we saw, the more we hungered to see. And we hungered to paint, to sculpt what we saw."

Master Ghirlandaio was aflame. His hands, his fingers danced, with each word he stressed, his hands chopped through the air, his eyes shone and sparkled, he was entranced with the words, with the ideas he expressed. He now stopped in front of Master Ficino and made an awkward little bow to him. Catching the Lady Riario's slightly amused expression, his face turned pink, and he quickly tucked his hands into opposite armpits.

"And then…" he talked in almost hushed tones, "then arrived the great men of thought, to bring their gifts to those who had been starving for reality and truth of thought, starving for an escape from—I beg Your Holiness to forgive me—the dictums of ancient church customs."

He cast an inquiring glance at Pope Sixtus, and when that one inclined his head with a kind half smile and a slightly raised brow, continued, or he would have, would Masters Ficino and Poliziano together not have interjected.

"Aye." Master Ficino nodded, beginning to walk back and forth in the room. "Like a fresh brook bubbling down from mountain passes, which becomes a rushing stream during the spring rains, these ancient and now new-again ideas erupted, began to flourish after a neglect of thousands of years." He made an eloquent and thoroughly

Italian gesture to accompany his oration and continued, with a little self-deprecating bow to His Holiness. "As the much overworked saying goes, truly, nothing is new under the sun! The great wisdom of the ancient Greeks should not be altered but admired and adopted into our current lives to enrich our thinking, just as our forebears, the ancient Romans did. We are learning to celebrate the reality of what we perceive, the God-given specialness, the human individuality in each of us!"

*****

His Holiness, Sixtus IV, was breaking his fast after his privately said sunrise mass. By this time, as usual, he was enormously hungry, more so, he always claimed than at any other time of the day. Reaching for some beautifully purple-glowing grapes to go with the soft sweet almond-studded yeast cakes he favored, he nodded to his secretary, the Dominican friar Brother Michel, who stood before him with a stack of assorted documents in hand. Sixtus nodded vigorously.

"Just so, just so! We no longer can delay to start the interior work for the Cappella Maggiore. We have been waiting for this rebuilding of the ruinous old structure for near ten years. It's done. Finally. Done! But we are not inclined to stop at a point which we consider to be the middle point of the labor."

Sixtus leaned forward, taking another yeast cake, slathered butter on it, then, with great attention not to let it drip, drizzled honey onto the butter. His face in profile showed the aristocratic long narrow nose, the softly curved chin, finely drawn lips, and slightly hooded but observant eyes.

"There is all the interior work to be completed, my son. Take note. We wish to assemble only the best of the fresco artists. Masters Botticelli, Ghirlandaio both reside in Firenze. We wish them here, first and foremost. We shall give you a list of the second-selection artists later. But Ghirlandaio and Botticelli for certes. We command their presence and at the soonest. Send messengers to them immediately, my son!"

Brother Michel bowed, then made some notes. Many were the orders from his master, and since he was relatively new to his position, he was anxious to keep track of all of them. Finally he turned the topmost page under and, looking up, read off the next page.

"Your Holiness told me to give you a reminder that you wished to contact Lord Riario with reference to the transfer of the lordship of the city of Forlì from the Ordelaffi family into his hands. If—"

He stopped as the pope raised his eyes and made a slight gesture for him to stop, and then rose from the table to slowly traipse to the window and look down into the gardens. He lifted the same hand higher and pinched the bridge of his nose while squeezing his eyes shut, as though to clear away all the debris to find the particular piece of information that was crucial to him. After a brief contemplation, he lifted his eyes and turned back to his secretary.

"Yes, yes, by all means, do as we have already discussed. Send a note to our nephew that I wish to discuss certain things with him. It is best if we keep those 'certain things' to ourselves, the two of us, my son. Outside these walls, other places have big ears."

Slowly His Holiness wound his way back to the table to continue with an earnest contemplation of the bowl of fruit. His hand hovered over the bowl with momentary indecision, then he selected a golden-rosy apricot. The nail of his thumb scored down the length of the fruit which fell apart to present the brown pit in the center, while the two halves of fruit, glistening with juice, were slowly, one by one, popped into the pope's mouth.

Brother Michel shifted his weight from one foot to the other. Ever since he had slipped and fallen on a patch of ice last winter, while crossing through the Alpine mountains from France to Rome, his back insisted on hurting when he walked or especially stood in one place for a longer time. He repressed a sigh, but evidently not totally. His Holiness's eyes, which could look so sleepy, so lazy, flew sharply to the friar's face. His mouth curved into a light smile.

"Ah, forgive us, my son. We have been woolgathering while you are getting more and more tired of standing…" His hand shot out in an expansive gesture, encompassing the whole large room. "Please, sit, sit. Truthfully if we wish to work together successfully, we need to pay attention to these little comforts." He pushed the bowl of fruit closer to Brother Michel. "Please, please, have some, they are ripe and quite good." He raised his so expressive Italianate hands. "No, no, no, don't be shy, my son, all of us are hungry or tired at times, no? Actually"—he looked down on his manicured hands crossed on top of the inlaid marble table—"actually we only have one more item to mention. And that is"—he smiled hesitantly—"that is to request that you, my son, remember to remind us, Friday next, to have a one-on-one conversation with Cardinal Della Rovere. And now you may leave us, my son."

Brother Michel, wrestling the documents down from his hands to under his arm, knelt and kissed the pontiff's ring. Without asking, he knew that when his master mentioned "one on one," he still meant for his secretary to be present as well, and to record the conversations and noteworthy observations.

He was almost at the door when His Holiness once more detained him.

"My son. We would like to see our niece, the Countess Riario. And the infant, the latest little addition to their family and mine. The little boy has been named Cesare, and we need to discuss the date and time for little Cesare's christening. We would like for the ceremony to be performed in the new Cappella Maggiore. Of course, while that holy place is very much incomplete, a work in progress as it were, we do wish for the *cappella* to be in use in the service of our Lord during the road to its completion. Arrange a visit from mother and child quickly."

*****

With a sigh of weariness and a groan of discontent, Lord Girolamo pushed the velvet covers away from his body and swung his long legs over the side of the bed to the floor. The darkened bedroom was inordinately warm and stiflingly saturated with the cloying smell—certainly not a scent—of some damn flower. Was it really a flower? Maybe cinnamon? Or cloves? A cheap smell. A nasty smell. An overpowering smell. Not like the gentle floral scent which his

Caterina—his Caterina. Was he crazy? He really, really did not want to be here. He was, he thought with irony, a fairly fastidious person at least. This—this woman, this, this—och, he did not even wish to dwell on the search for a proper word to describe her—came so highly recommended by some of his knowledgeable friends. Were they crazy? Or did they wish to get even with him for some particular reason, some particular slight or offense on his part? Or perhaps they were so unhappy under the sheets at home?

But he idiot! He was not or certainly should not be. He had a perfectly lovely young wife at home. One who had been educated in matters of sex and bed play by him and was not a shrinking shy little flower when confronted by her man's specific desires. One who did not mind another pregnancy and claimed that "she never felt better than when carrying" and sailed through birthing like others did through a bout of the sniffles. One who did not go into days of hysterics and tirades when he strayed from the marital bed but just shrugged her shoulders with a secret little smile like she knew—she knew—that he would return to her.

What in God's name did he do here in this slut's bedroom, paying for her service, when he could get vastly better at home? As soon as he got home, he would ask Caterina to stop nursing little Cesare, call the wet nurse, and have this whole church ordained pregnancy-delivery-nursing interdiction done with. Actually, he thought with a smile, she would probably be pleased, and knowing her, she would dance a little jig with her arms above her head and then throw herself at him because she missed having sex just as much as he did!

Truly not much to his surprise, his prediction proved true. Caterina had just returned home from some lecture on Greek philosophers at the Vatican Library, newly established by his uncle, the pontiff, with whom, he had to admit, she had a much more cordial relationship than he did. He was an impatient person, and his uncle's measured slow speech always irritated him. Caterina, he guessed, was either more patient or more calculating. At any rate, when he arrived home, she was in their bedroom, peeling off her riding gloves while her wardrobe mistress helped her to divest herself of the small jaunty riding hat. The riding hat was made of royal purple velvet, a gift from him to his wife, and had a most provocative purple ostrich feather, a single one, curving down to her shoulder and then farther down to the valley between her breasts, just barely visualized by the riding habit's neckline.

Mistress Angelina Maria Lazzari had been wardrobe mistress to her ladyship, the Countess Caterina Riario, since her arrival in Rome. She congratulated herself for understanding her mistress's taste, likes, and dislikes, albeit she was quite aware that she was far from understanding the lady herself. She shrugged and just told herself that there was probably not one person who understood her, and, that for a certainty, included her husband, Girolamo.

For one thing, she liked other children well enough but looked at her own with cool eyes and just made a face each time they misbehaved. Then there was her marriage. Husband and wife had a cordial relationship, without arguments, and with occasional tender moments and quite frequent passionate ones. Also Girolamo strayed. It did not seem to upset Caterina a whole lot. On the other hand, she had little interest in other men, although she could have had her pick. Her beauty and position, her connections and intellect all recommended her to men of her choice—she chose none, in contrast to what most of the other high-placed ladies in her position would have done. Without a doubt, husband and wife not only got along well but desired each other, a rarity among couples who were past the early years of their marriage.

She was passionate about learning, about reading, about learned encounters and intellectual exchanges. She loved beauty and surrounded herself with exquisite paintings, glass objects, statues of gold, silver, and bronze but was not at all upset to wear last year's clothes, "As long as they were not too outdated, soiled, or threadbare," she would say.

People complained that she was judgmental, critical, easy to anger, and fierce of temper, but to her, she was invariably kind and considerate. Even through her pregnancies, her temper did not change. Actually she always maintained that she never felt better than when pregnant, and her deliveries went so smoothly that she laughingly referred to them as "whelping." Och, she did have a very unsavory tongue, that one! Angelina Maria smiled slightly. Too bad, she thought sourly, that there wasn't anyone to wash her mouth out with soap. But then, she grew up at the court at Milano, and och, the wicked things she had heard about them, especially about her father, such a lecherous monster, he—'tis a true miracle that she grew up as well as she did, then.

Things actually, she supposed, were not much better here. The things which husband and wife discussed openly! The good Lord be thanked she was married herself, and to such a good man! Aye, indeed! For were she not, she would already have turned gray and dropped all her teeth from grinding them so much. Like even now, she wanted *so* very much to disappear into the sewing room but couldn't!

Girolamo, throwing himself into one of the two armchairs in their bedroom, petulantly watched his wife divest herself of most of the outfit she wore to the Vatican. When she was done, she turned to him.

"And how did your day proceed, husband? As pleasantly as did mine?"

Girolamo, brows bent inward, shook his head, his brown hair scattering about his ears.

"Not nearly, my love, not nearly. Not successful nor pleasant at all."

She looked puzzled.

"But how so, my dear? I thought the woman you visited came recommended from some of the highest places. Were they wrong or were you too demanding? Or was it just an off day altogether?"

Girolamo laughed, stretched himself out of the chair, and caught her hand. He pulled her over to the huge bed, its drapes tied back for the daytime. They both sat, eyes each on the other.

"How in the name of all that is holy do you know how my day went, you little minx? I see no one following me. I see no one reading my messages."

"Ah, husband, I have my methods. Nothing as obvious as you think. But think on it, do you ever see me act on such information? They serve only to order my days, love."

Girolamo bent to kiss his wife's forehead, then her cheeks, and finally feathered a kiss upon her mouth, then down her neck, to that luscious little ridge of her delicate collarbone. His fingers moved in little circles upon the side of her neck under her ears.

"It is obvious, my love, isn't it, that success has a pattern. There is also a reason for my lack of success today. You, I believe, my dear, would feel just as much bereft of pleasure as I was, would you go out to search for it! It is to your eternal credit, wife, that you don't and perhaps because what I can—could—provide is so much more greatly desirable. Conversely what you, love, would provide would be equally so much more desirable for me."

He got up and did a short tour of the room, then came back to the bed. He looked down at her, not knowing if he should yell at her or kiss her senseless.

"Get that damned wet nurse, wife! Today!"

Caterina threw her head back and laughed so loud that finally she fell back onto the bed, with only her legs and her voluminous skirts dangling. Rolling her head against the pillow, she turned her eyes to face Girolamo, standing in front of her, almost between her legs, his obvious erection pushing against the fashionable tight hose he wore.

"Ah," she said, still smiling, "then there is no sweetness in the devout pain of pleasure denied, all in the name of our holy church?" She burst out in another bout of laughter as she looked at him.

"Angelina, Angelina," she yelled, rolling her body side to side now with laughter, "do come quickly to help me be divested of all this clothing. His Excellency is in great pain!"

"There now, there now, my lady, all right already! Be patient just a little, I pray. You have so many layers on to be fashionable, it will take a little—" And she tried to tug at the ties on the side and, once loosened, turned with haste to the ties which attached the puffed sleeves to the overdress. Finally the one sleeve, then the other, could be slipped down her arms, revealing the embroidered kirtle underneath the velvet overdress.

By then Girolamo was getting truly impatient and finally strode over to Angelina Maria and pushed her hands away from her efforts.

"Begone, and quickly, woman! I know the ins and outs of your lady's finery much better than you do—best you start practicing that what you do here!"

With that, he pulled out the small ornamental dirk he wore at his sword belt, and his brow furrowed with the effort, started to slice open the little ties holding Caterina's kirtle.

Angelina Maria fluttered about for a short while but then, realizing that her presence had become not just superfluous but actually irritating and undesired, bent to gather scattered pieces of clothing from the carpet. With a stack in her arms, she walked to the door leading into the wardrobe, her face stormy, casting her eyes to the heavens. At the door, she turned back, but by then things had progressed with surprising rapidity to a point where she did not want to even take a peek, so she withdrew, crossing herself several times before closing the door on the eager couple and their godless behavior.

*****

Three years to the day after little Cesare's christening, performed in a "family" ceremony as His Holiness demanded, a courier on a lathered horse rode down the narrow rutted cobbled street from the Vatican to the Campo de Fiori and stopped in front of the Orsini Palace, the home of Girolamo Riario and his family. The courier was lucky, the family was in, having just returned from a prayer of the rosary with Brother Rabanus, their confessor, in their chapel, a prayer for the recovery of the Pontiff. His Holiness, Sixtus IV, was ill. Four days past, he fell ill and took to his bed, then yesterday he seemed to better, only to grow weaker again on this day. But now, the courier's sweaty face contorted, and his shoulders began to shake as he pulled his palm in front of his eyes. Despite his valiant efforts, he began to sob so that he could barely speak.

Speech was unnecessary; both Girolamo and Caterina could hear the tolling of the great bell of what Sixtus IV liked to call "our tired old Basilica of St. Peter's." He had so much hoped and wished for tearing down the over-twelve-centuries-old structure in favor of building a new basilica, which would have been the glorious magnum opus of his life; and now, in no time at all, all the innumerable bells of Rome's churches began to toll, some faster, some slower, some higher-sounding, some lower, in an ultimately magnificent melding of sound which rent the air to make people tremble with fear for their own fleeting mortality.

The pope, His Holiness Sixtus IV, was dead.

Despite both Girolamo and Caterina's attachment to their uncle and their genuine sense of loss and grief, both of them were realists enough to know that within one blink of the eye, the political winds had changed. Their political fortunes would undoubtedly change with those changing winds. Words were unnecessary between them. Their eyes slid toward each other; in matters of self-preservation more than in any other area, more even than their very acute sexual appetites, their thoughts ran in parallel tracks.

Caterina summoned the household staff and gathered her children. She ordered clothing, necessary household items, and valuables to be packed into large bags and sacks, their tops to be stuffed with her and her children's so innocuous-looking underclothes and sleeping shifts, or with the stuffed dolls of which her daughter, Bianca, had a staggering collection, and her two little boys' rag-stuffed and wood-carved toys. She also ordered the horses to be saddled and brought out from the stables to be ready to move at any time. Her children were too small to ride, and so the household retainers were to lift them into the saddle in front of them.

Caterina would have done the same, but she was heavy with her most recent pregnancy, which was in its seventh month. Angelina Maria was stridently adamant about not letting her mistress ride a horse, who was equally adamant to ride. Of course, Caterina won the argument. She always did, didn't she? She was directing all her efforts to the preservation of her family and of her own power of influence. She knew enough not to have to worry about Girolamo being less than adequate to the demands of self-preservation. He was a condottiere, for god's sake, a commander of armies, let him go out there and command! Her efforts were entirely focused upon getting herself and her household—her children and retainers—from the Palazzo

Orsini in Campo de Fiori to the Castel Sant'Angelo on the banks of the Tiber River.

Castel Sant'Angelo would be key to keeping an eye on goings-on at the Vatican, and that was now becoming imperative because cardinals from all corners of the Christian world would be converging for a conclave to elect the next pope. Who, in turns, was one of the most important, nay, the most important figure in the world of power politics, both figuratively and geographically. The pope ruled over all Catholics, but he also ruled over the Vatican States, a strip of land which literally bisected the boot of Italy. No commerce, no goods or armies, not one single artist, painter, sculptor, poet, scientist, no soldier, mercenary or other, not even a single pin could move from the north to the south or back but with His Holiness's knowledge and permission. And Caterina, from her position at Castel Sant'Angelo, appointed herself to be the one to oversee the process of who that next pope would be.

The next days, weeks, ultimately a whole month, turned out to be hellish. She walked the walkways on top of the ramparts, irritated with everything, feeling unwieldy and heavy with her pregnancy and cross with the world. She sent a messenger to Girolamo, who was negotiating with the Sacred College of Cardinals, those of the members, at least, who, so far, had arrived. The cardinals refused to go even near the Vatican, where they felt to be under Caterina's eye and within sight of her guns. Eventually Girolamo sent the messenger back, informing her that the Sacred College requested his withdrawal from Rome, sweetening the request with a bagful of ducats, also giving him the military post of captain general of the church and promising to confirm him in the lordships of both Imola and Forlì. In all of that, the beast, Caterina thought moodily, forgot to even ask her about her state of health. Hah!

Not to be outdone, she dispatched a blistering letter to him, addressing it to "oh, dearest husband of mine" and continuing with, "perchance you forgot to embellish your last message with such trivial niceties as, 'I pray you fare well, wife,' and even 'hope our children are in good health,' howbeit at the end, a little 'affectionately, your husband' would have gone a long way." The ensuing tug-of-war was the first, but certainly not the last, falling out between the spouses.

Finally—this time, and this time only, she assured her husband—Caterina consented and moved herself and her family out of Castel Sant'Angelo. She traveled to Forlì with her whole brood, this time husband included, with outwardly no ill feelings toward each other. After all, both husband and wife were pragmatists. At Forlì, shortly after her arrival, Caterina took to her birthing bed and gave birth to her son Giovanni Livio. As ever before, it was an easy and eventless birth. As she looked down drowsily upon the round little downy head of her newest son, she had her first genuine smile in a long, long time. Surely he should deserve the appellation "much traveled" during the last months of living in her mother's womb and now into the outside world!

Caterina tried her level best to settle in, but after the excitingly heady cultural atmosphere of Rome, it was a stretch, levelheaded as always, striving to make do with what life would offer her at the moment, a trait which she probably learned as a very young child. She looked around her and found nature. Forlì may not be able to offer exhibits of the recently acquired classical Greek statues brought in from the now-dissolved Byzantine Empire. It could not offer entrancing meetings with the greatest minds in philosophy and alchemy to discuss the ancient philosophies of Greece or the advances in astronomy from Al-Andalus. But Forlì did have something else—the loveliest landscape she could order up. Toward the west, softly rolling hills rose up into a mountain range, stretching from north to south. Like a curtain, they shut off from view the world beyond, toward the left to her beloved Rome and to her right toward Milano. The countryside offered one other thing she dearly loved and had almost totally neglected during her years in Rome. Hunting. Aye, hunting. Lots of it.

She remembered how she once had loved hunting. Her father, Galeazzo, first introduced her to it, and loving sports and exercise as she did, she was happy to be reminded of this. She pulled a face. Honestly it was rather easy to keep him as he lived in her memory, when one saw that selfsame father no more than five to six times a year. Each time, though, she recalled those lovely events of riding out with him. Be he as much an ogre as he was, to her he was ever a kindly loving father. And so she once again rode to the hunt. Girolamo joined her but rather haphazardly, claiming a surfeit of work. She hardly minded. By nature independent, she felt that she did well enough alone in the hunt. Of course, "alone" was a figure of speech, she was always accompanied by her bodyguards, as well as her ladies, and, when riding out, by some stable hands as well.

Not only did she love the hunt, she loved horses. Really loved them. On horseback, she could think uninterruptedly because etiquette demanded that her retinue keep in back of her. Girolamo, she mused, was beginning to be such an absentee father, just as her father once was! Also more and more an absentee husband. Perhaps? Perhaps because he chose to, perhaps because he really was so busy. One thing he insisted upon, though, whenever he could not join her, was that a detachment of soldiers accompany her and any guests she had with her. When she looked at him, her eyebrows raised in question; he shook his head. "Times are dangerous, my love, and the danger can lurk at any corner or behind any tree." As though she didn't know! But he disarmed her by taking her hand, turning it over to kiss the tender inside of her wrist, and then running the tip of his tongue over it.

She warmed immediately and shook her head. *Oh, that devil! How well he knows my fallibilities!* she thought.

Indeed, he did, for he smiled at her like a wolf looking at an easy meal. She was going to be an easy meal, she thought with a little sigh, *When I return home after the hunt and divest myself of all this... these layers of materials dictated by stupid fashion.* She knew how almost effortlessly easy it was for Girolamo to get her into the mood. She withdrew her arm from his captivity and rose on tiptoes to kiss his cheek.

"Tonight," she whispered into his ear.

The single predictable outcome to the short-lived but equally predictably passionate second—or was it now a third—honeymoon that followed their arrival at Forlì was the birth of a fourth little boy, Galeazzo Maria, born the winter of 1485. Since sufficient length of time had elapsed between her father, Galeazzo's, murder and this little boy's birth, she felt safe enough to name him after her father. Girolamo, as always, greatly pleased with the news of having sired another son, did not mind, perhaps he did not even notice. He liked children at fits and spurts and was a believer that children should be seen rarely and heard even more rarely.

Is this happening again? Angelina Maria wondered. No sooner than did her lady relinquish suckling the babe and regain her slim figure, then *wham!* She became pregnant—again! And here she was, so proud of her lady's slim girlish figure, a bragging point when discussing their mistresses with the other ladies' maids from the other noble houses. She was indeed the envy of them all, for her lady was lovelier and more graceful than the whole lot of the others put together! In her mind, somewhat disdainfully, she called the Forlì ladies provincial clodhoppers.

Working on dressing her lady to ride out to the hunt, she shook her head without any comment. She, by now, had learned that comments only lead to more comments and, eventually, to temper tantrums, especially when her countess knew that she was right. Caterina hated to be in the wrong in any argument, regardless who the argument was with. Angelina Maria did not need her lady screaming at her, not just at a very loud voice but also with a very vulgar vocabulary.

She—her lady that is—was pacing back and forth in the couple's spacious bedroom, her silk skirts swishing, moving her fan furiously, and scattering imprecations upon her husband and herself, like salt on stew.

"Stupid, stupid, stupid!" she raged. I don't have time for another pregnancy. Damn! It will slow me down for months and months. And now, when I really need to..." She took another breath for a continuation of the tirade, and Angelina Maria saw her opportunity.

"Forgive me for saying so, my lady." That, of anything she had ever uttered, was the most ridiculous one! She could only get away with it because she knew that Caterina paid scant attention to what she said but also because, angry or not, her lady was always honest with herself. With a scrunch of her brows, Caterina turned to her and demanded with a curt tongue, eyes snapping with anger.

"What now?"

"My lady, you should long ago have learned to put a gold ducat between your knees when in bed with your husband!"

Caterina ceased her angry pacing, stopped, and looked at Angelina Maria, her mouth falling open. Her gaze was still angry and her eyes snapping as she stared and stared again. But then her eyes softened, and the corners of her mouth began to twitch. Slowly her gaze transformed into laughter, and she threw her head back to burst out in raucous laughter. The laugher floated in the air up to the ornate ceiling and seemed never-ending, but in time, she quieted, moved her fan at a more languorous pace, and sat down upon the armchair placed by her inlaid dressing table. Hesitantly at first, slowly shaking her head, she began to play with the jewel-encrusted combs lined up one by one on top of the dresser, laid there to be placed into her hair. Absentmindedly she shuffled the combs from right to left and left to right. She shook her head and her fingers at Angelina Maria.

"Maria, Maria, you devious person you! For shame! To think such things! And then a whole ducat? Can you not find something cheaper to put there to serve the same purpose, eh? A whole ducat, my word!" And she once again collapsed in giggles. A sudden thought popped into her head, she stopped rearranging her combs and slanted her eyes to Maria.

"God Almighty, how many will this one make, Maria?"

Angelina Maria was quite unfazed by the question. Countless were the times she had counted up the children.

"One girl, my lady, and then nothing but boys, boys, boys. No wonder His Grace, your husband, is never upset by another pregnancy. Would he not be surprised if a little girl popped out, eh? But nay, we have four boys so far, and maybe more to come." And as an afterthought, she added, "Does Your Grace know if there are twins running anywhere in your or His Grace's family?" And she started laughing at the horrified look her lady gave her.

"Oh, God Almighty, no-no-no, that could not be possible!" Caterina groaned.

Eventually, though, the dust settled, and life proceeded as before, bringing better days and not-so-good ones.

In slow stages, problems popped up, like unwanted mushrooms, during this, what should have been the couple's, "peacefully settled years." It was well known that the new pope, Innocent VIII, a member of the Cybo family, was no friend of the Riarios. Right after Girolamo withdrew from Rome to Forlì, and as the saying goes, "the coast was clear," the new pope, albeit reasserting Girolamo in his title, refused to pay him. To Girolamo's credit, though financially strapped, he denied to collect taxes from the population of Forlì. Duke Ludovico Sforza, Caterina's uncle, had minded the shop at Forlì for the young Riarios before their arrival from Rome. Under his management, the local population quickly learned that he was a great deal more adept at what needed to be done than Girolamo. Sadly the sand in the clock was fast running down now to more and more loss of popularity, especially for Girolamo. Caterina's saving grace were her beauty and, when needed, her graciousness, both together masking her deeply inherent ruthlessness.

The outside problems continued to multiply. Girolamo, finally running out of money, needed to institute taxation. This was understood and accepted. But everyone was unhappy with the rate of taxation; everyone accused each of the other classes of the citizenry of collusion with Lord Riario. Conspiracies, one more fanciful than the other, reared their ugly heads, all having one single thing in common—the ever-increasing hatred of Girolamo. Within two years after the Riarios' arrival, emotions peaked to the heights of mountains. Elevated emotions bred dark plans, with more and more enemies willing to concoct ever darker ones. In April of the year of the Lord, 1488, barely more than six months after the birth of the fifth little boy to the Riario family, named Francesco but later called Sforzino, or little Sforza, things came to a head.

Girolamo was assassinated and his body cut to pieces. The mob entered the palace and imprisoned Caterina and her children.

Caterina was perhaps more incensed than distraught. After all, she had grown up in an age, a country, a stratum of society where assassinations abounded. Her father had been a victim of assassins. The brother of the great Lorenzo de Medici, ruler of Firenze as well. And now, regrettably, so was her husband.

She found out in short order that Ravaldino, the fortress sitting almost atop the town of Forlì, through its castellan, Sir Tommaso Feo, had refused to surrender to those who held her and her children. Without hesitation, she offered herself to go there, to persuade Sir Feo to surrender the *castello*. She would, she pointed out, do this out of a spirit of cooperation. She was shattered by the loss of her husband, and while mourning, she wanted to offer her help. She would, she also pointed out, go alone, leaving her children and retainers with her captors as hostages.

This she did, with the approval of the Orsi family, the leaders of those who had murdered Girolamo. No sooner did her riding boots alight upon the cobbles of the massive courtyard of Ravaldino, when she had all the gates locked, the portcullis lowered, and, upon meeting Sir Feo, had him accompany her to the battlements. Once installed there, she jeered down to her adversaries and unleashed a long-enough string of curses to have merited a place in history. When she was reminded that her children were hostages, she shrugged, pointing out that she already carried the next one. With her hand directed to her nether area, she yelled, "Should they die, here is my equipment to produce more!"

She may have quite shocked the onlookers but nevertheless achieved her purpose. After her outburst, nobody had dared to lay a hand on any of the five little ones.

God help her, a decade of living in the shadow of the Vatican had made her into an extraordinarily foul-mouthed in-your-face bully! Or was it part of her genes, an inheritance from her Milanese Sforza blood?

Caterina, smiling behind her hand over the success of her scheme, arranged almost immediately to become regent for her oldest son, Ottaviano. She returned to Forlì where, in the name of her son, she commenced to create a virtual vendetta to avenge her husband. No one even remotely associated with the assassination was spared. Families, including wives and children, were imprisoned, their homes razed, their properties confiscated. Following the nightmare time for her, she created what was truly a nightmare time for all.

After her anger had abated, Caterina, in all honesty and seriousness, strove to do good by her people. She voiced her dictum that the assassination was the product of a small group lead by the Orsi family. Whether true or not, it would calm and reassure the population that she bore no ill will toward the population of Forlì.

Caterina turned out to be a hands-on ruler, striving to achieve control over spending, friendly relationship with neighboring city-states, overseeing the training of Forlì's army, and sorting through the convoluted and antiquated system of taxation. Out of her own pocket, she bought several Greek marble statues from the Vatican, knowing that they were in storage and mostly in the way, and gifted them to Forlì. In return, unfortunately with little success, she expected some civic pride and gratitude for her gifts, peace in her little realm, and just maybe, a little bit of thanks.

About this same time, like a thunderclap striking her, something unexpected happened to the Lady of Forlì. She fell passionately in love—or lust? She could never really tell. The subject of her passion was a young stable groom who happened to be the younger brother of Tommaso Feo, her loyal castellan of Ravaldino. Giacomo, handsome and passionate, excited Caterina's passion and stole her heart in short order. Since all sorts of gossip swirled about with regard to a next husband for the young widow Riario, the lovers decided to marry in secret. Tommaso stood in as witness for his brother and Angelina Maria for her mistress. Once again, the sun shone down upon Caterina, even if only temporarily.

*****

Madeline was literally skipping down the circular stairway on her way from their bedroom to her husband's solar. She was late! Overslept! And if there was one thing—well, one of a long list of things—that Jean-Luc hated, it was when she was late for breakfast. Once upon a time, he had preferred to take his meals alone, and she remembered having flaming arguments with him about just that. About allowing her to share his meals. It broke her heart when she thought how once he had been so alone, surrounded by an angry world breaking against his hilltop aerie, like angry waves against rocks, and also so painfully alone in his heart.

Aye, the man she had met on arrival at Montchateau thirteen years ago, in such a horrible state in every way, was so tragically different from her husband now.

Lord, but it had been an enormously difficult uncomfortable travel! Obviously she could not go unaccompanied. Since her father had been unable to secure permission from King Louis, ultimately her half brother Etienne, with endless grumbling, had been designated to do the honors. Nominally he was in command of a detachment of French soldiers, commanded, in fact, by a very handsome and obliging young officer, Capitaine de Sévrellac, who formed a sharp contrast to her sullen scowling brother.

Of course, it was necessary that an elderly lady acting as chaperone also accompany her. After some searching and arranging, one of her numerous aunts on her father's side had been recruited. Her father had seven sisters, all of whom collectively adored and spoiled their only baby brother. Her aunts Cécile and Héloïse were available. Widowed, wealthy, and eager to embark on something adventurous, they agreed, but only if they could both go.

Finally things got sorted. Escorted by the detachment of soldiers, endless supply wagons, not only for the travelers but also for the coachmen, footmen, valets, ladies' maids, Madeline had no idea that things would get this complicated! Then on course, in addition to the three ladies, there needed to be coach for their attendants. And then there was Etienne, who elected to ride in a coach or, at least, to alternate between riding horseback and being in the coach, but not—definitely not—with the ladies. Good Lord! Finally the whole caravan left Milano.

In her memories, the trip was exceedingly tiring and stressful, not only physically but, most especially, emotionally. She did not think that she had been close to her father, but their farewell was still wrenching, both to him and to Caterina as well. The two aunts alternated between complaints, emotional outbursts, hysterical fear once the caravan began to tread its way through the mountains, then again gently snoring, with their head lolling to the rhythm of the coach.

Etienne unfortunately did not ever deviate from his sullenness, making her amply aware that this whole thing was her fault. He did not ever really specify what exactly he meant by "all this."

Finally, finally! They arrived. At that point, Madeline was endlessly thankful for that, no matter what awaited her.

What awaited her was a man leaning on two crutches, and assisted by a servant, who slowly treaded his way down the steps of the castle. One side of his face was heavily marred by newly healing scars, which pulled his one eye, eyebrow, and mouth to the side in a disturbing grimace. On the same side of his body, his hand was also disfigured, the fingers, still red with new skin, curling inward to the palm of his hand.

She remembered climbing out of the coach and standing there, looking at him, looking endlessly, her heart thundering in her chest. All the introductions, the polite greetings, the equally polite conversations in a drawing room all the following days, became a blur in her mind. What had slowly evolved over quiet conversations devoid of emotions or grand gestures, when she was finally allowed to be with him one on one, was that she discovered, under all the visible destruction, a soft-spoken man, barely holding on to his humanity and to thoughts beyond his desperation. She was a thirteen-year-old girl going on young woman, he an adult who had lost two wives to childbirth, in each case the marriage not lasting longer than a year. Madeline discovered that she felt a warmth, a closeness to this man she had never felt before to anyone.

She didn't know if this was love, certainly not passion, but the thought of leaving this man was worse than any farewells she survived before. Without logic, without passion, she knew, she knew that this was where she wanted to be, this was there she belonged. And so it was decided that under the watchful eyes of the two aunts, she would remain, remain until the officially recognized marriageable age of fourteen years. At that time, considered to be an adult, her betrothed and she would decide if they wished to spend the rest of their lives together.

She learned much during that one year. She learned how Jean-Luc was neglected by his attendants and neglected himself as well.

She learned that the new pink skin and damaged tissue underneath pained him enormously but that the pain was caused by the contraction of the burned tissues. She started a series of endless gentle massages with warm oils, first his hands only, his fingers all the way to the tips, then the arms. In slow stages, she managed to decrease his pain and increase the movements of the arms, legs. She started on his face and managed to restore most of the softness, suppleness there. Oh, it was an endless battle with his pain, his ill-tempered desire to just give in, give up. In the end, when he gently pulled her into his arms, which he could move as well now as he once did, to thank her, oh, the thought of giving her up was a pain worse than all the other pains he had suffered! But he needed to be sensible and responsible for this girl child who should not hide herself, her beauty, her charm, with such an old bear of a man in the backwoods of—

In the end, she won. And she felt that she was entitled to consider him hers, from his newly grown toenails and fingernails to his regrown hair, as dark as the shell of a chestnut. She remained, not inclined to give up what was already hers.

Madeline had smiled to herself. It was a relaxed, happy, but also secretive smile, as though she held some wonderful secret clutched to her heart. Aye, somehow by the time this one more year was up, there was no question in her heart but that this was what she wanted, that this was the man she loved, that this was the place she wanted to be more than anywhere else. Jean-Luc, at first, angrily fought her decision, called it and her irresponsible, a romantic, a child, until she marched over to him and, rising on her tiptoes, curled her hand around the back of his neck to pull the big man down to her, and, without hesitation, kissed him on his lips. As far as she was concerned, that was that, and Jean-Luc's arguments and contradictions were blown away with the breeze blowing in from the westerly sea.

And so she and Aunts Cécile and Héloïse, who had settled in seemingly for the duration, embarked on planning a wedding. Madeline was adamant that she did not want to wait beyond her fourteenth birthday. According to church doctrine, that was the permissible minimal age for marriage or, at least, for the consummation of a marriage. For some mysterious reason, mysterious even to herself, starting from the day that they met, she was not in the least repulsed by her husband. She somehow had the ability to look beyond the still sadly marred hand, neck and face, feeling neither pity nor some kind of a false kindness toward him. Somehow she saw him as he once must have been, and she had to agree with herself that however that happened, it was truly a gift of God.

She also knew, knew for certain, that Jean-Luc loved her without wishing to voice his feelings. She felt that his reluctance was due partly to not wanting to influence her decision, not to put her under any obligation, and also to shield himself from bitter disappointment. Surprising even herself, she found that these two years have not only matured her but also armed her to push when needed and to do battle when that was called for. The starry-eyed young girl of the Milano days was gone for good.

And as far as Jean-Luc was concerned, her devoted care for his afflictions, the endless massages and exercises she forced upon him, over the course of time, performed their own miracle. By the time they stood in front of the priest, she was a mature young woman, and he was a battle-scarred, but despite the scars, a handsome strong man.

They were made for each other.

*****

The Marquise of Landes rounded the corner after stepping off the last rung of the stairs and rushed to her solar, which she had furnished in obedience to the latest fashion as a sitting room, also called a dayroom. The door was ajar, and there was an inviting fire crackling in the fireplace. She loved this particular fireplace, the mantel elegantly embellished with the gray-streaked pink marble from the mountains around Montchateau. Jean-Luc rose and pulled out a chair for her, but before allowing her to sit, he pulled her to himself and kissed her.

"I missed our morning get-together, dearest, alas, you were burrowed so deeply in the pillows that I did not have the heart to wake you." He smiled. Their "mornings together" was usually a euphemism for an early morning session of loving before the couple actually faced the day.

Madeline gave him her sweetest smile and, rising on her tiptoes, kissed her giant of a husband's cheek. "My dearest, there should be no worry in your heart on that account. I believe I will feel the need for a restorative nap right after dinner, and you will be able to find me in our bedroom!" To which Jean-Luc threw back his leonine head and let loose a bark of a laughter.

She vividly remembered their wedding—how long? Oh, God, not true, was it more than ten years ago? It was a quiet affair, by mutual decision of bride and groom. Her father managed to arrive despite a snowstorm. Etienne, who had left shortly after her decision to stay for the required year prior to church permission for a physical marriage, did not come back; not something that surprised her. Jean-Luc had one disabled aunt who was pushed by her handyman in a most peculiar and amusing-looking chair, or rather a cart, with two large wheels attached. The wheels, just like in a barrow, were in the front, except much larger than the wheels of a barrow. The "cab" of this contraption had an awning to shade against rain, or bright sun, and a deep and comfortably cushioned seat. Behind the seat were two handles, connected by a crossbar, which could be let down to the ground when the chair was not pushed and propelled ahead. Aunt Élise, whom she liked immediately, was thus transported in comfort and safety from place to place.

Ah, she thought with sadness, Aunt Élise died quietly in her sleep just a few months ago.

After their wedding, there was a quiet celebratory dinner. She remembered little of it; her stomach was churning with apprehension of the coming wedding night. She did not need have apprehension, she thought now. Her husband's accident and the ensuing pain and suffering, both in body and soul, had burned away his arrogance, his impatience, his thoughtlessness, and negligence toward others. What had been left was a man with infinite patience, an infinite sense of gratitude to God, to life, and, most of all, to his young wife, and an infinite capacity to love her with all the tenderness and passion of his wounded soul. No one could have been more patient, gentle, and understanding with the concerns of a fourteen-year-old virgin bride than Jean-Luc. His slow loving introduction of his wife to the pleasures of sex established a relationship of trust in her which had never waned. She had, in the deepest sense, been forever grateful to him, this gratefulness only feeding her love, her burgeoning desire for her husband, just as his gratefulness was feeding his for her.

In slow stages, her inhibitions and shyness with a man, who was more than twice her age, dwindled, and she could receive and even make little jokes and sallies about their bed play. And then one day, she overcame her inhibitions and told Jean-Luc the story of how she and Caterina found that sinful book in the library of the Sforza Palace, that book from the Orient with all those not-to-be-believed drawings and watercolors of ladies and gentlemen. But Jean-Luc just laughed at her and kissed her and urged her to tell him in more detail which of these drawings she supposed she liked more than some of the others.

At first, she just gave him a look of disbelief but complied after more of his laughing urging. After a minute of her hesitance, he gathered her into his arms, sending his lips wandering down her body from her lips to her little toes, kissing, tasting, licking, and sucking and finally laid his mouth next to her ears.

Brushing her blond hair away from her ear, he whispered, "Well, love, we need to start on this chore today! You will choose the one most to your liking, and then we'll need to practice diligently to achieve perfection. We can move the number two on your list only after we have really, really perfected number one. Mind you, this will require a lot of time, work, my sweet, and attention to detail. Thank God we have a lot of years left yet, especially since I, for one, intend to continue practicing into my ripe old days."

And when she balled her hand into a fist and hit him on his arm, he only laughed that much louder. He pulled her that much closer to himself and, rolling her under him, proceeded to make slow sweet love to her.

As so often in the past, thinking of the past, Madeline just wagged her head with a secret little smile on her lips.

She shook out her napkin on her lap and, in silence, allowed the footman to serve her. When he was done, she dismissed him and the butler with a nod of her head. Well trained as the employees were, these two knew that husband and wife liked to have their breakfast privately and informally. Madeline dropped her gaze to her lap and smiled her secret smile. What a mountainous man she had garnered herself, and with such a mountain of frustrating contradictions! Courteous, tender, thoughtful, passionate, capable of apocalyptic explosions of temper and equally apocalyptic bursts of laughter, deeply buried resentments, and eager intelligence—it would take her three lifetimes to get to know this man.

Then she looked at her food and wrinkled her nose. The smell of smoked meat hit her during the next inhale, and she was almost done for. She was actually surprised when she put the two and two together—the need for ever-longer hours of sleep, the distaste to food in the mornings, dear god, not again! How stupid of her! Another pregnancy—of course it would thrill Jean-Luc, but honestly, she could do without.

She debated with herself. Her first impulse, as always, was to blurt it out. But then she thought that the breakfast table, from which, at best, she would pretty rapidly excuse herself or, at worst, run desperately to the garderobe, was maybe not the right place. Before she knew it, though, the words were out of her mouth. And even before all the words were said, that big mountain of a husband of hers had her swinging around, holding her by her waist, then took her up onto his lap to ask that eternally tiresome and mostly unnecessary questions of "are you sure?" and "do you feel all right?" and even more ridiculous, "darling, is there anything I can do?" To this latter, her standard answer was, "You have already done everything you could do."

In their eleven years of marriage, she gave her husband two little boys, twins, who looked as alike as two eggs but were vastly different in their personality and behavior. Bérnard, named after his paternal grandfather, the older by eleven minutes, was serious and studious, spending endless hours in weapons training and reading of history and laws as befitting the future heir of the name, title, and estates. Marcel, named after Madeline's paternal grandfather, was fond of books and studying but in a different way. He was the inventor, the alchemist, the boy who was always either showing up in torn or singed clothing, with big abrasions, lumps, insect bites but with eyes sparkling with excitement and endless stories of what he would be doing, building, scaling, or digging up next. He loved the new spirit in the air, the sense of questioning and exploration, of the newness of new and newer information reaching even their quiet corner of France.

Over the years, she had given birth to three little girls. The oldest, Marie, was nine years old, and the two younger ones who would now be, she supposed, eight and six years old. Both younger girls had succumbed to a wave of disease of children causing them to break out in fiery-red rashes, accompanied by high fever and a vicious and endless cough. Within less than a week, both of them were in their graves.

She wondered what it would be this time, while in her secret heart of hearts, she wished for a dainty little girl for her to spoil.

True to her promise, and also because she now craved rest as much as she did not crave food, she retreated to their bedroom after dinner.

That was where Jean-Luc rather predictably found her. He sat by her bedside, eager to discuss this wonderful new development in their family's life, to ask her if she wished to inform the boys and little Marie as yet, or even the household staff who were in the need to know, first among them her wardrobe mistress, but also their seneschal and the master of the table perhaps?

He held her hand, kissed each of her fingers, then, turning over her hands, kissed each of her palms, fragrant with the oils of lemon and thyme, which she regularly rubbed on her body. He bent, gently tasting her lips, tasting the raspberries-flavored wine she always loved to drink with the sweets served at the end of the meal. His lips moved to her eyes, kissing her eyelids, her nose, the gentle slope of her neck, and felt her pulse thrum faster. He slid his lips along her collarbone and felt her shudder with passion. Her arms wound around his neck as she tucked her face into his neck. She whispered his name, and they looked at each other for a long loving glance.

Something unnamed passed between them. It was the flicker of a feeling so powerful that it took his breath away. With a sharp pang, almost painful in its intensity, he realized this unique moment of his life—never did he, never could he, love Madeline more than at that moment. He never even knew that feelings—love—of such intensity existed!

Madeline shifted herself to be able to feel the length of her husband's body against her, pressing down on her. The weight of his body felt so wonderful, so absolutely right, and as always, it just inflamed her desire that much more.

"Husband, please, please, come to me, love me, I need you now!" she whispered. "God, I want you so much. I want you always. Always!"

Jean-Luc ran his hands down her body, her as yet flat belly. His mouth left her face, her neck, and followed his hands, visiting all the familiar, familiarly beloved places. She shifted herself to him with as much desire as she had ever felt. When they united, it was as lovely, as wonderfully fulfilling as always. Their pleasure crashed over them like a thundering wave, tossing them into each other again and again until both of them felt that they would die of the exquisiteness of their shared passion.

The next day, after Jean-Luc had endlessly kissed her lips, her hands, her fingertips, coddled her, questioned her how she felt, ordered more and softer pillows for her seat in her solar, worried about her walking too much up and down the stairs, and, in general, made more of a helpless nuisance of himself than being of any real help, she sent him to go hawking, which he dearly loved. Probably understanding that she wanted to get him out from underfoot, he finally agreed, and Madeline found some quiet time to sit down and write a letter to Catherine.

She wished to congratulate her on her recent marriage. Judging from such distance, she thought the marriage was rather precipitous, but then who was she to judge? She was too far away to come to any kind of a decision other than wishing her best friend a great deal of happiness; finally maybe this marriage would be all that she would wish for. After recently enduring the horror of her husband's assassination, something Madeline could barely even imagine, she hoped with all her heart that this time, Caterina would be happy!

*****

Catherine received Madeline's long and euphoric letter a month later. She smiled wryly. Only someone like Madeline would be thrilled to go through another pregnancy and birth, she thought. But then, Madeline was always enchanted by being a woman and delighted by all womanly things. And that, of course, first of all, included pregnancy and children. Catherine sighed. Why could she not be like that? Satisfied with her lot of doing the expected things and not minding to say yes-yes to a man just because he was a man? Oh, how calming such a life would be! And how boring! Boring!

By now, she sensed that her marriage to Feo was not all she had expected from it. Slowly it was beginning to fray. Studiously she attempted to ignore the first warning signs. In the beginning, his shallowness, his vanity, his constant need for reassurance and admiration were only irritating. Within a year of the marriage, she gave birth to Giacomo's son and had high hopes that this little boy, christened Bernardino, would help turn the corner of the shaky marriage. Unfortunately that did not happen, and wryly, Caterina reminded herself of the saying "act in haste, repent at leisure." Years passed with such an impasse during which time Caterina, much to her regret, discovered in addition to the other less-than-desirable character traits of her husband, such as his insolence, his pronounced cruelty.

God knew, Caterina thought, she was cruel on occasion, mostly to satisfy her anger and need for revenge, but most frequently just to intimidate. Though often an absentee mother, still her children were close to her heart. The day she witnessed Giacomo publicly slap his stepson, her oldest son, Ottaviano, the heir and future lord of Forlì, became, in her mind, a watershed event. To her surprise, it also was that for a number of the noble families of Forlì, so much so that two plots were hatched in short order, one after the other, to do away with Giacomo Feo. Neither of these murder attempts were successful, though.

Giacomo, obviously having the bit between his teeth, did not heed the warning signs. Finally the leaders of Forlì had enough. In the seventh year of their marriage, returning from a hunt outing, Giacomo was separated from the remainder of the hunt party and mortally wounded and killed.

Whether Caterina, deep in her heart, welcomed this solution of her marital problems, she never confessed to anyone. She did behave in the expected accepted fashion of her time and executed everyone even remotely associated with her husband's murder. Her revenge bloodbath ultimately caused only a temporary ripple in the life of the city of Forlì but probably served to further alienate her subjects.

*****

At the same time when Caterina de Sforza de Riario de Feo started to struggle with the problems which her second marriage, her second husband, began to present to her, in the city of Torun, kingdom of Poland, a fifteen-year-old teenager entered the Cathedral School at Wloclawek. He was preparing for admission to the University of Kraków. He was a most eager student, anxiously awaiting the hoped-for admission but had a serious problem of choice. He could not quite decide among physics, mathematics, astronomy, philosophy, medicine, economy, foreign languages, diplomacy, classical studies, or Greek literature?

By the time Caterina lost her second husband to assassination, the young man did receive his university degree from the University of Kraków and was contemplating a study tour to Italy, specifically to the world-renowned University of Bologna.

It was many years later, after the young man had furthered his studies in Bologna, Padua, and Ferrara and returned to Poland, that he acquired a French student by the name of Marcel de Landes, son of the Marquis Jean-Luc and Marquise Madeline de Landes.

The young Polish man's name was Nicolaus Copernicus.

*****

The year after Giacomo's assassination, Caterina received a visit from the recently appointed Florentine ambassador to Forlì, Giovanni de' Medici. The handsome twenty-nine-year-old ambassador, a descendant from the junior branch of the powerful Medici, calling themselves *il Popolano*, or "those of the people," sent a message to Her Grace, the Countess Caterina, Mistress of Forlì, to ask for her gracious consent to present himself to her in his official capacity. She immediately accepted his request, anxious to be on good terms with Firenze and the Medici family.

Giovanni was handsome, well mannered, gracious, of an engaging nature, and exceedingly well educated. That was only to be expected of a child growing up under the tutelage of Lorenzo, called also *il Magnifico*, "the Magnificent," and his younger brother, Giuliano. The court and the classroom for the little ones, regardless whether male or female, abounded with the best educators, painters, sculptors, philosophers, poets, the best books and best knowledge available to anyone in Europe.

Two days later, Ambassador Giovanni de' Medici presented himself to the ruler of Forlì, Countess Caterina Sforza, and offered her his credentials to represent the state and city of Firenze to Her Grace. The only other two persons present were the ambassador's assistant and Caterina's secretary, one Monsignor Amadeo Fratti, a Benedictine monk and priest.

Before receiving him, Caterina had grumbled to her secretary that she was really too busy to spend too much time "with the Medici guy." Upon seeing him enter, though, her mind changed rapidly. When she so wished, she could charm, indeed. When Giovanni so wished, he could be irresistible. What happened thereafter was perhaps inevitable. These two were literally destined for each other. Their ages, their positions, their influence and power, their interests, all of these things drove them to each other. It was little surprise that Caterina and Giovanni fell in love—actually genuinely and most ardently in love.

Giovanni was a bachelor four years Caterina's junior, much chastised by his family to marry finally. After his young betrothed died at an early age, Giovanni had never felt the inclination to search for a new bride. Caterina, on the other hand, was firmly convinced that she had sworn off marriages. But this time, Caterina's children, as well as her uncle Lodovico, Duke of Milano, were applauding the decision to wed.

Early on, as the courtship turned serious, another decision was made by all the various and far-flung relatives to keep the marriage hidden from the public view. Considering the merging of the Medici, Sforza, and Riario family interests, with the intrusion of the Borgia pope, who inserted himself regardless if asked or not, there were entirely too many high-powered interests to be satisfied or, at least, appeased.

And so, just barely two years after the assassination of Giacomo Feo, Caterina and Giovanni de' Medici il Popolano were married in a quiet ceremony. Her oldest son, Ottaviano, who had just been appointed condottiere of Firenze, was elated, the younger children clustered around Giovanni, liking him immediately, and the families applauded even, at least temporarily, the grasping old Borgia pope. Ottaviano expressed it most succinctly—at eighteen, one is painfully aware of anything "inappropriate" which one's elders dare to do—"These two behave like two overaged kids, holding hands and smooching and kissing at every opportunity. Yech!"

If the twice-widowed bride was unabashedly giddy with happiness, Angelina Maria was literally floating on air. She adored—adored—the "gorgeous" young Lord Giovanni, not the least of which was because he plied her with little honeyed spice cakes studded with pine nuts and was unfailingly thoughtful and polite with her. To be honest, though, she thought that given "that scum she married before" and even "that oversexed guy who kept her forever pregnant," Lord Giovanni was a vastly great improvement. She was not in the least shy about voicing her opinion to her lady.

Caterina laughed at her, eyes sparkling with happiness.

"Dearest Maria, how can I chide you for your forwardness, for I can only agree with your opinion. And your opinion is of value to me. You have always given it to me freely, without fear of any repercussions or chastisement from me. Yes, yes, and yes, he is a great improvement over the two others and also, I do believe, over anyone else walking about in this land of ours, maybe walking about anywhere. He is adorable, isn't he!"

She was letting Angelina Maria arrange her hair before joining her husband at the supper table. She, who really did not much care about her appearance before, was now acutely vain, eager to please. No wonder Angelina Maria did not know quite what to make of all of this.

Caterina, as soon as she was released from Angelina Maria's ministrations, could not move fast enough to hurry to the large dining hall. Even though there was a smaller, more intimate chamber available to the young couple to eat privately, tonight they were expected to host the papal delegation from the Borgia pope, Alexander VI, in the splendor of the beautifully frescoed and decorated great hall.

Giovanni was waiting for his wife at the bottom of the stairs she had to descend. When he saw her, his eyes lit up as he extended his hand and then kissed hers fervently, as soon as she was within touching distance. Once she stepped off the last stair, he pulled her to him and dropped his chin to rest on the top of her head.

"May the good Lord bless me, but do you not look again more beautiful than the last time I had seen you, an hour or two ago, my love!" He breathed. "Do I but bewail the bad fortune which forces us to go into the public and not to our bedchamber, lady! But since we must, shall we try to talk little and eat fast?" His mouth curved into a smile while he was talking, and by the time he finished the sentence, he was outright laughing at himself. Caterina, less restrained than her husband, tilted her head to the side and rocked with laughter. Both husband and wife were barely able to suppress their mirth as they entered the banqueting hall. As all the guests rose and applauded their presence, the Lady of Forlì and her spouse settled at the head of the main table. There was a loud universal scratching and scraping of chair legs and a rustling of silk as everyone seated.

Then the doors opened, and the servants, one after the other, entered and paraded around the various platters they carried, offering their platter to any of the guests who raised their fingers to indicate that they wished to sample that dish. So as not to make any mistake about what each platter contained, the master of the table, standing at the entrance, loudly announced each dish. The procession of food seemed to be almost endless. There were partridges stuffed with peppercorn and scallions roasted in honey, roasted mutton with onion and spices stewed in wine, roasted pheasant in its feathers, rabbit roasted with ginger in verjuice, capon in plum-flavored almond cream, broiled eel with creamed leeks, grilled bream in a sauce of verjuice, ginger, and wine, a whole baked sturgeon with its roe, goat's kidney pies, cheese lasagna, golden cream with cheese and onions, precious rice with almond milk, cream custard tarts, and a selection of small fruit pastries. Assorted wines and ale were poured with abandon. To eat fast and then to disappear, as Lord Giovanni wished, was not an option.

Actually it was hours later that the young couple made their way up the curving stairs to the large master's bedroom. They were pleasantly tired from the food, wine, and the vigorous dancing of their favorite, the favored dance of all the youth of the land, the la volta. But they were happily not too tired to engage in their other most favored activity, making love. Both dispensed with the assistance of the ladies' maid and butler but undressed each other with mounting impatience. As soon as he could untie the little ribbons to pull the heavy puffed sleeves off her arms, then liberate his wife from the confines of her gamurra and farthingale, he eagerly gathered the hem of her silk chemise to lift the garment and pull it over her head. As soon as her head emerged, he discarded the chemise, dropping it to the floor, and, with his other hand, reached for Caterina's waist to pull her as close to him as possible.

The two kissed with increasing hunger, Caterina becoming more and more aroused by the restrained power in Giovanni's gentleness. He was a muscular man who enjoyed weapons play and physicality as much as any young warrior. What endeared him to his wife even more, though, was his sparkling curiosity and intellect toward anything that surrounded him. Finally he raised his mouth from hers and, picking her up as fast as he could, dropped her on the bed, shedding the remainder of his clothing, and fell upon her, supporting himself with his bent arms.

"I do love you so, Caterina," he whispered, nibbling on her neck and earlobe.

"And I, you." Caterina sighed.

After, the only sounds emanating from the room were their occasional sighs and moans and the rhythmic slapping of bodies against each other.

They needed no one else and found their endless happiness in each other.

*****

Seven months after the wedding, Caterina and Giovanni became the parents of another little boy. Caterina, once again breezing through the delivery, laughingly commented that apparently, once she learned really well how to bear boys, did not wish to break the mold. Giovanni floated on air, and Caterina was happy for the child but mostly for her husband's happiness. Both parents agreed to name the little boy for his most famous relative, the great Lorenzo de' Medici. But the child, even without such an illustrious name, could look forward to a reasonably secure and successful future, or so the devoted parents prayed.

But Europe, and especially Italy, were a cauldron forever bubbling over with freshly sealed and then quickly overthrown allegiances and alliances between the city-states of Venice, Genoa, Firenze, Milano, and the Papal States. The latter, especially now, in the Borgia hands of Pope Alexander VI and his son, Cesare, the recently created Duke of Valentinois, elevated by Louis XII of France, created ceaseless friction. The very latest of such "difference of opinions" erupted between Venice and Firenze. Giovanni, of course, as well as Ottaviano, had to depart to participate in any subsequent scuffles and battles on the side of Firenze—Giovanni, by virtue of all his family connections to the Medici, and Ottaviano because he was the standard bearer, the leader of the army, the condottiere of Firenze.

Caterina hated to part with each of them, but she had gone through so many such events that she only took this one with a half-hearted seriousness. She minded her work, minded baby Lorenzo, listened to various and sundry complaints from the people of Forlì, and altogether attempted to busy herself, to the point of exhaustion, in order to fall into her—their—bed and descend into a dead sleep. A short while back, Giovanni had insisted that she get a permanent wet nurse for the baby, whereas in the past, she used one only, on and off as needed. Giovanni wanted her as much as she wanted him, and both of them devout Catholics, of a sort, they were forbidden from any sexual activity while the woman was breastfeeding.

One of the next sunny days, during the week, her secretary brought her a letter which he did not open, as he was authorized to do with correspondence in general. Extending her hand, Caterina took the envelope addressed to her and bordered with a thick black band. It was addressed to her from the Marquis de Landes. Her stomach took a sudden somersault. She knew, knew that it was Madeline. Swallowing deeply, trying to control the shaking of her hand—her hand never shook—she returned the letter to Monsignor Fratti to open. As soon as he had the letter in hand, she rose and went to the open window, looking down with blind eyes into the courtyard and taking big gulps of air.

Monsignor Fratti began talking, then reading in a slow soft voice.

"This letter, milady, is written to you by His Grace, the Marquis's hand. I read:

> "My dearest Caterina. Finally after days of suffering the agonies of hell, I try to find the strength to write to you, dearest friend to both of us. The Almighty, in his will, has seen fit to take from me my friend, my support, my love, my life, my everything for close to twenty-two years and forever...I know that she wrote to you earlier of our delight, the expectation of another child. Boy or girl, we were ready to welcome this, our

fourth child, into our family. And since Bérnard and Michel are now both gone their own ways, we thought the little one would be a baby to coddle for our ten-year-old daughter, Marie.

Alas, the birth was more than difficult, for the baby—who would have been another little boy—was in a breech position. There were two midwives and an apothecary in attendance, and all of their skills were naught. My dearest, dearest once-and-forever love labored on for three days, until I, even, thought to go mad from her suffering and screams. She labored until she had not voice left, no breath left, and all her blood had finally drained her body. I was with her, holding her listless white hand until it turned slack and cold.

I live in a fog. Do I ever want to leave this fog? I think not. I want nothing, nothing but to follow her. You must understand that I have no fight left in me for more, for more of this life… You must forgive me for this, and I pray and hope the church will forgive me as well! For I cannot do other—I must follow her. Do not worry about me, for I trust in God that he will be gracious to me, and, in his infinite kindness, perhaps once again unite us? Marie will be well taken care of. She has been betrothed years ago to the son of my dearest friend and comrade in arms. Louis-Robert de Ronscevalles, the only son of the Duc and Duchesse Ronscevalles de Haut Terre, is well known to her and has been a playmate and friend of hers, just as his parents are friends of mine. They love Marie like their own child.

For the loss of my forever beloved, beloved dearest wife, companion of my life, I can only add this, my belief with all my heart. I believe that our Lord's most precious gift when he wished to show his child, Adam, his complete love was the one gift, more wonderful than any other, most precious of all—the gift of a woman!

Farewell to you, my dearest Caterina. You have been a loving, true, and constant friend to us both. I wish for you to have in your current marriage the love that we had and which you could not find in your two earlier marriages.

I kiss your hands most devotedly,

Your true and grateful friend, Jean-Luc, Marquis de Landes."

Caterina's fingers were cramped and turning white, so desperately was she grabbing the window ledge. For a moment, she thought she heard Madeline's voice, Madeline's laughter, a whisper in the hollow silence of the room. She lifted her hand to cover her eyes, her face, as her shoulders shook in silent sobbing. Monsignor Fratti made a gesture toward her, but she shook her head and waved her palm to him to send him away from her and her grief.

The very next day, though, after that shattering letter, she received a most surprising and lovely present, sent to her from her husband who, along with her son Ottaviano, was encamped in the hills of Tuscany. He wrote how he missed her, and how, on one of his little visits to Firenze "to see family," he went to the workshop of Master Pollaiuolo who, however, was not personally present as he was now old and ailing. After explaining what he was looking for, one of his apprentices presented him with the little statue which he is now sending her. To Giovanni, it looked exactly what he was looking for, and he only hoped that she would be pleased with it. Knowing her penchant for Greek antiquities, this should interest her. According to legend, the little statue of a dancing woman, cast in pure gleaming gold, had been dug up on the island of Crete, where it had lain for thousands of years, going back in history to a time when, according to great Plato, the continent of Atlantis was destroyed by a volcano, such as caused the destruction of Pompeii.

"You will also see, my dearest, that it carries some kind of insignia, maybe the stamp or the cipher for the name of the sculptor, who must have been one of the greatest artists of any age!" And then the practicality of a Florentine merchant family heritage surfaced. "I had it assayed, my love, and it is indeed pure gold." He added as a postscript, "There is a strange legend attached to this piece, and of course, it is not very believable, especially since verification is not possible. For many generations, the legend attached to this small gold figure is that it was poured by a hideously ugly deformed dwarf who was desperately in love with the woman represented in the statue… Interesting, is it not?"

Caterina fell in love with the little statue, no larger than two hand spans, and decided that her husband was right. It was a small antique masterpiece, the elegance and beauty of which certainly was equal to, just possibly overshadowed, the works of the current greats Ghiberti, Verrocchio, and Donatello. She ordered a little marble pedestal made for the statue. Statue and pedestal then became the focal point of her very large and very cluttered worktable, standing there right next to a miniature of her Giovanni.

She struggled endlessly with a letter of condolence to Jean-Luc and finally gave up. Somehow in her heart of hearts, she felt certain that no letter from her or anyone else would now reach him.

Word came to her that there was a somewhat half-hearted battle in Tuscany, under her husband and Ottaviano's leadership, against the army of Venice, the battle bringing no conclusion to the antagonism between the two city-states. The next day, however, a much more frightening message arrived with an anxious courier. Giovanni was to be brought back to Forlì in a very bad state of illness. He had not been wounded on the battlefield but carried off the field in a swoon and fell off his horse. He had a high fever and was in and out of consciousness. He was declared by the army's astrologer-surgeon as having contracted evil humors at the battlefield. Caterina rushed everyone about to get a comfortable sickroom ready for him and prepared herself—or tried to—for any eventuality. Nevertheless, when he arrived and she saw him, she was utterly shocked. He had lost a lot of weight, he could barely eat, had an almost-constant high fever alternating with chills, and his breathing was extremely loud and labored.

Slowly Giovanni improved a little. At his own anxious insistence, he was transferred to Santa Angelina in Bagno, a seaside place of healing, much to the south of Forlì. To transport a sick man across bad or often nonexistent roads across the mountainous terrain was a most desperate plan, but Caterina was willing to do anything, anything! Giovanni survived the trip and rallied full of hope in the miracle of the waters of Santa Maria, where several members of his family had supposedly recovered their health. But it was not to be. Caterina was summoned with great urgency when she went to take a little nap after being up with him all night. She made it back to her husband's bed.

She was by his side as he died. She held him close, loved him, and watched him as his soul flew elsewhere.

*****

She was caught in a bubble. She was caught, locked in, and couldn't get out.

In the bubble, there was a tightness and a lack of air so that she could barely breathe, every breath an effort with little result. It was not dark in the bubble, but not light either, and nothing could get to her, though she could see all that went on around her. The bubble was filled with heavy fog. Voices were muted. What was around her was meaningless, though, and what was in the bubble, well, there was nothing else but she, and everything else was separated from her by the bubble. No sound, no sense of touch or feeling, just ear-shattering, soul-destroying silence.

But she did not want anything else but the silence. She was so tired! Tired of people, tired of moving, even to move her lips to talk, and if she tried to talk, no sound came out with the effort, anyway. She was so very tired, she wanted to please, *please*, be left alone. But no! Not that! She was so afraid to be alone, and oh god! She was alone and afraid and tired. She closed her eyes and tried to listen to the sounds, which she knew were around her but could not get through to her inside the bubble.

She wasn't quite sure when she started to recover enough to start eating and feel the taste of the food she ate. To look at her infant son and realize that he was hers and—oh god—hers and Giovanni's. Little Lorenzo, little Lorenzo who now was an orphan, and the first time, a hesitant slight little smile flitted over her face. Poor little Lorenzo who would not be really an orphan because he had a passel-full of siblings and other relatives. If anything, he would eventually turn around and be running away from them just to find some peace and quiet!

She sighed and took a cautious look about. She felt like awakening from a deep illness or a nightmarish dream. But life, inexorable life, intruded and poked a little hole into her bubble, and the bubble slowly started to deflate and, finally, collapse at her feet. She was standing without any protection from her bubble, standing on the rubble of her life. She felt powerless to stem the intrusions, so for the first time in her life, she closed her eyes to life, too tired to do battle.

Her reawakening from grief, from mourning, happened in slow stages, and much of it, at first, without her will, for she had no will left to do anything. Then she remembered something Giovanni told her in some connection or other, she no longer could remember when or why? Mayhap it was premonition?

"Do not ever be unwilling to engage life, only be ready for whatever it brings, good or bad. We all only have our allotted time here. Think of it as a river. Just as you cannot touch flowing water twice, because the flow that has passed will never pass again, so it is also with our lives, with each day, each hour, each minute, my love! Use them, clutch them, and treasure them all! Remember, my love, always, that there is no one else I have ever loved or will ever love, here or in my afterlife!"

And so she lifted herself into the saddle again, going from skirmish to skirmish, becoming more and more well known for her fearlessness, her military and political acumen, famous enough to be called by the population *la tigre*, "the tigress."

Ultimately she was defeated, though. Captured by Louis XII's French Army, imprisoned, she lost Forlì to the Borgias. Cesare Borgia, Duke of Valentinois, brought her to Rome and imprisoned her at Castel Sant'Angelo, the very place where she had resided long, long ago, at the death of her uncle, Pope Sixtus, before fleeing Rome with her children to shelter her family in Forlì.

At the end, she was allowed to leave Rome and go to Firenze. Her children, under the wing of their Medici relatives, were there, waiting for her.

*****

One century after the great Ghiberti commenced his monumental labor on the baptistery doors, a beautiful elegantly dressed great lady alighted from her carriage in front of the Cathedral di Santa Maria del Fiore. She took the hand of the young boy who followed her from the carriage and hurried him across the planks laid over the muddy walkway toward the baptistery. The young boy fidgeted, finally managing to pull his hands out of those of the woman. He clasped the short sword at his side.

"Please cease, *Bell'ammá*. You do not see me often enough to know how I have grown! I am not a child to be led by the hand! I'll be six next April, you know!"

The lady released his hand and flashed him a big conspiratorial smile.

"Och, aye, I know, my boy, I was there!"

The boy looked up at her with a giggle. She grabbed the rim of her large hat, which a sudden gust of wind almost swept off her head. Her long reddish-blond plaits swung down her back with the sudden movement.

"Really, Bell'ammá! You are again—"

"Treating you like a little boy, when you are almost grown-up!" The lady's tinkling laughter floated above shouts coming from the masons hammering away on the north side of the duomo's massive wall, where water seepage had been detected, endangering the exquisitely laid flooring.

She had indeed not seen her son for a while. He was at the select military academy for young boys from the highest echelons of Firenze's society, trained to become a great soldier, a condottiere, a leader of the armies, which were to defend the precious city against her enemies. Just because he still called her bell'ammá', as he did once, when he could not pronounce *bella mamma* without stuttering, did not mean that she should lead him by his hand. Her son was right. But she could not help her feelings of desperate possessiveness for her youngest child. She had been deprived of seeing him all during her imprisonment in Rome, missing his early growing years, and even after she returned to Firenze, a bitter battle for the child's custody continued for a while. Her brother-in-law, Lorenzo di Pierfrancesco, only grudgingly relinquished guardianship to the child's mother.

They stood before the two doors, each door with their ten panels of gilded bronze, the magnificent incomparable doors which the divine Michelangelo had named the Gates of Paradise. Lady Caterina Sforza and her youngest son, renamed Giovanni after his father. She stood transfixed by the beauty in front of her, folding her hands together, forgetting about the little body who stood by her side, scuffing his feet in the dust. Finally he reached up and pulled on her skirts.

"Bell'ammá, you said you wanted to show me something and tell me about it?"

Caterina stirred, as though awakening. She smiled at Giovanni. With good reason was she famous for her open and generous smile. Putting her hand on his shoulder, she pulled her son close.

"These doors, my son, were created close to a hundred years before you were born, Giovanni. They were made by a sculptor-goldsmith-painter, truly one of the first all-round God-gifted citizens of this city. His name was Ghiberti, my son, Lorenzo Ghiberti. Can you believe that Signore Ghiberti worked over twenty-five years to complete just these twenty panels you see here? His father, who was also a worker of gold, helped him, but still! Over twenty-five years, son! Think of it!

"And look at how marvelous the workmanship is! Look at the people that are represented there! And then think of the Madonna who sits enthroned at our Church of Orsanmichele, where we usually go for our Sunday Masses! Recall the beautiful Madonna sitting there above the altar in her dark robes, holding the Christ child. Does she strike you as a real human figure? No, I think certainly not! Signore Orcagna has represented her as a woman enthroned, with a golden background behind her and angels with bright round halos."

"Tell me, my son, don't you feel that this picture, though beautiful for its workmanship, does not represent a real flesh-and-blood woman? She is a gorgeous two-dimensional representation of a living person. Do you know what is meant by two-dimensional?"

The little boy, his dark-blond hair blowing here and there with the gusts of wind around the huge structure of the duomo, nodded excitedly, jumping from one foot to the other and eagerly pulling on his mother's skirts.

"Aye, Bell'ammá, Maestro Lorenzo de Credi, who comes once in a while to lecture us how to look at and value paintings and sculptures, explained to us. Told us how we really live in a world which has three dimensions, and that third dimension disappears way, way back, after getting to be smaller and smaller. That's why when I stand on the opposite side of the river and look for the duomo, it looks much smaller than when I stand next to it, see?"

Caterina's smile lit up her face. She squatted down to be at eye level with her son, her skirts billowing and spreading out in the dust of the street.

"What a smart boy you are, my sweet! Aye, that is exactly true. But now think back to many other beautiful paintings that surround our lives. Do you recall Signore Orcagna's other painting at Saint Mary's New Church? Our Santa Maria Novella, where we occasionally go to pray the rosary in the Strozzi chapel, do you recall the altarpiece? There also, you will not find a third dimension! And do you, my so smart son, do you know what this mysterious third dimension is called in painting?"

And when Giovanni shook his head to make his hair fly, she lifted her gloved hand and leaned to his ear, almost whispering.

"It is called perspective, darling, yes, perspective. Or if you will—distance. Now if you look, darling, you will see that this is the first of two most interesting things to be shown us by Signore Ghiberti. People are shown in three dimensions. People in the back are smaller than those in the front. Scenes such as these draw the eyes of the spectator in, don't you think so?"

The little boy, forehead furrowed, eyes big, and his rosy lips open, nodded eagerly.

"And then, look here, darling, when we think back to the peoples of Signore Orcagna's paintings, does it not strike you that those depicted do not, at all, look like real persons? Living flesh-and-blood people? Don't they but look as though they were the generalization of a certain group of persons—the Madonna who represents young, loving, saintly mothers, the man lifting the whip against our Lord represents the evil, brutal, repressor soldiers. But here look, darling, each person represents a real human, an individual. And look, also look, the background is not just a layer of gold but like a gold curtain. In front of this curtain, we see humans who sit or stand or talk, one to the other in poses which are not generalized, but real representations of real individuals and the real behavior of those individuals. Do you understand what I am trying to tell you?"

Giovanni, by now all excited by his mother's explanations, released his hold on her skirt and hopped from one foot to the other with greater speed.

"Yes, yes, of course, Bell'ammá, what you mean is that this guy, um, ghib—Ghiberti made real landscapes in the back and real ladies and gentlemen in the front. And they all were themselves. Right?"

Catherine smiled and wagged her head in a typically Italian manner.

"Well, yes, yes, more or less, son. But that should be enough of my lectures for you today! Shall we walk slowly around each side of the baptistery and look at the doors once more? That way, Giovanni, you can really fix them in your mind's eye.

"And how would you like to walk from here to Orsanmichele, to pray the noontime Angelus together? You can then also look at Signore Orcagna's Madonna there and form a comparison between perspective or lack thereof. I shall tell the coachman to go there and then take us home to eat. We'll sup together, just you and I, and, of course, my ladies. How is that? Come, darling!"

And young Giovanni, delighted to be able to be with his bell'ammá a little longer, continued to hop and skip from foot to foot, as he followed his mother. Then out of an overflow of childhood energy, which needed to be channeled somewhere, he pulled his short, child-sized rapier out of its scabbard, and holding it horizontally with both hands, he pirouetted about, making short slashing motions.

"Do you not want to paint with perspective, you stupid fellow, you? Off with your head! Off! Off! You are too damn old-fashioned…yes, you! Too old-fashioned, you!"

Caterina looked at him, shaking her head, her laughing eyes gently softening as she kept looking at her youngest child, her only child a heritage of her beloved husband Giovanni. She could see so much of him in this little boy, the same profile, already transforming into the strong jaw, high forehead, and long narrow nose of her dead husband. Only the eyes were different, her husband's a soft hazel, while little Giovanni's were dark with an intensely inquiring and challenging gaze. And of course, the mouth, but then no one could ever have lips as soft and sensuously curved as her husband had.

*****

Nikki Copernikk, or Nikki-Nikk for brief, as his friends all called him, albeit running the risk of being brained by the tall thin but very agile young Copernicus, felt that he was wearing down the cobbles of the road between Warmia, his hometown in Poland, and Padua, Ferrara, and Bologna, three university towns in Northern Italy, mercifully more or less on a straight road a fairly short distance from one another. It seemed to him that he and his horse had treaded that road back and forth more times than he could count. Now he was coming back to Padua, which was the center, really, for anyone who wanted to become well learned these days. He was going to get his education and doctorate in medical learning. Sometime during those studies, he would pay just a short side visit to the University of Ferrara—so he hoped—to receive his expected doctorate in canon law.

Finally his much maligned "scatterbrained" interests, hopping from here to there, were paying off in gathering doctoral degrees. He was thrilled to find that included in the educational curriculum for a doctorate in medicine at Padua was the study of astronomy and astrology. They were actually considered important parts of the study of medicine. By sheer coincidence, they were also among Master Copernicus's primary interests. At least astronomy was, while secretly he pooh-poohed astrology, embraced so fervently by many with medical and healing aspirations. He had great difficulty in being convinced, or even imagining, that some constellation—an immense distance away from earth—would have any bearing upon someone's illness after all! He was hopeful that by spending some time in Padua, in one round-trip swing from Poland to Italy, he could kill two birds with one stone, as the saying went, or rather get a doctorate in both medicine and astronomy.

He was well aware that his capacity for learning and for the employ of this learning was not as most other students, but other than having this pointed out to him, he felt in no way different from his classmates. Well, perhaps he made an effort of hiding the quickness of his brain and his exceptional reasoning abilities—just to make himself fit in better.

But now, standing in the narrow little entryway of the walk-up fourth-floor dormer-room he occupied, for what he knew was too much money, even for a university town, he was sorting through his mail given him by his landlady. He had just made his monthly rent payment and, in return, received his mail. His landlady, Donna Clementina, out of a surfeit of caution, never gave out his mail before seeing his rental coins in her palm.

There was one slim longish envelope with a crest showing in the red wax seal. The crest somehow tweaked his memory, a shield with five circles or balls? Then a flash of illumination—ah, of course, the Medici crest. Lord! What did the Medicis want with him? He knew none of them in person, albeit had ample knowledge of the various members of the famous—or was it infamous—family. Curious now, he ripped open the envelope, written by a scribe, or secretary, and signed by Her Grace, the Countess Caterina Sforza de Medici.

Her Grace sent him an invitation to go to Firenze to join her and others invited in a weeklong exchange of opinions and discussions of the newest currents in the sciences, alchemy, and arts. All those invited would be Her Grace's guests at her home, the Villa Medici di Castello, for the duration. She also sent her greetings and indicated her eagerness to meet with such a variety of persons with great intellect or artistic gifts.

Nikki-Nicolaus, personally born into a family with power, prestige, wealth, and connections, including many prominent noble families of Poland and an uncle who was the bishop of Warmia, nevertheless felt exceedingly flattered and looked forward to comply with the invitation. It also gave him, he felt, an opportunity to—well, to show off his education, his knowledge. At this point in his life, he felt he needed to further his fortunes, his future, both of which, of course, depended greatly on broader public acceptance of his name. Once that was accomplished, he could garner the acceptance needed for his many challengingly novel ideas about the round shape of the earth, its rotation around itself, and its path around the sun, and many, many more!

With a happy smile on his face, Nikki-Nicolaus sat down at his writing table stuck in the corner of his very, very small cramped room, delaying only long enough to light a candle, and then eagerly began to sharpen a writing quill. He pulled a sheet of paper in front of him and commenced to write his grateful acceptance letter to Her Grace, making every attempt at graciousness and scientific condescension in equal degrees.

*****

In the great city of Venice, there were two artists, friends and competitors at the same time, who were acknowledged to be the leaders of the new school of painting called the modern art. They were born within a few years of each other. Giorgio Barbarelli was the older of the two, and for a while, he was also Tiziano Vecelli's teacher. Eventually that relationship developed into a close friendship, although it also fomented acute competition between the two. But by then, they had become famous and known simply as Giorgione, or little George for his slight built, and Titian.

Both of them were occupied with work and certainly not of a mind for travel, when an almost-identical letter, except for the appellation, reached each. For each of them, it was a gracious invitation to go to Firenze and be guests of the Countess Caterina Sforza de Medici at the Villa Medici di Castello for a week of discussion and exchange of opinions. There would be a number of like-minded scientists, philosopher-writers, and artists present. Her Grace was anxious that they would feel themselves freed from their daily commitments and thus able to attend.

Needless to say, the two quasi friends met at the earliest opportunity to compare the same letter with each other. Somewhat nonplussed, they looked at each other. It was a true aha-you-too moment. They checked the feasibility of suspending their work for a while and making the pilgrimage to Firenze. Actually was there ever even a doubt? Once that was established, the friends and potential co-guests at that illustrious gathering in Firenze agreed to temporarily suspend any competitive animosities. They agreed as well to then travel in each other's company. In that fine spirit of friendship and cooperation, letters of acceptance were sent and travel arrangements made.

Actually in retrospect, both little George and Tiziano agreed that they had a splendid time in Firenze, where the gracious hostess had invited them—probably reserving bragging rights to her adopted city—to remain for a while to take in all the "new things her town had to offer." Even more surprising, both agreed that their travel turned out to be most enjoyable and illuminating.

Her Grace, Countess Sforza Medici's, plans were developing quite the way she had planned. But well, most of the time, they had a way to do so.

*****

Master Ludovico Ariosto, poet, on numerous past occasions, diplomat to His Grace, Alfonso d'Este, Duke of Ferrara, was actually, so to say, on loan from His Grace's brother, Cardinal Ippolito d'Este. Both of the brothers employed his services, albeit neither of them had made his appointment to the diplomatic career official. That meant that he was, he felt much to his chagrin, never adequately compensated. The whole of this was becoming a more and more unwelcome item in Ludovico's emotions. Since his father's death, Ludovico's family commitments had become critical; unfortunately it was a very large family and included an invalid sister.

And now here he was, once again summoned to the Ducal Palace of the Dukes d'Este of Ferrara. There was evidently another mission for him, one that would take him to Rome, to the throne of Pope Julius II. Master Ludovico knew already, without speaking to His Grace, that it was to be a difficult mission and potentially also a dangerous one. His Holiness, the Pope, and Duke Alfonso were, had been for a while, at loggerheads with each other.

Not feeling very well yet, while recovering from an earlier illness, Ariosto tried in every possible way to evade the assignment. The duke insisted. Ariosto evaded. Of course, ultimately Duke Alfonso prevailed. After all, he was the duke and Ariosto in his employ. The best that the on-again-off-again diplomat could do was to get a concession to rest a while on the way from Ferrara to Rome and to go to one of the highly recommended famous medical clinics in Firenze. This little detour, almost no detour at all, he fervently hoped, would cure him of his affliction or, at least, benefit his health since Firenze, just as Bologna, were great centers of medicine and healing. Firenze even had a great innovation—the Ospedale degli Innocenti, an orphanage and special hospital devoted to the care of children! A great new development in the annals of that forward-thinking city, indeed!

What Master Ariosto neglected to mention to his employer was that by some fortuitous sleight of hand, or so it seemed, only a week ago, he had received a kind and gracious invitation from the Contessa Caterina Sforza de Medici, known to him from some earlier encounters. The invitation was to attend a meeting of like minds, and minds interested in the arts and in alchemy and science, for a week at the lady's residence at the Villa Medici di Castello. He had been torturing his brain how to escape Ferrara and the d'Este, and lo! The Lord performed a miracle.

He would go to the Villa Medici di Castello, participate in the discussions, and also take advantage of Firenze's medical knowledge before embarking on the last leg of his travels, from Firenze to Rome.

Indeed, indeed, he was a very lucky man! So much so that he felt inspired to compose a poem of his good fortune and to the gracious and beautiful lady who, as hostess, provided him with this good fortune. He composed it in ottava rima, stanzas of eight lines, which was his favored expression for short poetry.

Her Grace Caterina was exceedingly pleased when, albeit with some delay, she finally received the letter of thanks and acceptance from Master Ariosto. She had considered his presence a quasi feather in her cap; she loved poetry, and she loved to show off famous poets.

*****

Niccolò Machiavelli, firstborn son of a well-regarded Florentine attorney and his lady wife, was evidently born precocious, as his proud parents would assert. He learned languages with ease, spoke Latin, German, and French before he turned ten, did beautiful calligraphy, but also began to write short treatises, little plays, and verses while not even a teenager.

He was intensely interested in the turbulent politics of his day. Politics was everywhere, and often it seemed, the more turbulent, the better. Two of the most important hothouses were Rome and the Vatican embedded in the heart of Rome, and of course, his own hometown of Firenze. More than anything else, Niccolò admired power and strength. It was not surprising that he greatly admired the Borgias, especially the Borgia pope's son Cesare.

Building on that admiration, Niccolò conceived of a standing militia for his city of Firenze. Actually he did have a good reason for doing so, in addition to his self-interest. Most city-states were forced to rely on mercenaries. Regrettably, well-qualified, dependable mercenaries led by a well-trained condottiere were understandably both expensive and unreliable. It was well known that they first and foremost obeyed the prevailing wind of the day.

Actually for a time, Niccolò's citizen army proved quite successful, but then it turned out that the city-state of Firenze was too small to provide sufficient numbers of soldiers for a homegown army. And thus, for at least a short while, Niccolò was at loose ends. When he received an invitation from the woman he admired more than any other for her bravery, her cunning, her political bravura, and he did not even have to venture farther than the outskirts of Firenze to the Villa Medici di Castello, he was more than happy to comply with her request.

Actually, and regardless of the nicety of the invitation to her home, Niccolò persisted in his admiration of Lady Caterina to her, unfortunately so premature, dying day. He also transferred his admiration to her youngest son, Giovanni, the Medici son, who later, when he grew into manhood, became a most renowned condottiere and actually earned Niccolò's admiration. Little did Niccolò know that he would be given an opportunity to meet the man he would later so admire, the young then-eleven-year-old boy, at the same gathering he was just invited to!

Ah, the surprising twists and turns of lives can indeed be more amazing than the best of stories.

Once again, Caterina, the hostess, had struck gold!

*****

The Marquis de Landes requested his family's confessor and both the Abbott of the nearby Benedictine monastery of Saint-Sever, as well as the bishop of the Diocese of Aire and Dax, to which Landes belonged, to arrange for the customary prayers to be said over the body of his lady wife, the Marquise de Landes. The custom was a vigil of three days and nights before entombment. This was necessary to give sufficient time for everyone wishing to say their farewell to the departed, to come to Castle Montchateau. Friends, villeins, and many others not immediately recognized by the castle guards formed a long line, patiently waiting their turn to say a prayer for the great lady and to look at her for a last time. She had been known as the benefactress of the abbey and of many other worthy causes she had instituted during her lifetime. Following the example of the city of Firenze in Italy, she had caused a hospital for children to be erected in Saint-Sever. She was the patroness of the orphanage in Mont-de-Marsan and of the leper colony deep in the moors and forest along the little river Douze. There was hardly anyone who would not have thought of her with respect or gratitude, or both.

Her husband had spent most of his days and nights of these final three days of farewell and separation sitting in a dark corner of the castle's great hall, where his lady's body lay on a flower-encrusted bier, illuminated by the light of rows and rows of fat beeswax candles. He was barely even noticed in the darkness by any of the visitors to the chapel. The monks and sisters chanting their prayers during those endless hours became accustomed to his dark shadow over the days. The marquis barely stirred, only occasionally would he rise from his armchair to shuffle away for a while, presumably to eat or to refresh himself with a glass of wine, or both. Perhaps he went to the garderobe to take care of necessities, or perhaps he went to get some rest for an hour or two? Nobody dared to ask him; the few who did, at first, just received a blank stare behind a brow severely narrowed to a scowl.

After the interminable three days, the cortège wound its way to the chapel for interment in the family crypt. The marquis laid the required red rose, signifying his love, and a white rose, signifying his wife's soul, now cleansed and innocent once again of any sin, on her coffin, then he turned around and walked out of the chapel. He was also notably absent from the repast held in the great dining room of the castle. His firstborn son and heir, Bérnard, and his young lady wife, Sabine, played host and gave thanks to the assembled family, friends, clerics, and other dignitaries. Bérnard explained that his father was too grief-ridden to be present and thus begged to be excused.

Jean-Luc, Marquis de Landes, dragged himself up the winding stairs to his and his lady wife's bedchamber. Noting that her side of the bed had not been turned down, nor her night rail laid out, he slowly walked to a high-carved chest and, opening the lid, removed a lacy silk night rail, one of Madeline's favorites. Carefully he laid it out, just so, on top of the goose-down coverlet. Then he walked over to his side of the bed and slowly undressed; he had told his valet that he would dispense with his services for this night and sent him away. His wife's wedding ring lay on the night counter by the bed; he picked it up, almost in a daze, held it, and turned it this way and that. Finally he pushed it on his little finger, the only one that was small enough for the ring, where it lodged just as far as his first knuckle. There he let it rest. For a moment, he looked around, hesitantly, looking for something. He found it right away, hidden by the folds of his gold-embroidered black velvet doublet. It was his short dirk, the one always at side, tucked into his belt. He pulled the dagger out of its sheath, tested the blade's edge against the tip of his tongue, as was his habit. It was as sharp as he wished it to be.

His wife's prie-dieu was lodged in a small recess in the corner of the room. Slowly he turned toward the large crucifix above it. He crossed himself and murmured the words of a brief private prayer, then crossed himself again.

Finally he lay down on his side of the bed. His hand reached over and pulled his wife's frilly lacy night rail over to cover himself with as best he could. He reached for his dagger, holding it in one hand, his fingers curled around the hilt. His other hand's fingers expertly pinpointed the large blood vessel he could feel pulsing in his neck, just under his jaw.

Carefully, slowly, and with great precision, he pushed the tip of the blade through the skin, muscles, and tendons. The pain he felt was no more than that of a sharp pinch. He let out a big sigh, which seemed to have been lodged in his body for the last three days. It felt as if a huge weight were lifted off his chest. He began to smile and closed his eyes, letting the images of Madeline fill his mind. The dirk slipped from his clumsy fingers and clattered to the stone floor, only to roll onto the Turkish carpet. Just after that, Madeline's night rail floated down to lie next to the dirk.

He felt endlessly calm and happy.

Then he saw and felt nothing at all.

*****

He still remembered running across the bridge, which his mother always called the Roman Bridge but which people nowadays began to call the Ponte Nuovo, the "New Bridge." Running up the hill to his favorite lookout from a crumbled-down cross, a reminder of some unfortunate traveler's long-ago death, probably due to some evildoer, either soldier or thief. From there he could see the great growing city of Firenze across the Arno, and if it was a clear view, even his uncle's house, where he had been growing up until he was six and also the house where he now lived with his mother and the younger children from her earlier marriages. He would guess that they were his stepbrothers, or more correctly, as his bell'ammá explained to him, his half brothers, but he never thought of them in such way, for they were strangers to him. And his only stepsister, Bianca, by then was already married, so she truly was a stranger.

It was not an easy thing to grow up in that household; certainly not, for it required endless lessons in all the things which his father would have considered important, and then also in those things which his mother did indeed considered important.

Yet it was not as difficult as living in his uncle Lorenzo di Pierfrancesco's house. His mother, never a friend of his uncle, used to say that in that family, all the charm was gifted to his father and all that was disagreeable to his uncle. He had no way to tell, but surely, it was difficult to be more sour-faced than Uncle L. P., as he secretly called him. Uncle L. P. made him go to a junior military academy for other noble youngsters, but oh Lord, how could he have liked it? They were so far behind and beneath him in the knowledge of things military! No finesse in swordplay, even with wooden swords. No gift for archery. Och, he was sorely bored by all that they tried to teach him, all of which he already knew—probably knew better! Even without overhearing Uncle L. P. one day complaining that he was an exceptionally precocious child, he was well aware that he was smarter than most, for sure!

As a child, he had wondered about the curious reversal of roles between his parents, even though he was, of course, not so certain about his father's likes and dislikes. He was less than a year old when his father died! Most of what he heard came from his uncle L. P., who was not a champion of his brother, Giovanni's dad, ever since he had "the poor judgment" to marry his bell'ammá. The same year when his mother had finally been able to return from imprisonment in Rome, she and her brother-in-law made a great effort to get along. They should have, well, most of the time. They had very much the same interests, but there was also a lot—a lot—of arguments between the two of them. Alas, his mother, beautiful and famous for her strength of will and her valor, valor, mind you, for a woman, was entirely devoid of pliancy or gentleness.

His uncle Lorenzo, L. P., in whose house he spent the first six years of his life, did value education, culture, the arts, including the burgeoning art called the science of arts and alchemy much more than warfare. Growing up in such haphazard way, between the two poles represented by uncle and mother, he did have, at first, difficulty to find a balance. As a very young teenager, he struggled mightily with this, his mother's influence outweighing that of his uncle. His good friend Pietro, known by all as Aretino, who was six years his senior and thus in the enviable position of knowing everything, teased him mercilessly about the seriousness of his struggle to achieve balance. Aretino had, at that time, no such problems. By his own admission, he was totally lacking either balance or serenity. He was an unabashed tease, an unrepentant gossip, and a self-avowed lover of beautiful men.

Thinking back, he had to smile and shake his head. Was it any wonder he grew up to become an offensive, aggressive, foul-mouthed, confused teenager? Good Lord, he thought, the confusion started long before, for barely had his father been buried when his mother decided to rechristen him and rename him from Ludovico to Giovanni! Good Lord, think of it! Was he really no more than two and ten years when he was banished from Firenze because of a murder he supposedly committed? He didn't even recall any of those circumstances; he was so falling-down drunk! At two and ten! And then when he was allowed to return a little over a year later, had he really participated in the rape of an older boy, a boy of fifteen or sixteen? Again, totally befogged recollection.

That was when he had first met Pietro and was so greatly impressed by his urbane behavior, which, of course, included his being a sodomite. Lord! It's amazing and a miracle of God Almighty that he finally had his head turned around, turned a corner, and became a serious and successful person. And moreover, a respected pillar of the community. On his own merit, not just coasting on his illustrious family name. That was the part he was most proud of!

His employer was no less a personage than the pope—His Holiness, Leo X, who, in his earlier life, had been Cardinal Giovanni di Lorenzo de' Medici. Finally he was able to use his military training and liking, assemble a most worthy group of mercenaries, and become their condottiere in the service of the pope. He smiled wolfishly. The Lord indeed worked in miraculous ways.

Ah, yes! Did he ever remember that glorious afternoon which, for many years and into his adulthood, became the best afternoon he ever had! He was maybe ten, no, eleven years old, almost an adult, or so he thought of himself. His bell'ammá had invited him to join her in entertaining a variety of famous men whom she was assembling at her receiving hall each day of the following week. He was still living at home with her but spent as little time there as he could possibly manage. At first he was reluctant to agree, but when he heard the list of those attending, his chest puffed up, and he almost burst with pride. That she would even consider him to help her play host, well, he felt more adult then than at any time since, except probably at his wedding to his sweet Maria!

*****

That week of gathering was like magic. He was a smart young man who could not help but listen, watch, and occasionally nod. At first, he only made hesitant polite comments. Then Master Ariosto—oh joy, he thought, the best—not only deigned to stop and listen to him but actually was willing to engage him in conversation. Taking him in tow, Ariosto drifted toward a conversation group, including Master Machiavelli, and that already-famous young genius from—where was it—ah, yes, from a place called Poland, Dr. Copernicus, Nicolaus Copernicus. He noted that his mother had turned around to listen as well, and then she also stepped up to join the group. He could hear from some distance already that the conversation revolved around all those opinions, both negative and positive, bandied about that this earth was actually a globe and that that globe ran a never-ending course around the sun.

Professor Copernicus, tall, thin, serious, and very young-looking, was nodding toward his bell'ammá and drawing imaginary circles with his arms, and then mimicking a spinning top by raising his pointer finger toward the ceiling and twirling it around and around, was trying to explain his concept of the Earth and the other planets simultaneously revolving around their round bodies and also running an endless circle. Amazing! And that all the while, when it was doing it, the Earth was as round as a ball? But how could that be? We were, after all, not ants to crawl right side up and upside down! Does that mean then that on the bottom side of this ball, nobody lives? All the people and all the waters are only on the upper half of this rotating ball? Amazing, amazing, amazing!

Giovanni sighed with longing. Lord, we live in such a confused but such an interesting time! Never bothered too much by shyness, he finally had to enter into the conversation with his own comments and questions.

"Messer Copernicus, can you please tell to me if what you are explaining is what has motivated our great seafarers? To go farther and farther and see if there is, in fact, life or anything on the bottom side?"

Copernicus turned toward his side and gave Giovanni a little bow. His eyes, with all seriousness, looked him up and down.

"Excellency, I compliment you on the astuteness of your mind. Indeed, as I have already found in my younger years, young age is not an enemy of true intellect. To the first question you posed, I have to answer you with an unequivocal yes. Ah, but then, the second question is quite difficult. The great Ptolemy of Alexandria, and those before him, had described a model of planetary globes, including our Earth, circling around the sun. He does not consider our Earth to be the center of the known universe, which he calls the cosmos. However, the explanation of how everything on this, our planet Earth, remains in place no matter how this Earth rotates, ah! That explanation awaits more thought, more experiments to unravel its mysteries. As much as that sentence has been and always will be the bane of my life, I have to honestly answer you, young Excellency, for the time being, it is so because it is so.

"Some think that perhaps there is a mysterious force emanating from our soil which has the strength to hold everything in place when actually, it should fly away into this cosmos." He lifted his bony shoulders and shrugged. "A mysterious force which pulls on everything that exists on top of our Earth's surface, even liquids, like water from the lakes, rivers, and oceans!"

"Of course, Excellency, all of these ideas are quite opposite to the dictums of our holy mother church, as my uncle, the bishop of Warmia, had warned me innumerable times in the past."

Ariosto eagerly approached the group, as he followed the young Giovanni. His eyes gleamed with anticipation to join into the discussion.

"Ah, yes, my dear friends, I for one have no doubt at all that the new dictums are the right direction to proceed in our knowledge. Has not new knowledge at first been always maligned, distrusted, and outright persecuted? Perhaps, just perhaps, we have passed that age of humanity's progress where we no longer have to cower and fear the persecution of the holy mother church, albeit I would not bet even one piece of silver on it! We must recognize that whatever advancement knowledge uncovers must, by its nature, be new, and new is always threatening the accepted and comfortable ways."

Before young Nicolaus could even voice his agreement, except by nodding vigorously, Master Giorgione picked up the conversation. Giovanni did not notice him before for he was hidden from view, leaning against the wall next to a deep recess of a window. He moved out, and as he did, Giovanni was struck by the romantic handsomeness of his face but even more so by his dark eyes, which seemed to see through you.

"Gentlemen, look here, look at this object I have been contemplating, at first bereft of speech and now totally entranced in my admiration for its beauty. This treasure has been, perhaps, overlooked by all of us because of its small size! May I?"

And giving a hesitant look to his hostess, receiving her smiling nod, he lifted the small gold figure of a dancing woman from its pedestal. Reverently cradling it in the shelter of both hands, he walked around, offering each a look.

"Has anyone seen anything of this size with such perfection? I cannot even guess who would have attempted—and succeeded—to produce such a miracle, but it must have been borne far from our land, in the south of Greece perhaps? Ah, no, that could not be, for the Greek artists were not renowned for gold pouring. Hmm, perhaps farther south? But I do not believe that it would be the north of Africa. What a mystery!" he then exclaimed, shaking his head, his brow drawn tight.

With a smile of mystery, Caterina drew close to him.

"Master Giorgione, allow me to clear your mind of this mystery! Let me also compliment you for your widespread knowledge about where and what kind of art was once practiced."

And seeing her young son Giovanni coming closer to her, she extended her arm and clasped his fingers with hers.

"About two months before his death, my beloved husband Giovanni Medici, while he was away from me, doing battle for our city of Firenze against Venice"—she stopped and bowed her head graciously in Giorgione's and Titian's direction—"he sent me this little statue because he thought that it would bring me joy. So it did, very, very much so, to this day every day of my life, for I recognized its exquisite beauty. It has become my custom to visit my little statue every morning upon waking and sending a thank you to my love, who has so soon been torn from my arms…But I digress, sirs! The story of the little statue is that it was made, many thousands of years ago, on the island of Crete, according to great Plato, perhaps the home of mysterious Atlantis before it sank into the sea…And to add spice to the story, the myth continues that it was made by the greatest goldworker of all the ages, a deformed dwarf, who made it in the likeness of the lady who was the only love of his life!"

Giorgione listened intently, along with most of the gathering. When the hostess finished, he pivoted as he raised the little figure once more to everyone's view, then carefully, almost reverently, replaced it onto its marble stand. Turning around, his soft eyes, which still felt like they looked through the person, pinned each of them one by one.

"And may God make us grateful for such great art and for giving humanity the means to preserve such greatness forever, that glorious metal we call gold!"

While the two Venetians, Titian and Giorgione, were lost in the admiration of the little figure, Ariosto, as though having a sudden thought, turned to Giorgione with a question, grabbing the younger man's arm.

"Good sir, I have heard of the beauty of your painting which you, I believe, have decided to call *The Tempest*! Your talk about beauty reminded me that I was planning to ask you as soon I would encounter your presence. I beg you, good sir, please give us the particulars!"

Giorgione's eyebrow rose halfway up his forehead.

"The particulars, sir? Those I can summarize for you very quickly. It has a size of seventy-three by eighty-three centimeters, my good sir, and is simply oil over canvas. It shows three human figures, a young woman nursing an infant in the middle distance and a young man leaning on a lance in the extreme foreground on the left. Neither is looking at each other, there is no connection between the two human figures. There is also an animal present, a stork on a rooftop. I am at a loss what else to add to the 'particulars,' my good sir." And with that, he turned away abruptly, not hiding his annoyance.

Fortunately his friend and travel companion, Master Titian, as much of a deft diplomat as artist, sauntered over to the pair who, at this point, were eyeing each other with decided distaste, and wrapped his beefy arm around Giorgione. Shaking his head, he laughingly squeezed little George's shoulder.

"Master Ariosto, pray do forgive my friend's curtness of answer. He is a shy fellow, that one, and when asked, especially after such a fulsome praise as yours, sir, he becomes tongue-tied. I, however, find that I never suffer from that condition, my dear Master Ludovico, and knowing his work almost as well as he does—maybe even a little bit better—I will be happy to oblige you with more information."

He released his hold on Giorgione and proceeded to manhandle Master Ariosto in the same fashion, with the intent to gently lead him away to an unoccupied corner of the large receiving hall. Caterina, heaving a relieved sigh and with a mental note to send a message of thanks for Master Titian, followed the two, drawing her son and Dr. Copernicus with her. The group listened to Titian's lengthy explanation of the novel idea in stage setting of a painting by bringing nature to be a main player, equal in importance to the figures drawn. Titian was warming to his subject.

"Since my friend Giorgione has been just that, my friend, and also my teacher once, I am fair certain that I can interpret his intentions with reasonable assurance. The painting's features seem to anticipate a storm. The colors are subdued and the lighting soft, greens and blues dominate. But what fascinates most, especially for such a small canvas, is that probably for the first time in the history of painting, the landscape is not treated as a mere backdrop. Indeed, it forms a theme of an importance equal to, or perhaps even greater, than that of the young woman feeding her suckling child and at the very opposite of the canvas, a soldier with a lance.

"Neither of the figures are involved with each other, and without that involvement, their placing apart from each other without interacting only stresses the great significance of the landscape. I've heard some pronounce that the painting is a great curiosity, in that one becomes so engaged in the landscape and the mood and illumination of the stormy sky that the two unrelated figures become of secondary interest, quasi an interruption in the enjoyment of the painting. But I believe not so. This canvas is a pathfinder in the art of painting, a whole new avenue which I am certain shall be enthusiastically followed by many future painters. Thus are the first stones thrown into a new direction, whether in the arts, in literature"—and

Titian made a polite bow to Ariosto—"or in the sciences"—there was the bow again, this time to Dr. Copernicus—"which will be admired, appreciated, and applauded by our children, grandchildren, and great-grandchildren to come." Messer Titian had indeed warmed to his subject. "This is the beginning of a whole new avenue of paintings, those of the glorious landscapes which surround us everywhere!"

Not willing to allow the discussion to evolve only in the direction of the arts, Caterina, well known for her interest and activities in alchemy, turned to Dr. Copernicus, whose studies in astronomy and medicine more closely approximated hers in alchemy.

"My dearest Dr. Copernicus, nay, forgive me, for I must call you Professor Copernicus! I have heard that Bologna accorded you the distinguished title of Professor Mathematum for which I beg you to accept my most heartfelt congratulations, sir! Now I pray, my dear Nicolaus, you will allow me to call you thus, will you not?" And she flashed an enchanting smile at him, enough to melt any male heart this side of eighty. "Pray explain to me in more detail the long-lost theory of great Ptolemy regarding the rotation of the moon, and even supposedly our Earth as well, all of which you have alluded to before. However much holy mother church wishes to disregard, distrust, and even entirely disavow such findings, I am a great believer in all things new and challenging in the study of science and alchemy. And I pray you, Nicolaus, explain your findings in that area and how they were derived by your most excellent brain!

"Is it not wonderfully challenging and refreshing to live now, as compared to even in the days of our grandparents? We have so much that is exiting and entirely satisfying to our intellect. I swear to you, my dear sirs"—and she turned slightly to her right to acknowledge Master Machiavelli who now had also joined the small discussion group—"I am beginning to comprehend how stimulating it must have been to live in ancient Greece and Egypt's Alexandria, in the days of its great library, for I wake up each morn eager to face the newness of the day!"

At that, almost on cue, the double door to the reception room opened, and servants brought in a huge silver bowl filled with the rose-colored wine of Tuscany. The wine was filled with thinly sliced berries and apples which grew in profusion in the woods and gardens around the Villa Medici di Castello. Several other servants carried silver trays with the newly fashionable glass goblets blown on the island of Murano, just across from the city of Venice. Goblets were distributed and filled with the fruit-fragranced wine. When everyone had a goblet in hand, even young Giovanni, the hostess moved into the center of the room, inviting her son to join her as the host of the affair, and asked that all those present raise their glasses to the wonderful new movement, blowing off the dust of centuries past.

As a good hostess should, her eyes everywhere, she noticed two of the guests, the painter Messer Sandro Botticelli and the politician and writer Messer Niccolò Machiavelli, engaged in animated conversation, leaning against the casement of the windows in a small alcove. Of course, Messer Machiavelli was deeply involved in the politics and defense of his hometown of Firenze, and she knew as well that Messer Botticelli dabbled in hometown politics, so she was not surprised that the two had converged toward each other. She took two swift steps toward them, waving one of the servants with the glasses in their direction. She addressed them directly.

"Come, come, gentlemen! Pray suspend your so intense conversation for just a little while. Join the rest of us for a toast. Then you can return to your discussions with a vengeance!" She took a quick breath and continued.

"Gentlemen, masters, and professors of your specified fields of work. In the name of humanism, shall we all drink to it and bless its achievements done and also those yet to follow, a blessing to the human intellect, the human spirit, the human soul!

*****

Three of the men, elegantly dressed, the fourth seemingly travel-worn in clothing and appearance, sat outside, enjoying each other's company, at ease around several small tables set up to hold refreshments for them. The combination arbor and garden, aromatic with the scent of flowers and herbs, provided shade, the food and wine on the tables sustenance, and the view out through the lagoon to the sea offered a feast for the eye.

The oldest of the three, at thirty-three, the host of the gathering, a man with piercing dark eyes, a long narrow nose, and a high forehead showing the beginnings of a receding hairline, compensated for by his sparse long hair, was, at the moment, bending to the soldier, obviously the honored guest. In order to emphasize what he was saying, he nodded but also lifted his hand, extending his index finger to tap the back of the soldier's hand for emphasis.

"A great lady, indeed, and a valiant one at that. Nobody could dispute either attributes, ever! Ever!"

The man who was so addressed smiled and nodded. He turned to his host and, without rising from his seat, bowed to him slightly.

"Ah, Master Titian, how right you are, indeed. No one could fault my mother, God rest her soul, for being hesitant or less than—well, calling a spade a spade—bellicose. As I understand from my friend Professor de Landes, who tells me that his mother and mine were the best of friends growing up in Galeazzo Sforza's Milano. His mother, Madeline, used to tell him and his twin brother stories about this militant friend of hers named Caterina." He shook his head, still smiling. "Even then…she could not have been older than twelve or thirteen!"

The man addressed as Titian threw back his head and emitted a laughter like a short bark.

"Well, yes, it is not to be denied that blood will tell!"

The soldier, youngest of the group, adjusted his cape and, extending one elegant leg, leaned forward.

"My dearest Master, once again let me be able to express my gratitude, and that of Professor de Landes, to you for kindly extending your invitation to him as well. As I pointed out, he had, last eve, arrived at my house's door in a rented gondola. I had no idea that he was even en route from Poland to Paris and wished to see me to do just that which we are doing here, to reminisce. You see, he was unaware that I have now temporarily changed my residence from Firenze to Venice. I did that simply for my own convenience. You may be aware of my upcoming marriage to my betrothed, Maria

Salviati. The Salviatis and Medicis together are making such a hubbub that I thought best to flee Firenze until just before the ceremony! It was fortunate that Marcel, lodging for the night in a small inn, happened to hear about my presence here in town!

"As I have indicated to you, my dear Master, Marcel is the younger of the twins of the aforementioned Madeline, who had been such good and loyal friend of my mother, as she was to her. Marcel has ever been a scientist, thinker, mathematician, and astronomer who had not only studied under Professor Copernicus but also worked with him for years. He has now been favored with the appointment by the University of Sorbonne to set up a chair for the new science of mathematum and medicine. I have to confess, I am excessively proud of him!"

The fourth man, thin and taller than average, with tightly crinkled reddish hair and beard to go along with his ruddy coloring, had risen and sauntered to the water's edge. There the tiny waves from a passing boat were lapping at the stone steps leading down from the garden to the water. A brightly painted gondola was moored to the yellow-and-red-stiped post. The gondola, responding to the gentle waves running toward the stone steps, swayed with the soft lap-lap of the water. For a while, he watched the play of the water, then turned around with suddenness. There was an evilly teasing gleam in his eyes, which alternately swept each of his companions but ultimately settled on the youngest of the four.

"Perhaps you will all forgive me for returning to the praise of this young man, the friend of my youth, Giovanni's mother, for just a little while. Aye, who could dare to dispute either her boldness or practice of the martial arts, pray tell? But you, dear Master, forgot her beauty, her great beauty which, sadly, I was deprived to see except in my thoughtless youth!" He bowed slightly to the young man. "My friend, may she rest peacefully until the angel sounds the final trumpet, as she rises to the throne of God!

"Is there any doubt at all that out of all the beauties that abound in our land—as our maestro can attest with greater aesthetic knowledge than any other—there are none to compare! And as far as being valiant"—he lifted his shoulders—"tell me who could outdo the beautiful Lady of Imola and Forlì, standing on the ramparts of the *castello*, and, when threatened with the lives of her children to force her surrender, exposes herself to the enemy army and tells them, 'Go ahead, for lo, here I have what I need to make other children!' Truly an incredible act of bravery and is it not a gamble as well!"

At this, the traveler, the one named Marcel, sucked in his breath and raised a troubled eye toward the young soldier. "What," he stammered, "what is it I hear about my valiant Aunt Caterina? Lord, Giovanni, *dit-moi*! You must tell me about this event in detail! *Ce soir, n'est-ce pas*?"

Giovanni just sighed as one who has told the story a hundred times already, then nodded good-humoredly.

The host turned to the thin man, shaking his head in disapproval.

"Ah, Pietro, Pietro, cease such talk. Perchance your words will offend his Excellency?"

The young soldier to whom Master Titian addressed himself, again adjusted his position in the deep armchair, and shook his head with a smile.

"Master, Master, suspend your worry, I beg you! Only an obtuse idiot would take that scamp's words amiss. As we all know, that which leaves his lips is only allowed to leave from there if it shocks. Even the way he structures his sentences are designed to do so, for he constructs them with great convolution and most always leaves them dangling without finish! Feigning shock only incites him to more of his atrocious verbiage! But let us be honest here. As much as I honor my dearest mother's memory, what Aretino says is God's truth! Or so I have heard repeated many times. Sadly, at that time, I was short of being born yet by ten years. I swear, I would have liked to witness it."

The guest of honor was a man only one year short of twenty and dressed as a soldier. He was a devilishly handsome young man. His torso was covered by a finely gold-embroidered black silk doublet. His black leggings hugged him, presenting well-shaped calves and muscular thighs. He had removed his sword belt and, with it, the lethal-looking narrow Italian sword, with its elaborately worked square hilt. Both rested on the ground by his seat. A short rapier rested against his hip, threaded through a thin braided black leather belt. A cape lined with bright-red silk hung from his shoulders. His black leather gauntlets were tucked into the front of this narrow belt. He wore a dark mustache, and his dark hair was shorn short to cool his head when he had to wear a metal helmet. Today he wore a hat. It lay at his feet, a red ostrich plume waving gently in the slight breeze coming in from the Adriatic.

Lodovico de' Medici, rechristened Giovanni by his famous and famously volatile mother, Caterina Sforza, was a distant cousin to the great Lorenzo de' Medici, "il Magnifico," the de facto ruler of Florence, except that he descended from the junior branch of the family. At least, Giovanni thought with irony, his side of the family liked to stress the cousinship. And to be fair, his father, Giovanni "il Popolano"—another Giovanni—when orphaned, had grown up and been educated in the Palazzo Medici alongside the young Lorenzo, learning from such giants as the great humanist and linguist Poliziano and the philosopher priest Ficino.

Giovanni slid farther forward in the seat of his cushioned armchair. Impatiently pushing the cape back from his shoulders, he extended one long leg and angled his arm, his fist upon his muscular thigh.

"Gentlemen, let us pass over such more famous statements and actions of my lady mother. They are surely known well enough up and down the two coasts of our peninsula! Certainly she was a bawdy lady but a great lady, nevertheless. My father and she fell in love, truly, greatly in love, and were very happy during that brief period when I was born and before my father's untimely death. I like to think that they have now found each other in the afterlife and, as the saying goes, do live happily ever after!

"Howbeit, I feel compelled to tell you that she had an uncanny ability to draw out people, aye, and not only just to do so but also to find relationships, intersecting points between seemingly totally dissimilar personalities and interests and to—to—well, to mold such dissimilar people's minds around a common interest. Her interests and education extended into many fields, and mind you, not superficially either! At the Milanese court, she grew up with no restrictions placed upon her mind, and having a very precocious mind, she truly leaned and learned."

He stopped himself with a little chuckle and a slight shake of his head. "Aye, I'll grant you that her precocious mind absorbed the loftiest learning, along with all the smut that tends to rise to the surface to float around in such august places."

"I must tell you, gentlemen, I was no older than ten or eleven years at the time. It was just one year before my dear mother had so unexpectedly and prematurely been taken from this life. I was beginning to grow into a veritable 'bad boy,' but I am certain that both of you have heard—ad infinitum—of my early exploits which eventually got me banished from Florence! Well, Mother sent me an invitation, engraved and heavy with Latin and calligraphy. I want to call it to your attention, gentlemen, that at that time, I lived in my mother's home, but she went all out to make me feel an adult and sent me that invitation, to one of her intimate gatherings. I had heard about them, she cultivated the best of the best of the men and women of literature, the arts, the humanities, the burgeoning fields of astronomy, and the study of plants and the human body. I was thrilled, felt like quite the adult, and hoped against hope that my then-greatest idol, none other than the great Master Leonardo, would be present. Alas, no such good fortune.

"Nevertheless, I must tell you, gentlemen, that the small select group were made up of Professor Copernicus, who came expressly to visit Mamà, and made the detour from Padua, where he had just left the university, to journey home to his country of Polonia. The other two guests were our gracious host Master Titian and your dear friend from your student years at Master Bellini's studio, the incomparable Giorgione. Also the equally incomparable Master Botticelli. Both of these great painters now lamentably departed from us too soon, too young! Master Ariosto and Master Machiavelli were there as well. That one afternoon gave me more education than would two years at the academy for the science of war in Firenze!"

Titian, the host, stirred. He threw out his hands in a typical Italianate gesture of supplication.

"There you go, gentlemen! Excellency, you dink my wine and eat my oysters, and you call them incomparable in my home! Hmph!"

Giovanni turned to his host. With a self-deprecating gesture of his hand and wrist, he rose slightly from his seat.

"Ah, Maestro, I only called them incomparable"—and he raised his eyes heavenward—"because they no longer are here with us!"

Titian nodded his head with a slight smile. "*Ebbene,* I understand, Your Excellency…I do, indeed." And with his smile in place, he reached for his jewel-encrusted gold-decorated goblet.

Aretino, feeling deplorably neglected, an entirely unusual experience for him, turned from the canal's edge and sauntered back to the others. His eyebrows narrowed slowly as his alert eyes slanted from one to the other of his companions. When he looked at them again, he raised a questing eyebrow.

"Forgive me for asking, Giovanni, my old friend of childhood, when he still looked up to me and not in reverse, whom I will steadfastly refuse to address as Your Excellency, tell us, if it is not too painful, how did the death of your gracious mother come to pass?"

Giovanni sighed and adjusted his body in the armchair, then pulled both legs under the chair. With another sigh, he reached for his goblet and drank deeply.

"She had been feeling weak and poorly for a while, not desiring to eat, really. She was losing weight and strength, more so from each day to the next. By then a while ago, she had made her arrangements for her death and burial, confessed to her confessor, did all of those expected things, but we, her family, her children, and grandchildren, were not really taking all those preparations seriously. Neither did I, but then I was barely past childhood. I was only eleven, albeit a precocious eleven. She was, after all, only forty-six years old and in full bloom of her strength until just two weeks before. But she developed a deep hacking cough and started gasping for air. At the end, she became feverish and had a heavy and labored breathing. She died on the twenty-eighth of the month of May of last year. Most of her family were there and surrounded her. I was the one who closed her eyes. And also folded her hands together in prayer. I was told that it was supposedly a Medici tradition…" He shook his head and took a deep shuddering breath. "She was, my friends, a great, great and valiant lady, truly the tiger of Forlì...Truly her actions, her life were worthy of the life of a great person!"

There was silence for a moment, once again, all that was heard was the soft rhythmic lapping of the small waves against the pier.

Aretino was the first person to regain his voice.

"Our generous, illustrious, honored, and most prolific host"—with a bow toward Titian—"and, sir, when I say the word *prolific*, of course I am only alluding to your art! That is understood! My impression for the purpose of this gathering led me to believe that we were selected to view the progress of your latest work, Master. Is that exquisite pleasure still on our agenda?"

Titian smiled with seductive mischievousness. He rose from his seat and walked to the door leading into the house, partly obscured by opulently gathered sunset-pink draperies. At the door, he stopped and shook his head, throwing his hands out in one of his favorite gestures.

"My friends, I assume you already know that I am not a man plagued by modesty. Thus I may as well confess that I am currently working on two items, of which one is in its final phase of completion, while the other is only an early concept for a commission I have recently accepted. However, please be at ease, my friends. It will cost you no more to view both as one!" And throwing his head back, he barked his characteristic short laughter. "I pray, please follow me, and I beg you watch where you are stepping! There is clutter everywhere, and I wish you not step into a pot of paint! It would only spill, and paint these days is far too expensive for that!" And there was that bark again, this time accompanied by a shake of his head.

The master continued his explanation, while his guests carefully wound their way in the semidarkness across a veritable obstacle course of tables and chairs filled to overflowing with boxes of chalk, charcoal, rolls of parchment, lengths of wood for framing of canvases, while pieces of clothing and scraps of paper littered the floor, along with a flutter of canvas, odds and ends thrown away carelessly in what appeared to be a fit of irritation. Finally they reached the entrance to one of Titian's workrooms currently dominated by one large sketch of the Madonna floating up to the heavens, looking up to God's extended arms and benevolent gaze. There were also a number of smaller sketches, studies of faces, hands and draped materials scattered about.

"This, my friends, is a collection of my initial sketches to work on the commission of our good Franciscan friars to paint the altarpiece for the Basilica Santa Angelina Gloriosa dei Frari. The requested piece was to be the miraculous assumption of the Virgin into the heavens, into our Lord's arms. I must confess, it is a magnificent and munificent commission and that much more appealing since this is my first commission for a painting to occupy the eye from the main altar, not one of the side chapels. I must also confess feeling flattered and desire, above all, to do justice to the assignment! It is a huge work, and I had indicated to the directors of the basilica that the production will be quite time-consuming. Of course, they were not pleased with that..." And there again, he emitted his barking laugh. "But pray tell, was there ever a commission for an artwork which was finished quite at the desired timeline?"

With great attention, the little group paced by the various parts of the developing painting, but other than for the eyes of another artist, there was not all that much to see. It took a trained eye to perceive the subtleties of even a masterpiece in its early stages of *unfolding*, a term which Master Giorgione, a lover of all things plant and nature, had loved to use. In short order, the master shepherded his small group to the opposite end of the room, where an almost-finished wood panel stood on an easel, under much better illumination than the altarpiece.

Drawing close, Pietro Aretino, sharp-eyed and trained to view many of the master's works quite frequently, exclaimed with surprise, "Ah, my dear friend, but I perceive this work is panel painting, is it not?"

Master Titian nodded eagerly. "Yes, yes, my friend, I must applaud your powers of observation from such a distance! It is, indeed. But remember, wood panels painted with oils is still used with equal frequency as is canvas. In some cases, it is the preferred support for oil paints because of its durability and also the ease with which the paint can be adhered to it. Canvas is, after all, so much softer and looser, no matter how well it is stretched!

"Howbeit, in this case, wood panel was specified since the commission I received from His Grace, Duke Alfonso d'Este, from Ferrara indicated that what His Grace wanted was a wooden door panel for a cabinet in which he wishes to store antique classical coins. I traveled there, for much of the panel needed to be painted in Ferrara. I have only brought it with me to do some finishing touches on it. And so here it is, gentlemen, for you to see it before it is taken back to Ferrara and becomes off-limits to all eyes except the duke's and his circle."

Master Titian felt the need for more fulsome explanations. He could not hide his joy and pride in this product of his brain, his eyes, and his hands.

"If you will recall, Your Excellency, my good sirs, there is a parable in the Holy Bible. It concerns itself with our Lord encountered by some Pharisees. I wanted to depict Christ and a Pharisee at the moment in the Gospels when Christ is shown a coin. Christ takes the coin that is shown to him and says, 'Render unto Caesar the things that are Caesar's, and unto God the things that are God's.' I have called the painting *The Tribute Money*. As best as I could establish, this is a subject not yet represented before in art."

Once again, the guests stood, this time quite absorbed by the view of the painting. It was a most elegantly executed and, at the same time, touchingly human scene between two men, that of Christ, in an almost frontal view, looking at the Pharisee with kind, pitying, and all-knowing eyes. His elegant fingers are hovering over the gold coin without actually touching it. In contrast, the Pharisee looks to grovel, wheedle, and insist, while the hand holding the coin almost pushes it into Christ's hand.

The guests watched and looked, transfixed. Finally Captain Giovanni recovered first, shaking his head.

"My friend, Messer Titian, in truth, I have a difficult time to recall when I have seen any painting this eloquent, this elegant, and so wondrously earthy and ethereal at the same time. This, I believe, is where the essence of great art shows itself. Duke Alfonso will truly be a lucky man to gaze at this wonder any time he wishes!"

Aretino leaned closer to the painting. With ruffled eyebrows, he squinted into it.

"Do I perceive correctly, or are my eyes deluding me, is there a signature of 'Ticianus f,' for 'Ticianus fecit,' painted on the Pharisee's collar?"

The host nodded his head with a pleased smile. "Aye, you are quite correct, my eagle-eyed young friend. That's where I signed the work. I thought few, if any, would see it!"

Not to be outdone, Captain Giovanni shook his head, then began to laugh.

"My good sir, you are not only an incomparable artist and a wonderful host with a never-ending supply of food and drink, but I hazard to think, you are also a scamp, sir. Or will you deny that that face of the Pharisee is the visage of none other than the great Venetian painter Titian?"

Once again, that bark laugh of the host floated up into the air. He shook his finger at Giovanni.

"Aye, aye, you are as right as our friend Aretino! Begone, begone, the both of you. Shall we repair out into the bright fresh air in my loggia or the garden? Try as I want, I cannot get the musty moldy air out of this building of mine, too many old musty canvases, I believe, and too much wet air from the canals! It is a deadly combination for clothing, painting, furniture, and the human body!"

*****

Angelina Maria sat in the little garden in the back of the little house she shared with her widowed sister, Celestina. Celestina had begun to be very confused and forgetful at times, and she needed looking after, so after her brother-in-law's death a year ago, Angelina had decided to take her in. She had a house spacious enough for two. If necessary, her daughter Lucia, who lived next-door to her with Matteo, her son-in-law, and their three little ones, could help out, just as she helped out whenever necessary for them. It was a nice arrangement all round, and after all, family was family and came first in one's life!

And once again, right now, she was doing for her family, attending the little ones, two girls, three and five years, and a baby boy, gurgling and babbling in his basket. The girls were chasing each other and laughing, and the baby, Matteo, had just been suckled by his mother before she dropped off the lot of them on her mother. So Angelina could have some time to herself with only half of one eye cast occasionally at her charges. Lucia went to her once-a-week work for the Contessa Bianca Gondi. Lady Gondi was the young sister-in-law of Angelina's beloved Giovanni de' Medici, sister of Giovanni's widow, Maria.

Countess Bianca needed someone to launder, steam, stretch, and reshape her prized lace parts to her costumes, lace that had been imported at great expense from faraway Alençon, in France. The French lace was considered to be the queen of laces, and rich ladies vied with one another to possess it. Its maintenance, however, required great skill, and Angelina Maria was proud of her daughter's skill in doing well with it.

The good Lord be thanked, through word of mouth from Lady Bianca to her lady friends, Lucia's trade now prospered well above what they initially expected. Lucia was usually gone for at least part of every day of the week, except for Sunday.

Thankfully her mother lived next-door, and thus Angelina Maria's presence helped with overseeing the children. Lucia's husband, after whom baby Matteo was named, was gone long weeks at a time. He was one of the supervisors of the marble quarries at Carrara; and Lucia was quite proud of him. With three little ones, and one sickly confused aunt living with her mother, the combined household needed all the income they could gather.

Howbeit, the gracious Countess Maria, her Lord Giovanni's widow, saw to it that Angelina Maria lacked nothing. She understood that her dearest husband had cherished Angelina Maria and had considered her sort of a nurse, nanny, and aunt at the same time. Many a times, he would tell her how he had felt her as close to himself as he did his mother, Caterina; and that was understandable, as the mother had been absent from her son's life so often and then left him an orphan at a child's age of twelve.

And so now, Angelina Maria sat in her garden, occasionally looking at the children and then again at the fruiting apple and cherry trees. Her eyes would wander over the well-tended vegetables, bordered by blooming flowers. On the garden side of the house, pink and red roses climbed up on lattices attached to the walls. In the sleepy quiet of the afternoon, interrupted only by the glee of the children, bees hummed about, busily visiting the selection of flowers available to them.

Angelina Maria rose from her chair and went into the house. No more than a minute later—she dared not leave the children alone for long, after all—she came back carrying a small box. She sat, put the box onto her lap, and carefully lifted the lid to the box. With great care and caution, she lifted out a velvet-wrapped object and, with the same care, unwrapped it. She had looked at this wondrous object many times, but each time she saw it, its beauty twisted her heart. It was a delicately small gold-gleaming statue of a dancing woman, her eyes closed in the ecstasy of the dance.

This, this was the treasure which Angelina Maria received from her darling Giovanni before his death. Oh, she had committed to her memory every moment of those horrible, horrible days!

As soon as news reached them, at the Villa Medici di Castello, that Giovanni had been wounded in a battle near Governolo and been taken to the Gonzaga Palace in Mantua, to be treated for his injuries, she was called to the presence of the Countess Maria, Giovanni's wife. She was ordered to take their young son, seven-year-old Cosimo, and to travel posthaste to Mantua. Maria was unable to travel, she was heavily pregnant at the time. Delivery was actually expected within a week or two. Maria was adamant, if she could not be near her dangerously wounded husband, she knew he would want nobody else but his Auntie Angelina, and as they did not know the seriousness of the injury, she insisted that nine-year-old Cosimo, young as he was, should be there to give pleasure for her husband, his father, or God forbid, see his father for the last time.

When Angelina Maria saw Giovanni, he already had his injured leg amputated, cut off just below the knee. He was greatly pleased to see both his son and his Angelina Maria, and made light of the surgery, repeating time and again that he would be healed because the great surgeon Abramo did the cutting. Abramo, it seemed, had treated His Excellency before with much success, and this trust kept Giovanni in good cheer. But within a day, he complained bitterly of severe pain and became feverish. By the fourth day, he suffered raging fever and was in a state of delirium.

Angelina Maria sat by his bedside and incessantly bathed his face and all the rest of his body with cold water she insisted would be drawn from a mountain brook and kept cold while it was transported to Mantua. Miraculously she was obeyed, being looked upon as a representative of the Countess de' Medici herself.

On the fifth day, Giovanni rallied, and Angelina Maria thought that things would now begin to turn around. He talked to her for a while, calmly and with total lucidity, and denied having any pain or even discomfort. He summoned her closer to his bed and bid her reach under his pillow. She did and pulled out the little box, the self-same one she now held in her hand. When he told her to open the lid, she knew quite well what was contained within, and when His Excellency told her to take it—this was to be his mother's inheritance to her—she could not believe her ears.

She fought with him, literally, until he caught her hand and shook it, telling her that it had been his mother's wish to will the little figurine to his auntie. Caterina had maintained, that other than her son Giovanni, it would not have the same meaning to anyone who did not know her dearest husband Giovanni, the man who gifted her with the box and its contents! Finally, when she again opened her mouth to argue, His Excellency told her that no one else, no one, at this time lived who still knew his father, she was the last bond, so to say, to his mother, Caterina's, and his father, Giovanni's, love, and it was for her to keep it and to treasure it or to use it as she would need, perhaps.

As always, when she had arrived to this point in her musings, her tears were already falling, and she needed to mop her face busily so that the children would not notice their nonna crying.

Aye, God had been good to her. She had served a loving kind family for many years, who truly became her family as well. For she had served them faithfully, and they had been grateful to her and considered her to be more than a servant. She had loved them all, the lady as well as her children, well, all except her first two atrocious husbands. Especially the second one! He was a despicable, vain, and shallow man! She still had to shudder each time she thought of him. She had said goodbye to many of them in that large family and buried them and mourned them. And she was now keeping the little figure, to give it to baby Matteo when he was old enough and tell him all the stories, oh Lord, so many stories to tell; and it was her obligation to pass on the stories, for who else would now listen to her?

Her darling boy, Giovanni, had after all succumbed to his wound. He died no more than half a day after. She had been heart-broken, and little Cosimo cried bitter tears for his babbo. When finally the news reached Her Excellency, Lady Maria, she collapsed in grief. She had a miscarriage and spent a long and perilous time in recovery. Widowed, once little Cosimo was grown, she withdrew from life and wore the black and white clothing of a novice nun, which she never gave up. She had hardly any contacts with the world, except asking for an occasional visit from her son and from Angelina Maria, mostly to reminisce about her husband, Giovanni.

And now here she sat in her little garden of the comfortable cozy little house she owned; it was hers and nobody could take it away from her. The sun shone down and warmed her. Her grandchildren gathered around her. She was well known, well regarded not only for her work but her person and position as well. She had become a person in her own right, a personage, a citizen of Florence. She was now Donn' Angelina, or Donna Maria, a woman of the middle class, the daughter of sharecroppers and serfs. She knew nothing of humanism and its political meaning, but she was not a stupid person, and the weight of history was not lost to her.

This was truly, truly a new world that has been awakened in such a short blink of an eye, she thought, just in one short lifetime!

New Worlds Rising

Triton, Largest Moon of Planet Neptune, the Outer Reaches of the Solar System

AD 2050–2080

Introduction

Gold. Chemical sign Au. When mined, brought out of the earth in the desert of Nubia, the mines of Great Zimbabwe and those of South Africa, the ancient Indus Valley civilizations, in California or the Yukon, or anywhere else on this globe, it was, it is, and it will still remain Au.

Worked into shapes for trivial embellishments or gloriously beautiful adornments, for decoration of homes, temples, churches, palaces, it was, it is, and it will still remain Au.

Its immutable nature was exactly the reason why this miraculously unique metal was chosen to be included in *Voyager 1* and *Voyager 2*. Both probes were launched in 1977 to study the planets Jupiter and Saturn, although *Voyager 2* also traveled past Uranus in 1986 and Neptune in 1989. Aboard, the probes included two phonograph records which contain sounds and images selected to portray the diversity of life and culture on Earth; they are, in fact, a cosmic time capsule. The great Carl Sagan, astronomer, planetary scientist, cosmologist, astrophysicist, astrobiologist, and the primary voice in the design and implementation of the project, chose gold to be the carrier of these messages.

"The spacecrafts," he wrote, "will be encountered and the record played only if there are advanced space-faring civilizations in interstellar space, but the launching of this 'bottle' into the cosmic 'ocean' says something very hopeful about life on this planet."

The probes have since passed out of our solar system and will pass within 1.6 light-years' distance of the star Gliese 445. Gliese 445 is currently within the constellation Camelopardalis, an estimated 40,000 Earth-years' distance away. As the saying goes, the probes have far exceeded any expectations.

Since those days of hope and idealism on Earth, the progress of science has allowed greatly more advanced and sophisticated spacecrafts to be sent here and there on explorations of neighborhood planets and especially some of their more promising moons. Mars, our neighbor, has now viable colonies established. Probes have been sent and had arrived on two of the moons of Jupiter, Europa and Callisto, also on two of the moons of Saturn, Titan and Enceladus.

Now it was time to strike out into the farther outer reaches of our solar system, the realm of the "ice giants," Uranus and Neptune.

Prologue

The IIPA, the great and revered International Inter-Planetary Agency, had been at work for decades on this quasi-cryptic project. Everyone was very hush-hush about it in the beginning, but then, as the first two Mars colonies had started up, became established, and the prospect of interplanetary travel became more accepted and, well, sort of a near-future certainty, the project was openly discussed and publicized. Everywhere. And published. Everywhere. An avalanche of learned and popularized information snowed down on all those who were interested to read up on the subject.

It became widely publicized that the project was aimed at a moon of one of the great ice giants, either Uranus or Neptune. In the eyes of those who were at all knowledgeable about such things, this meant probably, as next best guesses, either Titania, a moon of Uranus, or conversely Triton, one of the moons of Neptune. Innumerable bets were waged, and as the project was reported to progress well, people everywhere, even those on the two Mars colonies, were caught up in the excitement.

Most of the bets favored Titania, simply because it was "closer." In itself, of course, that was a ridiculous concept. The distances to either moons were such that the idea of closeness became irrelevant. Especially since cryobiology had already advanced sufficiently to be available, not only for such mundane projects as the replacement of certain selected body parts but had great potential for cryobiological means of dealing with the lengths of travel for biological bodies. Additionally AI would presumably be employed, albeit at this stage, most scientists were inclined to combine a mix of AI and cryostasis. But of course, those were mostly theoretical consideration, for the early probes to be sent would, without question, use only AI to be made a part of and to direct these probes.

It was a surprise to most lay persons when they were informed that the probe IIPP-1, or international interplanetary probe-1, scheduled to depart Earth in 2052, was directed to Neptune's largest moon, Triton. Its expected arrival was to be 2078–2080. The probe was filled with all protective mechanisms against the dangers of its interplanetary journey and filled to capacity with every conceivable piece of survey equipment.

After its launch, once the probe successfully passed by Mars, and the gas giants Jupiter and Saturn, it was on its way, through the icy distances of the solar system, to its destination.

IIPP-1 settled with all the gentleness and care it had been trained to do onto the wide flat rocky surface selected by its guidance system, poking out from a giant surrounding sea of water ice.

Any sounds it would have emanated in an atmosphere of air to carry sound waves were, of course, nonexistent. The atmosphere, as such, consisted mostly of frozen nitrogen, water ice, and carbon dioxide. But IIPP-1 did not need these sounds, actually they meant nothing to its functioning.

IIPP-1 surveyed its neighborhood with curiosity. Its curiosity was warranted; its life depended on precise evaluations of all the information received and transmitted by its sensors. Its further activities did as well. Its ability to transmit information to its faraway home planet as well. It had a great deal of activity and decision-making awaiting it within the next critical time.

The immediate information was apparently satisfactory because IIPP-1 proceeded to release its side arms and open its port to liberate the IIPR, or international interplanetary rover, which it carried on board. The rover, in turns, carried the TTES, or Triton terraforming evaluation surveyor. This cargo onboard was most essential to the mission for which IIPP-1 had been designed—the part of the probe expected to assay the moon for the potential of future terraformation.

After all of these primary chores were accomplished, the IIPP-1 opened a side port and, through this port, extended a long bar. Attached to the bar were two gold discs pointing into two directions of space. The cradle on which each of these discs rested was capable of both vertical and horizontal rotations as dictated by the probe. On each of the discs, a continuous storytelling play ran with displays of all types of hominids, including ancient to modern humans, animals beginning from unicellular beings to the largest sea-living mammals, also every kind of plant as well as microscopic and submicroscopic organisms. Symbols of all sort, mathematical and linguistic, chemical and cosmological, biological, such as the double helix and its components, ran side by side, accompanied by all of the known dialects of speech and all varieties of music and other noises from Earth.

The probe had accomplished the initial steps of its primary mission and began transmitting to its home base, the planet Terra, as well as in all directions of the vast expanse of the Milky Way Galaxy.

Glossary

Historical Names, Persons, Places, and Objects
The Pyramid Builders

Abydos. City in Upper Egypt, close to current-day Assiut.

Akhet. Season of Nile flooding. Rise of the water level began in the south at Aswan in July to September. High flood waters were reached in the north at the delta region from October to November.

Anubis. Jackal-headed god, guardian of the dead who helps the souls reach the afterlife and, there, assists Osiris in their final judgment.

Ba. In Egyptian theology, the soul.

Book of the Dead. Manuscript of instructions, dated circa 2800 BC and ascribed to the poet and scribe Manetho. Contains directions on how to avoid the many dangers which the dead may encounter on their journey to the afterlife, as well as instructions on how to answer when Osiris and Anubis examine the dead and assign their guilt or merit.

Byblos. Seaport and commercial center on the Mediterranean, not far from Beirut.

canopic jar. Sealed container into which the embalmed internal organs of the dead were placed, to be buried alongside the mummy. Named after the Nile Delta city of Canopis, located in the Canopic branch of the river (the second main branch of the river at the delta being the Rosetta branch).

cartouche. Oval-design enclosure surrounding the name symbols of important personages in Egyptian hieroglyphics.

Cush. In modern history, probably Ethiopia. The land south of it is the current-day Danakil, south and east of Sudan, and across the Red Sea from Yemen. Extensive salt flats there have been mined since antiquity.

Danakil. Desert in northeast Ethiopia, southern Eritrea, and northwestern Djibouti. Its huge salt flats are harvested to this day.

deshret. The flat-topped cylindrical red crown of Lower Egypt, somewhat wider at the top than at the base. Later the hedjet and deshret were combined into a single crown, which retained the shape of each of the two original crowns.

Djedefhor. Son of Khufu.

Djedefre. Son of Khufu, whom he succeeded. Married to sister Hetepheres II; ruled ten to fourteen years; succeeded by Khafre. Recent archeological information indicates his buried [?] pyramid on which extensive work is in progress.

Djoser or Zoser. Pharaoh of the third dynasty, builder of the step pyramid at Saqqara, design of which was attributed to the architect Imhotep. Architecturally it is considered to be an intermediate between the early bench-shaped funerary buildings, or mastaba, and the true pyramids of the fourth dynasty at Giza, built by later Pharaohs Khufu, Khafre, and Menkaure.

Eastern Sea. Red Sea.

Edfu. City in Upper Egypt, later burial site during the New Kingdom (1800 BC–AD).

Eye of Ra. symbolic name and title of Pharaoh. The symbol has later become assimilated into Christianity as the all-seeing eye of God.

First Cataract. Northernmost of the Nile cataracts; has been eliminated due to the construction of the Aswan Dam and subsequent inundation of the area south of the dam, resulting in the development of Lake Nasser just south of Aswan.

Geb and Nut. In archaic Egyptian mythology, sibling gods of earth and sky.

Giza or Gizeh. Burial site on the west bank of the Nile, north of the funerary sites of Saqqara, Maidum, and Dahshur; across from and adjoining Cairo. Consists of the three pyramids of Khufu,

Khafre, and Menkaure, and [?] possibly the buried pyramid of Djedefre, also their funerary or valley temples, along with several hundred minor mastabas of royal concubines, other dependents, and lesser functionaries of the royal households. The Great Sphynx is located in front of the pyramid of Khufu.

Hathor. Cow-headed or shaped goddess of prosperity, health, and fertility, protector of the family.

hedjet. The white elongated barrel-shaped crown of Upper Egypt. Traditionally Upper Egypt was thought to be a more aggressive warrior state than Lower Egypt; this crown symbolized valor and military might.

Heliopolis. Nile Delta city in Lower Egypt.

Henutsen I. Daughter of Pharaoh Sneferu and his consort, Hetepheres I; sister and consort of Pharaoh Khufu.

Hetepheres I. Queen of Egypt, principal wife and sister of Sneferu, daughter of Huni and (probably) his principal wife, Meresankh I, mother of Khufu, grandmother of Khafre. Artifacts excavated from her tomb are in Cairo and include exquisite jewelry and furniture.

Horus. Falcon god of Upper Egypt; son of Osiris and Isis. He avenged his father's murder. Symbol of royal rule and the emblem of the pharaoh.

House of Eternity. Pyramid or other mortuary monument.

House of Purification. See House of the Dead.

House of the Dead or House of Purification. Temple and workplace for embalming rites.

House of the Living. Temple with hospital and medical school attached to it.

Huni. Considered to be the last pharaoh of the third dynasty. Father of Sneferu and Hetepheres, husband-brother of Khamere-nebti I.

Imhotep. Architect, scientist, and artist of the third dynasty, Old Kingdom, assumed architect of Djoser's step pyramid at Saqqara. Regarded as one of the great minds of antiquity.

Isis. Wife and sister of Osiris, mother of Horus and of his sister Nephthys. After Osiris was killed by his jealous brother, Set, and cast into the Nile to be eaten by crocodiles, Isis brought back pieces of his body and, together with Nephthys, reassembled his body by wrapping (embalming). Symbol of womanhood and wifely devotion.

ka. In Egyptian theology, the essence or personality of a body. Each ka has a twin in afterlife, and after death, the two have to become united in order for the body to achieve eternal life. After death, the ka will occasionally visit the grave of the body to partake of food, drink, and other amenities left there for its use. Life-size representations of the dead, thought to house the ka during these visits, were usually buried for this purpose, along with the body.

Kanefer. Son of Sneferu and Hetepheres; became second vizier to Sneferu. Twin brother to Nefermaat.

Kawab. Son of Khafre.

Keftiu. Refers both to the island of Crete and its inhabitants.

Khafre or Chephren. Son of Khufu, brother or [probably?] half brother of Djedefre, grandson of Sneferu and Hetepheres I. Builder of the second largest middle pyramid at Giza. Ruled twenty-six years. Successor to Djedefre. Father of Menkaure and his sister-wife, Khamere-nebti II.

Khufu or Cheops. Second ruler of the fourth dynasty. Builder of the Great Pyramid of Giza. Son of Sneferu and Hetepheres I, father of Pharaohs Djedefre and Khafre, also of Kawab, Khamerenebty, Hetepheres II, Meritites II, and Meresankh II, husband and brother of Henutsen and Meritites. Ruled approximately forty-six years.

Lagash. Modern Telloh, one of the most important capital cities in ancient Sumer, located midway between the Tigris and Euphrates Rivers in Southeastern Iraq.

Land between the Two Rivers. Mesopotamia; current-day Iran and Iraq and parts of Jordan.

Libya. In the Old Kingdom, the area between the First Cataract and the Second Cataract; approximately the area of present-day Lake Nasser.

Libyan Desert, Desert region from Cairo to south of Aswan on the west side of the Nile.

Lower Egypt. From the Nile Delta to approximately current-day Assiut. Originally a group of delta cities united by Narmer.

Ma'at or Mayet. Goddess representing the world order under the divine rule of the gods, justice, and peace of the gods under the god king. Her statue was found in many of the temples of other deities of the period.

Maidum and Dahshur. Burial sites located south of Cairo on the west bank of the Nile.

mastaba. Tomb built out of sun-baked mud bricks with sloping slides and a flat top, resembling a truncated pyramid. These were the first accepted shapes for funeral monuments. The true pyramid shapes used in the Old Kingdom were developed out of these by successive building up of the sloping sides to a point at the apex. These more massive constructions were only possible after stone was adopted first in Djoser's step pyramid to be included into the building materials.

Memphis. Capital of the Old Kingdom and of Lower Egypt, circa 3600–2400 BC.

Meresankh I. Queen of Egypt, wife (and probably sister) of Pharaoh Huni, mother of Sneferu and of Hetepheres I.

Meritites I. Daughter of Pharaoh Sneferu and his consort, Hetepheres I, sister and consort of Pharaoh Khufu.

Mut. Goddess, especially worshipped in Upper Egypt, symbol of life and health.

Narmer, or Menes. First pharaoh to be recorded, warrior king, and founder of the first dynasty, who supposedly united Upper and Lower Egypt to lay the foundation of the kingdom of Egypt.

Nefer. Wife of Prince Rahotep; she was Hetepheres's and Sneferu's daughter-in-law.

Nefermaat. Son of Sneferu and Hetepheres, became first vizier to Sneferu. Twin brother to Kanefer.

Nephthys. Daughter of Osiris and Isis, sister of Horus. She helped her mother resurrect her slain father. Symbol of the child's duty and devotion to the parent.

nome. Geographic and administrative unit, usually supervised by an appointed nomarch.

Northern Islands. The Greek islands in the Mediterranean, especially Cyprus and Rhodes.

Northern Sea. The Mediterranean.

Nubia. Area south of the Upper Kingdom, from approximately the First Cataract (current-day Aswan) to the Fifth Cataract (in current-day Sudan).

Nubian Desert. Desert region from Cairo to south of Aswan on the east side of the Nile.

Old Kingdom. First dynastic period founded by uniting Upper and Lower Egypt by Narmer (Menes). Most important rulers: Narmer (Menes); Djoser (Zoser); Huni; Sneferu; Khufu (Cheops); Khafre (Kephren); Menkaure (Mykerinos); Pepi I; and Pepi II.

Osiris: Lord of the Underworld, master of eternity. "He who judges the souls of the departed." By custom, all deceased were called by the prefix *Osiris*, as one would nowadays say, "The late *X*." In life, each pharaoh was the human embodiment of Horus. After death, he became one with Osiris and reigned supreme in the next life.

Peret. Spring season of planting after floodwaters receded, from approximately October to January.

Pharaoh. Original meaning of the word is "great house" or "he who is from the great house." Hereditary ruler of ancient Egypt with absolute powers. He was believed to be divine and to control the Nile through the magic powers of his godliness. He was the commander of all Egyptians, the source of all justice, dispenser of all wealth, and regulator of all trade. He was "superintendent of all things which heaven gives and the earth produces." His powers were at the zenith during the Old Kingdom and thereafter gradually eroded over the centuries.

Place of the Dead. Burial sites on the west bank of the Nile, customarily regarded as the direction in which the sun, as well as dead souls, went.

Ptah. Son of Ra, husband of Sekhmet. Worshipped, especially at Memphis.

Punt. Probably modern-day Sudan.

Ra. Supreme sun god, in the Old Kingdom, creator of the universe.

Rahotep. Younger [? or youngest] son of Sneferu and Hetepheres I, brother of Khufu, Meritites, and Henutsen. High priest of Ra at Heliopolis and commander of the army. He and his wife, Nefer, or Nofret, are buried at Maidum. Larger-than-life-size statues of the couple are preserved in Cairo.

Ranefer. Son of Pharaoh Sneferu and his consort, Hetepheres I.

Royal Beard. Goatee-shaped beard, usually made of precious metal, which Pharaoh wore, tied to his chin, on ceremonial occasions. Along with the two crowns (hedjet and deshret) and the crook and flail, symbols of kingship.

Saïs and Bhuto. Nile Delta cities involved in the initial unification of Upper and Lower Egypt by Narmer.

Saqqara. Burial site, location of the step pyramid of Djoser. Located south of Cairo on the west bank of the Nile.

Sekhmet. Lion-headed goddess, daughter of Ra, and wife of Ptah, defender of the gods' rule and symbol of the desert and the destructive power of the sun.

senet. Game played with board and pieces similar to modern-day chess.

Shemu. Drought season and season of harvest from approximately February to June.

sister and brother. Terms of endearment indicating love and physical closeness; not necessarily used in their original sense of sibship.

Sneferu. First pharaoh of the fourth dynasty, Old Kingdom (ca. 2680), successor to Huni (presumed son of Huni's and Meresankh I's). Father of Khufu, grandfather of Djedefre and Khafre, brother (presumed) and husband of Hetepheres I. Warrior king who initiated the first economic contact with the Levant through imports of wood and other commodities from Lebanon. Built three pyramids: the first at Maidum, the second ("bent pyramid") and third ("red pyramid") at Dahshur. Red pyramid is considered to be the first true pyramid-shaped tomb and, in dimensions, only surpassed by the pyramids of his son Khufu and grandson Khafre at Giza. Presumed buried in red pyramid.

Syene. City in Upper Egypt, close to current-day Assiut.

Syria. Includes portions of current-day Turkey, Syria, Lebanon, and Israel along the Mediterranean.

Taueret. Hippopotamus-headed goddess of pregnancy and childbirth.

The Fayyoum or Faiyooum. Region of rich farmland southwest of present-day Cairo. Well-watered, thanks to Lake Fayyoum, canalization of which and irrigation of the region on a larger scale first accomplished by Senusret, pharaoh of the Middle Kingdom (ca. 2400–1800 BC).

Thebes. Capital of Upper Egypt, the site of current-day Luxor and Karnak.

Tinis. Early Old Kingdom capital in Lower Egypt in the Nile Delta, established by Narmer.

Two Kingdoms. Name of Lower and Upper Egypt.

Upper Egypt. From Assiut, south to current-day Aswan. Original territory ruled by Narmer and his ancestors.

uraeus. Ceremonial crown or diadem worn by royal persons only, shaped like a snake, usually a cobra with a raised head.

Uruk. Ancient city of Sumer (and later of Babylonia), situated east of the present bed of the Euphrates River, on the dried-up ancient channel of the current Euphrates.

ushabti figures. Miniature figures to accompany the dead into the afterlife. They usually represented a specific type of work or occupation and were intended to assist, should the dead person be asked to do any kind of work or service in his or her afterlife.

valley temple or funerary temple. Temple built close to the shore of the Nile and attached to the pyramid by a causeway. Its function was to receive the embalmed body after transport by barge from the House of Purification, where the embalming process took place. Secret death rituals were conducted at the temple before laying the body in its sarcophagus into the pyramid's burial chamber.

Fictional Characters

Pyramid Builders

Ahhotep. First lady and unique friend to Queen Meresankh.
Ankh-haf. Childhood friend of Sneferu, high priest of Ra.
Atet. First mistress of the royal daughters.
Heri-hor. Merneptah's father, royal scribe, and master of the royal archives.
Itethy. Master of the royal archives and library, successor to Heri-hor.
Keser-khaf. High priest of the Great Temple of Ptah in Memphis.
Khnumet. Half sister and one of Sennefer's favorite friends.
Menkau-hor. Royal architect of Sneferu's Dahshur Pyramid (bent pyramid), uncle to both Sneferu and Hetepheres.
Merit. Sneferu's mistress, later one of his wives, from the south of Egypt.
Merneptah. Commander in Sneferu's army, son of Heri-hor, and Hetepheres's lover.
Methety. High priest of Ra in Saïs.
Radji. Khnumet's sister.
Sahure. Brother-in-law of Lady Ahhotep.

Historical Names, Persons, Places, and Objects

The Bull Dancers

Achaean. Native or inhabitant of Achaea, i.e. Greece.
Byblos, Sidon, and Tyre. Coastal cities of Asia Minor on the Mediterranean Sea.
Cypros. The island of Cyprus.
Gournia. Site of a Minoan palace complex situated on the north-eastern coast of Crete.
Great Sea. Mediterranean Sea.
Knossos. Largest Bronze Age archaeological site on Crete; has been called Europe's oldest city. Settled as early as the Neolithic period.
labrys. Minoan double-headed ax.
Malia. Coastal town on the northern coast of Crete, dating from the Middle Bronze Age, was destroyed by an earthquake during the Late Bronze Age.
Mount Ida. Highest elevation on the island of Crete.
Mycenae. Located on the Peloponnese peninsula of Southern Greece. In the second millennium BC, Mycenae was one of the major centers of Greek civilization, a military stronghold which dominated much of Southern Greece, Crete, the Cyclades, as well as parts of Southwest Anatolia. The period of Greek history from about 1600 BC to about 1100 BC is called Mycenaean, in reference to Mycenae. At its peak in 1350 BC, the citadel and lower town had a population of thirty thousand.

Phaistos. Second largest city of Minoan Crete.

Phoenicia. Parts of modern-day Syria and Lebanon. Named for the Greek word *ponikoi* or "woodcutters," for cutting and processing cedarwood, much in demand for decoration and wood carving of interiors of buildings.

rhyton. A conical container for drinking, typically formed in the shape of an animal's head.

Sicani. One and probably the oldest of the three tribes inhabiting the island of Sicily.

Thebes. Current-day Luxor. During much of the Middle and Late Kingdoms, capital of Upper Egypt.

Thera. Now called Santorini. The Minoan eruption of Thera, also referred to as the Late Bronze Age eruption, was a major catastrophic volcanic event. Dated to the midsecond millennium BCE, the eruption was one of the largest volcanic events on earth in recorded history. It devastated the island, the Minoan settlement at Akrotiri, as well as communities and agricultural areas on nearby islands and the coast of Crete with related earthquakes and tsunamis. It caused turmoil in Egypt and has been alluded to in a Chinese chronicle.

trireme. Ancient Greek or Roman war galley with three banks of oars.

Zakros. Located on the east coast of Crete. Believed to have been one of the four main administrative centers of the Minoans. Its protected harbor and strategic location made it an important commercial hub for trade to the Levant.

Fictional Characters

The Bull Dancers

Annina. Nursemaid to Naïs and Patinos's children.
Athenis. One of the most popular female bull dancers; Ido's lover and, later, his wife.
Athinos. Naïs and Patinos's oldest son.
Emeris. Oldest of Naïs's sisters.
Helia. Naïs's and Patinos's first daughter.
Ido. Main fictional character; young man of a more middle-class background, who becomes Naïs's lover. He is an important teacher at the Sacred School of the Bull and is instrumental in securing an appointment there for Naïs.
Ilyo. Naïs and Patinos's newborn son.
Itaio. Delegate of the High Commissioner for Maritime Affairs.
Kyana. Naïs's younger sister.
Milo. Naïs's younger brother.
Miro. Ido and Athenis's younger son.
Naïs. Main fictional character; young woman raised in poverty with several siblings, who becomes the most famous bull dancer of the city.
Naïs. One of twin daughters of Ido and Athenis.
Ninno. Odaro's secretary. Comes from a well-known family with good connections which had met with bad fortune.
Novoro. Ido's and Athenis's oldest son.
Odaro. Rich merchant who takes Naïs as his mistress after she becomes famous in the bullring. He dies in a shipping accident when his ship sinks in a storm.

Oneyo. Tutor to Naïs and Patinos's oldest children.
Patinos. Goldsmith and gold sculptor, frequently employed by the royal palace to the pleasure of His Majesty, the king, as well as his royal household.
Saphero. One of Ido's teacher colleagues and close friend. The handsomest man in Knossos.
Somiro. Patinos's valet and helper.
Taïs. One of twin daughters born to Ido and Athenis.
Tannis. Nursemaid to Naïs and Patinos's children.
Tomo. Oldest of Naïs's brothers.

Historical Names, Persons, Places, and Objects

Nest of Eagles

Akkad. Succeeded the Sumerian Empire in third millennium BC. Later the northern portions became Assyria and the southern portions Babylon.

Ashur. Chief god of the Assyrian pantheon.

Assyria. See above, under Akkad.

Atalyā. One of Sargon II's main wives, mother of presumed crown prince, Sennacherib. She had been a gift to Sargon II from King Marduk-apla-iddina of Babylon.

Babylon. Capital of Babylonia.

Babylonia. Cultural heritage of the Sumerians and Akkadians adopted by their successors, the Amorites, a western Semitic tribe that had conquered all of Mesopotamia by about 1900 BCE. Under the rule of the Amorites, which lasted until about 1600 BCE, Babylonia became the political and commercial center of the Tigris-Euphrates region, and a great empire, encompassing all of Southern Mesopotamia and part of Assyria to the north. The ruler largely responsible for this rise to power was Hammurabi (ca. 1792–1750 BCE), the sixth king of the first dynasty of Babylonia, who forged coalitions between the separate city-states, promoted science and scholarship, and promulgated his famous code of law.

Cimmerians. Kingdom defeated by Sargon II, 716–715 BC. Geographically the country lay between the Caucasus and Sea of Azov. Sargon was killed during his 705 BC campaign against Cimmerians.

Colchis. On Black Sea in Asia Minor, part of current-day Georgia and Turkey. Associated with legend of the Golden Fleece.

Cyme. Current-day Nemrut, city in Aeolia on the coastline of Asia Minor.

Damodice. Wife of King Mita of Phrygia, born in Cyme.

Dur-Sharrukin. New city built by Sargon II, king of Assyria, north-northeast of Nineveh. Today's Khorsabad, Iraq.

Great Bay. Persian Gulf.

Half man. A castrated male; a eunuch; a male allowed in the women's house other than the husband of the women.

Ishtar or Inanna. Wife of Ashur, goddess of the earth, also of love and fertility.

Judah. Iron Age kingdom of the Southern Levant under Assyrian vassalage. Prior to this era, the kingdom was probably no more than a small tribal entity which was limited to Jerusalem and its immediate surroundings.

Land of Ashur. Assyria; all other gods and goddesses are aspects of Ashur and subservient to him.

Levant. Approximate historical geographical term referring to a large area in the Eastern Mediterranean region of Western Asia, equivalent to the historical region of Syria, which included present-day Syria, Lebanon, Jordan, Israel, Palestine, and most of Turkey.

Marduk-apla-iddina II. Crowned king of Babylon in 721 BC. In 710, Sargon II waged war against him. He was eventually captured, after which Sargon proclaimed himself king of Babylon.

Mesopotamia. "Between the rivers." Encompasses the land between the Euphrates and Tigris Rivers, both having headwaters in the Taurus mountains. The two rivers have numerous tributaries. The whole river system drains a vast mountainous region. Overland routes in Mesopotamia usually follow the Euphrates because the banks of the Tigris are frequently steep and difficult. The climate of the region is semiarid with a vast desert expanse in the north and a southern region of marshes, lagoons, mudflats, and reedbanks. In the extreme south, the Euphrates and the Tigris unite and empty into the Persian Gulf.

Mita or Midas, king of the Mushki. He married Greek princess Damodice of Cyme. At war with Assyria over eastern Anatolian provinces. Subjugated by Sargon II. Committed suicide later when he was defeated by the Cimmerians.

mitra. High cylindrical hat, often embellished with feathers and embroidery worn by court officials and the king of Assyria.

Mushki. Eastern Mushki (approximately current-day Georgia) and Western Mushki or Phrygia (most of current Turkey).

Narrow Sea. Red Sea.

Neo-Assyrian Empire. From approximately 900 BC to the fall of Assyria, approximately 600 BC; current-day territories of Iraq, Syria, Jordan, Lebanon, Iran, parts of Turkey, Egypt, Saudi Arabia, Kuwait, Palestine, Israel, Cyprus, and Armenia.

Nineveh. Traditional capital of Assyria, on the eastern bank of the Tigris (across the river from current-day Mosul, Iraq). Assyrian kings Assurnasirpal II, Sargon II, and his son and grandson, Sennacherib and Esarhaddon, added to construction and enlargement. Abandoned in 612 BC.

Phrygia. See above, under Mushki.

Ra'īmâ. Possibly mother of Sargon II's son and heir, Sennacherib.

Samaria. Central region of the ancient land of Israel, also part of Palestine, bordered by Galilee to the north and Judaea to the south.

Sargon II. King of Assyria, ruled 722–705 BC. Supposed son of Tiglash-Pileser III and younger brother of Shalmaneser V, whom he succeeded in 722 BC. Alternate tradition assigns him the position of turtanu or grand vizier under Shalmaneser V, took the throne upon Shalmaneser's death. In Assyrian literature, also referred to as Sharru-kinu ("true king").

Scythia. Located along the Northern Black Sea coast, occupied part of current Moldavia, Ukraine, and Crimea. Related to the Cimmerians.

Sea at the Center of the Earth. Mediterranean Sea.

Sethos. Egyptian Pharaoh ruling Egypt concurrent to Sargon's rule in Assyria.

Sennacherib. Firstborn son of Sargon II. Ascended the throne on the death of his father and ruled from 505–681 BC. Father of Esarhaddon and grandfather of Ashurbanipal.

Shalmaneser V. Ruled 727–722 BC. Son of Tiglath-Pileser III.

Tiglath-Pileser III. Assyrian general (see turtanu) named Pulu, who seized power and proclaimed himself king (ruled 745–727 BC).

turtanu. Equivalent to grand vizier or prime minister/military adviser to the king. The turtanu serving under Sargon II was also named Sargon, or possibly this reference is made for Sargon II, who may have been the turtanu under Shalmaneser V, adding to some historical confusion. Other records indicate that the turtanu serving under Sargon II may have been his half brother.

Urartu or Ararat. Kingdom defeated by Sargon II. King Rusa committed suicide. Geographically the country lay in the foothills of the Taurus Mountains and from the river Euphrates in the west to the Caspian Sea in the east.

Fictional Characters

Nest of Eagles

Adad-Nirani. Architect supervising Bagtu-Shar's work.

Ahnaputta. Bagtu-Shar's second and minor wife, a former bond woman.

Akh-Merami. Sargon's personal Egyptian healer; a gift to him from Pharaoh Sethos.

Bagtu-Shar. Highly skilled and valued stonemason active on the construction of Dur-Sharrukin.

Borsuk-annam. Supreme overseer of building works, delegate of the king.

Empyades. Crown Prince Sennacherib's Greek slave.

Enheduanna. Bagtu-shar's chief wife.

Himene. Second and last queen of Sargon II. Daughter of King Mita of Phrygia.

Maleanna. Sennacherib's first concubine in his new household.

Neghanna. First queen of Sargon II.

Shammuramat. Newborn daughter of Bagtu-Shar and his chief wife, Enheduanna.

Shutur-Nahhunte. Turtanu or grand vizier of Sargon II.

Simirrah. First wife of Shutur-Nahhunte, Sargon II's turtanu.

Tiglath-Pileser. Newborn son of Sargon and Himene, named after his grandfather, King Sargon's father.

Historical Names, Persons, Places, and Objects

Wind from the East

Alba. Kingdom formed by union of the Picts and Scots under Kenneth MacAlpin in 843. Their territory ranged from modern Argyll and Bute to Caithness, across much of southern and central Scotland. It was one of the few areas in the British Isles to withstand the invasion of the Vikings.

Álmos (ca. 820–895). Father of Árpád. Was, according to the uniform account of Hungarian chronicles, the first head of the Federation of Hungarian tribes at approximately 850. Died—possibly a ritual death—for the success of the Magyar tribes' colonization of the Danube basin. Emperor Constantine VII recorded that Álmos was the first grand prince of the Federation of the seven Magyar nations.

Aquincum. Ruins of the city can be found today in Budapest. Emperor Marcus Aurelius wrote *Meditations* there. Aquincum became the capital of the province of Pannonia Inferior after AD 106. By the second century, the city had at least thirty thousand inhabitants in the area today known as the Óbuda district of Budapest. Excavations show evidence of the luxurious lifestyle of the period. Decline of the Roman Empire included Aquincum. Germans and the forces of Attila the Hun invaded the region during AD 409. It probably became part of what was known as Attila's capital.

Arcadianae. Shopping arcade in Constantinople.

Arnulf of Carinthia (ca. 850—December 8, 899). The duke of Carinthia. Overthrew his uncle, Emperor Charles the Fat. Became king of East Francia from 887, then king of Italy from 894, and then disputed Holy Roman emperor from 896, until his death at Regensburg, Bavaria.

Árpád (ca. 845–907). Head of the confederation of the Hungarian tribes at the turn of the ninth and tenth centuries. He may have been the sacred ruler or kende of the Hungarians, or their military leader or gyula, although contemporary sources contain differing information. Most Hungarians refer to him as the founder of the nation, and Árpád's preeminent role in the Hungarian conquest of the Carpathian Basin has been emphasized by later chronicles. The dynasty descending from Árpád ruled the Kingdom of Hungary until 1301.

Attila (ca. 406–453). Was leader of an empire consisting of Huns, Alans, and Ostrogoths in Central and Eastern Europe, and one of the most feared enemies of the Western and Eastern Roman Empires. His unsuccessful campaign in Persia was followed in 441 by an invasion of the Eastern Roman (Byzantine) Empire, the success of which emboldened Attila to invade the West. He also attempted to conquer Roman Gaul (modern France), crossing the Rhine in 451 and marching as far as Aurelianum (Orléans) before being defeated at the Battle of the Catalaunian Plains. He subsequently invaded Italy, devastating the northern provinces, but was unable to take Rome. He planned for further campaigns against the Romans but died in 453.

Basil I. Leo VI's father.

Basileia. Greco-Roman term for empress.

Basileus. Greco-Roman term for ruler or emperor.

Basilica. Meaning literally "royal laws." Collection of laws, completed circa 892 in Constantinople by Leo VI the Wise of the Macedonian Dynasty. Started by his father Basil I. Simplified the original law texts of Emperor Justinian I's Corpus Juris Civilis ("body of civil law).

Boris of Bulgaria. See Tsar Boris.

Bosporus. Narrow strait connecting the Black Sea with the Mediterranean Sea.

Braies. Pants generally hanging to the knees or midcalf, resembling what are today called shorts. They were made of leather, wool, or, in later years, cotton or linen.

Bureau of Barbarians. Department of government in the Roman/ Byzantine Empire. It handled all matters of protocol and keeping records for any matters dealing with barbarians. Also the office exercised supervision over all foreigners visiting Byzantium.

Byzantine Empire or Eastern Roman Empire. The Byzantine Empire, also referred to as the Eastern Roman Empire, or Byzantium, was the continuation of the Roman Empire in its eastern provinces during late antiquity and the Middle Ages. Its capital city was Constantinople (modern Istanbul, formerly Byzantium). It survived the fragmentation and fall of the Western Roman Empire in the fifth century AD and continued to exist for an additional thousand years until it fell to the Ottoman Empire in 1453. During most of its existence, the empire was the most powerful economic, cultural, and military force in Europe.

Carpathians/Carpathian Mountains. Are a range of mountains forming an arc throughout Central and Eastern Europe. The range stretches from the far eastern Czech Republic in the northwest, through Slovakia, Poland, Hungary, and Ukraine, Serbia, and Romania in the southeast. The highest range within the Carpathians is known as the Tatra Mountains in Slovakia and Poland, where the highest peaks exceed 2,600 m. The second-highest range is the Southern Carpathians in Romania, where the highest peaks range between 2,500 m and 2,550 m.

chausses. Armor for the legs, usually made from mail. They could extend to the knee or cover the entire leg.

cotun. Padded and stitched shirt/jacket worn by a soldier as body protection against arrows or sword. The cotun prevented or, at least, made difficult being pierced or sliced through to reach body parts. In concept, a precursor for metal protection.

Cumanians. The ethnic origins of the Cumanians are uncertain. The Cumans had blond hair, fair skin, and blue eyes (which set them apart from other groups and later puzzled historians). By the eleventh and twelfth centuries, the nomadic confederacy of the Cumans were a dominant force over vast territories, stretching from the present-day Kazakhstan, Southern Russia, Ukraine, to Southern Moldavia and Eastern Wallachia.

Danubius. Latin name for the river Danube.

djellaba. Long loose-fitting unisex outer robe with full sleeves that is worn in the Maghreb region of North Africa. It has a Moroccan origin.

documentum. Written document.

Elöd. Chief of a Hungarian tribe. Scar-faced, scar running from ear to mouth.

Formosus, Pope. Pope Formosus (ca. 816–896) was cardinal bishop and pope, his papacy lasting from October 6, 891 to his death in 896. His brief reign as Pope was troubled, marked by interventions in power struggles over the Patriarchate of Constantinople, the kingdom of West Francia, and the Holy Roman Empire.

Grand Prince of the Hungarians. (Hung. *Nagyfejedelem*) Title used by contemporary sources to refer to the leader of the Federation of Hungarian Tribes in the tenth century. Elected by the leaders of the seven Hungarian and the three Kabar tribes. The grand prince is both the spiritual leader (Hung. kende) and military commander (Hung. gyula) in one person.

gyula (Hung.). Military commander of the Federation of Hungarian tribes.

Huba. Chief of a Hungarian tribe. Short, shriveled up, toothless.

Jenö. One of the seven Hungarian tribes forming the Federation of Hungarian tribes.

Kabar tribes. Three tribes, originally members of the Khazar Khaganate, which separated and joined the Magyar tribes. After that they traditionally formed the advance and rear guard of the consolidated ten tribes.

Kér. One of the seven Hungarian nations forming the Federation of Hungarian tribes.

Keszi. One of the seven Hungarian nations forming the Federation of Hungarian tribes.

kende (Hung.). Spiritual leader of the Federation of Hungarian tribes.

Khazar Khaganate. Were a seminomadic Turkic people with a major commercial empire in the late sixth century AD, in the southeastern section of European Russia. Khazaria became one of the foremost trading empires of the medieval world, in the western marches of the Silk Road, as a crossroad among China, the Middle East, and Kievan Rus (see below). For some three centuries (ca. 650–965), the Khazars dominated the vast area extending from the Volga-Don steppes to Eastern Crimea and Northern Caucasus.

Khazaria. Medieval kingdom, 652–969. Over a thousand years ago, the far east of Europe was ruled by Jewish kings who presided over numerous tribes, including their own tribe, the Turkic Khazars.

Kiev. Capital of the Ukraine.

Kievian Rus. Loose federation of East Slavic and Finnic peoples in Europe from the late ninth to the midthirteenth century.

kilij saber. A type of one-handed, single-edged, and moderately curved saber, later also used by the Timurid Empire, Mamluk Empire, Ottoman Empire, and the later Turkic Khanates of Central Asia and Eurasian steppes.

koboz. Ancient Hungarian string instrument of the lute family. Still in use in the sixteenth century. Similar instruments are used even currently, e.g., the guitar.

Kristos Pancreator. Greek terminology for Christ the Creator or Christ the Omnipotent.

Kond. Chieftain of one of the seven nations.

Kürt-Gyarmat. One of the seven Hungarian tribes forming the Federation of Hungarian tribes.

Leo VI the Wise. Leo VI Sophos, called the Wise or the Philosopher, was Byzantine Emperor from 886–912. The second ruler of the Macedonian Dynasty, he was very well read, leading to his epithet. During his reign, the renaissance of letters, begun by his predecessor Basil I, continued, but the empire also saw several military defeats in the Balkans against Bulgaria and against the Magyars.

Levente. Árpád's oldest son and heir.

Marcus Aurelius. Roman emperor (161–180) was a Stoic philosopher. He was the last of the rulers known as the Five Good Emperors, according to Niccolò Machiavelli thirteen centuries later. Last emperor of the Pax Romana, an age of relative peace and stability for the Roman Empire.

Martinike. Family name of the Empress Theophano, Emperor Leo VI's first wife.

Magyar. Hungarian name for Hungarian.

mead. An alcoholic drink of fermented honey and water.

Megyer. Ancient word for Hungarian. Probably the dominant one of the seven Hungarian tribes forming the Magyar Federation, naming the entire union and the later nation.

Meknès. City in Morocco.

Minoan. Culture developed on the island of Crete and some associated islands. Flourished between 3000–1450 BC.

Myceneans. The last phase of the Bronze Age in Ancient Greece, from approximately 1600–1100 BC. Represents the first advanced and distinctively Greek civilization in mainland Greece with its palatial states, urban organization, works of art, and writing system. The most prominent site was Mycenae, in the Argolid area after which the Argonauts were named.

Moravia. In the ninth century, Moravians founded the Realm of Great Moravia, ruled by the Mojmír Dynasty until the tenth century. It emerged into one of the most powerful states in Central Europe. After the death of Svatopluk, the last ruler able to hold together a centralized Great Moravia, most of the country fell into the hands of the Hungarians.

Naissus. Modern name, Nish (Niš) or Nissa. Moravian town on the Nišava River, a tributary of the Morava River which flows from south into the Danube.

Nišava. River, a tributary of the Morava River which flows from south into the Danube.

Nyék. One of the seven Hungarian tribes forming the Federation of Hungarian tribes.

Parthia. Historical region in Northeastern Iran. Conquered and subjugated by the empire of the Medes during the seventh century BC, incorporated into the subsequent Achaemenid Empire, under Cyrus the Great in the sixth century BC, and formed part of the Hellenistic Seleucid Empire following the fourth-century-BC conquests of Alexander the Great.

Pechenegs. During the late ninth century, under the pressure from the Turks and Khazars, the Pechenegs, a nomadic Turkic-speaking tribal confederation, migrated from the Volga-Ural region and occupied the area stretching from the Don-Donets to the Danube.

Pontus. Is a region on the southern coast of the Black Sea, located in modern-day Eastern Black Sea Region of Turkey. The name was applied to the coastal region and its mountainous hinterland (rising to the Pontic Alps in the east) by the Greeks who colonized the area since the Archaic period. The extent of the region varied through the ages but generally extended from the borders of Colchis (modern Western Georgia) until well into Paphlagonia in the west, with varying amounts of hinterland. Several states and provinces bearing the name of Pontus were established in the region, culminating in the Byzantine Empire of Trebizond. Pontus is sometimes considered as the original home of the Amazons, in ancient Greek mythology.

Porphyrogenetus. Latin appellation for one who "is born to the purple," i.e., son of the previous ruler.

Rus. Scandinavian people trading and raiding on the river-routes between the Baltic and the Black Seas, from around the eighth to eleventh centuries AD. They were often referred to as Viking Rus. The consensus is that the Rus people, around the eighth century, came from what is coastal Middle Sweden.

scimitar. Curved single-edged saber used mostly by Arabic peoples.

Scythians. Were a nomadic people who dominated the Pontic steppe from about the seventh century BC until the third century BC. They were part of the wider Scythian cultures, stretching across the Eurasian Steppe, which included many peoples that are distinguished from the Scythians.

seven nations (or tribes). The seven original Magyar tribes were Magyari, Nyék, Kürt-Gyarmat, Tarján, Jenö, Kari, and Keszi. These were probably the tribes who, among themselves, elected Árpád. Along the way from current Ukraine, they absorbed three disaffected Turki or Ugrian tribes (the Kabars) and organized a federation of ten tribes (Onogur or "ten arrows").

Simeon. See also Tsar Simeon of Bulgaria. King of Bulgaria from 893–927. Third son of King Boris.

Svatopluk (840–894). Ruled 870–871, 871–894, see also under Moravia.

Tarhos. Middle son of Árpád and Alán.

Tarján. One of the seven Hungarian tribes forming the Federation of Hungarian tribes.

Tas. Chief of one of the seven Hungarian tribes under Árpád. Face hideously marred by a long and poorly healed cut from his left earlobe almost to the corner of his mouth.

Theophano. First wife of Byzantine emperor Leo VI the Wise.

Tisza. One of the main rivers of Central and Eastern Europe. Flows from its beginning in the Ukraine due west, then west southwest through Slovakia, due south through Hungary, and eventually joins the Danube River in Serbia.

Töhötom. Chieftain of the nation Tarján.

Tripoli. Capital of Libya.

Tsar Boris of Bulgaria. Father of Tsar Vladimir.

Tsar Simeon of Bulgaria. Third son of Tsar Boris.

Tsar Vladimir of Bulgaria. Oldest son of Tsar Boris. Boris had him blinded and put into a dungeon where Vladimir's trail ended.

turul. Mythological falcon sent by the Great Creator God, ruler of all, to guide his creation and specifically the destiny of the Hungarian people. Symbol of tribal unity of the Federated Hungarian tribes. By tradition, the turul was the guide of the nomadic Hungarians to lead them westward to the sacred land of their ancestors, the Huns, and of their ruler, Attila. More specifically, the turul was the emblem of Árpád's tribe.

Üllö. Youngest of Árpád and Alán's sons.
Tunis. City in Morocco.
Vladimir of Bulgaria. See Tsar Vladimir of Bulgaria.
Wisent. European bison or Caucasian wisent
Zaoutzes, Stylianos. Emperor Leo's adviser, father of Leo's mistress, later the second wife, the Empress Zoe Zaoutzaina.
Zoe Zaoutzaina. Emperor Leo's mistress. After the death of the emperor's first wife, Theophano, she became his second wife and empress of Byzantium.

Fictional Characters

Wind from the East

Adair. Árpád's junior scribe, from the island of Alba (Scotland).
Alán. Chief wife of Árpád and mother of Levente, his first son and future grand prince.
Alaricus. Freed Visigoth war prisoner who remained with the Hungarian tribes. He speaks many languages and thus is of value to Árpád.
Beni Mellal. Chief slave of Sidi Ben Moussa, sold from him to Alaricus, the freed Visigoth war prisoner.
Botond. Messenger who brings news of Vazul's death to Árpád.
Contantinos Baïana. Leader of the delegation from Leo VI to Árpád.
Dörge. Messenger to Árpád from the tribe of Megyer.
Emö. Árpád's chief female healer.
Fajsz. Árpád's stablemaster.
Goldilocks. Virág's mare, gift to her from Árpád.
Ingerinus, Alexander. Master of ceremonies at Leo VI's Byzantine court.
Jenö. Árpád's chief scribe.
Jenö. Guide and commander of the detachment of soldiers accompanying Virág to visit her father.
Julia. Empress Theophano's sister, Leo VI's sister-in-law.
Kouronos, Aristophanos. Jeweler in Constantinople.
Margo. Healer, Emö's assistant.
Marót. Lieutenant of the advance guard/scout.
Megyeri. Árpád's senior squire.
Servilius. Vazul's Roman interpreter.

Sidi Ben Moussa. Merchant owner of caravan of slaves and camels, dealer in goods and information.

Szabolcs. Vazul's second-in-command and shield bearer. Short, muscular built, round shaved head.

Szárnyas. Árpád's favorite horse. Name translates to "winged."

Szilárd. Son of chieftain Előd. Spent some time in Bohemian captivity. Sent as emissary to Rome.

Taksony. Jenö's younger brother, and Árpád's junior scribe.

Törs. Árpád's senior arms bearer, graying stocky man with a chest like a barrel and disproportionately short legs, for which, behind his back, he had earned himself the nickname "Sitting Dog." One of the best swordsmen in the seven nations.

Ugron. Árpád's junior arms bearer.

Ügyek. Zalán's shield bearer and second-in-command. Handsome, curly-haired, dimpled young man.

Uruk. Chief Huba's groom, a tall bony man with an enormous beak of a nose and gentle blue eyes.

Vazul. Árpád's emissary to Byzantium. Short stocky man with long tumbling brown hair turning gray, tied at the nape of his neck with a leather thong.

Virág. Árpád's youngest and most recent wife, daughter of the former tribal chieftain Töhötöm, of the tribe of Tarján. In her childhood, betrothed to Zalán. The name translates to "flower."

Záhony. One of Arpad's squires.

Zalán. A leader of the nation of Nyék, friend of Nyék's Chieftain Huba, and betrothed to Virág, daughter of Töhötöm, the chief of tribe Tarján.

Zombor. High priest of the Hungarian tribes.

Historical Names, Persons, Places, and Objects

To Repel the Dark

Abbey Saint-Sever. Benedictine abbey in Saint-Sever, Landes, France. Founded at the end of the tenth century by William II Sánchez of Gascony. It was listed by France as a historic monument on November 18, 1911 and in 1998, it and other sites were jointly designated as the Routes of Santiago de Compostela in France's World Heritage site.

ad infinitum. Latin for endlessly.

Al-Andalus. Was the name given by the Muslims during the Middle Ages to the Iberian Peninsula. At its greatest geographical extent, its territory occupied most of the peninsula and a part of present-day Southern France.

Aretino, Pietro, (1492–1556). Born in Arezzo, Republic of Firenze. Author, poet, satirist, playwright. Supported by Agostino Chigi, Cardinal Giulio de' Medici, Giovanni de' Medici, Pope Adrian VI, Federico II Gonzaga, Pope Clement VII, King Francis I of France, Charles V of Spain, Pope Julius III.

Ariosto, Ludovico (1474–1533). Italian poet. Born in Modena. He is best known as the author of the romance epic *Orlando Furioso*, which later inspired playwrights, painters, opera composers, and many others. He also had a diplomatic career under the rule of Alfonso, Duke of Ferrara. Ariosto also had coined the term *humanism* for choosing to focus upon the strengths and potential of humanity rather than only upon its role as subordinate to God. This led to Renaissance humanism.

Arno. The river running through Firenze.

Arte di Calimala. Guild of the Cloth Importers of Florence.

babbo. Father, dad, pop, in Italian.

bas relief. Relief is a sculptural technique where the sculpted elements remain attached to a solid background of the same material. To create a sculpture in relief is to give the impression that the sculpted material has been raised above the background plane. What is actually performed when a relief is cut in from a flat surface of stone (relief sculpture) or wood (relief carving) is a lowering of the field, leaving the unsculpted parts appear to be raised.

Basilica of Santa Maria Gloriosa dei Frari. Is, after the Basilica of St. Mark, the most important ecclesiastical complex in Venice. Originally built between 1236 and 1338 by the Franciscan Conventual Friars, it was thoroughly remodeled in Franciscan-Gothic style in the fourteenth century. Over the centuries, the basilica has become a veritable treasure chest of works of art. Any discussion on the art within the church has, of course, to start with what is perhaps the most famous masterpiece of Titian's early maturity—The Assumption (1516–1518).

battlements. Parapet at the top of a wall, especially of a fort or castle, that has regularly spaced squared openings for shooting through.

Beau père and Belle mère. French for father-in-law and mother-in-law; literally translates to "beautiful father" and "beautiful mother."

biblioteca. Latin for library.

Bona of Savoy, Duchess of Milano (1449–1503). Second wife of Galeazzo Sforza. Married 1468. After the death of her husband, she eventually adopted Galeazzo's illegitimate children by Lucrezia Landriani.

Borgia, Cesare, Duke of Valentinois (1475–1507). Son of Pope Alexander VI. Title given to him by King Louis XII of France. Was an Italian politician and condottiere whose fight for power was a major inspiration for *The Prince* by Machiavelli. He was an illegitimate son of Pope Alexander VI and member of the Spanish-Aragonese House of Borgia.

Botticelli, Sandro (1445–1510). Born and died in Firenze. Painter, belonged to the Florentine School under the patronage of Lorenzo de' Medici. Initially trained as a goldsmith. Apprenticed with Philippo Lippi. Opened his own workshop in 1472. Worked in Rome (Sistine Chapel) in 1481. In old age, was a supporter of Savonarola.

Cappella Maggiore. Original name for the Sistine Chapel.

Cappella Sistina. Sistine Chapel.

Castel Sant'Angelo. The Mausoleum of Hadrian, known as Castel Sant'Angelo, is a towering cylindrical building in Parco Adriano, Rome, Italy. It was initially commissioned by the Roman emperor Hadrian as a mausoleum for himself and his family. The building was later used by the popes as a fortress and castle and is now a museum. The structure was once the tallest building in Rome.

Ce soir, n'est-ce pas. This evening, right?

chemise. Linen, cotton, or silk shift worn underneath an overdress or gamurra.

Church of Ognissanti. In Firenze. Completed originally during the 1250s but almost completely rebuilt around 1627 in Baroque style. Soon after, a new facade (1637) was erected. Ognissanti was among the first examples of Baroque architecture to penetrate this Renaissance city.

Church of Orsanmichele. In Firenze. Building constructed on the site of the kitchen garden of the monastery of San Michele. Between 1380 and 1404, it was converted into a church used by Florence's powerful craft and trade guilds. On the ground floor of the square building are the thirteenth-century arches that originally formed the loggia of the grain market. The second floor was devoted to offices, while the third housed one of the city's municipal grain storehouses, maintained to withstand famine or siege.

Comte. French for count.

Comtesse. French for countess.

condottiere. Italian captains contracted to command mercenary companies during the Middle Ages and multinational armies during the early modern period.

Copernicus, Nicolaus (1473–1543). Astronomer who proposed a heliocentric system, that planets orbit around the sun, that Earth is a planet which, besides orbiting the sun annually, also turns once daily on its own axis. Studied at the Jagellonian University at Krakow (1492–1494) at the astronomical-mathematical school. Sent to Italy and studied at Bologna (1496–1500), Padua (1501–1503), and Ferrara (1503). Also obtained a doctorate in canon law and was also a mathematician, astronomer, physician, classics scholar, translator, governor, diplomat, and economist. His book *De Revolutionibus Orbium Coelestium* (On the Revolutions of the Celestial Spheres), just before his death in 1543, was a major event in the history of science.

d'Este, Alfonso I (1476–1534). Duke of Ferrara from 1505, during the time of the War of the League of Cambrai. A noted Renaissance prince of the House of Este, an engineer and patron of the arts.

d'Este, Beatrice (1475–1497). Duchess of Bari and Milan by marriage to Ludovico Sforza (known as "il Moro"). She was reputed as one of the most beautiful and accomplished princesses of the Italian Renaissance. A member of the Este family, she was the younger daughter of Ercole I d'Este and the sister of Isabella d'Este and Alfonso d'Este.

d'Este, Ippolito (1479–1520). Italian Roman Catholic cardinal and archbishop of Esztergom, Hungary. Member of the House of Este of Ferrara. He spent much of his time supporting the ducal house of Ferrara and negotiating on their behalf with the pope.

d'Este, Isabella (1474–1539). Marchioness of Mantua and one of the leading women of the Italian Renaissance as a major cultural and political figure. She was a patron of the arts as well as a leader of fashion, whose innovative style of dressing was copied by women throughout Italy and at the French court.

de' Medici, Cosimo I (1519–1574). Second duke of Florence from 1537 until 1569, when he became the first Grand Duke of Tuscany, a title he held until his death.

de' Medici, Giovanni, "dalle Bande Nere" (Lodovico; later renamed Giovanni by his mother [1498–1526]. Born in Forlì. Only child of Giovanni Medici "il Popolano" and Caterina Sforza. Became condottiere for Pope Leo X (Giovanni di Lorenzo de' Medici). Eventually formed his own company. As a symbol of mourning, his relative Pope Leo X's death, Giovanni began to wear black bands on his uniform, giving him the name *dalle bande nere* ("of the black bands"). Died of wounds obtained in battle. Thought to be the last of the great condottieri.

de' Medici, Giovanni, "il Popolano" (1467–1498). Giovanni "of the People," third husband of Caterina Sforza, father of Giovanni delle Bande Nere.

de' Medici, Lorenzo di Pierfrancesco, "il Popolano." Older brother of Giovanni, Caterina Sforza's third husband.

della Rovere, Bianca. Caterina Sforza's mother-in-law; her first husband, Girolamo Riario's, mother, sister of Pope Sixtus IV.

Di Credi, Lorenzo. Italian Renaissance painter and sculptor, known for his paintings on religious subjects. He first influenced Leonardo da Vinci and then, in turn, was greatly influenced by him.

Diocese of Aire and Dax. The bishopric of Landes.

dit-moi. Tell me.

Donatello (1386–1466). Sculptor. Born in Firenze. Studied under Lorenzo Ghiberti.

Duomo Santa Maria dei Fiori. Cathedral of Saint Mary of the Flowers, main church of Firenze. Construction started in 1296 in the Gothic style. Completed in 1436 in the Renaissance style.

Ebbene. Italian for *well*; a conjunctive or connecting word.

en route. On his/her way.

facade. front (of a structure).

farthingale. Ladies' skirt stiffened with reeds encased in silk or linen for protection against rubbing the skin.

Ficino, Marsilio (1433–1499). Italian scholar and Catholic priest. Was one of the most influential humanist philosophers of the early Italian Renaissance, an astrologer, a reviver of Neoplatonism in touch with the major academics of his day, and the first translator of Plato's complete extant works into Latin. His Florentine Academy, an attempt to revive Plato's Academy, influenced the direction of the Italian Renaissance and the development of European philosophy.

Forlì. City in Emilia-Romagna, Northern Italy, the capital of the province of Forlì-Cesena. It is the central city of Romagna on the crossroads between Venice and Firenze. It was ruled by a succession of lords from the thirteenth century, the last being the Riario family, until it was taken by Cesare Borgia in 1499 and incorporated with the Papal States.

Frari or Order of Friars Minor. Also called the Franciscans, the Franciscan Order (postnominal abbreviation, OFM). Is a mendicant Catholic religious order, founded in 1209 by Francis of Assisi.

galliard. Dance consisting of choreographed patterns of steps, which occupy one or more measures of music. In one measure, a galliard typically has five steps. These steps are right, left, right, left, cadence, posture. The main feature that defines a galliard step is a large jump, after which the dancer lands with one leg ahead of the other. This jump is called a cadence, and the final landing is called the posture.

gamurra. Italian style of women's dress popular in the fifteenth and early sixteenth centuries. Consisted of a fitted bodice and full skirt worn over a chemise. Usually was unlined. Early styles were front-laced, but the fashion later changed to side-laced styles. The fashion for sleeves also changed, though sleeves earlier in the fifteenth century are attached to the bodice, after 1450 were usually detached and laced or pinned to the bodice.

garderobe. Indoor toilet room without plumbing.

Ghiberti, Lorenzo (1378–1455). Florentine artist of Early Renaissance, best known as the creator of the bronze doors for the Florence Baptistery. Trained as a goldsmith and sculptor, he later established important workshop for metal sculpture. His book *Commentarii* contains important writing on art, as well as what may be the earliest surviving autobiography by any artist. Worked concept of point of vectors=perspective into the designs. Michelangelo likened the gilded bronze doors of Florence's baptistery of San Giovanni to the Gates of Paradise. Combining the goldsmith's training in delicacy with a foundryman's training, sculptor Lorenzo Ghiberti condensed the Old Testament into ten panels and produced one of the defining masterpieces of the Italian Renaissance. Since their installation in 1452, the doors have withstood a variety of near-biblical catastrophes: a torrential flood, vandalism, overzealous polishing, and caustic air pollution.

Ghirlandaio, Domenico (1448–1494). Born in Florence. Learned metalwork from father, a goldsmith, then painting and mosaic work from Andrea del Verocchio. Was part of the so-called third generation of the Florentine Renaissance, along with Verrocchio, the Pollaiolo brothers, and Sandro Botticelli. Ghirlandaio led a large and efficient workshop training many artists, including Michelangelo.

Giorgione/Giorgio Barbarelli (1470s–1510). Born in Castelfranco, Republic of Venice. Studied painting under Giovanni Bellini, also associated with Titian. One of the most influential artist of his era.

Giovanni Pico della Mirandola (1463–1494). Italian Renaissance nobleman and philosopher. Famed for the events of 1486, when, at the age of twenty-three, he proposed to defend nine hundred theses on religion, philosophy, natural philosophy, and magic against all comers, for which he wrote the *Oration on the Dignity of Man*, which has been called the *Manifesto of the Renaissance* and a key text of Renaissance humanism.

gonfalonier. Translates to "standard bearer." Appointed military leader of the Papal States or any of the various republics, especially in central Italy. The office later became largely ceremonial and political.

humanism. Revival in the study of classical antiquity, at first in Italy, and then spreading across Western Europe in the fourteenth, fifteenth, and sixteenth centuries. It was based on the study of worldly subjects rather than religious ones in the arts, literature, and philosophy and a new interest in the branches of science.

Humanists studied the subjects taught in ancient Greece and Rome and believed that education should stimulate creativity.

Imola. Town and episcopal see, in the district of Emilia-Romagna, Northern Italy, southeast of Bologna. An independent commune from 1084, it was ruled by a succession of lords from the thirteenth century, the last being the Riario family, until it was taken by Cesare Borgia in 1499 and incorporated with the Papal States.

Landes. Region bordering the Bay of Biscay in the Aquitaine Basin of Southwest France toward the Garonne Estuary.

la volta. This dance was associated with the galliard and done to the same kind of music. Its main figure consisted of a turn and lift in a sort of closed position, which could be done either to the right or to the left.

Leonardo Da Vinci (1452–1519). Widely considered one of the most diversely talented individuals ever to have lived. His initial fame rested on his achievements as a painter; he also became known for his notebooks, in which he made drawings and notes on science and invention. These involve a variety of subjects, including anatomy, astronomy, botany, cartography, painting, and paleontology. Leonardo's genius epitomized the Renaissance humanist idea, and his collective works compose a contribution to later generations of artists rivalled only by that of his contemporary Michelangelo.

linear perspective. Method of creating the illusion of space on a two-dimensional surface using lines.

loggia. The Italian word for *lodge*, *loggia* is a covered space running along the length of a building similar to a porch, but with columns or arches on the open side. Loggias have been incorporated into palaces, museums, and other grand buildings for thousands of years, particularly in Italy, Greece, and Spain and in the Americas as well.

Lucrezia Landriani. Mother of four of Duke Galeazzo Sforza's illegitimate children, including Caterina Sforza. Wife of Count Gian Piero Landriani, a friend of Galeazzo.

Machiavelli, Niccolò (1469–1527). Born in Florence. Italian Renaissance diplomat, philosopher and writer, best known for *The Prince*, written in 1513. Served for many years as a senior official in the Florentine Republic as a diplomat and also in military affairs. Writer of plays, poetry, and songs in addition to scholarly works. He has often been called the father of modern political philosophy or political science.

Madonna: The Virgin Mary. It can also be the appellation of a high-class woman ("my lady").

Malatesta, Carlo I (1368–1429). Italian condottiere and Lord of Rimini, Fano, Cesena, and Pesaro. Member of the powerful House of Malatesta.

mamma. Mother, mom in Italian.

Masaccio, Tommaso (1401–1428). Born in Florence. Studied or associated with Brunelleschi, Donatello, and Felice Brancacci. One of first painters to use linear perspective, technique of the vanishing point. Employing a more natural mode, he was pathfinder of using perspective and chiaroscuro (technique of employing lightness and dark in painting) for greater realism.

mathematum. The science of astronomy.

medieval astronomy. Three of the most notable Andalusian astronomers were Ibn Tufail (died 1185), Ibn Rushd (died 1198), and Nur ad-Din al-Bitruji (died 1204). All lived around the same time and focused their astronomical works on critiquing and revising Ptolemaic astronomy. Instead they accepted Aristotle's model of the theory of homocentric spheres.

Messere or Messer. Italian; obsolete form of signore or English for *sir*.

Michelangelo di Lodovico Buonarroti (1475–1564). Was an Italian sculptor, painter, and architect of the High Renaissance, born in Florence, who exerted an unparalleled influence on the development of Western art. His artistic versatility was of such a high order that he is often considered a contender for the title of the archetypal Renaissance man, along with his rival, the fellow Florentine, Leonardo da Vinci. Several scholars have described Michelangelo as the greatest artist of his age and even as the greatest artist of all time.

Mont-de Marsan: Capital city of the province of Landes.
nonna. Grandma, nana, nanni, granny in Italian.
nonno. Grandpa in Italian.
Old St. Peter's Basilica. Predecessor of the current one. Consecrated in AD 360 and eventually demolished in AD 1505 to be replaced by the current basilica.
Orcagna: Andrea di Cione di Arcangelo (ca. 1308–1368). Italian painter, sculptor, and architect, active in Florence. Consultant at the Florence Cathedral and supervised the construction of the facade at the Orvieto Cathedral. His Strozzi Altarpiece (1354–57) is noted as defining a new role for Christ as a dictator of Catholic doctrine and papal authority.
Ospedale degli Innocenti. Is a historic building in Florence, originally a children's orphanage. Regarded as a notable example of early Italian Renaissance architecture. Features a nine-bay loggia, built and managed by the Arte della Seta or "Silk Guild of Florence." That guild was one of the wealthiest of Florence and took upon itself philanthropic duties.
ottava rima. Rhyming stanza form of Italian origin. Originally used for long poems on heroic themes, it later came to be popular in the writing of mock-heroic works. A form of poetry consisting of stanzas of eight lines of ten or eleven syllables, rhyming *a-b-a-b-a-b-c-c*. Its earliest known use is in the writings of Giovanni Boccaccio.
Palazzo Ducale. The residence of a duke.
panel painting. Painting made on a flat panel made of wood, either a single piece or a number of pieces joined together. Until canvas became the more popular support medium in the sixteenth century, it was the normal form of support for a painting not on a wall (fresco) or vellum, which was used for miniatures in illuminated manuscripts and paintings for the framing.
Plato (428–347 BC). Athenian philosopher during the Classical period in Ancient Greece, founder of the Platonist school of thought, and the Academy, the first institution of higher learning in the Western world.

Poliziano, Angelo Ambrogini (1454–1494). Italian poet and humanist, a friend and protégé of Lorenzo de' Medici and one of the foremost classical scholars of the Renaissance. He was equally fluent in Greek, Italian, and Latin and was equally talented in poetry, philosophy, and philology.

Pollaiuolo, Antonio (1429–1498). Born and died in Florence. He and brother Piero dissected human cadavers to learn anatomy. Studied with Lorenzo Ghiberti. Popes Sixtus IV and Innocent VIII supported his work.

Polonia. Poland.

Ponte nuovo. See Ponte Vecchio.

Ponte Vecchio. "Old Bridge." The bridge spans the Arno at its narrowest point where it is believed that a bridge was first built in Roman times. The Roman piers were of stone, the superstructure of wood. The bridge first appears in a document of 996 and was destroyed by a flood in 1117 and reconstructed in stone. It was swept away again in 1333, except for two of its central piers.

Pope Alexander VI. Born Rodrigo Borja, father of Cesare Borgia and Lucrezia Borgia.

Pope Innocent VIII (1432–1492). Born Giovanni Battista Cybo. Son of the viceroy of Naples, spent his early years at the Neapolitan court. Elected pope in 1484. King Ferdinand I of Naples had supported Cybo's competitor, Rodrigo Borgia, the future Pope Alexander VI.

Pope Julius II. Born Giuliano della Rovere (1443–1513). Head of the Catholic Church and ruler of the Papal States from 1503 to his death in 1513. Nicknamed the Warrior Pope or the Fearsome Pope, he chose his papal name not in honor of Pope Julius I but in emulation of Julius Caesar. One of the most powerful and influential popes, Julius II was a central figure of the High Renaissance and left a significant cultural and political legacy.

Pope Sixtus IV (1417–1484). Born Francesco della Rovere, head of the Catholic Church and ruler of the Papal States from 1471 to his death. His accomplishments as pope included the construction of the Sistine Chapel and creation of the Vatican Archives.

A patron of the arts, he brought together the group of artists who ushered the Early Renaissance into Rome with the first masterpieces of the city's new artistic age.

portcullis. Heavy vertically closing gate typically found in medieval fortifications, consisting of a latticed grille made of wood, metal, or a combination of the two, which slides down into grooves inset within each jamb of the gateway. Portcullises fortified the entrances to many medieval castles, securely closing off the castle during times of attack or siege. Every portcullis was mounted in vertical grooves in the walls of the castle and could be raised or lowered quickly by means of chains or ropes attached to an internal winch.

prie-dieu. Kneeling bench designed for use by a person at prayer and fitted with a raised shelf on which the elbows or a book may be rested.

ramparts. Defensive wall of a castle or walled city, having a broad top with a walkway and typically a crenellated stone parapet.

Ravaldino. Fortress near the town of Forlì.

Riario, Bianca (1478–after 1522). Daughter of Girolamo Riario and his wife, Caterina Sforza.

Riario, Cesare (1480–1540). Son of Girolamo Riario and his wife, Caterina Sforza.

Riario, Francesco (1487–after 1509). Called Sforzino ("little Sforza"). Bishop of Lucca, son of Girolamo Riario and his wife, Caterina Sforza.

Riario, Galeazzo Maria (1485–1557). Son of Girolamo Riario and his wife, Caterina Sforza.

Riario, Giovanni Livio (1484–1496). Son of Girolamo Riario and his wife, Caterina Sforza.

Riario, Girolamo (1443–1488). First husband of Caterina Sforza, assassinated. Lord of Imola and Forlì. Served as gonfalonier, chief of the army, and standard bearer for his uncle Pope Sixtus IV.

Riario, Ottaviano (1479–1523). Son of Girolamo Riario and Caterina Sforza.

rocca. Rock, as e.g., a base for a castle.

Roman bridge. See Ponte Vecchio.

Salviati, Maria (1499–1543). Italian noblewoman, the daughter of Lucrezia di Lorenzo de' Medici and Jacopo Salviati. She married Giovanni delle Bande Nere and was the mother of the Duke Cosimo I de Medici. Her husband died on November 30, 1526, leaving her a widow at the age of twenty-seven. She never remarried; after her husband's death, she adopted the somber garb of a novice, which is how she is remembered today as numerous late portraits show her attired in black and white.

seneschal. Senior position filled by court appointment within a royal, ducal, or noble household during the Middle Ages and early modern period; historically a steward or majordomo of a medieval great house.

Sforza, Caterina (1463–1509). Born in Milano, illegitimate daughter of Galeazzo Maria Sforza, Duke of Milano, and his mistress, Lucrezia Landriani, wife of the courtier Gian Piero Landriani, close friend of the duke. Descendant of a dynasty of noted condottieri, distinguished herself through her bold actions taken to safeguard her possessions from usurpers and defend her dominions. Privately she was devoted to experiments in alchemy and a love of hunting and dancing. She had many children, but only the youngest, Captain Giovanni dalle Bande Nere, inherited his mother's forceful militant personality. Her fearless resistance earned her the title La Tigre ("The Tiger"). Caterina's resistance to Cesare Borgia meant she had to face his fury and imprisonment. Once she gained freedom in Rome, she moved to and led a quiet life in Florence. She died there of pneumonia at age of forty-six.

Sforza, Galeazzo Maria (1444–1476). Fifth duke of Milano, from 1466 until his assassination a decade later. Notorious for being lustful, cruel, and tyrannical. He married into the Gonzaga family; on the death of his first wife, Dorotea Gonzaga, he married Bona of Savoy.

Sforza, Ludovico Maria (1452–1508). Sixth duke of Milano, also known as Ludovico il Moro (Lodovico the Moor), was an Italian Renaissance prince who ruled as Duke of Milano from

1494, following the death of his nephew Gian Galeazzo Sforza, until 1499. He was the fourth son of Francesco Sforza I, famed as a patron of Leonardo da Vinci and other artists, and presided over the final and most productive stage of the Milanese Renaissance. He is best known as the man who commissioned the da Vinci mural The Last Supper.

Sorbonne University. Considered the second-oldest university in Europe. It was established as a university in Paris, France, from 1150–1793, and again 1806–1970 as a corporation associated with the cathedral school of Notre Dame de Paris.

tabard. short coat commonly worn by men during the late Middle Ages. The coat was either sleeveless or had short sleeves or shoulder pieces. Usually open at the sides, it could be worn with or without a belt. Though most were ordinary garments, often work clothes, tabards might be emblazoned on the front and back with a coat of arms, and in this form, they survive as the distinctive garment of officers of arms.

Ticianus fecit. Done by Titian.

Tiziano Vecelli (1488–1530). Known in English as Titian. Italian painter, considered the most important member of the sixteenth-century Venetian school. During his lifetime, he was often called da Cadore, "from Cadore," taken from his native region.

umanesimo. Italian for humanism. The movement to choose the focus upon strengths and potentials of humanity rather than only upon its role as subordinate to God. This led to the Renaissance concept of humanism.

Vasco da Gama (1460–1524). Portuguese explorer and the first European to reach India by sea. His initial voyage to India (1497–1499) was the first to link Europe and Asia by an ocean route, connecting the Atlantic and the Indian Oceans and, therefore, the West and the Orient.

Verrocchio, Andrea (1435–1488). Florentine sculptor and painter and the teacher of Leonardo da Vinci. His equestrian statue of Bartolomeo Colleoni, erected in Venice in 1496, is particularly important.

Villa Medici di Castello. Near the hills bordering Florence, became later the country residence of Cosimo de' Medici I, Grand Duke of Tuscany. The gardens, filled with fountains, statuary, and a grotto, became famous throughout Europe. The villa also housed some of the great art treasures of Florence, including Sandro Botticelli's Renaissance masterpieces *The Birth of Venus* and *Primavera.*

Visconti, Bianca Maria (1425–1468). Born in Lombardy. Mother of Galleazzo Sforza, grandmother of Caterina Sforza.

Fictional Characters and Names

To Repel the Dark

Angelina Maria Lazzari. Caterina Sforza's wardrobe mistress and ladies' maid.
Bérnard. Jean-Luc and Madeline's elder twin son.
Brother Michel. Pope Sixtus IV's private secretary.
Capitaine de Sévrellac. Captain of the detachment of soldiers accompanying Madeline to her husband-to-be.
Cécile. Madeline's aunt.
Celestina. Sister of Angelina Maria Lazzari, Caterina Sforza's wardrobe mistress and ladies' maid.
Chateau de Landes. Jean-Luc, Marquis de Landes's ancestral home.
Comte de Saint Salieu. Madeline's father.
Contessa Bianca Gondi. Sister to Maria Salviati, Giovanni de' Medici's wife.
Donna Clementina. Nicolaus Copernicus's landlady in Padua.
Élise. Jean-Luc, Marquis de Landes's, disabled aunt.
Etienne de Saint Salieu. The Comte de Saint Salieu's son, Madeline's half brother.
Father Rabanus. Confessor of the Riario family.
Héloïse. Madeline's aunt.
Jean-Luc, Marquis de Landes. Madeline's husband.
Lucia. Angelina Maria's daughter.
Madeline, Marquise de Landes. Wife of Jean-Luc, Vicomte de Landes, and daughter of the Comte de Saint Salieu.
Marcel. Jean-Luc and Madeline's younger twin son.
Marie. Jean-Luc and Madeline's only daughter.

Matteo. Lucia's husband, Angelina Maria's son-in-law, a supervisor at the marble quarries of Carrara.
Monsignor Amadeo Fratti. Benedictine monk and priest, Caterina Sforza's secretary and confessor.
Montchateau. Ancestral castle of the Marquis de Landes family.
Sabine. Bérnard de Landes's wife.

New Worlds Rising

AI. Artificial intelligence.

Carl Edward Sagan (1934–1996). American astronomer, planetary scientist, cosmologist, astrophysicist, astrobiologist, author, and science communicator. His best-known scientific contribution is research on extraterrestrial life, including experimental demonstration of the production of amino acids from basic chemicals by radiation. Sagan assembled the first physical messages sent into space, the Pioneer plaque and the Voyager Golden Record, universal messages that could potentially be understood by any extraterrestrial intelligence that might find them. Sagan argued the now-accepted hypothesis that the high surface temperatures of Venus can be attributed to and calculated using the greenhouse effect.

cryobiology. Cryobiology is the branch of biology that studies the effects of low temperatures on living things within Earth's cryosphere or in science. Cryobiology is the study of biological material or systems at temperatures below normal. Materials or systems studied may include proteins, cells, tissues, organs, or whole organisms. Temperatures may range from moderately hypothermic conditions to cryogenic temperatures.

cryostasis. The hypothetical use of cryobiology for the long-term conservation of tissues or bodies, to be used after the cessation of cryostasis.

IIPP-1. International interplanetary probe-1.

IIPR. International interplanetary rover.

Milky Way Galaxy: The term Milky Way is a translation of the Latin *via lactea*, from the Greek. The Milky Way is the galaxy that contains our solar system. The name describes the galaxy's appearance from Earth: a hazy band of light seen in the night sky formed from stars that cannot be individually distinguished by the naked eye. From Earth, it appears as a band because its disk-shaped structure is viewed from within. Galileo Galilei first resolved the band of light into individual stars with his telescope in 1610. Until the early 1920s, most astronomers thought that the Milky Way contained all the stars in the universe. Following the 1920 Great Debate between the astronomers Harlow Shapley and Heber Curtis, observations by Edwin Hubble showed that the Milky Way is just one of many galaxies.

Terra. Earth.

terraformation. Planetary engineering designed to enhance the capacity of an extraterrestrial planetary environment to sustain life.

TTES. Triton terraforming evaluation surveyor.

About the Author

At the age of six, Ildiko received a birthday present from her father, his old portable Olympia typewriter. "Portable" then certainly was an exaggeration; these things weighed about ten pounds. However, this present delighted Ildiko above all others, and she cherished and used it so much that it became the basis for a lifetime habit of writing. The portable typewriter eventually died, others followed, then a PC, and eventually a laptop computer. Many times, paper and a pen worked just as well.

Ildiko, born in Budapest, Hungary, eventually made her way to Southern Germany with her parents, then to the USA. She has been an American citizen for many years. Her education included elementary schools in Budapest, secondary education in Germany, college in the USA, then back to continue her studies in Germany. Her fields of interest were the sciences, especially mathematics, physics, and the biological sciences of immunology, microbiology, and molecular biology.

Writing, however, was ever-present in her life. The manuscripts kept piling up, mostly in the area of historical fiction. Retirement finally afforded her the opportunity to accomplish what she had always dreamt of, to turn one of her manuscript into a book.

CPSIA information can be obtained
at www.ICGtesting.com
Printed in the USA
BVHW081355081121
621076BV00005B/29